More praise for
THE CHILDREN OF FIRST MAN

"A fascinating book which manages to tie up two continents and seven centuries of history, adventure, and fantasy into one epic tale . . . Thom writes with an amazing sweep through time that makes characters and places come alive."

—JACK WEATHERFORD
Professor of Anthropology
Macalester College
Author of *Indian Givers*

"Well-researched and intriguing . . . [A] sweeping historical novel . . . Thom is wholly convincing as he depicts the history of Welsh settlement being distorted down through the ages."

—*Kirkus Reviews*

"Fascinating . . . James Alexander Thom has told an old and almost forgotten story about movement between the Americas and the Old World long before Columbus."

—PAULA GUNN ALLEN
Author of *Spider Woman's Granddaughters*

"In a style and with a scope akin to James Michener's, James Alexander Thom traces the history of the Mandan tribe of American Indians through several centuries."

—*Indianapolis Star*

By James Alexander Thom
Published by Ballantine Books:

PANTHER IN THE SKY
LONG KNIFE
FOLLOW THE RIVER
FROM SEA TO SHINING SEA
STAYING OUT OF HELL
THE CHILDREN OF FIRST MAN

THE CHILDREN OF FIRST MAN

James Alexander Thom

FAWCETT GOLD MEDAL • NEW YORK

A Fawcett Gold Medal Book
Published by Ballantine Books
 Published in the United States by Ballantine Books, a division of Random House, Inc., New York, and simultaneously in Canada by Random House of Canada Limited, Toronto.

Frontispiece:
George Catlin, *Four Bears, Second Chief, in Mourning,* 1832. National Museum of American Art, Smithsonian Institution. Gift of Mrs. Joseph Harrison, Jr. Scala/Art Resource. Reprinted by permission.

Library of Congress Catalog Card Number: 93-42240

ISBN 0-449-14970-6

Manufactured in the United States of America

First Hardcover Edition: July 1994
First Mass Market Edition: September 1995

10 9 8 7 6 5 4

For Dark Rain,
my other wing

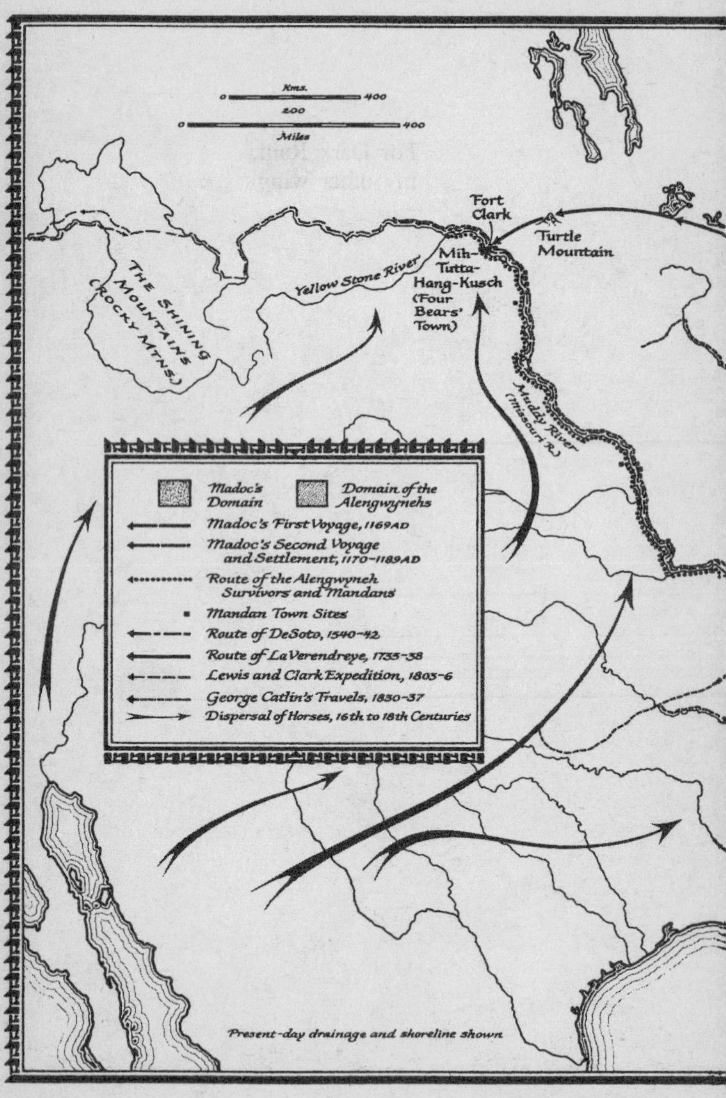
Kms.
0
400
200
0
400
Miles
The Shining Mountains (Rocky Mtns.)
Yellow Stone River
Fort Clark
Turtle Mountain
Mih-Tutta-Hang-Kusch (Four Bears' Town)
Muddy River (Missouri R.)
Madoc's Domain
Domain of the Alengwynehs
Madoc's First Voyage, 1169AD
Madoc's Second Voyage and Settlement, 1170–1189AD
Route of the Alengwyneh Survivors and Mandans
Mandan Town Sites
Route of DeSoto, 1540–42
Route of LaVerendreye, 1735–38
Lewis and Clark Expedition, 1803–6
George Catlin's Travels, 1830–37
Dispersal of Horses, 16th to 18th Centuries
Present-day drainage and shoreline shown

N
Cahokia Mounds
Falling Water (Louisville)
The Beautiful River (Ohio R.)
ALENGWYNEH MOUNTAINS
(ALLEGHENY MTNS.)
Mother of Rivers
(Mississippi R.)
Castle
(Chattanooga)
Etowah Mounds
Madoc's First Colony (Mobile Bay)
The Gulf Stream
Atlantic Ocean
Gulf of Mexico
©A-Karl/J-Kemp, 1993

PROLOGUE

WASHINGTON, D.C.
APRIL 1838

BACKSTAGE IN THE OLD THEATRE, GEORGE CATLIN THE ARTIST kept darting from his wife's side to make nervous adjustments in the array of canvases, deerskin costumes, weapons, tools, buffalo robes, warbonnets, shields, and hoops, whose odors of musk and smoke and linseed oil permeated the cramped space. From beyond the curtain came the drone of voices from the eager audience of Washingtonians who had been filing in to claim seats since seven o'clock. The theatre was small, and it would be crowded.

Having adjusted his grand portrait of Chief Four Bears in center stage until he could not see how to adjust it another half an inch, the artist came back to his pretty wife and stood beside her, nibbling inside his lip, glancing over the display for anything else that might need a final touching or tilting or dusting. From beyond the curtain now came an excited surge in the noise of the audience, even a pattering of hand claps.

"Listen how excited they are!" his wife exclaimed in a breathy voice, hugging his right elbow to her side and gazing up at him in adoration.

He shook his head. "That, Clara, is the sound of a crowd recognizing somebody important. Pray it's Daniel Webster coming in."

"Daniel Webster indeed! Can't you admit, my dear modest celebrity, that *you* are probably the most talked-about man in America just now?" Even though she fairly shouted into his good right ear, he could barely hear her words over the hubbub.

"Talked-about!" He chuckled. "Well, if being talked of were all I wanted, I should be well-satisfied by now. I'm their Freak of the Moment, the man who's slept among savages and eaten dog meat and whatnot. . . ."

"Nonsense, George, you're not their freak. They praise you to the heavens. As they well should! You're as famous as Webster himself now."

He grinned, then winced at a twinge of pain under his left eye. He pressed the heel of his thumb on the old deep tomahawk scar on his left cheekbone to diffuse the ache. That old scar was an irony; seven years he had roamed among the wildest Indians on the North American continent, and his only scar was from a tomahawk badly thrown by a white playmate in his childhood. It had glanced off a tree, fractured the cheekbone and knocked him unconscious; festering for months, it had eventually cost him the hearing of his left ear. The scar was the only imperfection on his youthful but weathered face.

Two men in dark frock coats came onto the stage from the opposite wing and approached, glancing at his display as they came. In the half-light, George at first recognized only the theatre manager. But then he straightened and smiled when a splendid, imposing gentleman with a familiar high forehead came through the glow of an oil-lamp sconce.

"Mr. and Mrs. Catlin," the manager said, "I have the honor to introduce Senator Webster. He's asked for a word with you before you go on."

"Of course, of course!" George exclaimed, extending his hand. The senator's grip was strong and warm. It was still as much the hand of a New England farmer as that of a Whig politician. Webster's brow was high, broad, and noble, and his eyes, under thick black brows, were intense and sparkling. It was wryly said in Washington that no man could be as great as Daniel Webster seemed to be. He kissed the hand of Clara Catlin.

"We were only just speaking of you, sir," she exclaimed. "My husband was hoping you could come!"

"There is certainly nothing else so compelling in town this evening," said Webster, and when the artist heard the timbre of his voice, he was surprised to feel a wave of nostalgia for his old friend Four Bears, whose voice had resonated just like this. Webster's was the voice that so often wrung tears and cheers from the whole Senate, and his oratory had turned tides of opinion. "I have your letter concerning your Indian Gallery," Webster went on. "I'm intrigued by your notion of making it a national resource. The newspapers can't seem to praise it enough. So I've come this evening to see it, to hear you present it, and I pray that after the program you'll have leisure to honor me with your company, and we'll talk of what might be done by Congress to obtain it."

"Thank Heaven! Oh, sir, I am so relieved! Thank you, thank you! This is a sacred cause with me, you understand. I've passed by two lucrative careers in order to do my part of it, and I've made the paintings and the collection, and written a lot . . . but now it must be used to influence national policy, before it's too late. . . ." He paused, even in his excitement afraid he might say too much, then went ahead and expressed it: "President Jackson scattered the tribes out of their homelands like leaves before the wind, and if his Indian policies go on uncorrected, entire peoples—splendid peoples!— will perish in our lifetime, with all their knowledge and lore!"

At the name of Jackson, Webster glowered, and then said, "Young friend, your heart and mine may stand upon the same center point." He took George's hand again and squeezed it warmly, and as he leaned close, his breath reeked of whiskey. Even so, his speech was impeccable. "How I envy you," he said fervently, "having had such grand experiences to put into words and pictures!"

George laughed. "What? Envy a man who now must try to be an orator in front of *Webster*?"

They parted with laughter, and then, as the senator left the stage, George Catlin pulled his handkerchief from his sleeve and wiped his brow. He was flushed with hope and anxiety. "By Heaven, Clara! Pray for me to be convincing this evening, for if I can win his heart for the Indians, *that* man in turn can win the hearts of Congress for them!"

"My dearest," she said, "you are *always* convincing!"

They heard the audience buzz again as Webster passed among them. The heat and presence of the crowd seemed to have penetrated even the thick velvet curtain. George put the handkerchief over his mouth and nose to shut out the dense stinks of white civilization: the stale, sweaty wool of people's clothes, their breath redolent of onions and liquor and rotten teeth, the women's cloying perfumes, the stench of masticated cigars, the acrid coal smoke, the musky whale oil of lamps, the reek of street filth on people's shoes and hems. His senses had grown too keen in his seven-year odyssey beneath the immense, fresh skies of the Great Plains. His heart had been stolen by the red people, and now he perceived the world through their senses. Their so-called wildness he had come to regard as the natural freedom of man, a freedom so clean, so beautiful, so vast, that his own teeming, unwashed society seemed utterly oppressive. Though still a respectable Christian, George had assumed the preservation of their freedom as his life's own sacred mission. And if he had not needed to be here in this noisome civilization to wage his fight for them, he knew, he surely would have stayed out on the Plains forever.

George thought of Webster, who was known to be a hunter and fisherman and man of the countryside; surely the senator would be in sympathy with the clean and spacious freedom Catlin so wanted to protect forever, out beyond the Mississippi frontier. . . .

"I wish," he blurted to Clara, "oh, I wish I could take Webster on a buffalo chase! On some of those wonderful Indian ponies . . . letting him feel that headlong pursuit . . . sweeping miles and miles over that sea of grass. . . ."

"It's time, Mr. Catlin," said the stage manager nearby. "Seven-thirty."

Clara squeezed his arm and kissed his cheek, then stepped back into the wing. He put his handkerchief in his sleeve, straightened up, took a deep breath and prepared himself to persuade. With a whispery rumble the heavy curtain rose, and like a dawn the blaze of footlights rose upon the vivid display of colors: quillwork, painted parfleche, furs, beads, carved wood, dyed feathers, polished horn and shell, silver and copper. The awed murmur of the audience pleased his soul. They were never quite prepared for their first sight of the splendor of Indian decorations and craftsmanship.

George Catlin went to the center of the stage, stopped beside the single painting that stood there upon an easel, and bowed his head until the greeting applause died. He looked about at the many faces, dim and attentive beyond the footlights, until he found Webster nodding reassuringly at him from a box seat, then began:

"Ladies and gentlemen, welcome, and thank you for coming this evening. I am George Catlin, painter. Once I was a lawyer, then a portraitist of the well-to-do. But for the past decade I have been exclusively a chronicler and friend of the original peoples of this continent—those you are accustomed to call 'the wild Indians.' Thus far, it has not been a lucrative profession, as my subjects know and care nothing about money." He paused, and a ripple of laughter swept through the theatre.

"But it has rewards greater than money. Standing with me here," he went on, turning and extending his left hand toward the portrait on the easel beside him, "is the man I consider my best friend—surely the noblest and bravest man I have ever known. He is Mah-to-toh-pah, which means 'Four Bears.' He is the most revered chief of the Mandan tribe—the so-called White Indians—dwelling near the Great Bend of the Missouri River, some twenty-five hundred miles from here. He comes this distance with me only in this painted form, which is my poor effort to portray his grandeur. He will not personally come to Washington. Why will he not? For this reason: His predecessor was brought here some thirty years ago, to meet President Jefferson, in an entourage by Captains Lewis and Clark on the return from their great voyage of exploration. That chief's name was Shahaka, and by his sojourn here he was ruined: changed from a beloved chief to an anomaly, a freak among his people." Catlin paused and let the audience wonder about that; it was a story he would tell them in due time.

"Four Bears would not come here because of what happened to his predecessor, Shahaka. I would not want Four Bears to come here—though I sorely miss him—because I could not stand to see Four Bears ruined, as he surely would be if he came here. This is not his world, as his is not ours. Here is how I saw Mah-to-toh-pah, five years ago, and here is how I choose to remember him. He was taught by Lewis and Clark to trust the American white men, and I pray we shall never betray his trust."

George paused again, stepped aside and joined the audience in admiring the portrait. The chief was stately, calm-looking, aristocratic in bearing, and light-skinned. His knee-length tunic was of soft, smoked deer hide decorated with quillwork, painted pictographs, feathers, and scalp locks. A warbonnet of white buffalo wool and red-fringed eagle feathers trailed to his heels, and he held in his left hand a lance festooned with eagle's plumes and dyed horsehair. The head of the lance was painted red, signifying the blood of Four Bears's brother, who had been killed with that lance by an Arikara chief, and also with the blood of the Arikara, whom Four Bears later had killed with the same lance. It was one of the stories George would tell this audience before the evening was over. Now he reluctantly turned away from the portrait and told his murmuring audience, "For his generosity, chivalry, elegance, bravery, and good looks, I do consider this chief the most extraordinary Indian now alive on this continent. In his world, he is esteemed as highly as, say, Daniel Webster is in ours—and justly so. Unlike Osceola and Black Hawk, whose portraits I'll show you presently, he has never fought white men. I pray that someday I'll go back and see this man again—though quite likely that will never happen. . . .

"Look at him! Do you really think there is any king in Europe, or any emperor in the Orient, who is as grand in stature, or as handsome in face and figure, as this man? And certainly there hasn't been a king in a thousand years with the strength and personal courage of Four Bears. Let me tell you some stories about his bravery—the . . . the *chivalric* sort of bravery, as you'll see—something to make you recall the Arthurian legends!" He beckoned offstage. "The robe of Four Bears, please."

A stage assistant carried out the rolled buffalo-hide robe, and held one edge of it while George unrolled it. It was covered with fourteen rows of stylized Indian drawings in many colors, each row representing an episode of combat in the chief's life. George cleared his throat.

"This beautiful robe, with his personal history painted upon it by his own hand, was Four Bears's most prized possession. But he gave it to me simply because I admired it. I say, not *sold*, but gave it to me, and wouldn't let me refuse it." A murmur rose from the audience, for the robe was obviously a treasure. "Many of the handsome costumes and accouterments I have in my possession—and you see, there are hundreds of them—were given to me in just that spirit. Imagine a people to whom friendship and the act of giving are more important than the owning and keeping of things! Think of that!" He wanted his audience to be moved by such kindly attributes of the Indians, rather than titillated by the usual exaggerations of their ferocity. But whenever he dwelt upon their codes of honor and hospitality, their cheerfulness and reverence, his audiences would start shifting and coughing, impatient for some kind of bloody excitement. Rather than let their attention slip away, he now extended his hand along one of the rows of drawings.

"This incident represents a mortal clash between Four Bears and a Shienne war chief; in terms of personal glory, it rivals anything in the *Iliad*. Let me tell you that story. . . ."

Then he began it, telling it just as Four Bears had related it to him beside a cook fire in the chief's earthen lodge five years before, a tale of two chiefs who jousted like knights on horseback and ended hand-to-hand in the dust with daggers, in a personal duel to death to spare the lives of their warriors; and like any tribal storytelling, it carried both teller and listeners away into the vivid, violent images, ending as a proof of Four Bears's gallant bravery. After the robe was rerolled, George displayed a drawing of a broad-bladed dagger with a claw-tip handle. "This," he said, "is the very knife that Four Bears wrested from the Shienne's grip and drove into his heart." The people almost climbed over each other to get a closer look at the legendary blade. Immediately, then, he turned to the story explaining the crimson point of Four Bears's lance, leaving the audience gasping with amazement—but inspired, too, as these were not mere accounts of violent battle and revenge, but tales revealing a strict code of honor befitting the knights of legend.

By nine-thirty in the evening George Catlin was two hours into his lecture and had shown and explained scores of portraits, landscapes, and action scenes, as well as countless weapons, tools, and works of fine native art. Despite the miasma of tobacco smoke and stale breath, the heat of lamps and candles and crowded bodies, his audience was wide-awake, nearly off their seats leaning forward to see the next picture, the next object. They were captivated; their imaginations were abroad upon the High Plains. Once George looked over at Webster, and the senator gave him a wink, nod, and smile of approbation.

Soon the formality of the lecture yielded to the comfortable exchange of questions and responses, and a robust, smirking, brown-clad figure in the third row bellowed a query that he had obviously brought to the theatre preformed in his mind:

"Mr. Catlin! Them Injuns eat dogs, don't they? Y' ever eat dog meat with 'em?" A chorus of laughs, groans, *bowwows*, and *ruff-ruffs* swept the theatre; George set his jaw and waited for it to subside.

"Sir, I have dined like an epicure in the Indian camps, on the inexpressibly delicious meats of buffalo tongues, of beaver tails, elk, antelope, goose, bear, turtle. And, yes, I have been invited to feast on dogs."

"And you *et* 'em?" the man prodded, still smirking.

"Some tribes never eat dog flesh," George said. "But among those who do, it is seldom—and it's considered to be the most honorable food that can be offered to a guest. You see, the dog is quite a useful animal to the Indian: a burden carrier, an aid at hunting, a sentry, a companion. When you are offered dog, you know that a good, useful animal has been sacrificed in your honor. You would have to be an utter boor to refuse it—and Indians don't like boorishness." He quickly turned while the audience gasped and groaned and laughed, and he pointed toward a raised hand near the back of the theatre. "Your question, sir?"

"Mr. Catlin, sir, it's getting late. You are planning to tell us about their torture ceremony, aren't you, the one advertised on your playbill, about them stickin' things through their flesh?"

The audience clamored, and so with a nod and a sigh George undertook to describe the undescribable: the Okeepa ritual, by which young Mandan men appeased the Good and Evil spirits and attained manly status through voluntary endurance of torture. This was always the part of the evening in which Clara would have a carriage cab summoned to take her to the hotel because she could never stand to hear it.

"Only I and one other white man, a fur company trader who was with me, have ever been invited in to witness this excruciating spectacle," he began. "Having expected that my account and pictures of the Okeepa would be met with incredulity, I obtained affidavits from fur company agents to confirm that I did indeed witness it, and the truth and accuracy of what I am about to present to you. As you have probably read, I have been challenged already by certain scientists and self-styled Indian experts, who declare that no one would, or could, endure such agonies—no, not even the dervishes or the drugged infidels of Islam.

"But I have indeed recorded, as eyewitness, the Okeepa ceremony, in these two paintings, without exaggeration, and my telling of it needs no embellishment, for the bare truth of it is all I can speak. . . ."

And when he proceeded with his account of Mandan youths hanging above the ground from cords skewered to their shoulders, backs, and nipples, the groans and grimaces of the audience were ecstatic. Two women had to be revived from swoons before the Okeepa narrative was done, and one squeamish gentleman rushed out into Louisiana Avenue to throw up. It was a fine program of entertainment that night in Washington's Old Theatre.

IT WAS HALF AN HOUR AFTER THE END OF THE PROGRAM BEFORE ALL the lingering question-askers and arguers and well-wishers were out of the theatre. Webster had had to slip backstage to elude the last of his own dogged admirers, and George found him prowling among the artifacts and paintings onstage behind the curtain, touching, smelling, and gazing at them. He stood for a long time in front of the fresh, glowing oil portrait of Osceola, the famed Seminole warrior, alternately nodding and shaking his head. Finally he said to George in a voice of tender wonderment:

"What a sweet and poignant visage it is! Those tragic eyes! *This* is the terrible warrior who led the United States Army on a goose chase for seven costly years? He looks more like a martyred saint than America's most dangerous enemy!"

"He *was* dangerous," George said. "Men get that way when you try to run them out of their homelands. But I agree with you; I can scarcely reconcile what I read in the newspapers about these fearsome bogeymen with what I see when I stand before them to paint their portraits. So it was, too, with Black Hawk—an immensely dignified and gracious old fellow despite his defeat . . . and Tenskwatawa, the old Shawnee Prophet: a pathetic, disenchanted wretch dying bit by bit in a hovel in Kansas. But as I told our audience: this portrait of Osceola I finished the day before he died of captivity. What you see is a trapped creature resigned to its end."

Webster shook his head and scowled. "And you say that Army surgeon at Moultrie severed this handsome head from Osceola's corpse for a *souvenir*!"

"What's more, he uses it to intimidate his own children when they're naughty."

"God in Heaven! And we call the red men savages!" Webster kept gazing at Osceola's portrait, his eyes moist, his fingers entwined behind his back and twisting hard. Then he sighed. "This is a magnificent portrait, Mr. Catlin. Perfectly executed in every detail. Second to no one's work, in my estimation."

"Thank you." George often chafed under the disdain of critics who, even while praising his Indian Gallery for its content, disparaged his painting techniques as crude. "I had the unaccustomed luxury of painting Osceola at leisure in a sheltered place, with no cold prairie wind congealing the paint or shaking the canvas on its easel. In prison, the subject's ball and shackles do constrain him to sit still as a model. Nevertheless," he added with an expression as sad as Osceola's own, "I had rather paint a restless Indian free in his own world than one in the ideal studio conditions of a prison—just as I'd rather paint a noble animal in the wild than in a zoo."

"A painfully apt analogy," said Webster. "By the way, young man, you are no mean orator, either! Like you, I may have produced gooseflesh now and then—I hope I have—but to my knowledge I've never made any of my listeners rush out and vomit. I envy you!"

They laughed until their eyes were streaming, were still laughing when the theatre manager and night watchman closed the doors behind them, and were still chuckling with pleasure a few minutes later when they were seated in a private cubicle in one of the senator's favorite taverns nearby. Late though it was, the establishment was crowded and full of tobacco smoke. Customers in the next room were roaring about dog meat and Indian tortures, apparently having come straight over from the Old Theatre.

"Weren't you ever in real danger?" Webster asked as he poured whiskey from a bottle into two glasses. "In all those years, surely?"

"Once I got pretty sassy with a grizzly bear, and had to be hurried away in a canoe."

"But I mean from the Indians."

"My father-in-law used to try to discourage me from going out there," George said. "He'd warn me that he didn't want his daughter a young widow. I simply told him, 'Sir, the farther I go, the safer I'll be.' And so it was. The only troublesome Indians I ever met were those along the frontier—those who'd rubbed up against the white man and bootleggers, and been lied to and cheated."

"Remarkable! But I suppose I understand."

"In all my years among them," George said, "I was never hurt, or robbed of so much as a button, though there were no laws to prevent either. Sir, I was never even allowed to go hungry! Do you wonder that I love such people, that I think they have much to teach us? My God, Senator, and you can't imagine how refreshing it is to live among a people who don't live for the love of money!"

"Money, yes," said Webster. "Damnable stuff, but you and I are going to have to talk about it quite earnestly, as you know. Senator Clay and I have discussed the acquisition of your Indian Gallery."

"Yes. He was another one I wrote to about it, because he always seems to be a champion of needful peoples. And . . . like you, sir, he is a persuader."

"He is that," agreed Webster. "And one of these days his luck might turn and he'll be President. That would be a good day for all freedom-loving men. And for you. Anyway, Henry Clay agrees with me that your paintings ought to be acquired by the government as an educational resource. And we concur on the reasons for doing so." Webster tossed a shot of whiskey into his throat and swallowed it as easily as if it were water. George sipped from his own glass, set it down, searched Webster's eyes and said with fervor:

"If only the citizens of this nation could study my pictures of those people, and my writings on their customs and beliefs, *surely* they would realize that the western tribes and their way of life *must* be preserved! Sir, if I could make it so, all the Great Plains would be left to them and their buffalo herds, and they could prosper without money there, as they are accustomed to do. It's not a kind of land meant for farming, except as they do it in the river bottoms. They are a glory on this continent, sir! Should they go the way of the great tribes on this side of the Mississippi, ruined and run over by our greed and progress, until they are obliterated, too? And all their beauty and knowledge dispersed like smoke? No! It is a tragedy what has happened here, and it must not be repeated there! But unless public attitude and government policy change very soon, those knights of the Plains, their unexampled freedom, their gallantry—all they could teach us about true liberty on earth!—all will be gone in a few years, and they will be drunken wretches living in hovels, without dignity or name, just like those are now whom Andrew Jackson drove out of this land! Sir, to erase such a glory just for the sake of greed, that would be a crime I do not want on the conscience of my country. I want them let alone!"

His hand was shaking from this outburst of passion. Webster laid a palm on George's wrist as if to still the trembling, and the sympathetic touch almost brought tears to George's eyes, so agitated was he. Webster said, "Senator Clay and I are on your side in this, for those very reasons. May I ask, what other allies do you have, in places of influence?"

"None that I know of, except General Clark."

"William Clark? The Indian Superintendent, you mean?"

"Yes, sir. He has been my friend and mentor in the West. I couldn't have done what I've done without his indulgence and his faith in me. And his love of the tribes."

"Ah, yes. But being in St. Louis, he's too far away to have influence with Congress. And I hear that his health is failing."

"I know! That news shakes me to my very soul. What will become of the poor Indians when General Clark no longer stands between them and the traders' greed? And the damned bootleggers?"

As George said this, Webster was pouring more whiskey into the glasses, and the thought passed through George's mind that any Indian who had consumed as much as Webster had in the last ten minutes would be out of his senses and howling with inner demons.

Webster, however, was still lucid and planning. "I shall try to champion your cause in both houses of Congress," he said. "It would be good for you to curry some support in the White House, too. If you have no friends there, let me think awhile on that. . . ."

George chuckled and shook his head. "I've been gone for so long that most of the friends I have left are two thousand miles away. Indians and fur traders."

"Don't forget this senator from New Hampshire," Webster said with a fatherly smile, pushing George's newly filled glass toward him.

"Thank you, dear sir!" George sighed.

Webster squinted at a wall sconce and seemed to be listening to the hubbub in the other rooms, but then said, "Van Buren doesn't care much more about Indians than Jackson did. To him, too, they're a nuisance wherever they live. If he thought of your collection as a means to help them, I think he'd veto a purchase. . . ." Webster's voice trailed off and he sighed. "I'm afraid, m' lad, that it won't be easy getting any appropriation for the purchase, because of the Panic. We are in awfully hard times. Don't expect this to happen right away. Maybe when the country's a little better off . . . Well, now, I suppose you're going to have to talk about money, and tell me what sort of a price you have in mind."

George took up his glass and had a substantial swallow. Webster's mention of the depressed economic conditions, he felt, put him in an awkward position. He cleared his throat. "It represents seven years of my life," George began. "It was all done at my own risk and my own expense. I am in debt. I never thought of undertaking this for profit, you understand, but out of admiration for the Indians, and so it is alien in my mind to try to set a monetary price on it. I . . . I feel that at fifty thousand I would be giving it away, but I hardly dare ask more. . . ." He sighed again and looked down at the glass he had begun rolling to and fro in his hands, and fully expected Webster to grow either cool or indignant.

"Fifty thousand! Fifty thousand?" Webster exclaimed. "I should have expected you to ask twice that much, at least, for such a treasure. Seven years of your life . . ."

"Really?" George felt immensely relieved.

"Certainly! Yes, indeed! However, please be aware that fifty thousand, or even twenty thousand, might be as unattainable as a million in these times. We might get an agreeable expression of interest if we—if you—stay below the figure of fifty thousand."

George's face fell again. "Below fifty? Senator, I have lately started writing and illustrating a book on those same travels, and it, like my gallery itself, will all be done at my expense, with no return in view for a long time. How should I support my family in the meantime? Fifty thousand will scarcely cover my present debts, let alone carry me till the book starts earning! Why—Why . . ." For the first time since he had been in Webster's heartening company, George felt anger and frustration heating his face and ears. "This country profits by millions off the Indians and the lands it has taken away from them! By God, sir, excuse my indignant tone, but couldn't this nation afford fifty thousand out of those millions to acknowledge the first Americans and to teach its public to care about them? Why, this country spent more than fifty thousand every day for years, I'll wager, to hound the poor Seminoles and chase Osceola through the swamps of Florida! *Damn* it!"

Webster was sitting back gazing at him, and George fell still, afraid his outburst had been unseemly, afraid that he might have offended his hard-won ally. Webster said in a quiet tone, "I'm sorry to say it, but the public usually feels it can afford much more for fighting than for educating itself. That's the way of it."

A jab of pain in his cheekbone made George wince. It was his reliable old warning that he was far too tired. "I will offer my collection to Congress for forty thousand, in that case," he said. "If they don't think it's worth that much, then perhaps England might. Or France. Or Holland or Austria. *They* have a healthier interest in American Indians than Americans have, I well know!"

"Oh, my!" breathed Webster. He bolted down another mouthful of whiskey. "Be assured, my young friend, I shall do my very best to convince my colleagues of its value. I shouldn't want an American treasure carted away to a foreign museum!"

"Nor should I," said George. "Over there it could do the Indians no good whatsoever. Here, it might. Believe me, if I could afford to, I would just *donate* it to our citizens. If my book does well, perhaps someday I can. In the meantime, I'll continue for a while showing it as I have been doing, and try to educate a theatre full of people each evening about the importance of preserving what's left of the red race. . . . I'll tell you a strange thing," he said after a pause. "The women and the medicine men of the Mandan tribe had a premonition: they warned that soon the only thing that will remain of them will be my paintings of them. You know, I have a dreadful feeling that their augury is right!" He sighed heavily, and extended his glass for refilling.

"The Mandans. That's the tribe of your impressive friend Four Bears?"

"Yes. The Mandans. The White Indians. The Children of First Man, Nu-mohk-muck-a-nah. Or Madoc the Welsh prince, I'd almost swear to it."

"You do believe they are the lost tribe from Wales?"

"I believe their remnants are among them. General Clark thought so; I think so. I've gathered much evidence. I intend to make a convincing theory of it in the book."

"Ah, what a saga that was, if true! White men here three hundred years before Columbus! Jefferson used to carry on about it, I remember. What a wondrous mystery that would solve!"

"It would indeed. But it will be futile to try to plumb that mystery any further if the Mandans go the way half the Indian nations on this continent already have gone: white men—whiskey—scalping knives—guns, powder and ball—smallpox—debauchery—*extermination*! In God's name, Senator, and for the sake of a splendid, doomed people, help me!"

PART I

A.D. 1169 — A.D. 1201

MADOC WYF, mwyedic wedd,
Iawn genua, Owen Gwynedd:
Ni fynnum dir, fy enaid oedd
Na da mawr, ond y moroedd.

MADOC I am the sonne of Owen Gwynedd
With stature large, and comely grace adorned:
No lands at home nor store of wealth me please,
My minde was whole to search the Ocean seas.

—Hakluyt's *Navigations & Discoveries, 1589*

CHAPTER 1

Forty Days' Sail West of the Pillars of Hercules Summer A.D. 1169

There was no breath of a breeze. The striped mainsail of the *Gwenan Gorn* hung like a curtain. The sea was mirror smooth, and the ship would have sat becalmed except for the lethargic labors of the twenty naked oarsmen on their sweat-wet benches amidships in the sail's shade.

Madoc the yellow-bearded prince, their captain, seven feet tall, peeling from sunburn, stood in blazing sunlight on the afterdeck, holding in his hands a pigeon cage of wicker. His brother, Prince Riryd, broad-faced, a head shorter, stood before him. Both princes were stripped to their sweat-soaked linen tunics, and they wore sandals so the sunbaked deck would not blister their soles.

Madoc squinted up at the masthead, drew a golden-haired forearm across his brow to wipe away his sweat, then loosed a thong to open the lid of the cage. The pigeon chortled, raised its head and looked about, and up at the blazing blue. Madoc tapped the cage from underneath, smiling, and said in a voice soft but deep as far summer thunder, "Go. Fly away and find us Iarghal!"

"Lead us to the Land Beyond Sunset," Riryd said to the bird. "My brother swears there is such a land."

Madoc tapped the cage again and the bird rose with a flutter, circled the masthead, and vanished in the glare of the afternoon sun. Madoc pinched sweat out of his eye sockets and nodded.

"Westward he goes, as I told you he would do," he said. "And this day I do not expect he'll return. I tell you, I smell land, I feel it!" He turned, teeth clenched and bared, gazing at all quarters of the horizon. There had to be a landfall soon. All the sheep had been cooked and eaten, and there was nothing left but bags of barley and lentils and rotting onions, not enough of them to feed the crew all the long way back to Europe. There had to be land. Madoc was almost sure he was within a day of it.

He had seen shore birds in the last two days, two of them, one something like a sparrow, that had come and rested awhile, perched on a stay line; and another, a large, bright-plumed green bird unlike any bird of the homeland, but no sea bird. The sailors had netted a frond floating northward on the blue current, something resembling a great fern but very tough-fibered, certainly a land plant. Madoc, long a sailor of all the known seas, had an uncanny sense for landfalls, and he believed almost without doubt that the continent of legends, called Iarghal, known to Plutarch as Eperios, known to the ancient African seafarers as Asqa Samal, lay ahead surely just under the horizon.

For had not Plutarch written, a millennium ago, that five thousand stadia west of Ice Land lay a continent long ago visited by Greeks?

Had not the Iberian Celts, centuries ago, mined copper on that continent, and traded with its nut-brown natives for the hides and furs of its game animals?

Had not the mariners of Phoenicia and Carthage and Libya traded across this great ocean with their colonists in that forgotten land mass of Asqa Samal?

And had not Norsemen been there, too, within the last two centuries, calling it the Land of Vines?

Madoc knew most of this from the Irish monks, who had long guarded the proof of those ancient explorations: proofs recorded in the forgotten Ogam alphabets, writing like claw marks. The monks could read them; Madoc had studied these old mysteries with the monks. He was not just a seafarer, he was a scholar of the seas. As he had cruised to Venice and Genoa, to Marseilles and Portugal, to Alexandria, to Denmark, he had also studied maritime history with his grandfather, Gruffyd ap Cynan, a great navigator, and had burrowed in the scrolls and manuscripts of a dozen monasteries. Most of the old sea lore that had been generally forgotten, Madoc had rediscovered.

And thus there was hardly a doubt in his mind that the Land Beyond Sunset would rise soon from this deep blue sea beyond the figurehead—Mermaid and Harp—of his ship the *Gwenan Gorn*.

Hardly a doubt.

But of legends there could always be a doubt, and doubts can grow large as stomachs grow empty.

At the outset of this voyage, Madoc had told no one but Riryd how he planned to sail, and Riryd had been astonished and dubious.

Two months before, they had embarked from a stone quay in the mouth of the little river called Afon Ganol on the border of Caernarvon. Madoc had steered not northwest toward the familiar Norse route—Ice Land to Green Land to Vine Land—but instead had left blue Plymlimon Mount behind on the port quarter and sailed southward through the Irish Sea, down past the great rocky headland of Saint David's, then had put in at Lundy Isle for a day to get pigeons and sheep in crates, and a mysterious wooden box. Then down the coast, past Brittany, southwest for days offshore of Iberia and Portugal. Anxiously Riryd had watched the Guide Star sink lower and lower astern, finally asking Madoc one night if he planned to forsake the star altogether. For what sort of madman would think to cross the vast Mare Atlanticum out of all sight of land without the Guide Star in view?

"Nay," Madoc had replied. "West of the Pillars of Hercules, we shall find a westering current to speed us on our way, star or no."

"You know of that said current, do you, or only think there is such a one?" Riryd had been skeptical enough to ask.

"I believe in it, as I believe in the God I have never seen," Madoc had replied, to which response Riryd had rolled his eyes.

Madoc had deduced, from his studies of the ancient voyages, that the old traders from the Levant must have used such a favoring current. It was only a deduction, and to go by it required faith, for even the best of mariners relied upon only familiar currents, not hypothetical ones.

For two days then, bearing southwest and ever farther from land, Madoc had sniffed and gazed about, and then one fine morning had said to Riryd with a nod, "Do you feel it, brother? We are on our current." Riryd, sensing not a thing, had rolled his eyes again. Since then the sturdy *Gwenan Gorn* had sailed and drifted along and along for forty days on that invisible river of current, while the Northern Star hung low off the starboard beam. Days were hot, sunrises and sunsets glorious, nights balmy; to sail was easy, and time hung ripe. Some evenings Madoc had sat on the high afterdeck, head tilted over a harp, and sung of the sea and of home, sung badly, while Riryd leaned on the tiller and watched the constellations. The crew every night had gambled by lamplight in their forecastle, which was really only a roof made of four inverted coracles lashed together above the deck in the bow, half hearing their prince's doleful songs. His voice was too deep and rough for the harp.

Madoc was intent upon reaching the legendary land, obsessed by it, but he was also a lusty husband, five-and-thirty years of age, and like any sailor yearned homeward as well as onward. His comely wife Annesta and little daughter Gwenllian were now hundreds of leagues behind, and on such beautiful evenings, unless one sang, melancholy could overwhelm him.

There had been a period of three days and nights of cloud and rain, with no star to steer by, and Riryd had complained with growing alarm. But Madoc then had brought forth and opened his mysterious box from Lundy Isle. With a sly smile, he had taken out a bowl, set it on deck and filled it with water, upon which he had floated a thin wooden disk and laid on it a needle of iron. The disk had rotated a quarter of a turn upon the water, then held still with the needle pointed toward starboard. "If the clouds were now to blow away," he said, pointing that way with his hand, "just there would you see the Northern Star still standing."

"Ah!" Riryd had exclaimed. "I have heard of this! A lodestone?"

"A lodestoned pointer, true as the Star itself. Remember that I built the *Gwenan Gorn* with staghorn pegs, not iron nails, thus not to confuse this pointer. I always know what I do, brother."

Riryd had been soothed a bit by that, as well as amazed. He had known a little of the mysterious principle of the lodestone, but had never known it could be applied to navigating the open sea. For fear of encountering uncharted islands of lodestone, some shipbuilders had been using staghorn instead of nails, to prevent the vessels from being drawn onto the rocks or pulled apart by the mystic force. But young brother Madoc had thought even beyond that. Riryd himself was a fair ship's captain, along coastal or familiar waters. But he was also Lord of Clochran, in Ireland, and thus more attached to land, and no such sea scholar as Madoc, nor as bold, nor as inventive.

Their father, King Owain Gwynedd, had begot twenty-seven known children upon two wives and several mistresses. Madoc, born of a mistress named Brenda, was, though a prince, a bastard with no royal aspiration, no estate. Since their father's death the year before, the many sons had feuded and intrigued over succession. Madoc had turned his back on all that, to face this Western Sea. He had persuaded Riryd:

"Our father's kingdom is crowded and blood-soaked from a thousand years of fighting; now our brothers drain each other's veins upon it. Brother, I want to find the unpeopled land beyond sunset, where, surely, men untainted with the lust for power can make a paradise to inhabit, according to God's will. There we, you and I, might rule fairly over an able people, and build a kingdom free of the vices of our poor homeland. Listen, Riryd, brother:

"I do honor the memory of our father. Cambria never had a greater king. But I swear that in that new place I will be more merciful than our father was. I shall never castrate, or gouge out the eyes, or cut out the tongue of anyone who opposes my wishes. I shall not put any one of my kin down to rot in a dungeon, from fear of his thoughts. Need one do such things to be a king?"

Riryd had looked at his younger brother with a mocking smile. "Then you expect to have only benign and trustworthy subjects and relatives in that kingdom of yours?"

"We will be free to choose only the best to start our colonies. We will lead them with mercy and justice, and teach them and their children the words and ways of Jesus the Savior. In a spacious land they can multiply without stepping one upon another, and all eat without denying others their fill. I do believe, brother Riryd, that a devout people in a spacious land can make a paradise."

"Aye, do you, then? Would it were, young brother. Let us pray so. But—ha ha!—did not the First Man and his Rib live uncrowded and still get themselves cast out of their Paradise? Ah, to have Saint Patrick go ashore before us when we find that Paradise—*if*—and assure that this Iarghal Land have no serpents! Ha ha! Ha ha ha!"

Except for those three days of rain and cloud, the weather had stayed mild, with silver-edged clouds piled heaven high but never bringing storm. The sheep had bleated pitifully in the heat, a strange sound on the open sea, but day by day their voices had diminished as they were slaughtered to feed the crew, roasted on a spit over a brazier of charcoal before the mast. If the crewmen were fearful about their constant westering beyond the sight of land, being Welshmen they would not show fear. They had lived out the long days obediently, rowing when there was no wind, watching dolphins play and distant whales spouting on the shining blue waters, and lately seeing big fish with sword noses leaping above the waves, but not one had seen any of the monsters they had feared to see—though one sailor, Mungo, swore on his own good name that a smiling mermaid had watched him piss over the gunwale one day at sunrise, and beckoned. Madoc their captain and prince was esteemed a fair and easy man, but he was a giant, and the son of his ruthless father, not the sort of man before whom one would whine one's doubts about sailing too far in one direction. His own absence of doubt was an inspiration. If their mariner-prince believed they were going to Paradise, so did they.

And so they had sailed on like this, ever westward in the warm sea, until three nights ago when Madoc had observed with his astrolabe that the Guide Star was ascending again. "The current is bearing us northerly now," he said with quiet satisfaction. The Norsemen had found their Vine Land in a northern latitude, and if any one thing had worried at Madoc's confidence on this voyage, it had been that the course of the southern current and the winds might bear his vessel too far south and below the continent—for the extent of the legendary land was known to no one. What would become of us, he had wondered, if we sailed under the new land and went ever onward beyond it? Madoc had faith in the reckonings of Eratosthenes of Alexandria, that the world's surface was curved, and that the world was thus likely a globe. If so, he thought, finally we would return to a place south of home. But by the ancient Alexandrian's calculations, the world would be more than eight thousand leagues in circumference. No ship could carry provision for so long a voyage. We are down to two days' food.

We *must* make land on Iarghal, he thought. And so this northward drift heartened him. Many were the ships in legend that had sailed outward never to return. My *Gwenan Gorn*, he thought, will not be one of those. Today let us make a landfall on that continent I smell.

Or so *want* to smell that I think I smell it!

BUT THE SUN WENT DOWN AND SANK BEYOND A LANDLESS HORIZON once again. Still no breeze came up. The rowers, thirsty and exhausted, shipped their oars and drank water, rinsed themselves with seawater and sat to eat, wondering whether their prince would put them back on the oars in the cool of the night. They were aware that the ship's food stores were all but gone. Riryd sat on a cushion on the afterdeck sipping wine from a goblet, and watched Madoc pace to and fro with his hands clasped behind his back, gazing westward into the rosy afterglow.

"Are you looking for your pigeon," Riryd said, "or smelling land? Or, mayhap, praying? Ha ha!"

"Praying? Aye. Any man on the great sea in a small ship should always be praying. Smelling land? Aye. But I do not look for a pigeon. He is on land somewhere."

"If you smell land," Riryd said with his one-sided smile, "what sort of a land do you smell?"

Madoc did not hesitate to answer. "Marshland."

"Marshland, is it?" Riryd mocked. "You can say by your nose that it's marshland, even before you see it with your eyes?" But even as he mocked, he was flaring his own nostrils and trying to detect a trace.

"Aye, marshland," Madoc repeated. And he was sure of it, though there was scarcely a breeze to bring a smell offshore. But Madoc had a nose as keen, it seemed, as a fowling dog's—indeed, Dog was his nickname in the family—and he had sniffed the marshes off the Nile and the Adriatic long before landfalls, and he was sure he was smelling sea marsh.

"Perhaps," Riryd scoffed, "you're smelling nothing more than the body sweats of our rowers, which are swampy enough to me. Ha!"

Madoc smiled patiently. "I smell those well enough, as well as yours and my own. But beyond those, I smell marshlands, and my nose cannot deny it. You will see." He shut his eyes and his nostrils quivered. Behind his closed eyelids he envisioned reeds and waterfowl, tidal flats dark with rot, crab shells, estuaries of green grass and dun muck, cranes wading. "And," he said, opening his eyes to the purpling sea, the last trace of rose petal in the western sky, the bright point of the evening star, "if there be marshlands, then the land is surely large. Rare is an island with sea marshes."

Riryd proceeded to drink until he was sleepy, and went to his bunk in the cabin after the evening star had set. A slight breeze arose, and the sail rustled and bellied, and at last the tiller under Madoc's hand felt alive, with its steady little pressure against the moving water. The sweat had dried on his face and body, and his eyelids were dry and felt rough. But the breeze was good and soothing on his sun-scorched skin, and it brought the land smells stronger to his senses. His heartbeat quickened.

After one hour a glorious half-moon came up astern, big and orange. As it climbed and grew whiter, it cast his shadow forward onto the sail, his head and shoulders outlined on the moon-pale cloth. Now it seemed that only Madoc himself, and the lookout sitting in his hooped perch above the mainyard, were the only two awake on the vessel. Madoc secured the tiller with a looped line and went to lean with his elbows on the rail, looking down at the waterline a few feet below. Along the shadowed hull the seawater purled and gurgled faintly, and the tiny blue starlike specks of the mysterious waterglow fell away and swirled. He wondered, as he often did, whether there was a similar force in those underwater lights as in the invisible pull of the lodestone. And he wondered whether there was a way of understanding God's mysteries besides just wondering about them.

The sea, he thought, makes you wonder why you wonder.

He felt his ship, felt its strain and easy motions as if it were alive, as if it were a horse he was riding. The *Gwenan Gorn* had grown out of a picture in his mind, a picture of what a vessel for the open seas should be, a picture created from the many things he had learned of the strengths and weaknesses of other ships. Madoc made it a planked ship, like those of the Norse seafarers, but longer, and had decked it over and raised a high, roofed cabin on the afterdeck. Both stem and stern had tall, carved posts, the stem ornamented with a mermaid and harp, the sternpost in the form of a mermaid's raised flukes. Because of the decking, the *Gwenan Gorn* would not ship water even when heeled far over, and he had faith that she was unsinkable. The keel and ribs were all drilled and laced together with fiber cordage, after the old Mediterranean fashion, which he thought sturdier and more resilient than a frame drilled and pegged. He had chosen planking over leather-covered wicker to sheathe the hull, believing it more durable, and fastened it with staghorn, which would not rust away like nails.

Thus with his sleek vessel's hull waxed to slip through the seas, her rudder fixed to the sternpost on pintles, with a main yard maneuverable by only two men, Madoc had a proud and nimble deep-sea ship, and the *Gwenan Gorn* had proven herself on many a trading voyage through storms and doldrums in both northern and southern waters. And she was almost as much a home to Madoc as was Cambria, his father's bloody kingdom.

With a sigh of appreciation, the prince straightened up, clasped the rail with one hand, released it and patted it twice, and returned to the tiller. There he stood and steered with the halfmoon climbing behind him, and now and then raised his head to sniff for the land smells, and tried to sense his location in the universe. He had sailed far over the curve of the sea. He wondered, as he often had, what could hold the earth's waters upon a curved surface. Was the globe like a giant lodestone, hugging the sparkling seawater unto itself? And what of the stars?

I have come so far, yet they have hardly seemed to move. They must be farther off than we think! How high, really, *is* the canopy of heaven?

That thought caused him a shudder of fearsome humility, and he prayed:

Lord of Heaven, forgive me for trying to pry amongst thy secrets!

But then he reminded himself that by sailing to a mythical new land, he was still trying to examine God's secrets.

Once, in condemning philosophers and wizards, Madoc's father Owain Gwynedd had pronounced: "Man will destroy himself by seeking to know the unknowable!"

And Madoc thought now: Is that true? Will we destroy ourselves? Or can we, by seeking to know, become immortal? Might we not find upon this world a place where no one dies?

That itself was one of the legends of Iarghal, the Lost Land Beyond Sunset, one reason why it could never be quite forgotten: it was believed that Everlasting Youth was to be found there. How many ships had sailed off in search of that, never to return? And why had they not returned? Because they had been lost on the great ocean, or because they had fallen into an Abyss—or because they had found Eternal Youth and refused to return from it?

Madoc himself was not of the turn of mind to believe strongly in Everlasting Youth or Immortality. That had not been the prime lure of this quest; he was looking only for a peaceful and bounteous place to found a better civilization. But still, never to die . . .

"Ho, my Prince!" came the lookout's voice. "I hear a surf, and thought I saw it, too!"

Madoc's heart was pounding. The voices of crewmen were querying in sleepy tones; figures were rising in the moonlight. Madoc lashed the tiller again, calling up, "Where? Which quarter?"

"All along, Highness!"

His legs stiff and clumsy from long standing at the tiller, Madoc lumbered to the portside rail and peered off at the dark waters. Riryd's thick voice, slurred with sleep, came from the cabin hatch: "What? Is it land?"

"Wait," Madoc said, staring off. "Be still and listen!" he

shouted to everyone in his booming voice, and all the talking stopped the length of the ship. Now there was just the soft hush of the wind, the murmur of water against the hull, the creak of stays and wood.

Yes, I believe I hear it, he thought.

It was like the slow breathing of a sleeper, out in the night ahead. The land smells he had detected during the calm of the day were gone now; the gentle wind was blowing onshore and smelled only of sea.

And now Madoc began to see the long, pale line of luminescent froth, ghostly, now seen, now not, but very extensive, as if on a long shore ahead. He darted to the starboard rail, peered forward and saw that it stretched off to the north as well. His scalp prickled. Now there was danger. As he jumped to the steering post and unlashed the tiller, he hissed to Riryd:

"We must come about or we'll be aground! Get them hauling the sheet!"

"I see no land, though!" Riryd said.

"Haul it!" Madoc shouted. Riryd went forward, calling. Soon the mainsail began to haul in, and Madoc leaned left on the tiller. The vessel swung northward, heeling down on her port side, and the high moon came around from behind Madoc to hang in the sky at his right. The swash of the surf was louder now. Though the *Gwenan Gorn* was no longer sailing toward it, but parallel to it, Madoc knew she would drift toward it in the onshore wind.

It was not a strong wind, and no one was alarmed. Only Madoc considered the hazard of hauling along an unknown coast in an onshore breeze. And so he said, "Put the crew on oars. We shall have to row to windward, or we'll go aground!"

Riryd understood at once and complied. The crew, groaning, began to row, and Riryd returned to the sterncastle. Standing beside Madoc in the moonlight, his tunic flapping in the wind, Riryd said to him, "Damn me, though, if I can see land!"

"Lookout!" Madoc called up. "No land yet?"

"Nay, Highness, only a surf close by, and others beyond!"

"As I feared," Madoc said to Riryd. "Yon breakers roll over an outer bar, or a tidal island, or in this moonlight we'd have seen land ere we came so close. If we don't go aground tonight, what we'll see at morn, I'll wager, is a very low land." For a moment the frown of anxiety vanished from his brow and in the moonlight his face was creased with a broad smile. "And that land will be Iarghal!" Riryd was shaking his head, but he, too, had a smile he could not hide.

Soon Madoc said, "But if this is only an island, we'll not want to lose it. I'll try to get us a safe way off from the bar, and perhaps we can set a firm anchor for the rest of this night!"

Until the moon was above the masthead, Madoc steered northwestward, outside the seething breakers, still seeing no land. The oarsmen glanced time and again in murmuring wonderment toward the west, themselves now certain that land lay just beyond, or, if not land, some frightful force that churned the sea. At times Madoc himself, as he grew more weary, would begin to wonder if this landless rush of white waters on his lee side might be the precipice at the world's edge where the waters must flow off. His notion of a global world had after all been obtained just by reading and reasoning; it did belie all the evidence of one's senses, which said that water must lie level, must overflow an edge.

Once, about the middle of the night, the lookout called that he thought he saw a point of yellow light, like fire glow, about the level of the invisible horizon. But none of the excited men on deck could see it, nor could Madoc or Riryd from atop the sterncastle. And then the lookout himself could see it no more—if he ever really had.

Madoc thought of yellow light. Warm light, not the cold light of stars or moon, but the glimmer of a distant fire. And of course then he could only think of man.

If this were Iarghal indeed, what sort of men would be here? Strong men? Weak? Hostile, or friendly? With two eyes, two arms, two legs? Hairy men, or scaly, or smooth-skinned? Hunters of meat or catchers of fish? Shepherds, and of what sorts of beasts? Men with horned heads and long claws, as lived in legends?

Cannibals?

Madoc knew that if he were thinking such thoughts about that glimmer of warm light, then surely his men must be, too. Even in their own Welsh land they were familiar with mermaids, Bwcas, and Coblyns, and other malevolent spirits of legend, and were ever watchful for the enchantments and fatal tricks of wood and water sprites. And, now having sailed ten times farther into the unknown than they had ever dreamed of, into a new region of the world, they likely were fancying all manner of grim monsters of great size and grotesqueness on that hidden horizon. Their fears he would have to heed and deal with, no doubt, as this adventure went on.

Thus thinking, Madoc was for a while unaware that the breakers were no longer seething on the leeward side. The lookout, perhaps lost in his own reveries, failed to call down. It was Riryd, finally, who suddenly gripped Madoc's arm, pulling him from his reverie, and pointed to windward, querying:

"How comes this? Are we inside the shoal?"

For a surf was boiling pale and loud off the *Gwenan Gorn*'s starboard bow, perhaps a furlong ahead. Madoc glanced about in amazement and saw that the vessel was moving through dark waters.

And he realized that, by sheer chance, the vessel had entered an inlet through the bar. In a moment he felt the stern rise slightly, and the ship seemed to be slipping swiftly downhill.

Then she was in calm water, gliding through the moon-silvered dark on an even keel, the rowers still pulling.

"We are," he said to Riryd, "inside the shoal indeed!" He had an impulse to scold the lookout, but he himself had failed just as badly to observe. Madoc's father, and most other nobles, would have had the lookout flogged for this. But Madoc meant to rule his own people fairly, and thus would not punish an underling for negligence of which he himself was guilty.

And now there were more urgent moves to be made. The ship was in shallows now, and surely nigh shore. He ordered the oars shipped and soundings taken, and finding a mere fathom of water here, dropped anchor. The vessel swung around on her anchor chain and lay prow to the breeze. And then in the light of the descending moon, while the crew's excited talk dwindled to sleepy grunts, Madoc and Riryd stood on the sterncastle and tried to get a sight of a shore.

The moon cast a shimmering path across the water, and at last dropped low enough to silhouette the western horizon.

"Ah!" Madoc said in a soft and happy voice, pointing. "There is land! As I said, it is low!" Riryd peered toward the moonset. "See?" Madoc said. "Trees there." He turned toward the southwest. "And trees there. And the water between, I'll wager, is a bay, or perhaps a river's mouth! Brother, I am going to try to calm my soul and sleep now till daybreak. Then, we shall see the sunrise shine on Iarghal! My brother, dost thou realize what it is we've done? We've come to the Land Beyond Sunset! Here it is! Here are we!"

"Aye," Riryd said with a great yawn, turning toward the hatch, "aye, *if* that's Iarghal."

MADOC WAS DREAMING OF A SHEEP-SHORN MOUNTAIN MEADOW overlooking the twin towers of Dolwyddelan Castle, his childhood home, when a long, squawking cry began to wake him. In his dream he was with his mother Brenda, a concubine of King Owain Gwynedd, sitting on a ground cloth; his mother was tenderly holding him on her lap and feeding him a morsel of squab when the note of a trumpet rang far below, and they looked down in the valley to see sunlight flash from shields and armor: Owain Gwynedd returning from defeating still another Norman army.

The blare of the trumpet became the squawk of some waterfowl. Madoc opened his eyes and sat up, seeing daylight outside the hatch. Farther off there were other squawks, and whirs and whoops, and a steady rasping whine of insects. Madoc scrambled groaning with stiffness from his high-sided bunk and, already wide-awake and heart racing high, emerged from the hatch onto the deck, turning and hungrily staring about for his first daylight look at Iarghal, the fabled land on the far side of the world. Already some of the swarthy crewmen were on their feet gazing about or pissing over the side. Overhead, white gulls turned and mewed. An ebbing tide had swung the *Gwenan Gorn* on her chain and she faced landward. There was no wind, and the hazy, delicate-hued scene before Madoc's eyes fairly made him think he had gone to Heaven.

"Dear God, our Father!" he gasped, dropping to one knee and clasping his hands under his chin, gratitude rushing from his heart. Then he stood again, arms outstretched, turning and blinking to try to see the whole spacious vision around him. His bladder was morning-full and tingling for relief, but not yet; first he must *see*.

His nighttime guess had been correct; the anchorage was in an estuary, where a broad river emptied from lush lowlands directly into the ocean. Streaks and puffs of cloud were tinged the colors of ripening peaches by the dawn light, and wisps of river mist hung over the limpid water, so that the distant wooded shores of the river seemed to float. White birds the size of storks passed over the gray-green waters on slow wingbeats. To seaward, the golden arc of the rising sun was just now peeking over the horizon. Foam was churning on the shoals and bars through which the ship had passed by such happy chance the night before into this haven.

WHEN THE TIDE TURNED LATER IN THE MORNING, THE ANCHOR WAS weighed and the rowers took their places. Without sail, the *Gwenan Gorn* began moving up the green river, her twenty oars rising and dipping at a slow cadence. Rhys, the ship's mate, manned the bow with a knotted sounding line, but the water was so clear that the line was not needed; the bottom could be seen. And the *Gwenan Gorn* had a shallow draft. Madoc expected she could navigate far up this river before it would be necessary to launch the coracles for further exploration.

Atop the sterncastle he stood with Riryd and they watched the shores, amazed. There grew trees like the great oaks of Britain, but festooned with something that looked like seaweed or hanging moss, as if a freak tide had covered the whole land and left its wrack hanging high. There were lagoons where glades of thick-boled trees stood rooted in water. Long reaches of the riverbanks grew in nothing but rushes. As the vessel glided slowly up between the narrowing banks, countless long-legged wading birds, blue ones, white ones, gray and brown, stalked the shallows, warily moving upstream with an eye on the vessel, it seemed. In some big trees, so many of the huge white birds stood amid the dark green foliage that they looked like great white orchard fruits. Flocks of waterfowl would rise splashing on drumming wings, veer off, and splash down on the river farther upstream, squawking and clucking in a thousand strange voices. In the higher reaches eagles and vultures swept and turned, silhouetted against the hot pearl sky.

"Is this Iarghal a land ruled by birds?" Riryd once asked.

But as the banks closed in on both sides and sloped higher, opening to reveal tributary creeks, dense shrubbery and thickets, the Welshmen began seeing more and more game animals. Drinking deer raised their heads and stared at the strange thing coming up the river, sometimes standing stock-still until it was past, sometimes darting up the banks or into the thickets, flashing the white under their tails. The banks were alive with small creatures like muskrats, otters, and a chunky brownish beast like a small bear with black stripes on its tail and what appeared to be a black mask across its eyes. One of these creatures, on a half-submerged log, seemed to be washing its forepaws; it paused and watched the moving ship with disconcertingly intelligent eyes.

By noon the heat and oppressiveness in the river course were stifling. Every man shone with sweat; the rowers were gasping. At the mouth of a creek on the right bank, Madoc brought the *Gwenan Gorn* close enough to shore that it could be moored to tree roots. He jumped down, waded to the sandbar and planted a banner there. "Before God," he said in solemn tone, "I proclaim this a land of peace, to be ruled by the sons of Cambria!" After a minute of silent prayer, he dispersed the crew, sending them to clean and refill the freshwater butts, gather firewood, and go hunting and fishing. Their faces were animated by eagerness, but also trepidation. They had debarked from the safety of their ship onto the soil of an entirely new world, which, though it looked beautiful and hospitable, might have dangers unimaginable, creatures invincible, powers demonic. As if that were not daunting enough, Madoc now warned them of something that had not yet even entered among their timid imaginings:

"All this day in this land we have seen no sign of men." At the word *men*, the crewmen glanced about and at each other, fearful. He went on: "We must not suppose that this is an uninhabited land. From what is said of Iarghal in the old tales, there are people here. Mostly they are fishers and hunters and fur takers. Among them came Egyptians and Carthaginians, Celts and Libyans, who made colonies here and traded with them, long ago. They were many, but if 'tis as large a land as I think, we might see no one in this part, but might yet meet them in another.

"We are few. And though brave Welshmen all, and well-armed, we must walk softly on their land, and befriend them if we meet. So I charge you: Give no offense if you meet them in the wood. Be firm and show no fear, but raise your hand against them only if you must protect your life. Coax them if you can to come to me at the ship here, where we might hold council with them—or here defend ourselves if we are forced to. Each of you who goes forth to hunt or fish, I shall give strings of our blue glass beads. Offer them beads in friendship, and encourage them to come meet your princes." That, he knew, was a method of diplomacy long used with natives of Africa. "Is this all understood?"

The men nodded and looked at each other. Then one, a shipwright named Idwal, with black pores in his nose, raised his hand toward Madoc and asked, "Your Highness, how large do these men be?" The others seemed to hang on to that question, and searched the prince's face in wait for his reply.

His visage softened into a smile. "Why, I have never seen one. But I've heard not that they are larger than, say, an Irishman."

And so, in apparent good spirits, ten of the men went out in pairs, with their bows and shields and bronze helmets, up and down the riverbank. Others were put to work sand-scouring the scum out of the water casks and refilling them from the crystal-clear creek, gathering wood, and sluicing salt off the *Gwenan Gorn*'s deck and rigging with pails of fresh water. The pure, fresh water was a delight to them all, after the long voyage on rationed water and the morning of hard rowing in the sultry heat. The men worked naked, rinsed out their clothing, and waded in often to refresh their bodies. Two sailors unleashed and launched one of the coracles, outfitted themselves with a bow and one long, barbed fishing gig, hooks and fishing line and a short sword, and paddled upriver to find a quiet place to fish, with Madoc's blessing. The princes Madoc and Riryd then stripped, gave their clothes to a crewman to wash, and waded into the creek's mouth to bathe at leisure. Onshore at the end of each mooring line stood a spearman on guard, and one crossbow archer climbed to the lookout's rest on the masthead to watch over the surroundings.

And so the hot afternoon, the first afternoon ashore on a mythical land proven real, was spent in light chores, splashing, laughter, a growing familiarity with the new place, while the surrounding woods and marshes rang with the shrill rasp of cicadas and the tunes of songbirds.

Madoc reclined in the shallow water, leaning back on his elbows, eyes shut, the sunlight on his eyelids creating patterns of drifting yellow and red, and daydreamed of his wife Annesta, slim and pale and half a world away. He was in a state of well-being, almost bliss, but hungry. Pray the hunters luck, he thought. Just then Riryd's voice crooned nearby where he lolled in the water:

"Ai, but this is a seductive land! Oh, for a woman to bathe me! Even my Danna would do!"

"*Only* your wife would do," Madoc replied. "Among the corruptions of our homeland I intend to leave behind are adultery and fornication. Each man to his own wife, each wife to her own husband. I mean for God never to find cause to expel us from this Eden!"

Riryd rolled his eyes.

* * *

THE TWO SAILORS WHO HAD TAKEN THE CORACLE UP THE RIVER were also under the spell of the lush countryside, and for their own reasons were thrilled to be out of sight of the crowded ship.

The older of them, a black-bearded, white-toothed, and hairy goat of a man called Mungo, near thirty years of age, was an insatiable wencher on land and a predatory pederast at sea. Ewen, the red-haired boy with him, had come under his spell and his wing. Like the other sailors on the *Gwenan Gorn*, they had been warned that their Christian Prince Madoc abhorred the sins of Sodom and well might kill or castrate anyone caught at it, and they had had to steal their pleasures. But now finding themselves alone together in an Eden of warmth and solitude, they soon had the coracle beached in a brook's mouth and were locked together in the manner of mating dogs on a mossy bank under a willow tree.

Suddenly, through the panting of his own lust, the man Mungo heard the sweetest music his soul knew: the giggling of girls.

Pausing in his motions, he opened his eyes. There, in the ankle-deep water of the brook not five yards in front of him, was a vision beyond his fondest dreams: three brown-skinned, smiling, black-haired girls, totally nude, carrying baskets. They were not children; their breasts and hips were shapely, but their genitals were hairless, and his eyes focused there, nearly bulging out of their sockets.

Instantly, even before allowing himself time to think, Mungo forsook the orifice he had been tending with such heat and leaped off the lad to go in pursuit of the girls. Ewen himself had just opened his eyes at the sound of their laughter; his response to the sight of them was the shock and shame of one caught. He scrambled up to flee from these intruding witnesses; Mungo collided with him and fell. Mungo was on his feet again in an instant, howling with satyr's laughter, but the girls had turned with the alertness of does and were sprinting, splashing, up the creekbed into the foliage, now squealing with fright, not laughter. For a few yards Mungo chased them, a desperate Priapus hot after the quarry of his dreams. But they had vanished and their voices had fallen silent. Turning his ankle in creekbed sand, Mungo stumbled to a halt and stood there breathing deeply, his organ still erect, his expression changing from lust to anguish, and at last to fear:

Where these wild girls were, surely there must be wild men nearby.

Or, as quickly as these beautiful creatures had vanished, might they not as well be Asrai, or some other dangerous enchantresses of the wilds of this new land? Mungo suddenly felt that he was in gravest danger. He turned and limped back down the creek, where he found the boy Ewen standing fearful and sulky beside the coracle, ready to flee.

Mungo did not try to remount the boy just yet. He motioned toward the boat and muttered, "We had better catch fish."

"Are you going to tell the prince we saw people?"

"We might say we saw savages onshore while we were fishing. . . ." Mungo sighed. He knew he would never forget what he had seen. He would never stop wanting them; they would return forever in his dreams. Surely they had been enchantresses, after all. He sighed again and looked at the boy, who was pouting and wouldn't meet his eyes.

After they had been wordlessly fishing for a while, Ewen stammered, "Why did you leave me to chase them?"

"Ah, that's why ye sulk, is it, then? Why, my darlin', I only meant to catch one and give her blue beads and take her back for our prince to see, as he asked of us, now didn't he?"

AS THE SUN SANK INTO THE TREETOPS, A PAIR OF HUNTERS returned to the ship with a fawn hung between them, its legs trussed over a pole. They had hidden themselves beside a tracked place at the river's edge and shot a bronze-tipped arrow when the fawn and its dam came down to drink, and had missed the doe. The fawn was scarcely a meal's meat for the two dozen men, and when the other hunters came in empty-handed and downcast, Madoc abandoned his hope of a shore banquet of spit-roasted venison. He ordered instead that a side be boiled in the ship's kettle with the rest of the barley, to make it go further. Then, as the fire was built up on the sandbar and the kettle was being rigged over it, the coracle came into view around an upriver bend, with Mungo and the boy in it looking grim and worried. A few of the sailors who knew Mungo well nudged each other in the ribs with winks and leers. In the bottom of the boat lay no more than a dozen mulletlike fish they had speared, all quite small, black with flies.

Madoc thought, as this paltry catch was being tossed ashore: these sailors of mine are nearly useless for anything but hauling a sheet or pulling an oar. To colonize this land I'll need to bring hunters and fishers and serfs, ironsmiths and weavers, shepherds and builders and craftsmen, not just sailors.

And women, he thought. Useful men and their useful wives. Potters and tinkers and tailors . . .

"Your Highness . . ." A voice broke through his thoughts. It was hairy Mungo coming forward on the sandbar through the drifting smoke of the bonfire, limping a bit. "A word with you, my Prince?" The boy Ewen came along behind him, looking furtive.

"Yes? Speak."

Mungo glanced at the other sailors all about, then nodded toward the end of the sandbar, as if he had a secret. So Madoc strolled out toward the river with Mungo and the lad following. He stopped, looked down at the seaman from the corner of his eye and said, "What, then?"

Mungo licked his red lips, glanced at the boy, then said in a low voice to Madoc, "We saw people, sire."

Madoc took a sharp breath. "People?"

"Savages, aye, brown people! Eh, Ewen?"

The lad nodded, then glanced down and aside as Madoc's eyes met his. Quietly but intensely, Madoc demanded, "Where? How many? Did they see you? Were they hostile? Tell me something, man, this is important to us all!"

"Your Highness, not half a league up the river, on this side. We saw them on the bank, eh, boy? When they saw us, they ran off."

"W-we saw three," mumbled the boy.

"At least three there was, aye, sire," Mungo repeated, nodding with vigor, "that is to say, three is how many we saw at the edge of the woods, though there might have been many more within, sure, Your Highness."

"And had they weapons? Did you threaten them to make them run off? Tell me if there was trouble, man!"

"Oh, no trouble, sire!" Mungo exclaimed. The boy kept looking at the ground, and Madoc felt that Mungo was lying in some way about this.

"Boy," he said sternly, and drilled the youth with his eye when Ewen looked up. "Is this just as you saw it, too?" The lad nodded. Madoc glanced all around at the edges of the woods, half expecting to see an army of savages coming from anywhere. He said, "How long ago did you see these men?"

The boy glanced at Mungo and replied, "They were no men, sire, they were girls, all naked. Carrying baskets. It was when we first went up, at midday, sire."

Madoc's mouth dropped open and he seemed to swell up before their eyes. For a moment he was speechless, then he hissed: "*Midday!* And only now you come down and tell us? By Heaven!" He turned his wrath toward Mungo. "Did you not think they might be hostile? Why did you not come and warn us at once?" He started toward the camp, to prepare a defense, then stopped and turned slowly to glower at Mungo. "Naked girls, were they? Perhaps you did *not* chase them away, but frolicked the day away, to straggle in all pale-faced, with hardly enough fish to feed two men? What did you, eh, trade them the blue beads for their favors, Mungo, you knave?"

"No! No, sire, I only saw them from afar! I still have the beads—"

"*Pah!*" Madoc barked, and stalked toward the ship, calling for Riryd, calling for Rhys, the mate. Then he called back over his shoulder to Mungo and Ewen, "Get you up here! I want to know exactly how you treated those creatures, so I might know what to expect if their men come and find us! In the name of my Lord God! How can my own countrymen be so dim-brained, so heedless of duty?"

Within minutes Madoc had all the men except the cook standing guard in a half circle around the *Gwenan Gorn*, all facing the woods, wearing helmets, bucklers on their arms, and holding spears, bows, and battleaxes, all warned to watch with all their attention for savages. They stood sweating in their armor in the humid heat, wondering what such people would look like, how big they would be, how they might fight if they should attack, and, especially, how many they might be. Riryd suggested that the ship should be anchored in mid-river for safety.

"Not yet," Madoc said. "Not until we have cooked the meat. We cannot sit besieged in the water without food. And . . ." He paused, thoughtful, then said, "My hope is that if these people show themselves, they will come in peace and will make themselves our friends, if we conduct ourselves with merit. . . ."

Madoc winced and slapped himself on the cheek. Riryd slapped himself on a bicep, then his thigh. The men all around the perimeter were becoming agitated, slapping themselves and murmuring. The very air of twilight seemed to vibrate and hum, and Madoc heard high whinings around his ears. In a moment he felt himself being bitten on every exposed part of his body and face by the mosquitoes, which had come forth in a cloud with the passing of the evening sunlight. They were so thick they had to be wiped off one's eyes constantly, and to inhale was to draw them into mouth or nostrils.

"God's blood!" cried Riryd, dropping his sword and using both hands to brush and wipe at his face. "Ai! Ah! 'Tis a plague of them!" Even the cook standing amid the blue smoke of the cook fire was whirling and cringing and slapping at himself as if in a fit.

Welshmen traditionally fought naked except for their armor, and so the sailors' bodies were vulnerable everywhere except under their helmets and the soles of their feet. Through his own wincing, Madoc saw several of them flailing at themselves; others had turned about to look to him with beseeching eyes, as if he could somehow rescue them from this torment.

At first he thought there was nothing for them but to endure it. But Riryd gasped: "Brother! We must make for open water! Or we shall go mad! No man can stand this!"

"Yes! Yes," Madoc agreed in relief. His skin stung and tingled in a thousand places and his heart was racing. Though he believed that he could through force of will stand this for as long as it might continue, he knew that these common men of his had no such moral reserve to fall back on, and might indeed go mad one by one.

And so he shouted for the men to get the cook kettle and meat and the fish and coracle on board, cast off the shore lines and man the oars. With shouts and howls they all scrambled to do so, every one moving with twitching, quick motions.

Within minutes the *Gwenan Gorn*, with oars dipping and dribbling, pulled stern first out of the creek mouth and turned slowly into the river current. She withdrew from the vibrating cloud of mosquitoes as if from a veil of dark smoke, trailing wisps of them until she was midstream and the air was clear. The men were gasping and jabbering, needing desperately to scratch but wanting to row until they were far beyond the range of such tormentors, even if they had to row to the North Sea.

In the afterglow of the sunset, the ship was anchored that night in midstream a league down. The cook burned charcoal under the half-cooked stew, and skimmed a few hundred dead mosquitoes off the top of the broth, and the men at last sat, squirming and scratching and wincing, faces and fingers swollen, and gulped the one repast of their first day in the Land of Iarghal.

Sleep was nearly impossible that night; everyone writhed and moaned, itching and swollen. In the stillness of the sterncastle, very late, Madoc said to Riryd in a low voice:

"Do you know, I suspect that Mungo fellow of buggery. He'll bear watching."

Riryd groaned. "If he was stung on his cock by those bedamned mites as I was, he'll likely be buggering knotholes to relieve his itchings."

After a moment of silence Madoc replied, with no trace of mirth: "There are no knotholes in this ship! I built her of flawless timber!" Riryd snorted in the darkness, and his bed shook with laughter—or scratching. The ship was still except for the small thumpings and shiftings of restless men on the foredeck. Then Madoc's voice again:

"How do you suppose the savages protect themselves against those bug mites? Ai! Whatever they do, I should like to find it out!"

He was eager to encounter the inhabitants of this lush new land, which seemed to him so like an Eden, despite the insects. So much could be learned about the hunting and food-growing on this particular part of the globe. They could tell him more about the extent and the nature of their continent. Perhaps they would even have a knowledge of the history of Iarghal! Even answers to his questions about Carthaginians, Libyans, Greeks, and other seafarers of old who were said to have been here, so many hundreds of years before! Madoc's head was so full of racing thoughts, of satisfactions and triumphs and expectations, that even the intense itchings from his head to his toes could not distract him.

A new world! he kept thinking. Here we—I!—can begin to build a new and better world!

Great Lord on high! That Thou hast chosen *me* for this!

FOR THE NEXT MONTH, MADOC CRUISED UP THE COAST, PUTTING IN nearly every day at river mouths and vast bays and little coves. The coastline ran generally northeastward, and for much of its distance, offshore islands and bars formed a naturally protected waterway, as if God had meant to make his exploration safe from the whims of the unruly sea.

He found the coastal lands low and rich, with limitless marshlands or dense woods, and sometimes on clear days, high hills were visible far inland. The shores were bountiful with waterfowl, beyond counting and in glorious variety. The crew lived largely on fish, which could be taken with ease by hook or spear or net, and on crabs and clams and oysters, which they were learning to harvest as they became familiar with these waters. Huge middens and mounds of shells, mazes of weirs and net poles, and fire rings on the beaches, showed that many, many people harvested the sea life along this coast at times, but the camps were always abandoned when the Welshmen arrived.

Madoc took the *Gwenan Gorn* up three major estuaries; in two of them he went as far upriver as the ship would navigate, then launched the coracles to scout farther upstream, going far enough in one valley to mount foothills covered with magnificent hardwood forests, a shipbuilders' paradise.

The men grew more skillful as hunters, finding deer plentiful and almost tame, learning to get waterfowl in throw nets, even cornering and killing a small bear with their pikes. In places they found wild grapes and berries profuse, and tasted strange but delicious fruits. The scrawny crew waxed healthy, and as time went on, there was enough surplus that foods could be smoked or dried to replenish the ship's stores. The climate seemed benign, though there were a few days of squalls and deluges and treacherous fogs.

Entering a churning inlet one day, riding in between cresting swells during an ebb tide, the *Gwenan Gorn*'s bow got down in the undertow while a crest was lifting the stern, and the vessel stood on her nose for a horrible moment, on the verge of pitchpoling, everything and everyone sliding and crashing forward on the nearly vertical deck. Somehow, though, the crest rode under and lifted the bow, the stern wallowed down, and, so it seemed to Madoc, God's merciful hand guided the ship, rocking and careening, the rest of the way through the churning turquoise froth into the calm water inside. His hair stood on end as he remembered that this must have been just the same luck that carried them safely through in the blind of night when they first reached Iarghal's coast. Madoc held a prayer service for this day's deliverance, which all agreed had been a miracle; not a man had gone overboard or suffered a broken bone.

"I am learning more about the capricious might of the sea on these harmless-looking beaches and cays than the cliffs of the Irish Sea ever taught me!" Madoc exclaimed to Riryd.

They saw people on the distant shores several times during this exploration of the coast, sometimes a few figures fishing in the surfs, and once, it seemed, hundreds running along a gray-sand beach, watching the ship's passage. But when the *Gwenan Gorn* veered toward shore, they all disappeared. Twice Madoc saw smoke rising from among the dark green trees, but, going ashore, could find not a trace of fire or even a footprint. He said to Riryd, "There are souls aplenty here, but are they flesh or are they ghost?"

The man Mungo was sure they were flesh. He craned over the rail and scanned the shore like an eagle whenever the *Gwenan Gorn* was prowling the inlets. "If I see another naked wench like those before," he told a seaman, "by God I shall jump overboard after her! True I cannot swim, but I would walk to land on the sea bottom!"

As the vessel worked northeastward along this coast week after week, Madoc came to believe that this continent must be larger, much larger, than the Isles of Britain; the *Gwenan Gorn* had sailed farther along this one shore than it had in circumnavigating the whole of Britain in other voyages. His conception of his discovery grew almost overwhelming in his mind. He was beginning to suspect that it might be even as large as all Europe, or perhaps Africa. And yet so thinly peopled, it seemed. Whoever should colonize this land would have a veritable Eden full of illimitable game, wild fruits, forests for shipbuilding and town-building, grazing lands without measure, rivers and streams of pure water. And it was he who had discovered it: Madoc!

HE ACHED FOR SOME SORT OF CLOSE MEETING WITH THE ELUSIVE NAtives. As he came to know and love their land, he yearned to see them, to observe what sort of specimens they might be, and how content living in such abundance, whether they had kingdoms or fiefdoms, whether there were artisans or masons among them, whether they had spices and perfumes and remedies, whether they had horses or sheep or cattle, whether they used money, whether they worked in gold, or in the baser metals, or had gemstones, whether they had navies, what weapons their armies used—aye, whether they even *had* armies!—what or whom they worshiped, whether they had a literate priesthood with libraries or arcane knowledge like the Irish monks who had taught him so much of what he knew, whether they observed the stars and solstices as did Druids, whether they remembered the history of other seafarers who had been here in ages past . . . Madoc kept Riryd's head awhirl, wondering aloud.

"Have you observed," he said one bright, windy day as the ship returned toward the sea on the smooth waters of a bay that seemed as big as the Irish Sea, "that the land and its clime have changed their very nature in the time since our first landfall?"

"Changed?" Riryd said.

"Aye. Feel and smell this fresh and salubrious wind, and remember the steamy vapor we breathed when we first came, can you? Remember the soil there, all sand and mold? And now look at the loam we find on shore, the higher banks, the stony foundations of the earth! And the woods, how they have become taller, oaks and maples and nut trees, not soft wood. What ships could be built upon these shores we've come to!"

"Yes, yes," Riryd replied with a thoughtful nod. "I have noticed. We seem lately to be by lands more like those of home."

"Aye. Those before seemed to me more like the shores of Africa. It seems to me, brother, we have come upon a land so vast that it might have every sort of terrain and plant and animal that exist in Europe and Africa together! Think of it! And if we kept sailing northward along this very coast, might we not meet even an iced land like Thule? Think what must exist inland, where those rivers begin! And how far south might we have followed land if we had set out that way rather than this! Oh, how I want to know the length and breadth of this great Iarghal!"

"Iarghal," Riryd mused. "Or should it not be called New Cambria!"

Madoc squinted across miles of sun-glittering waters toward a hair-thin horizontal silhouette which was the seaward shore of the vast bay. With his fingertips he absently rubbed off some of the peeling skin from his sunbaked forehead. "Riryd," he said in a quiet tone, "I think every day of how this land and this discovery would have looked through the eyes of our father, who for all his excesses was the greatest Cambrian king. And I think that this should be called Owain Gwynedd Land, to honor him."

Riryd took a deep breath and gazed far. "You are modest," he said. "When I think of our brothers, they who would kill each other for the crown of our father, I am sure that if one of them had discovered this land, he would name it for himself. Have you never," he said with a mocking grin, "thought of this as Madoc's Land?"

Madoc tossed his leonine head back and uttered a short, derisive laugh. But he was flushing even under his sunburn. "Nay. 'Tis Owain Gwynedd's land."

" 'Tis good you're such a fine mariner, brother." Riryd chuckled. "Thy head isn't big enough to fit a king's crown!"

* * *

"HO!" SOMEONE CRIED FROM THE DECK. "YOUR MAJESTY! THERE is smoke!" It was Mungo, pointing forward off starboard. Madoc peered in that direction, heartbeat quickening, as ever hopeful of finding a village.

Above the treetops on the landward side of the bay hung a smudge of gray, drifting. Madoc stared hard at it to be sure; so profuse were the waterfowl and other birds in this land that several times the lookouts had mistaken rising flocks for smoke clouds.

But this, he was certain, was smoke. That shore was perhaps a league distant, ahead and downwind. "Let us go and look for people," Madoc said to Riryd, and leaned his left flank against the tiller. "Mungo!" he called, "get you up on the bow with a sounding line!" White teeth shining through his whiskers, Mungo darted forward.

Running on the wind, the *Gwenan Gorn* sliced through the choppy water toward the place where the smoke stained the sky. Madoc looked back and saw a pair of porpoises playing in the wake, jumping over each other to change sides, their snouts appearing to show smiles of the simplest pleasure; Madoc himself smiled, infected by their goodwill. Forward, most of the crewmen were leaning on the gunwales, watching ahead and chattering excitedly. The sun baked Madoc's shoulders but the wind was cool. He wore no tunic now, only a loincloth and a scabbard belt. His brawny back was still mottled with patches of peeling skin, but at last had begun to stay brown. His hair and beard had been bleached almost white by the constant sunshine.

Mungo's cry startled him. "I see boats, Majesty!"

Madoc squinted forward. There, a mere furlong ahead, lay low in the water several long objects that might have been floating logs, but with four or five people riding each one. And at the moment when Madoc saw them, they seemed to have noticed the *Gwenan Gorn* bearing in their direction. Two or three of the figures started to stand, then crouched back down, and in a moment everyone was active over a paddle. The vessels, which now could be seen to be log dugouts, all of a piece, turned toward the shore and moved with surprising swiftness in the direction of the smoke, as if pursued by the ship. "Ah, that is bad," Madoc muttered. "We've given them a scare." But it's no wonder, he thought. What must they think we are, a thing this size coming after them under a square sail!

"There is a town," Riryd said, pointing. "There where the

smoke is!" The shapes of roundish huts could be seen on the shore.

"Before God, yes!" Madoc exclaimed. "At last we'll meet these people and see how they live! And, God willing, make us some friends in this lonely land!"

But again that was not to be. Mungo raised his sounding bob and cried, "One fathom, Majesty! We're going on shoals!" And before Madoc could change course or order down the mainsail, there came a sliding, rumbling jolt that threw Riryd to his knees and made Madoc stumble and nearly fall over the tiller. The *Gwenan Gorn* was fast aground, groaning in her joints.

And the natives in their dugout boats sped on to hit the shore, leaping out and running into the town with cries of alarm that could be heard even here above the wind, two furlongs from the beach.

"Damn me!" Madoc muttered. "What an ignoble arrival! Get that mainsail in!" he shouted. It was flapping and booming, still drawing enough wind to nudge the ship more solidly onto her muddy trap.

Riryd rose and went down on the main deck to direct the work with the sail. Then he called up to Madoc: "Can we wait and float her off with the tide?"

"The tide is going out. We must pull her off now or we will be aground for hours. I want to get to that town before those people all flee. Or," he added after a pause, "if they choose to come out and attack us in their boats, we must not be sitting here helpless. To oars, all! And you, Mungo! You, Idwal! Get in the bow with poles! Now, all! Lean on!"

The oarsmen sat at their benches and, pushing instead of pulling their oars, tried to back the ship off the mud, while Mungo and Idwal set long poles against the shallow bottom of the bay and strained upon them to lift and push the bow. Mungo's muscles shone with sweat and quivered; he had his own reason for wanting to continue the pursuit of the natives as quickly as possible.

The oars churned the water; the setting poles bent. "Ai! She moved!" Mungo shouted in a groaning voice.

But scarcely a foot did the *Gwenan Gorn* back off, and then felt just as lodged as before. Madoc, impatient, glancing toward the shore, observed that hundreds of figures were scurrying and milling about among the huts, all reddish-brown-skinned and mostly naked; some people were standing on the beach looking out at the ship, while others ran northward on the shore.

At least, he thought, they probably don't realize the ignominy of our plight.

Still, he felt embarrassed, and wanted desperately to get afloat before the ebbing tide stranded the ship higher.

And so he ordered two more men to set poles in the bow, and the rest all to get aft, to shift weight in the vessel and help raise the bow. "And move those water casks back as ye come!" He had strong hopes for this maneuver, and stood expecting to feel the bow rise and slough free. But the trim did not change perceptibly, and he began to fear that the grounding might have been hard enough to stave in the bow and open seams. "Ewen lad," he said quietly to Mungo's laddie, "slip down below-deck and see if we're leaking anywhere. Then come up and tell me privately, not to alarm the crew. Do ye understand me?" The boy nodded and was gone. In the bow the four strong men were still straining on their poles, resetting them, pushing, groaning, cursing.

And on the shore there were fewer people.

Madoc sighed. Riryd came and stood close, and Madoc said to him, resignedly, "If we've sprung leaks, then we shall just have to wait here and be glad the tide's going out. We might have to make repairs at low tide. But, before God, I hate to see all those people slip away. It does look as if they're deserting their town, does't not?"

"Aye. And most swiftly."

Ewen came back up, smudged with pitch and bilge slime. "Majesty, I saw no water coming in. None at all."

"God be thanked for that. So, then, Riryd, let us not wait out the tide here! We are seaworthy!"

"No? Well, brother, you have already tried every measure I could have dreamed of to get off. Have you something else in mind?"

Madoc nodded. "Kedge on our anchor."

"Ah-ha!"

"Quick about it, though. The tide's still going, and we grow ever more firmly planted on this spot."

The little coracles were launched over the side and lashed together. The ship's anchor was lowered and hung on a beam between them. Then the anchor chain was fed out over the stern of the *Gwenan Gorn*. The boatmen paddled several yards out behind the ship, the weight of the anchor making their little coracles ride deep in the water. They managed to heave off the anchor without swamping themselves, then paddled back to the ship, where they boarded and joined the rest of the crew in hauling at the chain.

The stern rail creaked and chafed up in splinters as the iron chain strained across it. Madoc felt the stern dip slightly. At last came the soft tremor as the keel slid in the silt. He cheered the pullers. Another tremor, a few more inches. And then the ship came free so suddenly that the crewmen staggered backward with the slackened chain, and all cheered and laughed.

But with the tide going, there was scant hope of taking the ship any closer to shore. Indeed, much of the distance to the beach was now revealing itself as a tidal flat. Madoc had the men retrieve the anchor and row to a deep channel, where he anchored the *Gwenan Gorn*, then stood pondering the distant village. It now looked quite deserted.

"Before God I'll swear I want to meet those people!" he exclaimed. "But they're timid as mice!"

"I see not one living soul," said Riryd. "But I think I feel a thousand eyes upon me."

"Brother," Madoc said after a while, "I am going into that town." The resolve in his voice obviously unsettled Riryd, but he was determined. "Tomorrow when the tide is in, I want to go ashore to that town. I shall take two armed men in each coracle. You stay with the rest and keep our ship ready for flight, should events not go well."

"Brother," Riryd said in a voice strained with dread, "I would deem it safer to wait here until their curiosity brings them forth, just a boatload of emissaries. We might thus catch a few for hostages. They may seem as timid as mice, as you said, because they know not what this ship is. But if eight men walk into their town, they will see that you are merely men, not gods, and that you are only eight. They are *hundreds*!"

"True, it would be less risk to stay aboard, all of us. But I fear that if we wait for them to approach us, nothing will happen. We cannot wait forever."

THAT NIGHT THE *GWENAN GORN* LAY AT ANCHOR IN THE BAY OFFshore from the town. In the darkness before moonrise not a speck of firelight shone in the town or anywhere on shore. There was no sound but the hush of the cool night breeze and the lap of water on the hull. The moon rose enormous and yellow-orange, laying a sparkling reflection across the waters of the bay. Madoc posted a sentry in the bow and one on the sterncastle. Then he tried to sleep.

When the moon was high and white, he was still wakeful. He got up and went out into the moonlight. He murmured to the sentry who stood leaning on his spear, then stood at the rail and gazed toward the darkened town. The people had all left. Where would they be now? he thought. Hiding in the woods?

He tried to send his thoughts to them across the water.

Please stop running from me, vanishing like wraiths!

I need to know you! My destiny is here, in this same land!

I have come far to meet you. I can bring you the enlightenment of the Savior Jesus and the True God. Let us be brothers and share the bounty of this magnificent country of Iarghal . . .

Or Owain Gwynedd's Land. . . .

I wonder what they themselves call it? he thought.

It was then that he saw something on the water, not a hundred yards off.

The moonlight had reflected off something for an instant. He tensed and peered across the distance. There was a low, dark shape there, indistinctly moving. Then something near it reflected moonlight. Turning his eyes toward that, he saw that there was another long, low shadow on the bay. He heard a slight, hollow knock come across the water.

The sentry appeared at his side, helmet gleaming with moonlight, and whispered, "Sire, I heard a sound."

Madoc put a finger to his lips and pointed out over the water. "Boats," he murmured. "Now, very quiet, my man, do this. Wake my brother and bid him make no sound. Tell him the natives seem to be having a closer look at us. Then help the other sentry wake up everyone else—just as quiet, no alarm—and have them stand to arms. Very quick but quiet, I say."

By the time the sailors were all awake and posted along the gunwales with their bows and spears, Madoc had determined that some ten or twelve of the hollow-log boats were floating at a distance around the *Gwenan Gorn*. When he looked toward the east where the moon's light reflected off the bay, he could now and then see one of the boats in silhouette, with five or six people in it.

That could mean, he thought, that they are three or four times our number. God our Father, may they remain too mystified and intimidated by our ship to think of attacking us.

The moon rose to the top of the sky and began its descent while the circle of dugouts prowled at a safe distance around the ship and the Welsh sailors stood, weary but tense, waiting for something to happen. Now and then one or two of the vessels would part from the others and come slowly forward, silent, as close as a spear's throw away, then linger, with someone standing up in the boat for a better look. By the moonlight Madoc could see that the native men were erect and well-formed, that they wore only loincloths, and that they all seemed to have long, dark hair. After a few minutes, then, that particular boatload apparently would lose its nerve and the silent paddles would remove it to a distance again.

Every time one came so close, Madoc's impulse was to call out a greeting, an invitation. Riryd's notion of grabbing a few hostages had merit, if there was no other way to begin a contact, he thought; at least we could learn how to converse, if we had them in hand.

But as the night and the tension wore on in this way, Madoc's patience began to wear thin. It seemed that perhaps only the sight of the armed sailors was keeping the prowlers at their distance. He said to Riryd:

"Have the men crouch out of sight. If those savages creep closer because they think we've gone to sleep, then, by Heaven, we shall know their intentions better."

For the next hour, then, with no spearmen standing up in view, the natives did bring their boats closer. But for some reason they stayed perhaps twenty yards off. Their patience, their ability to keep their boats clear of each other without breaking silence, was ominous. Madoc could hear his own men shifting and bumping about, clearing their throats, sometimes sneezing, sometimes talking to each other, but not a breath of sound did he hear from all those brown men all around.

He saw a man stand up in one of the boats and make motions with his hands and arms. Others in the other boats did the same, and then Madoc saw paddles move and the ring of boats soon was a little tighter around the *Gwenan Gorn*. But at about ten yards out there were more hand signals, and they stopped there. Now Madoc could see that half of them held paddles, and the others crouched with bows and clubs and spears.

"This wears me ill," Riryd whispered beside him. "I've a will to shoot a crossbow at the next one who stands up."

"No. I don't want to start a conflict, I want to talk with them. My God, what I would give to know only their word for peace!" He sighed wearily. "I don't want to hurt them. I just want them to go away till daybreak. . . . Ah! I have it now, a notion to do something that will greaten their respect without hurting them.

Here's what I intend to do, and you go tell the men to stand ready in case it doesn't scare them off. . . ."

He told Riryd what he meant to do. Riryd's moonlit face broke open in a voiceless laugh, and he went down on the deck to ready the men.

Madoc went into the darkness of the sterncastle, and emerged carrying the ship's long, curved bronze sounding horn. As he stood in the moonlight placing the mouthpiece to his lips, he saw the sailors looking at him, then out at the log boats.

He took a long breath to fill his deep chest.

The purpose of the ship's horn was to sound in fog along rugged coasts and listen for the echoes from looming cliffs; sometimes it was used to summon lost shore parties back to the ship, or to call ships of a fleet together in fogs.

Riryd in his bawdy way had once compared the noise of the sounding horn to the cry of a dragon in rut. Madoc fancied it as the roar of the legendary Minotaur in the Labyrinth. Either evocation would do for an effect on the natives. Madoc blew hard.

Even before the note trailed off, the waters around the *Gwenan Gorn* had erupted in splashings, bumpings, and frightened cries. Several of the savages apparently leaped from their dugouts. One boat turned over in a flurry of splashing. Wild paddle strokes flung water as the dugouts were propelled away from the ship by their terrified occupants. As Madoc filled his lungs to blow another bellow, he could hear a chorus of screams and wails even from the distant shore.

By the time Madoc had put away the horn, all the log boats were out of sight and the night was still, except for the chuckles of Riryd and the crew.

Madoc in his weariness felt a twinge of regret. Should I have done that? he wondered. I didn't want to scare them so badly I'll never see them again; I *want* to see them!

But at least the men of the *Gwenan Gorn* could sleep.

THE FOUR LITTLE OVAL CORACLES LEFT THE SIDE OF THE MOTHER ship as the sun rose. The water of the bay was calm, smooth, pewter-colored.

The boats wallowed along slowly, each being moved by one paddler and carrying an armed passenger. Madoc himself rode in the leading coracle, paddled by Idwal the strong-armed shipwright, who moved his hook-handled paddle in a figure-eight stroke, never lifting it from the water. Madoc would have been a heavy passenger even without armor. Now he was clad in a bronze breastplate embossed with the Harp and Mermaid, a set of bronze greaves, and a bronze helmet with a plume in the peak. Under his legs lay his round bronze shield, chased in silver with another Harp and Mermaid. Across his legs lay his broadsword in its jeweled scabbard. With all that, and his own armor, Idwal had a load to pull, but he was inspired by his devotion to his prince, and the honor of being his boatman and bodyguard, and he rowed hard and steady.

Madoc watched the shore for signs of the natives, and scanned the water for their boats. But he saw nothing. There was not so much as a wisp of smoke from the town. And yet it was as Riryd had said: He felt as if a thousand eyes were upon him.

When the coracles reached shore, the armed men heaved themselves up and stepped out into the water. The boatmen pulled the vessels onto the beach and then donned their own armor. One with a bow and a spear was left to guard the vessels, and Madoc led the other six across the brownish sand toward the village. He kept his sword sheathed. Behind him came Idwal, bearing a long lance upright with a small gonfalon fluttering from it, embossed with the Dragon of Cambria. One of the other armed men, coming behind, was Mungo, and he was peering intently toward the village, seeming to penetrate the doorways of all the huts as they drew near. Mungo was looking for naked girls and women, but he was disappointed. The village was truly deserted. The only sounds were of songbirds.

Madoc led his men silently, slowly, along the shoreward side of the town, never getting out of sight of the coracles, or of the *Gwenan Gorn*, which lay, a stout and tall silhouette, on the sun-silvered water of the bay. He tried to imagine how she might be perceived by someone who had never seen a ship. They might think she was a house on the water, a large house; certainly she was far bigger than any of these dwellings here. He looked back at her again, letting his eyes unfocus.

She might be perceived an island, he thought, remembering tiny islets he had seen along some coasts and bays, islets no more than thirty or forty paces across. A moving island, they might think.

Then he remembered blowing the sounding horn last night.

Nay, he thought. With that noise, and with her figurehead, if they could see it, they must, rather, guess that she's a living thing—a monster of a sort, a water dragon.

He walked on alongside the huts, which were of poles, covered with slabs of tree bark, or some with woven-grass mats that swayed a little in the morning breeze with rustling sounds. He could smell the ashes of dead fires and the pleasant odors of the herbs and leaves of various kinds that could be seen hanging from the roof poles of some of the huts whose sides were open. He could smell rank meat now and then. That odor came sometimes from deerskins and other pelts that stood half-flensed on stretching racks, apparently abandoned when the ship had caused such alarm.

But if they took the *Gwenan Gorn* to be a water dragon, a living beast, he thought, then what must they think when they see men upon her, or coming ashore from her?

That we are her children?

He laughed silently on his breath and shook his head. It was hard to see the world through the eyes of a strange people.

He stopped at the doorway of a hut that was half again as large as most of them and stooped to look in.

The room was dim, the air musky, a pleasant aroma of herbs, earth, animal hides, smoke, none of the sour odors of body waste one would have smelled in the huts of serfs back in the homeland. In fact the whole village was devoid of the kinds of street stench that prevailed in any of the European or Mediterranean towns he had been through in his travels. The room was tidy. The few implements and decorations left in it by its occupants in their flight were off the floor, hung on poles. A few pots and baskets sat on stones around the fire pit in the center. The floor was of packed and swept dirt, so worn that it had a sort of polish to it. Along two walls of the oval dwelling there were beds, set about a foot off the floor level and covered with animal skins. The room looked very comfortable, though there was not a thing in it made of metal or cloth, and he imagined he could feel the life of the family that dwelt here. As his eyes grew used to the dim light, he made out certain objects: a drum, a pretty ornament made of feathers and colorfully dyed fur, a pouch covered with artful patterns in red, white, and yellow quills, delicate as some Levantine mosaic. He thought of how Annesta his wife, a wizard of weave and stitchery, would admire it.

"I think I should like these people," he said thoughtfully to Idwal. "So clean they seem! And fond of ornament."

"That is so, sire, now as you mention it."

"I wonder if this is the home of a king or a headman. Let us see if the smaller houses have such things in them."

Madoc poked into a few more huts, followed by his little

group of bodyguards, who were more interested in keeping an eye out for the savages themselves than in examining the things they made and the way they lived. But they already knew that their prince was a curious man, who made it his business to notice far more than they would ever think of noticing, whether he was looking at the sky or the sea, at a landscape or a plant or animal upon it. His was a princely and scholarly mind; theirs were not. Such was the order of things.

Madoc was even more eager to see these people for whom he had looked so long, now that he had seen how they lived. And so, with a glance back at the beached and guarded coracles, he turned and led his men deeper into the heart of the village. Stepping among the huts along the well-trodden grassy streets, he suddenly emerged upon a wide, open area with a large post in the center, a circle of smaller posts around it. Somehow he at once felt that this was a place of worship or ceremony. It reminded him of ancient Druid sites he had seen in his homeland. Beyond it stood an enormous house, perhaps thirty paces wide, made of a framework of poles, roofed with bark. Idwal the shipwright wandered toward it, open-mouthed, intrigued by its ingenious bracing of posts, beams, and struts. Madoc followed him and went in.

"Majesty!" Idwal exclaimed. "Such a building, for not having one nail or peg, that I can see! Do ye suppose their king lives here?"

"I wonder, rather, if 'tis their church, or meetinghouse. See you, there are no beds. And those emblems hanging about, methinks they might be religious emblems of a sort." On each post there was something, a mask carved in wood, a hawk's wing, a set of antlers painted in bright colors, a great tortoiseshell, a cluster of deer hooves, the shell of a whelk, a skull of a bear, the whole skin and feathers of some glorious bird, beautiful and iridescent in the pale light from the smoke hole in the roof. Madoc inspected a shield which was made of heat-hardened leather on a hoop and painted in garish circles, surely tough enough to deflect an iron arrow point.

They must be warriors, he thought, timid though they seem. We must not presume them easy, and be off our guard . . .

A distant shout broke his musings. It came from the sentry he had left on the beach. It was repeated, "*Na! Nagash!* No!"

The boats! he thought.

He ducked out through the low doorway of the great lodge, calling his six men. Drawing his sword, he led them at a hard run back across the ceremonial ground and among the huts, now realizing how careless he had been by getting out of sight of the coracles. If these many savages cut his little band off from the boats, there well might be no escape from the hundreds of brown men. His short-legged Welshmen followed their long-legged prince, their armor and weapons clanking and clacking as they lunged to keep up, dreading the sight of hundreds of savages beyond every hut.

Madoc emerged on the beach at full tilt. The place where the boats had been drawn up on shore was crowded with dozens of native men, all tall and sinewy and long-haired, carrying clubs and spears, who were milling about, talking fast, some laughing, some sounding angry. Madoc could see in their midst the helmeted sentry he had left to guard the coracles. This sentry was grimacing with anger or fear, and dodging back and forth shouting at the natives, *"Nagash!"* and once in a while calling, "Help! Please my lord, *help*!"

Madoc stopped ten paces from the scene, uncertain whether the people were attacking, taunting the guard, or just curious and excited. He did not want to charge among so many with his few, who had abruptly stopped with him and were gaping at the mob. Just then some of the natives, hearing the clatter of their arms, turned to see them, and for the first time Madoc was gazing into the faces of the people he had sought for so many weeks along this lonely coast. His eyes widened and he gasped at their remarkable appearance. In his many voyages he had seen many peoples of strange aspect, but these were surely the most striking of all.

They resembled most, he thought, Egyptians, but craggier in their facial structure, and more muscular and erect. On seeing Madoc, they tilted their heads back and stared with intense black eyes for a moment. Then, apparently astonished by his enormous size and golden beard, they began backing away, crying, "Hai! Haya!" until even those still taunting the sentry had stopped and turned to look.

At that moment the sentry took advantage of their distraction and thrust his spear into the back of one of his tormentors. The savage emitted a loud gasp, dropped his club and slumped forward, blood gushing from his mouth.

In an instant another warrior leaped six feet with a pulsating scream and swung a club with such force that it caved in the Welshman's helmet and crushed his skull.

Madoc bellowed in dismay at the sight of that tragic violence.

Everything he had hoped for with the natives had been ruined in an instant by one quick-tempered Welsh sailor with a spear!

But there was no time to think about it. Even as the savages by the boats hesitated, and his own men stood stunned, Madoc heard voices and rushing everywhere around. He glanced back toward the village and saw hundreds—it seemed like the whole population—moving among the huts and coming toward the beach.

He had no choices now, not even time to think about a choice. If there was even the faintest chance at all of living beyond this moment, and there seemed to be none, it was by charging through the smaller number of savages, those around the coracles.

"To the boats!" he roared, and lunged down the slope toward the water's edge, his shield before him, broadsword up. He shouted at the top of his voice, that terrible, deep-lunged, growling monotone of a battle cry before which Flemings, Irishmen, and King Henry's very own Britons had quailed. At once his six armored sailors were running with him, howling their fierce Welsh rage, and for a moment it looked as if the sheer menace of their charge would clear the savages away from the boats.

But he had presumed right; they *were* warriors, and they sprang to action with incredible agility, their dark eyes wide, a yodeling sort of wail rising from every throat.

Madoc collided with them a mere ten paces from the boats. Their clubs and stone spear points slammed against his shield and glanced off his helmet, nearly stunning him, and then he was not running but wading through the mass of them, his sword whistling and slashing, slinging blood spray in every direction. "Fight in a circle!" he cried. "Guard your backs! Let none behind you!"

In that way the Welsh swung and hacked and grunted and howled through the storm of blows and screams, stepping over the forms of natives they had struck down, and in a minute were at the water's edge, among their own boats.

But they could not pause in their struggle long enough to clamber into the frail craft and shove them off. And the horde of villagers was now streaming and screaming down onto the beach: more warriors, boys, then even gray-hairs and women, and their hundreds of voices had risen to a shrill din. All were armed with sticks and clubs and rocks and were in an obvious fury.

It seemed hopeless now. For a few moments the Welshmen

fought shoulder to shoulder on the water's edge and felt charmed and indestructible, their metal shields fending off and shattering the stone projectiles that pounded them. But then a sailor toppled into the shallows, blood from a hamstrung leg reddening the water, and even before he was down there was a fatal stone spearhead in his groin. Madoc himself had swung his great bloody sword until the muscles of his right arm burned with fatigue. Then the brave Idwal the shipwright, fighting at Madoc's left side, suddenly began spewing blood from the mouth and sank to his knees, drawing his shield up over his head as he went down. Madoc could not turn his face from the assault even long enough to touch one of the coracles behind him. The brown faces were a blurring, jolting wall now, crazed eyes, white teeth bared, glossy black hair flying. Madoc felt the sting of a cut on his left shoulder but had no way of knowing how severe it was. His hand was sticky with blood from the hilt of his sword, his throat sore from thirst and shouting. He felt scarcely enough strength to swing at one more befeathered savage, but they were countless beyond the rim of his shield, all hammering and thrusting at him and pressing him farther into the shallows. There was not respite even for a prayer.

Then, through the clangor and the howling, there came a throb of deeper sound, a long, low moan.

Bit by bit the activity of the savages relented; their screaming diminished. The fury in the faces turned to panic.

The reprieve was like a miracle of deliverance given by God, and Madoc was bewildered. He stood panting as the natives began to turn, scream, and run as a frightened mob toward their village, pausing only to drag away their wounded warriors.

In the ringing pause after the struggle, Madoc realized what he had heard, and now he heard it still again: the doleful sounding horn of the *Gwenan Gorn*!

Before him on the beach and in the water's edge lay perhaps a score of fallen brown men, badly cut, their blood darkening the sand and staining the water; one or two were still moving slightly and groaning. Several wounded were limping after the fleeing mob. Among the dead savages there lay also four of the seven Welshmen who had come ashore with him. Only Mungo and two others stood near him now, their chests heaving, their bloody weapons dangling at their sides, watching the astonishing retreat. Madoc groaned with pain for their loss.

He turned. The *Gwenan Gorn*, with sail spread and oars rising and falling like walking legs of some huge beast, was racing straight in toward the shore on what was left of the high tide, her sounding horn being blown every few seconds like the roar of a dragon.

"Ha! Riryd! God bless you my brother Riryd!" Madoc cried aloud. "Ah, that man is a savior this day! Now, move, my boys! Catch our boats and put our poor dead in!" The coracles, drifting off the beach during the mayhem of the battle, were a few feet offshore, bobbing empty and light. Madoc, though just spared from certain doom, knew that not all was safe yet. The natives might rally their courage and rush back. As for the ship, she might run hard aground again even closer to shore than last time, plowing shoreward as fast as she was coming now. *Turn away*, he thought, as if to send the thought to Riryd's mind.

As if Riryd had received the thought, the vessel swung her prow around to lie broadside to, heading down the shore, and the oars shipped and mainsail coming down. Madoc could just hear Riryd's commanding voice on the wind, and it sounded sweet as the song of a bard.

Saved! There would be much praying after this—when there was time.

THE NEXT MORNING THE *GWENAN GORN* LEFT THE NEW CONTINENT astern and sailed toward the sunrise, toward Cambria. A league offshore, Madoc prayed over Idwal and the other slain sailors, and their pale bodies, weighted with ballast stones, were dropped off the side into the deep. Then Madoc mounted to the sterncastle and stood there braced on widespread legs, facing aft, his hand on Riryd's strong shoulder, watching the low, dark blue line of the shore recede. Through the sunny haze he could barely see the shapes of the mountains farther inland. His left shoulder, throbbing in its bandage, and the ache of strained sinews in his sword arm, with the weight of the burials in his heart, were reminders of the sorry outcome of his first encounter with the natives of Iarghal—Owain Gwynedd's Land—which had cast the only shadow over the bright triumph of the journey.

But that unfortunate affair with the natives, those handsome, clean, sprightly people, could be overcome on the return voyage.

"Next year," he said to Riryd, "we shall come with enough strength of numbers to meet them in council and establish a peace. Shown the True Light, they can become Christians. We will bring clerics to convert and teach them—and to uplift our own people, too—and turn their dextrous hands and healthy bodies to good industry. What a plentiful source of labor they'd be for building colonies! Aye, there's space enough in Owain Gwynedd's Land for two races to dwell together!"

"We've not got out of sight of the place," Riryd mused, "and already you're back next year building colônies! As for me, I yearn for Clochran Castle, roast lamb, mead, and the comfort o' fair flesh, ere I return to wilderness. Assure me, brother, if you can, that you can find our wee homeland across this awful great sea!"

"I am as sure of that as I was sure I'd find Iarghal."

Riryd grunted and grinned. "Eh well! Good to hear!" he said. "At least we go a-knowing there *is* a Cambria!"

CHAPTER 2

Dolwyddelan Castle, Caernarvon, Wales
Spring A.D. 1170

The little girl Gwenllian was awakened by shouts and bangs and clashes, to the smell of smoke. Her mother was there in nightdress, holding a candle that lit up her face, wild with fright.

"Get up! Hurry!" her mother hissed. "And make no cry!" The girl obeyed, mute with terror. The stone floor was cold under her bare feet. Her mother was grabbing up things in the bedchamber and hastily bundling them into a cloak. A scream from some far room of the castle echoed, quavering, and there were sounds like metal clashing on metal, far-off reverberations like furniture falling.

Meredydd, her father's bard, trembled at the door, holding in one hand his precious harp and in the other a smoking torch. He looked like a frightened hare, with his big front teeth biting his underlip and panic in his eyes. At once he led them down corridors, away from the terrible noises, down steep stairs, past the deserted scullery, down more stairs into a dank and foul-smelling passage leading past an iron dungeon door. At the end of that passage was a hatch in the wall with an iron ring, which Meredydd strained on and pulled open. The three slipped into the hewn-rock tunnel behind the hatch and huddled there in the torchlight, waiting for something. The eyes of rats glinted. From somewhere behind and below there came a chilling draft and a constant hiss, and water dripped and trickled. Gwenllian was scarcely able to think in her wordless panic, but it came to her mind that this was the terrible secret tunnel down through the mountain to the waterfall, a legend whispered about by children who lived at Dolwyddelan Castle. Never in all the six years of her life had Gwenllian been scared by anything so much as by her imaginings of the Tunnel, and now she was in it, and something unimaginably terrible was happening in the castle above.

She heard running footsteps, heavy, grating footsteps, approaching the other side of the hatch. It swung open and a huge figure, panting loudly, came stooping in.

It was her father, Madoc the Prince. The first thing Gwenllian saw of him in the torchlight was his great sword, longer than she was tall, its broad blade red with fresh blood. Then the light illuminated his face, its whole left side hideous with blood and dirt, that eye swollen shut. Gwenllian gasped, speechless. Her handsome father looked ruined; he stank of sweat and fire, and his own blood was dripping from the golden chin whiskers she had always loved to stroke. He pressed the hatch shut and locked it with its rusty iron bar.

"Go on, bard," the prince panted, "lead us down." Meredydd, who was so young that his own auburn beard was spare and flossy, bit his lip with his hare teeth once, nodded, and turned with the torch to start down the tunnel.

In the tunnel's dank updraft the torchlight wavered on the wet stone ceiling, a ceiling so low that they had to walk stooped, crabbing along sideways down the slimy slope. Gwenllian hung onto her mother's hand and followed her, trying not to fall on the steep, slippery, cold floor. Behind her came her father, still breathing desperately hard. The air was dense with rat smells and the oily smoke from the torch.

Her mother slipped and fell hard, uttering a little cry and then a groan of pain. Gwenllian, gripping her hand, almost fell, too. Her father came scrabbling down to help, his sword grating and clinking on stone. Bent almost double in the cramped space, he soothed and shushed them both, and helped his gasping, sobbing wife to rise and continue on.

"Meredydd, ye craven, wait for your betters with that light," he called down. The bard's spidery figure halted and held the torch back to light the family's way.

From the upper end of the tunnel behind them there rolled indistinct but terrifying noises, sometimes sounding like muffled shouts, sometimes like the clash of metal on metal, all distorted by echoes along the tunnel, the scuff of footfalls and hissing updraft, the constant trickle of water and the chittering of rats. Something more dreadful even than dragons was up there in their castle, Gwenllian was sure, because she had never believed her father, Madoc, would flee and hide from mere dragons. She might have thought this was just one of the bad dreams that she sometimes had, but the chill of her bruised little feet was too real. She clung to her mother's hand and, gasping and whimpering, stumbled onward and downward, inside the mountain beneath Dolwyddelan Castle.

MEREDYDD THE BARD, QUAKING, RUNNY-NOSED, BLADDER FULL TO bursting, held up the torch and picked out footing gingerly. Every emotion he had ever tried to fabricate from his poetic soul while living as a pampered court pet at Anglesey was now real and rampaging through him: anger, dismay, passion, devotion, love, and fear—fear most of all, by a hundredfold.

Meredydd had never been in danger before. Since boyhood he had been apprentice to the king's own bard, the famous Gwalchmai, fully protected by the sovereign. He had never had to think of violence, except the remote violence of the legends of which bards sang, but now he was fleeing from violence whose echoes he could still hear. Meredydd loved this giant prince whose bard he was, and Annesta whose confidant he was, and their daughter Gwenllian, whose tutor he was, but always he had loved them idyllically, loved them with the elegant phrases they inspired, loved them with dreamy songs and gleaming metaphors; his fingertips had caressed them only through the harp strings he strummed as he sang panegyrics of them. Meredydd since his apprenticeship had happily served his prince as a blithe idolater, and as a family pet while Madoc was gone a-sailing. But now that he crept quaking down a dripping, sepulchral rat hole, about to besmirch and besprinkle himself from fear, Meredydd found himself a flinching skinful of dread and bewilderment. The world as he had always thought it to be was all overturned; its enchantment was gone. He was caught in Madoc's plight.

In the year past, Meredydd had seen his charmed world begin to quake and tilt. After the king's death, while Madoc had been away discovering the Land Beyond the Sunset, the throne-crazed sons of Owain Gwynedd had turned once-united Cambria into a field of blood. First, Howell, Gwynedd's son by his Irish queen Pyvog, had ascended the throne. But his half brother Daffydd, born of Queen Chrisiant, had risen up with an army of thousands to try to unseat Howell, even though Daffydd's birthright was condemned by the Archbishop Becket because Chrisiant's marriage to her cousin the king was incestuous. Then other sons of both queens had plotted against each other, and hired assassins, until blood stained the Cambrian streams at every bridge and ford, and the smoke pall from burning castles and ports and towns had smudged the skies over all the countryside. Meredydd as poet had penned epic phrases about this upheaval: prince against prince, the clash of sword on helm and pike on shield, fumes of intrigue and boiling schemes of fratricide. But Meredydd had written it all from hearsay, safe in Madoc's Dolwyddelan Castle, which was a neutral place because Madoc, son of the king's concubine Brenda, had no claim to the throne.

Then to this ravaged country Madoc had returned last autumn, sailing in from the Irish Sea after twice crossing the Mare Atlanticum, and had clasped Meredydd's narrow shoulders between his huge hands, exclaiming, "My bard! I should have taken you with me on that voyage, to write of the great discovery and describe that glorious land! You shall come with me when we go back!" At once Madoc had set about building a fleet of ships and recruiting strong and able men and women to colonize Iarghal: carpenters and masons, weavers, farmers, shepherds, fishermen and hunters, ironsmiths, potters, charcoal burners, kiln makers, tanners and cobblers, glassblowers, jewelers and armorers, priests and scribes. With Riryd's help Madoc had acquired six seagoing ships and built three more, and these now all lay by the quay at Afon Ganol: ten ships, including his own redoubtable *Gwenan Gorn*.

But it had been this fleet-building that had at last drawn his half brothers' wrath down upon him. Each had suspected the others of plotting with Madoc to build them a navy, and so each had decided on his own to kill Madoc before he could create such a power. Thus it had happened that here at Dolwyddelan Castle, Madoc's birthplace, someone had betrayed the family this night and had let assassins in. Only by his memory from childhood had Madoc been able to send his family to this ancient escape route.

Yet even now escape was uncertain. The tunnel seemed so damnably long, the descent so slow, and perhaps the intruders themselves knew of the tunnel, for all of the princes had lived or visited at Dolwyddelan sometime in their lives. The moment of the attack, Madoc had sent a thegn running to the stables to get horses ready for the family's escape, but in these times no one could be trusted.

Meredydd was terrified. With every shaky step he took downward, he expected to meet some of Daffydd's helmeted murderers coming up. The clangor of their mayhem sounded as if it could be reverberating from either end of the tunnel.

The torch was flickering more wildly and the air smelled cleaner, like a stony mountain stream. Suddenly the cramped, hewn tunnel opened into the spacious, craggy jumble of a natural cave. Beyond, there was a steady, loud rush of falling water.

"Ah!" Madoc exclaimed, and stepped ahead. "Stay here, dear ones, with the light. I must see if our exit way is safe." He stepped into ankle-deep water and waded into the gloom, toward the rushing of the cascade. Meredydd stood shaking, torch in his right hand, harp clutched to his narrow chest. He was almost dancing with agitation; his bladder was so full that the sound of the cascade was a torture.

In less than two minutes Madoc came back into the cave. He was drenched. Water streamed from his clothes and hair and beard, and the old blood had been rinsed from his face to reveal the gash on his forehead from which bright new crimson was seeping. He was smiling.

"Come," he said. "Horses are there for us!" As they splashed toward the mouth of the cave, he said, "We have to walk through the waterfall and wade a few yards, then climb the right bank. We will be very wet and cold. Daughter, will you be brave for me, and not cry?"

Gwenllian, eyes wide with fear and bewilderment, stared at her father's wound, but did manage to nod and make that promise.

Meredydd asked timidly, "My lord, how am I to carry a torch through a waterfall?"

"Cast it away when we're out. We'll not want a light to give us away."

Meredydd stood last inside the cave mouth while the others passed, gasping, through the curtain of falling water and disappeared. Then he thrust the torch into the cascade, stood with pounding heart in the roaring darkness, wrapping his cloak around and around his harp, then stooped and stumbled forward into the waterfall.

The icy water took his breath away as it pounded on his head and shoulders and poured down through his clothes, its power almost forcing him to his knees, the cold shock making him start to piss right in his clothes. He gasped and floundered through, eyes shut. When he was out of the cascade the night air was no warmer than the water, and he stood, shuddering, just letting his bladder drain. With a sigh, then, he wiped his eyes and opened them. To his surprise, there was enough light, a lurid, foggy half light, to see by, although he knew it was past midnight. He could make out Madoc on the right bank, helping Annesta and Gwenllian climb the rocks.

"This way, bard," Madoc called to him over the rush of water. "The horses are above."

It was not until they were all mounted, shivering, with Gwenllian on a pillion behind her father's saddle, that Meredydd at last understood the reason for the dim, ruddy light that colored the mist. He looked up the face of the crag as dark horsemen led them along the rocky trail.

There at the top, whence still issued distant banging and shouting, one of the two square towers of Dolwyddelan Castle was burning like a red torch, with a halo of reddish fog. Madoc saw him looking up and said:

"My own brothers burn our birthplace. That blaze up yonder fair signals my farewell to this accursed country. God help us get safe to our ships. I am sick at heart, and yearn for my pure new land!"

THREE DAYS AFTER THE ESCAPE FROM DOLWYDDELAN CASTLE, Madoc's ten ships were being rowed down the Menai Strait toward Caernarvon Bay. South of the sunrise loomed the blue-hazed mass of Snowdon Mountain; close by on the starboard lay Anglesey's low bluffs. Here the strait was no wider than a river, and upon the bluffs, no farther away than a longbow's shot, islanders were running, watching, wondering, shouting. Never had they seen ten ships at once, except navies, and this obviously was not a navy, its ships being crowded with serfs and townsfolk, not fighting men. The people in the ships, their own faces alight with wonder, smiled and waved timidly while holding the rigging or gunwales with one hand, unaccustomed yet to being off solid land. A few were already hanging over the sides, vomiting.

Because of the narrow strait, the ships were in a single file, Madoc's *Gwenan Gorn* leading, and Riryd's *Pedr Sant*, the Saint Peter, following the line. Riryd himself captained the *Pedr Sant* this fine morning, having fought his way out of Daffydd's trap at Dolwyddelan and shown up at Afon Ganol quay riding in an oxcart under a load of hay.

The forecastle of each ship was roofed with coracles lashed on upside down; under these the passengers, some thirty to each vessel, would live for the duration of the voyage. Amidships there were bleating sheep and goats. Bags of grain and bundles of hay had been compacted into every cranny in hopes of keeping the beasts fed until they reached their new pastures beyond the Western Sea. They, too, were unused to the lack of firm ground underhoof, and their bleating was constant and pitiful. Hunting and herding dogs were tied to the ropes and rails, and they barked, whined, and howled in their misery, and dirtied the decks faster than the boys and girls assigned to the task could clean up their waste. Thus on this very first day the ships had begun to stink by midmorning. The people aboard had pots or pans to relieve themselves in, and their contents were emptied overboard instead of on the decks, but as much as they did not shit upon the decks, they vomited.

"Thanks to Heaven, anyway," Meredydd muttered, scraping his shoe soles on a cleat, "there's not room aboard for bullocks and kine, with their great puddling stools!"

In Caernarvon Bay that afternoon a briny breeze arose, and ten square sails were set, ten sails of bright striping bellied taut, and the *Gwenan Gorn*'s weathered, carven prow gashed the bay's blue water. The vessel ran ahead as if she knew the way, southwest along the peninsula of Lleyn, past Bardsey Isle, and into the chilly chop of Saint George's Channel. The brick-red sun went down behind the far-off Irish Mountains, seeming to dissolve in purple haze, and cast a ruddy path of quivering light across the waters. Then the last warm ray winked out, and the ten ships sailed on through blue dusk. Madoc would not put his fleet in anywhere in Wales now; he had bade that bloody land farewell, and he did not fear to sail at night. Each vessel burned a lantern high on the sterncastle, a constellation of ten lights on the darkened sea beneath the constellations in the sky, lights to hold the fleet together until the morning's sun.

The passengers slept ill this first night, being cold and damp from spray, sick from the rise and fall and roll, crowded with strangers and beasts on a swooping, bucking little world of decking not seven paces wide. Most were more than a league from their homes for the first time ever, and heading toward a future which was unimaginable, though it had been described to them as a paradise. Most were wretched and heaving with seasickness as the sun rose up next morning over the Cambrian Range. But Madoc was thrilled by the sight of the other nine ships' sails off afar to left and right, burnished by the golden glow of sunrise, and the familiar headland of Saint David's rising from the sea due south. They had sailed near thirty leagues since embarkation the morning before, would leave sight of

Cambria this day, and by tomorrow ought to clear Land's End. Then would come the days and nights of open sea with the Guide Star falling astern, the days growing more balmy, and the winds and finally the miraculous current, that current which seemed to be Madoc's secret possession, to carry his people westward to the new land, the paradise he had promised them. Of course, the people were wretched now, and full of fear, and he felt pity for them. But though they knew it not yet, they were a select and blessed people, he knew, the forerunners of a great race of New World Welshmen.

IN FAIR BUT WINDY WEATHER, THEN, DAY AND NIGHT, MADOC'S fleet sailed southward, past Brittany and then Iberia. Madoc's blue eyes squinted over the glittering waves. About his head the lusty winds sighed and the riggings creaked. Meredydd the Bard would sit near him and watch him hold the tiller, and listen to him tell of that western land whose legend he had proven true, and would dip a quill in ink and write down things to remember. Meredydd was now even more eager than he was fearful, which was a great deal.

Sometimes Annesta, too, would sit nearby and listen to her husband, but the sunlight was too fierce for her milky skin, and usually she would come out only at such time of day that the sterncastle deck was shadowed by the sail. On the stern they were upwind of the stinking welter of people and animals on deck.

Gwenllian their golden-haired daughter would lie on a tuffet and hear her father's tales, or watch the swaying masthead scribe the sky. Sometimes Meredydd would sit before her and teach her to play the harp, and though her hands were small and her fingers soft, she would pluck at the strings and sing a plaintive little song the wind would snatch away. Never had this family known such happiness and hope. As Madoc's head wound healed in the clean ocean air, so did the horrors of the escape from Dolwyddelan Castle fade in Gwenllian's memory like an old nightmare.

Gwenllian loved books and tales as much as she loved song. As often as she could, she persuaded her father to let Meredydd get the Bestiary out for lessons in reading. This book, which she had seen for as long as she could remember, was one of the precious objects her mother had gathered up in their flight from Dolwyddelan. Another was a Bible. The Bestiary was written in Welsh and she could read much of it herself; the Bible, in Latin, could be read only by Meredydd and her father. The priests could read it, but they were on the other ships. The books were kept in the sterncastle, in buckled wraps of leather. Madoc would allow them to be brought out only on fair and calm days, when there was no risk to them from spray or rain. Gwenllian had been taught the proper reverence for their great value. She knew that each book had required years of work to make. Once, watching Meredydd write on his poetry, she said, "You could make a Bestiary, or a Bible, could you not?"

"Why, yes, if I had a lifetime like a monk's, with nothing else to do, perhaps I could. But I am your father's bard, and so it is the Saga of Madoc the Prince that I write."

"And will't be a book like those when you finish, with pictures inside, and covered with leather and gold?"

He smiled his odd little rodent smile. "Perhaps, my dear Princess, it will be. But may it never be finished, nay, not for a long, long time!"

"What, sir!" she exclaimed. "I should think you would want it to be finished and be a book!"

Meredydd laughed his whinnying little laugh. "But, you see, the Saga of Madoc the Mariner Prince can never be finished, as long as he lives. And may he live long and long, eh?"

"Oh yes! Long and long!" Then she bent her head over the Bestiary and turned pages until she came to her favorite picture, which was a woodcut of a nobleman on horseback. She looked at it for a long while, then called to her father at the tiller:

"Oh! You forgot to bring horses to ride in the New Land!"

Madoc, golden beard full of sunlight, looked down at her and laughed. "My child, I did not forget. But our ships have not enough room for horses or oxen, nor any beasts larger than goats."

"But," she protested, "you will be king there, and the king of a land should have a fine horse to ride, but you have none. A princess should have a fine little horse, too, but I have none!"

"Nor shall any other man or woman of our kingdom have a steed. And so I shall walk the ground on my own feet, taller and more proud than any other soul, and have no less pride than any mounted king.

"And mayhap," he went on with a broad smile of happiness and well-being, "there are already horses in that vast country, that we may catch and tame to the saddle."

"Or, better," she cried, pointing to the next page, tossing her head back and laughing into the sun, "even unicorns!"

* * *

DAY BY DAY THE SUN SEEMED HIGHER OVERHEAD. ONE DAY, SNIFFing the air, Madoc declared that his fleet was at last upon the favoring current to the westward, and so then began the weeks of sailing toward the sunsets.

For a month they sailed upon that smiling sea without bad weather. Sometimes a sheep would die from heat or some sickness, and would be butchered on deck and cooked. One carpenter and an elderly smith came down with agonies in their guts and in a few days died and were buried at sea, their bodies weighted with ballast stones to make them sink. But in general the people remained well. Few were seasick anymore, except on rough days, and their spirits were good. As the ten ships plowed westward, their bright, striped sails swollen with wind and trimmed alike, the people on each vessel liked to gaze in admiration at the other nine, and often would wave at people they knew when the ships were close enough for them to recognize each other. Sometimes on calm days the captains would put men on the oars, and their rowing chants could be heard across the water. The people grew sun-browned, and the sun and spray bleached their hair and clothing, and Madoc could see that they were growing to love the sea that they had so feared at first. He would see some swarthy man or strong-jawed woman squinting at the far horizons with a serene smile, wind whipping their long hair, and his heart would swell with Welsh pride.

On a few days there were squalls and heavy seas that would bash over the sides and make the ships leap and buck, and the people would be sick and scared again, intimidated by the sea's senseless might, and children would wail and sob. But Prince Madoc knew his vessels and his captains well, and knew there was no danger on such days. After such storms the people would be relieved and cheerful, and a little less afraid of the next rough day. They were being tempered by the sea, as he could remember being tempered when he was a very young sailor-boy on his grandfather's ships, in cold seas and warm.

Little by little the people were learning when not to be alarmed, and Madoc's kinship with them increased. And every morning he would lead them in a prayer for safe passage, reminding them to respect the sea and revere God even as their hearts grew bolder. The time went by in a long succession of such heartening days, until Madoc judged that his fleet was more than halfway across the sea.

Twice on calm days Madoc summoned the nine ships' masters by his sounding horn, and they brought their vessels close by and then came in coracles to the *Gwenan Gorn*, where they conferred about incidents on their respective ships and tallied their provisions. The voyage had gone well, without delays, and so there was as yet no crisis in the quantity or condition of foodstuffs. Each crew had collected rainwater on the stormy days, and the water butts were half full even after all these weeks at sea. On all ten ships there had been some fevers, and six men and women had died of sicknesses, and one woman and infant in childbirth. But those were no more than would have died among a similar number of people ashore in their own towns—perhaps even less, with the war of princes going on back in Cambria.

In the darkness Madoc sat up suddenly. Something, he knew not what, had awakened him from a deep slumber. Annesta murmured beside him in sleepy alarm, and he heard many querying voices outside the sterncastle. He seemed to hear or feel a rubbing on the hull. He rose at once, went to the hatch and looked out onto the moonlit deck. People were crowding the gunwales, looking out and jabbering in worried tones.

There was enough wind to ruffle the sail and make the yard groan against the mast, and the ship should have been moving, yet it seemed becalmed, as if lightly aground. But it was not aground; Madoc could feel the easy rise of swells. And still there was that rubbing feel.

He hurried to the rail, just as the night steersman, the veteran Rhys, came from the tiller, breathing fast. Even in the moonlight his face showed his anxiety.

"My Prince," he murmured, "something hath hold on the rudder!"

"Aye? What!" Madoc replied. As he leaned over the rail, he could hear faint shouts from the other ships, whose lanterns he could see glowing at varying distances.

He was mystified by what he saw at the waterline.

Where moonlight burnished the water, there seemed to be floating matter everywhere. The moonlight's sheen was flecked and glinting over dark specks.

Whatever on God's ocean this is, he thought, it must be what is rubbing our hull. His scalp was tingling.

"Bring me a gaff," he told Rhys.

Madoc reached down into the water five feet below with the gaff, and through the long handle he felt the hook touch something, something firm but not hard. It was as if he had hooked something alive, and despite himself he recoiled a moment in fright. But then he turned the hook and, bracing its handle on the gunwale, began to lift. Something heavy came up from the sea, dribbling. The steersman leaned over timidly with a torch.

"By heaven, my Prince, 'tis but weeds!"

"Ah!" Madoc exclaimed, and began drawing the gaff pole in. "Be calm!" he cried to the murmuring people. "It is only sea-weeds!" But he was not so calm himself. In the legends of the sea recorded by the Irish monks, there was that of a horrid sea of weeds in mid-ocean, a mass of weeds that clogged the headway of ships and crushed them or dragged them under, a monstrous tangle of vast size, teeming with dragons, horned whales, and poisonous serpents. Many a ship that had ventured into the Western Sea was supposed to have been becalmed and engulfed in its tentacles, or swallowed by the leviathans. This legend, which he had only half believed, now came back up in his memory. If the people on his ship knew of it, they would go into panic. Madoc would not speak of it. He wondered whether Riryd, or any of the captains and mariners on the other ships, knew the legend. If they did, and spoke of it among their crews and passengers, the people might well go mad with fright.

They were even now all jabbering in fear; babies were crying. Madoc called for attention, and when they were still, he spoke.

"All my people! I tell you that you must have calm hearts and lie still. This is only a field of seaweed. When day comes, you will see that it is harmless to us, and we will row our ships out of it. I forbid you to frighten yourselves, or each other, or your children, by foolish talking. You can see that all our ships lie calm about us. Go back to your beds now. God keep you till the day comes." He ordered the mainsail lowered.

When the ship was still, Madoc stood in the moonlight for a while and tried to feel confident. He could still hear people whispering, and from the ships in the distance there was wailing and shouting. But there was nothing he could do about the fear aboard those other ships. He went back to his bed. Annesta clung to him, trembling.

"I fear," she whispered, "that there are monsters just under our ship!"

"Hush you! Gwenllian might hear!"

"She is asleep still."

"Then," said he, "be you likewise."

But no one slept.

When day dawned, the lookout called down from the masthead that the weeds lay as far as he could see in any direction. The men and women, in a sudden wave of fear that they were entrapped, thronged to the gunwales to look down, then gasped and began crying out about creatures they thought they could see swimming in the shadows under the ghastly brown-green vines and furling leaves. They howled that they were seeing dragon fish, great snaking motions, scales glistening, slitted eyes, slimy polyps.

Madoc himself peered down, with Meredydd beside him; Annesta was afraid to look for fear of what she might see. Madoc once again held his stout gaff, and kept a trident spear close by. The slimy polyps proved to be no more than air bladders branching off the seaweeds. When Madoc hauled up another great strand of weed and plopped it onto the deck, it yielded a flopping fish about the size of a hand, sharp-finned, speckled and ugly, with horns and spines; a brown crab with white spots; and a long-snouted, snakelike pipefish, two yards long and scaly. These odd little creatures Madoc thought would make the people laugh with relief at their own imaginations. Instead, many of the people at once presumed that these were only babies of the huge and equally ugly monsters they thought they had been seeing, and they grew quiet and preoccupied with dread.

As for himself, Madoc found the sea of weeds both an obstacle and a fascination. The waters here were very warm, clear and calm, and there seemed to be innumerable forms of small animal life dependent upon the mass of plants. He saw flying fishes, sea horses, snails, jellyfish, and water bugs of many kinds everywhere he looked, and he presumed that larger fish would be all about, feeding on this bounty.

If we were truly entrapped here, he thought, we'd need not starve. Net and spear would keep us fed forever.

But here the ships could not sail, and they were still far from the shores of Iarghal, their promised land. While they lay here, the people would grow deranged from fear and imaginings.

And so Madoc put the men on oars. He had the rudder lifted from its pintles and laid on deck so it would not drag in the weeds. Then he blew the sounding horn, to call the other captains' attention to what he was doing, and set his rowers to work. They were reluctant at first, as if afraid that monsters would grab their oars and pull them overboard. But Madoc urged them on, and when their chanters started, they tried to row with vigor. It was hard work indeed. Weeds entangled the oars, hung on or slithered off, making it impossible to keep a rhythm.

For a fortnight then, the ten ships of Madoc and his people flailed their oars, and the ships crawled across the seemingly endless expanse of weeds. The draft of the ships was just enough that they could pass over the weeds, but the barnacles encrusted on the hull of *Gwenan Gorn* and the other older ships created a terrible drag in the vegetation. The sun bore down, the rowers were burned and dehydrated and exhausted by mid-morning, and they began to look like skeletons. The food supplies steadily declined in the ships' larders; sheep were killed for food. And though countless little creatures were netted from the sea, they proved to be mostly shell and bone and scales. Eventually even parts of the seaweeds were being eaten, but few of the people could keep them on their stomachs. There seemed never to be a rain cloud over this steaming sea jungle, and the water in the butts was low and stagnant.

God our Father, Madoc prayed each night, deliver us to the open sea again!

THREE DAYS AFTER THE FLEET HAD CRAWLED OUT OF THE SEA OF Weeds, the setting sun vanished not on the horizon but several degrees above it, behind an enormous pile of purple clouds. For the next hour the dark mass grew higher, flickering incessantly with lightning bolts. The people watched the oncoming weather with dread in their faces, sometimes turning to look at Madoc at the tiller, as if studying him for signs of how frightened they should become. His face was set without expression, but its very stolidity was ominous.

A chill wet blast of wind parted Madoc's whiskers and whipped his hair and tunic straight out behind him. The sail boomed and split. The sailing lantern blew off its standard and spun into the sea astern. Women and children screamed at the sight of the flapping sail above them and tried to crowd all at once into the shelter under the coracles on the forecastle.

In a moment dire black and tattered clouds were blowing overhead, whipped by a howling wind, and the sea was driven up into frothing peaks that overtopped the mast. With no sail, the ship threatened to go broadside and roll over. Madoc, only by seeming more ferocious than the storm itself, got the cringing men onto the oars and made them row to provide headway; then he crawled back up the sterncastle ladder and roped himself to the tiller. Twice the *Gwenan Gorn* stood on her beam ends before the oars and rudder forced her forequarter against the mountainous waves and she could ride up and over them. It was on one such swooping, rearing lift into the spuming gale that Madoc squinted for a sight of any of the other ships. Through the blur in his salt-stung eyes he thought he glimpsed one spar festooned with shredded sailcloth, just as it slid out of sight beyond a white-topped hill of water. The air was already darker than dusk, and there were no lanterns to be seen. The entire fleet except the *Gwenan Gorn* might well have been capsized already, he knew; in fact he was certain they already were, as they were less seaworthy and their captains less sea-wise.

Nine ships, each carrying thirty brave Welsh souls, all lost in moments because of his ambitious dream of a new kingdom! His heart dropped and felt as if it would shatter if it ever stopped falling. And he was not certain that he could even keep the *Gwenan Gorn* and its thirty people out of a briny dark grave. Now and then in the shrieking wind he thought he could hear his daughter and wife crying within the cabin below. He thought of the deep, cold maw of the sea waiting below to swallow his loved ones, the fish waiting to pick their bones. He squinted and tried to see, through the whipping, gloomy spray forward and below, whether the rowers were still able to work. He saw glimpses of them, momentarily lit by lightning flashes, and they seemed to be clinging to the oars for life as much as rowing with them.

Those same lightning flashes revealed the carved oaken figurehead of the *Gwenan Gorn*, rising against the white foam, climbing, climbing, until the vessel would surmount the spraying crest, tilt sickeningly forward and plunge down as if to the floor of the ocean. The vessel would shudder as if it were being twisted apart, then in another flash of white light Madoc would see the prow smash into another wall of water, and the next flash would show cataracts of brine rushing from the forecastle and back among the rowers like a mountain river.

Madoc could not even guess at the passage of time as he struggled at the bucking tiller. Even though he had roped himself to it, he was flung time and again to the deck, until his knees bled. Often he would gasp for breath and suck only water, and would weaken himself with coughing and gasping. He felt as if he had drowned a hundred times; passing under the Cave Falls at Dolwyddelan had not got him as wet as he was now.

"My God, my God!" he cried against the roar. "If Thou'lt

spare my poor people through this . . . I shall gladly die tomorrow, to satisfy the hunger of the sea for human bones!"

He squinted for an eternity into the heaving, hissing maelstrom in hopes of seeing a pale shred of sail, the black mass of a ship's hull, or some other ship's lantern that by a miracle might still be burning, but he really had no hope. He could only try to keep his own ship headed into the wind as long as human strength, his and his rowers', endured.

I am stronger than my people, he thought. But the sea is far stronger than us all. Mercy, almighty God! We were only trying to serve Thee, in a new Eden Thou discovered unto us!

SOMETIME IN THE NIGHT MADOC BECAME AWARE THAT THE LIGHTNING was no longer flashing, but the wind still howled and the sea kept piling high.

Aching everywhere, legs and hands bleeding, he wrestled the tiller and watched the blackness of night fade to gray of morning. Seeing was almost worse than imagining had been. The sail's shredded remnants, though heavy wet wool, stood straight out, crepitating in the wind. One coracle was gone and two were smashed. The crow's nest on the masthead looked like a smashed basket. The mainstay and shrouds at least were still unbroken, though they alternately stretched and sagged as the stress on the mast endlessly shifted. The sea kept pounding and shoving the ship, like Poseidon's gray-green fist, and the decks boiled with milky froth, washing casks and oars and men like flotsam to and fro. Those not rowing struggled to bail, fought to stay on foot, hung on ropes to keep from being swept off into the green-glass mountainsides of looming swells. They were fighting the battle of their lives, and had been all night.

Now, even as he watched in horror, a man Madoc knew to be a shepherd was crushed, screaming, against the gunwale by a loose water cask, and when it rolled away with the ship's motion, his broken body was floated to the other side and went writhing into the sea, to vanish. The ship's mate crawled painfully up the ladder, clinging to any handhold, and shouted to Madoc that three other men had been washed overboard during the dark hours, and that three were under the forecastle with broken fingers or limbs. A child was dead, apparently having drowned in her bed.

"Alas! Ah, alas!" the mate groaned. "Will this storm end?"

"I am praying," Madoc yelled into his ear. "But this is the sea!"

* * *

SOMETIME IN THE AFTERNOON, THE RAIN CEASED. THE WIND NO longer blew the tops off the waves. It grew darker, but at last Madoc could see a streak of yellow daylight, then a fleeting sunbeam, on the western horizon. In the dying light of day he had the sailors tighten the stays and shrouds and raise the spare mainsail. And though the seas were still as high as hills, the sail steadied the *Gwenan Gorn* so that she could again cleave the swells as she was meant to do, and truly sail. As dusk fell, Madoc had another lantern hung on the sternpost. It blew out several times in the steady wind, but at last stayed lit. He searched the night in every direction, his vision blurred by salt and fatigue-burned eyelids, but saw no other lantern anywhere. A star peeked through the dispersing clouds. The sea noise now was a steady rush, and he could hear the voices of the people below, the cries of men as their broken bones were set, the wails of children still terrified.

Then in the darkness Madoc had the sounding horn brought out and blew a long, bellowing note, stood for a while and listened for reply, then blew again. Once he thought he heard a mournful answer from afar off, a similar moan all forlorn just over the rush of wave and wind, but then heard it no more, though he blew the horn again and again for nearly an hour. Dropping down on his knee, his strength all spent, wife, daughter, and green-faced bard nearby, he prayed aloud with thanks for deliverance, asked mercy for the four souls lost at sea, and then at last beseeched:

"Our Lord God, bring into our view at break of day a sail . . . two sails . . . or happiest of all Divine gifts, all nine!"

Then he gave the tiller to a trusted sailor and went down into the sterncastle cabin, whose deck was slick with the vomit of Annesta and Gwenllian. He fell onto the damp bedding beside Annesta and plunged into exhausted sleep even while she was talking to him.

The watch pounding on the hatch awoke him at dawn, as he had ordered done. His limbs and back ached as if broken, and even his heart felt cracked. But he struggled to rise, groaning, soothed Annesta's brow with his hand, and hobbled in the lamplight like an old man, eager despite his pain to mount the sterncastle and search the horizons at first light.

The edge of dawn was silvery astern as Madoc hauled himself groaning onto the high stern deck. The ship's mate was on the tiller, and Madoc was surprised to see the man's face creased in a great grin.

"Look ye, my lord," Rhys said, and pointed off the starboard quarter over the now-tame sea. Madoc looked, and his heart leaped with joy.

Silhouetted against the silvery rim of the world, a league astern, was a tiny, square speck of sail.

His heart clenched with love and gratitude, Madoc gave a quick prayer of thanks, then rubbed his eyes and, breathing deep, searched on around the pale horizon, which now was taking on a hue of peach.

"There!" he cried, leaning forward and peering into the distance at a speck, far off the port side. "A green sail, it is! It would be the *Gryphon*!"

But the mate, staring in that same direction, exclaimed, "Nay, my lord, I beg your pardon, but it is red, and would be the *Pen Mawr*."

"No, green . . . Ah!" Madoc realized that he and the man were looking at two ships, not one, far to the south, one with a green sail, the other red. Still muttering prayers of thanks, he searched around, and around again, and again. The people on the deck below were clamoring and pointing now, having seen at least one of the distant ships. Finally Madoc had to admit that there were no more sails within the rim of the horizon. "But four of us," he cried, his face a mask of both agony and joy. "Four of our stout ships, at least, did come through that maelstrom!"

"And perhaps," Meredydd the Bard interjected, having tottered up, quavering with nausea, "perhaps, my lord, the other six did live it through as well, but were blown farther off."

"That," said Madoc, "is the best we can want, and let us pray 'tis so." But his heart ached terribly, and he had little hope that Meredydd was right. The other ships were less seaworthy than his own, and the *Gwenan Gorn* had barely survived. "Ah, my stout brother," he groaned. He was certain that Riryd must be dead, and that certainty, upon his great weary pain, was too enormous to bear if he meant to go on. He could not afford to think upon it now; too many were depending upon him for everything.

The three other ships were perhaps too far away to hear the sounding horn, but he blew upon it anyway. At this distance those on the *Gryphon* and the *Pen Mawr* might not have seen the *Gwenan Gorn* and might sail on out of sight forever. The one astern, whose sail color he could not yet make out because it was in silhouette, was closer, but its crew might not have seen the *Gwenan Gorn*, either; one could never assume.

Madoc told the mate to veer a little southward, to draw closer to the two ships there, and repeated the note of the horn. And now on the wind from astern he barely detected one low, long note; the ship astern had answered.

Good, he thought. Ah, good! Now follow me, he thought across the distance toward that distant sail. Follow me while I try to close on those two!

As the morning wore on and the sun rose, he saw that the following vessel bore a sail of brown and white stripings. Thus it would be the *Ysprid*, or Spirit, one of the new-built vessels. That gave Madoc a little hope. If the *Ysprid* had been sturdy enough to come through the storm, perhaps the other two new ones had as well.

But that would depend, of course, on the skill of their captains, and on plain luck.

Not luck, he told himself. Upon the grace of God.

By the late afternoon, Madoc had hailed the *Gryphon* and the *Pen Mawr* and overtaken them, and the *Ysprid* had caught up. The four ships lay near one another as the captains came aboard the *Gwenan Gorn* to report to Madoc how they had fared in the great storm. Five men and two children had been crushed, drowned, or washed overboard from those three ships, and four had suffered broken bones. All the coracles had been destroyed on the *Gryphon*, and two damaged on the *Pen Mawr*, but not beyond repair.

"That storm has afflicted us sorely," Madoc told his weary captains. "Six ships and their hundred and eighty souls are lost to us, and eleven of our own we saw perish." He shook his head sadly.

"My Prince," said the *Gryphon*'s captain, "we are now little more than an hundred, going to make a colony where thou hadst meant to use three hundred. Pray, dost thou think of going on? Are we enough? Wouldst thou turn back to the homeland for more ships and men? Or forsake thy plan?"

Madoc stared at the man through fatigue-sunken eyes, weighing the question. Strangely, he realized, such a reasonable question had not even entered his own mind, though he should have asked it of himself already.

"We are but days from that new land," he replied at last. "All the hazards of the terrible ocean, that we have just seen, lie between us and Cambria—and that itself a country we just escaped with our lives. No, my brave captains. I have not even thought of yielding under that blow. The founding of a peaceful state in Iarghal was given me as a sacred duty, by our Lord God who discovered it to me. An hundred strong Welsh men and women *are* enough to colonize a land!"

AND SO THEY SAILED ON.

For two bright days in bracing winds the diminished fleet plowed through the blue sea. The crow's nest of the *Gwenan Gorn* had been repaired, and manned by a sharp-eyed lookout, but he saw neither the black sail of Riryd's *Pedr Sant* nor those of the other five ships, and hope began to die. In their hearts the people resigned their countrymen to their briny graves, and tried to begin their slow recovery from grief. The ships moved swiftly westward on that unseen current through the sea that Madoc knew so well, and by the night of the second day Madoc's strong body and heart had rested until he felt himself a whole man again, though in the darkness of his cabin he lay beside the sleeping Annesta with tears in his eyes, thinking of his stalwart brother Riryd, to whom he owed his life.

Just then he heard the lookout's cry from the crow's nest: There were lights ahead!

Madoc sprang from his bed and clambered out into the windy night under a star-filled sky. He saw three yellow lights far ahead, not the white cold light of stars, and bade the crew trim the sail to pursue them across the dark. Climbing to the sterncastle deck he looked back and saw the lanterns of the *Gryphon*, *Pen Mawr*, and *Ysprid* not far behind. He could catch the lights ahead without being lost to the three ships behind. His heart beat high, full of hope. Surely among those ships ahead would be Riryd's *Pedr Sant*!

It was a long, hopeful chase through the early hours, and before dawn the distance had been so closed that Madoc blew the horn, waited, blew it again, waited, and then a third note. Then he heard a note of reply, and though it was faint, he knew the sonorous tone to be that of the *Pedr Sant*, most surely!

AT SUNRISE THE SEVEN BATTERED SHIPS ALL LAY CLOSE, BELOVED voices calling all the tidings to and fro, while Riryd was paddled across to the *Gwenan Gorn* in a coracle. He clambered onto the deck grinning with teary eyes, and he and Madoc clamped each other in a mighty embrace. Then Riryd told his tale.

"We each thought the others lost, through that first night and then the day. We saw so many planks and spars and wooden chests adrift, we thought all the other ships and folk had gone to rest below the stormy waves. But as the gale blew out, I saw first the *Bonedd*, limping with a broken spar, and then just before nightfall, the *Offa*, sailing sound and solid, though with her captain lost overboard and her mate in charge."

Madoc shook his head, his face changing from joy to remorse and back again. "Now we have three ships lost instead of six," he said. "We are some two hundred souls, many strong and skillful hands to make our colony. And, God willing, we may have another such miracle as this today, and find still another ship—or all the rest. My notion of our Lord's beneficence grows greater once again, now that my brother has been restored to life!"

"Hah!" exclaimed Riryd. "*My* brother restored to *me*, rather, for *I* knew *I* was alive!"

Madoc laughed. "Come," he said. "Today I am going to throw a pigeon into the sky. Land cannot be far ahead!"

THE NEXT EVENING A PIGEON DID NOT RETURN, AND THE FOLLOWING morning at the break of day, land was seen—but it was astern. The fleet had sailed past an island during the night, Madoc realized at once. He brought the *Gwenan Gorn* about and led the fleet south and east for a look at the land, which appeared at a distance to be mainly a low range of hills, hazy blue in the morning light.

As the ships approached, Madoc observed that the hills were overgrown with gray-green scrub, and that the low land along the shore was covered with spike-leaved shrubs and tall, fernlike trees, and edged with a beach of sand white as the snow on the Snowdonia Mountains in winter. Most remarkable in beauty, though, were the reefs and shallows that extended far offshore, ranging from limpid turquoise and aquamarine to an intense cobalt such as he had not seen since his boyhood on a voyage to the Aegean Sea. Dolphins, harbingers of good fortune, cheered the families by frolicking around the ships.

The ships were anchored in the beautiful shallows, and Madoc went ashore with sailors in three coracles. Their quick exploration proved that the island had no people, nor any source of fresh water, and so he returned to the ships and set sail again in the afternoon.

The next day three small islands were seen. One of them had a narrow, clean stream, from which the water casks were replenished. The hunters caught bright-plumed birds in cast nets. Growing on tall trees were clusters of large, hard-husked fruits, which required the use of carpenters' tools to open. Madoc, praying that they were not poisonous, tasted the juice inside, which he declared to be rather like goat's milk, and the flesh, which he thought similar to walnut, and he named them goat nuts. The crew then gathered hundreds of these and they were ferried in coracles to the anchored ships, where they were added to the diminished larders. The next morning at daybreak the fleet was again afloat, still heading westward through the incredibly blue sea, and all hearts were high. Children and adults feasted on the goat nuts, fully delighted, and the women taught themselves to make bowls from the shells. Another island was bypassed in the distance this day, and Madoc wondered why no islands had been discovered on the first voyage, there being so many.

Perhaps, he thought, the great storm blew us into a different part of the ocean. That night he did a careful sighting on the Guide Star and determined that his fleet indeed was considerably farther south than it had been on its first landing.

That deduction was strengthened by his observation the next day that the sea's current, which should have been northward now, was against the ships' bows, and warmer, and not so clear as before.

Beginning to worry about the possibility of sailing under the continent, he put the rudders over the next morning and trimmed the sails to set the fleet on a northering course, in hopes of recovering the favoring current.

On the next morning a pigeon flew and did not return. The fleet bore northward by wind alone, on no discernable current at all, in waters slightly murky and more green than blue. "I believe," he told the ship's mate, "we are near the outflow of rivers." His heart was yearning for land; he remembered the intriguing rivers he had explored the year before, and sniffed for the odors of woods and marshes. This was a very warm part of the sea, and calm, and was alive with porpoises and sharks, with fins cutting the water everywhere.

And then there came the lookout's cry:

"Land! Land ahead!"

This, Madoc soon saw, was not just another little isle. Off starboard lay a low, dark, green-gray land, stretching, it seemed, forever, without a mountain, hill, or even ridge to be seen. Madoc was mystified and a bit alarmed that it lay to the east instead of west of his fleet, but at last reassured himself that he must have sailed under some cape or peninsula and then come up its western shore when he veered northward two days ago. Indeed, this warm, murky, and calm sea in which he now sailed did seem more like a bay or gulf than like open ocean, though it was vast, with no sign of another shore to the west. The crew and the people on board, however, seemed not even to have noticed, and were simply crowding the gunwale, talking excitedly and gazing toward the coast.

"Aye, then," he said to the mate. "Let us bear in closer and follow the coast awhile, and look for a harbor."

Iarghal! he thought. *My country!*

BUT THE LAND THAT LAY UNDERFOOT WHEN THEY TOOK THE CORACLES ashore was not the lush, seductive land that he had found on the first voyage. It was instead a nearly intolerable kind of Hell, a prickly, steamy anvil upon which the sun beat down like a smith's hammer. Half the land was swamp and jungle, where roots and vines made walking impossible; the rest was hot gray sand, studded with spiky ground plants whose spear-tipped leaves pierced clothing and skin. There were fields of tough, saw-edged grasses crawling with reptiles, droning with clouds of flies and mosquitoes. For as long as they could endure the insects, Madoc and his dozen men tried to penetrate this coastal desert to see if there were better land within. In many places they could move forward only by wading in the beds of sluggish streams, and in these their sandals, and then their feet, were slashed by the oysters and barnacles that encrusted everything under the tidewater line. Snakes swam away, or hung in the trees before one's eyes at every turn. To walk was to gush sweat from every pore and gasp for breath, and every inhalation filled the mouth or nose with gnats. Once, brushing insects from his eyes, Madoc caught a glimpse of what appeared to be a long-nosed dragon, longer than a horse, scurrying into the swamp a few yards ahead. He would have thought it was his imagination, but for the distinct sound of its splashings and the cries of terror from men behind him who had seen it, too.

Because the monster had plunged into the same water they were wading, the men would go no farther forward. Madoc himself wanted to turn and head back for the safety of the ships, but felt it was imperative to keep probing for better ground. While he was trying to harangue the men into a bolder state of mind, one of them pointed to a small deer that had crept into the stream a few yards ahead and started drinking. A bowman, temporarily emboldened by the sight of game so close ahead, nocked an arrow. But before he could step forward and draw, the deer splashed violently in the water, trying to turn to land and flee. To their horror, the men saw that the dragon had seized the deer's neck in its great jaws and was trying to drag it under. A few moments of thrashing and splashing and nothing was left, except bloody foam drifting toward them on the surface of the stream, and even Madoc was discouraged from going farther. The men were completely unnerved and had scrambled out of the water onto the mucky bank, wailing and gasping. Now they imagined the streams full of such monsters and would not wade even to return to the coast. Thus the rest of the day was spent in climbing, crawling, and stumbling among vines and roots and spines as they retraced their way. In some places Madoc had to hack a way with his great sword, while the sweat poured stinging into his eyes and blinded him.

If this place seemed a Hell for man, it was a paradise for birds. As the Welshmen floundered along, they started up great flocks of wading birds the size of storks. White ones by thousands thundered up from the water's edge or flapped out of trees where they had been perched. Pink and scarlet ones lumbered skyward or simply rose to skim and sail a few feet above the water and land again in the shallows farther away. Huge gray pelicans sat on snags and stumps everywhere. High above flew eagles, hawks, falcons, kestrels. Amid the foliage, long-plumed birds as bright and iridescent as gems flashed as they darted through the dappled sunlight. Even in their fear, exhaustion, and discomfort, the men seemed astonished by the constant thunder of feathered wings and flashes of flying color. The thought crossed Madoc's mind that perhaps the only life that could flourish here was that whose wings could carry it quickly above the danger-infested waters.

Madoc's men were gasping and stumbling and moaning by the time they reached the lagoon where the coracles had been beached. Every man was stained by the sweaty blood seeping from grass, thorn, and shell cuts, and insect bites.

To their dismay they found that the coracles now were nowhere near water. A receding tide had taken all the water out of the lagoon, leaving between them and the sea a mucky tidal flat half a league wide, all squirming with horseshoe crabs and starfish. They would have to carry the coracles to the sea or wait till after dark when the tide returned. The ships were visible on the calm breast of the sea in the distance, now silhouetted against the sparkling water under the late afternoon's glaring sun. The mosquitoes whined over the mud flat in clouds, biting everywhere every minute. There would be no waiting here, not among these tormenters on a coastline infested with dragons.

"Pick up the coracles," Madoc said, "and let us go on."

Plodding, slipping and wheezing, sinking to their knees in the hot slime, cut again and again by the crustaceans of the tidal bed and almost maddened by the mosquitoes, the Welshmen, two on each side of a coracle, carried and dragged the little boats toward the setting sun, toward the little flotilla of anchored ships where their comrades and families waited; and those cramped hardwood decks, of which they had grown so weary in the weeks at sea, now beckoned them like a paradise of safety and comfort. Madoc slogged ahead, carrying the banner staff, grimacing and gnawing at his lips, trying to force himself to believe that he had not sailed into some insufferable purgatory instead of his dream land, Iarghal.

FOR A WEEK MADOC SAILED HIS FLEET UP THE COAST, LOOKING FOR more hospitable land. There were many pretty islands off this coast, islands with low green woods and white beaches. But the waters were full of low-tide shallows where the ships ran aground, and the coastline was confusing because what seemed to be harbors were merely straits between islands and the coast, and what seemed to be straits sometimes proved to be the wide mouths of shallow rivers. At last Madoc decided to set out for deeper waters and sail outside the coastal islands. After a few days of northerly progress with the land lying to starboard, he found the coastline veering westward, and soon was sailing that way in a milder clime. The land along this coast looked better, less like desert and jungle, and not so flat, but whenever he would land a party on what seemed to be a forested shore, it would prove to be swamp, the trees growing in fresh or brackish water. He began to wear a frown, and paced the deck with hands clasped behind him, staring at the distant shores.

Madoc was trying to envision the shape of the coasts of Iarghal, trying to imagine how he had turned up on the wrong side of a country he had first reached from the east, a land whose eastern shore had extended nearly a thousand leagues north and west, ranging from rich soil and dense hardwood forests to granite mountains and bold fjords.

Most terrible was the bothersome notion that he had, perhaps because of the great storm, missed the beautiful continent of Iarghal entirely and had strayed onto this untenable hell of a land—perhaps another continent altogether, or, at best, some huge island, the size of Britain or Thule—which could block his way to Iarghal. His thinking was further troubled by the memory of all the little islands he had seen on the way here but not on the first voyage to Iarghal. At last he sat at a table in the cabin one drizzly day as the ships sailed slowly westward, and with a piece of charcoal and two sheets of parchment before him, went through his memories and tried to create a map of the coast of Iarghal as he recalled it, and a map of this coast. When the two sketches were finished, he laid them on the table and moved them back and forth, up and down, beside each other, above and below each other, and tried to comprehend by sheer concentration, and intuition as well, how the two coastlands must relate to each other. He thought of currents and sailing times, of Guide Star measurements, of the colors of the sea and the look of the skies, all the details that were logged in his memory from the two voyages. When he had thus pondered it all several times, he was convinced in his heart and head that it was the same continent, and that he had landed farther south and west this time. He placed the two sketches where he thought they should be in relation to each other. The map from the first voyage was above and to the right of the other.

Yes, he thought. We are farther west and farther south than we were before. This wasteland we have explored must be a peninsula, perhaps the size of Italia, or so it would seem from our cruise up its western coast. The first voyage landed us somewhere on or above its eastern coast, and we went north from there. This time we must have sailed under the tip of the peninsula all unknowing, and then made our first landfall on this side. Did I not presume just that, days and days ago, before I allowed myself even to ponder upon it?

He softly pounded his great fist on the tabletop once, twice, and nodded.

To go back to that other coast we would have to sail for weeks back down and around that peninsula, recover the current, and sail northeasterly.

If my deductions are right, he reminded himself.

If not, who knows where we might sail off to in vain and never find Iarghal?

Or, he thought, looking again at his crude drawings, if I presume aright, our present course is along the underside of Iarghal Land, and that lovely eastern coast might be reached overland from this side.

But no, he thought. Where we go to make our colony, we shall go with these ships. They are our home until our colony shall have been built.

And so it seemed that there was but one thing to do. If a few more days along this coast revealed no good harbor or favorable land, he would have to turn the fleet about and retrace a way around the long peninsula, back up to the eastern coast. And he would have to do so on the faith that he had made a true deduction from his wretched, smudged-charcoal maps.

He leaned back from the table with a great sigh. Such headwork wearied him; he was a man who thought best on his feet.

His daughter Gwenllian had been hovering nearby, watching him concentrate and draw lines, and now she came forward and looked. "What is that?" she asked. He took a moment to try to explain what a map was and why he was making it.

"Then over here," she said, pointing to a drawn coastline, "draw a *krokodilos*, for this is where he lives."

"What? A *krokodilos*? Why?"

Gwenllian asked Meredydd to fetch the Bestiary, and she opened it to a page and showed him a picture. "I heard the sailors talk about the dragon in the swamp. I just knew it was a *krokodilos*."

Madoc smiled. Despite all his obsession with the fear of being lost in the new world, he finally felt calm, somehow reassured. "Very well, then, daughter," he said, and as well as he could with his large and unskilled hand, he copied the picture of the crocodile on the map in charcoal. She clapped and said:

"Now 'tis a useful map, for it shows where things really are!"

"Ah," Madoc said, and with quick strokes he drew seven little hulls with crosses for masts, under the coastline that ran westward, saying, "Here is our fleet. Now, on our first voyage, to that eastern shore, my good men killed a bear. Hast that wondrous book a picture of a bear I can draw upon that other coast?"

THE NEXT DAY BROKE WITH GLORIOUS SUNRISE AND CRYSTALLINE air, and by mid-morning Madoc could see higher ground along the shore, slopes and gentle hills. Here at last was substantial land, an end to wretched swamps, and his spirits rose. He watched intently for a harbor.

For ten or twelve leagues, then, he sailed west along an unbroken bar, looking for an inlet but seeing only sand and scrub. The lookout kept reporting that there was a calm-water channel on the inside of the bar, but hours passed with no sign of a place to enter. When the sun went down and dusk fell, there was still that uninterrupted white line of surf, barring the way to the handsome terrain beyond. Madoc's frustration was rising again. He wondered if this maddening continent had been placed in his way to punish him for the sin of Pride, after his discovery of a new world. He remembered that he had indeed felt very full of his own importance, even while acting modest for Riryd.

And so that night, as the seven ships lay at anchor with their seven lamps gleaming on the waters and the distant surf whispered on the bar, Madoc knelt on the sterncastle deck and made himself humble under God's brilliant stars.

Show me an inlet and a good harbor soon, he prayed. Do not require me to turn about and retrace that accursed shore! To turn backward would seem to show that I doubt Thy guidance!

The restive bleat of goats on the crowded deck below seemed to be the only response, and it was a mocking one.

AS IF IN ANSWER TO HIS PRAYER, AN INLET WAS REVEALED IN THE first hour of sail the next morning. It was a gap a league wide, and looked directly into the mouth of a deep, tranquil harbor flanked by wooded slopes. With high heart Madoc dropped sail and put the rowers to work. The seven ships entered the harbor in single file, their oars munching the water, bright pennants snapping in the wind, the women and children crowding forward to see the beautiful bay open around them, and Mungo the sailor standing in the bow with his sounding bob, calling out the depths.

The bay was more than two leagues wide and seven long, its northern end so distant that it could at first be seen only from the lookout's high nest. Its waters were brackish and green, obviously fed by some considerable river, and even though the tide was ebbing, there were at least two fathoms of water. Here and there on the shore, or on pilings in the shallows, stood dilapidated huts of thatch or mats, but not a person was seen. Madoc presumed these were the huts of seasonal fishermen, as the shallows were arrayed with poles in patterns that suggested fishing weirs and crabbing platforms. Along the green shores, flocks of gulls and egrets and ibises drifted like snowflakes, and pelicans skimmed over the water.

The sky over the bay was hot and pearly, and the sun beat down on the decks, baking them. The rowers poured sweat. Children were naked and sunburned, so far from their gray Welsh climes. The women's ragged shifts were sweat-sodden and clung to their skin.

By afternoon the ships, accompanied by lively escorts of dolphins, had reached the northern end of the bay, which proved to be a maze of islands, sandbars, and the mouths of several rivers and creeks meandering in through swamps. Madoc ordered the fleet to be anchored close by a long sandbar far enough offshore to avoid the clouds of mosquitoes that could be expected to infest the twilight. Then he ordered the crew of the *Gwenan Gorn* to unlash the coracles from the ship, launch them, patch their seams for watertightness, and set out two men in a boat for a quick exploration up the mouths of the tributaries. "Come back before sundown," he said. "If you can kill any game at the water's edge, do. But do not wander from the shores and get lost."

The coracles, each with a paddler and a bowman, had scarcely disappeared into the shady green jungle before a commotion of excited voices came back across the water, and Madoc's heart leaped with fear of another skirmish with natives, like that on the beach the year before. He rushed toward the sterncastle to get the sounding horn and alert the captains of the other ships, but stopped suddenly and peered over the rail.

The coracles were coming back, but not in any undue haste. They seemed burdened, low in the water. Then sharp-eyed Mungo, standing on the gunwale shading his eyes with his hands, exclaimed, "By the dink o' Saint David! They've caught some brown people!"

"Mungo, your blasphemous mouth will get you flogged!" Madoc shouted at him, but his anger was fleeting, because he was delighted to see that the boats did indeed carry one captive apiece, lying down wedged between paddler and bowman.

"They were seining in the river, sire," said a paddler as the trussed captives were lifted aboard. Two wrinkled old men, a mature woman, and a girl of about fourteen, they wore only shell necklaces. They stood huddled close together on the *Gwenan Gorn*'s crowded deck, surrounded by the curious, gaping Welsh men and women and children. One of the old men was bleeding from the corner of his mouth, and the older woman's torso was marked with welts. "They were easy to catch but hard to hold," explained the boatman.

"Were these all, or did you see others?" Madoc asked.

"Not a sight of any others, my Prince."

The captives were slender and straight with shapely limbs, even the old men. Though their dark eyes glanced constantly about in fear, they stood dignified and not cowed. The woman's hair was parted in the center and lay in a thick single braid down her back, while the girl's hung free to shoulder length, neatly cut across the front at the level of her eyebrows. Both old men had thick white crowns of hair, cut off at eyebrow level all the way around their heads. All had their wrists and ankles tightly bound, hands behind their backs.

The swarthy sailor Mungo, leering like a satyr through his glossy black beard, stooped like a troll, had pushed his way through the crowd to get next to the captive women, whom he was ogling lustfully. Now he thrust one hand into the girl's crotch and cupped the other over her buttock. In the next instant he lay facedown on the deck, gasping to regain the breath that Madoc had knocked out of him with a blow of his fist and forearm. "Tie that knave to the mast and brand his palms," Madoc growled.

The captives watched with widened eyes as that was done, and at Mungo's screaming, tears even ran down their faces. On the sterncastle, Annesta covered her mouth with her hand and turned her daughter away from the spectacle.

"Now," Madoc commanded, "loosen these people's bonds and offer them food and water. With a bit of kindness, perhaps we can make them ours, to good use."

While Mungo slumped groaning at the mast, the ship's mate put the branding iron back in the smoking brazier and knelt at the feet of the woman captive. He untied the knot and slipped off the rope. Her face showed Madoc nothing. The mate then stood behind her and tugged at the knot on her wrists. The instant she felt it loosen, she crouched and sprang through the encircling crowd, bowling over several women and children, and leaped headlong over the side. Madoc, mouth open in astonishment, watched her tawny body arch through the air, shining like gold against the dense green of the distant forest. By the time he reached the rail there was no sight of her beyond the ripples of her plunge widening on the green water.

While ordering the boatmen away to go after her, he kept

searching the intervening water, expecting to see her surface somewhere.

But he never did see her come up.

He decided that this was not the time to untie the others. Instead he had them put into an empty goat cage made of wooden poles. They were offered dippers of water through the bars, but would not drink. The coracles moved away around the sandbar and again disappeared into the green shadows of the shore.

And for much of the afternoon Madoc remained almost silent, only giving necessary orders and answering questions. He was somehow haunted by what he had seen, the golden woman arching through space without hesitation from captivity to, presumably, drowning in green water. In a strange way, it was the most beautiful thing he had ever seen. It had been a vision, meaning much.

THE DESCENDING SUN SILHOUETTED TREETOPS ACROSS THE BAY. AN evening breeze soothed the people's sun-scorched bodies. Ropes were hung over the gunwales so that those who wanted to bathe could let themselves down into the water, but few did, because of the general fear of reptiles and dragons. And many were still haunted by the thought of the native woman who had not surfaced.

It was a beautiful and comfortable evening, sky ruddy-tinged, with a sliver of new moon following the sun down. Madoc felt that the curse on this voyage was broken. Here was a good harbor in a beautiful place, with fresh water and solid ground at last. It had the same hospitable appearance as those other bays and harbors he had discovered the year before, and surely it would be just as bounteous in fish and game and wild fruits as those places on the eastern coast had been. True, it was an oppressive climate, whereas on the other coast he could have sailed northward to a more moderate latitude. But, he presumed, winters here would be more mild, and wild foods thus more plentiful; it seemed a good place to build at least a temporary colony, and Riryd was so tired of wretched landing sites that this one appeared acceptable even to him.

"We have time, and good people," Madoc waxed on, "and a world of resources to discover. Our prisoners may come to serve us well and guide us about, once we teach them our language and the priests secure their souls. Doubtless there are more of their tribe nearby, who could be taught to perform some of the labors our lost ones would have done. If in one year we do not find this place suitable, by then we shall have learned our way in this new land, and can sail off to any part we choose, and there start anew. By the good Saint David!" he exclaimed, gripping Riryd's thick wrist as his gaze swept the darkening bay and the crescent of the setting moon. "I can scarce embrace the grandeur of this notion in my head yet! We are a new race, set down by God's grace in Eden, all anew, perhaps to undo and redeem the folly of our first ancestor!"

Just one thing stained his exuberance that first night as his fleet lay sleeping at anchor under brilliant stars. The old men in the goat cage began softly singing some kind of a lament, nasal syllables ending in throaty gasps, which awoke all the people and made scalps prickle. At last he had to have the captives gagged, their mouths stuffed with wads of raw wool. The last thing Madoc noticed before he returned to the sterncastle was Mungo, still bound to the mast with his branded hands wrapped in pale linen, his eyes burning like a predator's in the lantern light, glaring at the naked captive girl in the cage. That night in his dreams Madoc saw the golden woman flying off the side of the ship to freedom, and in the dream she did not dive into the bay but became a bird and disappeared over the forest, never to return to the ship, never to be caged.

CHAPTER 3

Madoc's Colony
Late Summer A.D. 1171

Meredydd the Bard dipped a quill into the new ink he had made and wrote a word on the parchment. He squinted at it, grimaced, and whined in frustration. Then he sighed, dipped the quill again and continued the line, stopping now and then to wave away the flies and mosquitoes that droned under the thatched canopy. He was wearing only a ragged loincloth, and his bony torso was covered with mosquito bites and scabs where he had scratched his itchings. Gwenllian, where she sat nearby on the ground scribing letters in the earth with a sharp stick, looked up at him and said, "Why are you whimpering, good sir?"

He wiped the quill and sighed. "Oh, every new ink I make is a different color! Those berries I last used make it red. The ones before made it purple. This air, damp as mermaid breath, fades it in a fortnight!" He sighed again. The girl got up and stood by his shoulder. She was modestly dressed in her last silken dress, but it was soiled and torn, and clung to her sweaty skin. She looked at the page of parchment upon which he was writing.

"It is pretty," she said, "with so many colors of ink."

He turned and looked into her blue eyes, and his vexed expression dissolved. "Ah," he murmured, "how would I bear these miseries without thy childish cheer!" He sighed again. "I can make ink—after a poor fashion—but what shall I do when there is no more vellum to write upon?"

"Why," the girl asked, "would there be no more vellum?"

"Because I have about used up what we brought on the ships, and the beasts and dragons have eaten all our lambs, and so we have no lambskin to make more vellum." She looked at him in full concentration, and so he continued with the litany of worries that had been on his mind. "The very last one of our sheep was dragged off today by a *krokodilos*. Henceforth we can no longer make wool for our clothing, either. That is why our people all go about shamelessly naked, and will ever more so."

Gwenllian pursed her lips and looked at him from the corners of her eyes. She was thin and pale-skinned, affected, like everyone else in the colony, by worms. She said, "I should enjoy to go naked myself, like the other children. It is too hot to wear clothing here."

"Child, child!" he hissed at her. "Never let your father or mother hear you say such a thing! You are a princess, and must be proper!"

Putting on a prim expression, she replied, "I am quite proper. And someday when nobody has any clothing, even I, then surely they will have to say it is proper for me to wear none, either!"

Meredydd shook his head and chuckled. "Sweet child," he replied, "winter will be coming, as ye know't does even in this cauldron. By then, pray, we'll have learnt to make clothing from something, if't be only grass. And learnt to make pages to write on, too. And ink all of a color."

"If not," she said, "I shall give you this gown to write on!"

WHILE MEREDYDD AND GWENLLIAN WERE MURMURING IN THE shade, Riryd limped by. Madoc had summoned his brother, to propose another voyage. Riryd, grown thin and wearing tattered clothes gone gray with stain and mildew, came hobbling in sunlight across the beaten dirt courtyard within the palisade of pointed stakes. The ground reeked of trampled excrement and urine. Though Madoc had encouraged his people to relieve themselves in pits outside the village and keep the streets clean in the example of the native towns, they feared the world outside the palisades and reverted to their lifelong custom of emptying their chamberpots in the village streets.

Riryd entered the shade under the thatch roof of Madoc's pavilion. The buildings of the colony needed no walls, except in winter, when bark and mats were attached under the eaves. Riryd was limping from the recent bite of one of the dark-scaled swimming vipers. He had nearly died of its venom. His foot and leg were still mottled blue.

Madoc rose from his wooden throne and greeted his brother. They seated themselves on hewn benches in the middle of the room, facing each other over the fire pit, which on this hot day had no fire in it.

Annesta's handmaiden, the native girl captured the previous

year, shuffled in, bringing bowls of a spicy red tea made by steeping the root bark of an aromatic tree. She still wore nothing but her necklace, and the chain hobbles on her ankles to keep her from running away. The men sipped the tea wordlessly. Madoc found it a good tonic for the blood; it helped alleviate his lethargy in this sultry place. He had, in the year since landing here, come to ascribe all sorts of evils to the oppressive climate.

What little decorum the Welsh people had known before had loosened almost to the sort of wantonness and indolence that Madoc had always ascribed to Mediterranean and African peoples. Sometimes Madoc and Annesta felt that only they two and their daughter, and Meredydd the Bard, remained above the savage state. Going half naked in the heat, the men and women had grown lewd and promiscuous. The clergymen managed to keep themselves in some degree clothed, having had more vestments to begin the voyage with than anyone else, but they too were in patches, and went about like old, tattered vultures with their eyes raised toward the skies to avoid seeing everyone else's nakedness.

Yet, though the people copulated promiscuously in every corner, the population of the colony in its first year by this bay had not increased. Instead it had decreased by thirty souls. Six babes had been born to wives and unwed girls, but five had died in infancy. Only one had survived beyond a fortnight, that being the first son of Riryd and his wife Danna.

In that discouraging first year in Owain Gwynedd's Land, some thirty of the colonists had died. Four had been killed by the poisonous vipers, three by accidents during the building of the wharf, the church, and a food warehouse. Then twenty more had been suddenly swept away by a plague of fevers and flooded lungs, which had nearly killed thirty more. The other deaths had been of children caught and devoured thrashing in bloody water by *krokodilos* of the swamp, and one boy stung to death by some creature he had stepped on while wading.

The palisade that had been built around the village to defend it against hostile natives had been of no use, for not one savage had been seen since the arrival in the bay, except those caught the first day. Of course, the fortification had been useless against serpents, and rats from the ships, and stinging insects.

The palisade had not even succeeded in keeping the captive natives in. After a few weeks of forced servitude, or rather, resistance to it, the two elderly men had grown so sick and bony and wasted that they had simply slipped their shackles off and stolen away one night. Only the serving girl had remained, and she was sullen and silent, refusing to learn her masters' tongue or to wear clothing.

Now Madoc, with heavy heart, began his counsel with Riryd:

"Brother, this place is worse than unhealthful. Reluctantly I have come to believe it is accursed. If we stay here another year, surely we shall all be dead, or so reduced that our colony will be doomed. Our very brains I believe are mildewed. It is time to sail for that other coast." Riryd was silent, and Madoc continued:

"I should like us to begin fitting the ships and filling their larders. In ten days I believe we can be provisioned and the ships seaworthy, and sail for that salubrious eastern coast. What say you?"

Madoc had expected his brother to have little enthusiasm. Though Riryd complained constantly of the place, he showed little spirit for anything. Riryd sat studying his discolored foot and the boils and insect welts on his sweaty bare legs. Then he fixed on Madoc's eye.

"Brother," he said, "if I were to set sail from this pit of Hell, I'd not go somewhere else to build hovels in a wilderness. No, I would want to catch that northeast current that takes us home."

Madoc's eyes widened. "Go home?" he exclaimed.

"Aye! Home to Cambria, where a Welsh prince belongs."

For a time there was no sound but the murmur of voices and the squalling of children in the distance, and the irritating rasp of the insects that shrilled away ceaselessly in the oppressive heat. Some great bird emitted the shriek of a lunatic. Madoc finally began speaking, with a growl, his voice starting to rise:

"Art thou such a great fool? By Heaven! We hardly got out of that bloody land with our skins on! Surely 'tis even worse there now than then! A prince? You would be a dead prince when your foot touched shore!"

"I would go, then, to Ireland. My Clochran Castle stands there awaiting me, and I can fairly feel its cool stone walls about me."

"Damn you, Riryd! You have gone small on me!" Madoc rose from the bench and towered over his brother. "So this is the rot that has softened your head as you turned into a half-dressed sloven!"

Riryd's eyes blazed, but he did not stand up. "Indeed I am half dressed, as we all are in this improvident slough of a land! What have we to wear, when monsters unheard of devour our sheep? Indeed, what have we to eat that is palatable, when those very monsters grab our lambs? I am sick to death of fish and bottom crawlers, and scrawny venison and fowl!"

"Sick of those, you say? Why, in thy idleness as Lord of Clochran, you hunted deer and fowl as if lambs were unfit for thy stomach! Riryd, what has become of you, my ally, my boon fellow in our mission?"

"Our mission," Riryd snarled, standing up to get out from under the looming tension of his brother, "our mission has failed!"

Madoc's eyes blazed; he recoiled at the statement, which sounded to him like blasphemy.

But Riryd went on, sweeping a hand toward the little enclosed village: "This you call a kingdom? This is Owain Gwynedd's land? Our father would *cringe* at such insult to his name! A pole-and-straw hamlet, ringed by stinking waters and by green monsters that bolt down our lambs, and our children as well, you would call it by the name of Cambria's greatest king? This is your new Eden? By my great God, no, it has too many serpents for Eden! This is *exile*! And as for me, my last hope is under sail, with this detestable wilderness farther and farther astern! Remember that I, like you, am a Welsh prince, and free to do as my heart and head compel me!"

Madoc was trembling, with clenched fists, but he kept his voice low. "Yes, we are princes, and our people must not hear us quarreling like fishmongers. But even though I whisper it in your ear, brother, hear me well: If thou wouldst betray our dream even before it can begin, thou shalt have to sail away alone. You do not know the stars and the great sea as I know them. Winter's storms would catch you in the northern sea. I will not be there to guide you if you desert me. I stay in Iarghal."

Riryd replied in an equally vehement, hissing murmur. "I and my crew of the *Pedr Sant* would take our chances on the sea. I, too, am a mariner. If you deem me low and lazy, it is only because of this bedamned wasteland. I am fired now with a passion to go! My baby son will be a prince in silk and armor, not a naked heathen mucking for shellfish and roots!"

With that pronouncement, Riryd turned quickly and stalked out into the sunlight. Five strides and his blue leg began to hurt even through his indignation, and he limped out of sight toward his own pavilion, which was built in a corner where two palisade walls met.

Madoc stood glowering after him, his spirits sinking lower than they had been during any of the colony's relentless misfortunes. Will Riryd actually do as he threatens, he wondered, or is he only venting his misery? He wondered whether he might dare arrest his brother and forcibly detain him. With half a sneer he thought of how his brothers and uncles and ancestors had always handled such things in Wales. They would have beheaded him, or cut out his tongue or eyes and put him in a dungeon. But of course he could do no such thing. It was not in his heart and never had been. He had come to this new land to build a kingdom untainted by such machinations. Even to dispute openly with his brother in this depressingly intimate little colony would further demoralize the whole people, perhaps even precipitating mutiny. Madoc sighed and paced, twisting his hands behind his back.

This confrontation had confirmed his belief that unless some drastic action were taken, the colony was doomed. It needed a more hospitable place, and a climate more like that of Cambria. It needed sheep, or some other livestock that could be domesticated, and it needed more people—strong, skilled, industrious people who still acted and thought like Welshmen.

Madoc silently reviled himself for his own lack of leadership. He had been bold and resourceful at sea, and in starting to build this settlement. But the sultry, bad spirit of the place, and the evil magic of its strangeness, had gotten into the people before he had seen it happening, and he had failed to remedy it by either inspiration or discipline. To govern in this land was a task he had not learned to do. The feudal structure on which old countries stood did not exist in this colony, and could not. Between the vassals and their prince there stood no barons, no thegns, no ministers, no magistrates, no channel for handing down authority. Aside from directing construction and adjudicating disputes, Madoc realized, he had not governed. He could only admit that he was a mariner, not a ruler. It was perhaps true, what Riryd had said, that the mission *had* failed already. Madoc sighed, his heart aching. He wanted to smash or kick something—a totally alien impulse for him.

He felt a soft hand in the bend of his elbow. Annesta stood beside him, still regal and modest in a threadbare but clean robe of old velvet, wearing a gold brow band set with emeralds. Her skin was still untouched by sun, though there were welts where insects had bitten her everywhere. Annesta was the only person in the colony besides himself who let bites itch and resisted the impulse to scratch at them; thus, unlike the others, she was not covered with scabs and open sores. She alone, perhaps even better than he, had remained fully civilized, not half a savage. He realized with a pang of gratitude and love that she must be his only confidant now—she and, perhaps, Meredydd the Bard. Madoc had never been inclined to trust the priests, who seemed like ineffectual capons to him, mere chanters and confession-takers with no conception of the colony's purpose, and of no help in governing. Besides his own family, and Meredydd and Riryd, they were the only ones who could write, but what was there to be written? Anything worth noting, Meredydd was writing down in his free hours, or so he said, though Madoc had seen or heard none of it, and never demanded to, because the bard's primary duty just now was the education of Gwenllian.

"Forgive me, I did not mean to overhear," Annesta said, "but I did hear your brother's threat."

"Aye." He patted the back of her hand, and was surprised to feel a wave of such delicate self-pity that he had to bite his lip to keep tears back.

"What will you do?" she asked, and he realized that he had no ready answer. He said after a moment's thought:

"If he really does intend to return, I cannot stop him. Perhaps I could persuade him to raise another fleet over there and send it back to us with more sheep and people. He would not bring them back himself . . . unless he found the homeland even more untenable than it was when we left. Even Ireland might be all flames and blood by now. If 'twere, he would probably flee to Europe, not come back here. But . . ." He sighed again. "Even if he crossed the sea safely and could raise help to send us, what chance is there that they could return to find the place where we would be? Even I failed to land us within a hundred leagues of our former landfall, I am sure." He sighed again and returned to sit on his throne, which now seemed like nothing but a large, rough chair, so feeble was his authority. "I thank you, beloved consort, for thy soothing hand. Now, leave me awhile to ponder on Riryd, and on sailing away from this sorry place."

For the next three days, Riryd came and argued with Madoc about sailing plans. He contended that all the ships should be sailed back to Wales, or to Ireland, and that if Madoc then still wanted to return with more livestock and skilled colonists, he could do so and reestablish another colony in a more favorable part of Iarghal. This more reasonable tone made it plain that Riryd wanted to retire to his estate at Clochran, but that indeed he did not have any confidence about navigating the Great Sea without Madoc.

For a while Madoc seriously considered Riryd's proposal. Perhaps, he thought, a whole fresh start should be made, one in which the tragic mistakes of this first year could be avoided. If all went back to the homeland, then a returning mission would not have to cruise endless coasts searching for the original colony.

But then Madoc remembered the bloody, torchlit flights and escape from Cambria, and doubted that there was even a wan hope of raising another expedition. He remembered, too, the great storm at sea, the loss of his three ships and ninety souls. To return in this season would expose the ships and people to even greater hazards, both going and returning. Finally he rejected such a plan. Riryd left, muttering viciously, and that night Madoc slept with the problem still unsolved in his head. When he awoke, he seemed to have an answer. He told Riryd:

"Let as all sail together for the eastern shore. There we will rebuild, in that benign clime.

"Then, next spring, when fair sailing weather returns, I shall sail to Cambria, or Ireland if need be, and raise another fleet, and you govern the colony until my return—"

Even before he finished, he saw Riryd virtually swelling and reddening with fury.

"Ah! Ah!" Riryd jumped to his feet, waving a fist. "By my eyes, now I see your black stripe! Dupe me? Go seize my Clochran and reign there while I rot in this stinking bog?" His mouth drawn into a trembling sneer, he poured out accusing words in a spray of spittle, calling Madoc a cutthroat as sly as their murderous brother Daffydd.

Madoc lost control of his temper. Springing up from his seat, teeth bared, he slammed his forearm across Riryd's chest with all his might, sending him flailing and sprawling across the beaten-earth floor in a clatter and clanging of flying benches and pewterware. As Riryd lay there gasping for wind, Madoc hulked over him, grabbed him by the hair with one hand and under his arm with the other, hoisted him with one great heave to his feet, snaked a powerful arm around his neck and propelled him to the threshold, where he released him and watched him tumble five paces across the courtyard in a cloud of yellow dust. When the veil of fury faded from over his eyes, he became aware that people were watching from everywhere in the courtyard, some aghast, mouths hanging open, others beginning to slap themselves with laughter. Instantly his fury drained out of him and he was filled instead with self-disgust. But even then he could not bring himself to go and help Riryd up or apologize.

"He is a true son of Owain Gwynedd!" Madoc exclaimed to Annesta, who had come running in with her fingers over her mouth. "A paunch bag seething with suspicion, like all my brothers!"

He saw not another sign of Riryd that day, and would not unbend to send him an apology. He went to bed in a mood of frustration and resentment, now seriously thinking about arresting Riryd merely to get him out of the way of the decision making.

"Does even the Lord God know who of us will sail, and to where?" he muttered to Annesta, who lay tense and forlorn beside him in the darkness. It was a long time before his misery and the maddening hoots and howls and caws of the night creatures let him drop into sleep. Once he woke up just slightly, thinking how silent the night had become, but slipped back into exhausted slumber.

He was startled from his sleep by a din of roars and shrieks. The cover blew off his bed, and he was stung by driven rain. Before he could move or even think, a terrible rending and crackling sounded all around, and in the dimness he saw the thatch roof and its framework of poles and rafters lift up and fly aside. Immediately he was being drenched by a cold deluge. Annesta and Gwenllian were screaming. He grasped his wife's arm and tried to scramble with her toward their daughter's cot, but the bed at the moment was overturned by the swirling wet wind. He and Annesta were dumped onto the floor—but the floor was all fast-flowing water. They could barely cling to each other, and were tumbled and immersed whenever they tried to rise. The flow swept trunks and furniture against them and shoved them against posts and splintered poles. When he tried to encircle her waist with his arm, she was naked. Her nightdress had been torn off or swept away.

Madoc kept trying to get to the sound of his daughter's voice without losing his hold on Annesta, but the girl's cries were fainter every moment.

And then he could not hear her at all above the rush of water, the howl of wind, the crack and roar of destruction all around. The noise now was so overpowering that he could not even hear what Annesta was screaming into his ear. It sounded as if forests were falling.

The water on the floor was now flowing hard like an undertow, pulling in a direction he thought was toward the harbor, though uncertain in the tumultuous darkness. He had just gotten to his feet and lifted Annesta to stand beside him when he became aware of something massive rising and rushing close by, coming toward him. It was like the feeling in a storm at sea when a massive wave is coming, and now he thought he could see it in the charcoal darkness, a pale wall of foamy water, higher than a rooftop. Clamping an arm around Annesta's body, he gulped wet air and was immersed, lifted, and swept backward, helpless, not knowing up from down, his limbs and back pounded and scraped by hard things in the water.

Nothing was in his control except his grip on Annesta, his hold on her precious life. At one time he felt that his head was above water, and he gasped a breath. Salty water gushed into his throat and he coughed, then was underwater again before he could take a breath. His lungs felt as if they would cave in before he had another chance to gasp air, and he could only pray that Annesta was not already drowning in his arms as they tumbled blindly in the surge.

Desperate moments later he felt his feet and legs being dragged over objects, and then he and Annesta were again on the ground, being rolled and tumbled by swift water and pelted by spray. So much spume was in the scouring wind that he could breathe only by turning his face away, but he could breathe. He ached everywhere and felt the sting of salt water in cuts on his legs and back.

Annesta was still alive. She sagged in his arms, but she was coughing. Though the high water had receded from the village, the wind still howled and it was too strong to stand up in. He crawled in mud, dragging her, and eventually found the stump of a broken tree. He hugged her to it and pressed his body over hers to keep her from being blown out of his grasp. He hooked his fingers into fissures in the bark and hung on, and he prayed. Objects as big as houses rolled and scooted in the murk, but their shapes were blurred by the blown spray and the stinging brine in his eyes. Never, even in the fiercest storms at sea, had he known such powerful winds. He hung on with his cramped fingers and felt his naked wife shuddering and gasping under him, and strained for the sound of voices—particularly Gwenllian's, though he dared not have hope for her.

He prayed with an intensity beyond speakable prayer, and he hung on.

* * *

WHEN GRAY DAWN CAME, THE WIND HAD DROPPED ENOUGH THAT one could walk without being blown down, but water was still gushing and gurgling back down the shore into the bay, carrying a flotsam of vegetation, splintered wood, broken furniture, chests, shreds of cloth, thatches of grass, tree limbs, fronds, goat nuts, kegs, mats, sheepskins, and grain sacks. It was as if all the waters of the bay had been blown onto the land from west to east and now were draining back. That was all that Madoc could yet presume. Through the sheets of blown spray he could now and then glimpse the gray silhouettes of broken trees, jutting posts, jumbled wrack, tilting sections of the palisade, tangles of twisted and splintered roofing poles. Once Madoc thought he saw a person in rags climbing over something, but after a veil of spray blew through, he could see that person no more. There seemed not to be a foot of ground that was not strewn with wreckage, and water was still draining through it all. The surface of the bay was still obscured by blowing mists and sheets of rain. No part of the ground was recognizable; Madoc did not even know which way to look to see if the wharf still stood. As for the ships, he would not even let himself think of them.

THE HURRICANE WAS GONE BY MID-MORNING. MADOC FOUND A soaked piece of bed linen to clothe Annesta's nakedness, and they set out through the sodden ruins with agonized hearts to look for their daughter Gwenllian. At once they were shocked by white, blood-and-mud-smeared bodies pinned under poles and trees. Bleeding, gashed, broken-boned people were crawling and stumbling through the mud, crying the names of their mates and their young. Half-conscious, coughing children were being pulled out of the muck. Madoc could not even guess how many of his people had been killed or swept away; he was surprised to see any still alive. He stopped to help here and there, but was driven by his desperate need to find Gwenllian. Every little limb he saw protruding from the slime or debris he expected to be one of hers. To compound the horror, the land and muddy pools everywhere were squirming with the dark, poisonous water vipers, so numerous that he dreaded every step he had to take.

He recognized the broken foundation posts of the storehouse, and knew that all the colony's food, roots and nuts, dried meat and fruit, must have been strewn and lost, as well as many of the precious iron tools that had been kept there.

Then, raising his eyes once from the snake-infested ground,

he saw the direst sight of all, which wrenched from him a bellow of despair:

The ships lay stoven and skewed amongst the fallen trees, the whole fleet reduced to crushed hulls, splintered planks and booms and muddy shreds of sail, shattered spars and snarled rope, a gigantic windrow of broken hopes.

It was while he stood gaping open-mouthed and heartsick at this smashed fleet that Meredydd came toward him, leading by the hand the naked little girl Gwenllian, her delicate skin covered with blood-seeping scratches, and one eye swollen shut.

Madoc and Annesta embraced her and soothed her, and praised the bard, all of them streaming tears of relief until their hearts felt drained.

Riryd appeared soon, with his wife Danna and their infant son Owain ap Riryd. They had escaped harm because their pavilion, built within a sturdy corner of the palisade, had been only unroofed and flooded but not smashed.

A while later the captive native girl was found, huddled unhurt under a pile of thatch. Only her hobble chains had kept her from escaping in the chaos.

Madoc and Riryd examined the ships. They climbed among the wrenched hulls, then sat together on a fallen mast, looking at each other. Madoc was in his torn loincloth, legs and back stinging with untreated cuts and tormented by flies. At last Riryd said, in the most subdued tone he had used in days:

"God has settled for us our dispute."

"Aye," said Madoc. "Neither of us shall sail for Cambria."

"Nor even to the other shore of Iarghal."

"If we leave this cursed place, we must leave it by walking."

"Or," said Riryd, "by crawling."

FOR TWO DAYS THE SURVIVORS PULLED SWOLLEN WHITE CORPSES from the shallows of the bay, and muddy, bloody, broken bodies from under trees in the fallen woods. Wailing with grief, they buried them in shallow graves scooped out of the sand and muck. A steamy stillness prevailed in the hurricane's wake. Madoc drove the gravediggers to get the cadavers covered before they became too putrid and flyblown to handle. They fought buzzards and crows, crabs and insects, for the bodies of their friends and relatives. The priests had been drowned, and so Madoc had to say the rites over the graves.

Only a hundred and twenty souls had survived. Half a hundred had drowned, or been crushed, or lost. Several more seemed moribund with festering wounds. Three died from bites of the water snakes. Rats from the wrecked ships scurried everywhere, and children were bitten. The people were stunned, defeated, full of morbid fear. There was nothing to eat. The hunters were too lame or dispirited to go out into the shattered woods, among the snakes and swamp dragons. The muck of the ground was silver-specked with dead fish blown from the bay, but already those were too putrefied to eat.

It was Madoc who, at last disgusted and alarmed by the people's lethargy and self-pity, began to stride among them bellowing, "Look ye! There is food crawling at your very feet!" He showed them how to pin a water snake down with a forked stick and kill it, and told the people to build fires to roast the meat. Though loath to taste it at first, they soon found it to be palatable. Children were set to the tasks of catching crabs and killing rats. Thus starvation was staved off and soon there was not a live serpent or rat to be found anywhere.

As the people regained their strength and their will, they began to probe about, hunting lost tools and belongings. They repaired and made coracles, and began to fish again in the bay and the rivers.

Life resumed amid the wrack of the shore, but only the most rudimentary shelters were put up, mere lean-tos of wreckage, because the two princes had agreed to leave this bedamned place beside the bay. Though it had seemed a favorable site discovery more than a year ago, it now seemed to have a poisonous pall of death and evil over it. It was not a safe harbor after all, not in the face of such storms as this, and the brothers now believed that by its heat and swamps and bloodsucking midges and its murderous reptiles it would eventually sicken everyone.

IN THOSE SULTRY AND FEARFUL DAYS, ONLY MEREDYDD THE BARD gave thought to written language. Now that the priests were dead, only Meredydd, the two princes, and Annesta could read and write, and Gwenllian had half learned to read the Bestiary in Welsh and make a few words of letters, but couldn't yet read any of the Bible, because it was Latin. Meredydd knew that he would yet have to teach her to read and write in Latin. He dreaded that, because his mastery of Latin was poor. And without the priests to help him with it, he was not sure he could teach her correctly.

And so, for the time being, the whole burden of the colony's literacy was on Meredydd's shoulders. Madoc and Riryd and

Annesta had no time to think of it. By a miracle, the chest containing the Bestiary and Bible and Meredydd's harp had been found after the hurricane, undamaged, not even wet enough to have been ruined. Meredydd could play the harp in the shade of a roof of fronds and marvel that it was still intact after being carried through a waterfall in Cambria and tumbled by a tempest in Iarghal. Aside from a few flutes the people had made of cane, his harp was the only instrument of music, and it was revered among the colonists.

One day while the people were working to store foods and make coracles for the migration inland up the rivers, Meredydd made ink of charcoal, berries, and weed sap, and resumed the writing of the Saga of Madoc that he had begun on shipboard the year before. He labored over verses that told of the fearsome journey up the coast and the discovery of the bay, the year of sickness and misery, and then the storm, a tempest such as had never been seen in the Old World. He told of Madoc's valiant effort to prepare his Welshmen to move onward, to the interior of a vast and unknown land.

Madoc our Prince then didst command
All able souls to turn their hand
To gather tools and weaponry,
Such foods and clothes as yet might be,
All these in small boats to be stowed,
And in each, one strong man who rowed,
Whilst all the rest should march our way
Up rivers from that swampish bay,
To higher, cleaner, firmer land
Where Cambrians might proudly stand
On hills and meads, in fresher air,
And build Madoc his kingdom there.

CHAPTER 4

Valley of the Ala Bamu
Autumn A.D. 1171

Up the green river where Madoc had not even expected to find life, he now found towns and cities—but they were empty of life and full of death.

At the edge of a deserted village of about forty huts, he gazed up at a castle-sized mound topped with fresh earth. Sticking out of the top of the mound was a pole decorated with feathers, hawks' feet, bundles of grasses and herbs, and long, narrow strips of a fine woven cloth dyed red or black. When Madoc told some of his soldiers to go up and dig in the mound and see what was in it, they were afraid, and he had to lead them himself up the mound's steep, grassy side to the bare earth of the summit. Only a few spades and hoes and picks had been found after the hurricane, so only a few men could work.

When ten soldiers started to dig, the captive native girl began shrilling, and a sudden gust of wind made the cloth streamers flutter and writhe about the pole. Then, just as suddenly, the wind passed and the air was as close and still as it had been. The soldiers paused and looked at Madoc. "Dig," he commanded, though his nape tingled.

Barely under the surface they broke into fresh graves. Their outspillings of bones and putrid flesh, pots and jewelry, made the soldiers throw down their tools and run stumbling down off the mound. The native girl wailed and gnawed off her little finger at its first joint. This so unnerved the Welshmen standing nearby that many of them started to run. Madoc drove them back by sheer force of menace.

A few hours of digging revealed that the top of this mound was a mass grave of many men, women, and children who had died recently. Leaning close despite the stench and horrid decomposition, Madoc saw that every skull had been crushed by a blow to the right temple. Riryd, standing beside him with a rag over his face, mumbled through it, "Were all these killed in a war?"

That had been Madoc's first thought, too, but he answered, "I think not. All the blows are the same. That is never so in battle." Madoc picked up a pot and with his dirk pried out a disk of wood that sealed its opening. To his astonishment, pearls rolled out into his palm. The pot contained a fortune. Heart slamming, he plugged the pot and looked about for more. The girl below renewed her wailing and tried to run away from the mound, but could only hop and stumble with her chain hobble, and an impatient soldier knocked her down. She got up and squatted there, rocking on her haunches and sobbing, her face hidden in her tangled hair.

"Bard!" Madoc called to Meredydd, who was near her. "Can you calm that wretch and try to learn what might have happened to the people here?" Meredydd, and only Meredydd, had learned to convey and to understand a few simple words and ideas with her through vocal sounds and hand signs. Usually the girl would neither ask nor answer anything, but a few times in the year of her captivity Meredydd had penetrated her surly solitude.

So now he knelt by the naked, trembling, weeping girl and patiently, kindly, tried to get through to her attention, while Madoc and Riryd and the diggers on the mound continued ransacking the stinking graves for more treasures.

Eventually all he got from her was one sign. She put her two index fingers side by side in the sign meaning "together" and pointed them at the mound, then put the two fingers in her mouth, meaning "those who eat together with me." Then she shrieked and put her head down and ran her hand with its bloody finger stump through her hair. Meredydd left her and reluctantly climbed the mound. A skull with patches of decayed flesh still clinging to it rolled past his feet, making him dance aside. He found Madoc and Riryd huddled together over pots of pearls amid the dirt and bones, hissing in another of their whispered arguments. Riryd was saying, ". . . worthless! What value have pearls in a land of no civilized people? Nay, in a land of no *living* people!"

"Damn your gloomy vision!" Madoc snarled. "Pearls are valuable because they are pearls! They—" He saw Meredydd and stood to face him. "What, bard?"

"Excellency, the slave says only that these dead folk are her relatives. I mean that is what I think she meant. She was overcome and said nothing more. I doubt she knows more, having been held by us so long. . . ."

Madoc glowered and thought. Beside him the feathers and streamers on the pole trembled and swayed in a wisp of breeze and then hung still again. "Aye," Madoc said, "probably this was the village she and the others had come from when we caught them. But who . . . *who*, do ye suppose, killed and buried all these people?" He shook his head in perplexity, his eyes ranging over the distance.

Suddenly he leaned forward, squinting toward the horizon in the northeast, and then pointed. "Look ye yonder! There, and there!"

At first Meredydd saw nothing but the drifting dark flecks in various quadrants of the sky that he knew to be vultures. There were many drifts of them, and Meredydd said, "Do you suppose, my lord, we shall find more and yet more dead up the river as we go on?"

"I mean," Madoc said with a quiet intensity, "those . . . are they structures, or are they hills?"

Meredydd's vision was not keen, but he now could make out something extraordinary beyond the treetops, perhaps a league distant, something too level and regular in silhouette to seem a part of the terrain. Riryd, too, was looking now, and some of the soldiers as well. In the humid haze the faint outlines showed no detail. But they were like flat-topped, steep-sloped hills, or castle ramparts. Two of them stood close together in the north, and then through another gap in the trees the bard saw what seemed to be another grouping of them, farther away and more eastward. From anywhere down in the riverside village those distant shapes would not have been visible. But here where the befeathered pole stood atop this high burial mound was a height that seemed as if made for viewing those distant massifs.

"We shall go there," Madoc said softly. "If men made those, we shall meet a kind of men I did not expect to find here." Madoc said that with his usual firm confidence. But Meredydd saw something new in Madoc's eyes, something a bit fearful. . . .

A fear, Meredydd thought, suddenly feeling it himself, that they might be coming into a settled country that already had kings and castles and monuments of its own.

That would not be a comforting thought, Meredydd realized, for one coming into the country of a continent that he had hoped to found and rule.

* * *

AS THE WELSHMEN MOVED ON UP THE MEANDERING GREEN RIVER IN the next several days, their women and workmen paddling the loaded coracles and the soldiers walking in file along the well-worn riverbank paths, Madoc was astounded by the number of native villages they passed through, sometimes two or three within a league's march. They were neat villages of ten to forty huts, well-crafted of poles, woven mats, bark, fronds, and thatch, most still furnished with pots and beds and grinding stones, tools, even caches of dried foods and animal skins.

But the dwellings were empty; only the graves were full.

At each town Madoc wondered: Has there been a war? If so, where are the victors? The survivors?

At each town, the captive girl went into new paroxysms of grief, and her moanings and shrieks made everyone's hair stand on end. The long succession of lifeless communities was having its own eerie effect on the superstitions of the Welsh people. Some of the women suggested that the slave girl should be killed, or thrown ashore from the coracle in which she lay, to be left with the ghosts of her relatives, if that was indeed what these corpses were.

Two of the communities were not towns, but cities—palisade-walled cities, with hundreds of dwellings around open plazas—and in those cities stood the gigantic flat-topped earthen pyramids that Madoc had seen from atop the grave mound of the first village.

One morning Madoc, Riryd, and Meredydd stood atop one of these pyramids, gazing out over the misty green forests that stretched to every horizon. Madoc held a thick hank of strung pearls and a wide sheet of copper cut in the shape of an eagle—treasures of the kind he had found in several of the mounds. In the distance, blue with haze, he could see the flat tops of the two great mounds of the first city he had led his people through two days before, southwest of where he now stood. Far, far northward lay ranges of upland hills. In the middle distance were smudges of smoke. From all these mound tops he had espied distant smoke, but whenever a community was found, it was, like this one, abandoned.

In every direction, clouds of vultures spiraled in the sun-tinged sky. Higher, so high they were almost invisible, flew solitary eagles. Madoc looked down at the copper eagle in his hand, then gazed down into the city. In the plaza a hundred feet below, beyond the base of the long earthen staircase that he had climbed up the eastern slope of the pyramid, his people were babbling and murmuring, sitting, pacing about, looking up at him. On the riverbank a hundred yards away lay his little fleet of coracles with their cargoes, and a big, new two-wheeled wagon. Madoc gave a long sigh and shook his head.

"Death!" he exclaimed. "A whole kingdom of *death*! Not one living soul have we met in twenty leagues' marching through villages and cities! Are we to believe that corpses build cities and plant crops and then lie down in their graves to rest forever?"

Riryd shuddered. The passage through one eerie, deserted village after another had made him increasingly sullen and furtive. "We escape from a whirlwind of death, into a land where it seems no one escaped death, though the whirlwind was never here. Cursed land! In Saint David's name, why did I follow you on this voyage?" he snarled.

Madoc glowered and reminded him still again, "Your skull would be grinning atop a pike if you had stayed in Cambria, brother." He sighed again and swept another gaze around the horizons. "I do not comprehend it. These thousands of people were living this close to our colony for more than a year. Surely they knew we were there! Why did we never see them? Why did they never come?" For an instant he saw in the eye of his memory the sun-gilded form of the older captive woman diving over the side of the *Gwenan Gorn*, an image that still sometimes visited his dreams after more than a year. Perhaps she had not drowned after all, and had instead fled up this river warning these populations about the newcomers in their big boats in the bay.

Or the old men who had slipped their shackles and disappeared—perhaps they, too, had come this way, telling of their imprisonment in animal cages, telling of a man's hands being burned with a brand. . . .

How naive he had been in his hopes for an easy intercourse with the native people, Madoc thought. They were as wary and touchy as wild animals.

And yet they had been, apparently, a richly provided and civilized people. In every town, the food caches had been full of grains, roots, seeds, and vast varieties of dried meat and fish. Near every town the river and creeks were laid out with weirs and fish traps of stone or wicker. Near the towns there were huge middens of fishbones, scales, and mussel shells. Well-crafted clothing and ornaments had been left everywhere, and had been gathered up by the passing Welshmen. In the well-built temple buildings atop the mounds, Madoc had found decorative treasures like this copper eagle, or crowns made of mica. And pearls! Pearls were so plentiful they had become a burden to carry. Indeed, Madoc had ordered a wooden tumbrel wagon made to carry the accumulating treasures and foods, for the coracles were full.

The wagon had become one of the most visible, and audible, features of the migration of Madoc's Welshmen. It incorporated planks and fittings from the wrecked ships. Its wheels were as tall as a man, and each solid wheel weighed as much as two men. The wagon's tongue was fifteen feet long, and drilled with holes enough that as many as thirty workmen could be harnessed to it with pulling ropes. Smiths had fashioned wheel hubs from some of the ships' metal fittings, and though these hubs were greased several times a day with fat, they emitted squeals and squeaks that could be heard half a league away as the tumbrel banged and clunked along the riverside footpaths. The wagon was a great impediment to progress, particularly in places where the paths narrowed and axmen had to clear brush and trees to make a way for it.

By the time the Welshmen had moved through several of the abandoned native towns, it had become apparent that the natives did not make or use wheels, and that this tumbrel might well be the only wheeled vehicle in the whole land. And the sweating, staggering, exhausted men who had strained in harness to pull it along commiserated while tending their strained sinews and chafed shoulders at the end of each day's march:

"It's work for oxen, not men!"

"Or horses! Aye! These savages don't have beasts o' burden, and no roads. No wonder 'tis that they've no wheels!"

"I m'self should like to be rid o'wheels," groaned one burly laborer, whose skin had been cut through to the seeping flesh by the pull ropes. "No, by good Saint David, I am no ox, to be pulling that damned cruel burthen!"

Madoc's wife Annesta and Riryd's wife Danna, being princesses, were carried along the riverside paths in sedan chairs, each borne on the shoulders of two strong men, and were thus spared the indignity and discomfort of walking, or lolling in the coracles where bilge water and sunlight would have soiled and freckled them. The sedan chairs were made of saplings and rope. They provided a springy, swaying ride, and could be covered with light cloth to shade the women, provide privacy, and keep out the hordes of biting insects. Danna carried her baby son,

Owain ap Riryd, in her lap as she rode. One other small sedan chair had been built to convey Gwenllian, but the girl was too active and curious to enjoy being toted along like a piece of material cargo, and she preferred to walk along the riverbank paths with her mentor Meredydd, talking with him about the wonders of this country they were passing through, or learning legends, songs, and Biblical stories from him. Thus her sedan was usually available for carrying things found along the way, or sometimes adults or children too sick to walk.

Gwenllian and the bard usually paced along some thirty or forty feet behind Madoc and Riryd, where they could see the sun dapples flash off their helmets or shimmer down their broad backs and glint on their weapons, and always the girl and the bard walked in the protection of half a dozen of the princes' roughest and most dedicated thegns: burly, brindle-whiskered Celts with bulbous noses and hairy backs, who wore antlered helmets and glanced constantly into the woods as if hoping for enemies to fight. Meredydd knew these men had small brains and would be happy to die protecting the princely families. There was a strain of brutality in them that Meredydd both feared and disdained, but it was comforting to have them on all sides when walking through a land of unknowns.

Gwenllian, like her father, had been continually mystified by the disappearance of all the populations from their excellent, comfortable communities. There being yet no answer to the mystery, she now was asking Meredydd:

"We are looking for a good place to live, are we not?"

"Aye, that we are, says your father."

"And when we find a likely place, we shall have to build a town?"

"Aye, child, that we shall."

"Pray, then, why do we not just stop in one of these pretty places, whence all the people have gone away, and live here?"

Meredydd tilted his head back and looked at her along his nose, his gray incisors protruding in a smile. "Why, little Princess, that is a very canny question that you might ask your father!"

"I have asked him, and he says only, 'Because they are not ours.' "

"Then that must be his answer, Princess," Meredydd said.

"But it is not a good answer. Such a city as that last, it could be ours if we were only to move into it. No one else is there anymore!"

"I suspect," said the bard in a murmur, "two reasons he has. Those places are too full of the spirits of a dead people to make us comfortable there." Her gray-blue eyes widened, looking up at him, and he went on, "Another reason being that your father wants to build a proper castle like Dolwyddelan, on some high, rocky place by a waterfall. That is how a Welsh prince lives, you know."

She argued, "He could build a fine castle atop one of those mounds."

"Aye. But what then would he do for a waterfall?"

Gwenllian walked unspeaking for a while, thinking of what he had said. The coracles moved slowly along the sun-flashing green water, pulled by their durable paddlers. One of the bodyguard thegns walking just ahead broke wind loudly. Gwenllian snatched up the frayed hem of her gown and fanned it ahead of her, making a mock grimace that caused the bard to chuckle at her. After a while she asked the question that she had obviously been pondering: "Friend Meredydd, sir, do you really think my father fears ghosts?"

"Ghosts? What ghosts?"

"The spirits of those savages in the mounds, as you said."

"Ah! No, I think your father fears nothing. He is a brave and canny man, canny as is his daughter. But most of our people, child, they are not so. They are most superstitious. You remember how they were on the sea voyage, fearing monsters under the ship and all the like." He didn't mention how frightened he had been then.

She nodded. Then she said, "The people who lived in these towns—do you suppose they were superstitious, too?"

"I suppose all simple folk are superstitious. And our slave girl—I suppose biting off her finger was due to some dreadful urge of their enchantments."

Gwenllian sighed. "I wish they were not all dead. I so wish we could meet them and be friends. They are such a clever people, and could teach us how to eat well in this land. And I think they are pretty, too, do you not agree?"

"Pretty? I've seen only our girl . . . and two old men and a woman. But yes, the ones I have seen are handsome enough."

"Did you notice, even the old men still had teeth?"

"I had not noticed."

"They did. And I think the slave girl is beautiful. She would be very beautiful if she were happy. I saw her smile once."

"Truly? I cannot imagine when she would have had a cause to smile, the poor creature. When did you see her smile?"

"It was when one of our soldiers was flogged," Gwenllian said. "One of those who had captured her."

"Ah!" Meredydd looked aside at Gwenllian's proud and thoughtful little face as they walked along. It often surprised him, how much she noticed about the heart of a matter.

She went on: "I wish Father would set her free. He ought to."

"Why?" Meredydd inquired. "It is the right of a noble to have lesser people serve him."

Gwenllian pursed her lips and looked ahead through narrowed eyelids, thinking deep. Finally she said, "I do not think people should be made to serve others, if it is not in their nature."

"And pray tell me, child," Meredydd mocked, "why do you think it is not in her nature?"

"Because her people go naked and free as animals and birds, as you saw. Do you remember when the other woman leaped off the ship to her freedom?"

"Mm. Mhm. And so, does nakedness have something to do with freedom?"

"Oh, but yes! Anyone can see that!"

"Well, now, Princess! There is a philosophy the philosophers have never written down, not to my knowledge! If 'tis so, why does your father Madoc not go naked? He is free, having no authority above him."

"You are so silly, Sir Bard! He is not free at all. He has to carry everything. He is more a servant of us all than even the slave girl is."

"My, my!" the bard mused, afraid that she was more right than he would like to admit. "Would you say then that a king is not free?"

"A bad king could be free. But not a good one."

He walked for a long time pondering what she had said. Finally, expostulating as her tutor, he challenged her: "One day you may be Queen of Iarghal. As such, will you want to serve, or be free?"

"Good sir," she replied, "as I have told you, I wish I could go naked. That girl in her skin is more pretty than I in my gowns. Probably I would not be a good queen."

"Then, my dear Princess," he admonished her, "perhaps you should ready yourself to be a good one, and think most of all about learning to serve. It is born in a noble queen's nature to serve her people."

"Oh, of course you would say that, being my tutor!"

Meredydd smiled. He relished the child's ways of thinking. Sometimes it seemed to him that she was the most intelligent person who had come to Iarghal on the voyage—perhaps more intelligent than Madoc himself. It was true, as she had said, that much could be learned from the ways of the natives. It was obvious that they lived a bounteous life, a clean and healthful life, not by husbanding livestock, but by collecting and hunting everything the wilds provided. Without any sign of metal tools or weapons, the natives had built comfortable houses, made fishing nets and weirs and boats, carved ornaments and statues of bone and wood, formed pottery, and made beautiful jewelry of clay beads, seeds, shells, bones and feathers, copper and mica. It was remarkable that they could wrest their living from a wild land and yet have so much time left to spend on the crafting of beautiful things. He remembered the year just past, by the bay, where the Welshmen had wasted all their time in futile efforts to feed and clothe themselves in the old way of their homeland, with the meat and wool of sheep. No one had had either time or inspiration to make anything of beauty. Sometimes the entire population had lain ill with puking and runny bowels, having eaten poisonous fruits and roots. In this country the Welshmen were always hungry and knew not what was good or bad for them.

Now in this trek through the hastily abandoned towns, Meredydd had been amazed at the variety and quantity of foods that the natives knew how to gather apparently from the wilds, and also by the many remarkable crops they cultivated in the fields around the towns. In some of the houses were stored baskets and pots of meal and white grain, of larger kernel than wheat or barley or oats. There were roots and nuts of many kinds, many of them left in the mortar in the process of being pounded into flour or hung under the ceiling to dry in the air, and there were cakes of dried fruits and berries bonded together with some kind of meal and shaped by hand. There were great quantities of the seeds of grasses that the Welshmen had never thought to use, apparently harvested with great patience. These people also had harvested the leaves, stems, and flowers of certain weeds for fresh food.

In the gardens were many plants of sorts that he had never seen before. Vines grew profusely on poles and racks, bearing pods full of plump, colorful seeds. On other vines, growing along the ground, there were globular or egg-shaped things whose flesh was succulent, firm, and a little sweet. Some of these were larger than a man's head—one single fruit adequate for a day's repast!

While the procession of Welshmen had been grabbing up and devouring everything edible, Meredydd had memorized and written notations about the various foods, and where and how they seemed to have been grown and used, and had gathered seeds of many of the food plants. Something in the back of his mind had advised him that it would be prudent to do so, and Gwenllian agreed.

Evidence of the natives' skills as hunters and fishermen was everywhere. On pole racks and hoops were stretched the skins of every kind of animal large and small—deer, small mammals, birds with their complete arrays of feathers, and even bears—and, to everyone's astonishment, whole skins of the long, rough, gray-green *krokodilos* dragons that had eaten most of the Welshmen's sheep and intimidated the colonists so thoroughly. Here were a people who could kill dragons and skin them! As for fishing, there were such immense middens of fishbones and mussel shells in some places that it was apparent the natives must have dwelt here for hundreds of years.

"These people are so wise about their land and everything on it!" Meredydd had exclaimed. And he knew that Gwenllian in her childish wisdom was right: To survive at all in this new land, it would be essential to learn from the natives how to use the land's bounty. And to learn from them, the Welshmen would have to befriend them.

If, he thought, we can find any of them alive!

NO ONE WANTED TO FIND LIVING NATIVES MORE THAN DID MUNGO, Mungo of the branded hands. Not for one day in more than two years had Mungo failed to daydream about the copper-skinned women and girls who surely, he believed, must live everywhere on this continent. He did not believe they could all be dead, despite the many mass graves found in every town. Surely, many still lived beyond the greenery.

For most of the year in the colony beside the bay, Mungo had shared the bed of a bawdy young woman who was a daughter of one of the Welsh woodwrights, keeping up a semblance of a marriage though they had never been wed. She was lewd and randy enough that the priapic Mungo was the likeliest man for her. But even when thumping away in her moist white saddle, Mungo was always seeing the obsession of his mind's eye: the nude brown nymphs of the forest. Several times every day of that year Mungo had contrived to desert his duties and drift toward Madoc's pavilion, and station himself in some position to spy upon the slender slave girl who wore nothing but her shackles and a necklace. He had kept a distance from her, of course; the memory of the branding iron was still too intense in his hands. But the glimpses of her kept his dreams alive.

Until the day of his branding, Mungo had been a faithful enough subject of Prince Madoc: a bold sailor and hunter, a vanguard scout. But the red-hot iron sizzling in his palms had undone his loyalty, and now he was a man all separate from the interests of his prince, just obedient enough to avoid more punishment, his silvered black beard always concealing a sneer of mockery.

Mungo just now was perched on a brookside root, emptying the blood-tinged flux of his bowels into the brook below. He was sick in the bowels, as was everybody, and had been for so long that it had come to seem normal. Mungo also had a constant crawling sensation in his scrotum and groin, a sort of tickling that was not altogether unpleasant, and indeed usually kept him half aroused. This he suspected was a souvenir of his past whoring in sailing ports throughout Europe and the Mediterranean. His filthy gray loincloth was perpetually stained with his shits and seepages. Head almost between his knees, Mungo dully watched his waste splatter in the water under him, staining it red. It was troubling, but there was nothing to be done about it.

From beyond the foliage came the awesome squealing of the tumbrel's hubs, the thud and rattle of its huge wooden frame, and the cursing and grunting of the wretches who had the duty of pulling it this day. Like every able-bodied man, he had spent his share of days in the traces of what he had christened the "Prince's Great Behind" for its position behind everything else in Madoc's procession. Like all the others, he had hauled against the lumbering monstrosity until he fell and could no longer rise, and with every rasping breath he had whispered curses upon Madoc and everything Welsh—including his thick-waisted slattern, who complained as if every difficulty and discomfort were his fault instead of Madoc's. And lately she had been professing that she was pregnant. That, too, she called his fault, as if her own great rutting appetites had had nothing to do with it.

Mungo sighed with his miseries and arose, grunting and clambering over the roots, then hopped off onto the soft ground and wrapped his loincloth around his middle.

Something moved nearby.

He paused, stock-still, peering into the brush and ferns just up the brook from where he stood.

Someone had moved there. Mungo had caught a glimpse of brown skin lit by one ray of sunlight that penetrated down through the trees.

He stared, crouching, craning. He saw some foliage move slightly, though there was no breeze.

His heart began to hammer. The black hair that grew profusely on his back prickled and seemed to stand, like a dog's hackles. Mungo slipped his knife from the sheath he had just belted onto his waist and crept forward two steps, three, four.

There was a flicker of swift movement in the left corner of his eye, and he saw a bare, muscular back vanish into the shadows of a thicket. He crept to the place. In the soft humus beside the brook, water was oozing into fresh footprints.

Now all was still. He took a slow, long breath and stood up out of his tense crouch. He was smiling and his eyes were blazing.

For days, from pyramids along the riverside trek, Mungo had observed something that no one else, even Madoc, seemed to have noticed: that wisps and columns of smoke could be seen above the distant treetops not only ahead to the north and east, but also behind.

Mungo was certain the natives were not all dead, though many obviously had been wiped out by some disaster. He had come to suspect that the surviving ones had fled their towns only because they knew the Welshmen were coming. And, that soon after the column had passed, the natives were returning to their villages and cities.

They are all around us, Mungo thought. There are still many of them, and for some reason they are afraid to meet the few of us.

And just now he had seen one of them, and realized how closely they hung about.

To Mungo this realization was more thrilling than frightening.

AT THE NEXT VILLAGE, A STONE WEIR HAD BEEN BUILT ACROSS THE river shallows to entrap fish, and as the coracles were being hauled over the stones, the one carrying Madoc's fortune in pearls collapsed and its leather skin tore. By scrambling valiantly in the waist-deep water, the boatman managed to save all the bags of pearls, and Madoc rewarded him with great praise.

The boat being beyond easy repair, it was decided to make room on the overburdened tumbrel cart for the pearls.

The exasperated wagon pullers did not want to haul one more pound than they were already. And so, as soon as Madoc's back was turned, they took it upon themselves to compensate by throwing off into the bushes one of the iron kettles.

Mungo, who was wielding an ax to cut a path for the tumbrel, saw them discard the kettle. He smirked, knowing why they had done it, and he said nothing about it to anyone.

MUNGO HEARD A BUZZ OF VOICES FROM THE CENTER OF THE TOWN. Hurrying among the huts, he found Madoc and Riryd examining a large, open-sided shed with enthusiastic interest, with a small crowd of the Welshwomen craning to look on. Madoc came out into the sunlight to examine a pale sheet of woven fabric he had draped over his arm. Some of the women clutched handfuls of white fluff, and Riryd was looking at spindles wound with white strands.

" 'Tis not wool," Madoc was saying.

"Nor flax," said a woman. "Majesty, see these seeds in the fluff."

"By Heaven!" Madoc's voice boomed. "I've seen this in Egypt; this is what they call *qutn*, and make into cotton. This then is cotton cloth I have here! Riryd! These people make cotton! Riryd, what a boon to us, whose fleecing sheep were lost to us! You women, gather all the seeds you can find!"

Mungo sneered. Any pleasure Madoc displayed was a rasp on his soul.

WHEN THE COLUMN OF WELSHMEN LEFT THE TOWN, MUNGO WADED into the river to help launch the coracles. As the last one was paddled away, he did not climb back on shore. Instead he slipped out of sight among the roots of a tree at the river's edge and sank until just enough of his face was out of water that he could breathe, and stayed immersed there until the boats and marchers and the tumbrel were out of sight.

It was the most reckless thing Mungo had ever done in a lifetime of rash acts. Not only was he slipping out of the world of his people and into that of the natives, he was forsaking his allegiance to his royal masters—a crime for which he could be not just branded, but killed. Even as he did it, he kept open in the back of his head an excuse he could give if he should lose his nerve and go catch up with his countrymen: that he had got lost while scouting.

Mungo did not intend to rejoin his people. He hated the authority that had branded his hands. He was sick of the labor and hardship of this migration. He had got the carpenter's daughter with child, and she was stupid and tedious. She had lately begun whining to him about rashes and seeping sores in her female parts, lumps in her groin and pains in her bones, for which she blamed him. Mungo desperately wanted to be away from that tiresome dull bitch.

Now, submerged in the tepid green river, hearing the din of the squeaky tumbrel fade away, he felt both free and afraid, but wholly excited, excited in a way he had not been since that day two years ago when he had chased the naked brown nymphs through a green creek valley.

He waded out of the river. Looking around, he took off his loincloth and wrung the water out of it, then put it back on and crept cautiously up into the deserted village. He was both desiring and dreading the return of the natives to their town. He went to the brushy place beside the trail where the wagon men had discarded the iron kettle. He picked it up. To his surprise, he found a red silken banner in it, embroidered with a Welsh dragon. With his ax, which he had hidden near the kettle, he cut a limber long pole and hung the banner on it. What an impression he might make upon these savages when and if they returned, what advantage he might gain, by having a kettle to give them, and by having a glorious banner to wave. That was what Mungo was thinking as he walked into the plaza in the center of the village. He set the kettle down and stuck the banner pole in the ground. Then he put the ax in the kettle, its handle sticking up for easy reach, and gazed all around, chewing his lips. Now in the silence he really began to wonder what plight he had put himself in. If these savages disappeared when the Welshmen were near, they obviously did not like the Welshmen. What might they do to him, catching him here alone? He was a veteran of the battle on the eastern shore two years ago, so he knew the men were quick and strong warriors. What if they were cruel? What if they were cannibals?

Mungo had let that part of him between his legs lead him into this. He had presumed that a people with no shame whatever about nakedness must be a free and easy people with no compunctions about fornication, and he had dreamed and daydreamed about such wanton freedom. He had envisioned naked women and men copulating wherever and with whomever they met, without a moment's hesitation. That had been Mungo's concept of heaven, and he had imagined that it was here, in a land where all the native people he had seen had been healthy and good-looking and shameless.

But now the sun had gone below the treetops, and in the shadows the air was cool. He shivered in his wet loincloth. He thought of going into a hut and getting a deerskin to wrap himself in, or a sheet of the material Madoc had been holding. And he thought about setting off at a run up the trail to catch up with his own people. It might not be too late. . . .

He saw that he was no longer alone. The profuse black hair on his back prickled.

In every corner of the shaded village people were moving, in utter silence. Men with lances and clubs were slipping toward him among the huts, their eyes intent upon him. Every warrior wore a forelock pulled through a hollow bone or bead to hang between his eyebrows.

They stopped and stood all around him, but at a distance, around the edges of the plaza, murmuring, their lances pointed his way, looking at him with as much wariness as he felt in himself. Turning, he saw that the ring of men was completely around him. And now children and women and old people were moving up behind the warriors.

Mungo licked his dry lips and the roof of his mouth. There were the creatures of his dreams, nude and shapely. Like the men, they wore strips of hide or cloth of woven grass that hung from waistbands to cover their organs, and nothing else but jewelry—ear bobs, necklaces, bracelets, and anklets of shells and pearls and fashioned bone, bright against their dusky skin, skin gleaming with ointment. Here stood Mungo seeing the nymphs of his fantasy. But between him and them were tall, sinewy warriors who looked nervous and held stone-tipped lances pointed at him. It was exactly the plight he should have expected himself to be in after deserting in their country, but now he could hardly comprehend that this really was happening, and he had not the slightest notion what he should do. He just kept turning, looking around, nape tingling, always expecting to find one of those tall warriors close behind him.

But they were keeping their distance. They stared at him and stared. Never in his life had he been looked at so long and so intently by so many people. Mungo, whose forearms, legs, chest, face, and even back were covered with thick black hair, was aware of the contrast between his hairiness and the smooth skin of the natives; perhaps that was the cause of their wonder. They might well have thought he was a bear.

These people seemed to have no end of patience. Mungo's nerves were screeching inside him. Shadows were creeping as the afternoon aged, but nothing else was happening.

Mungo heard a shuffling, a murmur of low voices behind him, and turned to see an impressive, elegant figure moving toward him through the crowd, which parted to make way. It was a large man in a white robe, wearing colored plumes in a headband and carrying a lance decorated with feathers. He appeared to be a king or a bishop or some such thing. His face was flat and broad, deep-creased, dark brown, and shiny; his eyes were black slits between thick brows and pouches of flesh, and each eye was circled with a ring of white paint. A necklace of pearls and small conch shells hung on his breast.

This giant, who looked as tall as Prince Madoc, walked slowly through the circle of warriors, looking stern and dangerous. But as he came into the center where Mungo stood, his steps slowed. When he was within five paces, Mungo, desperately fearful, plucked the banner pole out of the ground. The little flag swayed, and the white-robed man stopped where he was, his eyes on the embroidered dragon. Mungo sensed, to his surprise, that the big man was suddenly afraid, and he took a short step toward him, making the bright banner sway. To Mungo's astonishment, the big man backed off toward his warriors then, eyes bugging at the banner. The whole population then gave a sort of moan and began to cringe back.

Mungo was not a bright man, any more than he was a brave man, but he began to suspect that they saw the banner as a magic thing, just as African natives, timid and superstitious, had been frightened by things they had never seen before, as when he had scared some away with a bronze bell, once long ago near Tunis.

Another great and unusual notion bloomed in his wild brain: that perhaps they took him to be some sort of a god! If they had stayed hidden from the Welsh column for fear that the Welsh were gods, might not they presume that he, too, was a god? White-skinned and hairy, so different from them, and waving this magic pole before them, might he not be taken for some furry man-beast god?

With luck and bluff, perhaps he could make them believe so.

Staking his perilous fate on that notion, he bared his teeth and strutted forward a few more paces, sweeping the dragon banner back and forth before their eyes. They backed farther off. But only a little way. When the women and children began to scatter with frightened cries, the warriors murmured ominously and stood their ground. Then, at a word from the robed man, they began to edge toward Mungo, spears bristling, clubs raised. He edged back to the place where the kettle lay on the ground. He had lost advantage; the whole circle was closing down on him. They might not have thought him a god after all, but perhaps only a dangerous animal.

Then, by God, he thought, heart pounding, a dangerous animal I am!

Snarling, he whirled and stooped and grabbed the only weapon at hand, his ax, which was in the kettle.

When he snatched up the ax, its head struck the rim of the big iron kettle with a resonating clang. At the sound, all the natives cringed, yelped, and fell back, clapping their hands over their ears.

Mungo was so astonished that it took a moment for him to realize that it was the noise that had frightened them so. With a fierce surge of spirit, he stuck the banner pole in the ground, snatched the heavy kettle up by its bail and gave it such a resounding rap with the ax that the ring of it hurt even his own ears. The natives all but stampeded away from him.

Amazed that he could use mere noise as a magic weapon, Mungo rushed at the retreating king of the natives, striking two more ringing blows as he went. Now the king actually fell to the ground, bawling, one arm clamped around his head. Mungo stood over him, eyes crazed. He struck another bell-like blow on the kettle, and the king, sobbing in pain, reached up to surrender his feathered lance to Mungo, abjectly proffering its haft to him.

Mungo, blinking with amazement, put the ax in the kettle and took the lance. He raised it triumphantly overhead and strutted back to the center of the clearing, his turbid brain only beginning to suspect what he had wrought through sheer bravado and luck. "By my bloody eyes!" he exclaimed aloud. "Have I made myself their king, eh?" A joyous sense of power stirred him throughout and he began beckoning to the women who cringed in the shadows. "Come out! I'd like a good look at your maids!"

AS MADOC'S NOISY COLUMN OF WELSHMEN LABORED ALONG THE river paths north by east, they passed broad, open fields in the bottoms where white fluff clung to standing stalks, and he understood that these must be the *qutn* plants from which the natives made their fabrics. He sent women through the fields to glean fluff and seeds.

The column proceeded on at the tumbrel's laborious pace as the sun descended. Armed men walked the shore while workingmen strained in the wagon harness or paddled the coracles or carried the sedan chairs of the princes' wives. Meredydd and Gwenllian strolled and chattered, talking mostly now about cotton and its uses and the process of weaving. The column passed no more villages this afternoon.

Later, Madoc climbed a bluff onto a meadow and stood resting on his spear staff, gazing along their route, when he became aware of a distant sound, which was strangely like that of a bell, a bell far, far away. The tumbrel had been stopped momentarily for an adjustment of its load, or he might not have heard the sound at all.

He listened with all his concentration. The noise had been so faint that he was not really sure he had heard it. He stood there thinking about iron, wondering how he could have been hearing a ringing of metal here in the wilderness. All the iron he knew of was what the smithies had salvaged from the ships' fittings and anchors to bring along. The iron was a burden for the procession, but it would serve as their resource until ore could be found in this land. Madoc was confident that some would be found, somewhere, eventually. The discovery of the *qutn* plants had put him in that state of mind.

Two or three more times he thought he detected the ring of iron reverberating across the distance.

Perhaps I imagine it because I have been thinking of iron, he mused.

Then the tumbrel began moving again, and its squealing and the shouts and curses of its haulers filled the valley, so Madoc turned and strode down the bluff to take his place at the head of his people. He asked Riryd and then Meredydd if they had heard anything like a distant bell, and they only looked at him askance.

SEVERAL TIMES MUNGO HAD NEARLY LOST, THEN REGAINED, HIS spell over the warriors of the village, breaking their will by the clangor of his ax and kettle, showing them the dragon banner, baring his teeth, and even bellowing a Welsh drinking song, anything to frighten and bewilder them, and finally they had lain their weapons on the ground and stood submissive, as if afraid to provoke any more of his head-hurting noises, those high, ringing thunders he called down by striking two things together. The native king sat in shadows, seeming defeated, but watching keenly everything that the hairy creature did.

Now that Mungo for the first time in his life had power over people, he did not intend to waste time waiting for a chance to use it or to figure out the subtleties of their ways.

He had picked from the crowd one tawny, full-lipped, dark-nippled maiden of about thirteen, the sight of whom made his knees weak, and he went to her, led her to the center of the plaza by pulling her necklace, and then thrust the point of the lance into the dirt. He unbelted his loincloth and let it drop to the ground. He grasped the hair at the back of her head and made her bend over. The cowed natives stared dumbstruck at Mungo's pride, which protruded from his black belly hair, as if they were watching some spirit-visitor in a vision. No one made a move toward rescuing the girl from this sacrificial fate.

Mungo had dreamed for two years of doing this, but had never imagined he would be doing it with a whole village looking on. But he was bursting with desire and with a power which he knew might be snatched from him at any moment. His contempt for these timid people was so thorough that they might as well not have been there. This was his most intense moment.

The girl quivered and convulsed. Mungo's teeth were bared and his eyes rolled and he grunted and moaned. His spasm was instant; the natives babbled in amazement at the quickness of it. Mungo released her hair and she dropped to her elbows and knees, face on the ground, sobbing, bleeding from the breech.

Now they might become so outraged that they would rush him and kill him, but Mungo was above fear. There could never be another moment like this. Even that bedamned Madoc the prince could not have cowed a whole people and humiliated their king and taken one of their virgins like this right before their eyes! Mungo raised his hands before his face and looked at the burn scars Madoc had put in his palms, then made fists at the sky and howled.

WHERE NIGHTFALL CAUGHT THE PROCESSION, THERE WAS NO NATIVE village nearby, so the Welshmen had to make an unsheltered camp and eat from the grains and dried foods they had brought along from other towns. They gathered nuts. One hunter killed a young doe at the river's edge, providing enough meat for a big kettle of venison and broth. Somebody complained that one of the iron kettles was missing from the tumbrel; the wagon pullers shrugged and replied that the vehicle was so overloaded that it probably had just fallen off somewhere along the way, and nothing more was made of that.

While the venison was cooking, a buxom young woman came to the princess, to say that all afternoon she had not seen her husband. She feared that he might have drowned in the river, or wandered into the bush and fallen into the hands of savages.

This woman Madoc knew to be no man's wife. She was a daughter of one of the good carpenters, and through the year had shared the bed and mess of the old hand, Mungo. Madoc was at once suspicious. Mungo was too canny a man to have got lost; Madoc presumed he had deserted, a bitter and branded man. But Madoc did not say such a thing to the distraught woman. Instead he bade her to go and stay near her father's fire and not to raise alarm or cry about the camp. The wretched woman was far pregnant, and had sores on her mouth, and a sickish look. Doubtless she had contracted from Mungo the poxes of his quayside whorings. After she slouched away, Madoc shook his head and told Riryd: "I suspect the poxy satyr has fancied seeing wood nymphs again, and gone in pursuit of them. Damn him! He is a valuable man, though a knave. I am sorry to lose any of our people." He considered sending back an armed party to look for him, but decided not to risk worthy men for a churlish deserter. If Mungo was drowned indeed, it was too late to help him; if he had deserted, he would never let himself be found.

Though fatigued by the day's march, Madoc could not calm himself for sleep. Mungo's disappearance filled him with forebodings, and he kept remembering the bell sound he had thought he heard. He brooded about the great and inexplicable wave of death that had swept through the populous native civilization. At dusk Madoc had heard wolves chorusing in the distant hills, an ominous sound. The night was cool, and a thin overcast of clouds diffused the light of a nearly full moon. On clear nights Madoc often could soothe himself to sleep by lying on his back and studying the familiar constellations, but this night no constellations were visible.

Finally he arose from his bed on the ground beside Annesta, tucked the blanket of salvaged woolen sailcloth close around her and Gwenllian, and went to sit by a bonfire. Beyond the fire sat Meredydd the Bard, who was too bony to sleep well on the ground and usually sat up very late hooded by his blanket, running thoughts and rhymes through his head until he was fatigued enough to lie down and doze off.

Madoc sat rubbing his huge hands by the fire, thinking how few his people were in this vast land, and worrying about their slow attrition. They seemed to die faster than they could multiply in this strange land where death appeared to prevail over life.

Meredydd started and blinked when he saw that Madoc was beckoning to him. He rose stiffly and hobbled over to sit near him. Madoc said, "Bard, help me weigh a notion that is heavy on my soul."

"Thank you, my Prince."

Madoc was speaking low. "I am sorely troubled by our small and dwindling numbers. We have been cursed by storms, at sea and in our colony by the bay. . . . We've lost so many! Thegns of good blood, with knowledge of governing."

The bard nodded and bit inside his lip, watching his master's face. Madoc went on: "Riryd and I had spoken of sailing back to Cambria for more good people, ere the whirlwind wrecked our ships. Bard, listen: to multiply enough to survive in this land, and build a population, I wonder if we shan't have to interbreed with natives."

Meredydd swallowed and his eyes widened. " 'Tis not such a thought as had entered my mind, my Prince; I know not what to say yet. But meseems we should have to find some of them, to do that; I mean some living ones."

"Surely they are not all dead throughout Iarghal. Those on the eastern shore were as robust and vigorous a people as any race I ever saw. As we have seen, by their familiar knowledge of this land, they flourish as in Eden, whilst we stumble and starve. By intermarrying, we could not only increase, but ally ourselves with them and be aided by their comfortable knowledge of the place. We could repay them by teaching them the righteous way of the One True God, our Lord and Savior."

"Our clergy all died in the whirlwind, my Prince."

"Aye. But we have our Bible. And you, bard, know as much as they knew. None of them taught the Creation or the Flood or the Christ's story so well as my bard."

Meredydd was almost rocked by his prince's appraisal. "Thank you for believing that."

"What say you about this notion of intermarrying?"

Meredydd thought long, before replying with the one doubt

that had entered his mind. "But then, my Prince, we would no longer be a colony of Welshmen."

Madoc nodded, and glanced beyond the fire glow to the place where Annesta and Gwenllian slept.

"*We* could not interbreed, God forbid it," Madoc said. "I mean Riryd and I and our families, we the offspring of Owain Gwynedd; we must certainly keep the blood of our father pure."

Meredydd feigned deep thought, though he was too fatigued to do more than wonder idly whether he himself would have to keep his own blood pure—if it was pure to begin with. Madoc and his ruling family were fair Celts who could recite their lineage for centuries past with no mention of any blood-taint from outside; indeed, it was esoteric among bards that these rulers would rather breed among close cousins than let inferior blood come in. But Meredydd himself, like most Welshmen, was Celt and Pict and Saxon and Nord and whatever else had washed up on Cambria's shore—including sheep and goats, as the old Welsh joke had it.

But now Madoc was not talking like a Welsh noble. He mused, "In the world I've sailed, there are people exceeding handsome and vigorous who are the influx of many bloods. I should not be surprised, if our burly Welshmen mated with these natives, to see their offspring an improvement."

"Thou'rt my prince," said Meredydd. "Thy wisdom I deem flawless. Any offspring of mine could only look better than I." He hoped to hear Madoc chuckle at that, but the prince apparently was too serious just now.

"Aye," Madoc mused on, "a colony of healthy, handsome people, trained as artisans and obedient to the teachings of our Savior, resourceful in a familiar land, all pious and industrious, multiplying as the Scripture decrees, and governed by the untainted bloodline of Owain Gwynedd!"

"A noble dream, and lovely," said Meredydd. But he remembered what Gwenllian had said about these native people and their pure freedom, and he wondered about such governance being put upon them. However, he said nothing about that doubt to his prince.

"Thank you for your ear," Madoc said. "I value thy wisdom and discretion. 'Tis late. Go sleep. I shall do likewise. My heart's a bit less burthened, thanks to thy counsel."

"For me, my Prince, 'tis easier to sit a-counseling than to sleep on bare ground. I shall sit awhile yet and watch the fire burn. I should have been born to the sentry class. God rest ye, beloved lord."

He watched Madoc ease off beyond the firelight, heard him pissing on the ground, and watched him lie down with Annesta and young Gwenllian. The bard sighed. He loved his Madoc and Annesta and their child; they were his only family, they were the beauty in his homely little life.

He tried to imagine himself breeding with a native. It was an uncomfortable thought. He had so little drive of that sort that he was almost without yearning; he had thought often how alien was a goatish man like Mungo: Mungo, wherever he might be now!

The only native Meredydd could envision was the captive girl, so sullen, so withdrawn. A bird in a cage can sing, he thought; obviously a woman cannot. He thought of what Gwenllian had said about nakedness and freedom. He wondered why Madoc had not freed the girl, even when they passed through the towns of her people.

Probably he just did not even think of it.

The girl is comely, he thought. Even tepid-blooded Meredydd at times had looked at her with desire, as well as pity.

I wonder what her name was? he thought.

THE RIVER GREW NARROWER, MORE SWIFT AND CLEAR; THE BLUFFS were higher on either side of the river course. The air was less sultry every day, the trees taller, straighter. They were at last coming into the kind of country Madoc had hoped to find in the interior, and he gazed ahead into the distant foothills for a proper site for a winter stronghold, some protected high place well-timbered, with access to freshwater springs, perhaps even a waterfall. The winter season was but weeks away, and though he expected the winters to be mild in this latitude, good timber would be needed for good houses.

When Madoc spoke of that to Riryd, who was plodding wearily beside him, Riryd vented his feelings:

"Brother, what perversity is it that makes you do everything the hardest way? Why do you want to go up in the hills and labor to build another colony, when we have already passed through a score of good towns well placed, and without a living soul in them? Why should we build another town? This country, meseems, has more towns than people! Let us just stop somewhere and move in for the winter! Then in spring we can proceed, to the eastern shore, or to seek a perfect castle site—whatever your fond ambition shall have become by then!"

Madoc replied, in a harsh whisper: "I do not want our people to hear you speak to me in that tone! Now, as I told you, I want us to get out of this ill climate. I do not want us dying one by one from the fogs and the miasmas of swamps. And, whatever evils exterminated whole populations of those natives may still lurk in those villages. Finally, brother, this caution: If by chance those people are not all dead, should they try to return to their homes and find we've usurped them, we shall have made enemies. We few Welshmen need no enemies in this hard land; we scarcely know how to live as it is.

"I should pray, instead, that when we have built a stronghold in clean air, with clean waters, and show that we do not invade their places, natives will come at last by curiosity to us, and trade their beautiful cloth and furs, and their foodstuffs, with us, for such tools and treasures as our artisans can make. And if they will thus learn to trust us, we shall have allies, and helpers, and—"

He stopped short of mentioning his notion of interbreeding with natives. Riryd was so disgruntled that he spat back even ordinary suggestions. That of interbreeding with savages would be too much for him yet.

For another week in mild autumn weather, the foliage glorious with color, Madoc and his people toiled onward into the hills along the narrowing river. They found here and there little abandoned hunting and foraging camps. Most significant was that on three different days of that week, Madoc's huntsmen, ranging ahead, caught glimpses of native men armed with bows, who vanished in silence.

Twice the Welsh hunters had seen smoke rising from distant hilltops. Madoc, presuming that smoke meant occupied towns, both times went out with armed parties to find them, but in vain; he never found the fires. Meredydd suggested to him, "Perhaps those are not village smoke at all, but instead a way of sending messages afar. Perhaps those smokes speak of us, of our passing through."

Madoc shuddered. "Sinister thought! How come you by that notion, my bard?"

"Why, my Prince, I presumed it from what I saw in the slave girl's eyes when she saw the smoke. She watched it as keen and long as someone *reading*!"

Madoc tilted his head. Once again the bard's alert intelligence had impressed him and produced a useful notion. "Speaking by smoke indeed!" he exclaimed. "If 'tis so, what a good way to signal afar!" He shook his head wistfully, suddenly remembering the sweet winking lanterns of his fleet of ships on the vast sea: distant signals, silent as stars, yet bearing messages of life and death. For a moment then Madoc felt a bittersweetness, a yearning for the motion of the *Gwenan Gorn*'s deck beneath his feet, reminding him that at the core of his heart he was a mariner, who should have found and claimed this land, and left its colonizing to others, while himself sailing away to seek whatever other places there might be as yet unfound upon this world. He sighed for the sea.

But, he told himself, you, Madoc, son of Owain Gwynedd, wanted to found a new Paradise and be its king!

THE NEXT DAY ANOTHER SMOKE COLUMN WAS SEEN ABOVE A FORested mountain to the northeast, and Madoc, determined to find these people who would be his neighbors for the winter, set out climbing with a dozen armed men to find the fire signalers, despite Riryd's grumbled warnings.

They went up creeks and freshets, clambering up steep slopes and around boulders among the grandest trees Madoc had ever seen, trees of immense girth and crimson foliage. The air was cool and clear, the sky as deep a blue as the Aegean Sea he remembered from so long ago. He was still yearning for the seas, even while climbing the greatest mountain he had ever felt underfoot. Here and there stone escarpments rose high above the treetops, and when Madoc looked back down toward the river's narrow course, he was awed. Surely, he thought, we are twice as high as Plymlimon or Snowdon Mounts!

By now he had lost his bearing on the place where the smoke had been seen. But it had become even more important now just to reach the summit of this mountain, and to see what such a height could show him of the lay of the Land of Iarghal. Surely no Welshman has ever climbed so high before, he thought. His men were gasping and stumbling and sweating as they tried to keep up, and his chest was heaving with hard, dry breathing.

As he neared the top of the mountain, the woods dwindled to scrub, then there was only rock, mottled with lichen. The wind whipped his tunic and blew his hair about his face, and soughed in the treetops below, making them sway, blowing off leaves.

At last Madoc stood upon a bald-rock crest. He seemed to be

at the top of the world. Forested mountains stood in ranks, each hazier and bluer until they faded into the invisible horizon.

Chest heaving, legs quivering from fatigue, Madoc stood and peered into vast distances. His men began sinking to the ground to rest.

To the north and east, the way he had been bearing, he thought toward the eastern seashore, there was an infinity of mountains to match this one he had just climbed so laboriously. If he and his able-bodied men could so exhaust themselves in climbing one such mountain, how could the women and the children and the feeble climb an infinity of them? How could the tumbrel and the sedan chairs be hauled through such country?

Turning to his left then, he saw a different panorama, which nearly took his breath away, and this view lifted his hopes. To the northwest, beyond foothills, lay a broad valley, a descending series of forested slopes, with what appeared to be a great river course meandering through it. It was on the opposite side of the mountain from the river they had been ascending. He looked at it for a long time, so long and so intently that some of his men rose and hobbled to where he was standing.

"See that!" he exclaimed to the veteran soldier Rhys. "One must presume that yonder river drains the other side of these mountains from the way we've come."

Rhys, who had not enough conception of lands and waters to presume anything from what he saw, agreed with Madoc because one never disagreed with a prince. Madoc went on:

"And so, my thegn, likely it is that yonder river is our way to the eastern shore we seek!"

"Ah!" exclaimed Rhys, pleased by his lord's hopeful face and tone.

"So we must bring our people across this mountain," Madoc said, "and launch our boats in that river." He pointed down toward the valley they had just left and then into the broad one on the northwest side of the range.

"Majesty!" Rhys responded, trying not to groan out loud. Not only would that require climbing this mountain again, but bringing over the women and children and boats and goods—and maybe even that bedamned tumbrel!

But one dared not disagree with a prince.

ON THE WAY DOWN FROM THE MOUNTAINTOP, MADOC LOOKED FOR a pass by which he could lead his people over the mountain without having to take them to the top as he had his soldiers. He found a saddle several hundred feet lower than the ridge tops. This would be their way.

When he returned to the people, the dusk was deep and they had already lit campfires and were watching anxiously for his return. That night he sat by a fire with Riryd and, using the old parchments upon which he had made his coastal maps the year before, he sketched the river they had been following, the mountain range, the pass, and as much as he could remember of the river valley he had seen to the northwest. Riryd immediately raised a troubling question:

"You suppose the river over there runs to the northeast and will flow to the eastern coast. You so presume because you so fondly wish it to be. But may I suggest, dear brother, that you could not tell from the mountaintop which way that river flows, and it might instead flow the other way?"

Madoc frowned. He was getting the drift of this intelligent query and hoped mightily that his brother was wrong. Riryd went on.

"By the look of your chart here, if the river ran southwestward, instead of the way you prefer, it very well could carry us right back past the way we have come with such toil these many weeks, and deposit us at that same warm sea, perhaps near that same stinking bay with all its monsters and storms." He stared at Madoc over the fire, then asked, "Had you not better go over and see which way that river flows before causing our weakened people to cross a mountain to it?"

For a while Madoc frowned into the fire. His insides were churning with the doubts Riryd had raised, and he knew he was right to doubt. He considered setting out again in the morning and crossing the pass to investigate the river.

But then he shook his head and straightened up, his mouth set in a thin line. "I thank ye, canny brother, for those cautions. But I want to move our people over into that beautiful valley, no matter where that river leads. I doubt it goes anywhere other than to the eastern shore. You know that in our homeland, if you ascend the Severn unto its source in the mountains of Cambria, then cross over, all of the waters off the other slope flow quickly to the sea. So it is also with the Wye. Thus it is with rivers everywhere, my brother. Being off the other side of the mountains, that river will not go back to the place whence we came."

"So say you. But this is a big land, and rivers do twist like snakes and seem not to go where they are going."

"Even so," Madoc replied, very weary and not wanting to dispute because he had made up his mind, "I want us to go to that valley, for it is a finer-looking place than anything we have seen. Its lowlands are wide, and there are bluffs and plateaus fit to build a Dolwyddelan or a Clochran Castle upon."

"Build castles!" Riryd exclaimed, his face revealing both anger and astonishment. "Pardon me, but I thought you said you intend on going to the Great Sea!"

Madoc leaned close to the fire and grinned intently at his brother. "Do remember," he said, "this whole great continent is ours, to settle and people as we please. If a land is more inviting even than the eastern shore, might we not build a seat there before going on to search for the eastern shore?"

Riryd's eyes widened, then narrowed as he, too, leaned close over the fire. "And do you remember, Madoc, that I like not this new world, and have spoken my desire to return to Cambria!"

"So you were saying," Madoc mocked, "before God smashed our ships with a great whirlwind, and made that argument a moot one."

"We can build another ship. Any day in this land, we walk through more forests than there are in all of Cambria. We could build a fleet of ships. We could," he said, "*all* go home to a civilized land."

"Cambria," Madoc said softly, "is not a civilized land, if you choose to remember. *This* land, *we* shall civilize, all anew, and according to our own vision!"

"*Our* own, is it? Or just *thine* own, medoubts!"

IN THE DARKNESS BEFORE DAWN, AN UNEARTHLY YAWPING SCREAM from one edge of the camp threw everyone bolt upright in terror from fitful sleep on the cold ground. The scream was followed at once by a man's voice ejaculating howls of horror. Children in the camp began screaming, adults moaning and querying. There followed a rustle and crashing in the brush, and one of the sentries came flailing, bloody-faced, into the firelight, eyes crazed. As the men in camp grabbed their spears and tried to steady their quaking hearts to fight demons, Riryd and two men overpowered the sentry and examined his wound—a slanting gash across forehead, nose, and cheek—and tried to get a coherent word from him about the attack. It was almost daylight, the people still cringing and fearful, before the man regained enough sense to tell what had happened. And by the time he had described it, the coming of daylight was very welcome.

The sentry had seen, he said, a face with a beak above him,

glowing red, with eyes burning like green stars. Then that terrible shriek had sounded right before him. Yelling in terror, the sentry had jabbed at the glowing face with his spear. A wind had blown on him, a wind, he said, that smelled like the dead, and then the slashing blow had cut his face, and he had turned and bolted toward the fire glow of the camp. The man had no apologies for his abject panic. "It was a *coblynau*," he insisted. "No man can fight a demon with a spear in the dark." No one called the man a coward then. Even Madoc, whose reason urged him to believe it had been a wild animal or a native warrior, could not fault the man's panic, and he himself kept envisioning griffins until daylight drove them out of his mind. Even he, with all his enlightened faith, was beginning to lapse sometimes into dread intuitions about the spirits that guarded this beautiful but strange land. Sometimes he even wondered whether the native people were real or spirit, so elusive were they. Even their smoke left no ashes.

As the hubbub of terror prevailed in the camp, Meredydd the Bard observed the behavior of the native girl. She had drawn herself up like a fetus and was trembling violently, whispering fervent syllables as if praying. Meredydd knelt beside her in the dim fire glow, pitying her, and began to stroke her hair. To his surprise, she did not recoil from his touch, but seemed to be a little comforted. He put his blanket over her, and himself sat shivering in the predawn autumn chill. Now and then she murmured something, and he knelt closer to listen, still stroking her thick tresses. The word, or phrase, was *win-ti-goh*.

Meredydd, by sign and facial expression, could by now ask the girl a question meaning, broadly, "What is?" and sometimes she would try to respond. He thus inquired. And by her expression and a few hand gestures she told him what seemed to mean "bad wind." He already knew from her reactions at the mounds that "wind" sometimes meant not just "wind," but "spirit." And so he concluded, and went to tell Madoc soon, that the apparition had been some sort of a bad spirit the girl called *win-ti-goh*.

Madoc nodded and crossed himself. But the daylight world now had to be dealt with. Riryd must be persuaded to acquiesce, and the people had to be led over the mountain pass to that great valley beyond.

THE MEN ON THE HARNESSES KNEW, LONG BEFORE MADOC KNEW, that the tumbrel wagon would not go over the mountain.

They strained until their harnesses cut their flesh and their shoes were torn from their feet, while soldiers braced their backs and shoulders behind it, and yet it could scarcely be moved up the slope an inch at a time.

And when at last it was a little way up, there was no way to brake the enormous wheels, so there remained a constant tension, a desperate certainty, that it would get away at any moment and roll backward over somebody or drag its pullers down the hill after it. The men were afraid to stay in harness, and got out and simply pulled with their hands until their hands bled.

At midmorning it happened. A wheel slipped a mere hand's span off a rock on the slope, and that jolt overpowered all their tenacious might. The harnesses were yanked from their hands, taking skin and fingernails as they went. The men fell on the slope or dove left and right from behind the wheels, and lay there yelling in dismay as the monstrosity plunged and careened down the mountainside, thundering, smashing bushes, spilling freight and shaking itself apart. Finally it broke itself to wreckage in a ravine, and some of the men could not restrain themselves from cheering. Madoc, looking down on the debris and drifting dust, was gray-faced.

And so then it was necessary to gather up the cargo strewn along the slope and redistribute everything onto people's backs or into the coracles, and then carry the coracles like huge baskets. Workmen were sent down to salvage all the metal from the shattered hulk, and the harness ropes. For a long part of the morning, women and children crawled on the slope picking up pearls that had scattered from a smashed treasure basket.

Carrying the loaded coracles up the slope required four to six men on each boat. Women and even children carried sacks and clanking utensils. In steeper places along the mountainside the people were almost crawling, clutching at tree roots with fingers and toes as they drew themselves and their burdens up. Sometimes a coracle's weight would wrench it from the men's grasp and it would go sliding or tumbling, ribs snapping, hides tearing, contents spilling, knocking down people in its way. Several suffered bad sprains or were cut and scraped. Several such shouting, groaning mishaps had slowed the ascent and damaged three coracles by early afternoon of this cool day. The people had had to stop and rest so often that they were not much more than halfway up by the time Madoc had thought they would be at the top of the pass. He had hoped they would be descending the other side by afternoon and reaching a water source for camp by dusk. But now there loomed the unpleasant probability that a waterless camp would have to be made on or near the top of the pass. A tangy, chilling wind was whistling through the hardwood trees, making more leaves swirl away like golden snowflakes.

In midafternoon, as the column struggled near the saddle of the pass, a line of bruise-purple clouds coming down from the northwest blanked out the sun.

And when the staggering column of Welsh men and women at last surmounted the pass, Madoc had not even the pleasure of pointing out to his brother Riryd the beautiful valley on the other side. Everything but the windswept rock they stood on was invisible in whirling, stinging snow.

The people retreated, wincing and shivering, a few yards down the sheltered side of the ridge, into the scrub. There they tipped up the coracles and lashed them to the bushes in a line, to make some shelter for the children and the sick. A few small fires were built, with great difficulty in the howling snow gale, but little wood was to be found at this height. One man went fading into the curtain of snow with an ax to cut wood. By dusk he had not returned. Now no one else dared to go forth in that whirling gray oblivion. The fires burned down and the wind scattered, then doused, their bright embers and sparks. Riryd growled, "A pity 'tis we could not get thy cumbersome wagon here to the top. I and many others would have taken joy in seeing *that* abomination burn for fuel!"

Madoc's wretched people burrowed together, huddling three and four in a bunch under tattered sailcloth blankets for each other's body warmth, and tried to rest. Their moans and curses and their children's crying mingled with the howl of the wind, and when the total darkness had enveloped them, all their wailings were as forlorn and terrible as the voices of the demons they felt around them. Meredydd shared his shabby blanket that night with the captive girl, who for the first time in her captivity was too cold and scared to huddle alone. It seemed as if the *win-ti-goh* had virtually broken her spirit. As he comforted her and tried to communicate with her, he learned what no one had learned in all the time she had been with them: that she had a name. It was, as well as he could discern, Toolakha, and it seemed to mean something like Daughter of Earth.

When Meredydd spoke her name several times, she began to weep, perhaps because she had not heard it spoken for more than a year. He murmured and stroked to comfort her, and she burrowed close to his bony body for warmth as the wind howled. A strange, melancholy sweetness invaded his heart.

Someone really needed him.

Before they slept, Meredydd had for the first time in his lonely life come to a true understanding of the affections and yearnings that bards wrote about, and the carnal knowledge they did not write about.

As soon as it was light enough in the morning to move about, Madoc went shivering around through the blizzard to appraise the condition of his people. All were shaking and coughing, glassy-eyed and torpid—all except homely Meredydd, who rose with glowing countenance from under his snow-covered blanket, and left it for the native girl to wrap around her nakedness. Madoc, seeing her deep in the blanket and the new demeanor of his bard, raised his eyebrows and said to him: "Good fellow, when I spoke of interbreeding, I was only posing a notion, not giving an edict!" Meredydd smiled, and kept smiling as he and his prince went about bestirring the benumbed people.

The last of the snow swirled down and the wind began to abate. All the mountains were white, and the trees had been stripped.

Madoc's feet were cold, wet, and tingling in his battered leather boots. Many of the people had long since lost their shoes and worn out their buskins on the long march from the bay, and their feet were bare or wrapped in rags or animal hide. Of all the worries that beset Madoc in his fearful misery this morning, the desperate need for footwear kept nagging him most.

He sent several men out to find wood for fires, and told them to look for the woodcutter who had disappeared into the storm. Starting a blaze was difficult because of snow and wet wood, but soon a bonfire was blazing and the people were beginning to seem alive. They crowded so close to the flames that their wet clothes steamed. Then they began dragging out firebrands to make cook fires of their own. They scooped snow and melted it in their pots and kettles, and in the boiling water they threw whatever grain and seeds, roots, bark, and meat scraps they had. That morning the people drank some of the grayest, vilest swill that had ever passed their lips, but they revived on it. As for the woodcutter who had disappeared the night before, he was not found. Madoc made the people gather at the bonfire for a prayer for his safety, or his passage to Heaven, whichever it might be. Then he told them to break camp for the trip down the other side of the mountain. Through all this, Riryd just hunched by the bonfire with his wife and baby, looking sullen and disgusted. Madoc went and stood beside him, seething with anger, and said in a low, hissing voice:

"Listen well. Your moping steals heart from our followers, who need all they can muster. I know you would rather be wallowing in a satin bed at Clochran, but you cannot be there, you are here, and you were born a Prince of Wales. You want to mock me that the hole is in my end of the boat, but, by Heaven, Riryd, thou'rt in it with me and must help me keep it afloat. If you slouch about here sapping our people's resolve, I might be forced to make you vanish as completely as that poor useful man who vanished last night. Even though you are my blood brother, I shall not drag you along anymore!"

Riryd's eyes widened, then narrowed. "You threaten me!"

"If you act inimical to me, I threaten you. If you act like a true son of Owain Gwynedd, I vouchsafe you life and honor. Look at thy wife Danna, all resolute and protecting your baby son from these elements. *There* is Welsh spirit; study it!"

Saying that, Madoc left him. Riryd did nothing for a while, but as the coracles were reloaded and the people got ready to set out, he began moving among them, advising and encouraging them, and kicking up laggards. Madoc smiled grimly and hoped it would last.

Meredydd came to Madoc and asked him to have a smithy cut the shackles that chained the native girl's ankles. The request surprised and annoyed Madoc, coming as it did in this moment of discomfort and urgency. "She will flee," he argued.

"My Prince, I swear she'll not. Please, I beg. Yesterday she had to crawl up this mountain because of the shackles." He did not mention how inconvenient they were during copulation. "She has a name, my lord. It is Daughter of Earth."

The name did it. With a nod and an impatient wave, he sent them away, and Toolakha's hobbles were removed, leaving a ring of scar tissue around each ankle which probably would never disappear. Wrapped in Meredydd's blanket, then, the girl stayed close to the bard as the column began to move up the slope. Madoc glanced now and then at the pair of them. He expected her to vanish at any moment. But for the moment that was not a matter of any great importance. Then he watched as his daughter Gwenllian ran through the snow to Meredydd, and he heard her say to him, "Oh, good tutor! How happy I am! She is free!"

* * *

THE SKY WAS CLEARING WHEN THEY REACHED THE SADDLE OF THE pass again and looked over. The snowy valley was vast and beautiful, and down in the lower lands the trees had not been wind-stripped. The valley was white and blue-white, and seemed burnished with gold leaf, with the shadows of dispersing clouds moving over the far slopes. Madoc cast a glance at Riryd and saw that he was transfixed by the vista of the magnificent valley. Even the shivering, shabby people seemed to be braced by the splendor of it.

And then Madoc, as he moved ahead scouting for the easiest route down, paused and looked afar at something that had caught his attention.

Along the deepest part of the valley, in the river course itself, there hung two distinct smudges of smoke.

Villages! he thought, spirits rising again. Villages of *living* people, not dead! People with food, people to trade with us and be our neighbors for this while!

Though the wind was very cold, the snow was on the verge of melting, and it was slippery. The people, letting the coracles slide on the snow instead of carrying them, constantly lost their footing and fell sitting in the snow, sometimes sliding some distance until they could catch branches or roots and stop themselves. Their clothes and gaiters and foot rags grew sodden, and only their exertions kept them from chilling. Madoc stepped carefully, digging his heels into the snow to avoid the indignity of a princely tumble.

He heard a shout and screams and laughter behind him. Turning, he saw a coracle come sledding toward him at a quickening rate with two pairs of legs sticking up from it. The people from whom it had escaped were running, skidding, or sprawling behind it, some yipping in dismay, others howling with hilarity.

Realizing that it would collide hard with any trees or rocks down the slope, Madoc lunged to get his hands on it as it came careering by. The two upended people already riding in it were boys who apparently had flung themselves in as it started sliding. Madoc got the gunwale with one hand, but its momentum pulled him off his feet, and then he was prostrate behind it, hanging on.

At that marvelous sight, some of the people hauling other coracles apparently saw this as an easier and more exhilarating way of descending the mountain. Without heed for the consequences, three or four at a time piled onto their loaded boats, hooting with joy, and the vessels slipped faster and faster down the slope. Others thought better of it, held their boats in check and anxiously watched the others go.

Madoc's dragging weight gradually slowed the coracle he was hanging on, and it came harmlessly to a stop on the very lip of a cliff. As he rose from the snow, holding the coracle anchored above the precipice so the two shaken boys could safely get out, Madoc could only watch helplessly as two other boats went by over the cliff and sailed off into space, their occupants screaming. Two other boats smashed against trees before reaching the cliff. The occupants of another, seeing the void ahead, leaped out and dragged it to a stop a few yards short of the edge. Now below the cliff Madoc heard a frightful thudding and crackling, then sobs and groans. He staggered to the cliff's edge and looked down.

One of the boats, smashed out of shape, hung tangled in the branches of a leafless oak twenty feet below. Someone was still in it, clutching feebly about, only an arm showing. Two men lay unconscious and bleeding on the ground at the base of the tree, amid the boat's scattered cargo.

The other boat had landed on its bottom on clear slope and was still sliding, now a hundred paces farther downslope from the cliff. One man had fallen out and lay in the snow, but a man and a woman were still in it, their howls fading into the distance. As Madoc watched with racing heartbeat, the man swung out over the side and hung on, his legs plowing up a shower of snow until the boat was stopped.

Dragging the coracle he had saved away from the edge of the cliff, Madoc heard more excited screaming from above. He looked up the snowy slope, and what he saw almost stopped his thudding heart:

Skimming at high speed down from above was Gwenllian's little sedan chair, coming like a sled—and she was in it, shrilling with exhilaration. And when she saw that she was heading for the cliff, her scream of delight changed pitch to a screech of terror.

It was aimed to pass far from where Madoc stood, perhaps ten paces away, and there was nothing he could do but try to get in its path and hope that when it hit him it would stop, instead of bowling him over the edge with it.

He sprinted, kicking up snow, as the little conveyance came slithering fast, too fast, toward the place where he would have to be.

Gwenllian had enough presence of mind to try to get out. Her weight tipped the chair forward, and its carry poles dug into the snow. The sedan chair somersaulted, spraying snow, and she tumbled and rolled. The upset slowed her enough for Madoc to be at the edge of the cliff and dive into her path, where he caught her with his right arm. The chair whirled on by and vanished below. Madoc and his daughter lay in the snow and gasped and sobbed.

THAT EXCITING FOOLISHNESS HAD COST THE PEOPLE SEVERAL BROken arms and legs, three coracles smashed and one badly damaged. Madoc was furious, though thankful that no one had been killed. In particular he was furious at Meredydd. He strode through the snow in a rage, yelling for him, and when the homely little man came forward bewildered, Earth Daughter trailing after him, Madoc slapped him to the ground with a single blow, bellowing: "Blackguard! My princess near perished because you let her out of your care!" He drew back his foot to kick Meredydd's ribs, but paused in astonishment when Earth Daughter, in the shabby blanket and barefoot in the snow, leaped into his way with crooked fingers ready to go for his eyes and her teeth bared.

Madoc was stunned; his face reddened with rage and he drew back a fist to deliver a blow that likely would have killed the girl, but Gwenllian threw her arms around him, sobbing and begging him to have mercy on both the poor creatures. Panting with contained fury, Madoc relented, even though he was sorely insulted by all this, in particular the audacity of the savage girl who had been ready to assail him. Annesta had run up, hearing the commotion, and stood trying to comprehend the whole tense confrontation. Meredydd had put a gentling hand on Earth Daughter's wrist to keep her from gouging his prince's eyes, and the girl was simmering down like a boiling kettle taken off a fire.

Madoc glowered at Meredydd and said in a flat tone: "If ever again you let my daughter out of your care, fool, I shall have thy guts for garters!" Then he paused, and added, pointing to the native girl, "Tame that vixen, since she seems to be yours!" Then he went off, growling and shouting, to get his battered procession back into order. Riryd, who had watched the scene from a few feet off, was chewing his lips with his hand over his mouth, obviously delighted to have seen so much defiance flung in his brother's face by someone other than himself.

Because of the delay caused by the setting of bones, reloading of the remaining boats, and salvaging the skin coverings of the broken boats, it was late afternoon before the column could proceed again. Two men with broken legs had to be added to the cargo in the serviceable coracles, which were now handled in the most gingerly way. Several times during the descent Madoc went out of his way to observe whether Meredydd was keeping proper watch over Gwenllian, and each time found them as a curious, happy, self-contained trio with Earth Daughter. They were almost like a little family in themselves. Grudgingly, he even found himself admiring the raggedy little savage girl who had sprung toward him in defense of Meredydd. Madoc reminded himself that he had been contemplating interbreeding between his Welshmen and native girls; her display of protective fury put another face on it.

Could it be that she *loves* my bard? he wondered. He had never thought of anyone loving Meredydd, except in the way he and his own family loved him, as a sort of highly talented and indispensable servant.

And Madoc even began to regret the ferocious scolding he had given him. Meredydd was, after all, the only intelligent man in the whole party in whom he could confide any important thoughts, since his own brother Riryd had become a mocking adversary.

I must mend my bard's feelings somehow, he thought. But he was not sure yet how to do that, as a prince would never deign to apologize to a servant—especially not a prince who was a son of Owain Gwynedd.

They camped that evening down off the mountain, in woods near a spring, with plenty of deadwood for fires. It promised to be another hungry camp for the exhausted people, until an uproar occurred in the woods downslope. A man was shouting. Several men leaped up with their spears and bows, looking in that direction. Rhys the thegn was scrambling desperately uphill through the snowy woods toward the camp with a small black bear loping in pursuit.

Suddenly sensing the smoke and the presence of many people, the bear halted and rose on its hind legs, looking about. Before it could turn and flee, two arrows were in its chest. It toppled, roaring and floundering, and as it regained its footing, two Welsh hunters were upon it with their bronze-tipped spears. In seconds the beast lay dead in the bloody snow and the hungry people were swarming around it, praising the hunters and clamoring for its immediate butchery.

Roasted over the bonfires, the bear's flesh made the best meal the people had eaten in days. Fattened for hibernation, it was juicy and greasy, most satisfying to the people in this cold evening. They were merry despite their fatigue and aches and bruises. The meal was scarcely done before some were laughing and shouting:

"Good, but not enough! Rhys, sir! Run out and bring us another bear!"

THE NEXT DAY THE SNOW MELTED AND THEY CAME SLIPPING AND stumbling down through the foothills, making mud roads as they slid and slogged. They often lost sight of the river, and followed creeks down steep ravines. In some places they had to hack through thickets with their swords, or turn back and go around. By afternoon they had descended from the last plateau and were almost to the banks of the river. Madoc could see through the woods that it was indeed a large river, and his heart seemed to be climbing in his breast as he felt the lay of the land and tried to confirm that the river would be running toward the northeast, from his left to his right, which would mean it flowed to the eastern shore.

At last, through a break in the undergrowth, he saw the surface of the river close ahead. A chill breeze was whispering through the woods and blew his hair across his eyes; he brushed it aside and stared at the river, breaking into a heavy trot down those last few yards. Riryd came running alongside him, his armor rattling and clanking.

"See!" Madoc exclaimed. "It goes that way, as I believed it must!"

"Aye," Riryd panted.

They stopped on the riverbank and stood together breathing hard. The column of people made a babble of voices in the background and their feet rustled the fallen leaves on the forest floor. Madoc gazed across the water with a grateful and hopeful heart. "And God in His goodness has led us straightaway to a safe launching place. . . ."

Suddenly his heart seemed to sink. He had been looking at an object floating in midstream, a small, forked driftwood log. And he began to perceive that it was moving upstream. It was moving to his left.

That was impossible, he knew.

He looked at the floating wood, confused, beginning to feel troubled again by the bad magic of this strange land. Riryd seemed not to have noticed yet that the log was floating upstream.

Then Madoc stared down into the water close to the shore. A fish was there just a few inches under the surface, moving its fins lazily, just enough to hold its place in the current.

But its head was in the direction Madoc had thought was downstream.

Then he slumped inside, realizing the truth, and sighed heavily. Riryd looked at him, questioning.

"The river," Madoc said, pointing to his left, "flows that way."

"What say you? No, it—"

"The wind blows the waves toward the east. The current, though, is west." Madoc, who had known waters and currents and their appearances all his life, had been fooled by the wind on the surface.

This river did not flow toward the eastern shore after all.

The people had brought their column to a halt nearby and were setting down the coracles and unloading their burdens, talking, laughing. Someone yelled:

"I'm hungry! Rhys, go bring a bear!" And everyone laughed . . . except the two princes.

AFTER A LONG, DEPRESSING COUNCIL TOGETHER, MADOC AND Riryd decided that there was nothing to do but make a winter quarters in this handsome valley, and perhaps resume their explorations in the spring of the next year. Madoc persisted in hoping that somehow this big river might wend its way to some shore besides that sultry place from which they had come. "We know not the shape of this continent," he said. Then he returned to his analogy of the Severn and Wye Rivers in Cambria, but this time with another argument.

"In their headwaters, they seem to flow east," he said. "But they make their way southeast and then south and at last flow westward under Cambria into the Channel of Bristol. Is that not so? And so this stream, though it seems to flow southwest, might wind among these mountains and return eastward."

Riryd shook his head. "Anything can be, aye. And no matter how unlikely, you will choose to have it be the way you want it to be."

Madoc laughed grimly, trying to lift his own gloom. "But even if my desire cannot make this river go east, we are in the midst of the fairest country man's eye has ever beheld. After all, by Heaven," he exclaimed, "did we cross the Great Ocean to Iarghal only to find our way back to the Great Ocean? No!"

The first task was to repair and rebuild coracles for fishing and scouting on the river. This place was pleasant and good land for a winter camp, but it offered no protection against attack, and Madoc, remembering the smokes he had seen from the mountain, was sure there were natives along this river. He wanted to locate their villages, but he wanted to find a place for a defensible winter camp first, in case they could not be made friendly.

That night, after a meager meal of fish, Madoc stood at the margin of his camp's firelight with a nervous sentry, and they listened to an ominous sound.

It was like a heartbeat. Sometimes in loving Annesta, Madoc had lain with an ear between her breasts and heard her precious and mysterious heart beating inside. PUM-pum. PUM-pum. PUM-pum. Steady but faint, muffled by her flesh. Now the sound in the night along the river was like that, but muffled by distance. Madoc, his breath condensing in the cold night air, told the shivering sentry:

" 'Tis but a drum, from one of the native towns down there. Have no fear. But be alert."

Soon another heartbeat of a drum was answering from upriver. Madoc's people lay wakeful in their thin blankets, shivering from cold and dread. Gwenllian was wakeful. She said to her mother, "Our bard has Toolakha in his blanket."

"Yes," replied Annesta, her lips set tight. She did not approve, but she did not want to diminish the tutor in the pupil's esteem, so she said, "The wretched girl is not used to such cold nights. He is a kind man, and keeps her warm. Put it out of your mind and go to sleep."

"I miss him lying near us, Mother."

"Never mind. He is not really of our family, you know."

Before the middle of the night the drums fell silent. Madoc lay with Annesta's warmth on one side of him and Gwenllian's on the other. The girl whimpered that she was cold. So they moved to put her between them, and thus warmed, she was soon breathing evenly in slumber. Madoc much later drifted toward sleep with the impulse of the drums still throbbing in his memory. He was sure that their message pertained to his people's arrival in the valley. Likely they were not mere music. He wanted to whisper something to Meredydd about the wondrous ways these natives had of communicating across distances; then he remembered that the bard had moved his blanket away from the family, and sighed. Better not to stir and talk anyway; he did not want to wake Gwenllian. He remembered how close she had come to death the day before. The warmth of her little sleeping body beside him then became such a comfort that he stopped thinking and went deep into sleep.

IN HIS BLANKET, MEREDYDD HELD DAUGHTER OF EARTH CLOSE, molding his body along the back of her curled figure, and reveled in her warmth, in her skin, in her closeness. He felt as if his whole being had turned into a smile. He wondered now how he had ever endured the spare, grim, aching separateness that had always been his lot, and prayed silently in his soul that he would never have to sleep another night without this contentment. He could touch her nipple with his fingers and feel it stiffen and change, and that seemed to be perfectly all right with her. She seemed to have affection for him; she seemed to have even admiration for him, and he had never felt admired by anyone in all his life. And although he knew nothing about how women feel about copulation, it seemed to him that she liked it. She was attached to him, he could feel, and to him alone; she seemed to have no regard whatever for anyone else, not even the prince.

With Toolakha warm against him, he felt at last at home in Iarghal.

AT FIRST LIGHT NEXT DAY MADOC LEFT RIRYD IN CHARGE OF THE camp, took Rhys and six other soldiers in four of the coracles, and set off on the dawn-silvered river, drifting silently downstream. He had sent no boats upstream, but had said any hunters going that way should scout carefully for native signs and take note of any outstanding sites for a fortified camp. Depending on what he might find below, perhaps he would himself explore upriver by boat tomorrow.

The river was swift and clear. Along its banks Madoc saw deer drinking in many places, most on the right bank. They raised their heads and watched the four boats drift silently past, and were not alarmed. Countless small mammals were busy along the riverbanks. Little chattering squirrels swarmed from treetop to treetop, crows cawed, and enormous flocks of birds passed over, hundreds of thousands, their wingbeats rushing like ocean surf. Just such a flock had gone over, pigeonlike birds of bright plumage, when Madoc's keen nose caught a trace of woodsmoke. He thought at once of the native villages, the drums.

We do not want to float suddenly down on them and be seen in so small a number, he thought. He wondered which bank of the river a village might be on. He remembered then that most of the wild animals he had seen had been on the right bank, which might indicate that the village would be found on the left.

It might also indicate, he thought, that native scouts were moving along the left bank. If they have been following and watching us, he thought, they already know how few we are. His scalp prickled. He suddenly had a feeling that he should turn the vessels about and return to the camp. It would be a hard paddle against the strong current, but his instinct was warning him, and he could not ignore it.

But at that moment he saw a sight that his mind's eye had envisioned a hundred times in the weeks of this trek. It was a spit of land on the right bank, fairly level, perhaps thirty feet above the river and almost treeless. Its banks were very steep, almost perpendicular. He saw, as the boats floated past, that it was formed by the juncture of a swift creek with the river.

It was the ideal site for a fortified camp. He told Rhys to steer into the creek.

While one soldier held each boat on the shore, Madoc climbed with Rhys and the others up the steep bluff, using roots and rocks as their ladder. At the top he looked about and saw that it was as good as it had seemed at first glance. He paced across from the creek side to the river side, looking in every direction. A palisade could be erected across here in a day's work, he thought, with a bastion for archers over it, and in three more days a dry moat could be dug outside. It would protect about three arpents of land, enough to build huts on for everyone. Steep bluffs of the river and creek would protect the other two sides, and water would be accessible even in a siege. Enough trees for the palisade and all the huts grew within two hundred paces of the site, and would not have to be dragged uphill. That is good, as we have no horses or oxen, he thought. "Come," he said to the soldiers, and they scrambled back down to the boats. He wanted to see which side of the river the native town lay on. He hoped it would be on the opposite side; that would be ideal. But even if it were on this side, he would still want to build his winter fort here.

As they clambered back into the boats, they heard drumbeats start up, and they were very distinct. They sounded as if they came from around the next bend in the river. Their rhythm was different from the heartbeat sound of the night before. These came in three quick beats, then two deeper thumps, and the rhythm was repeated over and over. After a few repetitions they stopped. Then there came faintly from upriver an answering series of rhythms, which stopped abruptly. Madoc's men were looking at each other, at him, and all about the riverbanks, with fearful eyes.

"Quick, now," Madoc commanded in a low voice. "Back up to our camp." The drums had made him desperately anxious about the people in the camp, about the hunters scattered all around. Taking up an extra paddle, Madoc helped Rhys apply power against the current, and the little blunt-prowed vessel plowed upstream, the three others close behind. From time to time Madoc thought he saw movements in the woods on the riverbank. Once he did catch a glimpse of a flitting figure moving with incredible swiftness among the trees on the shore to his right, going up toward the Welsh camp. Madoc felt such a sense of urgency that he could hardly endure the sluggishness of the little round boat.

"Ply harder, my good man!"

"Aye, my Prince!" panted Rhys, clearly inspired.

THE CAMP HAD NOT BEEN ATTACKED, BUT RIRYD'S FACE WAS GRIM when he came running down to meet the coracles.

The hunters, he said, had started the day well, getting four deer, a bear, a large elklike stag, and many squirrels and small mammals. But then they had begun to see natives in the woods all about, armed natives who had not attacked but had hovered closer and closer until all the hunters had deemed it prudent to retreat into the camp. Though the natives had not come within sight of the camp itself, Riryd had ringed it with a picket of bowmen. Hearing the drums, he had been afraid for the fate of Madoc and his boatmen.

"There is no time to linger," Madoc said. "We must march in compact order down this shore about a league. There we will ferry our people across to the mouth of a creek. There you'll see I've found a place we can fortify at once. That done, we can endeavor to meet with these people, and, I pray, befriend them."

THE NATIVES WERE ALWAYS PRESENT, IN FRONT OR OUT ALONG THE flanks of the column, but rarely was there more than a glimpse of them. The woods seemed vibrant with their silent movements. The few that Madoc really saw were astonishing: they were painted all over.

Madoc moved his Welsh people in close file down the animal paths along the riverbank, princesses in the chairs, with the coracles floating close along the shore carrying all the baggage. As they went farther along, the concentration of natives in the woods ahead seemed to increase. They may think we're marching against their town, Madoc thought. Sooner or later they will probably make a stand against us. Let it not be too soon.

At last he could see his chosen spit of land across the river. If only they will not attack us before we're opposite that place, he thought, and he prayed as he went along.

Finally he stopped the column. He told Riryd to load the coracles with women and children and a few armed men and ferry them across into the mouth of the creek. He sent Rhys across with them to show them the place to land and climb up. Then he formed the rest of the people into a semicircle with their backs to the river, to protect the rear of the embarkation. Now that he had gotten used to looking for the savages, he could better perceive their presence in the woods around. They were masters of concealment, making themselves almost invisible beside and behind trees and shrubs and fallen logs, but he had learned to watch out of the corners of his eyes for them. A man's face, Madoc realized, was as symmetrical and as out of place in the brush as an egg, but these natives marked their faces with dirt or pigments so that they did not stand out as faces against the forest background. And whereas a Welshman usually wore at least one or two pieces of armor—a helmet or breastplate—that gleamed very visibly, these natives clad themselves in materials taken from nature and were thus in no contrast to the surroundings. Even their bright paints seemed to blend them into the autumn foliage. In truth, one could hardly detect them except through movement and shadow. Perceiving their elusive figures this way, Madoc was able to estimate that the natives in the woods were at least three or four times as numerous as were his own people.

But still they did not come forward and attack, or even threaten, as the boats shuttled to and fro and the number of Welshmen on their side of the river dwindled to half a hundred, to twenty-five, to ten. The natives seemed indecisive, or lacked leadership, or perhaps were not even hostile. When Madoc climbed into the last coracle with two soldiers, he felt a huge sense of relief.

When the boat was in midstream, Madoc looked back and saw that hundreds of the warriors had come down to the riverbank he had just left and were watching the coracles cross. The sight of them was thrilling; it was the first sight he had seen of a large body of these mysterious people since the fight on the bay shore two years before. Where those had been naked in the heat of summer, these were colorfully and beautifully clad in decorated skins, and a few in garments of cotton, against the chill of late autumn. Those who were bare-chested had painted their bodies; all had paint on their faces. Their clothing and weapons were festooned with decorations, of feathers, shells, bones, even what appeared to be long locks of human hair.

Looking downriver then, Madoc saw, to his surprise and alarm, that several long boats full of natives were afloat in the river not far downstream, apparently having come up from the village below.

At first he was afraid that they had been launched to cut off his ferrying of people, or to attack them at the mouth of the creek. But as they kept their distance, he presumed instead that they had instead simply arrayed themselves across the river to keep him and his boats from descending to their town. Madoc's attention returned then to his people, who were working like ants to haul their tools and provisions up the steep creekbank to the plateau. Madoc himself finally stepped out of the last coracle and scrambled to the top. He told the men to haul the coracles up by rope.

At the top, Riryd had already begun organizing groups of axmen and sending them to cut posts for the palisades, while women and children dragged in deadwood for fires. Madoc then gathered a number of men with spades and paced off for them the line where he wanted post holes dug for the palisades.

"Now," he said to Riryd as the camp began to resound with the noises of industry, "if the pagans will keep their distance for a few hours, we shall have a place where no one can molest us. What think you?"

Riryd was nervous, his lips drawn down and teeth clenched in a grimace as he looked across the river toward the colorful array of lively warriors, but he was for the first time in weeks looking strong and intense like the Riryd of old. " 'Tis a fine site," he said. "And by Heaven, that ax work is more agreeable to my ear than their accursed drums!"

* * *

THERE WERE DRUMS THAT NIGHT. THEY BEGAN EVEN WHILE THE axes were still chunking and hammers pounding pegs at dusk. Madoc had fires built close to the palisade so that the work on the fortification could be finished after dark. In addition to the bastion at the wall's midpoint, he had two archers' platforms erected, one at each end, to prevent attackers from wading or climbing the bluffs at the creek end or the river end of the palisade.

When the work fell still, the drumming continued, very distinct; the native village apparently was around the next river bend. Even voices could be heard, chanting voices, and sometimes when the breeze was right, the soft, eerie notes of some flutelike instrument. These noises haunted the Welshmen even in the new security of their fort, and sleep did not come easy, exhausted though they were from the work. Madoc looked over his camp at midnight and saw people still sitting up by the firelight. The sentries along the bluffs and on the bastions were tense, their heads swiveling. When Madoc talked to them, they told him that they had not seen, but sensed, that prowlers were afoot not far beyond the palisade. Because of that, and because the people were so wakeful anyway, Madoc doubled the guard. Soon after they were posted, the drums and music fell quiet, and a still greater tension prevailed. Madoc finally was able to lie down and doze shortly before dawn.

He was awakened moments later by a boy who said a sentry needed him. Madoc groaned, slipped shivering out from under the blanket, kissed Annesta's brow and hobbled toward the sentry post, which was near the point of the spit. The sentry pointed downstream.

In the half-light he saw that the river was full of the long native boats. They were coming up the river, slipping almost silently along.

"Wake my brother," Madoc told the sentry. "Tell him to get all our fighting men under arms, but to make no noise about it. Get Rhys and tell him to pass the word not to build up the fires. I want our people all awake and ready, but to seem asleep. Do you understand?"

After the sentry had slipped away, Madoc stood on the point and watched the native flotilla, to see what their intentions might be. He expected them to go up the creek or perhaps to debark their warriors at the base of the bluff for a stealthy climb to the plateau. Probably, he thought, they intend to surprise us in our blankets. Eh! 'Twill be they who are surprised! Behind him he heard whisperings, mumblings, movements, as the camp was carefully awakened. He looked back over the camp. Figures passed to and fro before the glowing embers of campfires. He heard people urinating on the ground and breaking wind. He heard the querying voices of children, the shushing admonitions of mothers. His people could be so good when they needed to be. Surely they're frightened, but they do well. And the men were ferocious fighters, when actually confronted with an enemy. Superstitious and full of awful imaginings, Welshmen were as spooky as horses until they really saw what was in front of them. Then, none braver.

Horses, he mused. I wish we had horses. Fighting war without horses is like being crippled.

But those natives have no horses, either. There just seem to be no horses in this land. How odd that is.

Thus his mind roamed as he watched the dim shapes of the boats moving up the river and the sky in the east began to pale. Men started coming to him carrying their shields and bows and spears. Riryd came and stood beside him, helmet on, sword at his side, and watched the slow-moving boats. Rhys came, and Madoc had him post men along both salient cliffs. "And the palisade, the bastions? Are they manned?"

"Already so, my lord. With archers, crossbows, and pikemen."

"Good, then. See that the bastion gate is barred double and stay with those men and watch the woods. Keep a bright boy at your side to run messages to me."

By now the native boats were off the end of the spit, the leading ones less than a crossbow's range away. But they were veering away. "By Heaven," whispered Riryd. "What do you suppose?"

"I don't know. Probably they see that we're on guard. See, they hug the far shore now. Perhaps they're only going up to their other village, and have no designs on us at all. Though I doubt that."

Then he thought he understood their intent. If the natives landed upstream, they would not have to cross a creek to approach the fortress.

He told his brother of this notion, and Riryd nodded. He said, "If you intend to fight, you had better arm yourself, eh?"

"Aye, indeed!" Madoc had forgotten that he was still dressed as he had slept. He strode back to the center of the camp, where

Meredydd dressed him in his chain mail, greaves, and gauntlets and helped him strap on his sword belt. Meredydd then lifted from Madoc's armoire a close-fitting cassis helmet of brass with a riveted coronet around it and a burnished gold plaque above the brow. Pulling a woolen cap over Madoc's head, he then set the helmet on and stepped back. Meredydd's heart rose in his breast; he had not seen his lord prince so grandly bedecked, so dauntless, for years. Annesta stood nearby with Gwenllian, and both looked like wraiths in the dim light. "Guard them," Madoc told Meredydd, and then he went back toward the river.

By now it was clear that Madoc's notion had been correct. The natives' vessels had gone about a furlong up the river, then had crossed and put in on the near shore, where the warriors were climbing out and pulling the vessels onto the riverbank.

The sun was not yet up over the mountains, but the sky had grown light enough to show that the warriors were moving into the woods. "They must mean to strike us from our land side," Riryd said.

"Hasten. Put more archers on the bastions," Madoc said.

Within a few minutes that had been done, and as the eastern sky above the mountains grew peach-colored, the two princes stood on the shooting platform of the center bastion, waiting and watching the woods.

After a few minutes Madoc pointed toward the woods, beyond the stumps and brush piles the axmen had made.

There stood a tall and heavy-built man in a long, pale robe, perhaps a hundred paces from the bastion. He held a decorated staff of some sort.

As the Welshmen watched, the big man began to walk in a stately manner toward the fortress. On either side of him came three other men, all carrying spears. They walked forward among the stumps until they had come half the distance across the clearing. There they stopped and stood erect, looking at the palisade.

One of the men was holding something that gave off wisps of smoke. The first rays of sunlight slanting across the clearing illuminated the rising smoke. Madoc heard one of the soldiers exclaim:

"By my eyes! The man has fire in his hands!"

The big man tapped the ground at his feet with the butt end of his staff, and the man with fire in his hands stooped to set it on the ground in the indicated place. Two other men knelt there then and placed something on the same spot, and soon a small fire was burning there. Then one of the other men took a large, dark animal hide off his shoulders and spread it on the ground beside the fire. As the Welshmen looked on, mystified, the fire builders arranged some sticks on the ground and stood up. The seven now stood and gazed straight toward Madoc and Riryd and the archers on the bastion. The robed man had on his head something that Madoc had presumed to be a large, black hat, but now in the strengthening morning light it proved to be a ravenlike bird with wings outstretched. Madoc pointed it out to Riryd, who blinked and squinted and then exclaimed, "It *is* a raven, by Heaven, perched right on him! Heh! Heh, heh! Do you suppose it shits in his hair?" Several of the archers nearby laughed.

But now Madoc put his hand on Riryd's forearm and said, "Brother, meseems quite sure, they come in peace! I think they wait for us to come forth. Surely that big man is their king." Even as he said this, he thought how much the man's bearing resembled that of his own father, Owain Gwynedd.

But Riryd snorted. "Peace, you say? With half a thousand savages lurking in the woods behind them? Nay, don't be a dupe! Once outside this gate, we would be rushed and massacred!"

Madoc shook his head. "With due caution, but of course. I do mean to go out and meet that king. You *know* how I have yearned for a chance to know these people!"

Riryd hissed: "Don't you remember the battle on the beach?"

"I do, for 'twas I who fought it. I have no fear of going out to meet that man." Madoc was standing on Riryd's left and facing him, and when Riryd turned to glower at Madoc, he was momentarily blinded by the sunlight blazing off Madoc's coronet. He squinted and looked away. Madoc, seeing the light dance on Riryd's face, realized what had happened, and turned his head slightly. Then he said in a soothing voice, "I shall go out only to where they stand. I will take six tall men with me, just as many as he has with him. If there is treachery, and I doubt there will be, we will seize him hostage and bring him back in with us. You should keep the crossbows ready to let fly at any of their soldiers who emerge from the woods. But *only* on my command, for I am going out there in peace. Do you understand all I say?"

"I am against this," Riryd muttered.

"Of course you are, brother. As you are against anything I do," Madoc said.

Riryd sighed and slumped. "So be it. But first, pray, let us do something to impress upon them the hazards of tricking us."

"A prudent thought. And how would you do that?"

"Show them the strike of a crossbow." Riryd was a firm believer in the weapon. "Show them it will hit a man even there in yon wood where they lurk."

"No, damn you! I say we mean to create peace! Not start a war!"

Riryd sighed again, and flinched when the sunlight again reflected off Madoc's coronet.

"Never mind the crossbow," Madoc said. "I know how to make a strong impression upon them."

WITH SIX TALL SOLDIERS ARMED WITH PIKES AND SHIELDS, MADOC set forth from the opened gate and strode out among the stumps toward the group of native envoys, clad in mail and armor, sword at his side, carrying a pikestaff with a Welsh banner. His heart raced with excitement and admiration as he drew near them, but he kept his face stern and calm. He kept looking straight at the eyes of the man he presumed to be the king, and as he drew near, he saw that the man had immense dignity and resolve. His face was nut-brown, wide, flat, and hairless. Some sort of fine shell pendant hung before his lips from the septum of his nose. His headdress appeared to be the whole skin of a raven, with head, wings, and feathers on. He was not quite as tall as Madoc, but nearly so, and quite erect and imposing. The smoke from the little fire before him swirled up and away in the light of sunrise.

As Madoc approached them, he veered leftward, and they turned slightly to face him as he came. Then he turned right, and the sun's reflection off the plaque of his coronet flashed over their faces, blinding them. He kept moving his head slightly and saw the yellow light dancing and shimmering over them, from one to the other.

At last Madoc stopped three paces in front of the king and stood so the shimmering light stayed on his face, forcing him to squint. Then he said, in his deepest and most resonant voice:

"I am Madoc, son of Owain Gwynedd. I come to you in peace." He held up his right hand to show that aside from the banner pike, he held no weapon. The native king's stoic face was dissolving into confusion and awe, and the six men with him looked as if they were on the verge of flight.

Madoc presumed that he was creating fear and superstition in these natives, that the light flashing from his forehead might be having the same effect on them that the great bellowing dragon of the *Gwenan Gorn* had had on the natives on the bay shore two years before.

If indeed it were, the native king was proving himself a brave man. He still stood his ground, and now he uttered a few syllables apparently to calm or encourage the men beside him.

The native king raised his right hand as Madoc had. Madoc smiled and spoke to one of his soldiers. "Now give me the beads." The soldier came forth and gave him a necklace made of eight strings of blue glass beads. Madoc stepped forward and proffered them to the king, who hesitantly reached out with his palm upturned. He twitched when Madoc laid the beads across his palm, as if afraid they might burn him. Then he looked down at them, his face full of intense interest, and began to roll some of the beads between his fingers and thumb. The delight on his face grew until he was smiling broadly and making a kind of chuckling sound in his throat. He turned left and right, showing the gift to the six men with him, and they in turn chortled over it. Apparently they had never seen the like. They all examined it for a long time, like children, rattling it, holding it up to the morning light, smelling it, even tasting it with their tongues. When the king returned his attention to Madoc, he was smiling openly, revealing even, white teeth, which Madoc found to be amazing. Few men of that age in the civilized world still had teeth.

For a long time they stood facing each other at an arm's distance, looking at each other, sometimes nodding, sometimes smiling, trying to read each other's eyes and expressions, wishing they had words that could be understood. Eventually Madoc began to study the beautiful mantle the native king wore over his broad shoulders. From a distance he had not been able to determine what it was made of, but now he discerned that it was of whole skins of some brightly feathered birds, and that in the morning light it shimmered with rainbows of colors, like the fine feathers of pigeons he had seen in Europe, though the general feathering was much lighter in hue. And when the king saw that Madoc was looking at the mantle, he made a rather pigeonlike chortling sound, turned out a sort of bone toggle and removed the mantle from his own shoulders. Then, handing off his staff to the native on his right, he stepped to Madoc's side and set the mantle over his broad shoulders. Madoc smelled the same clean musky odor he had noticed in all the towns.

Then the king, apparently seeing pleasure in Madoc's face, did a surprising thing. He put his arms around Madoc and held him in a hug that grew so warm and strong that for one alarming moment Madoc thought it had been a trick, to crush him or break his back. Madoc's soldiers murmured in astonishment and were about to spring forward and save him. But Madoc, reading the king's throat sounds as true pleasure and affection, returned the embrace with his own considerable might, even until he could hear and feel the king's joints pop. Then both broke the embrace and the king stood back, holding Madoc's elbows and laughing with delight. At that, the king's six men came forth chortling and began embracing Madoc and his startled soldiers, which for one precarious moment almost started a fight, until Madoc exclaimed to them, "This is good! Embrace them! These are no enemies!" And, himself now almost giddy with relief and affection, Madoc poured up laughter from the very core of his breast and accepted the hugs of the other six natives. From the woods there arose a joyous clamor of hundreds of voices, and Madoc was astonished to see countless natives materializing there, where not a body had shown itself before.

"Praise God!" Madoc exclaimed to Rhys the soldier. "We have found a loving people! If only they can learn our tongue—perhaps our bard Meredydd could teach them. . . ."

Many of the native warriors were coming across the clearing now, some hesitantly but others on the run, howling with a childlike joy.

Suddenly several of them screamed and fell. The others faltered, turned in confusion, began shouting and keening. Madoc saw the native king grow tense, looking toward the disturbance, and was as bewildered as he was. Then a terrible notion struck him, and he turned agonized eyes toward his fortress.

What he had feared was true.

The bowmen and crossbowmen on the parapets were filling the sky with a hail of hissing arrows. Most of the missiles were falling far short of the warriors, who were still some two hundred paces from the palisade. But the far-flying crossbow bolts had already downed several of the natives. This triumphant moment of peace and goodwill had been ruined by a warlike impulse of his Welshmen, just as another moment had been two years ago on an eastern bay shore!

Now Madoc thought fast, wondering how to keep from being caught and killed by the onrushing horde of natives. For a moment he looked at the bewildered face of the native king, and thought of grabbing him as a hostage and dragging him, with a dirk at his throat, back to the fortress. But the man was obviously too powerful to be subdued in an instant; the warriors would be upon Madoc before he could do it.

The king shouted to his warriors in a trumpet of a voice, several words, and he and his six aides darted quickly out of reach, running toward the warrior mob. They in turn stopped where they were and then began running back toward the woods, their king following. The king kept looking back at Madoc with an expression of pure agony in his face.

"Come," Madoc said to his soldiers. "Slowly and show them no fear." And he began leading them back toward the fortress. He saw that the warriors had gathered up their fallen comrades in their retreat.

In his state of chagrin, Madoc could scarcely think. When I find out who ordered the archers to shoot, he thought, I'll have his head!

But something told him that the man responsible must have been his own brother Riryd. And for the moment at least he thought:

I would happily sacrifice that small-minded brother of mine for the boon of that king's embrace!

Then of course he was ashamed of the thought.

He wondered, as he strode back toward the palisade with its helmeted bowmen standing on the parapets, why the natives had been turned back so easily by a few wounds and the shouts of their leaders, which surely they could scarcely have heard in the din of their own onrush. Then as he looked back at the retreating warriors and their king, he realized that it must have been the range of the crossbows that had disheartened them. To have been hit by shafts at the distance of two or three hundred paces must have seemed like a terrible magic.

And, too, there had been the blaze of light from his coronet. They as well as their king must have been bedazzled by that seeming magic.

Magic! he thought bitterly. We need the affection of those people for our very survival, but all we do is confound them once and again with sham magic!

The soldiers inside the fortress were exuberant until they saw the murderous scowl on Madoc's face. Riryd at once sensed that he was in deep disfavor, and set his face defiantly.

"You told the archers to shoot?" Madoc hissed. "Could you not see that we were making peace with their king?"

"Peace? I saw them wrestling you, and their warriors charging! God in Heaven, man! Do you think I care not for your life?"

Madoc then could see it all through Riryd's eyes and could not condemn him. And when Riryd realized the consequences of his hasty command, he could no longer exult over the power or accuracy of the crossbows. For the rest of the day the Welshmen worked glumly on the structures of their fortress, watched in vain for any reappearance of the natives, and after sunset began to be haunted again by the monotonous drumbeats from down the river. Madoc lamented to Meredydd that night:

"How I wanted to cry to that elegant brown king that it was a mistake, and beg him to come back! Not to know another's tongue is worse than being mute! Meredydd, if you could have conveyed one word of my sentiment to that dusky lord, I would have made you my minister in the instant!"

"Perhaps, milord," Meredydd said, his heartbeat quickening, "there will be another chance to meet him. I am trying to learn hand-sign from Toolakha. Mayhap that will help."

A COLD RAINSTORM BLEW IN THE NEXT DAY, AND THE HALF-finished compound was soon trodden into a swine pen of a place where everyone was too miserable to give much thought to the natives, except the parties of hunters who had to venture forth. They returned with two deer and reported that although they had been stalked continually, none of the warriors had come within a furlong, evidently from fear of the far-shooting weapons.

Then through two more dank days of intermittent rain and snow, there was no more sign of the natives; even their drums were silent in the evenings. The skillful axmen made frames for the houses, which the women then interwove with wattle. After the roofs were covered, with everything from thatch to brush and dead leaves, the people began churning mud in pits to make daub, and plastered the walls with it. At last they had homes where they could kindle hearth fires, dry their sodden clothing and footwear, and sleep without shivering.

But even this brought little cheer, because winter was upon them, and the specter of hunger stood before them, stranded as they were in a stark land with no stores of grain, where the woods were haunted by stealthy warriors who had been turned hostile.

* * *

THE THIRD DAY BEGAN WITH A SETTING MOON EMERGING FROM BEhind the clouds shortly before sunrise, a reprieve at last from the dismal autumn rains. Before daylight a sentry sent word to Madoc that someone was kindling a fire out in the clearing. Roused from his bed, Madoc climbed up and gazed out over the stumpy field.

There in the weak light of morning stood the native king and about a dozen other men wrapped in robes, a small fire burning on the ground before them, exactly where they had met with Madoc before. They were watching the fortress and waiting.

Madoc's spirits rose like the sunrise.

"Rhys!" he called out, and when the soldier appeared, he said, "They have come back to resume our council! Quick, get the bard and my brother. And . . . go to my armoire and get the feathered cloak!"

He waited until the sun was above the horizon before ordering the gates opened. He did not think this was a native trick to lure him into danger, but he intended to seem as powerful as he could when he met them again, and so he wore his coronet, which would flash sunlight in their eyes as before. With him now were fifteen of his able-bodied soldiers, about all he could gather together from the sick and gaunt colony to make a formidable impression in their armor. With him this time was Riryd, who also wore a polished coronet. Madoc wanted Riryd at his side so that he might be properly impressed by the character of the native king—but also in order that he would not precipitate such a disturbance as he had the last time. Rhys was left in charge of the fortress.

Beside Madoc walked Meredydd, who swallowed nervously and crept fearfully out of the safety of the palisade. Meredydd could not in any way make a manly impression with his weak, narrow face and flossy little beard, but Madoc intended to use well the bard's abilities.

Meredydd carried his little harp, wrapped in leather, brought along because Madoc suspected that music and songs might somehow enchant these natives. The harp would not be more sham magic, but likely would create wonder with its sounds. Meredydd was a sorry sight of a man, but he sang like an angel, tones all dulcet and clear. Madoc thought there might be an opportunity to have the bard play and sing for the natives.

But his main reason for bringing Meredydd was his hope that the bard might, through his skill with words or his growing understanding of sign, be able to convey or understand meanings across that chasm between the two languages. Thus Meredydd was possibly, in Madoc's expectations anyway, a more important part of this entourage than even his richly armored and haughty brother Riryd the Prince.

Again Madoc approached the natives so that his coronet flashed in their faces, and Riryd played his upon them as well—a pair of god-men.

The native king's strong face was impassive when Madoc stopped before him. The king at once, with a sweep of his right hand, indicated the distant woods, and Madoc perceived that to mean that no warriors were hiding there in wait.

Several hides had been spread over boughs on the ground, on both sides of the fire. With a gesture the king invited Madoc and Riryd to sit on one side, and he and a few of his men seated themselves cross-legged on the other. When the princes and Meredydd were seated, the king nodded, though he still did not smile, and said something to one of his followers. The man held the skin of a small animal with dark brown fur. He reached into the tail end of it and drew forth what appeared to be a decorated handle with a carved stone on one end. Then he reached into a leather bag and pinched out something that appeared to be crumbled dead leaves, and with it he filled an opening in the carved stone. While he was occupied with this, the king sat beside him and gazed intently at Riryd and the bard. Then his eyes returned to Madoc's face and he waited. The morning was cold and the small fire gave off little heat; apparently it was a ceremonial fire only. It was fragrant, of cedar and some other aromatic fuels.

The man handed the long object to the king, who then did a remarkable thing. Putting one end in his mouth, he picked up a small firebrand and touched it to the stone end. Sucking on the stem end, he rose effortlessly to his feet. He turned to face east, raised the object to his eye level, and blew a cloud of smoke from his mouth. Then he turned to face south, sucked the stem again, raised the object and blew another cloud of smoke. He repeated the actions toward the west and north, then blew two more smokes, toward the sky and the earth. To the Welshmen it appeared as if the man were eating fire, and they were awed.

Now the king turned to Madoc and extended the object across the fire toward him, and with a nod seemed to be signaling him to stand.

Madoc rose, his heavy armor making him awkward. He took the object. A wisp of the smoke from the stone end was rich and fragrant, like an incense. The king pointed to Madoc's mouth and nodded, and with his finger indicated that Madoc was to repeat what he had done toward the four directions. He stared at Madoc with an intense appeal in his eyes, and nodded so emphatically that Madoc knew this was quite important. So, while his men gaped at him, Madoc put the stem in his mouth and cautiously inhaled through it, facing east.

The pungent smoke burned his throat and lungs as if he had swallowed fire. He went into a convulsion of coughing. His eyes watered and his nose leaked. Riryd looked terrified. The native king and his men put their hands over their mouths to conceal smiles, but they kept themselves from laughing aloud.

Madoc felt more humiliated than angry, as if the native king had proven himself stronger by eating fire with such ease. Madoc's convulsion at last died down, but his throat was raw and he was beginning to be dizzy. But now the king indicated that he should face south and do it again.

With the greatest dread, Madoc faced that direction and sucked the smoke again, with the same results. He began to fear that this was a trick, and he heard Riryd mutter, "They are poisoning you!"

By the time Madoc had finished his four turns he was miserable, so dizzy he had to sit down. His fingers and head were buzzing and his hands were cold and wet. His mustache and chin whiskers were full of mucus from his nose, and he could only wipe them on his sleeve. He had, he felt, fallen for a ruse and might die of this.

But now the native king had retrieved the smoke-breathing device and passed it to one of his own chieftains, who used it with no apparent ill effects, so it must not be lethal after all, Madoc thought.

Then the native king passed the smoke stick to Riryd and signaled that he should use it. Riryd gave Madoc a panicky glance, but Madoc could only cough and say, "They'll . . . think you no man . . . if ye refuse it."

After Riryd and Meredydd had choked and gagged through the procedure, Madoc realized that he was feeling better and had not really been poisoned. And by now the native king was smiling. He pointed at the birdskin mantle he had given Madoc and nodded, and nodded again in pleasure as he fingered the blue beads and held them up to show.

"I think," Madoc said to Riryd and the bard, "that we're forgiven for his people's wounds. Praise be to God for that! Perhaps he realizes it was a mishap."

"Or that this bedamned fire-breathing has punished us enough," Riryd rasped through his sore throat.

"Now," Madoc said with a grin at Riryd's joke, "it seems we have survived their ceremony. Let us see whether they can bear our bard's singing." That, too, was a joke, for Meredydd's voice was a pleasure to hear.

The natives looked on with intense curiosity as Meredydd untied thongs and opened the fleece to reveal the shapely little instrument. Its varnished wood and bright brass fittings gleamed in the morning light, and Madoc could only wonder what their untutored minds might perceive it to be.

Meredydd shifted to sit with his right foot tucked under his hip, his left knee up and crooked to serve as a rest, and lovingly, tentatively, laid his fingers upon the tight gut strings. His eyes took on that farseeing, dreamy look that always preceded his music, and the native king murmured at the sight of that look itself. Madoc himself had always found it almost mystic, that look in a bard's eyes.

Meredydd's fingers were ugly; long, knobby-knuckled, fishy-white, and weak looking, they were now sooty and abraded from tending campfires and handling greasy meat; his few unbroken fingernails were impacted with black dirt. But when they stood now upon the harp strings like spiders on webs and began to move, they transformed themselves.

The quivering chord of notes that sprang off the strings, like little invisible arrows off bowstrings, made the natives gasp; if they had not been seated, Madoc felt, they might have run away. Though the notes were thin and without resonance out in this open space under the morning sky, they obviously were so new a sound to these ears that they must have seemed like magic.

At once Meredydd's spider fingers shifted to new positions and shot forth another volley of sound arrows, then another; then he began plucking a melody. It was not one of the child-songs he had been teaching Gwenllian, nor one of the old ecclesiastical cantos, but something new, quite strong and lyrical. To Madoc's ears it was beautiful. To the native listeners it was astonishing; it was as if the arrow notes were piercing their hearts, but whether with pleasure or pain Madoc could not yet tell.

And now, even while they were still stunned by the experience of the harp music, Meredydd began to sing, in his clear, high voice, and Madoc realized at once that this was his own saga, the work Meredydd had been doing with crude pens and homemade inks, even the juice of berries, during this long and perilous adventure.

Madoc am I, King Owain Gwynedd's son,
With stature large, and comely grace adorned.
No lands at home nor store of wealth me please,
My mind was whole to search the ocean seas.
Toward the sunset sea I sailed,
My ship the *Gwenan Gorn*:
Her stays were sprung and sails were torn
By storms that surged and wailed!
But on came I undaunted still
By dragons of the deep;
Faith in our Savior did I keep
And bold was my heart until
At last like Noah's soaring dove
My uncaged bird espied
This fabled land ere hope had died,
Espied it from above,
And led me on to Iarghal's shore
Where dwells my Fate forevermore . . .

Meredydd's voice, richly modulated and sweet as a flute, transfixed the natives, and they watched his lips and tongue for the Welsh syllables as keenly as they studied the marvelous dance of his fingers on the harp strings. Madoc was charmed and touched to the depth of his soul by this communion between singer and hearers. He leaned over and laid his hand on Riryd's wrist.

"We have won them," he said.

CHAPTER 5

Valley of the Ten-nes-see
A.D. 1175

Madoc, tugging thoughtfully at his graying chin whiskers, watched the stonemasons mortar in the last capstone of the last bastion of his castle. At last a castle stood in the new Welsh land!

Dolwyddelan, he thought, with a deep sigh. My son is being born in Dolwyddelan Castle! As I was born in Dolwyddelan Castle, half a world away!

Standing atop the wall, Madoc turned slowly and surveyed his castle and his kingdom around it. The prospect of it was breathtaking. A hot summer wind stirred the treetops far below in the river valleys. Two hundred and thirty feet below him, around the base of the nearly vertical stone bluff, curved the seething rapids of the narrow river whose source was twenty leagues south along the ridge of the Long Mountain. In those rapids there were eddies and pools of crystalline water calm enough for even children to bathe in, and even now he could see, so far below they seemed the size of insects, the naked coppery bodies of several dozen of the native women and their half-Welsh children, the first generation of the mixed race of which he had dreamed in those desperate days of the migration.

There were not so many of these mixed-blood children as Madoc had hoped there would be by now, after four years of interbreeding. Few of the newborn had survived infancy, and hundreds of the native mothers had died in their pregnancies. Even men and boys of the native tribe had died of awful sicknesses in the first two years of their alliance with Madoc. Even their king had become profoundly ill and nearly perished. But his people had chanters and healers, and the king had survived and grown strong again, and he had vowed fealty to Madoc, and stood by his word. A most open and eager coition between the two peoples had been encouraged, and the population had begun to grow. These surviving children of that first generation were the beginning of a laboring and serving class. They, and their children in turn, would grow up learning the trades of smiths, masons, miners, and carpenters, and would be the builders of other castles as Madoc's kingdom spread. Madoc had elevated his best white Welshmen to thegnships, and they helped enforce his authority in his growing realm. Madoc still thought of himself as a prince, but he reigned now over a domain equal in size to his father's kingdom in Cambria. To his subjects, both Welsh and native, Madoc was King.

The castle walls contained a hectare of well-drained land, with houses and streets and a two-story manor house for his own family, another for Riryd's. Several houses had been built within the walls for chiefs and chieftains of the native people, who called themselves Tsoyaha Euchee, which Meredydd had translated to mean "Children of the Sun from Far Away." Their tribal king, lover of the bard's music, was Sun Eagle, who four years before had smoked the ceremonial pipe with the princes and listened to Meredydd's song in a clearing outside Madoc's wooden fortress, ten leagues upriver to the northeast. The alliance begun that day between the sons of Owain Gwynedd and the Euchee had made Madoc's colony flourish. Not since that glowing day had Madoc's people gone hungry or wandered lost in the mountains. Sun Eagle's people had fed them and taught them everything about the hunting, growing, harvesting, gathering, and preserving of foods in this land, and had shown them roots, barks, and leaves that could be used to heal wounds and snakebites and even diminish pain. They had taught the Welshmen to cover their skin with herb-scented grease to protect them from the maddening insects of summer. The native hunters had taught the Welsh hunters how to find, stalk, and kill game more effectively, how to build snares and deadfalls, how to trap fish in weirs, and even how to go fishing without hooks or nets but bare hands when need be. And they had taught them the profound pleasures of the pipe, that instrument that had sealed the friendship of their kings: both in ceremonies and for pleasure they breathed the fragrant smoke of tobacco, sumac, red willow bark, and hemp.

Madoc, now standing on his castle wall while Annesta was in the labor of childbirth in a room of their manor below, could see also in the river bottoms far below another of the wondrous provisions the Euchee had given his people: in every clearing and glade spread the yellow-green stalks of the grain crop they called *meejep*. Hard-hulled, durable, and nourishing, it was a kind of wealth in its own right. It filled the castle's granary and could feed all the colonists throughout the winters even if hunting was bad, and the Euchee had taught the Welshwomen scores of appetizing ways to cook and serve it. The winter before, there had been a surplus of the grain, and one of Madoc's thegns had fermented a mash of it to make a palatable sort of ale. It had proven to be so welcome that the princes had allotted a portion of this year's *meejep* crop for the brewing of ale.

And in those four years with the Tsoyaha Euchee, trading with surrounding tribes as well had been opened for the Welshmen and was expanding every year. Envoys from distant tribes would give almost anything for the blue Welsh beads, which they called "Little Night Skies." Those were in such demand by everyone, including the Euchee, that one family of Welsh glassmakers had been provided a kiln for their manufacture, and ordered to keep the process a secret even from the Euchee, so that the wealth accruing from blue beads would always stay with the Welsh.

And, much as the fame of the "Little Night Skies" had spread, the renown of Madoc's metalsmiths had, like a lodestone, drawn traders and admirers from outlying tribes, bringing still more wealth.

Madoc now strolled along the high castle wall as confidently as if it were a path on the ground, even though the wall and then the cliff below it fell away so sheer that a misstep would have pitched him to death in the river boulders far below. So firmly did Madoc feel set upon the top of the world that he now risked the height as he never would have before, and was exhilarated by it.

"Give me that tool," Madoc said to the mason who stood on scaffolding inside the wall he had just finished. The man handed up a pointing trowel he had been wiping clean of mortar. The mason obviously was frightened by his master's recklessness. He said:

"Pray, Majesty, do not step here where I have just finished, for the mortar has not set and the capstone would fail you!"

"Aye, of course." Madoc swirled, raised the trowel high overhead, and his voice boomed out, causing many people in the castle to look up:

"A sacrifice of iron, to God Almighty who delivered us from tempests and floods and guided us to make a kingdom here!" He flung the tool far out over the abyss, the motion almost costing him his balance, then steadied himself and watched it turning and falling, turning and falling, until it disappeared in the foam of the rushing river far below. Turning then and seeing the shocked look on the stonemason's face, he said, "Yes, iron is scarce. But our Lord thinks little of a sacrifice that's easy to give." He knelt and put a big hand on the mason's shoulder. "Your iron tool in the water will help us find ore somewhere in these mountains. I have no doubt of it, good man. The natives bring bits of ore—iron, copper, tin—and we shall learn whence it comes. Thank you for your excellent work and thank you for that tool. Ha! A great day! Dolwyddelan Castle has been done!"

The mason, looking both bewildered and delighted by this happy speech from his sovereign, replied, stammering, "Majesty, I . . . I offer you my shoulder to lean upon if thou wouldst climb down." To the worker's great relief, Madoc did climb down from his precarious place. But he stayed on the scaffold awhile, arms leaning on the wall, and gazed northward toward the deep, steep valley of the big river into which the fast little river flowed. The big river, called by natives the Ten-nes-see, was the river upon whose banks Madoc had built his winter camp near Sun Eagle's town, and the next spring he had floated his people down, exploring for a perfect castle site, which he had found here, on this jutting stone promontory flanked by a waterfall. Even while anchored here with the building of Dolwyddelan, Madoc had daydreamed about setting off someday to float down the Ten-nes-see to its end. The descriptions of its course, learned by Meredydd the Bard from native traders and chiefs, fueled Madoc's wanderlust in the way the Mare Atlanticum and the legend of Iarghal once had. Below Dolwyddelan, the natives said, the river ran through ranges of hills and then plateaus and woodlands toward the northwest, perhaps two hundred leagues and growing deeper and wider, until it poured into a larger, westering river, which in turn flowed shortly into the greatest of all rivers, which flowed south for a long, long way to a sea that was always warm, being so close to the sun.

Along those great rivers there had lived hundreds of hundreds of hundreds of people of many tribes, who traveled by long boats and traded with each other, and built hills of earth with temples on top, such as Madoc had seen in the lowlands of the south. Sun Eagle had said those hill-building people were as numerous as the leaves on a tree.

For all this knowledge, vague though it was, Madoc was indebted to Meredydd the bard and his concubine. She had taught the bard the hand-sign way of talking, which, amazingly, almost all tribes understood regardless of how their spoken tongues differed, and she had taught him the tongue of her own people, who were called the Coo-thah. Meredydd in turn had taught her enough of the Welsh tongue that she could be understood—though she still would talk to hardly anyone but Meredydd and Gwenllian. She seemed to have anger and contempt for all the other Welsh people, including Madoc and Riryd and their wives. She was indeed so aloof and uncivil to her masters that Madoc would have liked sometimes to pitch her over this precipice. But of course he could not do that because she was the key to virtually all the communication with the native peoples—and because she was the very love of Meredydd's life, a love through which the little poet had flourished and become perhaps the canniest man in Madoc's whole colony. Furthermore, Madoc's own daughter Gwenllian doted on Earth Daughter. Gwenllian and Meredydd and Earth Daughter had become like a tiny family unto themselves, usually cloistered together in a room with the Bible, the Bestiary, the harp, and Meredydd's handwritten sheets of vellum.

Madoc turned from the view and looked down into his castle, which was as usual thronging with people, voices, dust, movement: artisans working, carpenters building, white-skinned and brown-skinned children racing about and playing, Euchee men and women chatting, eating, trading. Madoc watched three young Euchee women cross the courtyard below his scaffold with baskets of tubers and beans balanced on their heads, wearing nothing but jewelry. The unabashed nudity of the Euchee women stirred and troubled Madoc. Though he continued to love Annesta with the most idealistic devotion, she had been with child for a full term, and Madoc, in the prime of his vigor, sometimes found himself gazing at these cheerfully wanton native women and envying his male subjects, whom he had encouraged to interbreed freely with them.

When Madoc had first seen the natives of this land, he had hoped to see them enlightened in the Word of God, but that goal seemed to be slipping further and further away. Since the death of the priests in the hurricane, the colony had been without an ecclesiastical rudder. Even Sir Meredydd, his minister and the kingdom's principal teacher, cohabited with a native woman who would wear nothing but necklaces above her waist.

But thank Heaven for that, Madoc would remind himself

sometimes. Without that woman, we probably would still be trying to talk to Sun Eagle by pointing and nodding and gaping like fish!

Still, he would think, I have knighted a man who has a naked heathen in his bed.

Madoc and Annesta had talked a few times about the women's immodesty. "Have we a right to try to teach them shame?" he had asked her. "These people seem not to have been put out of Eden!"

And Annesta had wondered, "Do you suppose that these are *not* children of Adam? I fear sounding heretical by asking, but might they have been created separately, and did not taste the fruit of knowledge?"

Madoc had pondered those questions often. According to the Scriptural teachings, Eden was on the other side of the ocean. How could any of the Children of Adam have come here?

This is an Eden, and these people remain in the state of innocence, he thought. Had this side of the world, Iarghal, been a separate creation?

Whatever the answers, he believed Iarghal to be a true paradise. He turned and looked southward. Beyond the castle wall, over the rim of the river gorge, rose the thin mist that could usually be seen above the waterfall just upstream. Built upon this high stony crest, with chasms on all sides, Madoc's Dolwyddelan Castle was impregnable. Any attackers coming to its gate would have to climb single file up a narrow cliff path, which, a hundred and fifty feet above the river, squeezed between two natural monoliths so that only one man at a time could pass through. Into the cliff adjacent to that tight passage, guardrooms had been quarried, big enough to hold perhaps twenty Welsh soldiers—enough to repel an attacking force of thousands, Madoc believed. Yes, Iarghal looked like a paradise. Madoc's homeland of Cambria had looked like a paradise, too, but had become a bloody and evil land. One might have faith in God's protection, but would also depend upon one's own devices as well to protect the people.

IN THEIR STUDY ROOM, GWENLLIAN AND EARTH DAUGHTER WERE trying to do their reading lessons, but it was difficult to concentrate because of the sound of Annesta's agonizing labor, which could be clearly heard from the next chamber. Gwenllian's heart raced with anxiety; sometimes the outcry was so terrible, tears would start in Gwenllian's eyes.

Earth Daughter, too, was being bothered by the sounds, but in a different way. Finally she glanced angrily in the direction of the door and muttered: "Queen not hurt so, if she get up as they tell her. Oh of course a mother hurt, trying to do birth lying on her back! Hnh!" Earth Daughter had been in that room with Annesta and the midwives and knew what was going on.

Meredydd looked up from his writing table and said with a wave of his quill, "I have told you, a queen does not bear the king an heir while squatting as if to relieve herself."

"She makes herself hurt so bad," Toolakha said. "Things not fall *up*! Not even babies who will be kings fall up! Hnh!"

Meredydd glanced at his woman with both admiration and annoyance, while Gwenllian simply gazed at her in wonder at what she had said. Both Meredydd and Gwenllian lived in dread that she was still wild enough inside, and angry enough at the white people, that she might just vanish sometime and flee back to the life from which she had been abducted five years ago. Neither Meredydd nor Gwenllian had ever spoken that fear to each other, but both had it. Earth Daughter was a good mistress and a remarkable student, certainly the only savage on this continent who was proving capable of learning to read Welsh. But teaching her the Welsh tongue seemed not to make her think or feel Welsh, and Gwenllian thought she was still like a caged bird.

Meredydd needed Earth Daughter in many and complex ways. She had made a happy and important man of him by giving him her affection. But she was also his window into the soul of the native peoples, and always was teaching him as much as he taught her. Though she was not a Euchee from the mountains but a Coo-thah from the southern coast, she understood what was important to the people of the tribes. Meredydd, as Madoc's minister, had done wonders as ambassador and interpreter between the Welsh and Euchee, but he doubted that he could have done it at all well without the insights and understandings she gave him. The old Tsoyaha Euchee king Sun Eagle lived in a stone house in the castle and did everything Madoc wanted him to do, and was not a free king of a free people anymore, but just a dignified elder who doted on a bearded young king who had bedazzled him years ago with blue beads and a flashing helmet. Earth Daughter seemed to have a special kind of contempt for old Sun Eagle, who not only had yielded up his whole people to the white-faces, but had not even tried to learn the language of his new masters.

Heavy footsteps were approaching in the stone corridor, and a thegn appeared in the door. "Sire," he said to Meredydd, "you are summoned to the Great Hall. Some men come, from a tribe unknown, and you are requested to bring . . . her." He tilted his head toward Toolakha, not knowing what to call her.

As they prepared to go down, Gwenllian got Earth Daughter aside and asked her, "How do you so surely know more than my mother about the way it feels, squatting down or lying abed?"

"Toolakha was a mother, with little son, before you came and caught us. I bore my son squatting down, so he could fall down, not fall *up*."

Gwenllian's eyes widened. "Where . . . what became of your son?"

Toolakha's eyelids grew hard and her nostrils flared as she remembered that day. "When you Welsh caught us that day at the river . . . I saw husband of mine up by trees, and he saved our tiny boy and ran away. They be dead now."

"Why?" Gwenllian exclaimed, her mouth like a flower bud, eyes swimming at the thought of such a sadness. "Why would you think that?"

Earth Daughter looked down and compressed her lips. "In my village we saw everyone was dead, do you remember?"

MADOC WAS AS AWED BY THE SIGHT OF THE SIX TRAVELERS AS THEY were by the Great Hall of his castle.

They were sick men, repulsively sick, beyond pity. Though they carried themselves with dignity as they were led before his throne, they were emaciated, and their bodies and mouths were covered with running sores. Their hair was gone in patches, two seemed half blind, several had twitching hands. They knew they were wretched, and would not meet the eyes of the warrior thegns who stood along both walls holding their blazoned shields, or of old Sun Eagle, who sat at Madoc's left on a cushion of furs. Next to him stood Sir Meredydd, the minister. His concubine, Earth Daughter, was beside him, and she was struggling with more emotion than she had shown since the day she had bitten off her finger at the mound graves so long ago. "*Coo-thah!*" she whispered. "My People!"

A bad beginning was made when Madoc and Riryd declined to smoke a council pipe with the visitors because of their leprous appearance. And the Coo-thahs themselves seemed to be so overawed by the echoing gloom of the cavelike hall that they could scarcely express themselves. Finally, one of them said by hand sign that it was not good to have a woman in a council of men. They were surprised to hear her explain to them in their own tongue, "Do not see me here as a woman in this council of headmen and kings; I am only a hollow bone for words to pass through between mouths and ears. My song is yours, your words are mine. Speak through me as through a hollow bone to this giant king with yellow face-hair, and all will be understood."

When Meredydd told Madoc what she had told them, Madoc was pleased, and nodded, and pointed between the men and Earth Daughter.

At last the Coo-thahs urged one of their members forward to speak for them, and he began, in a voice curdled by illness and interrupted frequently by pauses for breath, with Toolakha relaying their woeful tale in Welsh:

"We thank Creator for bringing us together so that we may say these things. We speak in truth and ask the hair-face king to listen with his ears and heart open.

"We are People of the Coo-thah. We are few now. Once we were as many as the leaves in the forest. Our towns were beside the river you came by to the mountains. You saw our temple hills that we made when we were many. Our paths led to Eh-to-ah, Great Temple Place, and back, and all around."

Meredydd listened keenly to this first explanation of who they were. This was preamble, he knew, and he hoped there would be time later to learn more details of their civilization, which evidently had been far greater than the Euchee had led him to believe. Toolakha had hinted that her people were part of a great circle of peoples, but he had presumed that she simply meant mankind on this continent. Now she continued translating the words of the sick man:

"Six summers ago we watched your big, winged canoes come. We hid, to wait. When your warriors caught some of us"—here Toolakha's voice paused and quavered, as she remembered—"we said, 'These are dangerous men,' and we watched you from far off. A woman you caught got away at once, and came to tell us you were bad, and we believed her. So we did not go to meet you, even when you built your town by the mouth of the Coo-thah, where we used to fish."

Madoc closed his eyes and nodded, remembering the image of the golden woman leaping off the side of the *Gwenan Gorn*, that image that had recurred so often in his dreams.

"After that," the Coo-thah continued, "two of our elders got away from you, and came up the river to tell us you had kept them in cages as children keep birds. Those elders were filled with spirits of sickness. They leaked dirty water from all the holes of their heads and bodies, and dried up dead.

"And then," he continued, his voice rising to a wail, tears streaming from his eyes, "a great wind of death swept among all our peoples!" Madoc at first thought the man was referring to the hurricane, but he went on: "All got full of pain! All poured dirty water out until they were dried up wrinkled and dead like the two elders, and our eyes sank back into our heads! Our people died faster than we could bury them! And when we who remained were too weak to carry dirt to make graves, we ran from our villages and many more died in the woods! We thought your god was punishing us because we had killed some of your four-leggeds to eat—"

"Hah! So!" Riryd cried. " 'Twas not all wolves and lions and swamp dragons after all, was it, that stole our sheep and swine!"

The Coo-thah waited silent until Madoc, with a grim smile, motioned for him to continue. But at that moment Toolakha poured forth a torrent of words to the Coo-thah in a querying tone. He paused for a long while, swaying on his feet, thinking, then answered her in a low voice with a few short syllables. She squeezed her eyes tight shut and sat there for minutes, head down, weeping silently. After a while Meredydd asked her if she could continue. She nodded, then fixed her wet eyes on Meredydd's face and gave him the explanation he had expected. "No more is my family. All gone to Other Side World, my husband, son, brothers . . . mother and father . . . all gone, from sickness!" Then she added what he had not expected: "All gone, from sickness of the white-faces of your Wales country!"

"What? Silence, wretched woman!" Madoc bellowed suddenly. "Bard, thy concubine has an evil tongue!"

And for once Riryd's indignation was aimed the same as his brother's. "*Her* people's sickness, not ours!" he snarled. "Her people got plagued, not ours! Muzzle thy naked slut, bard!"

Meredydd cringed before all this royal choler, but thought fast. The Coo-thah emissaries drew protectively together, glancing all about, as the princes' loud voices echoed in the stone hall and the dozen thegns grumbled and shifted their armor in response to their anger. "Majesties! Majesties!" Meredydd cried out. "Our translator is distraught, only just learning of this tragedy! Mercy on her, I beg you, lords! Mayhap, without the thunderclouds of thy disfavor rumbling over her, she would choose to apologize to you for what she hath said!" And as the furor subsided, he leaned close and softly implored her to do so, for her own sake.

Instead, Toolakha stood erect looking at the princes angrily. Though she had been prevailed upon to wear more than a mere loincloth as a member of the castle court, she still dressed only in a hip skirt and necklaces and whatever covering was provided by her cascades of ebony hair, and still seemed too primitive and savage a figure to be staring two princes in the eyes in their own court. Both knew, of course, that she could read, which none of their thegns could do, and that she and Meredydd were the keys to all their commerce with the tribes; still, the audacity of this barefoot, bare-breasted concubine was almost insufferable, especially to Riryd, who found virtually nothing to like in this alien country.

"Lords," Toolakha said, "the Coo-thah are long here, for generations you could not count. Always they know to make well any sickness spirits. They know all sickness here before.

"Then you come, all dirty people live with your four-leggeds. Catch me and elder men, and put in cage like birds. I feel your little biters all over my skin. What you eat is too old, is like what comes up from a sick stomach. Very soon I am sick, old men are sick, all so sick I pass through the sun, but I am young and strong and want to live and meet my child again, so I live! This man the bard be good to me, and comes he into my spirit with words so we both know. And teaches me to read the silent words in the books, so thus I go to your land, too, in my spirit. But all others of my Coo-thah, ah, no! By your swine animals or your sheep animals, or the rat animals, or the sick old men who got away, your Wales sickness pass through all the Coo-thah, and everyone dies almost! My husband and little boy, everyone of my blood, dies of your Wales sickness." She had started out with fire, and ended quietly. But Riryd leaped up, flushed with rage, pointing at her.

"That is nonsense, and calumny against Welshmen! This heathen slut accuses a Christian people! I ask, if it is a Welsh sickness, how comes it that our Welshmen stay well and her heathen people go down plagued? By God, make her answer me that!"

"Brother, sit ye and calm yourself," Madoc rumbled. " 'Tis not meet that a Prince of Wales haggle and point at a savage. We have emissaries here, and our Euchee king, and all our thegns. In God's name, hotspur, sit down and be seemly." Madoc's lips were hard and his teeth sawing but he tried to seem calm himself. But the allegations she had made about this plague troubled him. He had studied the ancient Greek physicians and historians, and knew that plagues had often followed invasions by armies from elsewhere. And he remembered, too, that soon after his arrival in this valley with his Welshmen, great numbers of Sun Eagle's people had fallen with vomiting fevers and milky fluxes and died. Riryd stood glowering at Toolakha for a long, defiant minute, then eased back into his throne, still livid. Meredydd's face was shining with cold sweat. Madoc said, "Let this outburst be forgot. Meredydd, sir, hereafter instruct your aide not to obtrude her person into manly councils; she is here at our leave only because she can convey the Coo-thah tongue, and I want these wretches to go on with their account." He looked at Toolakha now and said, "Have them continue."

The Coo-thah spokesman conferred with his peers for a while, and then his story resumed. "The great Sea Wind blew down your houses and walls and wrecked your big wing-boats. Soon you came marching up along the Coo-thah, do you remember, with your little skin-boats in the water? And men pulling a house that rolled on hoops and screamed like a panther? You came through our towns and tore up the graves of our many dead, and we thought the spirits would destroy you for that. But we watched, and they did not, and so we feared you more, and said, 'Their spirits that protect them are stronger than our spirits.' Our old shaman dreamed on you, and told us you were gods. And so we fled before you as you came on. There were few of us because of the Wind of Death earlier, and we who still lived were meek, and not strong. Yes, we fled before you, and went back to our towns only after you had passed through them. Then this happened:

"In our last town, the one most north, after you passed through, we returned there and found a Bear God. He looked like a white-skin man but was covered with dark hair. He had a magic of unbearable noise, and with it he seized the power of our king. That Bear God became the ruler of that village, and then another, until he had power along the whole Coo-thah. . . ."

Madoc and Riryd were leaning forward in their thrones, attentive and utterly mystified. The Coo-thah went on:

"We believed that Bear God to be one of you. We feared him because of his noise-magic, and because we thought he might get angry and make the rest of us ill again. But soon the Bear God told us why he had come. He would not rule us hard, he promised. He wanted only one thing: his choice of maidens to make fertile, and the right to plant his seed in any man's wife.

He made us words that all our Coo-thah nation would be given his great strength and vigor by the infusion of his blood, and we would be many again, and strong again. We counciled and our spirit leaders said this was a great gift from Creator, we needed this fertility, and Creator would scorn us if we did not accept Bear God. Thus we had many rituals. Bear God again and again showed his great power. Many girls and women got pregnant with his seed."

Suddenly Madoc's mouth dropped open. "Mungo!" he breathed. He said to Toolakha, "Ask them, did he say his name to them?"

She asked, and the Coo-thah replied, "Mnh-guh."

Toolakha said, "Mnh-guh. It is our name for bear."

"Aha! Tell them to go on."

"Soon," said the Coo-thah, "we were growing ill again. Not stronger as Bear God promised. But not the same sickness. Women who lay with Bear God began to rot in their woman-parts. Then their husbands got rotted in their man-parts. When children were born, they were dead, or crooked-limbed, or grew blind young. Most are dead now. And we are like this, as you see us." This last was said with abject sadness, the speaker spreading his fingers and sweeping them downward from his shoulders.

Madoc's jaw was clenched. He remembered the carpenter's daughter who had dwelt with Mungo before he deserted. She had died shortly after childbirth, covered with buboes and skin ulcers, and then her little monster of a baby, born without a nose, had suffocated in its own drool two months later.

"Mungo, knave of the Devil!" Madoc growled, slamming his fist on the arm of his throne. "I should like to send soldiers back to that valley of tears and bring Mungo here to behead him before the eyes of all our Welshmen!"

"Hah!" Riryd barked. "What? Send men a hundred leagues through mountain and forest, all to punish one sick man! Look you, virtuous King of a Wilderness! What did Mungo, that you have not got our own Welshmen doing: breeding upon heathen beauties, to give them Welshmen's vigor! All he has done that you do not condone is spread pox!"

Madoc clenched his fists ahd took deep breaths to control his temper. Meredydd studied his king and understood that much of his anger against Riryd was because what Riryd said was valid, as his sarcasms so often were. Finally Madoc said, "He deserted his countrymen, Mungo did."

Riryd retorted, "Aye, and good for us all, I'd say. How many of our own women, and these Euchee breeders of yours, would be all poxy by now, had Mungo stayed with us?" Now Riryd reached over and laid a hand on Madoc's wrist; Madoc refrained from jerking his arm away only because of the onlookers. "Anyway, brother," Riryd went on, "Mungo is probably dead or nearly so. Would it not be bootless to go a-chasing down a dying man? Is not the traitor punished already?" Riryd had softened his tone as he talked, hoping to bring Madoc down from the high dudgeon he had provoked in him. Riryd knew Madoc was indeed the king in this domain, despite his own equal title and greater age. Sometimes Riryd rebelled against Madoc with sharp and bitter words, but he knew that he only pushed himself down by thrusting up against Madoc's authority.

Meanwhile, Meredydd had whispered to Toolakha to ask her countrymen whether Mungo did indeed still live and reign. The Coo-thah's narrative took a new turn:

Coming to believe that Bear God was the source of their sicknesses, they had set their shamans to making magic against him. When that had failed to keep babies from being dead, a secret council had been held, in which it was decided that all the warriors would surround Bear God's hut, with their weapons, and beseech him to leave the Coo-thah valley and take his fertility power to some more deserving people elsewhere. But Bear God, angered, had used his great noise-magic against them again until their heads hurt.

"Stop," Madoc said to Meredydd. "Have her ask them about that noise-magic. I do not understand what that is, or could be."

The Coo-thah then, cringing and flinching, pointed toward the fire hearth at the end of the Great Hall. After a few questions, it became clear that he was indicating the iron kettle that hung in it from a hook.

At that moment one of the smithies at the castle's forge began working something on his anvil—a common daily noise here in Madoc's castle, so ordinary that Madoc would not have noticed it had not the Coo-thahs yelped in fear and huddled together with their hands clapped over their ears, cringing and looking about and murmuring, "Mnh-guh! Mnh-guh!"

After the Coo-thahs had been soothed, it was easy from those clues to understand that Mungo had terrorized them simply by striking a kettle with something to make it ring like a bell. Madoc remembered how his own Euchee subjects had been frightened and suffered extreme pain by their first hearing of the smithy's clangor, even though it was much less than the ring of an ax or hammer on a kettle would be. Thunderclaps were the only loud noise these people ever heard in their world, and their hearing was thus painfully acute. Meredydd had Toolakha assure them that the ringing noise was not the approach of their Bear God, and soon they were able to resume their tale.

For many moons after Bear God had frightened them back into submission, the Coo-thah people had stayed quiet, suffering their sickness and lamenting the pain and blindness and death of their babies. But then Bear God himself had fallen into suffering, and the Coo-thah had suspected that he might not be a god after all. In secret council they had agreed to try to kill him. One of his favorite maidens had been given a sacred knife and told to do it.

"But that girl was one who too much liked copulating with Bear God. She warned him and gave him the sacred knife. When the sun came up, Bear God's lodge was empty. Gone was Bear God, gone was his noise-magic. Two years' moons passed since then and no Coo-thah ever see Bear God again. Now Coo-thah live as in the days before Bear God, with no fear of noise-magic.

"But now, we are all dying. Once we died from the water pouring out of us, and died quickly. Now we who remain die this way. . . ." Again he indicated the condition of his body with that pathetic sweeping gesture. "Our healers cannot heal us. All our priests at Great Temple Place died in the Great Wind of Death before. We are lost people. Our Great Spirit left us. At last we have council and say, 'Go to the white-face people who passed through. Fear them no more; what could be worse than how we are now?' And so we six were chosen, and we have come to you. We remember, Bear God appeared on that day when you passed through, and so we suppose he was one of you. If he was, might this nation of white-face people have a power to make this sickness go away? We have come to ask you. You do not die of Bear God's sickness. Is your Great Spirit stronger than ours? Will prayers to your god make it go?"

Toolakha finished the translation barely above a whisper, tears for her people streaming down her face, and the Great Hall was quiet but for the uncomfortable shifting and throat-clearing of listeners and the wheezing, gurgling breathing of the sick Coo-thahs. Madoc, heavy with guilt and remorse, tugged his beard and thought hard about how to answer to these wretches. Their tale was a horror. He was reluctant to admit that the Bear God—

Mungo—had been one of his Welshmen. Where might Mungo be now? Among other peoples somewhere, making them die? Madoc knew, through Sun Eagle and his vast web of allies and kin, that the Wind of Death had blown through every known tribe, reducing most and even extinguishing some, everywhere the natives traveled to trade with each other. How much was due to the drying-up disease, how much to Mungo and his cock pox? Madoc, long ago in the libraries of the Irish monks, had read Galen and the other ancient physicians; he knew that the pox affected the Natural Spirits, Vital Spirits, and Animal Spirits of the human body, all three, and that it could never therefore be cured and always drove its sufferers to the grave, some sooner than others. Some of the ancient writings held that what the hideous lepers of old had suffered had been really this pox. He stared at the twitching, seeping, wheezing, half-blind Coo-thahs before him and pressed back against his throne in fear, suddenly almost afraid to breathe the air in the room. Why were his Welshmen still alive? Why had not Mungo died years ago?

Meredydd coughed and asked, "What shall we answer them, Majesties, about their queries?"

Madoc glanced aside at Riryd, whose eyes were closed, his chin on his chest, a sign that he was leaving this dilemma to him.

"Why, Sir Meredydd," Madoc said at last, "as you know I never lie to the natives, tell them that all we can do about their affliction is to pray, and assure them that our God is Almighty, the One True God.

"As for their Bear God, tell them the truth—and warn your concubine not to miscarry my words!—that we never saw a Bear God, nor until this day even heard of such a creature. And that is enough of this. Tell them that, and please get them out of Dolwyddelan! Thank your woman, Meredydd, for serving us so well here, conveying all these words. . . ." He rose quickly from his throne and drew his cloak across his front, covering even his mouth, and hurried out of the Great Hall toward Annesta's chamber where she still lay suffering in childbirth. He was troubled deep in his heart. This day that had begun with such high spirit and promise, with the completion of his castle and the birthing of another heir, now had a shadow over it, a shadow of guilt and foreboding, though the sun still shone over all the kingdom.

HERE, THE CLEAR POOL AT THE BASE OF THE WATERFALL, WAS Gwenllian's favorite place in the summertime. It was cool and pleasant, and the sound of the falling water was like music. She could stoop in the shallow, crystal clear water, where every pebble could be distinctly seen, and liked to pick up pretty ones with her toes.

Gwenllian had to bathe with her shift on; it was a strict rule in the royal family that they must never be seen naked by outsiders. Even her mother, still in labor in her chamber up in the castle, was being kept swaddled so that the midwives could not see her whole body. It had always been thus, from the tradition of the kings in Wales.

For a princess, Gwenllian was a ragged child, always in the same thin, patched linen shift, yellowed with age, a garment reduced from one of the queen's nightdresses. It was so ragged and stained that Gwenllian knew she would look more elegant in nothing but her skin. Cloth was scarce. The Welshmen's efforts to grow cotton had failed here in the mountains. There had been experiments with the various flaxlike and hemplike weeds found in the valley, but so far those had produced only rough fabrics that did not last. And therefore the colonists, like the natives, tanned skins and furs to wear when they needed clothing, and used little clothing at all when the weather was mild.

While the native women and girls waded and splashed and bathed in the free nakedness that Gwenllian envied, she waded in the waist-deep pool, white and modest, toward the waterfall. Its constant rushing motion fascinated her. In her dreams—more especially, in her nightmares—she was sometimes beaten down by falling water.

She clambered over a jumble of stones to a place where the water, falling from a rock ledge high above, roiled and foamed. Growing bold, she walked straight up to the sheet of falling water, letting it pour cool and fresh over her head and shoulders. She retreated, laughing and gasping. A few yards away the women and girls squatted on the rocks, rinsing garments or bathing themselves, the white-skinned Welsh women in one group, the brown-skinned native women in another. No one was watching Gwenllian at this moment.

She turned and pushed again into the curtain of falling water, and, holding her breath and squinting, went deeper. Suddenly there was no more water pouring on her, and she opened her eyes.

Where she had expected only the stone of the cliff, she was delighted to find instead a sort of grotto, all mossy stone, dimly lit, as big as a castle room. She felt magic and heard music, the music of water, rushing, hissing, dribbling, tinkling. She turned her wet face up, smiling with joy. Turning, she saw that the water of the falls, like a liquid curtain, shut off her sight of the whole world outside. She was utterly alone in the lovely grotto, and she realized that no one on earth knew where she was at this moment. It was a thrilling, almost frightening thought. There were not even flies or gnats; they could not fly through a curtain of water.

Gwenllian, in this unprecedented privacy, suddenly felt a soaring, exhilarating rush of personal freedom, fully unfamiliar, thrilling. She pulled off her water-soaked shift and laid it across a boulder, and stood in knee-deep water, wearing nothing but the little golden neck-pendant with a mermaid and harp engraved in it. Her heart was fluttering with her sense of freedom. She stooped to dash handfuls of water over herself. Though her wheaten hair was already drenched from entering the falls, she bent forward, put her whole head in the water, and wrung her tresses out. Then she waded about, sluicing water off her body with the edges of her hands, and went to sit on a mossy slab of rock to listen to the water music. She lay back and shut her eyes. It was a bit frightening, and she opened them and glanced around several times before finally closing them and listening. She began remembering dreamlike moments evoked by the rush of water.

She could recall vaguely a dark, dripping stone tunnel, going down, holding her mother's hand, shouts behind her, a torchlight ahead, and the dribble of water all around. She remembered slipping and falling on the wet rock in the tunnel, and the memory made her heart race. That, she knew, had been in Cambria, on the far side of the great ocean, when her father had had to flee with his family from evil people who wanted to kill them.

Then she remembered the sounds of the sea and wind, sailcloth rustling and drumming, sunny skies, a masthead above, and harp music. Then she could remember the howl of the sea gale and roar of waves breaking over her father's ship, and then in her mind there was the greatest of her nightmares: that thundering, deafening, shrieking hurricane in which she had been washed and flung about and dragged and cut, and waking to find a serpent slithering over her chest. Her scream of terror then had brought dear Meredydd sloshing to her side. . . .

She sat up, her heart pounding. She was in the grotto under the waterfall, and it was beautiful, but she was thinking of water snakes. She got up and waded to the place where her dress lay.

She reached, hesitant, dreading to see a serpent wriggle out, but at last snatched it up, shook it out, and pulled it on, having to tug to cover her wet skin with the wet cloth. Then, heart still racing, she stepped through the sheet of falling water, out into the sunlit pool.

The women were hurrying about on the rocky bank, even climbing on the rocky walls of the ravine, calling her name, searching frantically for her.

Not one of them had seen her emerge from under the falls. She was just suddenly there, wading toward them with her hair and dress soaking, clinging to her. The big native girl Duck Egg, who was supposed to oversee Gwenllian, came sloshing toward her, her brown face looking most severe, scolding, "Where were you? I shall tell their excellencies that you strayed away!"

Gwenllian did not want to reveal the wondrous place that she had found. And so she replied, haughty and shrewd:

"Did you not know that I can become unseen, just by wishing it?"

Though Duck Egg had been taught by Meredydd to speak Welsh, she had to pause and think what the words meant. Her eyes widened; perhaps she believed this. Gwenllian continued:

"Be careful what you ever say, for I might be right beside you, though you see me not." She added, thinking fast: "It is my secret that I can become unseen. You had better say nothing about it. It will go hard with you if you tell anyone that you let me out of your sight."

Now Gwenllian felt that the woman would not dare tell. And she hoped that soon she could come down and go under the waterfall again, perhaps as soon as tomorrow. At last she had a secret, sacred place in the world. For the first time ever in her life, she had been for a little while out of everybody's reach and ken. Like her golden memory of the woman who had dived off the ship, she had felt free and been naked. It was as she used to discuss with Meredydd, back in those days before his responsibilities had preoccupied his thoughts and made him dull: to be naked was to be free of spirit.

It was a wondrous new secret she had, this place, and just the thought of it made her laugh silently in her heart.

THAT NIGHT ANNESTA'S GROWLS AND SCREAMS IN THE BIRTHING chamber made Earth Daughter so impatient and angry that she got up from her bed and went in with the midwives. Gwenllian listened and heard scolding and arguing.

After a while Annesta's awful sounds abated a little, and Gwenllian dozed. She awoke when Earth Daughter returned, carrying an oil lamp, and went into the alcove where Meredydd slept. She heard her tell him, "You may go and say to your king that he now has a son."

The whole castle was roused to celebrate the news by torchlight. A barrel of *meejep* ale was unbunged for the thegns, who grew loud and maudlin. Riryd tried not to sulk, but his brother now had a male heir.

And Earth Daughter explained succinctly what she had done in the birth room: "I gave her *cohosh* to make baby come faster. And made them sit her up so it could fall *down*, not *up*! No need to tell king, please."

MADOC NAMED THE INFANT CYNAN AP MADOC. CYNAN, MADOC'S great-grandfather, had been Cambria's greatest king before Owain Gwynedd. Gwenllian stayed as close as possible to the baby for the first week of its life. She and Madoc would sit on a bench watching the infant boy suckling at Annesta's breast, and those were good times. Gwenllian loved to look at her father and see how quiet and blissful he was. It was good also to be in a room with him and hear him talk about matters concerning his domain. Gwenllian knew much about the governance of Iarghal because she spent so much time with Meredydd, but it was rare to have time to talk about the same matters with her father. Madoc encouraged her knowledge of such affairs, because until now he had presumed that she would inherit his throne.

"I saw Rhys and many men preparing to go somewhere," she said. "Where, Father?"

"They are gong to look for iron ore, my child. We have so little iron left, you know. For a long time our smithies used the same iron over and over, out of old ship fittings and broken kettles. But building this castle used up so much of our iron. Once iron has been used as a nail, or a hinge, or a spit in the galley, it is gone from the supply."

"Yes, of course," she said, nodding seriously. "And now does Rhys think he knows where there is ore, or is he just going out to wander and look for it, as you used to do?"

"In the hills up the Ten-nes-see—not far from the place where Sun Eagle's village was—there are said to be some red bluffs," Madoc said. "That may mean there is iron ore in those bluffs. He is taking some smithies with him, and some Euchee guides and carriers. God be willing, he will find the red bluffs and see if they bear ore."

"May he find it, then," she said gravely.

"And for our continued prosperity," Madoc mused on, "unless we find new iron, we cannot make the knives and hooks and tools and needles for which the tribes trade so generously. Much of our iron has dwindled that way, too. You see, my child, we prosper by knowing how to make useful things."

"Or pretty things," Gwenllian said. "How they love our blue beads!" She was excited always by talking with her father of the concerns of the colony. He always seemed so pleased by her knowledge, most of which she had gained from Meredydd. She said, "Our bard believes that we should find ways to make beautiful fabrics, not only to clothe ourselves, but to trade!"

"Yes, and he is right to say so," Madoc agreed. "And you as our bright princess might well put your mind to such matters. From your mother you have learned spinning and weaving. Think of it! Somewhere in this bountiful land there must exist something with the merits of cotton, or, aye, even the silks of the East! If you were the one to find it and make it, what a boon to your people!"

Gwenllian clapped her palms together in delight at that thought. "Ofttimes," she said, "I have looked at a spider's web, and thought how such substance even as that might be made fabric of!"

WHEN GWENLLIAN, DUCK EGG, AND EARTH DAUGHTER WENT down the cliff path that afternoon to bathe, they saw Rhys and his party, smithies and soldiers and a group of Euchee warriors, already moving down the riverbank on their way to seek iron ore. The armor of the soldiers flashed in the hot sunlight, but the Euchee warriors were more colorful, with their ornaments of dyed feathers and their quill-covered shoulder bags in which they carried parched meal and dried meat. Soon they vanished through the green foliage alongside the riffles of the fast little river, and Gwenllian and her escorts turned the other way at the base of the cliff, going upstream toward the falls. As they walked toward the sound of rushing water, Duck Egg led them along the path, watching for snakes so that Gwenllian would never be bitten while she was in her charge. Duck Egg's hair was in one thick braid hanging down her bare back, and there dangled from her earlobes two coins, drilled through to hang as ear bobs. The Euchee had several of these coins—at least a score of them were worn by members of Sun Eagle's tribe—and had no idea what they represented. They had been found in old stone ruins along the Ten-nes-see.

Madoc had been utterly mystified by the presence of these coins in Iarghal. They were ancient, with Roman profiles on them, and readable words such as ANTONINUS and BRIT. How Roman money had arrived in this land, Madoc had not been able to explain, but for weeks he had been haunted by them and had gone on an expedition with Euchee men to see if more could be found. None had, but a brass cup and part of a bronze lamp had turned up. Gwenllian's father had admitted that he should not have been as surprised as he was. "Of course people had come across Mare Atlanticum long before," he had said, "for how else could the ancients have conceived of a western land?" He had always believed that the Great Sea had been crossed before, but the actual sight of evidence seemed to have humbled him a little. To have had even a half hope that he had been the first here had heartened him; since the discovery of the coins, he had not spoken of his discovery of Iarghal.

Gwenllian was still thinking lightly on these matters when she waded into the clear water below the falls. She saw that Duck Egg was keeping half her attention upon her, as if she expected her to slip away, or become invisible, at any moment. So she did not stray toward her secret place yet. She smiled at Duck Egg's anxiety.

The waterfall drew her, and she meandered slowly toward it. It rushed and seemed to sing, inviting her. The desire to be alone and unseen was delicious. Glancing back, she saw that Duck Egg had relaxed her vigilance and was stooping, unbraiding her hair to wash it in the pool. Toolakha was hip deep nearby, cleaning her teeth with a green twig. Gwenllian suspected that Duck Egg also spied on Toolakha for Meredydd, who never lost his fear that she would run away. No one else was watching her now, and so Gwenllian waded into the roiling foam at the base of the cataract, glanced back once again, and slipped through the curtain of falling water with her eyes shut. At once she pulled up the hem of her shift to wipe water from her eyes, then, ecstatic over being invisible and in privacy again, stripped the garment off over her head.

It was then that she saw the troll. Her breath caught in her throat and she was paralyzed by horror.

He squatted six feet in front of her, as astonished as she was, as naked as she was, though covered with black hair that was wetly plastered to his body. His eyes were red and fierce, and even in the dim light of the grotto she could see that his mouth looked like a festering wound with a few snaggled white teeth in it.

He was rising and reaching for her. His huge man-organ swung before his hairy thighs, and it, too, was raw with sores. Even in the roar of the falling water she seemed to hear him growling.

With a scream, Gwenllian spun about and sprang back through the waterfall. The force of the water bore her down into the foam. She felt fingers clutch at her leg, then lose their grip. She thrashed in the water to rise, trying to scramble toward the sunlit pool where the women bathed, but was being tugged back toward the waterfall by the garment she held in her left hand; the troll had a grip on the other end of it. And so in stark terror and revulsion she let go of her dress and floundered into the pool.

Duck Egg was still preoccupied, stooped over in the thigh-deep water, wringing out a thick, glossy rope of hair. At that moment she straightened suddenly and threw back her head, and the long hair swung back behind her, flinging a spray of sun-sparkling droplets. Her ample flesh quaked as she shook her head from side to side.

Then Duck Egg opened her eyes and saw Gwenllian splashing toward her, gasping, naked, her slim body white as bone. Anger and fear flashed in Duck Egg's face and at once she began scolding, but Gwenllian was still too much in shock and fright to heed it; she kept glancing back at the waterfall, expecting the troll to emerge. She imagined that she was seeing the hideous face peering from within the falling water.

Only Toolakha saw Gwenllian come out from behind the cascade. She said nothing, and pretended not to have noticed.

As Gwenllian collected her wits, she made up her mind that she was not going to say anything about what had happened. Though her waterfall grotto was now a place of terror, not delight, she believed it was still her secret. She lied to Duck Egg, telling her that her flimsy old garment had simply torn and come off as she bathed. Duck Egg sent a young girl up to the castle to fetch a garment for Gwenllian to wear home, and meanwhile kept scolding her. At last Gwenllian got her to stop her tongue by threatening to disappear. Toolakha watched this screaming match with masked amusement.

That night in her dreams Gwenllian saw the troll's face again and again, and in some of the dreams he was not in a beautiful rocky grotto but a dark, slippery tunnel lit only by a weak, flickering torch and echoing with frightful shouts and clamors of violence. She woke up wanting to tell her father about the troll, who was, surely, dangerous to the bathers. But she was reluctant to yield up her secret about the grotto under the waterfall, or to confess that she had dared to go out of Duck Egg's sight. Her father and mother were already angry at her for having lost her garment and being naked in the eyes of the common people. It was a strange turmoil going on in the girl's mind.

But most strange to her was the notion, after having seen the troll's face time after time in her dreams and nightmares, that she had seen it sometime before, long ago, back in her childhood—had actually seen it, not dreamed it.

But surely, she thought, if I had ever seen a troll before, I would remember that I had.

MUNGO HUNKERED IN THE MOUTH OF A CAVE ABOVE THE WATERFALL, stared out at Madoc's moonlit castle and tried to think about what he could do.

For Mungo, thinking was difficult, and it grew ever more so. Pains in his head and chest, back and feet, were sometimes like lightning bolts followed by intolerable deep aches. But it was not just the pain; his mind simply would not stay upon a thought. Often when he was trying to figure out what to do, his thoughts would dance crazily in his head. He would totter and have to catch himself to keep from falling, and sometimes it would not even occur to him to catch himself, and he would simply hit the ground. Sometimes he would pass out and wake to find himself fallen and hurt.

He would be trying to concentrate, and one of his limbs would kick out or jerk so violently that the lesions on his flesh would open, and he would forget what he had been thinking.

But now the sight of Madoc's castle reminded him that he was trying to think of a way to get back with the Welsh people without being hanged for desertion. That was the problem he had been pondering, but he had not got far with it. Sometimes he could not even remember why he wanted to get back with the Welshmen.

But then he would feel the ache of desperate loneliness.

It all had changed so much lately. Once this land had been

like a paradise for him. Virtually every young woman he had lusted for had been allowed him. He had had so much power.

So many girls and women! Hundreds of them, all won by boldness and sham and craft. His children were countless. But . . .

Sometimes Mungo could remember, and sometimes he did not remember, that most of those children were sick or blind, that many of them had been stillborn or died in infancy.

He had traveled far westward through the country, even to the Mother River, as some tribes called it, finding new tribes, using his audacious wits to become a god or shaman among them, a fertility god doing ceremonies, lying with their women, spreading his seed. Such a career it had been, full of dangers and triumphs, a reputation like a comet.

But then time after time the people would say he had made them sick, and he would have to escape and go on. . . .

Eventually that leprous pox, which made him feel as if worms were eating everything from his navel to his rectum, had erupted on his skin, had consumed his own flesh and fiber, until women would run from him and men would back away.

Now when he thought of the great nations of natives out there along that great river, it was as if he had only dreamed them. . . .

They had lived in teeming cities, by tens of thousands, with temples and fortresses on top of huge earthen hills. In his years as a sailor in all the ports of the world, he had seen nothing bigger or greater. Paths ran from those cities for hundreds of leagues in every direction to countless towns, and there had always been commerce on those paths. Such byways in Britain or Europe would have been infested with robbers, but in all that empire Mungo had never heard of a crime. Along the rivers, those people had traveled by long boats, carrying foods to trade for treasures, or treasure to trade for foods. An elegant priesthood had performed thanksgiving ceremonies, and controlled everything from commerce to burials. The cities were built around market plazas, and in those plazas, heavily laden travelers from afar had traded beautiful items made of bone, fur, mica, carved stone, shell, pearl, and copper.

But everywhere Mungo had traveled in that riverine empire, plagues had raged, and peoples had fled and perished. It had been chaos and darkest fear, and far along in it, Mungo's own body and soul had grown chaotic and rotten, as if he himself were an empire consumed by its own plague. He had witnessed the deaths of empires, but he had begun dying like them.

Until finally in the midst of his sufferings and flights, only months ago, he had heard rumors of a tribe of white-faced men who lived among the Euchee peoples in mountains far to the east of the Mother of Rivers. He had presumed them to be Madoc's Welshmen, his own old comrades, and he had been swept by a poignant yearning to stop masquerading as a bear-god, to hear his own language again, to be secure among white men who were not perishing of plagues.

Surely, he had thought, if I go back to them and tell them of being captured and held in a cage, surely the prince will forgive me; surely all my knowledge of this land will be welcome to him.

And thus, his hatred for Madoc grown all vague, nearly forgotten like a bad dream, Mungo had set out along the valleys and ridges to seek the white-faced men. It had been a long, lonely, exhausting journey. Sometimes he had been unable to move for days at a time because of pain and fatigue and disorientation. The journey had been the hardest thing Mungo had ever done of his own choice in his life, something like those abject journeys of penitence that he had seen sinners do in many parts of the world.

But now, here at the journey's end, within sight of Madoc's castle, he had lurked and hidden for two days, full of doubt and afraid he would be hanged instead of welcomed. Yesterday he had found at the foot of a waterfall a place where women came to bathe, and had passed part of the day aimlessly spying upon them, troubled by his old lusts but afraid to show himself. And during that vigil he had been visited, or vividly dreamed he had been visited, by a naiad of astonishingly pure whiteness, in a cave under the cascade. But she had fled, or, if she had been but a dream, vanished. Such a melancholy her pale nudity had wrought in his wretched soul!

Mungo yielded a long sigh and gazed at the castle on the far side of the gorge. Its moon-limned walls were cold stone, but now and then he could make out the warm glow from the lamps or bonfires within, and it was this thought of communal fire glow that at last inspired him to rise and leave the cave. He had seen a water sprite, and, if he remained this lonely and desolate much longer, he would go utterly mad. He must go and sit by fire and hear his native tongue. The prince surely would believe his story and take him back in. He had after all been one of Madoc's ablest men.

Mungo stepped outside the cave. On the narrow stone ledge

above the falls he crept along, one hand against the cliff to steady himself, the roar of the water below growing ever louder. He was thus inching along on the moonlit path when dizziness swept him again. The ledge seemed to tilt under his feet. He saw the moonlight on fast water.

A moment later Mungo's pox-ridden body, bones broken by its tumble down the cliffside, slipped over the edge of the waterfall and was dashed on the jumbled rocks eighty feet below.

It was there on the edge of the pool that the women and girls found it the next morning when they came down to bathe and wash clothes. Madoc went down from the castle and looked at the carcass in pity and disgust before saying a rude and awkward requiescat over it, remembering the poor poxed Coo-thahs who had come to him with their tale of a bear-god.

The Welshmen who had to bury the body looked down into the grave with dumb revulsion, and remembered him as they had known him years ago, before he had been given up for dead, until one finally shook his head and chuckled, "Eh, what a randy bugger he was, remember? He should have stayed with us, eh, and helped us breed the Euchees! Why, Mungo, ye poor goat! Oh, what ye've missed!"

As for Gwenllian, though she knew now that he was their former sailor and not a troll, she did not yearn for her secret place under the waterfall, because it still seemed to her a troll's place, and she might never have courage enough again to step through a wall of water.

IN A FORTNIGHT RHYS CAME BACK WITH SOME OF HIS EUCHEE ESCORTS carrying something heavily slung in a bundle under carry poles, and went straight to Madoc to report on his search for metal ores in the hills.

He had found the red bluffs. His smithies had built a bonfire against one of the bluffs and kept it white-hot with a bellows. Then they had raked down the glowing ore and hammered it to drive out the slag. "Now, here, Majesty," Rhys said proudly, and he opened the heavy bundle and lifted out several rough ingots, all ruddy and gray. He handed them one at a time to Madoc, who hefted their dense weight with as great a pleasure as if he were handling gold. Rhys said, "This is but three days of their work. They are mining more, even as I stand before you. They wish to know whether to build a smeltery there, or raft ore down and smelt it here."

Madoc, chuckling, turned to Riryd, handing him an ingot so heavy that it twisted his wrist as he took it. "By the Lord God, brother," Madoc exclaimed. "Iron! We have iron again! For our needs, and to trade! Now you shall see my . . . our kingdom grow great and greater!"

Madoc our King grew white in beard and mane,
But vig'rous as in youth he ever seem'd.
And by the constant prudence of his reign,
His Kingdom was as great as he had dreamed.
King Madoc laid his law upon the land;
His subjects' cynosure he was, and they, full leal.
He held the native lords as in his hand
And caused their sons to serve his Kingdom's weal;
In trades, and labor, and in soldiering,
The native men did fealty to him.
Their women did each year the harvest bring,
And bore us children lithe and sound of limb.

More mines he found, iron and copper ore,
And tin from yet another place, and thus
Our smiths made Bronze, which ev'ry soldier wore,
And tools and weapons for each man of us.
Potters and jewelers 'gan to craft their ware
To trade with natives of the Tribes who came
Along the waterways to see us there,
All drawn to us by Madoc's glorious Name.

A castle for his brother he decreed
Be built to guard the mines, thus by and by,
By strong Welsh masons was it done indeed,
Great walls of stone, with moat, and crenels high!
Castle Clochran, the name from Riryd's heart,
He call'd that daunting keep of mortar'd rock;
There Riryd ruled as 'twere a King apart,
Ally but not a vassal of Madoc.

Fair Gwenllian, grown lovely, tutor'd well,
Was wed as wife to Owain ap Riryd,
Though cousins they two were, which fell
Because no other blood was there to breed.

Cynan, the Son of Madoc, was in sooth
Destined Heir, toward the Crown to reach.
This Cynan rose a golden, brawnie youth
Of warrior mien, whom Madoc sought to teach
The craft of Kingship he had mastered last,
And nurtured in him yearning like his own
To seek the far shores of Iarghal so vast,
For what can be ruled well unless well knowne?

And so it hap'd that in a score of years
Of having first set foot upon Iarghal,
Madoc set out, dimm'd by Annesta's tears,
To find the Mother of Earth's Rivers all!
In curragh ships with coracles in tow,
Five hundred men and boys, Euchee and Welsh,
Cast off the lines and caught the Current's flowe,
While drummers beat, and Women cried farewells.

Until her King and Prince were out of view,
Annesta, Queen, waved from the river shore.
But in her bosom, dreary darkness grew—
For She had dreamt of seeing them Ne'ermore!

CHAPTER 6

Valley of the Mother of Rivers
A.D. 1189

It fairly makes my hair stand!" Madoc exclaimed to his son. " 'Tis as if I have been here and seen this all long, long ago!"

Cynan looked at him, mystified.

"Aye!" Madoc explained. "Egypt!"

He stood at the tiller, his skin baking in the sunlight, squinting over the muddy water toward the pyramids on the lowlands of the eastern riverbank. He remembered moving up the Nile in a merchant ship half his lifetime ago, and seeing there the ancient pyramids shimmering in the heat, so like this: the sky hot and pearlescent, the river murky. In Egypt the pyramids were triangular in silhouette, while these were flat-topped, but coming upriver on an oar ship and seeing them felt the same; it was an eerie feeling of returning.

As the ship was rowed closer, the pyramids changed from the bluish tinge of distance to green. They appeared to be overgrown with grass.

Far beyond the bottomlands stood bluffs of pale limestone, steep as a wall, crested with forest, but the floodplain was all cleared, hundreds of hectares in fields and garden lands surrounding a sprawled city of houses roofed with thatch. Even the great mounds and towns of the Coo-thah country in the south were small by comparison.

His tall, fair-haired son Cynan stood sweating beside him, keeping a wary eye on the native dugout boats that had been patrolling at a distance around the fleet of ships all morning. Along the riverbank, hundreds of natives were walking, running, and milling, watching the curraghs come up. The sultry air throbbed with drumbeats. The lad was doing well at pretending to be unafraid.

Madoc saw the mouth of a small tributary, and put the tiller over to lead his fleet in. This Mother of Rivers was a mighty and capricious current, dotted with snags and whole trees afloat; already on this voyage two of Madoc's wicker-hulled curraghs had been gashed open and sunk by driftwood, and he had learned to shelter his fleet out of the main channel whenever he debarked.

Now as the fleet was tied ashore, down from a creekside village came a procession of decorated and stately men, led by a dignified brown chief with his hand held high, a spread comb of hawk-tail feathers standing erect in his topknot. As he drew close, Madoc saw that he was sick and that most of the men with him were also.

After greetings were exchanged onshore, through Euchee interpreters and hand-signing, Madoc and his thegns were led up through the city to a vast plaza, wherein stood one pyramid the size of a hill, and lesser ones twenty or thirty feet high. The plaza was so wide that the palisades, mounds, and houses on its perimeter trembled in the rising heat waves. The Welshmen were led up a long flight of steps to the lower terrace of the great pyramid, where they were perhaps fifty feet above the plain, with a breathtaking overview of the city. There they were seated in a circle around a fire ring, where an aromatic fire of red cedar was burning. Several hundred townspeople who had watched them come across the plaza now remained below, their voices a steady drone. Twice as high as this terrace the main height of the mound loomed above, and atop it was an enormous thatch-roofed temple building whose roof ridge was perhaps another fifty feet higher than the mound's summit. The place was enormous, soaring up to peaks and sprawling so far across the flatlands that its perimeters dissolved in smoke and heat waves. And yet he could discern, when he looked closely, much of it was half ruined. On many roofs the thatching hung on only in patches.

When at last Madoc and Cynan and the thegns had passed the pipe with all the chieftains, the head man told them the same story they had been hearing everywhere on the long summer's journey:

"You see by this place," he signed, "we were so many. This was a good land. Nothing did we want that Creator did not give to us. What was not of this ground, we would trade for with other peoples who came here by the rivers." The headman's jutting chin trembled while this was being translated, and Madoc had never seen such vast sadness in a man's eyes.

"Then, some seasons ago, traders came here from down the Mother River. Their blood was bad, and fear was in their spirits. Some of them died even while they were here. Those people said a wind of death had gone through their towns, and few had lived after it. And soon after that, a Bear God came to them, to make them fertile and strong again. But the children from the Bear God were born dead or blind, and everyone was sick again."

Madoc compressed his lips and nodded. Bear God! The terrible legend was everywhere. He remembered the repulsive corpse of Mungo lying in the clear pool below the falls. Some fourteen years ago that had been, but it was as clear as yesterday in his memory's eye. The headman went on with his hand language:

"Those people traded cloth and pearls with us, and then went home, down the river. In a few moons, then, our people were full of the bad spirits and dying. Our children were born with the evil, and were blind, and they died. Our priests could not make us well, and soon they were unable to bury the dead, who were too many, and then the priests were dead. Our own king"—he pointed up toward the steep-roofed building atop the mound—"even up there he, too, fell and passed over. He who then followed him as king, he died, too. Now I am headman of a dying people and children who cannot see.

"Who are you, Elder One? Your hair is white, but you are very strong. Your son beside you has white hair, though he is very young. I have heard of a nation living south of the sunrise, who have white bodies and know how to cut stone. Are you of those people?"

Cynan's blond hair, bleached by weeks of sunlight on the ship's deck, was indeed almost as white as Madoc's own. Madoc turned up the sleeve of his tunic to show his untanned shoulder. "We are that nation," he said, and when his words were translated, the headman's eyes widened with wonder, or hope. He said:

"It is told that the stone-cutting people do not die of the bad spirits. Can you share your power with my People?"

Madoc understood that the power this man was begging for was healing power. But of course he had no healing power. A plague, like those Saint Bede had written of in old Britain, was sweeping through the paradise of Iarghal, and he could do nothing about it. He could only hope that this headman did not believe his Welshmen had brought the plague, as the bard's woman once said they had. Mungo had broadcast his pox far and wide, and it had run far beyond and ahead of him. But Madoc refused to believe that his people had caused these other winds of death.

"No," Madoc had to answer, as he had had to do so often before, "I have no power to heal the pestilence that has felled your people. I can tell you that these evils do not last forever. Your sick and weak ones will die, and later generations will be strong again. That has already happened to the Tsoyaha Euchee who dwell with us in the south. I will pray to my God that your people will be well again, and I offer you my hand in friendship. I bring tools that will cut rock, and cook pots that will not break in fire. I offer these," he said, having the gift bundles opened before the dulled eyes of the headman, "in trade for food for my boatmen. And I wish you to tell me about the rivers that come into the Mother River above here, for my son and I are making a great picture of all this land."

With a sigh, the headman leaned forward to look at the kettles and tools. Hot summer wind blew steadily across the terrace of the mound, hushing, whirling the cedar smoke.

And Madoc, despite his deep sadness over the tragedy of the plague, was glad in the secrecy of his heart that there seemed to be no native nations left with strength enough to pose any threat to the growth of his kingdom. At least, he had found none yet.

THE NEXT DAY MADOC WAS ALLOWED TO GO TO THE TOP OF THE pyramid with the chieftains, most of whom were so weak that they had to stop and rest several times during the climb.

From this level, perhaps a hundred feet above the floodplain, the course of the Mother of Rivers could be seen for leagues upstream and down, and the entire plan of the mound city was apparent. Madoc saw perhaps a hundred of the earthen mounds, ranging in size from huts to castles. At the far end of the plaza, perhaps two furlongs distant, two of the larger mounds stood side by side, one a flat-topped square and the other in the shape of a wide cone. Their outlines were magnificent against the backdrop of a wide lake, which the headman explained had been the place where earth had been dug for the building of the pyramids; the depression had filled with water generations ago and was now a lake. The earth had been carried in baskets on people's backs, he said, and heaped higher and wider until they became what Madoc now saw and stood upon.

Hearing this, Madoc was nearly overwhelmed. He had seen ants building anthills, in the lowlands near his castle, thousands of ants scurrying to and fro carrying grains of earth and piling them up; this place must have required the constant efforts of thousands of these people carrying earth, antlike, every day for generations! Here was human endeavor on a scale that he had never contemplated before, even though he had seen Rome and Athens, and the Roman Wall across North Britain, and even the pyramids of Egypt. None of those had so impressed him with the immense capabilities of human labor. "There must have been tens of thousands living here!" he exclaimed to Cynan. "And now no more than a few hundred sickly people!" And that made him ponder on the futility of it all. It was like the Egyptian works, he thought: people do these things, then they are gone!

In the remaining light of late afternoon, the headman, through hand signs and interpreters, and by pointing out features visible on the horizons, helped Madoc and Cynan understand this region of the land.

Less than a day's travel upstream, he said, the Mother of Rivers was formed by the joining of one that began in the forests of the north and another that began in snowy mountains far, far toward the sunset. Several days' travel downstream there flowed into the Mother of Rivers from the east another great and beautiful river of clear water, which was said to begin in green mountains far toward the sunrise. Madoc knew of that one; his ships had descended a part of it to reach the Mother of Rivers. And it was the one most intriguing to him now, because it was the one he believed to begin not far from the continent's eastern shore. He wanted to know more about that river—how far his big ships might be able to ascend it, what sort of people lived beside it, and what sort of things they might have to trade. He asked the headman whether he could answer such questions.

"Peoples from everywhere came here to trade with us," the headman signed, "and here the peoples from the eastern rivers came to trade with people from the western rivers. Not so many come now. Many of them are dead. Many are afraid they will die if they come here. But we remember what they said about that river.

"Some of them are peaceful people, some are like wolves who do not want other wolves to come inside their markings. Some are our kin, who have made high places like these, though not so large. We know not if they are still living; we have not seen them in many seasons.

"I have looked at your great boats. Never have I seen boats so large. But that is a wide river, and your boats can go on it. But half the way to its source in the mountains, there is a Falling

Water, a sacred place to those peoples, and a place where they catch many of the fish they eat. Boats must be carried on the shore to go above that Falling Water Place. I think your boats are too big to carry around it, though you seem a very strong people who might be able to do that."

"I want to see that sacred Falling Water Place," Madoc breathed to Cynan with intensity. "And somehow I want to go beyond it, to that river's source! From those green mountains, surely, one could see the Mare Atlanticum, because from the Mare Atlanticum we could see green mountains!"

"Father, do you mean to try to carry *ships* around the waterfall?"

Madoc chuckled. "No, my son, but even where ships cannot go, men can go. Ah . . ." He had had a thought. He asked the interpreter to inquire whether any people anywhere in this land had horses.

The interpreter had no idea what a horse was, and so Madoc had to try to describe one. As he did so, he remembered horses, and realized how much he missed them. In his memory he could still hear and smell them and remember the feelings of riding.

The interpreter looked incredulous when Madoc explained that a horse was a hoofed beast large enough to sit upon, and obedient enough to let a man so use him. When this was conveyed to the headman, he looked equally dubious. His reply was that the only hoofed beasts that large in this land were of two kinds, neither of which was friendly or accommodating enough to let a man sit on them. With much difficulty he described for Madoc an animal that apparently was an elk, and another that Madoc eventually came to envision as a cattlelike creature perhaps similar to the wild *aurochs* or *bisont* of Europe. To help in his explanation, he sent runners down into the town, and after a long while they returned bringing a hide of each beast. The dark brown hide of the bisontlike creature was amazing to Madoc. The forward part of its back was thick with curly dark wool, and he knew he would have to trade for it so he could take it back to Dolwyddelan. "Feel that!" he exclaimed to Cynan. "Gwenllian and your mother surely could spin and weave woolen cloth from that!" Nothing yet had been found to replace sheep's wool or cotton for the colonists, though Gwenllian's experiments with yellow flax and some inner bark fibers had produced a serviceable linenlike fabric, of which the tunic Madoc wore now had been made. But how wonderfully this dark wool would do! Madoc asked if the beast was rare.

For the first time a bit of a smile appeared on the headman's face. "Out that way, on the grassy lands," he replied, pointing toward a dim red sun setting behind a dark, smoky veil, "so many of these there are that one might not see across them all. Many, but not that many, live in the woods and prairies, and travel far, many, many together, even crossing rivers where they know shallow places." This speech required much complicated signing and translation, after which the man added, "They are so many. If you have not seen any yet, you will. But do you think they would let you sit on them? Is that what you meant?"

"I wish," Madoc said to Cynan, "that we had foreseen to bring the Bestiary with us! How simple it would be then merely to open it to the page depicting a horse and ask, 'Milord, have you seen any of these?' And then this ignorant man who has never seen a horse could shake his head and we would know."

"Father," said Cynan, "except for that picture in the Bestiary, I myself am an ignorant man who has never seen a horse!"

By Heaven, Madoc thought, he hasn't! A Welsh prince who has never seen a horse! And likely never will, alas!

IT WAS HARD TO DECIDE NOT TO GO ON UP THE MOTHER OF RIVERS to the place where it was formed by two big rivers flowing together. These people had said that was a mere day's journey north. Madoc yearned to go up there and go on up the north river, all the way, and also up the west river, all the way. But of course he could not do both, or either, in the remaining months of good weather before having to return to Dolwyddelan.

And so now his fleet moved back down the Mother River toward the mouth of the beautiful river that came from the east. That was closer in the direction of home, and the eastern part of the country had been the mystery in his mind for twenty years. The other rivers were new in his imagination, and though they loomed large there, he decided that he would have to return in later years to explore those.

Madoc and Cynan labored over their first map of Iarghal with bits of charcoal as the fleet floated back down the Mother River from the pyramids. They sketched in the things they had learned from the doomed men there, sketching in the mouths of tributaries. Later they would ink in the features they were fairly certain of and scrape away the charcoal notations, but nevertheless the large parchment was a smudged and dirty-looking thing. Madoc knew little of mapping. Other than what the Irish monks had preserved of the ancient works of Eratosthenes and Hipparchus and Strabo, he knew nothing. There were perhaps no more than five or six maps of the known world in existence, and of course none of Iarghal except this one, and he did sense the great importance of it. A map was knowledge.

Those ancients had mapped by calculations and the tales told by mariners, while Madoc could record only what he saw or what he was told by savages pointing and making hand signs. Still, he was a fair judge of distances and directions, and could feel the lie of the land and the fall of the streams with the same keenness as he used to feel the currents and smells of the seas. He had begun this map nineteen years before, while cruising along that southern coast lost and perplexed. On the basis of things heard from Sun Eagle and other far-ranging natives, his great map had grown crowded with lines and symbols and words, the blank areas scribbled with such legends as *Mountains North to South, draining West to tributaries of Mother of Rivers, and East to the Sea of Atlantis*, and *Above here a Purport Fresh Water Sea*, and now, *Greate Meadows with Herds of Aurochs or Bison*^{t} *West to Snowy Mount*^{ns}. Parts of the map where he had lived and traveled were dense with detail, markings all cramped and scratched and reworked until the parchment was nearly worn through. One such a place was that surrounding a tiny drawing of Dolwyddelan Castle; another was the ore-mining country dominated by Riryd's Clochran Castle.

From those places his smudged lines and revisions wandered westward and northwestward along the course of the Ten-nes-see, noting shoals and chutes and whirlpools that had endangered the fleet on its way down in the springtime.

Now, with the melancholy, dying grandeur of the pyramids fading astern, Madoc directed his full attention toward the broad, deep, beautiful river from the east, which flowed between high, forested bluffs through rolling meadows. Here, looking up, the voyagers at last saw herds of the dark, humpbacked bisonts. Madoc went ashore with hunters, expecting the cattlelike beasts to be easy prey, but they were so wary and swift that he could not get within a furlong of them, and could only admire them for their powerful and shapely forms, and note that they were shadowed by packs of wolves. To obtain enough bisont wool for a profitable weaving enterprise might not be so simple as he had hoped. But that was a matter for later contemplation; now the beautiful river was his preoccupation.

"Those chiefs confirmed my notion," he told Cynan, tapping the unmarked portions of the parchment with his finger, "that this river doth begin in the eastern mountains, far north of Dolwyddelan. I am so deeply contented to know I was right. How often and vainly I tried to impress my conviction upon Riryd your uncle! Look. By the little space remaining beyond here and here, the Sea of Atlantis indeed cannot be far beyond those mountains! My son, how eager I am to fill in those blank areas north of our own present domain! In the season left us, we shall try to ascend the Beautiful River and do that!"

Cynan surprised him then by asking, "Might we not have spent the season easier by floating down the Mother of Rivers all the way?"

"Why, someday, perhaps. But there is no unknown there. It goes to that warm southern sea on whose shore we first landed. We have already seen that."

"Aye, Father, you have. But," he reminded him, "that was before I was born. I have never seen a sea!"

ON A CALM, SWELTERING AFTERNOON THE FLEET REACHED THE mouth of the Ten-nes-see, whence they had issued a fortnight earlier. There being hours of daylight left, they rowed on, gazing to starboard and thinking their longing thoughts of Dolwyddelan and home, which lay far up that river. Within two leagues Madoc was surprised to see still another large river emptying in from the starboard shore; he almost missed sight of it because of a large island lying in its mouth. At once he was trying to envision where its source might be. Surely the same mountains drained by the Ten-nes-see, he thought, looking at the blank areas of his map. But north of it and parallel, he thought, for rivers do not cross each other.

The huts of an unpeopled fishing camp stood on the lower point of the island, and here Madoc made their camp for the night; the village was so close upon the shore that the moored ships could be guarded in the light of the bonfire. Once during the night the sentries on board saw several native dugout boats hovering offshore in the moonlight, and their presence created some dread for an hour or so, until Madoc took down the old sounding horn salvaged from the *Gwenan Gorn* and blew it, and had his soldiers beat shields with swords and kettles with axes, to scare them off.

The fleet proceeded at dawn under power of oar, and soon a hot, steady, following wind began blowing up the valley and the leathern square sails were hoisted, and the vessels were pressed northward on the wide river, sailing easily through still more wondrous rich country, woodland, meadow, and swamp, overshadowed sometimes by flights of wild pigeons as long and wide as clouds, raining excrement on the ships and the river until every man had been marked by it.

Every fertile island and every grand bluff recommended itself to Madoc as site for another stronghold, and he daydreamed of a time when this magnificent land he had discovered would be peopled by flourishing Welshmen, as it once had been by the makers of the mounds and pyramids. The river made a wide curve to eastward and the wind continued to fill the sails, and the fleet ran before the wind, with hardly an oar ever needed.

One day a Euchee lookout pointed up toward a limestone cliff towering over the river. In it was a huge hole, like an enormous arched window in a wall. Putting ashore, Madoc and Cynan, with bodyguards, climbed the steep, rubble-strewn cliff toward the gloomy aperture.

It was a cave mouth, twenty paces wide, with a vault thirty or forty feet high, and was dense with the smells of soot and wood ash. The cave floor was packed with trodden earth, scorched bones, ashes, and fragments of pottery and flint. The walls and roof of the aperture were smoke-blackened and etched with images of game animals, grotesque elephantlike beasts, suns, faces, and marks that looked like letters and numerals. So dense was the accumulation of human debris and musk that Madoc shuddered. "I have the sense," he said to Cynan, "that people have sheltered here since the beginning of time! And 'tis not to wonder, as safe and farseeing a shelter as 'tis. . . ." Turning then to look out over the river, he went on: "Here is a God-made fortress! Think ye of a line of forts and signal towers along these river heights, my son. By bonfires or smoke, a king of this valley could send warnings and messages the length of this whole river in a day or a night. Our forefathers did that of old, 'tis said, when invaders came to Cambria's coasts—even when the Romans came, so say the bards."

Cynan looked thoughtful, gazing down on the moored fleet, then asked, "Who would be invaders here? Only you ever sailed to find this land, is't not so?"

Madoc gripped his son's forearm and led him out of the cave to return to the ships, saying, "So I should like to believe. But when I set out for Iarghal, I was but one of the many who have dreamed of this place. I doubt not others were here long before—Libyans, Phoenicians, Egyptians—Roman coins we found near Dolwyddelan. With our own eyes in this cave we saw alphabets, meseems. How doubt that others will come by and by. So vast a land it is, in fact, that others from Europe, or Africa, or Asia, may be here already, unbeknownst to us.

"Aye, even Welshmen! Our countrymen knew I had been here and was returning, that Iarghal is no mere myth! Who knows but that they, or others from Europe, might be on the eastern shore, where I first landed?"

Cynan was thoughtful as they clambered down from rock to rock, grasping saplings and shrubs to steady themselves as they went. Then he turned to his father and asked, "But if others should come from our homeland, would we not welcome them? Would we call *them* invaders?"

Madoc sighed. "That I know not. It would depend upon what lay in their hearts. I can tell you that few of our countrymen were our friends when we left to come here. I suppose that I should tell you about all that someday. But I am reluctant to taint your mind, here in this Eden, with knowledge of the old world's corruptions."

"I have heard Meredydd and Gwenllian tell of those evils. I have wondered."

Madoc paused on the slope. "I do not even know, after this score of years, which of my brothers are alive back there, if any, or who rules, who has won or lost that strife—or even if any Welshman does still rule. King Henry of Britain had a demon in him to conquer Wales. . . . Ofttimes I am happy not to know, not to grieve over it all. Conquering has been the whole sorry history of the world over there, ever since man fell from grace. I do not believe that man here hath so fallen."

Cynan startled him by asking then: "Are you a conqueror?"

Madoc frowned. "I came not to conquer, not to invade! No. I am not a conqueror."

"Meredydd said this whole land belonged to the native people, ere you came; now 'tis yours, and the Euchee are your subjects."

"I won their hearts in council, and they chose to serve me. I did not conquer them. Conquering is done by force of arms, by killing and enslaving. No. I have not done that!"

So Madoc answered his son. But when he thought of the countless dead from plagues, and his doubts about the plagues' source, he was less sure of his answer.

TEN LEAGUES UPRIVER FROM THE CAVE, WHILE MADOC AND CYNAN were still lettering its location upon their map, a lookout called, and they went forward to see what lay ahead. Here a broad river flowed in from the north.

"That," he told Cynan, "is the biggest tributary we've yet seen on the larboard. And from what wondrous place in the north comes this? Perhaps you will be the one to go see, someday, before you get anchored in one place as I did, building kingdoms."

The boy's face was happy and handsome and the wind blew his hair. "I wish you could leave governing to Meredydd forever, Father, so that you and I were free like this and could follow every river to its source!"

THE NEXT DAY THE FLEET PASSED SIX ISLANDS. SOME OF THESE ISlands were a league or more in length and beautifully forested. While ashore on one of them, Madoc paused and turned his head, listening.

"Those are drums," he said, and his scalp tingled as he remembered the ominous drumbeats he had heard day and night so many years ago before his encounter with the Euchee.

This day the river had led generally eastward, then had made a deep southerly loop before turning north again, and the drumbeats, though very faint, were from the north, upriver. Madoc guessed that an hour of rowing would bring his fleet to their source.

As the vessels approached a sharp bend, with the drums growing very distinct, Madoc saw natives flitting through the woods along the left bank. He ordered his crews to hang their shields over the gunwales. Being made of waxed leather over wicker frames, the curraghs' hulls could be pierced by even a stone-tipped arrow. As always, Madoc believed that the natives could be befriended, but he remembered the statement of the headman a few days ago that some of these people might act like wolves about their territories, and he was not such a fool as to approach them unprepared. The drums had an insistent sound about them which alarmed his instincts. He looked at Cynan, who had put on his helmet, and thought, He is so young. May we have no fight this day!

When Madoc's fleet made the sharp bend in the river, they met an impressive sight. On the left shore stood an array of earthen mounds with thatch-roof buildings on top. The elevations numbered perhaps a dozen along the bluff, and there were more than a hundred dwellings. Along the shore below were dozens of dugout boats, which were filling with warriors. The bluff and the slopes of the mounds were crowded with people who were moving to get vantage points for sight of the fleet. Their voices made a constant murmur through the hush of the wind.

Madoc had expected to stop here and parley with the natives, as he tried to do at every village, but the actions of these people gave him little hope for that. No headman was walking out to greet them on the shore, in the customary peaceable manner. The warriors rushing to fill their boats were all armed with lances and bows. Cynan, standing beside Madoc, was big-eyed with alarm. He asked, "Will we turn back, Father?"

"No. We'll not show fear. If they make no overtures to talk, we will simply pass them by. Or fight, if they try to stop us. But I hope they won't try that."

He called word back along the fleet for half the rowers to ship their oars and take up their longbows, and ordered a crossbowman to stand ready in the prow of each ship. Thus readied for battle, the fleet moved slowly upstream, and as it came opposite the lower end of the town, Madoc had the vessels veer toward the starboard shore, where they could make the curve of the river at the greatest distance from the town.

Now both flotillas were moving slowly up the river parallel to each other and about a hundred and fifty yards apart. Madoc's curraghs, being on the inside of the bend where the current was slower, were passing through the bend faster, even though the big vessels were blunt and cumbrous compared with the narrow boats of the natives. The drums and the excited drone of the natives' voices, and the intensity of the warriors bent over their paddles, created a tension that Madoc and his men could feel across the river. For a few moments Madoc was able to look over the town and the flotilla.

The mounds and their buildings filled a huge area of the bottomland—as much as a hundred hectares, he guessed—and much of the land surrounding the mounds was in rich gardens and grainfields. Around the town there stood a log palisade hundreds of yards in length, with towers at intervals of a bow shot. Above the town was an enormous field of yellow sunflowers. This did not seem to be one of those towns depleted by the plague; it was crowded and the people were active and spirited.

Now he watched the oncoming boats. There were perhaps forty or fifty, each with five or six natives aboard. He stared hard at the leading one, looking for someone who might be the war chief. The man in the prow was, like the others, naked and unadorned and using a paddle. Madoc squinted to see him better, but at this distance could not see him well; with age, he had noticed before, his eyesight was fading. Suddenly, Madoc's helmsman called, "Which channel, Majesty?"

He turned.

Ahead, beyond the curved spit of land his ship was now circumventing, the river was split into two channels by an island. The right-hand channel was narrower, and closer. Madoc saw that the native vessels would have to close in on him or fall behind if both he and they used this narrow passage. He looked at their line of boats and guessed that they were heading left of the island.

"The starboard way!" He pointed toward the narrow channel.

And it was not long before he saw that the natives were not going to follow him into the narrow channel. They were veering off to pass the island on its far side, paddling hard.

"If I judge them aright," he said to Cynan, "they mean to outrun us and be ahead of us at the other end of this island." Beyond that, though, he could not surmise their intentions—whether to head his fleet off and attack, or to continue alongside observing, or to signal for a friendly meeting. That did not look likely.

The island was low and densely thicketed with willow and shrubbery, and as Madoc began to see, it was long—a very long island, parallel with the riverbank. There were a few huts along its edge, and fishing weirs in the water, visible a few feet down, whose posts threatened to gouge the curraghs' leather hulls. As the ships moved slowly on and on, the channel narrowed, so much that the oars nearly touched both sides, and Madoc began to think that the natives had herded his fleet into an ever-narrowing trap, very like a weir itself.

But gradually the channel opened, widening to twenty yards, and to thirty, and that sense of desperation began to pass from Madoc's pounding heart. Then he heard the cry of a lookout:

"Look you! There they be!"

The thickets on the island shore ahead seemed to be alive. Hundreds of brown figures were running through the brush. They apparently had landed their dugouts on the far shore and run across the island to ambush the fleet in the channel ahead. It was a clever maneuver. Even in his alarmed and angry state, Madoc had to admire their cunning. At the place where they were appearing, the channel narrowed again, becoming almost as narrow as the strait he had just passed through.

There was nothing to do but row on, and fight through the funnel if necessary. Sails were useless in such narrows, and had been furled. If the rowers had to ship oars and fight from behind their shields, the curraghs would simply be adrift at a standstill, at the warriors' mercy. Madoc and his crews were pouring sweat. There was no breeze in the confines of this channel. He was mortified that he had let himself and his fleet into such a trap.

A hundred paces ahead the swarm of warriors had emerged from the brush onto the beach of the island, which was a sandbar, and leading them was the muscular man Madoc had seen in the bow of their lead boat. At that point the channel was a mere stone's throw in width.

Madoc watched with greater alarm as many of the warriors ran into the water and began swimming across to the right bank. That bank was higher than the island, and he realized that from there the natives would be able to shoot their arrows and hurl their lances right down into his ships. And with projectiles coming from both sides at such short range, even bronze shields would provide little protection. He had about five hundred men, all strong and well-trained Welshmen and Euchee, but they would be jammed together like sheep in pens.

Then, in his desperation, he remembered something.

"Cynan, fetch me the sounding horn," he said. He called an order for the rowers to back water, and the command was passed back through his fleet. Madoc went forward and told the crossbowman there:

"You see that large man standing in the edge of the water, shouting to them? I believe that man to be their war chief. He stands in the open because he believes himself out of bow range yet. Do you think you can hit him from here, and disillusion him?"

"Certainly, milord."

"Then do, and dare not miss him."

While the archer was winching to cock the bow, Cynan came up with the horn and gave it to his father.

At the instant of the crossbow's shot, Madoc blew a blast on the horn. The warriors saw their leader fall bleeding in the river as the apparent result of a monster's voice. After a few moments of howling in fear and dismay, they scattered into the foliage. "Pull now!" Madoc cried. As his ship passed the beach, the body of the chief was graplined and hauled aboard. Within minutes the upper end of the island was passed and the fleet of curraghs emerged into the full width of the open river, with no sign of warriors or boats to be seen anywhere. Madoc prayed thanks for deliverance, and then turned his attention to the war chief's bloody corpse.

Even in death the man was magnificent, and Madoc was sad that such a manly exemplar had had to be sacrificed. The man had been almost Madoc's own size. His skin was light copper, tight over lean but shapely muscle, and he was utterly hairless except for a topknot of braided black hair and his eyelashes; even his eyebrows had been plucked. The iron bolt from the crossbow had slammed through his torso, breaking the spine as it came out his back above the waist. It had been just exactly the shot needed, and Madoc commended the bowman before the whole crew.

As the fleet moved on up the river, Madoc pondered on the disposal of the corpse. Somehow, a strong impression should be made, he thought—an impression as stunning as the death itself. It had been powerful impressions that had won or pacified the natives in every case, and Madoc had come to the wisdom that what seems to be is more powerful than what is.

And so now he had the warrior chief's body washed and its wounds plugged, dressed in an old suit of chain mail and a brass helmet, and laid supine in a coracle. The coracle was lowered into the river and set adrift. Madoc knew that the natives at the big mound city in the river bend would be shocked, angered, or mystified by the appearance of their dead chief encased in metal. He did not know just how they would interpret it, but when he returned back downriver past that hostile village, he wanted to be treated with respect or left alone. If he were not, he might not be able to return to Dolwyddelan, to his wife and his kingdom, at all.

FOR THE NEXT FORTNIGHT MADOC LED HIS FLEET OF LEATHERN-hulled ships on up the beautiful river valley, ever marveling at its placid grandeur. The current was strong but not swift, and the river was broad enough for sailing before the prevailing winds, except when the stream wound and looped and the high, wooded bluffs baffled the breeze. When the sails were down, the rowers pulled steadily, shining with sweat, their arms and shoulders corded with steely muscle. Madoc and Cynan mapped tributaries and islands, mounds, caves, and villages, noting sites for beacon towers, filling in the blank spaces of their precious map. Every day the sinuous ink line of the river inched toward the drawing of the eastern coastline, and sometimes Madoc feared that he was charting on too large a scale, that his inked river was close to his inked seacoast while in actuality he was still far, far to the west of it. If the headman at the pyramids had described the land truly, there was yet a mountain range between here and the eastern coast; he was drawing too large to get the rest on the map. So he cramped his drawing of the great river, and let Cynan, with his clearer eyesight and steadier hand, letter in the information, in script so small that Madoc could scarcely read it.

The difficulty with his eyes was intimidating, and it was worsened by the glare of sunlight off the river. And some mornings the stiffness of his hip and shoulder joints would make it hard for him to rise from his bedding. Madoc knew that although he did not yet look like an old man and his heart was young, age was in his bones.

Great God, he would pray at night as he lay in his blanket and the falling dew cooled his sunbaked face, give me time to see Thy creations!

Every day he strained for sight or sound of the falling water. He had been told that it lay halfway up the length of the river. "But," Madoc said to Cynan, "we have not yet reached it, though meseems we have come up an hundred leagues. If we have two hundred leagues yet above us, we shall not make the headwaters in time to return home before deep winter." He sighed, gazing ahead. "The *distances*! My son, in this season alone we have traveled far enough to have crossed Wales ten times. Yet we are still as deep within the interior as we were at first! This is a giant's land!"

The next day the river course turned northward, and the curraghs were rowed all day long in that direction, the river scarcely bending for as far as Madoc could see. Dusk brought the fleet up just below an easterly curve. No villages having been seen all day, it was deemed safe by Madoc to make a hunting camp on low ground on the east bank. Three does were killed at a creek mouth and roasted whole on iron spits, over fires whose smoke helped fend off mosquitoes. The rowers, famished, ate every shred of venison.

As darkness fell, and the whispering of the breeze and the crackling of cook fires died to silence, Madoc reclined on the ground to sleep, wrapped in a tattered blanket made two decades ago from sailcloth of his ship the *Gwenan Gorn*. Milky light from a high, bright moon flooded the valley and infused the wraiths of river mist, making the moored curraghs and the sleepy sentries into vague silhouettes suspended in silvery vapor. He remembered a long trek two decades ago when he and Annesta had huddled together for warmth in moonlit mist like this, with sentries standing about. Young we were then, he thought, lost and homeless in a new land. He sighed again, and shifted his aching hip on the ground. He remembered how, on such nights, they would discreetly couple, almost without motion, so not to awaken their daughter who lay beside them, or the bard who lay nearby, or give unseemly thoughts to the sentries.

Those memories made Madoc pine so for their old joys that he stayed wakeful. His strong, good son lay here near him, but how he missed Annesta. And his daughter now was a married woman. He lamented for the child she was no more; she herself would likely be a mother soon!

And he thought of Meredydd, who had become so much more than a bard. It was humbling for Madoc to admit how much of his achievement was due more to that homely, scrawny man's talents than to his own leadership.

Silvery tufts of cloud moved by the moon. The river gurgled softly. Insects creaked and grated, fish splashed, the voices of wolves and owls echoed eerily in the distance. Fatigue hummed and tingled in Madoc's veins. Hours later he was so sensitive in the margins of sleep that the earth itself seemed to be thrumming.

Then, his mind suddenly cleared of utter fatigue, he recognized what it was that he was hearing or feeling. It was the sound ever present at Dolwyddelan Castle—at both the Dolwyddelans he knew: the sound of falling water.

Very near, perhaps around the next river bend, must be the Falling Water Place! Had he been lying within sound of that desired place for all these hours?

IT WAS A BRIGHT MORNING DAWNING WHEN THE EIGHT CURRAGHS moved out into midstream and plied their way against the current, following the bend toward the east. The bluffs rose steep and high on the north side of the river, and still higher, bold and knoblike hills rose above the bluffs, while the land on the south side of the bend was low, fertile bottomland, hazy still with mist. All the woods and undergrowth were of a lush green that reminded Madoc of Ireland, the Misty Land. Here the river was a mile wide; the water was uncommonly turbid and frothy. And as the vessels came into the arc of the river bend, the low, rumbling hush of water grew louder. Ahead, the entire river vale was cloaked in mist, mist that shimmered with the rosy-gold light of the sunrise beyond it. Madoc could feel the cool moisture on his face and arms.

He stood with his son and looked in awe at the vague, dreamy panorama that widened before him; bit by bit as the ships drew closer, the silhouettes of islets began to appear, then vanish and reappear, their shapes shifting in the brilliant vapors.

Soon the curraghs were bobbing in willy-nilly currents, surrounded by drifts of foam. The ships themselves seemed to dissolve, their shapes growing vague. The rowers gaped all about.

Suddenly, as a breeze stirred the mist, Madoc saw before him a long, low expanse of sparkling white water stretching between two green islets. It was a cataract rushing over a ledge and churning into a deep pool. The cataract was perhaps a furlong wide. Beyond the small islet at its north end, the river poured through a vast jumble of boulders—not a waterfall, but a huge, steaming rapids. Above, farther upstream, Madoc could now see the treetops of other islands. Built on the banks of the islands and shore were tiny fishing huts, and scaffolds made of sapling poles jutted precariously over the cascades.

Madoc had the rowers rest and let the ships turn and bob on the roiling water. He was as close to the thundering waters as he should safely go, he well knew, but he wanted to drink into his soul the whole, enormous grandeur of it. It appeared that the great river here, with all its immeasurable waters, simply plunged over a stone threshold. And it was apparent, too, that this Falling Water Place was an important fishery for the natives.

As he watched, several drifting trees, with huge, spiky root boles and splintered limbs, floated to the edge of the cascade, paused, turned, tilted, and plunged into the froth below, disappearing entirely for a few moments, then breaking the surface like whales before settling down to move slowly on. Father and son, king and prince, stood together, marveling at all this, and so absorbed by it that Madoc thought only fleetingly of the danger such driftwood might pose to the hulls of his curraghs.

By then it was too late.

With a jolt, Madoc's ship reared on her stern like a horse, throwing every man off his feet. Then with wrenching, ripping sounds her bow rose to starboard while her port gunwale went down. Through a jagged hole in the leather and the splintered wicker frame, the wet dark root of a tree protruded into the hold, turning and gouging as hull and tree strained upon each other.

Water gushed in through the ragged puncture, and Madoc knew it would be only minutes before the vessel foundered.

Scrambling to his knees, then to his feet, Madoc hoisted his son from the mess in the broken vessel—the bags, skins, ropes, tools, and weapons tumbling in the flooding bilge—and shouted to him and to the armored soldiers on board, "Out of your armor!" They understood at once, and he and all the others began fighting their way out of the helmets and breastplates which would drag them to the bottom. As the great drift log revolved, the frame of the ship kept crunching and twisting. Madoc shouted over the rush of water and the cries of his crew, calling for help from the other vessels. Several of them were already coming, oars rising and dipping.

The next three or four minutes were a chaos of shouting, throwing, leaping, splashing, and straining, as the nearest curragh came alongside and the crewmen of the broken one tried to get aboard. Madoc and Cynan, both strong swimmers, stayed aboard until the last minutes, throwing armor and food and every useful thing they could find over into the other ship, and helping the crewmen who could not swim. Some tumbled into the river but were grasped by strong hands and pulled aboard, and no man was lost. Cynan and Madoc were the last to spring off the wreckage, grabbing at the gunwale of the rescue vessel, and they were hauled aboard, soaked. They stood in the overloaded vessel and watched the great culprit of a log drift slowly away, the swamped and misshapen hull hooked to it, the mast tilted far over. Madoc groaned as he watched her go; she had been a fine vessel on these river journeys—and he was dismayed at himself for letting such an avoidable thing ruin her.

The tree that had destroyed her was of monstrous size, eighty or ninety feet long in the trunk and another forty or fifty feet of branches, and the root bole that had gouged the hull was as big as a house. But even a smaller snag would have sunk the curragh just as surely, though it might not have twisted her frame that way. A tree of that size, and it had been dropped down and tumbled in the deep currents like a twig! Not since his long-ago years upon the seas had Madoc been so aware of the might of moving waters. . . .

Suddenly remembering something, he turned to his son with wild eyes.

"Oh, Cynan! Our map!"

A terrible look of anguish twisted the boy's face. He turned and gazed at the drifting wreckage, his mouth working.

Then, without a word, he dove over the side into the turbid water, before Madoc could even reach for him. "No!" Madoc cried, and crouched to dive into the foaming maelstrom after him.

But Cynan surfaced at some distance, and with the powerful overhand stroke he had learned from the natives, he swam toward the floating hulk.

"On your oars!" Madoc cried to the rowers. "Bring about and follow him!" And as they stumbled and groped in the over-crowded vessel, Madoc sprang headfirst into the water to try to overtake his son before he could get into the wrecked vessel. If the giant tree rolled while Cynan was searching in the wreckage, Madoc feared his son surely would be caught and crushed or drowned. The map was a precious and irreplaceable thing, the work of half a lifetime, but the prince was his flesh and blood, his only son.

Madoc could not catch him. Cynan was hauling himself up onto the wreckage when Madoc was still twenty yards from it and growing winded. Half exhausted already by the chaotic transfer from the shipwreck, he found his limbs tiring quickly, reminding him that he was old. He paused to tread water and get breath, to call Cynan back from fruitless risk. Surely the map had been blown or washed overboard in the confusion; even if it had not, it would have been ruined by water, a mere ink-stained rag, not worth the risk of a prince's life.

"Cynan!"

But if the boy heard over the rushing of the falls and rapids, he paid no heed, and Madoc saw him disappear into a portion of the crumpled hull. The other ship was far behind, not making headway yet at all. Madoc, gasping air, began swimming again, fearfully watching the wreckage as he went.

Cynan's sinewy arm appeared, gripped a rope; his upper torso came into view as he pulled himself partly out of the hull. And then, as Madoc churned forward toward him, the dreaded rolling began. Madoc's heart cringed at the sight:

The huge tree, either through the ship's weight or the boiling current or snagging somewhere underwater, began rolling, one of its huge top limbs keeling toward Madoc, the trunk slowly revolving upon the mashed ship, turning it under with audible creakings and snapping sounds. Through eyes streaming with water, Madoc saw his son's shoulders and golden head disappear into the blue-green water.

His soul screaming within, Madoc stroked with sudden new

power of desperation toward the place where Cynan had been, paused for a gulp of air and dove under.

He could scarcely see anything in the murky water, but as he swam closer, Cynan's pale, flailing form became visible against the dark mass of tree and ship. Madoc kicked and tried to get to him through the current, but was already so desperate for breath that he was not sure he could reach him. For some reason the boy, though not trapped in the hull, was not swimming for the surface, and Madoc was afraid he might be unconscious.

He got his hands on the writhing boy and tried to carry him to the surface. Cynan was not unconscious, but his teeth were bared in pain and bubbles of breath were streaming out of his mouth and then Madoc saw why his son had not swum up: he was caught. Cynan was terribly caught, by his left arm, and bleeding.

Lungs almost bursting, Madoc pulled himself closer; he could not see through the dark swirl of blood. Then it swirled away and he saw: the hand was snarled in taut rope which was so tightly strapped around the tree trunk by the twisting weight of the ship that it was torn and bleeding. Worse still, the irresistible pressures had snapped the bone of the upper arm and it was at a right angle, with the white bone end sticking through and tearing the flesh. Another swirl of dark blood spread around it in the murky water. Cynan's last breath was going up in bubbles.

Madoc's little dirk knife was still in its scabbard strapped to his calf. He drew it and tried to cut at the rope. But the dirk was for stabbing, not cutting, and its dull edge was useless on the rope, which was a thick braid of wet strands of leather.

There was only one other way to free his son, and if he did not do it, the boy would drown. The rope was much too thick and tough to cut. The weakest thing holding the boy was the muscle of his own arm, and the bone was already cutting that. Madoc wrapped his left arm around Cynan's chest and then with the dirk in his right hand he jabbed and poked with its sharp point at the strands of his son's arm muscles. The artery was cut; the blood was too thick to see through now.

With his last strength Madoc got his feet against something solid, the tree or the ship, and with his arm tight around Cynan he shoved away with all the might of his legs. The rest of the muscle tore apart and Madoc and Cynan tumbled slowly through the water until Madoc dropped the knife and began stroking toward the bright surface. If he held his breath another second he was sure he would die. He expelled it and hung onto his son and fought for the surface.

Those in the ship above saw first the blood and the bubbles boiling up through it and then they saw their king's face break the surface, a desperate grimace, saw his mouth open and gulp air, and then his face went under a little way and then came up through the bloody water again. One arm thrashed out, and then they saw the boy's face on the surface, and he looked dead, but Madoc was keeping him afloat.

The crewmen strained over the side and gripped the king and the prince by their hair and pulled them close and got holds on them and hauled them aboard. They were shocked to see that the boy had only one arm and that blood was jetting out of the tattered stump of the other. When they had the boy halfway over the gunwale, facedown, water gushed forth from his mouth and it diluted the blood spurting from his arm. They put him facedown on a rower's bench. Several of Madoc's old soldiers knew about such bleeding and about severed limbs. They got a thong around the stump and tightened it until the blood stopped spurting. Others hovered around Madoc, who was on hands and knees in the bilge, retching.

TWO DAYS LATER, WITH THE FLEET ENCAMPED ON THE SOUTH SIDE of the roaring river, the shaky King Madoc looked at his pale son lying on a pallet with his arm stump seared and tarred and decided that, yes, his son was going to live. Madoc had thought several times about the lost ship, and several more times about the lost map, but those things did not seem very important now. Something in Madoc seemed to have broken. For now, at least, he had not the will to proceed up the great river, though he had come so far. He walked the shore and explored the islands by coracle. He saw that the rapids and falls extended less than a league, with smooth waters above. He saw that it would not really be impossible to pass the falls. The lightweight curraghs probably could be towed on ropes up through the rapids by men walking on the north shore, one ship at a time, with perhaps a hundred men on the ropes. It would be risky, with such torrents and rocks, but it could be done. Another recourse would be to dismantle the ships below the falls, carry them up piecemeal, and rebuild them and go on. Or, most simply, the ships could be left below with guards while a small party explored the upper river in coracles. Madoc had yearned to reach the headwaters of this great river, and the watershed beyond the mountains which would flow to the eastern shore. His heart ached at the thought of stopping this far short.

But Cynan's dreadful mutilation and the loss of the map had stunned him. He wanted ease from his exertions. This was indeed a giant's land, and for the first time Madoc felt like a feeble little old man in it.

While lingering at the Falling Water tending Cynan's recovery, Madoc found more evidence that it was indeed a giant's land. The great rock shelf over which the river poured was littered with enormous bones and teeth—great, thick bones as long as a man was tall, molars as big as a man's hand. The only animals near that size in the whole world, to Madoc's knowledge, were the great *olifaunts* of Indus and Africa. They were depicted in the Bestiary. Were such beasts in Iarghal, too? After the crewmen had seen the giant bones, they slept uneasy. Madoc wondered why none of his native informants had ever spoken of such giant beasts. Sometimes those people would not speak the names of the dead or mention powerful spirits for fear of summoning them. Meredydd would know. Madoc wished Meredydd was here. Meredydd understood so much.

The bisont beasts were much in evidence here at the Falling Waters. In shallows near the falls, great herds of them forded the river on their way from somewhere to somewhere along their wide, trampled migratory roads that seemed to lead generally from southeast to northwest. The trampled roads intrigued Madoc despite his dispirited state of mind, and he wondered whitherward their vast migrations must lead them. Do they wander through the eastern mountains? he wondered. Might it be possible to find one's way across this whole continent by simply following these broad, open paths they had trampled out through the ages?

His hunters still found the bisont hard to stalk and kill. Though they seemed placid as kine while grazing, they were alert and would go thundering off at the approach of a man, or a sentry bull might come charging the hapless hunter. If only we had horses to hunt them with, Madoc thought. Now and then the hunters would have the good fortune to intercept a herd at the fording places, where they could be shot coming out of the water.

If we came to live here, he thought, perhaps our herdsmen could domesticate these animals. What a wealth of meat and wool they would provide!

And at that, Madoc realized that he had been thinking of this as a place to live. This was a greater river than the Ten-nes-see, much more navigable, closer to the Mother of Rivers. He could envision a fortification built upon the limestone promontory at the south end of the falls.

He tried to talk of these grand notions with Cynan, to draw the boy's mind off its horrid fascination with his dismemberment. But in reply the boy said something that, for him, sounded unmanly and showed the pitiful state into which he had sunk. "Will we be going home to Dolwyddelan soon? Should we not go to Mother?" His eyes were puddling with tears.

"We ought," Madoc sighed. "And ere winter catch us out."

CHAPTER 7

Dolwyddelan Castle
Autumn A.D. 1189

Annesta the Queen of Iarghal, slight, pale, and tense, her face lined with fine wrinkles, was pacing when Meredydd came to her chamber, and quickly sat down and folded her hands when she saw him appear at the door. He could see that she was in one of her imperious states of mind, and he knew that this would not be a pleasant meeting. The heavy oaken door made its hinges squeal as he closed it. He smiled sweetly but braced himself behind the smile for whatever complaint or demand she might have for him. Annesta, ruling in her husband's long absence, had become domineering and rather peevish—both traits that she had seldom revealed in her husband's presence.

"Esteemed Minister," she said, "you might imagine that I hate to be so many leagues away from Clochran when Gwenllian's child is born."

So that was the issue, and Meredydd foresaw how the contention would unfold. With the most careful courtliness, he answered, "Beloved Queen, of course. Every woman who loves a daughter would have a longing to be nearer in her time of motherly travail. The sweet Princess Gwenllian has, as you know, been as dear to me as mine own could have been, had I ever had children. I fully understand and—"

"Good bard," she cut in, "rather than talk me a long poem of lyrical sympathy, please at once prepare an entourage to take me to Clochran Castle. I shall need to leave within two or three days if I am to reach my daughter's bedside in time."

Again his small bow of the head, but he was braced, and knew his responsibilities, and his eyes were harder as he replied, "Does my Queen remember her husband's strict admonition to me, before he left, that I must not let you travel between places, for thine own safety and for his peace of mind. . . ."

Now he saw her resolve set in her eyes and lips, but her words were still lilting and polite to excess. "My safety? Oh, dear and beloved bard, surely you do not believe any harm would befall me, as I travel with the usual armed retinue, in a land ruled by our king, and under thine own omnipotent trusteeship!" She laughed again, covering her mouth with a fan of bluejay feathers to hide the decaying remnants of her teeth. Nearing half a century in age, Annesta was still a beautiful woman until she opened her mouth. Even as he thought up his reply, Meredydd noted sadly the changes time had wrought in this loveliest of women.

"Beloved Majesty," he said, "our two decades of peace in this land have lulled our instincts. Our Euchee brethren do have enemies both east and west, with grudges going back to the dawn of memory. And though they have long stayed in their distant regions, lately those in the west have made incursions. Old Sun Eagle believes they are beginning to migrate toward us, unsettled by the plagues along the Mother of Rivers. . . ."

"Meredydd, you are a veritable fount of knowledge, and duly esteemed by us for your skill in controlling these wanton people. I am your queen, however, and do not mean to be prevented from going to my first grandchild's birthing a few leagues away just because some natives somewhere might or might not be squabbling. I do mean to go to Clochran, my dear bard and minister, and you will have my entourage ready three days hence. If you are so frightened for my safety, then give me a guard of twenty Welsh soldiers and eighty Euchee warriors, selected by yourself for their known fidelity."

"I shall send for Sir Rhys," Meredydd sighed, bowing. He hoped that the old soldier, now a knight and the Minister of Arms, might help convince the queen that she should not travel to Clochran.

But Rhys surprised Meredydd by sympathizing instead with Annesta.

"Surely, my liege," Rhys said, "our King Madoc did not mean that she should not travel when there is so good a reason." And then, his eyes dancing and crinkling, he told Meredydd why he felt it was so good a reason. His own wife, a beautiful granddaughter of old Sun Eagle, had this very morning borne Rhys a son, the first child he had ever fathered in his long life, and he was full of paternal sentiment; if anything now seemed worthy of a journey, it was the impending birth of a child in the royal line. Rhys said he could have a party ready to march within three days. And Meredydd, though still uneasy, decided that it would be useless to resist the queen's wishes.

MEREDYDD, NOSE TWITCHING, SAT LATER THAT DAY THINKING about the two births and what they might mean for the future of the colony.

The imminent offspring of Gwenllian and Owain ap Riryd would be truly a noble born, the issue of a prince and a princess, and thus could someday hope to rule. There was no archbishop here in Iarghal to condemn a marriage between first cousins as incestuous, as the Archbishop of Canterbury had condemned that of Owain Gwynedd and Chrisiant.

If there should ever again be a contact with the land of Wales, the child's legitimacy to rule might be challenged by the Church. But, Meredydd thought with a sigh, what likelihood is there of that? No doubt we're a forgotten people now, presumed drowned at sea, our names hardly remembered in our homeland. . . .

As for Rhys's newborn son, he would be just another half-breed, even though fathered by a Knight of Iarghal. Knights and half-breeds!

As mine would be, if Toolakha had ever conceived with me, he thought.

He sighed and absently mined in his right nostril with the long nail of his little finger. He did this unthinking when he was alone. Toolakha would hiss when she saw him do it, reminding him. He'd sometimes do it unthinking even when people were around, and find people staring at him. His mind was too full of the details of his post for him to be very conscious of his person, and he was not tidy.

No one really knew what a task it was to accommodate Sun Eagle and his easygoing people to the demands of a true kingdom, in which authority came down by orders and decrees from the top. Meredydd had studied to understand the natives' beliefs, and their chiefs trusted him. He respected their mysteries. He had long ago learned that any plans and arrangements with the natives had to be made with respect for their Spirit Messengers. In order for him to get up a retinue of eighty Euchee bodyguards as the queen wanted, Meredydd had to ask Sun Eagle, who would then have to consult with his shaman and his council to learn whether such a journey should be undertaken at the designated time. The shaman would need time to pray to the spirits and watch for signs, then advise the council, which would, or would not, recommend to Sun Eagle that he comply. None of it was as simple as Annesta, or even Madoc, presumed. They commanded, and their commands were fulfilled, and they had no notion of the delicate magic by which he changed their commands into requests and obtained compliance.

Meredydd was aware that without him the Welshmen would not have any allies in this land, and probably all would have perished by now. It had all begun when, one day long ago, he had enchanted the Euchee chief with a harp and a song, and he had been doing, ever since, various kinds of enchantments to keep the old chief smiling and honoring these white sojourners in his land and letting them think it was theirs. Sometimes Madoc seemed to have an inkling of how indispensible his bard and minister was, but Queen Annesta did not. As for Riryd, Meredydd was glad he now lived far way, for he was a man with no magic in his soul.

Where is Madoc? Meredydd wondered. May he be safe! May he be coming home by now!

Toolakha hissed, and Meredydd jerked his finger down from his nose.

If Madoc did not return this year, or if word ever came that he had perished out there in those distant valleys, Meredydd thought with a shudder, a contest for power would erupt between Annesta the queen and Prince Riryd, and it would be bloody, and whichever of them survived would probably alienate the natives despite all my best efforts!

THREE DAYS LATER THE QUEEN'S HUNDRED BODYGUARDS, EIGHTY of them Euchee warriors, wound their precarious way down the cliff path to the stony riverbed, with Annesta riding in a leather litter chair carried by four young women. The Euchee men would not carry loads; they saw themselves as bodyguards and hunters. "They are such haughty knaves," she had complained to Meredydd. "If I ordered Welsh soldiers to carry me, they certainly would."

"Please, Majesty, don't," Meredydd had advised, "for it would bring those soldiers down in the regard of the warriors, and our soldiers must have their respect. They believe soldiers and warriors are meant to carry only their weapons and be ready."

She had given in on the point, saying that it did not really matter to her, as the Euchee women were as strong-legged as the men anyway, and more sure-footed, and did not fart so rudely.

Now Meredydd stood on a rampart of the castle high above, watching the procession go, and he wished he could call them back.

The shaman had seen an omen, an owl gliding through treetops, and Sun Eagle had wanted the expedition called off. In order to avoid an outright confrontation with Annesta, Meredydd had assured Sun Eagle that he could do a ceremony with iron and fire that would protect everyone against whatever harm the owl forebode.

Sun Eagle, having never been lied to by Meredydd, had believed him and let his warriors go, with the reluctant consent of his tribal council.

Meredydd now felt ghastly about what he had done. He had no ceremonies. Out of weakness before Annesta he had lied to an old man who had believed in him since the first day he heard him sing and make magic sounds.

All Meredydd had been able to do was pray that no harm would come to Annesta and her entourage, and that God should forgive him for lying to Sun Eagle. And to try to undo the lie a little, he had done the praying in the light of an iron lamp, thus making it an iron and fire ceremony as he had promised.

But his prayer at the iron lamp had done little to ease his foreboding. He remembered something, a dream Annesta had told him of when Madoc and Cynan sailed away. . . .

He went down to his study and opened the leather covers of his Saga of Madoc, and ran his finger down to a place on the last page.

> Until her King and Prince were out of view,
> Annesta, Queen, waved from the river shore.
> But in her bosom, dreary darkness grew—
> For She had dreamt of seeing them Ne'ermore!

The procession of the queen wound its way through creek bottomlands and along animal paths around bluffs, always with running water visible below through the yellowing foliage, moving steadily northwestward toward the ford of the Ten-nes-see. The hundred Welsh and Euchee fighting men walked in narrow file before and behind the queen's litter chair. Footsteps hushed and crunched; necklaces and anklets of bear teeth and shells and deer hooves rattled and chattered the walking rhythm; the armor of the Welsh soldiers grated and clinked.

The queen in her chair was fanning herself sleepily with her fan of bluejay feathers when the air in the creek valley suddenly filled with whirring stone-tipped arrows like hornets out of a nest, and a chaos of screaming, running, falling. The queen was jolted sideways in her litter by an arrow that went through her left teat. The litter toppled over as one of the carrying girls crumpled with an arrow protruding from her neck. The litter chair tumbled down the steep slope among rocks, dead leaves, and tree roots, and the queen fell out. Another arrow slammed into her spine just at the waist.

The narrow valley was in tumult: demonic babble and screeching, the lurching and flopping of bodies, the slamming of wood and stone on metal, and metal on flesh and bone, the ceaseless whir and whack of countless arrows.

The valley was silent again an hour later, after every Euchee and Welshman lay dead in the ferns and the fallen leaves. The two hundred who had ambushed them with such complete success, Chiroki who had been their enemies since the time of the grandfathers' grandfathers, gathered their own few dead and vanished from the valley.

THE ROWERS PULLED EAGERLY, AND THE EIGHT CURRAGHS MOVED steadily homeward up the swift current of the Ten-nes-see, almost home. With a high and yearning heart, Madoc gazed up along the high shoreline. "Watch above the trees there," he told Cynan, pointing, "and ye'll see Dolwyddelan . . . a wee bit more . . . There! Home, my son!" The square stone battlements glowed yellow-gray in autumn afternoon sun glow a league to the south and high on its cliff—but Madoc realized that he was looking at it through a moving black cloud of vultures.

The countless black carrion-birds were circling and dropping beyond the treetops of the river bend ahead, apparently at the fording place just above the anchorage. This was a troubling sight to greet him on the return from his long season of exploration.

The Euchee crewmen had become agitated by the sight of the vultures, and before the vessels could be secured, they were leaping overboard into the water to run up the narrow creek valley. Never on the long voyage had they thrown aside discipline in this way. And before Madoc could get ashore, he heard their many voices rise into the pulsating wail that could only mean lament for the dead. As Madoc and pale, one-armed Cynan ran up the path, the eerie wail was confounded by the thundering wingbeats of scattering vultures.

He saw at once that this had been a battlefield. Carcasses lay all about on the wooded slopes, and broken arrows protruded from them and from the trampled ground. Shreds of clothing, stained with dried blood, were everywhere, and Madoc, gulping to keep from vomiting at the sight and smell of the flyblown carnage, presumed at first that Sun Eagle's Euchee had fought here, perhaps defending Dolwyddelan's river path against one of the tribes that had been encroaching from east or west. Then Cynan called to him and pointed at something on the ground. It was a dulled piece of metal: the broken blade of an iron sword. Then Madoc began to see metal weapons and pieces of armor all about—pikes, battleaxes, casques, here a greave, there a scabbard—and his heart plummeted as he realized that Welshmen, too, had died in this battle, his own men or Riryd's he knew not yet, but Welshmen, of whom there were so few.

Some of the Euchee, ranging the slaughter site and picking up arrows, were shouting, "Chiroki! Chiroki!"

It was a scene of grief and horror and madness: the Euchee and half-breeds of his crews stumbling about, howling, his Welshmen gazing about and just beginning to comprehend, the vultures fluttering reluctantly up, then settling back down nearby, the malevolent droning of thousands of thousands of flies. And as Madoc wandered stunned through it all, his eye was caught by a stained wad of cloth which, though familiar, at first meant nothing to him in his unthinking state. But he stopped and looked down at it, down amid the roots and rocks below the path, toward the creek, beside a smashed litter chair. It was the kind of cloth that Annesta and Gwenllian had learned to make from yellow flax. Madoc stared, and began quaking, gaping.

The lump of torn, decomposed flesh in that stained garment, eye sockets plucked to shreds, chin and cheeks gnawed away to show the rows of decaying teeth, tresses clotted with blood but unmistakably silvered blond . . .

It had been Annesta, his queen, his one beloved wife.

Cynan, who had stopped several paces behind his father to look at a corpse in armor, heard Madoc utter a bellow of pain and rage that made his heart cringe, and vultures went flopping away in every direction. It was a cry such as Cynan had never heard in his life and surely would never forget.

"Death to the Chiroki!" Madoc roared, shaking his fists at the sky. "I shall not lay down my blade, by my Faith, while one Chiroki still breathes in this mortal world!"

* * *

GWENLLIAN'S CHILD WAS BEING BORN IN CHAOS. SOMETIMES, IN the margins of pain's delirium, Gwenllian would think she was a little girl being rushed from her bed down a cold, dripping stone tunnel while the clash of arms and roar of voices echoed all around her. Then her mind would clear and she would know that those were memories from a childhood terror in Old Wales, and that the shouts and clashings here in Clochran Castle were the sounds of men hurrying to go to war while she, an adult, was squatting in her bedchamber in childbirth with midwives on both sides of her.

And when she would remember that, her heart would be crushed with grief again, because she knew they were going to war to avenge the death of her mother, Annesta the Queen. The news of the massacre had come to Clochran Castle just as Gwenllian was going into labor. Her mother, the messengers said, had been journeying to Clochran to be with her while her child was born.

"Milady, please," fussed one of the midwives, "you waste your strength with such weeping! You must work to bring this baby down!"

But her spasmodic sobs were uncontrollable. She tried to explain that her mother's death was her fault, but could not make words.

Gwenllian sometimes thought the rushing in her head was the sound of the waterfall where she had hidden at Dolwyddelan. In her delirium she saw herself there alone in her exquisite secrecy, and felt free and happy. But then she saw the troll there, the beast with rotting flesh, and she gasped and screamed with terror; then her mind would turn over and she would again know about her mother's death and would be wracked again with weeping.

Finally the effort of expelling the mass through her narrow hips became so great and painful and consuming that it took over every part of her mind and soul and nerves, and she could no longer slip into guilt or remorse or reverie; she could only hold the bedpost and strain down, the sight of her hands gone all blurred from tears and the sweat flowing over her eyes.

And then it was done, and after a while she came out of a dream of being on her father's ship in the sunshine with Meredydd's harp notes playing around her, and found herself lying in her bed with a livid-faced, dark-haired infant being laid upon her breast by a smiling, bedraggled midwife who said, "Ye have a fine daughter, milady, and thanks be to God Almighty she is sound. Shall I go fetch her father, if I can find him in all that uproar?"

When Owain ap Riryd came in, his father Riryd and mother Danna were with him, all looking flushed and hurried like bypassing strangers. Owain was already clad in full armor, and wild-eyed, and seemed no more connected to this event of childbirth than she felt to him as his wife; Owain was a dull and smelly brute with no passions but game-hunting and ale-swilling; he could scarcely read. Living as her young cousin's wife here, she felt utterly alone in her soul, far from her mother and father, far from Meredydd and Toolakha. When Owain copulated upon her, he always seemed like some ruthless intruder who had to be suffered patiently until he was spent and ready to leave. Now he said, "Pity 'tis a female. I should rather have had a son."

Gwenllian's heart sank, then leaped up again in anger. "Be thou thankful for something! She is a pretty child, no gnarly monster as might have been born of incest with a churlish cousin!"

"By God, little bitch!" roared Owain's father, purple with rage. "How do ye dare speak so of your husband!" Riryd's wife had grown white and clutched her bodice but said nothing, and only stood gaping like a pond fish.

Owain snarled, "We are setting out to avenge the death of your mother, at risk to our own persons. Pray thee remember our cause if we should not return: *your* mother, not mine! If I return, I mean to get a son upon you!"

"Of course, of course," she murmured. "As is thy right, whatever my desire. Before ye go, would ye deign to touch thy child, and suggest a name for her?"

Owain shambled toward the bed, surly, and touched the baby's head with a thick forefinger, and his face did not soften one whit. "Name her Dena," he said.

That struck Gwenllian like a knife in the heart, for Dena she knew to be the name of Owain's mistress, the bawdy daughter of one of the armorers. "By my God I shall not!" Gwenllian cried.

"By my God thou shalt!" Owain bellowed in her face. "She shall be Dena or I snuff out her wretched breath under a pillow ere I leave this room! I warn thee, I am in a dangerous mood; I am whetted to a killing edge!"

And though Owain's parents were shocked by his meanness, they stood by him, and the infant's name became Dena.

THE WELSH SOLDIERS AND THE EUCHEE WARRIORS STALKED NOISElessly across the moonlit snow toward the sleeping village of the Chiroki. The bark huts, shaped like loaves, about a hundred in number, were set in concentric semicircles, all the lanes between them leading down toward the riverbank. A veil of pale woodsmoke hung in the air above the town. As the Welshmen and their allies spread out across the snow, they passed through the striped shadows of leafless trees, and moonlight sparkled on the snow like tiny stars.

Madoc's stalking men were intent as wolves as they moved off, some upstream, some downstream to close off those routes of escape. Madoc felt like a wolf in his own heart, as hungry for vengeance as a wolf is for meat, and these Chiroki would soon be in his teeth. Since autumn he had destroyed six of their villages within the fringes of his kingdom, and now he had carried the war into their own country. These Chiroki people, as old enemies of his Euchee, had been his own enemies in the politic way for years, but until they had marauded into his country and murdered his beloved queen, they had been in no danger from him. Now he was beyond mercy or restraint; he would eliminate their entire nation, numerous and farflung as they were.

Sun Eagle's Euchee warriors were fast to Madoc's cause, heart and soul, burning to avenge the deaths of their brothers and sisters who had been massacred with the queen and the twenty Welsh soldiers in the ambush near Dolwyddelan. On the return from his explorations last year, Madoc had been feeling the weight of age. But now, even though he was bone-sore and shallow of wind in these winter marches, his heart was full of red fire again because he was an avenger. At last in his life Madoc could understand the war passion of his father Owain Gwynedd. The great king had known the hard truth that kings must know: one must be so powerful that no neighbor would dare transgress. If Madoc had cowed these Chiroki ten years ago on behalf of his friends the Euchee, they would not have dared raid into his kingdom.

And my queen would have lived to witness the birth of our granddaughter! he thought. And we would be together before our hearth fire at Dolwyddelan now, in peace and security. We learn so late the wisdom of our father! Only strength assures peace.

I was like a foolish lamb, all blind to danger because I imagined I was in Paradise!

But no longer a lamb. Now Madoc was ranging like a wolf here in the west, with Cynan at his side, while Riryd and his son Owain struck the neighboring tribes in the mountains to the east of the kingdom.

And as they subdued the tribes all around, their fearsome reputation grew. They were the Iron Warriors, the Stone-Cutting Men. Who would ever again trifle with a people who could cut stone, and make swords from the rocks of hillsides?

Madoc turned to Cynan, who walked at his right. His son's helmet and breastplate gleamed with moonlight, and so did his sword. Only Cynan among all the Welsh and Euchee fighting men bore no shield; without his left arm he could not carry one, and so he fought without. But he had so strengthened his sword arm that he was as swift and terrible in battle as a man with several hands, and his armor was protection against stone arrow points. Less than a year ago he had been but a boy, but the loss of his arm and the murder of his mother had tempered him, and now he was a most zealous avenger, with no fear of pain or death, and the wolf was in his heart, too, as he stalked with his father toward the huts of the sleeping Chiroki. Now they were within a few paces of the edge of the village, converging through the garden clearing, and still not one dog of the town had barked an alarm. At every village Madoc had struck so far, the first bark of dogs had been used as the signal to rush, and the attackers had sometimes had to dash as much as a furlong to reach the town; during the minutes of such a rush, the warriors in a town sometimes had time to snatch up weapons and come out to meet the attackers, though usually they were too thoroughly frightened by the bellowing of the sounding horns to offer much resistance. But this was the first night that Madoc had approached through snow, and it appeared that it would be a total surprise.

And so now Madoc raised to his lips the horn that hung from his shoulder and blew a long, fierce blast, that bellow that oft had served so well, and then with naked sword before him he plunged into the nearest hut through its leather door flap, and in the dim light from the fire pit, began hacking at the querying, crying forms of the awakening sleepers as they tried to rise from their bedding. Outside now, other horns were sounding, and footsteps thudding, men shouting, people screaming, dogs barking frantically. Madoc cared not whether a moving body was man, woman, or child; he struck every one. Then he took from his waist a short resinwood torch, ignited it from the fire pit, and torched the dry mats and barks lining the walls, kicked the embers from the fire pit in every direction, and lunged out of that hut and into the next one. Every Welsh soldier and Euchee warrior carried such a torch, and soon they were flickering yellow in the silvery moonlight throughout the town. Figures darted out of the lodges, only to be clubbed or slashed down or run through with ready lances. The horns bleated and lowed, women screamed, Euchee warriors trilled their excited kill cries, and the air was full of the clacks and thuds of fighting. In minutes the pale blue of moonlight was overpowered by the lurid flames of burning huts, by yellow-tinged smoke, by swirling columns of sparks. Soot and embers rose on the roaring heat and sifted down to speckle the snow, which now was also stained and tracked with blood.

For nearly an hour in this howling inferno, the slaughter went on. The Chirokis not slain in their bedding or burned to death in their collapsing huts were chased down in the streets, beaten until they were crawling, then speared, clubbed, or gutted. Cynan's sinewy arm could whirl his sword around his head and then flick it out like a whip to decapitate a running man or woman as neatly as a headsman's ax at the block. The snow melted between the flaming houses and the ground turned to a bloody, slushy muck. Most of the Chiroki were naked, having been surprised in their beds, and when the Welsh soldiers trapped a woman or girl still alive, they would hold her down and take turns raping her, sprawling upon her in the icy mud. Boys, too, were trapped and buggered, then slashed or clouted to death. The Welshmen would not have dared commit such brutalities a few months before, knowing the chivalric nobility of their King Madoc, but they now knew they had license from him to do their worst; they knew that in his eyes these Chiroki were to be eradicated like vermin, like lice, even the nits killed without compunction, hesitation, or mercy.

When the sun rose over the snowy valley, it was smeared over with drifting dark smoke. Madoc stood on a hill looking down with red-rimmed eyes and a face like sooty stone. Nothing remained of the hundred houses but charred poles and heaps of burnt furnishings. The whole area, perhaps three hectares, had been trampled and churned under hundreds of running feet and mortal struggles. Nearly half a thousand Chirokis lay naked and mutilated in death's awkward poses. There were poles stuck in the ground with severed heads on top. Near the center of the town lay a huge smudge of burned wreckage; it had been the tribe's Great House, where they met and worshiped. Madoc himself had flung down its altar and piled its sacred feathers, bones, skins, carvings, and totems into a heap and torched them, while the Euchee stood back, afraid to see such a thing done, sobered for a moment by the old white giant's act of unthinkable sacrilege. To take an enemy's tribal bundle by force, or to steal it through cleverness and daring, was a thrilling adventure, adding much to the prestige of whoever could do it. But who had so little fear of the Great Spirit that he would smash an altar and destroy a Sacred Bundle?

Some of the Euchee warrior chieftains looked today at the white grandfather called Madoc, and bad birds screamed silently in their souls. Of course they would have to tell Sun Eagle what this madman had done. Sun Eagle, they knew, believed this man to be a god; for a whole generation Sun Eagle had done what this mighty old man god had asked him to do, and usually Sun Eagle had allowed himself to be convinced that those were good things to do, and had in turn convinced his people in council that they ought to help the white-man god to do them.

But the gods of the Chiroki were powerful; the Chiroki were a numerous and powerful people. And even if this white old giant did kill all Chiroki, which would help the Euchee, he could not kill their Beyond World spirits, and those spirits could come and make evil for the Euchee who had helped this altar-smasher and bundle-burner.

The warrior chiefs of the Euchee were afraid now, beginning to be more afraid of their ally than they had been afraid of their enemies.

CHAPTER 8

DOLWYDDELAN CASTLE
A.D. 1201

AFTER TWELVE YEARS OF KILLING, MADOC'S WAR HAD TURNED back upon him, and he was now caught in a trap of his own design.

The old king lay in a dirty bed, propped up to keep his lungs from filling, listening to the dismal sounds of the siege outside his stone walls, and he thought, Yes, God abhors me, and I am to lose my domain.

"What, then?" he croaked to Meredydd and Rhys, who stood dejected beside his bed. The bard, whose hair was now white and whose skin was as smooth and yellow as parchment, looked with pity at this king of his, who in vengeful fury had offended all the sacred spirits of Iarghal. Meredydd was now a prisoner in his allegiance to his once-beloved king. He sighed and told him what he saw to be the truth:

"We must beg the Chiroki for peace, Majesty. We starve. Most of our people are sick. There is nothing more we can do but sue for peace, or stay in here until we all are dead."

Madoc sighed, and turned to Rhys, his old Minister of Arms. Somewhere in the distance a voice was shouting Chiroki words, in taunting tones. Madoc said to Rhys, "You concur with our bard, do you?"

Rhys looked down and nodded, his craggy, grizzled face morose and ashamed. "Your Majesty, I do." He shrugged and turned his palms up. "If only we could have gone down and fought them on the field, we might have won. But as Your Highness knows, we could not get down."

Madoc shut his eyes and groaned aloud. The terrible absurd irony of it stung him like the blow of a lash. He had designed this impregnable fortress in such a way that no more than one or two attackers could attack at the gate on the cliffside path at once. But by the same strait only one Welshman at a time could pass through the gate to go down, and the clever Chiroki had simply occupied the path on the outside of the gate, thus confining the entire Welsh and Euchee army in the castle. Rhys's soldiers had poured embers and hot oil down from the walls to try to dislodge the small band of Chiroki from the path, but the Chiroki had hung on until there was no more oil or even firewood in the castle, and then had successfully blocked the gate for three more weeks, while the besieged, now unable to cook or go out and hunt, ate raw their diminishing stores of grain, seeds, roots, and nut meal, growing sick from such fare—and now, because there were more than two thousand trapped in this mountaintop castle, the food was all gone and the cisterns were fouled and nearly empty, and everyone was sick. The Chiroki controlled the countryside and hunted freely over it, and fished the rivers, and the maddening smell of their feasts drifted up to the castle on the smoke of their cook fires, further demoralizing the helpless defenders. The outer walls of the castle and the cliffs below were caked with the excrement the people had been emptying over the parapets for this duration of the siege; now they were too weak and lethargic to do even that, and merely tracked it about in the streets and commons. The castle was aswarm with flies; everything seemed to vibrate with their crawling millions, and they darkened the air and droned relentlessly. And now there were people dying, a dozen or so every day. There was no way to bury them on the stone promontory, and there was no wood for funeral pyres. The Euchee would not let their dead be simply thrown off the walls because of their religious beliefs, and so the bodies lay decomposing in rows on the sunbaked rock, surrounded by their wailing relatives. Meredydd, out of respect for those beliefs, would not let the Welsh dead be cast off the cliffs either; to have done so would have further eroded any respect the Euchee still had for their allies.

There was not much respect left anyway. By pursuing his war against the Chiroki far beyond revenge in the last twelve years, by raping their women and slaughtering their children, and by destroying their sacred objects, he had become the scourge of the Chiroki and their related tribes, and had brought down upon himself and his Euchee a war without end. Five years ago the aged chief Sun Eagle had died, lamenting the day he had first smoked the ceremonial pipe with Madoc. This succeeding chief of the Euchee, a portly, middle-aged man named Sits on Much Ground, remained unenthusiastically loyal to the Welsh simply because he had no choice. He knew his nation was forever tainted by its association with the Big White King. As many as half of all Euchee children and youth had the blood of the white men in them and had been made to learn to speak their strange tongue. Sits on Much Ground had been on the verge of counciling with his chieftains about breaking off from the Welshmen and trying to become true Euchee again, but before that council could be called, the Chiroki had invaded Madoc's kingdom with a confederation of allied tribes, bands of thousands of warriors, driving the Euchee before them to this place on the rock mountain, and besieged them here. Sits on Much Ground was now waiting morosely outside the bedchamber of the sick old King Madoc, listening to the voices of the white men inside.

Old Madoc, feeble and lung-sick though he was, still had a big voice, and Sits on Much Ground now heard him ask Meredydd:

"What will it gain us to treaty with the Chiroki? Meseems that if we surrender, our deaths will be but a few days quicker than if we stay here and die as we are doing. Surely you do not believe they would show us any mercy." On Madoc's conscience lay the murders of thousands of innocents, and he thought more about them as he came closer to meeting his Creator. He knew he deserved no quarter from the Chiroki, and should expect none. What bothered his dreams now was that his vengeful excesses might have blocked his way to Heaven, that he was perhaps beyond atonement. How he had yearned in these last months for the priests who had seemed so useless those thirty years ago!

Old Meredydd's nose twitched elaborately as he thought of his reply. Then he answered:

"Your Highness, I can only parley with them and learn what terms they will give. If they promise none, then we might as well resist here until we are dead. But if they will allow us something—say, the lives of some to be spared, or will let us live as slaves—then you can decide whether to accept. That, Highness, is all we can do. I am prepared to ask them for a truce and go down and talk with them, and Sits on Much Ground has agreed to go with me to council on behalf of his Euchee people."

Madoc, hollow-eyed and grimacing, shook his head slowly, dubiously. "They . . . If you go down, my good bard, they might only kill you. . . . Or if they promise to spare us, any of us, they might then kill us all as we gave ourselves over."

Meredydd leaned closer to the bed, his face now very intense, and replied, "I beg you to remember, Your Highness, the admiration that you had for these native peoples in our earliest years in Iarghal, before this war with the Chiroki clouded our vision with dark smoke. Remember the trust and compassion you felt in your heart then? Had you not had so accepting and hopeful a heart, you would have not befriended the Euchee, and our miserable colony would have perished then. Please remember how you felt then, sire."

Madoc lay still, thoughtful, but said nothing.

"I know it from all the Euchee," Meredydd went on, "that these Chiroki are always true to their word as they give it. They are not treacherous."

"Not treacherous!" Madoc exploded. "They massacred Welshmen and murdered my queen!"

Meredydd made a calming motion with both palms down and said, "They were attacking their old enemies, the Euchee. Queen Annesta hap'd to be among the victims by her own will, going abroad against my considered advice! Rhys, is it not so?"

"It is so, sire," Rhys answered. "I do remember it just so."

"Aye, so you have oft reminded me," Madoc groaned. "And how near I came to beheading ye both for letting her go!"

As I well deserved, Meredydd thought, still remembering with mortal shame how he had ignored the Euchee shaman's warning of the owl omen. Had it not been for the Euchee lust for revenge on the Chiroki, old Sun Eagle probably would have forsaken and abandoned the Welsh that day, because of Meredydd's perfidy.

Madoc lay for a long time with his eyes closed, so long that Meredydd thought he had gone to sleep. But finally he began to champ his gums, making his white whiskers bob up and down, and then he opened his eyes and gazed at Meredydd.

"But thou hast always counseled me wisely, faithful bard. How often ye begged me not to war so mercilessly on the Chiroki, and I ought to have listened, as we see now. Thou hast been my truest friend and helpmeet. So . . . try, then, for a truce . . . but do not let them know how finished we are. . . . They will more likely concede us a little if they think we could still fight. . . .

"And, listen you: before agreeing to anything with them, find out the fate of Clochran—of my brother Riryd . . . my daughter and my granddaughter . . . whether they too are besieged, whether still alive or dead. . . ."

"I shall try, Your Majesty."

". . . And what you learn about that, bring back and tell me, for it will doubtless weigh in my decision." Madoc sighed again, shut his eyes, coughed wearily. "Take my hand awhile, old bard," he said, "and then go and call for a truce. Do all ye can for us. And . . . Godspeed."

WITH SITS ON MUCH GROUND AND TWO OTHER CHIEFTAINS, Meredydd hobbled down the cliff path, led and followed by Chiroki warriors. To Meredydd, being outside the stinking misery of the castle after so long a time was almost overpowering. The fresh air and open space seemed to make him feel old and weak and vulnerable, so light-headed that he felt he needed to lean heavily on his staff to fight dizziness as he went down the high, narrow path. The stony little river straight below muttered and gurgled, as if calling for him to leap into its rocks and white waters for a quick, clean end of everything. Meredydd felt he had been carrying the burden of the dying Kingdom of Iarghal on his own frail shoulders for many months, and he knew not what yet lay ahead of him to do or suffer on the behalf of the kingdom. Would the Chiroki torture him, humiliate him, as retribution for Madoc's cruelties? Terrible and confining though Dolwyddelan had become, it had at least been an armor of stone walls around him.

Meredydd watched the warriors in front of him to keep his attention away from the precipice. These Chiroki, he observed, were a stockier, squarer-built sort of people than the Euchee, very muscular. They wore little adornment, but had stained their faces and bodies with many colors in gruesome designs.

They led him and his chieftains down and across a fording place and a little way up into the woods on an opposite slope, to a war camp in a glade. A runner had gone ahead to announce the parley, and so a group of Chiroki dignitaries stood waiting. Their leader was apparently the very stocky, round-faced man who stood slightly ahead of the rest, draped in a creamy-colored toga of cotton trimmed down the bosom with the bright feathers of various tropical birds. Sits on Much Ground and that man obviously knew each other by sight; both stared at each other most intently. Both were mammoth in bulk, but the Chiroki chief emanated physical strength in contrast to the soft puffiness of Sits on Much Ground.

Soon all the chiefs and chieftains were seated on the ground, and with the help of Sits on Much Ground, who spoke the

Chiroki tongue as well as Euchee and Welsh, Meredydd was introduced to the Chiroki chief, Bear that Floats.

Floating Bear's intense attention soon shifted from the Euchee to Meredydd, and his eyes drilled him during the smoking of the ceremonial pipe. Then Floating Bear began asking questions, and Sits on Much Ground conveyed to Meredydd the essence of the discussions.

"He wants to know if you are leader of the white tribe. I told him no, you are second chief and the nation's singer, and that the king sent you. Floating Bear is angry that our king himself did not walk down. In my answer I tell him our king is too angry to talk now and trusts you to talk better."

Meredydd turned an astonished eye on the Euchee and demanded: "Why did you tell him that? You'll make him angrier than ever!"

"I dared not tell him how feeble our King Madoc is. We must seem stronger than we are as we talk here."

"Yes," Meredydd agreed. "Very well. Now tell him that we are weary of this war, which keeps us all from the good things of life, and that we want to know why they came into our kingdom and killed the wife of our king. Ask him what he must have in order to stop fighting us and go back to his own country."

Sits on Much Ground was an intelligent man and a good speaker, and for the next few minutes he carried on a lively and rapid exchange of words with the Chiroki chief, with enough hand signs being given on both sides that Meredydd could almost follow the discussion.

It was that the Chiroki who ambushed the Euchee so many years ago had not known there were white people in the column, that they had had no grudge against the white people and would not have killed the king's wife if they had known. "Floating Bear says that now he knows that happened, he is sorry for it," explained the Euchee chief. "But Floating Bear says that the accidental slaying of one woman was not enough to cause tens of hundreds of Chiroki men and women and children to be slain in their beds. And he says that the white men brought illnesses into the valley of the Mother of Rivers, so that the Chiroki had to move about the land to get away from the dying. He says that the white king is wrong to believe that these lands are his, for they are the old home of the Chiroki and their friends, given to them by the Creator, and that the white king came only a generation ago, so he should not think they are his lands."

Meredydd sat and listened and thought, and in his heart he felt that the Chiroki chief was right. These were things that Meredydd himself had tried to tell Madoc, who in his vengeful rage had refused to listen. So now Meredydd said, "Tell Floating Bear that I, the First Singer and Second Chief of the Welsh people on the stone mountain, find his words fair and easy to understand, and that I will take those words back up to our king and put them into his ears."

Sits on Much Ground translated all that, and the Chiroki chief nodded impassively, but the light in his eyes was changing and softening, and after more discussion, Sits on Much Ground told Meredydd:

"Floating Bear says that his people, too, are tired of war, and would like to go home to their wives and children."

"Good!" exclaimed Meredydd. "Tell him that if they go, we will have no more bad feelings about them, and that I will persuade our king never to strike the Chiroki again, unless they first do something bad again."

As Sits on Much Ground translated this, Floating Bear and some of his chieftains began to look amused, then angry, and soon were muttering among themselves. Then, with much finger-pointing and very sharp eyes, Floating Bear delivered a quick tirade, which Sits on Much Ground translated to Meredydd in a meek manner:

"This man Floating Bear says it is not just. He says that the white king has killed too many Chiroki women and children to remain welcome here. If there is to be peace, he says, the white people must go far away, and that my People the Euchee must go also, because we helped your king with those massacres."

Meredydd sat, stunned. How could he take such a demand as this back to Madoc? And before he could even begin to form a reply, the Chiroki chief began talking again. Meredydd knew from the hand signs that he was speaking of the people from Clochran Castle, and Sits on Much Ground confirmed that when he translated:

"Floating Bear tells us that his warriors have already defeated the other stone village of the white men"—he pointed to the northwest—"the one you call Clochran, they have defeated it and burned it, he said." Meredydd's heart had leaped up painfully, and now was slamming and fluttering as he thought of Riryd, of Gwenllian, of Owain ap Riryd, of Madoc's grandchildren. And Sits on Much Ground continued, answering the questions before Meredydd had to ask them:

"The Chiroki hold most of the white-face people who lived there. They killed many Euchee warriors and some white-face soldiers. He says the white-face king up there was killed . . . that that king's wife killed herself . . . that the young people and the children of the big stone house are all alive, and some white-face soldiers and their women. Floating Bear says for you to tell your king that he will kill all of those people unless we leave this country. That is all he said, Singer."

Meredydd was fighting against faintness and confusion. He had for a moment presumed that the end of the war could be gained so easily; he had forgotten how the politeness of a native council could lull one to forget that serious things were still unresolved.

And of course the death of so many Chiroki innocents was serious.

Floating Bear, for all his ceremonial politeness, had not forgotten that too many of his People had been slaughtered, and it was not only peace he sought, but justice.

At last Meredydd regained enough presence of mind to say, "If we leave this country, will Floating Bear promise to return those captives to us, unhurt? And will he allow us to take our . . ." Meredydd had to pause and think about how to ask for this. ". . . our Sacred Bundles with us?" To Meredydd the books and harp were as sacred as life.

There followed a few more minutes of vigorous talk in Chiroki between the Euchee and Chiroki chiefs, with interjections from the Chiroki chieftains, whose faces were hard with resolve. Finally, Sits on Much Ground sighed, looked at the ground for a while, then told Meredydd:

"This man Floating Bear says: When all the white-face men and all the Tsoyaha Euchee leave this country, he will trade all his captives for one man, your king, who killed so many Chiroki women and children that their spirits cry out for him to bear an equal pain; that only this will free their spirits to go on in peace to the Other Side World. They want King Madoc's life placed into their hands. If this is done, the rest will be freed to leave the country with us. And he says you may take your Sacred Bundle. Unlike your king, he says, they would never destroy a Sacred Bundle.

"Singer, that is the offer he has made."

IT WAS CYNAN WHO BROUGHT MEREDYDD AND SITS ON MUCH Ground back into Madoc's bedchamber now. Cynan was tall and bronzed by sun, a picture of what Madoc himself had been at the age of a quarter century, except for the one missing arm. Rhys followed the three in and shut the door, and they stood around Madoc's bed while a servant girl moved a feather fan slowly to and fro to keep flies from settling on the king. Madoc reached for Meredydd's hand, which made a huge knot swell in Meredydd's throat. "Thank God you are safe, my bard. Now tell me what you learned of those at Clochran. Was that place besieged, too? Do they still hold out? You did get answers, did you not? And tell me what seems to lie in store for our kingdom." He kept his grip on Meredydd's hand, and such a current was passing between the two old comrades that Meredydd knew he could not lie or gloss over any of Floating Bear's demands; Madoc would sense whether he was truly forthcoming.

"Highness," Meredydd began, "Princess Gwenllian, and Owain ap Riryd, and their children are safe, but are prisoners of the Chiroki. . . ." He saw Madoc's eyes widen with alarm and, perhaps, anger, but Madoc said nothing yet, and Meredydd went on: "Clochran Castle has been destroyed. Some Welsh soldiers and their women are held captive—"

"And Riryd?" Madoc interrupted, scowling. "Out with it, bard!"

"He died in defending the castle, Highness. And Danna his queen they say killed herself. . . ."

Madoc's lined face tightened in a grimace, eyes squeezed shut against tears, and he loosed a long sigh, which ended with a rattle in his chest, and then he groaned. For a moment, as he fought for control of himself, the sounds of misery from outside seemed to swell in through the narrow window: the lamentations of women, cries of starving children, the drone of millions of flies, and a desultory disturbance of yelling and fluttering as men tried to drive buzzards off the rows of corpses.

At last Madoc gathered himself. "Thank God my young ones live," he said. "And I suppose the Chiroki want ransom for them?"

"Ransom, milord?" exclaimed Meredydd. "Why, we have nothing they want, you know. They have no use for anything we call treasure." Even in his state of mind, Madoc realized at once the truth of that startling statement; he presumed, with shock and despair, that there was no way to buy their freedom.

But now, Meredydd knew, was the time to say the hardest things.

"Highness, the Chiroki chief, Bear that Floats, demands that we remove far from this country, and he cares not which way we go, only that we go far away. If we do that, he will release our people to us safe and well. . . ."

Again a succession of feelings, from anguish to anger, paraded across Madoc's craggy face. "I am too old," he muttered, hardly audible, "to rebuild our kingdom elsewhere." He shook his head, gazing down at the bedding across his lap, and at his flaccid, spindly, pale, blue-veined legs, from which he had thrown the covers.

"Dear and beloved king," Meredydd now murmured to him, squeezing on his big hand, "the younger ones will have to rebuild the kingdom, if they can. Your Iarghal, if it is to continue, must live on through them. For this, and listen, Excellency, is the very crux of our fate and the fate of Iarghal:

"You will have to sacrifice your own person."

It seemed to take Madoc a long time to comprehend what his bard had said. And Cynan, standing behind Meredydd, gasped when he suddenly realized what he had heard, and began shaking his head. In this confounding silence, Meredydd explained the Chiroki chief's demands. Then, after a long pause, Madoc asked in a low, intense voice:

"If I were to agree, what warrant have I that the Chiroki will restore our loved ones to us, rather than kill them, too?"

"His word, Your Highness."

"Only his word?"

"These are not Europeans, my lord; their word is their honor."

And Madoc, reflecting on his two decades of experience among the Euchee and other native nations, nodded in assent, and a wistful, calm light began to shine in his eyes.

"Aye," he said at last. "I do have a thousand murders to atone for . . . and if the sacrifice of one king can do that . . . Go, old bard, and tell the Chiroki that I bow to his terms, and I am his."

THE CHIROKI WERE GOING TO MAKE THE WHITE-SKIN PEOPLE WATCH, so that they would never forget this lesson.

All the Welsh prisoners had been stripped of their clothing and armor, and their hands were tightly bound behind them. They were made to stand in a half circle so they all faced the stake that had been erected in the center of the courtyard of Dolwyddelan Castle. All the day before, the Chiroki had made the surly Welsh soldier-thegns carry wood and brush up the narrow path to the castle, humiliating them with the work of women. They had let the Euchee carry their decomposing dead down the path to bury them in the forest. Now on this morning the Euchee were being held as prisoners in a streambed below the castle, all except their chief and chieftains, who were to watch the execution of the great murderer.

Tethered to one pole directly opposite the stake were all the members of Madoc's own family. His son Cynan was strapped to the pole by his right wrist. His large physique was made asymmetrical by the pink-stumped left arm and the atrophied shoulder and chest muscles, which he had always kept hidden by clothing and capes.

At the other side of that pole stood Gwenllian, wheaten-haired, long-legged. At thirty-six years, she was still narrow in the waist, though childbearing had thrust her lower belly forward and widened the set of her hips. Chiroki men and women gawked elaborately and made fun of the blond hair on her woman-parts.

Next to Gwenllian was her husband Owain ap Riryd, ruddy and thick-built at thirty years, with dark eye sockets and red beard, his face livid with rage and shame, never looking toward Gwenllian. Though handsome in features, he had never been clean in his habits, and thus his nakedness revealed a repulsive mottling and scarring from carbuncles, boils, and rashes. Dena, the twelve-year-old daughter of Gwenllian and Owain, and Gower, their seven-year-old son, both slender and beautiful children, stood in a paralysis of dread. Gwenllian had no way of knowing whether they had any comprehension of what was about to happen. She herself had come to believe that there would be executions, perhaps of all the white people, and had been praying for days not for their lives but for the salvation of their souls. The drums, which had been thumping like a heartbeat since dawn, had almost pounded her own proud courage out of her, and she had given up trying to encourage her children with words. She was heavy with fatigue. She and Owain had so long been hostile strangers to each other that they did not even look to each other for reassurance. She was more contemptuous of her husband than she had been when he was simply her rambunctious boy cousin. He was not even a mediocre father to their children, and she knew what he was in his man's world beyond their marriage: a bloody villain, slayer of children and ravisher of women and girls in the field, an ale-swiller and philanderer at home, and the leader of a brutish clique of thegns who wore antlered helmets and gloried in brawling, rape, and buggery. She believed that if any Welshman here deserved to be executed by the Chiroki, it was her husband.

Now and then the breeze brought the rush of the falls from the gorge below the castle, and Gwenllian remembered the cool peace and privacy of that place from her childhood, and she yearned to be there.

FAR BELOW THE CASTLE, WHERE NEARLY TWO THOUSAND EUCHEE sat under guard in the river gorge, one slender woman with keen black eyes began edging imperceptibly toward a tangle of vines at the river's edge.

Toolakha knew not what fate was planned for the Euchee, but she was not Euchee and did not want to die with them. And there was a possibility that someone might identify her as the woman of the Welsh king's First Singer; that would be unwanted attention.

When Toolakha was partially hidden among the vines, she slithered quickly into the stream without the least splashing, and swam underwater upstream to the rapids, pulled herself among the rocks through the rushing water, and when she was in the old bathing pool, she swam underwater again to cross it. She glided through the frothing turbulence until she knew she was in the secret place behind the falls, the place the Princess Gwenllian had discovered when she was a girl. Here Toolakha would hide until the Chiroki were gone and the fate of the Welshmen had been concluded in whatever way the Chiroki had decided to do it.

Toolakha had passed thirty summers, most of her life, with those white captors of hers, and though she had never stopped hating them for stealing her freedom, she had helped them in many ways, especially through their singer and subchief, Meredydd. He was not so bad a man as most of them; he was wise. Toolakha had shared his bed and assuaged his loneliness and helped him understand many things. She had endured his unclean ways and had tried to comfort him when he was tormented with shame for the brutality of his king's war of vengeance. Toolakha had never loved him, but he had never had to know that.

Now his fate would be whatever it would be, but Toolakha was free now, as she had not been since she was captured in the river by the sea. She stripped off her heavy, sodden deerhide dress, wrung the water out of it and spread it on the stones, sat upon it among the mossy rocks behind the roaring waterfall, and waited for a safe time. And in her heart she thanked the white princess for discovering this good hiding place.

Somewhere, perhaps, across the mountains and back down the green Ala Bamu River, there might still dwell some of her Coo-thah People who had not died of the Welshmen's ill spirits. She would go seek them.

AN EXCITED MURMUR OF HUNDREDS OF VOICES STIRRED Gwenllian's attention. People were emerging from the great door of the castle keep. When she saw who they were, her heart squeezed in her breast and forced a groan from her throat.

Stumbling ahead of them was a rangy, loose-skinned, sickly-pale graybeard. His face was so haggard that it was a moment before Gwenllian realized that it was her father Madoc. He had been stripped and his hands were bound behind him. She had never seen him except as a mighty and handsome king, and this ghastly reduction of him so stunned her that for a moment she forgot her own shame and wretchedness. She nearly cried out for him, but stopped herself because she did not want him to see her naked and dirty, and she bit her lips. Tears began to blur her sight, but she saw old Meredydd walking among the Chiroki and Euchee chieftains behind Madoc. Gwenllian realized that the bard was the only Welshman who was not naked and bound; he was in his usual plain robe and clearly not a prisoner, as were all the other white people. Gwenllian felt an awful suspicion that perhaps Meredydd had betrayed the Welsh people somehow, but that was too grave and complex a thought for her to deal with in such a moment as this.

The fearful drums throbbed as Madoc was guided toward the solitary stake. The Chiroki chieftains shoved him about until his back was toward the stake, and then they tied his wrists to the stake, so tightly that he grimaced, while the Welsh people began wailing, realizing that their king was to be subjected to some singular punishment.

When he had been tied and the chieftains stood back, Madoc raised his head and stood as tall as he could, and gazed about at all the prisoners arrayed before him. Dismay was plain in his face even at this distance in the dusty enclosure; then his brow lowered with anger. Gwenllian did not know whether his sweeping glance had even recognized her. She heard him shout in that unforgettable, bellowing voice:

"Bard! Why are my people bound up like that? You said they go free!"

Meredydd hurried toward him, and the murmuring and wailing of the captives subsided.

"They will be free, Highness!" Meredydd said. "They are trussed up only to restrain them during the . . . during this. Believe me, they will be freed!"

Madoc glowered around. Then he said loudly:

"I have words for my people. Bard, do not let me be interrupted. Cynan, my son!"

"Aye, Father!" Cynan called back in a hoarse voice, his eyes glittering, chin up and thrust forward. Madoc stared toward him.

"You are King of Iarghal after me, my only son!"

"Aye!" Cynan cried. He glared all around. "You have heard him!"

Suddenly Gwenllian found her voice and called out, "I was your firstborn!" People turned to look at her. Madoc's startled gaze found her, and he stared at this naked woman for a moment before a softening of his visage revealed his feelings.

"Beloved daughter!" he choked. He looked confused, as if he had forgotten her or thought her dead. "Yes . . . Yes," he said, "you are my firstborn. . . . You—"

Cynan's voice cried out. "I! I, Father, I! I am your male heir! There can be no queen while a male heir lives. . . ."

Madoc now looked completely confused, and the Chiroki chieftains were beginning to mutter and exclaim angrily. Apparently this crying out among the prisoners was disrupting their execution ceremony.

Madoc, who had kept himself aloof from the royal court all during his life in Wales, and now had not really thought about the problem of succession during all his life in Iarghal, turned a doubtful, desperate face toward Meredydd, his customary source of answers. But Meredydd was not aware, because he was being railed at now by Bear that Floats. Some of the Chiroki chieftains sprinted toward the bound prisoners. One swung a club and struck Cynan a blow that felled him, unconscious. Another grabbed Gwenllian's long hair, twisted it around and stuffed it into her mouth to silence her. A warrior bound thongs around her face to keep her from expelling the hair, and she could only writhe and murmur, unable to shout, barely able to breathe.

Old Madoc, seeing these attacks upon his children, bellowed his rage and struggled so hard against his bonds that the stake moved to and fro, though it was too firmly planted for him to dislodge it.

The Chiroki chief now looked furious with this lack of decorum, and he shouted several syllables at the top of his lungs. At once warriors came carrying armloads of dry branches, bark, and kindling, which they began stacking on the ground in a circle all around Madoc, about three feet away from his feet. Still raging, Madoc kicked at the piles, but the warriors rebuilt them, just beyond reach of his kicking feet. They made the piles hip high, then stepped back. Madoc stood, panting, and glowered about.

Floating Bear called out again, and now two lines of Chiroki women came forward into the courtyard, their naked bodies blackened with grease and charcoal. The two women in front carried between them a pot of sand upon which a small fire smoldered with much blue smoke. The rest of the women carried long, straight poles whose upper ends were wrapped with oily wadding, like torches. When Madoc saw these demonic-looking women coming toward him, he quit his struggles, quit bellowing, and stood erect. Meredydd had told him that it would be the mothers and sisters of slain children who would execute his punishment, and he seemed to understand that these were the ones selected to do it. He faced them with clenched jaw, trying not to show his fear.

But Madoc was afraid, afraid as he had never been. It was not that he feared dying; he had already agreed that he should and would die for his crimes. What he feared was what he saw in their eyes. In their blackened faces, what should have been the whites of their eyes were red. Madoc had never, to his knowledge, been hated. He had never been the object of anyone's fury or contempt, but now he knew that he was, and that he deserved to be, and he knew that he was not going to be executed swiftly and mercifully, but that these women were going to try to make him suffer as much pain as he had inflicted upon countless hundreds. And so he braced himself and began praying wordlessly, and looked up at the smoky sky so that he would not have to see the indescribably terrible eyes of the vengeful women.

Gwenllian moaned as she watched the women light their torch poles at the fire pot. She could only groan and whimper, with her hair gag, while all the other Welsh people screamed and wailed.

The women stood outside the ring of kindling and began poking Madoc with their torches. He convulsed at each touch but made no sound. Soon his skin everywhere was covered with sooty blisters. One woman held her torch to his beard until it was entirely burned off his face, and then she burned off his eyebrows and the hair of his head. Madoc's mouth, bubbling with blisters, kept moving in his silent prayer. Another woman held her torch against his genitals. When all that hair was burned off, she kept the torch there and roasted his genitals. His body was wracked with spasms and violent shivering, but he still did not cry out.

Gwenllian went dizzy and almost fell, but willed herself to be strong, too, and would not let herself faint, or even close her eyes. Not to have the courage to follow her father's fate, she felt, would be to fail him in his suffering. And so she stayed conscious and watched.

Eventually he was not anything she could have recognized as her father, or hardly even as a man. He was a tall, two-legged, scorched, twitching, writhing animal. At last Gwenllian fainted.

It was perhaps half an hour before the charred body gave one mighty convulsion, and the blackened women howled in exultation as the body slumped and the bowels emptied.

The white giant, the murderer of Chiroki women and children, was dead. He had died bravely, without a whimper, but the pain of their hearts had all been passed to his body, and they knew it, and were satisfied; they would have to mourn no longer.

They stuck their torches into the kindling around his feet. Flames built up, roaring and crackling. The rest of the skin of the dead king crisped up and charred, and the smell of his burning meat hung in the air of the courtyard of his Dolwyddelan Castle, and when those flames died down, only a frame of charred flesh hung from the blackened stake. A great howl of passion went up from the Chiroki. The Welsh people were silent now. Old Meredydd was pale as linen, swaying on his feet.

Floating Bear spoke to Sits on Much Ground, who turned to Meredydd and told him what Floating Bear had said.

"It is done fairly in the eyes of the Creator. Now your people must go to their big boats and go down the river, and never again come back to the lands of the Chiroki."

Now must it end, this Saga of a King,
For gone is that great Voyage-Maker's soul.
Silence shall reign where Madoc's Bard doth sing.
The Life is done; the Story must be whole.

Mayhap someday a younger Bard there'll be
To carry forth the tale of his Heirs;
This Bard who speaks shall never live to see
Whate'er the Destinies that shall be theirs.

Exiled they fled from Madoc's Land apace.
Cynan his son in ships led them afar
By rivers to this Falling Water Place
He'd once explored; here now their Castles are.

One-armed Cynan a wistful King is he.
His Welshmen and the Euchee do his will.
Surfeit with War, he reigneth peaceably,
And soothes his solitude from vat and still.

Fair Gwenllian her intellect, Alas,
Disordered was by seeing Madoc's end;
Simple and sweet she lives, like childish lass,
Become a Weaver while her heart doth mend.

Now doth this aging Bard retire his Quill
And henceforth gives his all to Ministry
Of Cynan's Kingdom. So be it until
Bard rejoins Madoc, for Eternity!

CHAPTER 9

The Falling Water Place
A.D. 1245

Old Gwenllian the Weaver Queen saw a shadow fall over her loom, and when she looked up, brushing her long white hair back from her temple to see who was there, Prince Gower was standing silhouetted between the loom and the window. She smiled, a profusion of wrinkles.

"My son, how good of you to visit. But kindly step out of my daylight. I see dim enough as 'tis, and you are so very opaque, you make a shadow, a very dense shadow indeed." She chuckled at what she had said. She often used words that Gower didn't know, and "opaque" was such a word.

"Mother, you must put away your shuttle awhile," said Gower, who at fifty was a sturdy graybeard. "Cynan sends for us . . ." He hesitated to state the reason.

"Oh, no," she fussed. " 'Tis much too much a bother to go over there. Tell—"

"Mother, it is but across the river."

"Tell the dear sot that I shall see him at Yuletide, as always. Now, please, you're still in my daylight."

"I am sorry, Mother, but we must cross over today. Meredydd is failing, and has asked for you."

"Oh!" The shuttle fell clattering on the stone floor and she put the fingertips of both hands to her lips. "Yes, we must go, at once!"

Gwenllian's castle, actually a small, fortified stone manor on the north end of the great waterfalls, was piled and cluttered with bales and shocks of linden bark, yellow flax, and various grasses, upon which the Weaver Queen and her helpers were always experimenting, in search of good substitutes for the wool and cotton that could not be obtained. The place stank of retting vats and dyestuffs, and one could not pass through the castle without sneezing from dust and fluff and getting covered with lint and fuzz and down. Though her people's expulsion from the old kingdom of Madoc had cut them off entirely from the wonderful stuff called cotton, Gwenllian had in the last forty years combined her experiments with the natives' methods to produce several grades of fabrics from plant fibers and animal hair, and the Weaver Queen's cloth was the basis for much of the peaceful trade with the tribes along the Beautiful River, both upstream and down from the Falling Water Place where her castle and Cynan's stood.

Now Gwenllian tottered down the long causeway to her wharf, leaning on Gower's arm, her lined, white face all puckered with distress, and was lifted aboard the long oar boat, which had a carved throne in the stern. Gower stood beside her and shouted to the rowers over the deep rushing of the falls, and the vessel moved southward through the frothy water below the falls, heading toward King Cynan's castle at the other end. From the boat the castle appeared to be floating upon the mist and spray of the falling waters, like a ship of stone. Gwenllian could not see it very clearly anymore; weaving had weakened her eyesight. But she had seen the castle rise there across the river over a period of nearly half a century, growing and changing as Cynan's masons built it of quarried limestone blocks and roofed it with great timbers cut from the forested lowlands in the river bend. It was in truth a greater castle than Dolwyddelan had been. Cynan's accomplishments had been magnificent; Gwenllian knew that. Bringing a defeated people, a few score Welsh and a few hundred Euchee, out of Madoc's Land and into this broad and fertile valley, one-armed Cynan had made a new Iarghal grow in the very place where the force of the river had nearly killed him in his boyhood. This was a valley of huge and ancient civilizations, of temples and fortified towns and trade routes, but it had been depopulated by the great plagues of death, and Cynan, knowing the watershed as well as the veins of his hand, had rushed into the void with his peculiar genius and his vow not to let his father's glory fade, and had filled the valley with building and commerce. He had linked the whole length of the valley with fortified beacon towers that could convey messages three hundred leagues in a night. He had created thegnships for his white Welshmen and given his thegns the power of life and death over the natives in the provinces. He had continued to train the Euchee and half-bloods in the stonecutting and smithing trades, and had explored for ores and other raw materials. Gwenllian was fully appreciative of all her younger brother had done, including his recent mastery of the arts of brewing and distilling, which now consumed most of his energy and intelligence. Yes, Gwenllian knew that her brother had been a great king. Timid and preoccupied though she was, she was aware of all that; it was told to her endlessly by Cynan himself and all his followers. But Gwenllian knew also that much of Cynan's greatness had come from the same source as her father's:

Meredydd. The wisdom and vision of old, homely Meredydd, who had lived a hundred years and now, she feared, was through. Throughout her long life Meredydd had been her teacher, mentor, and confidant, and when she thought of him, as she often did, she was as likely to see his face as it had looked seventy years ago as the map of pouches and wrinkles it was now. Ah, how she had loved and depended upon the bard; he was closer to her soul than ever her husband Owain ap Riryd had been. In fact, in the thirty years since Owain's death, she had erased his face entirely from her memory, as people tend to do to their most unpleasant recollections.

Though the boat trip below the falls was beautiful, when the vessel nosed into the slip below Cynan's castle, Gwenllian was damp from the mist of the falls—that being one of the reasons why she did not like coming across. Bearers were waiting with a chair to take her up into the castle, and they said that Meredydd had been moved to the room Cynan called his Elixir Room, which was the sunniest and most pleasant wing of the castle, facing out over a paved garden that ended right above the falls.

There the ancient bard lay, propped up on a padded couch and covered with a soft, white blanket of Gwenllian's finest Queen's Cloth, and there in the same room sat the king, with a silver goblet of his beloved elixir in his hand, his eyes in his pouchy face already half glazed by the liqueur. Gwenllian guessed at once that the real reason why Meredydd had been moved down from his own study was so that the king might attend his declining minister without having to be far from his vats.

Old Meredydd appeared to be asleep, his toothless mouth hanging open, his deep eye sockets almost as dark as his maw; everything about his face seemed to slope down and away from his long, pointed nose. His chinless jaw was lost in the wattles of his neck. Light from the window gleamed in sparse white hair so fine and thin it looked like a mist about his face. He hardly looked to be alive, but when he heard Gwenllian's voice, his eyes opened and bulged her way, pupils milky and faded.

"Ahhhh, girl, I have been thinking of you," he rasped. "Or dreaming? . . . I have . . . I must say certain things . . . to you. . . . Sit close and hold my hand. . . ."

His hand and hers were so fragile and knobby that they might have been the hands of skeletons clutching, but Gwenllian felt a current of warm power from his dry fingers.

"You and I, girl," he began, while Cynan drew a goblet of his elixir for Gower and more for himself, ". . . you and I remember Wales. . . ."

She hardly did, but now that he had said so, she drew up a castle from her memory, and hazy mountains, and the terrible, frowning face of an old man who must have been, yes, must have been Owain Gwynedd, her grandfather the king. And she remembered a damp, dark, sloping stone tunnel full of terrifying echoes.

Meredydd began again: "No one else . . . no one else on this continent remembers our homeland. . . . Do you realize that? Only old Rhys . . . and an old peasant or two . . . came from Wales. Everybody was born down . . . in Madoc's land, or here in Cynan's. . . .

"Who is there to . . . to remember the tempest . . . the great voyage?"

He sank back, exhausted, and Gwenllian wandered in her own cloudy memories for a while before she understood what he was really saying. She said, "Is there something I can do? Should do?"

Meredydd sighed. "How sad it is! . . . All the Welshmen living beyond the Great Sea . . . even Madoc's own kin . . . shall never know of the kingdom he built . . . the war he made . . . nor even that he had a son . . . a son who built another great kingdom here . . . Cynan. . . ."

Cynan, pudgy and bald at seventy, twirled his goblet and gazed into the beautiful amber liqueur in it, and if he was even hearing Meredydd's tribute to him, he gave no sign. Cynan loved this elixir he had perfected as much as he loved his life itself. This beautiful, bright room was a temple to it. In the old country, a liqueur of distilled mead had been the drug of royalty. But there were no honeybees, apparently, in the land of Iarghal, and thus no honey to make mead. But Cynan had discovered that the natives in this valley made an exquisite syrup by boiling down the sap of a kind of maple tree. For years Cynan had experimented with distillation of that syrup, as well as brews made of native grain or the fleshy plants they called *squash*, and wild grapes and berries, and in his putterings he had produced liquors and liqueurs of ghastly sweetness and numbing potency; some of them had proven lethal, or had produced blindness in his unfortunate still workers. After several disappointing years, in which the brewing and distilling had overpowered the maple syrup's subtle sweetness and left only a cloying liquid with a tannic aftertaste, Cynan had had his coopers make casks out of the same tree the sap came from, instead of oak, and at last there had come forth this incomparable amber spirit, which Meredydd himself had declared to be surely the nectar enjoyed by the immortals on Olympus. Now Cynan raised his eyes from the goblet and said, "Aye, 'tis a pity that no one in that old land shall ever savor this elixir of mine! Ah! Would that Father had lived to taste this!" He shook his head, and tears ran down the deep lines beside his nose.

Gwenllian looked at him, bemused, then turned back to old Meredydd, and her heart squeezed when she saw tears streaming down his desiccated visage as well. He coughed, swallowed, gasped, and at last was able to speak. "This has been a saga to sing of. . . . Oh, though . . . how't grieves my heart . . . that our glory here never can be sung of in the homeland! Oh, would that someone were a mariner like Madoc . . . and could sail a ship back home!"

And those were Meredydd's final words. Holding Gwenllian's hand, he let his eyes shut and mouth fall open, and his expiring breath was lost in the rush of the falls of the Beautiful River.

WHILE GWENLLIAN WEPT—LIKE A GIRL, NOT AN EIGHTY-YEAR-OLD woman—with her son Gower behind her holding her thin shoulders, Cynan the King wandered about drunkenly, sipping more of his wondrous and comforting liqueur, muttering to himself about how he would govern his kingdom without Meredydd. Cynan's body, off center because of the loss of his arm, had developed painful quirks and a limp during the past half a century, and he walked little unless he had drunk enough to subdue the pains. Now he left his sister weeping, hobbled out into the rocky garden over the falls and stood wheezing, watching the gold light of the sunset glow on the vast scene of green bluffs and spilling waters and mist. Lying about in the garden were the stone-hard bones of giant animals, and gigantic skulls as big as chairs; these ancient curiosities turned up everywhere in the valley, falling out of eroding creekbanks or turned up by quarriers, and they filled Cynan's garden like statuary. No one in the kingdom had ever seen one of the giant animals alive, and so it was presumed that they had all moved away, or perhaps been killed off by hunters long since. Most of Cynan's people had never seen the animals called sheep, either, but they were remembered as having been very important to the Welsh in times past; Cynan himself still padded his throne with an old fleece that had belonged to his father Madoc. The animal called Horse was remembered, too; Meredydd and Gwenllian and Rhys could remember having ridden upon those animals back in the Welsh homeland, and in the Bestiary there was a picture of a man on such a beast. The old tales said, in fact, that a king in the Old Land hardly ever walked outdoors, but always sat on a horse. . . .

Cynan stood at the edge of his garden and drank, a king who had never sat on a horse or seen a sheep, or stood on the soil of the land from which his sovereignty derived.

Nor had Cynan ever had a queen; he had been a king for nearly half a century, but was the only Welsh king who had never had a queen . . . because there had been no woman of royal blood for him to marry. He had had more women than he could remember: Euchee servant girls during his youth in Dolwyddelan Castle, Chiroki women and girls he had raped by the hundreds during his father's long war, and a long string of concubines and mistresses here in his own castle. He had countless mixed-blood children and grandchildren in the kingdom. Even so, he was a king without an heir.

This, then, was the old king who, having just lost the best minister a king could dream of, was standing in his garden looking into the very maelstrom where he had nearly lost his life more than half a century ago. Finishing the last of the elixir, he turned with drunken awkwardness to go in for more, stumbled over the hip bone of a monster's skeleton and fell sideways, dropping his goblet, and as the priceless vessel bounced clanking down the cliff, he made a desperate grab for it. He tumbled from rock to rock and plunged into the spilling, roaring water of the cascade, unseen.

Gwenllian's sobs over old Meredydd were interrupted by the voice of her son Gower, who was asking something. "What?" she gasped, opening her eyes to the sun-flooded, tear-misted image of old Meredydd's corpse.

Gower said, "I think Uncle ought to announce his minister's

death, but I cannot find him. He was here but a moment ago. . . . Eh, well, perhaps he has already gone to give the news. . . ."

For two days the greatest confusion prevailed in the valley kingdom over the king's disappearance, until some native boys fishing downriver saw a bright piece of cloth snagged on a branch of a driftwood tree; when they tried to retrieve it, they pulled up the bloated body of the one-armed monarch.

Thus did Gwenllian the Weaver, daughter of Madoc, eighty years after her birth in Wales, become Queen of all Iarghal. "Oh, no," she protested to her son. "I shall have to forsake my weaving and move to this side of the river?"

"You are the Queen of Iarghal, Mother. You may do whatever you wish."

"Then I shall abdicate at once, and let you be King, my son!"

"That," he said, "you cannot do, because I will not take the throne as long as you live."

And so with a sigh Gwenllian resigned herself to being Queen.

CHAPTER 10

THE FALLING WATER PLACE
A.D. 1250

MEREDYDD'S *SAGA OF MADOC THE KING*, THE STORY OF THE COLOnizing of Iarghal, had been stacked and bound crudely between leather covers, rather like the royal Bible or the Bestiary, and it was now one of the treasures of the royal family. It lay on a table beside Queen Gwenllian's bed. The covers of the book had been made of elk hides, folded, steamed, and baked in an underground pit until too stiff to bend. It was a technique the Euchee used to make arrow-proof shields, and it had created a nearly indestructible cover for Meredydd's book. The book lay in a pool of lamplight, and Gwenllian could vaguely see it there when she looked to her right.

She saw now that a man sitting in a chair beside the table was Gower, her son, his grizzly-bearded chin resting on his fist. She said, in a voice cracking and gurgling:

"Oh, my eyes! I hate them! I cannot see words on a page anymore. . . ." Gower nodded as she paused and thought. She went on. "I cannot weave anymore. . . . It hurts to look at the river with the . . . with the sun shining on it. . . . Oh, I hate how my eyes have betrayed me!"

Gower leaned over and touched the book.

"Be thankful you can see as well as you do, Mother. And you *can* see words on a page. I saw you only yesterday reading this book."

"Oh, would that I were! I was only holding it, thinking about the story in it, that wonderful story of your grandfather. And remembering how dear old Meredydd would sit and write his verse on it with berry ink, or whatever he could. . . . Oh, my, if only he had known what I learned later about dyes and colors for cloth! It would have made it easier for the poor bard. . . ." She sighed, head tilting, and remembered old Meredydd dying in a sunlit room five years ago. She drifted in that sad reverie for a while, then said, "Please read it to me. That book is splendid, but it is doing no one any good. . . . Oh, what a story is in it. I need to hear it in the dear bard's words!"

Gower's reply stunned her. "I cannot read, Mother. Do you not know that?" At first she thought he must be jesting.

"What say you! A prince, and cannot read? Did I not teach you to read? The Bible, the Bestiary . . . Did not old Meredydd—"

"No, Mother. He began to teach me the letters when I was a boy. But we were building this place, everyone was so busy. It just fell aside, I suppose. I cannot read."

Queen Gwenllian was annoyed with such negligence. She said, "Who *will* read for me, then? Send for someone! Nothing ever happens! I just lie here and I don't care to live. I want to hear the saga! My head is like an empty room without so much as a lamp in it! The bard's story is like a song!"

Gower leaned forward toward her bed, holding the book in both hands, and stared at the little puckered mask of indignation and displeasure that was her face.

As for Gwenllian, she could not see what his expression was. Whether close or far, he was all vague outlines, just bulk and shadow. But she could hear his voice, even through the endless whistling hum in her ears:

"Mother, who *can* come and read to you? Meredydd is dead these five years; my uncle King Cynan, the same. . . . I know of no one who can read, only you."

It took Gwenllian a long time to comprehend the whole weight of what he had said, and she did not want to accept it. At last she said, "No, I cannot read anymore . . . I cannot see the words. . . . Ah! Your sister Dena! She can read! I am sure we taught—"

"Nay, Mother. Not one whit better than I. She never did it, and does not."

Gwenllian the Queen felt in her bosom the heaviest agony she had felt since the awful death of her father the King. Here was a great saga of a book that had been written about the newfound continent of Iarghal, written in Iarghal by the kingdom's great minister who had known more about the land than anyone—and there was not one person on the continent of Iarghal who could read!

She mustered all her faculties, shocked into thinking harder than she had been accustomed to thinking for years. At last she exclaimed, "No! I will not believe that! Bring Rhys to me. He was with my father from the beginning. He has been our Minister of Arms for half his life. I am sure he reads . . . or he would know who does. . . . Bring him, please."

After Gower left, Gwenllian tried to concentrate on the awful realization she had just had about her only son. Gower was a good and vigorous man of fifty-six, a trader, hunter, and fisherman, and certainly not one of those profane and brutish thegns of the sort who had consorted with her husband Owain until his dying day; somehow Gower had avoided being corrupted by his father. But Gower was not possessed of much vision, or the qualities of leadership. He had had little to do with the building of this second Kingdom of Iarghal, having been but a boy when it was begun by Cynan and Meredydd. There had been no wars or even minor conflicts with the natives of the valley, so he had not become a fighting man, beyond the customary training in archery, swordplay, and quarterstaff. Refusing to take the crown while his mother the queen still lived, he had lacked royal ambition and any sense of purpose. Though he was the royal scion, and was one of the few people of Iarghal still with pure Welsh blood, he had casually sired scores of half-breed children, with no thought of who would succeed him. There was not a child in Iarghal anymore, to Gwenllian's knowledge, who was not of mixed blood. The few women of pure Welsh blood remaining were past childbearing, and even if Gower should desire to marry outside the royal line or even among the thegns' families to beget a pure-bred Welsh heir, it was too late.

But all that was insignificant beside the fact that he had never bothered to learn his letters, and was, incredibly, an illiterate prince!

And his sister Dena an illiterate princess! A quarter of a century ago she had married the half-breed son of Sir Rhys, named Dylan. Dylan was now sixty-one. Dena had borne to Dylan one son, called Llewellyn ap Dylan, who looked every inch a Welsh prince with his blue eyes and auburn hair and fair skin, but was in fact one-quarter Euchee by blood, his grandmother having been a native woman from Sun Eagle's people in the south. Gwenllian shut her eyes and shook her head and exhaled a long sigh, trying to remember so many things about which she had long ago lost interest. Gwenllian recalled that Llewellyn's birth was written down in old Meredydd's ministry papers with the notation that he had Euchee blood in his veins—but that mattered little now, if no one in the land could read it. Maybe people would forget that Llewellyn's father had been a half-breed, and he could someday be the next King of Iarghal after Gowan. That would not be good, Gwenllian thought; Llewellyn is a brute and a boor.

If only I had given more attention to Dena's tutoring, she thought, and seen to it that she could read the Bible, she might have brought up a proper son. . . .

Perhaps everyone will forget that the king is supposed to be pure of blood, she thought. If that, too, is a written truth, might it not be conveniently forgotten as well?

If a people can forget how to read, they can forget anything!

Gwenllian sighed with confusion and helplessness. As things were divinely meant to be, only her children Gower and Dena could pretend to the throne now, and for either of them it was a closed road, for neither could produce a royal Welsh heir.

Running out of royal blood is like running out of people who can read, she thought. There is no way to go on!

Dear God the mighty, she thought. If only someone with good name could come from Wales and find us here, or we could return there!

"Mother." Gower's voice came into her troubled thoughts. "Here is Rhys."

Sir Rhys was almost a hundred years old, or was more than that; he did not know, nor did anyone else. But he was still able to teeter along, and was usually clear in his head, and was still known as Minister of Arms. His cheeks were mottled with age spots and sunken from toothlessness, but his eyes were merry and alert. He bowed slightly, and with a sigh of weariness from walking, sat in a chair that had been placed close beside the bed that had become Gwenllian's throne. Gower sat nearby. Gwenllian gazed at the indistinct shape of the ancient man.

"Sir Rhys, my venerable thegn, I trust you are well?"

"Your Majesty, I am well for one of my age. What is't in this land that keeps us so long alive? I remember, they used to believe immortal life could be found here."

"Ah, but sir, then only you and I have found that immortality. Everyone else has gone."

" 'Tis true," he said, wagging his head with a sly smile. "But 'tis by falling off mountains and waterfalls . . . or such untimely accidents, or wars, more so than age."

"Sir Rhys, I have summoned you to help me remember some things we need to know. You and I are now the only souls alive, are we not, who came to this land with my father, Madoc the King?"

Rhys squinted, thinking hard, then replied, "That is so. Your Majesty and myself, we are the last of those! Think of that! There was a woman, Adyth, widow of one of our smithies, but she died sometime lately, a month ago, perhaps. . . ."

Gower exclaimed, "Ah! Alas! I had not known about that old woman!"

"Nor had I," said Gwenllian. "She would have been honored. . . . Now, Sir Rhys, do I presume aright that you can read?"

"Read, Your Majesty?"

"Read writing," Gower said, and picked up the leathern book of the bard.

The ancient soldier eyed the bundle reverently and said, "Why, after a soldier's fashion. I can count and make the numerals. Yes."

"But can you read words? The written language of Cambria, your homeland?" Gower persisted.

"Your Highnesses, I was only a soldier!" He shook his head. "No. Reading language was above me. I thought that only thy royal family, or the priests, were taught that."

Wistfully, Gwenllian said, "God help us, I am afraid 'tis so. Then you do not even know anyone else who can read?"

"Oh! No one!" The old man shook his head so emphatically that he seemed to dodder. It was as if he were being accused of knowing someone who had stolen the secret knowledge. "There are a few builders, and traders, who can make counting numerals . . . even a few of our Euchee can do that. But no one, certainly not the natives, can read language. Ah! Long ago, Meredydd taught that concubine of his to read, meseems. . . ."

"But she is long lost." Gwenllian sighed, sinking back; it was the answer she had feared. Everyone who could read her native language was across the mountains and seas back in Cambria.

Now Gower said, leaning close to the old man's ear, "Am I correct in thinking that you sailed on both of my grandfather's voyages?"

"Aye, I am proud to say! That I did. Three times across the Great Sea that mighty mariner led us!" He moved a knobby hand from his left knee to his right, back to his left, then to his right again, helping himself remember. "Three times across, yes!"

Gwenllian, grasping feebly for hope, asked, "Think you, venerable thegn, that one could sail a ship back to Wales? And return here again?"

Rhys, who had not been given so much to think about in this latter half of his century, sat with eyebrows raised, forehead wrinkled and lips slack, trying to stretch his mind to accommodate such a question. At last he began trying to give a truthful reply.

"Your father, our great king and the finest mariner that ever set sail, knew the way. Let me remember how he said it. . . ." He rubbed his flaccid eyelids and searched in dim memory. "From the east shore of this land, one finds a strong current—like an unseen river, he would say—and you might float upon it all the way back to the waters of Britain. That we did, the time we went back for everyone. But to find the way to that east shore, ah! Can I even remember what he said? For we never did do that, ye know. . . . He made a map, but 'twas lost, was it not? Let me think how he said it:

"One would float down this river to the Mother of Rivers, and down that to the Southern Sea . . . then down under that long shore of desert and swamp, where we met with the dragons . . ."

"Aye," Gwenllian recalled. "The *krokodilos*, those were."

". . . A ship might pass from that Southern Sea to the Great Sea and get upon that current," said Rhys. "That was how he said it, as best I remember. I have thought of it often, just to be thinking."

Gower, leaning forward with intense interest, said, "If the flow of the sea itself carries you to Britain's waters, need one be so great a mariner to make the passages?"

"Oh, Excellency, there is so much hazard! Only a true mariner can understand the seas. . . . Why, your grandfather Riryd, he had been a ship captain his life long, yet doubted he had skill enough to venture across." The old man shook his head sadly. "I, long ago, came to know that I would never see Wales again. When Madoc was alive, such a voyage might have been made. . . . But no, not since he died. 'Tis not just the storms, young sir, with waves higher than the walls of this castle . . . or the wind, that will shred your sails and snap your spars. . . . Unless you can read the stars and know where you are, you can lose yourself forever. Madoc knew the stars."

"Can you read those stars?" Gower asked the ancient soldier. "You say you crossed the ocean three times."

The old man chuckled and shook his head. "My lord, I can scarely make out the full moon above me, leave alone stars! And when I watched Madoc sighting on stars with his sticks and angles, I might as well have been watching a sorcerer, for all I could make of it."

None of this was encouraging in the least, and Gwenllian, worn out from thinking, felt tears on her face.

But Gower seemed to be fairly vibrating with an energy he had scarcely ever shown in his life. He now hefted the book of Meredydd's saga in both hands, and Gwenllian heard him say such things as she had never expected to hear from this commonplace son of hers:

"In God's name," he quavered, "what a void is my poor soul! There's magic in writing, and there's magic in the placement of the stars, and there's magic in the blood of kings. But I cannot read the history of our kingdom; I know nothing of the stars; I cannot perpetuate our royal blood! These were all kinds of magic that were lost in less than one century, though my grandfather was master of them all!" He squeezed the book so hard that Gwenllian could hear the leather creak, and his voice hissed with intensity: "*Surely* I could float a ship on a current back to Wales! There I could learn to read! There I could find star mariners to teach me! And there I'd find our relatives, with our very blood in their veins . . . and a wife of royal blood . . . and bring them here to perpetuate our line, the line of Owain Gwynedd and Madoc!

"If I could sail to Wales, I could make myself a sovereign as great in name as they were!"

He was up and pacing, with Meredydd's book squeezed between his strong fingers as if he might draw from its lettered pages of power of his grandfather's knowledge, while old Rhys gaped at him with his toothless jaw ajar.

"I *can* do it; I *shall* act: this sacred book I'll take, and in a strong curragh I'll sail back to Wales. And when they there learn of this rich land, and what my grandfather did do here . . . and that we are still alive here . . . all will want to follow!" He turned and leaned over the queen's bed.

"Beloved Mother, grant me leave to build a sea ship, sufficient for . . . two-score rowers. Weave me strong sails, and permit me to take this precious book from thy bedside, and I shall rejoin to us our homeland, with word-readers and all those sorts of magic that were ours, or perish happily in the endeavor!"

Gwenllian could hear her son panting from the sheer power of his life's first inspiration, and her heart swelled and ached, and she thought:

Dear God, he is a late-blooming fool, but a real Prince of Wales at last!

"For my mother's love of you," she murmured from her pillows, "I'd detain you from such long hazard. But, as I hear in your voice, your will has outgrown mine own!"

Queen Gwenllian lay on a couch in the garden above the falls and watched Gower's ship turn the great river bend and go out of sight while thousands of her subjects milled along the riverbanks. The ship was a blur on the greenish expanse of water, in her fading eyesight compounded by tears, and she could hardly make out the throngs onshore; only the far murmur of their cries and singing told her they were there. To Dena, her gray-haired daughter who stood by the couch, Gwenllian said:

"I shall allow myself just five years of hoping. If I leave this weary life before then, you count the rest of those years. When I am gone, you shall be Queen of Iarghal . . . unless he returns."

Dena had knelt to listen over the rush of the falling water, and she answered in her mother's ear, "I do not want to be queen, Mother."

"You have to, daughter. You are the only one of us left. And it isn't so very bad, just a bother."

"If I become queen, my son will take the throne from me."

"He cannot. He has Euchee blood."

"But he would. He would kill me for it!"

"Indeed! What! If ye believe that of him, he should be in a dungeon from this day!"

"How can a mother imprison her son?"

"How can a son kill his mother?"

"He could," Dena said. "I could never."

Gwenllian, her mind already in a turmoil from the excitement and sadness of her son's departure, could only think: That is a dreadful matter! If she will not do anything to thwart such a pretender, I suppose *I* must. And soon . . .

But it slipped away in the lassitude of her old head; it became another dark thread in the fabric of her ever-weaving thoughts by day, and sometimes troubled her dreams by night. But she would waken to the pains and twitches of her ancient body and would try to deal with such difficult things as using her chamber pot, fussing with servants, getting food down, looking queenly enough to deal daily with petitioners and ministers, whose concerns so easily slipped her mind. Day after day and week after week went by, all matters blending together like the dyes in wet cloth, so the ugly problem of Llewellyn the mixed-blood gradually faded, and Dena said no more about it. Gwenllian mostly felt that a long, long waiting count was in progress, a count of days until some word should come of her son Gower and his crucial mission. Sometimes Gwenllian could remember just what his mission was, and sometimes she could not remember exactly what it was, but that it was crucial to the sovereignty in Iarghal and had something to do with Wales, and she felt that she needed to live five years more. People who kept track of such things said she was eighty-five, and five more years seemed to her either unbearable or a mere lark, depending upon her mood when she thought of it.

But less than two months after Gower's sailing, a war party of the Chiroki arrived at the edge of a field of maize and sunflowers where Welsh and Euchee women were harvesting. They reminded the women that the Euchee and the white-faces had been forbidden forever to pass the lands of the Chiroki and their allies, even by way of the Mother of Rivers. They told the women to go to the great stone lodge of their rulers at the Falling Water Place and inform those rulers that the Chiroki and the Natchez had captured a big wing-boat on the Mother of Rivers and had burned it and everything it carried. They warned that the same would happen to any other boat that ever came down. Then they gave the women something to take to the rulers of the white-faces: a string of eighty ears, and the rotting head of a bearded Welshman stuck on the end of a lance. And quick as they had come, they were gone.

When Gwenllian the Weaver Queen saw the head and understood that it was Gower's, she gasped and sank back on her pillow, face as white as death. For a night and a day she breathed barely with her toothless jaw hanging open, and drooled, and twitched. On the next evening she opened her eyes for just a moment. Seeing many people standing by her bed, but not seeming to recognize any, not even her daughter Dena, she murmured, "Read . . . me the . . . story. . . ." Then she was gone, a mere silvery-haired skeleton in thin, yellowed skin, covered by a blanket of her own Queen's Cloth.

Later that night her daughter Dena drowned in her bath in the bathing chamber under the falls, and Llewellyn ap Dylan, grandson of Rhys, proclaimed himself King of Iarghal. A few Welsh people were troubled by a vague notion that only a pure-blooded descendant of a great king of Old Wales could ascend the throne of Iarghal. But it was only a notion, and there was no proof that it was so, and no one wished to challenge the brutal Llewellyn. And so that notion was never mentioned again. There were, after all, no other direct descendants of Madoc alive.

Part II

1404 — 1750

"I was under the instant conviction that [the Mandans] were an amalgam of a native, with some civilized race; and from what I have seen of them, and of the remains on the Missouri and Ohio Rivers, I feel convinced that these people have emigrated from the latter stream, and that they have . . . with many of their customs, been preserved from the *almost total* destruction of the bold colonists of Madawc, who, I believe, settled upon and occupied for a century or so, the rich and fertile banks of the Ohio . . ."

—*George Catlin*

CHAPTER 11

Town at the Falling Water
1404

Sweetgrass Smoke, daughter of Stonecutter, was in her thirteenth summer when her grandmother decided that she was beautiful enough to become one of the Maids of the Rain Room, and so Sweetgrass Smoke was circumcised with an obsidian blade to begin making her ready. She screamed at the incredibly sharp pain as the sheath of membrane was separated from her clitoris, but her grandmother told her she would later be glad of it.

"When I was young," the old woman told her, "I was chosen like this to be a Maid of the King's Bath in the Rain Room, and this family was favored in many ways because I so pleased the king of that time. One good thing was that when I had a son, who is your father, he was selected to learn stonecutting and castle-building, and thus he is now as important as a man can be who is not one of the thegns." Being important in the king's castle, Stonecutter could gain audience with the king and offer to have his daughter seen by the Keepers of the Rain Room, who would be the ones to select her. And so, one day in her fourteenth year, Sweetgrass Smoke and her grandmother were taken to the castle by Stonecutter and led to the Rain Room. "I already know the way here," Grandmother kept telling her son proudly as they went through the familiar tunnels and hallways. She smiled at Sweetgrass Smoke and said, "The best part of my life was when I was here as a girl!"

Stonecutter left his mother and daughter at the Rain Room door. Beyond was a steady rushing noise. The door was pulled open and a small, pretty Euchee woman wearing a long dress of the material called Queen's Cloth led them into a beautiful little cave lit by sconces, where water cascaded from a hole in the roof to fall melodially in a stone pool. Several other women wearing the same fabric were in the room, and they all greeted the grandmother. Then the first one turned to Sweetgrass Smoke and said, "Take off your garment, child."

She slipped the tunic of deerskin off and stood, lit from above by the beam of daylight and all around by the flickering light of the sconces. The women nodded, looking pleased, and went around her, examining her from all sides. The first woman knelt before her and with her fingers probed her to determine that she was a virgin and had been circumcised. The girl Sweetgrass Smoke had been told by her grandmother to expect that, but nevertheless she twitched and her eyes flashed.

The women stood, studying her, while the first one explained the Rain Room to her. "This cave is under the edge of the waterfall. Water from the river comes in up there, and that which overflows from the pool goes down that channel to fall into the river below. The king called Llewellyn discovered this cave, a hundred summers ago. Here he would come every morning to be bathed. Like him also did the following kings, Daffyd and then Cynoric, and now our present king, Alengwyned, does so. They have all been kings with a great need for pleasure. Your grandmother was a favorite of Cynoric. Therefore she can teach you the art of pleasing a king. When she has done so, we shall call you here to serve His Highness Alengwyned, and he will keep you as long as you please him. You may put on your clothing now."

"Then you have chosen me?" asked Sweetgrass Smoke.

"You have been chosen. It is an honor. Only the most beautiful are chosen, and that you are. But remember that only the king will decide whether to keep you, and if he does, you will come to live in the castle with the other Maids of the Rain Room, and you will be treated very well."

"Do you bathe the king?" Sweetgrass Smoke asked.

The woman's eye twitched and grew hard for a moment, and Sweetgrass Smoke saw the little lines in the woman's face that showed her to be older than she had seemed. The woman said, "For a long time I bathed Alengwyned. I never displeased him, and so I have become the keeper of this room. Your grandmother must teach you never to displease the king. Go home now, and learn what your grandmother can teach you."

SWEETGRASS SMOKE WAS KNEELING ON A MAT BY THE COOK FIRE that evening helping her mother mix corn dough when the doorway of their hut was shadowed and Stonecutter stooped to come in. Sweetgrass Smoke had been daydreaming of a time when, as a favored bather, she would live in the castle and not have to mix dough or pound meal or gather firewood or sew clothing. She looked up smiling at her father and started to tell him that the Keepers of the Rain Room had approved of her when she saw by his abrupt movements and his eyes that he was not in happy spirits. So she kept still and watched him.

After Stonecutter had eaten and smoked his pipe, his wife asked him if he wanted to say why he was so angry and silent. He sat staring in the fire for a while, and then said:

"The hairy-faced men of Alengwyned are too arrogant and cruel. The Creator surely cannot like what they do." He scowled at the fire for a while, squeezing his left wrist so hard with his right hand that the mighty muscles in his forearm were like ropes of sinew, then he went on talking low.

"They had a hunter of the Lenapeh People from up the river. They had caught him and told him he could not hunt in the Alengwyneh land. In the castle I was fixing a wall of a room where they repair their weapons. They brought the Lenapeh man in, tied up. They were laughing at him and sticking him to make him bleed, but he would not cry out. And so they tied a band of wet rawhide around his skull and let it dry. They laughed at him while he began to sweat and shake with the pain. At last he died without crying out, and they were disappointed, and threw him over the falling water into the river. His body will be lost to his People, they cannot bury it, and thus his spirit will be lost forever in this valley. There are too many unhappy spirits in this valley who have been made that way by the thegns of Alengwyned."

"Will not the king forbid such things?" Stonecutter's wife asked. "Could he not be told what they do?"

Stonecutter hissed. "When they were torturing the Lenapeh, it was that king himself who came and told them of the way to squeeze his head with rawhide. He said it was a way they knew of in the old land beyond the great water, where his ancestors came from long ago." Stonecutter now turned his gaze to Sweetgrass Smoke, who was listening with wide-open eyes. "Daughter, you are very beautiful, but I pray that you will not be chosen to be in the Rain Room of that king."

Her eyes like a startled deer's, she glanced at her grandmother and then back to Stonecutter. "Father, they chose me."

He slumped, and cast an accusing eye at his mother. "I wish you had not thought of this. You always loved the favor of the white-faced kings too much, and now our one child will be in cruel hands."

The old woman drew back with angry black eyes, even in age being beautiful, and snapped: "Be respectful in talking to your mother! And, listen. The king never hurt me."

"I respect my mother and honor her. But Cynoric was another king, perhaps not so cruel as Alengwyned."

Sweetgrass Smoke had never heard her father and her grandmother speak sharply to each other, and the sound of their voices, as well as what they were saying about the king, made her insides churn. She was becoming more afraid than eager to be a bather.

"Father, if he treats me badly, then I only have to displease him in some little way and he will not keep me there. That is what the Keeper of the Rain Room told me."

Stonecutter leaned back and gazed at his daughter with eyes tender and fearful, then he rubbed two fingers across his brow and said, "No, my daughter. You do not want to displease that kind of a man. Not even a little displeasure."

TWENTY QUARRYMEN OF ALENGWYNED'S LAND, BURNING LIMEstone to make quicklime in kilns at a new quarry beside the Beautiful River, were not aware that they were being watched from above by dark and angry eyes.

Four warriors and a chieftain of the Unam People lay in a thicket on the brink of a crag a hundred feet above the kilns and watched their strange labors. Heat made the air shimmer above the kilns, which to the Unam chieftain looked like little gray huts, and the quarry was dense with drifting woodsmoke. Some of the workers were cutting wood and dragging it to the kilns; others pounded limestone rubble with heavy iron hammers. Close to the river's edge, squared blocks of limestone, which had been hewn and chipped into shape by other workers, were being hauled out onto log rafts. Such stones, the Unam chieftain had observed, were constantly being floated down to the huge stone lodges at the Falling Water Place.

The chieftain, whose name was Wind Made by Wings, most keenly watched two workers who were tearing down earthen mounds near the river and picking out bones to throw in a pile and take to the kilns.

The warriors watched the working men with hatred, but also with some fear. These pale-skinned men from the Falling Water Place were thick-muscled, certainly very much stronger than ordinary men. They always worked so hard they created dust, as well as all the smoke of their fire huts. They were a strange and mighty people who did strange and terrible things, like smashing old ancestor bones and throwing them in with the limestone they crushed.

The Unam People of Wind Made by Wings were one tribe of the three making up the Lenapeh Nation. Once, the ancestors of those peoples had been as numerous as the leaves on a great tree in summer. Once, they had been as hardworking as this tribe of pale-skinned hairy-faces, and had built big storehouses and earthen pyramids with temples on top, but then Creator had sent a Wind of Death among them, and now the Lenapeh were like the leaves of a tree in autumn after the wind has blown away all but a few hundred. It was believed that the Death Wind was sent to punish the People for insulting the Creator. They had insulted him by working too hard to accumulate food and wealth, instead of having faith in the bounty he always provided them through their True Mother the Earth.

Now the Lenapeh had gone back to the old ways; they hunted and harvested just what Mother Earth gave them for each year, and spent the rest of their time making and decorating the few belongings they had, and teaching their children to be generous and to love the Creator.

Wind Made by Wings did not care that the pale people called the Alengwyneh worked themselves so hard; that was a mistake which their gods probably would correct eventually. But there were some things the Alengwyneh people were doing that needed to be stopped now, and Wind Made by Wings would speak of those things in the next council of his People.

Wind Made by Wings was one of the best of the young men of his People. He had reverence for his ancestors. He was a great hunter, and a fierce protector of his People. He was lean; all his muscles stood out clearly under his skin, and so did the sharp bones in his face. When he ran in the woods, he was like his name: he was like a whisper in the air and then gone before he could be seen.

He had been staring down into the stonecutting pit of the Alengwyneh with such intense anger and loathing that he felt hot inside his throat. His eyes glittered and burned. His black hair was parted along the center of his scalp and held back out of his face by a strap of leather decorated with black and white quills; that strap encircled his head, passing across his brow just above the eyebrows. A hawk feather, attached to a mother-of-pearl disk, hung beside his left ear, where it was tied into a thin braid of his hair. He carried a quiver of long, stone-tipped arrows, a longbow with a flint lance point affixed to the upper end, and a long-handled war club with a stone head.

Now Wind Made by Wings signaled silently to his four warriors, and they slithered back from the edge of the cliff, then rose in the concealment of the woods, and he set off leading them at a fast trot toward their village up the river.

SWEETGRASS SMOKE ASKED HER GRANDMOTHER, "WHY DID THE Keeper of the Rain Room want to know that I have never been with a man?"

"Because the king believes that he has the right to be the first inside you."

The girl's mouth dropped open. "What? A bather . . . one must do *that* with the king? You had not said this!"

"Your lessons begin now, because now you have been chosen."

"But if I do not like the king, I do not want him to go inside my body!"

Her grandmother hissed, "Child, do you think a man would not come to desire you as you bathe him? And the king always has what he desires! He can kill anyone who denies him anything. One time when a bather resisted the king, he cut her head off."

Sweetgrass Smoke was very frightened now and wanted to talk about this. She thought about the girl who had resisted, and wanted to know who she was and what she had thought.

"No one knows what she thought," replied her grandmother. "When her head fell off, it told nothing to anyone. So to keep your head on, you yield to the king's desire. You should be honored to lie with a king, silly child! It shows that you are one of the most beautiful. When I was young and was called to bathe King Cynoric in the Rain Room, everyone was proud of me, and envious. My son was then born and grew up favored by the king. That is why your father is a stonecutter within the castle."

Sweetgrass Smoke had a sudden astonishing thought. "Was Cynoric the King my father's father? Is my father the son of a king?"

The old woman shrugged. "Perhaps," she said.

"Do you not know? Surely you would know!"

"Such matters do not concern you," said the old woman. "We are talking about how you will please the king."

But Sweetgrass Smoke had more questions in her head. "Did my mother never get chosen for the Rain Room?"

"She never was," said the grandmother. "She was not pretty enough."

"My mother is pretty!"

"Perhaps," replied the old woman, with pursed lips and raised eyebrows, "but not quite pretty enough." The grandmother was, after all, speaking of a daughter-in-law.

Sweetgrass thought of the danger she was in, if the king was indeed as cruel as her father had said he was. It appeared that she was going to have to submit to the king in a way she did not welcome, and she wondered if she could please him enough to keep from being beheaded. After a while she asked her grandmother, "Did you like what the king did to you?"

"Like it?" her grandmother replied, looking amused and puzzled. "Doesn't everyone like that sometimes, but not like it other times?"

"I do not know, Grandmother. I have never been done it."

"Ah, true. Well, you will know soon enough whether you like how King Alengwyned does it to you. As to kings, I know only of Cynoric, his father. All men are different, a bit different, even though what they do is the same thing. I can only advise you to make him think you like his way, whether you like it or not."

"How often will he do it to me?"

"You will bathe him every morning, if he likes you above all the others. Except on days when you are in your blood moon; those days someone else will do it. If this king is like Cynoric, he will do it to you every time you bathe him. Even as he grew older, Cynoric needed me every morning." There was so much haughty pride in her grandmother's voice when she said this that Sweetgrass Smoke wondered if her grandmother might be lying in order to boast of her desirability.

The girl sighed. She wished her grandmother had never offered her for this; she even wished she had not been pretty enough, so that this would not have had to happen to her. But since it was too late to change that, she could only wish it was over. She dreaded things she did not know. Somehow it did not seem right that a man, even a king, could do to anyone he chose a thing that the king himself decreed only husbands and wives should do with each other. But, according to her grandmother, the kings had had that right through many generations. According to her grandmother, only a king could say that something was good or bad.

And so Sweetgrass Smoke could only keep learning from her grandmother, and wait until the time when she was to be called, and until then she would be thinking very much about the king. She had seen him before, at distances; he was big and powerful, perhaps even looking like a god. These Alengwyneh had been told, by the words in their Sacred Bundles, that they had been created to look like their god. If that was so, their god had a hairy face and blue eyes and wore shining metal around his chest, and a shiny metal helmet with antlers and plumes. Whenever he walked out of the castle, he walked surrounded by other thick-bodied men who also looked like their god. Those men were his thegns, because they had little of the blood of the True People in them, but mostly the blood of those who had come two hundred summers ago from beyond the Sunrise Water. Sweetgrass Smoke knew something of their legend, because her father had been taught it at the castle, and it was a part of the story of her own Euchee People as well. The present king, Alengwyned, was named after the God-King across the Sunrise Water, whose son Madoc had been the first to cross the Great Water and come to this land, riding on a huge swimming reptile with a roaring voice that could knock people down and even kill them.

"He is powerful everywhere in this land," her grandmother would tell her. "You must seem grateful for every privilege he gives you, and use it to its fullest!"

But the old storytellers of the Euchee also had another Circle of Stories they sometimes told, more secretively; these were stories of the days long ago before the coming of the Alengwyneh kings. Those were bright and happy stories, of a time when the True People had been free to come and go where they pleased, and do whatever they thought was right. The Ancient Ancestors, said the storytellers, believed that was the way it ought to be. Sometimes they said the Ancient Ancestors were sad and angry that the People stayed under the Alengwyneh. Sometimes in the wind Sweetgrass Smoke could hear the Ancestors crying over the lost freedom. She was not as happy as she was supposed to be about being chosen a Maid of the Rain Room.

WIND MADE BY WINGS, THOUGH YOUNG, WAS A FAVORITE ORATOR of his Unam People. The primary chiefs and the elders sat respectfully listening as he stood in their Great Council Lodge to speak to them. The smoke from the council fire and the ceremonial pipes rose out through the smoke hole in the high roof, carrying the prayers and words of the council out into the sunlight and toward Creator, who lived beyond the sun.

"Grandfathers, Fathers, Brothers," Wind Made by Wings began in his clear, deep voice, "thank our Creator for bringing us together here to speak of what we see in our path. Listen:

"In other councils we have talked over this everlasting fire about the presence of those people who now dwell at the Falling Water Place. When they came, our grandfathers made them welcome, as it is our way to make others welcome. Even now we enjoy some of the things they make and trade with us: the clothing they weave and trade to us, the tools and drilling points, and the hatchets and arrowheads they make from the melted-stone metal, for those do not break, and they make our lives a little easier to live. The needles and awls make the chores of our women easier."

Wind Made by Wings paused, looked around at his listeners, who were thinking and nodding, and went on:

"When those people first came to this valley, they were a fair and respectable people, with a good, honest, one-arm chief, who met with our grandfathers and asked for agreement with us before they did things. They told our grandfathers that they had been driven from the southern lands in a war with the Chiroki nation. Our grandfathers said that if they were enemies of the Chiroki, they must be good to have here. Then their old Weaver Queen lived awhile, and she was good, too.

"But then each generation's chief became worse than the one before. With those chiefs, the Alengwyneh forgot how to respect us. They began to come into our country and take what they wanted, without asking us. They dug the red stone wherever they found it. They cut down big trees wherever they pleased to make their big boats. For their making of cloth, they came and stripped bark from the heart-leaf trees everywhere. They killed our hunters in the woods and claimed the woods were theirs, and they even took over our salt licks and said we must trade for salt from them!"

Wind Made by Wings was talking with a growing passion. His eyes flashed, and met the eyes of every man in the council.

"Is that a good people to have nearby? I say no! And listen to what else they have done lately while we said nothing. I speak of those stone towers they have built on high places along the river bluffs. Their first chief told us those towers would help our people as well as his, for when our enemies the Iroquois came down against us, the high signal fires would warn us. That seemed good to our grandfathers, and they said yes because he asked them. . . .

"But in late years, you see that they build more signaling towers, without asking us. And you see that they build them on places sacred to our Ancestors, like the one on the Bird's Head Rock, a place sacred to us. There, do you not remember, their soldiers would not let our shamans go on the Bird's Head Rock for their ceremonies. That is a great shame upon our People! Why did we not rise up against those white-faced men and drive them out of our country when they did that? I, Wind Made by Wings, was not born into this world when that happened. If I had been a man then, I would have gone up onto the Bird's Head Rock and thrown those intruders down from there!"

The men in the Council Lodge murmured and squirmed. What this young chieftain was saying made some of them ashamed and sorry, and others angry. The ones who had been chiefs and warriors when that happened knew that they had not acted like men. They had been afraid of the white giants, who encased themselves in shiny material harder than turtle shell and could not be killed by stone points, and who had weapons that could shoot a shaft through a man's body from as far as two hundred paces or more. They had been afraid of the Alengwyneh and they did not like to be reminded of it.

But the younger warriors had not learned that fear of the white-faced men, and they grew tense with the anger they heard in the voice of Wind Made by Wings. He went on now, still angry:

"You know that those warriors of the Alengwyneh king with their hairy faces did other things that brought shame to our peoples—all of our peoples along this river. You know! They would come down from those watchtowers and take our young women out from the fields when they were hoeing the maize and harvesting the sunflowers, or grab them when they were gathering mussels in the rivers. And when they had made them pregnant, those young women could do nothing but live with the giants and bear their children, and then they and their children labored for those bad men. Even when they did such bad things, our old chiefs still were too much afraid of them to raise a hand."

Again, those who had been chiefs and chieftains during those times kept their eyes down, or tried not to look directly at the young orator. But he did not single them out to challenge them, because he was trying to make all the men in the council be of one mind.

"In my own lifetime," he said, "when I was a boy, our people fished at the Falling Water Place. That has always been ours to do. How many fish there are at that place! Creator made the fish come there, more than anyone can count, and our peoples have not had to be hungry, even if the hunting was unlucky and the gardens were bad, because we could go to the Falling Water Place and take fish.

"But now! Now the new chief of the Alengwyneh says no one but his hair-faces can fish at Falling Water Place! He says that whole place is his. He guards it with a great stone house on each side of the river, and has towns with stone walls, and if we dare to go there to fish, we are chased away by soldiers! I ask you today, all who sit here listening to my words: Do you believe our Creator gave that Alengwyneh chief the fishing place that has always been for our peoples since the Beginning?"

The scores of men in the Council Lodge were stirred by every emotion now, from anger to fear. Some of the older chieftains were as angry at Wind Made by Wings as they were at the white-faced people, because he was making them ashamed of themselves and challenging them to resist the powerful intruders.

"All that I have said, you know is true," the young chieftain said now in a strong voice that reverberated in the great lodge. "All the bad things those hairy people have done, you know they are things that have been so for a long time.

"But now I have come to tell you of something else they are doing. This is something I have seen with my own eyes." Many of the listeners leaned forward now, for they had long known of the other transgressions, but this, it seemed likely, would be new fuel for the embers of their indignation.

"You know," he said, "that they burn rock, to make a powder that holds their stone houses together. We have seen them do that for a long time. There is rock everywhere for them to use. But now hear what I tell you: I have seen them digging rock from places where the Ancient Ones buried their dead!"

Those words from the angry young orator stirred an immediate uproar in the Council Lodge. Men seemed to grow bigger, taking deep breaths and then moaning and growling in shock, their eyes wide and mouths open. They all knew that to disturb the bones of the dead was to trouble their spirits and baffle their long journey to the Other Side World, and they knew that when the spirits were troubled, bad troubles often came to the living.

In particular it was thought bad to disturb the graves of the Ancient Ones, who had been a people of great power, but had died in such great numbers from sickness that their priests could not bury them with the traditional care. It was believed by many people that the spirits of many of the Ancient Ones had barely rested in the hundreds of seasons since their deaths, and that if they were troubled, they might even bring the sickness back with them. And so there was near terror in the Council Lodge when Wind Made by Wings said:

"I saw them as they broke the stone tombs of the ancient chiefs. And when they hammered the stones, they even smashed the old bones, and burned them along with the stone dust!"

It was a long time before the council could settle itself enough to talk about the problem of this latest crime in a rational way. For three more days the council met, and everyone who had something to say about it was allowed to speak until he was finished. Wind Made by Wings offered to lead a delegation to all the other tribes of the valley and persuade them to unite for a war against the hairy-face men.

But the older chiefs said no. And finally, after two more days of discussions and arguments, the old chiefs told the council what they were going to do.

"Probably," they said, "the new chief of the hair-faces does not know what his people do to the graves of the Ancients. Or perhaps he does not understand why it is bad. But if we go in peace to his towns by the Falling Water, and tell him that his stone diggers are troubling the old Spirits, then probably he will make them stop, for he is a chief and must have wisdom. He must want to prevent bad things. If he listens, there need be no war."

Wind Made by Wings stood and spoke again. "Fathers, go then and try to put sense in that chief through his ears. I pray you will speak well and he will listen well. But remember that when we tried to talk with him about letting us fish there, he insulted our chiefs with his tongue and drove them out.

"And so while you go down to talk to that bad chief, I will be going to the other tribes. I will tell them of all this. I will even go so far as the Iroquois, whose cousins, the Chiroki, once had to stand up against the hairy-faces. Though they were our enemies before, they will understand that the smashers and burners of ancient bones are enemy to us all. And they fear them not! I will try to make all the tribes believe as we do. If the Alengwyneh chief listens to you and stops the bad things, we will all be happy.

But if he will not listen, then we will have many allies ready to drive him away. Fathers, I do not ask your leave to go and do this talking, because I must go and do it, and shall. But I ask for your blessings to speed me as I go."

And so the old chiefs gave him their blessing and began readying themselves to go down the river to talk to King Alengwyned, while Wind Made by Wings set out in the other direction.

THE OLD CHIEFS OF THE RIVER TRIBES WERE NOT TIMID MEN, BUT IN the castle at the Falling Water Place they were quiet and subdued in their manner, because the king and his soldiers were frightful men. In their breeding with the Euchee, somehow the mixing of the bloods had resulted in a race of people who grew larger and stronger with each generation, and most of the big men had blue or gray eyes. Many had yellow or light brown hair, and there were some families in which hair, even eyebrows and eyelashes, was white. To the chiefs these albinos were especially intimidating, because with their powerful physiques and white hair they seemed to be both old and young at once, and thus possessed of some disturbing magic. These white-haired men were favorites of the king, who kept many of them around him as guards. They wore helmets and body armor made of copper, brass, or iron. The helmets had nose guards and eye slits, and were decorated with antlers, which made the giant soldiers look so unlike anything familiar, man or beast, that the native chiefs could hardly bear to glance at them. The king of these giants could see the furtive dread in the chiefs' eyes, and acted scornful.

King Alengwyned stood in front of the semicircle of sitting chiefs, waiting for them to explain why they had come. This king knew some of his forefathers' legends, and in his mind they had grown to the size of myths, and the notion that the blood of First Man Madoc flowed in his veins made him fiercely proud. He had Euchee blood, being descended from Llewellyn, the first mixed-blood king. And although he was blond and blue-eyed and tall as his ancestor First Man had been, he had the broad, craggy, sharp-boned face and prominent brow of the Euchee. He stood straight and haughty, and stared with the angry look of an eagle. It required a strong man even to look him in the face. His mouth, through his flowing golden whiskers, was shapely but cruel. The chiefs who had come to talk to him about their discontent glanced at him and saw little hope for any civility or reason. This king looked like an angry god.

He started the council off badly by refusing to smoke the pipe with them. "Tell them," he said to the interpreter, "that it was they who begged for this council, that I have other things to attend to, and that I shall not waste time on ceremony. And tell them to speak their minds directly, that I have no patience to hear about their gods and their origins and everything they know from the beginning of time! Tell them I have no patience with old men who talk too much."

When the interpreter had translated that admonition, the faces of the chiefs hardened, though they said nothing in protest. They turned their eyes to their primary elder chief, Standing at Sunrise. He, though stiff with age and seeming to be asleep, felt their concentration on him and rose to stand before the king. Standing at Sunrise had white hair to his shoulders, a quilled band across his lined brown forehead, and a pendulous nose that nearly reached his jutting chin. To Alengwyned's surprise, the old chief spoke to him in Welsh.

"Brother," he said, "you, chief of the Alengwyneh People, have asked us to talk fast so you can go and attend to other things. Good. I am old, and I, too, have little time to spend. Maybe you and I agree that being polite wastes too much time. And so, like you I will waste no time being polite. I will tell you this, at once:

"When you hurry away from this council to do more important things, I ask you, please, brother, to go to your men who take stone from the earth, and tell them our wishes. Tell them that the world is full of stone, and they can take as much as they want, except in places where our ancestors' bones have been buried. Tell them it is dangerous to trouble the bones. It is very dangerous to disturb the bones of the Ancient Ones."

Alengwyned's lips moved in a smirk. He looked around at his thegns and bodyguards, seeing to it that they were smirking, too. Then he turned a mocking face back to the old chief and replied, "Thank you for that warning. But tell me, old man: How is it dangerous? Might a quarryman hit himself by mishap with an old thighbone and bruise his hand?" He snorted a laugh. His thegns and guards laughed after him, and, encouraged in his joke, the king went on, "Might some teeth in an old skull bite his foot and make it bleed?" Now the white men around the room were hooting and guffawing. The native chiefs in the middle of the room were silent, their faces growing harder. Though they did not understand the words, they could understand that the words of their chief were being mocked. To mock a chief who was speaking earnestly in council was unforgivable. It was something that no civilized man of any tribe would do. The chiefs sat, tense, their fury burning them up inside, though nothing showed but the tightening of their features and the stiffening of their spines.

Nothing at all showed on the face of old Standing at Sunrise. His eyes were blazing, but were so deep in their wrinkled old sockets that the white men saw nothing. Now the old chief said, in the language of his people instead of Welsh, "Be calm. Anger will not help us. While we are here, we must try to speak so he will understand us. . . ."

"Talk so I can understand you!" the king shouted in his face, stamping a foot.

The old chief nodded his head. Inside his robe of elk hide, which he held clutched around him, he grasped his flint knife and took it from its sheath, not sure he would need it, but afraid that he might. Then he looked up into Alengwyned's eyes and said in Welsh, "Brother, I ask you not to laugh when I speak of those bones. It is true when I say it is dangerous to move them. I say this to keep you from harm, as well as my own people—"

"I begin to wonder," the king said sharply, "if you are making a threat to me." His men around the walls began muttering ominously, as if they had perceived that, too.

Standing at Sunrise replied, "Brother, the threat is not from my mouth. It is from the spirits of those whose bones are broken and burned up by your stone diggers. Maybe you do not understand what we believe: until those bones become dust in the earth, as they used to be before they had life, their spirits are still in This Side World. Only when they become dust can those spirits go to Other Side World, and then they will no longer care what happens on This Side World. That is why we warn you of the danger."

Alengwyned had listened to this with a half smile of incredulity, and now he waved his huge hand in front of the old chief's face and exclaimed, laughing:

"Why, old man! Listen! Bones are good in lime, too, as good as stone. So, when we make dust of those old bones with the hammer and the kiln, your old ancestors don't have to wait so long to go to Paradise! Don't you see? Ha ha!" And again his giants around the room joined him in roaring laughter at his joke.

Seething with anger and shocked by the white king's irreverence, Standing at Sunrise exclaimed, "Then it is true that your stone diggers smash the bones, as our young men said? That you, their high chief, know they do that, and do not forbid them?" The old man quickly spoke to his chiefs in their own language, telling them of this incredible revelation.

Alengwyned shouted over his voice: "What foolishness! When a man dies, his soul goes to Heaven at once! Or to Hades! What do old bones matter?" The king did not know much about the religion of Old Wales, but stories of Christ, of Resurrection, and Eternal Reward had been passed down through the generations and he remembered them, though vaguely, with conviction enough to scoff at the superstitions of these befeathered little brown men. "And so," he shouted, "we will quarry where we please. If that is all you came to complain about, you are wasting my time, and I resent it!"

Standing at Sunrise stared, thoughtfully but without expression, at the king for a moment, then said, "No. That is only one bad thing you do. We want you to say you will stop that, and then we will talk to you about other things, about letting our people fish here at the Falling Water Place as we have always done. And about your signal fire forts on our sacred places. And about how your soldiers come and take away young women from our—"

"Enough from your unhappy mouth!" Alengwyned's teeth were bared in a snarl, his head was thrown back, and his eyes bugged in anger, the white showing all the way around the irises, which in the beliefs of the natives meant a man was crazy. "I am the sovereign of this land, and as that, I shall do and take, as it please me! How think you to come and challenge me!"

His voice and actions had alarmed the chiefs, and they were all rising swiftly to their feet, speaking softly and quickly among themselves. Several who considered themselves the bodyguards of the old chief were moving to get themselves around him, to protect him from the giant madman of a king. The others were turning warily, their eyes on the big armored soldiers around the room. The soldiers' sallow faces were beginning to flush. Every man's hand was instinctively clutching at a weapon.

Even at that point order might have been maintained. Truths had been stated and requests politely made, and there could have been agreements or promises. Even a stubborn discussion could reasonably have been pursued, as was often necessary in council. But the shouted declaration from the hairy-face king had not made sense to Standing at Sunrise, and he needed to explain why this land of the Creator could not be ruled by intruders from somewhere else. And so he cried out over the hubbub, "Alengwyneh king, this is not *your* country!"

The king struck with his fist at the face of the old chief, as if knocking away a pest. Before the old man's body had thumped to the floor, three chieftains were upon Alengwyned with their knives. One slashed his face open from left temple to right ear. Another stabbed at his abdomen, but his flint blade snapped off against armor. The third leaped and slashed his neck, but the king's flailing forearm hit him and flung him to the stone floor. The king stood, blinded by blood.

By this time all of Alengwyned's thegns and guards had drawn swords and dirks and flung themselves into the milling group of old chieftains in the middle of the throne room, and a shouting, grunting, thumping melee was engaged. But it was brief.

The few natives, with their stone knives and clubs, had no real chance against the metal-clad giants, and within the duration of twenty breaths, all the tribal envoys lay dead, unconscious, or crippled on the stone floor. Three had been beheaded. Five had been hamstrung at the knees and heels, and crawled desperately on the blood-slickened floor until they were hacked to death by battleaxes. While this slaughter was being finished, the king was led by two thegns to his throne. He could not see because of the blood flooding his eyes, and his tunic was soaked with the blood from his neck. Neither he nor they knew how badly he had been stabbed, but they presumed that he was mortally wounded.

By the time the blood had been wiped off of Alengwyned, the last groan and breath had been heard from the bloody figures on the floor. Twenty old Unam chiefs, chieftains, and bodyguards lay dead. Among them lay four big men in armor, bleeding to death from slashes inflicted by the old men's stone weapons.

That night, while King Alengwyned lay tied down and squirming and groaning and his face and neck were stitched up, the corpses of the native elders and chieftains were dragged and hauled out of the castle and tossed from a ledge into the rushing waterfall. It was the same ledge from which the good one-armed king, drunk with elixir, had tumbled to his death so many generations before—but that was a part of their legend that no one knew.

* * *

ABOUT A HUNDRED NATIVES, RELATIVES OF THE TWENTY CHIEFS, had been waiting in a camp on the south side of the river, keeping anxious eyes on the stone castle at the Falling Water Place, waiting for their elders to come forth from the council with the Alengwyneh king. These people had stayed at some distance from the big walled towns of the hairy-faces. As the day had turned to evening and the sun had set far down the river, they had made their little cooking fires and had grown more and more quiet, waiting for their old men to come out of the stone place. When night fell and no one had come out except the usual soldiers and traders, the people resigned themselves to believe that the elders had been invited to sleep overnight in the great stone lodge of the king. Uneasy, the people bedded down to wait for morning.

At noon the next day a fisherman from one of the native villages down the river came running up the shore, going toward the castle. When he saw the little camp, he stopped there instead and told them something very terrible.

Bodies and heads and limbs of old men had been discovered in the river by fishermen.

The little camp of people was quietly folded, and they all slipped away, and went down the river to the village. There, with wailing and howling, they recognized the remains of some of the old men.

And the next day they sent runners up the river to tell the young war chief, Wind Made by Wings, what had happened to the old men who had gone to talk to the Alengwyneh king.

CHAPTER 12

Headwaters of the Beautiful River
Autumn 1404

Wind Made by Wings stood beside a rock outcrop near the mountaintop in the half dark before dawn, and peered at the stone tower on the crest a few paces above. The tower was a silhouette under the setting moon, and smoke drifted off and across the moon's face. The air was cold, and hilltops and trees were white with frost, but Wind Made by Wings and his hundred warriors wore nothing but breechclouts and moccasins. Their bodies and faces were covered with grease and pigments, painted in patterns. The entire left side of Wind Made by Wings, including his face, was blackened with soot and grease; his right side was covered with grease and red ocher. These were the colors representing death and war. In his right hand he clutched the hickory handle of a long, decorated war club with a black stone head the size of a goose's egg.

Below this mountain and beyond a range of lesser hills, two rivers flowed together, and this was the beginning of the great, long river the People all called the Beautiful River. The stone tower on this mountaintop was the first, the easternmost, of the beacon towers that the Alengwyneh had built along the whole valley of the Beautiful River. The next visible beacon place was a hilltop near the river, where the faintest plume of smoke could just be seen. The third was out of sight down the valley, half a day's walk downriver. Most of the beacon towers were small, with five to ten soldiers. This one, being the farthest Alengwyneh outpost, was like a small fort, and was occupied by about twenty-five of the armored soldiers, and around it in huts there lived soldiers' women, some of them being yellow-haired mixed-bloods, others native women lured or taken from their tribes.

Wind Made by Wings was now primary chief of his people.

He had been elected after the hairy-faces murdered Standing at Sunrise. In the three moons since he became chief, Wind Made by Wings had traveled the full length of the Beautiful River, visiting every major tribal village and speaking to their councils. He had told those councils about the murder of the old chiefs, and had convinced every tribe that it was time to drive the hairy-face intruders away from the Falling Water Place, even to kill them all, if necessary; they had grown too arrogant. The giant King of the Alengwyneh seemed to think that he owned this whole river, that he could kill tribal elders, steal women, ruin burial grounds, and forbid the original peoples from hunting and fishing near the Falling Water Place.

The strong words of Wind Made by Wings had convinced the chiefs and warriors that the spirits of the Ancient Ones were troubled, and that they would not be satisfied until there were no more of the hairy-faces left in the valley. Wind Made by Wings had persuaded so many so well that he now knew he had a hundred hundred warriors ready and eager, even several hundred of the Iroquois, who had been his People's enemies of old.

Now, standing below the stone tower as the morning brightened, Wind Made by Wings was not thinking about all the armored soldiers his warriors would have to fight, he was thinking only of the ones on this mountain.

He hoped to catch them still in their beds, before they could put on the metal clothes that protected them from flint weapons. He had never fought a man wearing armor, and did not personally know anyone who had, but he had known since boyhood that it is hard to hurt a turtle that is all withdrawn into its shell.

Now it was just light enough that the rocks, trees, and shrubbery were becoming distinct from each other. Wind Made by Wings gave his signal, the call of the Little Owl with Ears, and started on silent feet toward the stone tower, in his mind making himself unseeable.

Most of the hundred warriors with him were out of his sight, moving up the mountain crest in a contracting circle around the tower and huts, closing in, and though he could see only a few of them, he could feel them closing in with him as the mass of the stone tower loomed nearer.

Wind Made by Wings had told his warriors that some of the soldiers would probably still be in the huts asleep with their women, and others might be asleep in the tower, but surely some would be awake. In any camp at any time of night or early morning, even in the sleepiest time just before dawn, there was always someone at least half awake, thinking about getting up to pass water, or men and women quietly copulating while their children were asleep. And of course most camps had dogs. All the warriors knew these things from their own lives. And so, he had told them, we will get as far into the camp or the tower as we can unseen and unheard, but the moment a dog or a person raises voice, start killing everybody. The spirits of the Ancient Ones will not rest, he had said, until the last of this evil race has been killed or driven far from the valley of the Beautiful River.

And now as Wind Made by Wings slipped around the edge of a bark-covered hut, he saw a movement along the top edge of the stone wall, outlined against the fading sky: a spearhead, and a pair of antlers which he knew were the decorations on a soldier's helmet. Wind Made by Wings saw that the ladders were still leaning on the outside of the tower, the ladders that the soldiers and women used to go in and out. The tower had no gate. If the soldiers wanted to keep anyone out, they pulled up the ladders and put them inside. But even if the ladders had been in, it would not be hard for the warriors to get over these stone walls. They were not high walls, being in some places little over head high, and they sloped inward a bit, being made with the biggest stones at the bottom; with a short run and leap and the use of his hands and toes, an agile warrior could swarm over this wall as easily as he could scale a stone bluff. A soldier with his turtlelike armor probably could not, of course, and so perhaps the hairy-faces presumed they were safe inside such walls. With stone walls and turtle-shell suits, they did no doubt feel much more safe than they were. Wind Made by Wings felt his hatred and contempt for these intruders growing with every step he took toward the wall.

From the door of a hut he was just passing, a woman came out crouching, her brown hair hanging forward and hiding her face, a deer-hide robe drawn around her shoulders. She squatted in the path and pulled up the robe, blew a little air noise and began making water. These people make waste right where they walk, Wind Made by Wings thought in disgust, standing invisible not two steps away beside her.

It was then that she raised a hand and drew her hair back from her face, and looked around, and she saw a warrior with black spots painted all over his body coming up the path toward her.

She gasped in a breath, but her outcry never came forth: she collapsed in her own urine, her neck broken at the base of her skull by the stone ax of Wind Made by Wings.

But the sound of the blow or perhaps the passing of her spirit made a dog bark nearby; then there was a yelp of terror off to the left somewhere, the clank of armor from above, a surly, querulous voice from up on the tower, and in the same instant grunts and thumpings and shouts, whacking and splintering sounds from downhill on the right.

This was the beginning. Wind Made by Wings emitted a pulsating shriek and scurried up over the tower wall like a spider. There before him in astonishment was the giant soldier with the stag-antler helmet, looking at him with bulging eyes. The warrior swung his stone ax in a wide arc that knocked off one antler, dented the helmet, and caved in the side of the soldier's skull. Even as the soldier was toppling sideways, Wind Made by Wings was instantly noting everything within the tower: the big signal-fire brazier high in the center, its embers still orange and smoking; perhaps fifteen soldiers lying down, getting up, or standing in startled postures, beginning to look his way. A huge, pale body lunged toward him from the side, and Wind Made by Wings felt a thick arm encircle his torso and a powerful hand clutch at his neck. But like a convulsing snake, he freed his greased body from his captor and killed him with an ax blow between the eyes. And now Wind Made by Wings saw his warriors springing up on the tower wall on all sides. They howled; he howled. And they all sprang like panthers onto the stirring, stumbling, bewildered soldiers.

Before the setting moon had faded on the horizon opposite the rising sun, every Alengwyneh on the mountain was dead. And by the time the morning sun was illuminating the red and yellow foliage on the mountainsides and melting the frost on the slopes, even while the river below was still in misty blue shadow, the warriors of Wind Made by Wings were loping downslope through the woods toward the next beacon tower. Some of them now were carrying Welsh swords, iron-tipped lances, and battleaxes with broad, sharp metal heads. All along the valley of the Beautiful River, beginning on this day, the forts and the signal towers of the white-faced intruders would all be struck by the allied tribes. When all these signal places were destroyed and the tribes could move unnoticed throughout the valley, then all the warriors together, a hundred hundred of them, would descend on the Alengwyneh castles and cities around the Falling Water Place and destroy them forever.

Wind Made by Wings had begun it all well on this day.

ON THE FIRST DAY SWEETGRASS SMOKE WAS TO BATHE THE KING, she was awakened before daylight by the pretty Euchee woman who was the Keeper of the Rain Room, led down clammy corridors to the Rain Room door and ushered in. Though the room was a dripping, splashing cave, it was hot and steamy. A deep brazier glowed and smoked, and kettles boiled upon it. In wall niches, little lamps and herb-burning censers glimmered and smoked. On the edge of the pool was fixed a narrow bench, padded with oiled leather affixed by gleaming tacks of metal. The other Rain Room attendant stood naked by a steaming basin near the brazier and whipped its contents rapidly with a whisk. Sweetgrass Smoke recognized the smell of the concoction; it was being made from soapwort root. Her mother made the same foam for bathing and washing clothes.

"Undress," said the Keeper of the Rain Room. "You must be bathed and clean before you touch the king."

The keeper looked her over for sores and to be sure she was not in her blood moon. She made sure no hair had been left unplucked from her genitals, verified her virginity again, and then examined the result of her circumcision. Cut free from its sheath, the girl's clitoris protruded visibly. The keeper tugged at it with her fingertips. "Your grandmother did well," she said. "But you must keep stretching it. The king delights in this if it is long."

The attendant then bathed Sweetgrass Smoke with warm water and soapwort foam, rinsed her, worked scented fat into her black hair and spread it on her skin, kneading it until her entire body was flushed and gleaming. By then a pearly glow from the morning sky was coming from the hole above, where the river water poured in, and the incense smoke curled and drifted in that pale light. The room was beautiful in a strange way, and Sweetgrass Smoke felt good from the bath and the anointing, and though she still was haunted by a vague dread, she was in a curious way impatient. She felt as she supposed a bride would feel. Now the keeper told her, "We go. It is soon time for the king to come down. Remember all your grandmother told you to do. Here is the dipper you will use. It is a treasure of great value." The woman gave her a beautiful, shiny vessel whose metal reminded her of the sides of a trout leaping in the sunlight.

Then, walking around her with a censer of burning herbs, the keeper swirled the smoke over the girl with graceful movements of her hands and told her: "You are pure. May you bring great pleasure to Alengwyned the King."

The two women departed by the tunnel door, leaving Sweetgrass Smoke alone in the beautiful, steamy grotto with the sweet odors and the music of the falling water. Her grandmother had told her to stretch and stimulate the circumcised part so that the king would notice it, and so she did that as she waited. Her grandmother over the years had so lengthened hers that it nearly hung to the floor when she squatted.

Sweetgrass Smoke waited, almost afraid to move or look about, as if the woman had left her standing exactly where the king expected to find her. And so that was where she was standing when she heard his footsteps in the tunnel.

But not just his footsteps. Several were coming; they were talking about something, and their deep voices echoed along the corridor of stone.

The first to appear in the Rain Room was not the king, but one of his armored bodyguards, a man she had seen passing through the village, one with slit eyes and no front teeth. He stopped and stared at her for a moment, then looked around the grotto as if scouting for dangers. He stepped aside to let the others come in from the tunnel. They were all so tall that they towered over her, and their great shoulders seemed to take all the space, and they all smelled of sour sweat. She thought of what the women had done to purify the place, and wondered why the king let his stinking men come in and befoul it. The big men all circled around her, looking her over with rude eyes, grunting and chortling, and Sweetgrass Smoke began to feel both angry and ashamed.

Then King Alengwyned entered. He was taller even than his bodyguards. He wore no armor, only a long robe of the fine fabric called Queen's Cloth. His guards milled aside, and he strolled up and stopped to look at Sweetgrass Smoke. His eyes widened and darkened, and he took a deep breath. She could see that he liked the way she looked.

His size was frightening. She had seen him only at a distance before. She knew he towered over most people. Now she saw that she stood scarcely as high as his ribs.

His robe was held by a toggle of horn through a loop. He unfastened it. He said, as he slipped the robe back off his shoulders, "Leave, all of you. All but you, Gruffyd. Sit and tell me about the trouble."

Sweetgrass Smoke, as the daughter of a castle stonecutter, knew enough of the Welsh tongue to understand what he had said. She stood, fingering the shiny dipper, unsure what she should do. She had not expected that there would be anyone else in the Rain Room. Her grandmother had never spoken of such a thing. She was glad to see most of them going out, but confused to see the one remain and seat himself on a stone ledge by the wall. The king flung his robe away and stood facing the girl. Her heart quailed at the sight of him, the size of him.

He was yellowish, sleek and thick-muscled. Each of his thighs was as big around as her torso; his midsection was padded with fat, so that it was almost as broad as his shoulders. There was a long scar across his face and another on his neck. His body was matted with light-colored hair. Sweetgrass Smoke was puzzled by the look of his physique; in armor he appeared to have the same hard chest and stomach muscles as her father the stonecutter; naked, he was shapeless. She had no way of knowing that the muscular shape was that of the armor itself.

Now the king went to the edge of the pool and stretched out on the padded bench, facedown. He summoned her with a wave of his hand, rested his bearded chin on his folded arms and started talking to the other man while she went to the kettle and filled the dipper. She came back and stood beside the great mass of his body. He glanced up at her and nodded, and as she poured the warm water over him, he sighed. She poured soapwort foam on his back and, as her grandmother had instructed her, slathered it over his wet skin, using her palms and fingers. Her heart pounded fast. She was actually touching the king of the whole Alengwyneh, who ruled everybody she knew, and for whom this whole land was named!

"Now, Gruffyd," he said in a deep rumble of a voice, and her fingers on his back could feel the vibrations of his speaking, "what is happening that so worries you?"

"Majesty, I was told this morning that there was no light from the beacon tower up at the great bend of the river."

Alengwyned, sighing with pleasure under the hands of Sweetgrass Smoke, muttered, "Someone fails to light a fire. Or someone else fails to see it. And for that you intrude upon your sovereign's pleasure? Why bother me? Send up to the tower and ask! If the beacon tenders were asleep on their duty, burn their hands. You know the penalty; they know it. . . ." Then he grunted and moaned as the girl's hands lathered the backs of his hams. The foamy water dribbling off his back and waist was cooling. "Hot water," he grumbled at her, and, afraid of his tone of voice, she went quickly for it and irrigated his backside with it.

"Majesty," the thegn was saying, "I have indeed sent to find that out." Steam rose, and fragrance; water dribbled over stone.

"Then," said the king, "are you through with my attention?" He wriggled and flopped over on his back, and when the girl's eyes widened at the enormous cockstand her caresses had aroused, he guffawed. "Wash it. Wash it well, do you understand me?" She nodded, and fetched more steaming water and lather. Hesitating a moment, she took it and began washing.

Gruffyd, his eyes devouring the meek little brown girl, cleared his throat. "Majesty, I hear that other . . . that other towers *down* the river have failed to show their fires. . . . Ah, that, too, I shall have to . . . see to . . . that, also . . ."

The king's eyes were closed and he was writhing under the girl's ablutions. So Gruffyd just fell silent. He did not ask to leave, but just slumped and watched and perspired.

To Sweetgrass Smoke, this was the ugliest and most repulsive thing she had ever touched, worse than animal intestines after a butchering. But when she tried to move her hands elsewhere, to his legs, his waist, he gripped her wrists and returned her hands to it. Then he began groping between her legs, pinching and rolling her clitoris so hard that she flinched. "Now, girl," he grunted, "let your lord and master in."

It was what she had known she would have to do, but had so dreaded that she had not let herself envision it. She did not believe a thing of that size could enter a place where even a finger had never gone.

"Do it!" he commanded, pinching harder.

She remembered the girl whose head had been cut off. She knew she would have to obey. Her grandmother had reminded her that babies passed through that same hole in a woman, and had assured her that the penetration by a mere man-organ would not really hurt her.

But it did hurt. As she straddled him and did what he had commanded, she felt stabbed, stretched, and torn all at once. Her body convulsed in trying to get away from it, but he had encircled her waist with his powerful hands and was forcing her down, even while thrusting himself up and farther in. Only her fear of being killed kept her from screaming. She bit her lips shut and began to sob and shudder. Her eyes were shut and the pain inside her was visible in her mind like a red demon animal with sparkling claws. She heard a rumbling voice in the watery hush. She opened her eyes and saw the king's face in a wild-eyed grimace, his teeth clenched, red lips twisted. The power of his hands was controlling her whole torso, and she, doll-sized compared with him, could not even resist. She shut her eyes again, bit her lips, gasped, and tried to endure.

Then something different was happening. The red demon of pain was suddenly withdrawn, seemingly pulling out her insides, and she was being lifted, shoved about, turned over. Her arms were gripped in merciless hands; her feet were slipping on wet stone; hot moisture was trickling down her thighs. She opened her eyes and saw blood running down her legs. The king had risen from the ledge and was standing, talking to the other man. The man called Gruffyd got up and came close, grabbed her by the arms, then bent her facedown and clamped her neck between the chain mail on his arm and the brass of his body armor. Her breath rasped as she tried to get air. She thought her neck would break in this grip. Now, obedience or no, she had to struggle. But this armored man was too strong for her.

The king was standing behind her, lifting her. She felt another rude shoving at her tender parts.

When she could come to realize what was being done to her now, she gave an infuriated scream that came forth as a half-strangled groan.

Among her People, this was an act so disgusting that anyone who was known to have done it was declared a No-person and put out of the tribe, and any woman who let it be done to her was likewise a No-person. The Creator had taught all animals, including people, that that hole was only for making waste, and that Creator would be enraged if any animals, including people, used it as this king was now using it. Other animals never did. But sometimes people did. The grandmother of Sweetgrass Smoke had confided to her that it was not uncommon for the hairy-faced men to do it to their women—and sometimes even to their boys and to each other.

Now the king himself was trying to do that unspeakable thing to her; he was making her a No-person.

The pain from this was even worse than the other had been. She twitched and shuddered. Her legs tried to run forward from the pain but her feet were dangling above the floor and both men holding her were too strong. More and more of the king's rigidity was wedging into her. She felt as if her insides were being scorched and shredded. And the king began going back and forth, ramming into her bowels, grunting and growling, his loins slamming against her rump.

She seemed to be nothing now but a clot of shame and pain, swelling and shrinking with blazing bursts of red and swirling sparks. Then came a gigantic spasm in the center of the pain, and through the shrieking of demons in her head she heard the king's voice growling and roaring.

Her soul seemed to rush out of her. At last she was escaping the pain. She seemed to be floating on the great Beautiful River, far, far, floating toward a vast yellow land with no trees.

ALENGWYNED'S FACE WAS DRAWN WITH ANNOYANCE. THIS NEW bathing girl had been no good for him. Her only response had been to struggle. Sometimes the new ones did that. Once he had beheaded one for fighting him. This one had embarrassed him by showing displeasure while a thegn was watching, and that was why he had become fierce and buggered her. He would get a new one tomorrow; there were always several in waiting. He seemed to remember that this one was a daughter of one of the castle's stonemasons; he would humiliate that man for bringing him such a squirming fish. He let her slump to the floor and went to fill the dipper, to wash her bloody mess off his loins. He growled, "Have at her if ye want, Thegn Gruffyd. Ye've slavered over her enough. When you have done, though, go see to that matter of the beacon. Someone must be brought to account; I'll not abide slovens."

So saying, he rinsed and dried, and by the time he had pulled his robe on, Gruffyd, still in mail and breastplate, had mounted the unconscious girl and was hunching away at her bloody breech. Alengwyned stalked out of the room and told the soldiers and bodyguards who waited outside the door:

"You may help your compeer Gruffyd finish off that morsel of meat. Go on. I've loosened her up for you. Ha!" Their eyes flashed and they tried to conceal their eager delight. This did not happen often, but when the king cast one of these pretty creatures to them, they were like dogs on a bone. He had no sooner walked by them than they were jammed in the doorway, all trying to get into the Rain Room at once.

THROUGH THE MIST OF THE BEAUTIFUL RIVER AS THE MORNING dawned, more than a hundred dugout and elm-bark canoes slipped silently downstream toward the Falling Water Place. Propelled by strong paddlers, they went more swiftly than the current. Each vessel towed several cedar-trunk poles with a few inches of their branches left on.

In the leading canoe's bow crouched Wind Made by Wings, war chief of the Lenapeh. Glancing right and left, he could see motion along both distant riverbanks, a motion such as a gentle wind makes in foliage. There ran the hundreds of warriors of the Iroquois chieftains, along the right bank, and on the left, more hundreds of his own people and some of their allies from the river valley tribes. All were loping swiftly and silently along the riverside paths, going to strike the Alengwyneh villages on both riverbanks and the old Weaver Queen's castle on the right bank. Wind Made by Wings would land with his warriors on the island where the white king lived in his stone castle. All the enemy's little forts and signal towers had been destroyed already in the last few days, and all the soldiers in them had been killed so that no warning would come ahead down the river. Wind Made by Wings was sure that the hairy-faces' nation at the Falling Water Place was unaware.

This morning he and the other tribal chiefs had bathed in the cold river and had made themselves vomit to cleanse their insides, and they had freshly painted their faces and bodies according to their tribal customs. He was red on one side and black on the other. All their hundreds of hundreds of warriors had also purified themselves for battle, and prayed the prayers of their respective traditions, and were ready to die if they had to die, for Wind Made by Wings had blown the smoke from their eyes and made them see that on this day they would be fighting to drive a great evil from their homelands.

These kings boasted that their castle could not be attacked, and the tribes in the valley had believed that boast. It could not be approached from across the river because of the falls and rapids. It could not be attacked from the other shore because it stood upon an island connected by a drawbridge, with a portcullis on the gate. And the island could not be approached from upriver because boats would be caught in the rushing current and swept over the falls.

Wind Made by Wings knew of all those dangers, and he knew that the hairy-faces with their armored soldiers and long-shooting crossbows had kept the chiefs of the river tribes timid for many generations.

But Wind Made by Wings in his boyhood had fished and

hunted near the Falling Water Place, and he knew every crevice and cave and current. He knew it was possible to steer a canoe out of the main current above the Falling Water and come to shore on the upper end of the castle island. And he knew of a hole in the rocks of the falls where river water ran into a cave, which was a sort of bathing room and was connected to the castle by a tunnel. He had never been in that cave, but some of the Euchee people who worked in the castle knew about it, and the Unam had heard about it from them. And Wind Made by Wings had already proven that by swiftness, surprise, and courage, beacon forts could be taken and Alengwyneh soldiers could be killed.

His fleet of canoes reached the place where the main flow of the river began to race, and he turned and told his paddlers to steer toward the left bank. He made a sweeping arm signal for those in the other canoes to do likewise, and soon they were all following him into the safer current that would deposit them at the upper end of the island. He faced forward again into the morning breeze. He could smell the woodsmoke from the Alengwyneh towns, and other familiar and disgusting odors: the body wastes, the sour, pulpy smell of garbage rotting outside their villages, the tangy stink of their tanneries, the rankling smell of their lime kilns and charcoal pits and the retting vats where they soaked flax and dogbane and heart-tree bark to make cloth fiber. These Alengwyneh were a stinking and ruinous people, as well as an arrogant people, and Wind Made by Wings believed that the Great Good Spirit wanted him to clean them out of the valley of the Beautiful River. He had prayed to be the one who would find and face the white-faced king, the king who had murdered all the old chiefs. In his dreams he had seen himself moving through battle, going straight toward the king, and in his dreams he had seen Alengwyned on a high place and had gone up after him, war club in his right hand and the power of the Creator vibrating in his arm. The dreams had never shown him the end of the fight, but Wind Made by Wings was sure that he would kill the king because the Creator's power was in his arm. He could feel it even now, and his hand trembled with it.

The mist was drifting and he saw the island's low, brushy shore close ahead, and the gray walls of the castle looking yellow in the first light of sunrise. There loomed the high tower, which in his dreams was the place where he would find and slay the king. To the right of the castle island he saw the clouds of spray that always swirled in the air above the Falling Waters, and he could hear the steady deep rush of the water. All the woods on the high, curving bluff above the right bank were brightening, yellow and red, in the light of sunrise, and they were beautiful, as they had always been beautiful in his life, but even more beautiful this morning because it was to be the day when the river nations would kill all the Alengwyneh and regain control of their Ancestors' homeland. He was thankful for the cloudless sky, knowing that the glare of the sunrise off the river would blind any soldier guards who might be looking up the river. His heart raced. He was fierce and happy. This was a day that the Lenapeh would remember in their legends.

He could see that the running warriors on shore were now close to the edges of the Alengwyneh and Euchee villages.

The Euchee would have to be killed, too. They had become too much a part of the Alengwyneh to be any good as Creator's children anymore. Most of them were blood-mixed with the white tribe now, and they obeyed that king, and dug stone and made iron and cloth like the hairy-faces. Long ago those Euchee had been driven from their homelands in the south for those same reasons. And they had doomed themselves by helping the Alengwyneh dig the Ancestors' bones out of the burial places.

Wind Made by Wings tried to will the canoe to go faster, so that he could get ashore on the castle island before soldiers could be alerted and rush to the landing place; they would all become alert when the killing and screaming started in the towns. The landing would be dangerous, because the upper end of the castle island was always a tangle of driftwood that the river piled there, and his warriors would have to clamber over and through it before they could overrun the island; while in that driftwood they would be easy prey for the arrows and crossbows of the white soldiers.

But the driftwood tangle was close now, and there were still no soldiers coming out.

Over the rush of water he heard distant shouts and screams. That meant the warriors were in the villages now. It would alert the Alengwyneh in their castle, but it might also distract their attention from this landing place as the canoes came in.

Wind Made by Wings stood and reached over the prow to grab a sun-bleached snag and hold the canoe off. His muscles strained as the current pressed the long vessel hard ashore and began turning it broadside. Paddlers then reached out and held the vessel steady, and Wind Made by Wings leaped onto the driftwood and clambered over it while the others pulled the canoe out of the water. Other canoes and dugouts had reached the shore and warriors were swarming out of them. Some were wrecked, thumping and crackling, as they hit the island.

In a moment Wind Made by Wings was out of the driftwood and flitting through the brush and weeds toward the castle wall, with the selected warriors from his own canoe running alongside him. Others in groups ran crouching toward the castle, carrying their canoes and the long cedar poles.

No arrows or missiles were coming from the castle yet, but a warrior nearby gasped and stumbled. He sprawled, groaning, grimacing, reaching for his foot. Others began to yelp and fall in the weeds and grass. Wind Made by Wings paused by one of these fallen ones. An iron spike had gone through the man's foot. Wind Made by Wings looked into the grass. Everywhere there were strewn iron things that looked like big burs, made in such a way that however they lay, one spike was pointed straight up. He clenched his teeth in anger and moved forward more slowly, searching the ground at each step. Now his warriors had to watch the ground as well as the castle walls. Some had cried out when the caltrops pierced their feet, and the sentries on the walls must have heard them.

On the stone wall just ahead he saw flashes of sun on metal, and now he knew there were indeed soldiers on the wall. He saw antlered metal helmets, shields, pikes, battleaxes glinting. An arrow hummed past his head. He heard the bellowing voices of the soldiers on the wall, and now it seemed suddenly to be raining arrows. Left and right, warriors began falling, or dropping into the grass for cover. But they kept moving toward the walls. Some gathered under the inverted canoes they were carrying, and the hulls began bristling like porcupines with arrows.

At its lowest place the wall was as tall as three men. Wind Made by Wings, knowing that, had instructed all his warriors on ways to scale a wall. He had told them to bring the canoes to the wall, lean them against it, and climb up inside the canoes to the top. And the red cedar poles, which had branches all the way up the trunks, could be leaned against a wall and climbed in moments.

Now many of the warriors who were not carrying canoes or poles were bending their bows and sending their own arrow storm back at the archers on the walls. Many of his warriors carried atlatl sticks instead of bows, and with these they could fling spears nearly as far and straight as the archers' arrows.

Wind Made by Wings paused long enough to see the first few

canoes and poles tilted against the wall and warriors swarming up, then he uttered his pulsating war scream, which was taken up by everybody, by the hundreds here on the island, by the thousands on both riverbanks, a wild, throbbing wail that drowned even the rumble of the falling water.

Then, with the thirty strong young warriors who had paddled his canoe, Wind Made by Wings sprinted toward the place where the river water ran into the cave below the castle wall. The running was like a dance as they dodged the ground spikes.

He led his warriors toward the right end of the castle wall, which ended on the limestone outcrop just above the falls. They ran crouched through willow and weeds, hoping not to be seen by the soldiers on the walls.

They reached the base of the wall without losing anyone. With his club in his right hand, attached by a thong to his wrist, and a flint knife in a sheath hanging by a thong from his neck, Wind Made by Wings crept around the corner of the wall and slipped down to the craggy face of the cliff just above the thundering water. Here the water over the years had carved ledges and handholds, and by going like spiders, Wind Made by Wings and his warriors made their way to the place where a shallow chute of water swirled down through the hole into the cave. He had placed great faith in his knowledge of this place, believing it was the one unguarded place where men could slip under the castle's defenses unnoticed and get inside.

Now, with the screaming, shouting, and clangor of the assault muffled by the hissing and thunder of the falls, his painted body wet from spray, he slithered onto the mossy rock and lowered his legs into the hole where the water poured underground. Warm air smelling of smoke and incense came up around him. He eased down, bracing his hands on the moss-slick sides, water pouring over him, until there was nothing under his feet. He had no idea how deep the hole was, or whether he would land on rock or in water. He clutched wet rock with both hands and hung in the rushing darkness, then let go and dropped.

He landed on his feet in a shallow pool.

He had expected no one to be in the cave, but the steamy, dim place was full of deep voices and harsh laughter, and even in the sudden dimness he could see that men were there, moving about and shouting, and there were small flames flickering in the gloom.

One man, a big hairy-face, had seen him splash into the pool and his mouth hung open. He was starting to raise his hand to point at Wind Made by Wings when the warrior chief sprang out of the pool and broke his skull with a blow of the stone ax.

He had dropped into a nest of the enemy soldiers, and they were just becoming aware of his presence, some turning toward him from the center of whatever they had been doing. Even before another of his warriors could come slithering down into the cave to help him, he was darting among the startled Alengwyneh, stabbing and clubbing. Soon one warrior was beside him, then another, and another, and the floor of the cave was running with blood and water. A warrior clubbed a big soldier who was trying to get up off his hands and knees, and when the body rolled aside, Wind Made by Wings saw a naked girl lying there facedown, all bloody and slimy and bruised, not moving. Obviously she was a Euchee girl and all these soldiers had been using her, as groups of them so often used the women of the river tribes. For an instant Wind Made by Wings felt a twinge of pity for the poor creature—but remembered that a part of this mission was to wipe out the Euchee as well as the hairy-faces.

The last few soldiers were fighting for their lives, swinging swords and knives and fists at the agile warriors, and some were trying to get out through the door. Wind Made by Wings wanted no one to get out and spread the alarm, and so, in the smoke and steam and flickering light of the cave room, he set himself at the doorway and killed every hairy-face who tried to get through.

At last they were all dead, and the rest of his warriors had dropped down into the cave. Two warriors lay in the pool where they had been slain by the desperate Alengwyneh.

Now Wind Made by Wings was in the cave with access to the interior of the castle by way of the tunnel. Eyes blazing, face alight with fierce joy, he praised them for what they had done so swiftly and so well here, and with a wave of his knife he cried, "Come, good brothers! Come and help me kill their evil king, and avenge our beloved elders!"

They followed him up a long tunnel that stank of pitch and urine and sloped upward, lit dimly by torches on the walls. They could hear shouts echoing along like the voices of gods, and soon emerged running from the tunnel into a large, smoky room with a high ceiling, with daylight slanting in through the smoky air. White people in long clothes were milling about in the room, perhaps a dozen people, and a woman among them saw the painted warriors and screamed. Among the people were some very big men in iron armor. Before anyone could move, the warriors were among them with clubs and knives. Only one of the men was armed, but his skull was cracked before he could get his sword out of its scabbard. Wind Made by Wings cracked the head of a man and then swung his club again and broke the neck of a tall woman with light hair, and when he looked around for more, they were all dead.

He did not know whether these people were kings and queens or chieftains or workers, but he did not believe King Alengwyned was among these, for he had dreamed that he would find and fight him on a high place. This did not match his dream.

Leaving the bodies strewn on the floor of the big room, he summoned his warriors and led them along another corridor, which reverberated with noise of battle. His eyes were glittering, his chest heaving, as he ran on silent feet down this corridor.

At a door that opened into the corridor, he saw a tall, muscular, handsome mixed-blood man who had stopped at the sight of the warriors. The man had in his hand something that looked like a weapon, but the weapon was smeared with white matter. When Wind Made by Wings charged toward him, the man sprang back into the doorway and pulled the heavy door shut with a bang. Wind Made by Wings shoved at the door, but it would not open. Other warriors paused to help him push, but somehow the door was blocked. There was no time to stand here shoving on a door that was as solid as a wall just to get at one man, unless that man was the king himself, and he was not, for the king was known to have long yellow hair on his head and face. So the warrior chief summoned his warriors on and they followed him along the corridor toward the sounds of fighting.

STONECUTTER, HIS HEART SLAMMING IN HIS CHEST, STOOD GASPING, his shoulder to the barred door and his mortar trowel still in his hand, listening as the footsteps and the voices of the warriors grew faint in the hall outside. Never in his peaceful life had he received such a fright.

This morning Stonecutter had been repairing some loose stonework in the small room where the king's Magic Bundles were kept. He had worked only fitfully, pausing often to brood and worry about his daughter, his beloved only child, Sweetgrass Smoke, afraid that she might somehow displease the king in the Rain Room—but at the same time troubled with shame to think how she might be pleasing him if she were. Often he had clenched his teeth in anger at his mother, who had put the girl in that situation.

And now some other fearsome thing was happening. While mortaring a block of stone in place, Stonecutter had started hearing yells and commotions. Stepping out into the corridor to listen, he had been run at by a band of armed and painted Lenapeh, and had barely gotten in and barred the door to save himself.

Stonecutter stood sweating against the door, confused and very frightened. He did not understand how there could be Lenapeh in the castle, but they had got in, and they were running wild, their weapons red with blood. Whatever was happening outside was obviously terrible. He knew nothing of battles, because there had never been a battle in his life, or in the lifetime of his grandfather, even. He knew about murders and torture, both of which the king indulged in, but always the king controlled all violence, and Stonecutter was under the king's protection as a loyal subject. But from the sounds he could hear even through the closed door, great violence was being done, and the king was certainly not in control of it all now, or there would not be Lenapeh warriors running loose in the castle. Groaning, Stonecutter thought of his wife and mother in the village, and of Sweetgrass Smoke in the Rain Room under the falls. If the king was there, he might not even be aware of what was happening.

Stonecutter felt desperate to do something but did not know what he could do. He was afraid even to lift the bar from the door; the Lenapeh might still be ranging in the corridor, waiting for him to come out. Rubbing his dry, callused palms together and chewing on his lip, Stonecutter turned about in the dim little room and looked at the king's Magic Bundles, as if to beseech them for some answer, some useful power for this dubious moment.

The room had no window, not even any aperture or vent, because the ever-damp air of the Falling Water Place made leather and parchment mold and decay. Four ensconced tallow lamps were always kept burning in the high-ceilinged room, and had been for more than a hundred years, to maintain a warm and dry climate for the preservation of the bundles. It was therefore the most comfortable room in the castle in wintertime, and some suspected that the long hours the kings spent in this room were not so much for prayer as for comfort. The constant burning of tallow, though, had created a rancid-smelling, dark greasiness on every surface, worse even than that in the castle's scullery or kitchen.

Stonecutter had been close to these Magic Bundles often in his life, and always he had seemed to sense a power that hung about them. He had never dared to open any one of them, although they were simply folded and held shut by leather straps. One bundle he had never seen open, but the other two he had seen after they were left open by old Cynoric, the king before Alengwyned. The bundles inside were full of pale sheets of parchment covered with lines of small, black specks of various shapes, so densely laid in rows that they seemed to tremble when looked at closely. The power of the bundles apparently lay in the arrangement of those black specks, which were said to contain silent talk. It was very mysterious to Stonecutter—but also to the kings themselves; it was said that no one, not even Alengwyned, knew how to understand the messages of the black marks.

One of the bundles contained nothing but the rows of marks, but another—and Stonecutter had seen this with his own eyes—contained images that looked like animals. One of the animals was plainly a deer, with antlers; another one he had seen had looked rather like the deer, but without antlers—a doe, perhaps, or an elk cow, rearing with its forefeet raised, and with a man on its back, sitting astride. That image was the most puzzling thing Stonecutter had ever seen. The man shown on the animal's back was clad in what appeared to be the kind of armor worn by the king and his thegns, and held a shield and some sort of a long lance. Stonecutter did not know whether that picture meant that somewhere fighting men actually did sit on the backs of elk, or that someday men *would* do so. Since the bundles were said to have been made by some sort of shamans of the old times, and since much of the work of shamans had to do with prophecy, Stonecutter tended to believe it must be prophecy—that someday men might do so. Surely no one ever had!

Now, crouched in fearful confusion in the stuffy room, Stonecutter felt the power of the bundles, and they seemed to pull at him, to entreat him with silent voices.

He knew they were treasures; he knew that they had great power, as did all the Magic Bundles of all tribes and nations. He knew that in times of fire or flood, the keepers of the tribal bundles would risk their lives to keep the bundles from being lost or destroyed.

Stonecutter looked at the old leather of the three Magic Bundles out of the corner of his eye, saw them seeming to vibrate; he looked at them and listened to the growing noise of tumult elsewhere in the castle. If, indeed, mayhem and destruction were coming in this castle, who would save these Magic Bundles?

Though he had spent his adult life working in the castle, he had never heard of any one of the Alengwyneh being called the Keeper of the Bundles, unless it was the king himself, who seemed to be the only person who ever looked at them. And so now Stonecutter thought a prayer to Creator, asking whether Creator had put him here at this time to save the bundles from whatever was happening.

Once he had thought it, the answer seemed to be yes.

He went timidly to the bundles. He put his hands on them, felt their warm, greasy surfaces, and seemed to feel strength coming through them. He put the three under his left arm. Then he returned to the door, lifted the bar, and opened it a crack, ready to shove it shut and bar it again in an instant.

No one was to be seen anywhere in the corridor. But at once he smelled smoke, the strong smell of wood burning. Glancing up toward the high ceiling of the corridor, he saw drifts and swirls of gray smoke, smoke so thick it obscured the beams and rafters. Surely, Stonecutter thought, the castle was afire. The smoke was swirling along the corridor from south to north, so the part that was burning, he presumed, must be that part near the gates and the bridge. In the opposite way, and a floor below, he knew, was the cave under the falls called the Rain Room, where the king bathed every morning. The Rain Room could not burn. The king was probably there, as this was his customary time to bathe. Also there would be Sweetgrass Smoke, who was supposed to bathe him. Stonecutter's sense told him to go to that place. He would find his daughter. He would show the king that he had saved his Magic Bundles.

It made sense to go there. It made no sense to stay here, or to go the other way. So, his sinewy body glistening with the sweat of fear and doubt, Stonecutter began trotting down the dim, gray halls with the leather-covered bundles under his arm, glancing backward and ahead every few steps.

THE KING WAS IN FULL FURY. THE STUPID LITTLE BROWN SAVAGES with their stone weapons had dared to come charging down into Alengwyned's Land, a kingdom of fortresses protected by iron-clad soldiers with crossbows and metal weapons! It had taken him several minutes just to comprehend that they were actually doing such a thing, even though he had looked out of a window and seen the darting savages, the flint-tipped arrows pelting his castle like hailstones. But once he had seen it, once he had seen his towns ablaze on both riverbanks and heard the screams of dying townspeople, and realized that such an outrageous thing actually was happening, he had hurried to his armory in a red rage, summoning his thegns and bodyguards as he went. While being draped in his chain mail he sent a runner down to fetch Gruffyd and the gang of bodyguards from the Rain Room. As his bronze breastplate, embossed with the Mermaid and Harp, was being strapped on, he sent another runner to order the soldiers on the east wall not to yield, and tell them that he would soon be at their side.

And while his helmet was being fitted with its plume of red-dyed feathers, a frantic, blood-splattered serving boy was brought into the armory to relate the discovery of a dozen battered corpses, men and women, in the Great Hall.

King Alengwyned stood dumbfounded for a moment, thinking that such news must mean that some of the natives were inside his castle.

No, he thought. That cannot be. There must be some other explanation: treachery, perhaps, by Euchee within the castle?

There was no time to think of that now. There was nothing to do but repel the attacking savages. "Come!" he shouted to the thegns and soldiers who were around him arming themselves. "Come with me to the walls!" Waving his sword overhead, he led them all at a jingling, clanking run up a corridor toward the parapets of the east wall. He knew nothing of war except what had been told him by his father and grandfather and other old men who had never fought in battles either. Battles had existed only in legend, because the native neighbors, for generations, had been so complaisant.

Yet Alengwyned esteemed himself an invincible warrior, because it was his legacy. Though the legends had grown vague with time, it was still known that his namesake ancestor of a dozen generations ago had been the greatest conqueror in the history of his homeland across the sea, which had been called Welege, or something sounding like that. And his forefather Madoc, first man to cross the sea to this continent, had been another great warrior, a man of such courage and fortitude that even when he sacrificed his life on the stake for his people, he had not yielded up so much as a groan. So the legends went, and so Alengwyned the King had not the slightest doubt that he was just as invincible.

* * *

WIND MADE BY WINGS CHARGED AT ANOTHER ARMOR-CLAD, yellow-bearded man, ducked a swishing, two-handed swipe of the man's sword, and struck back at him with his war club. The blow caved in the man's helmet and popped his left eye out of its socket. As his big body clattered to the flagstones of the parapet, Wind Made by Wings snatched the sword from his hand. Now armed with his club in one hand and the heavy sword in his left, he sprang toward another big hairy-face.

This melee in which he was now engaged was outside the castle, on the parapet of the wall. He and his bodyguards had raced through the dim halls and rooms of the castle, killing perhaps a dozen men and women who had chanced into their way; then, hearing the shouts and clangor just outside the wall of a big room, they had spilled out through an open door to find themselves among the soldiers who were still trying to keep the main force of the Lenapeh from scaling the wall. Few of the tribesmen had yet gotten over. Even with their canoes and cedar poles to climb, they had been held off. The soldiers atop the wall were able to withstand the rain of flint arrows and remain at the parapet shoving and throwing down the ends of the climbing poles and canoes as quickly as they were erected against the wall.

Wind Made by Wings, seeing at once where he was and what was happening, had led his thirty swift warriors in among the soldiers. With swinging clubs and thrusting lances, his warriors had diverted the Alengwyneh from their defense of the parapet. With this diversion now, some of the warriors from below were managing to clamber up the climbing poles and canoes and slither over the wall to join the melee. As more and more of them mounted the wall, their yodeling became more shrill, more exuberant. Once over, they flung themselves at any man they saw in armor. Some of the big yellow-beards had as many as three or four warriors clinging to them or swinging at them.

Besides the armored soldiers, there were other defenders on the parapet. These were lightly armed Euchee and mixed-blood warriors who wore only a kind of torso armor molded out of fire-stiffened rawhides, and a kind of helmet, made of the same material, that encased their skulls, napes, and jaws. These men were smaller than the yellow-beards, and darker, and most of them carried only pikes. Perhaps a hundred of them had appeared on the parapet soon after the attack, and with their long weapons, they had helped kill and wound the natives who had surmounted the wall. Their hide armor could not resist a well-aimed arrow, but would deflect a glancing shot, and many stone-tipped lances broke against the stiff leather. It was for this reason that Wind Made by Wings had grabbed up a sword. He knew it would cut the Euchees' leather armor without breaking. When one of the Euchee warriors came running at him with a pike, Wind Made by Wings speared him with the sword point. The Euchee fell, bleeding and squirming.

The white soldiers and Euchee warriors kept coming out of the castle doors, and even though the Lenapeh warriors were now coming over the wall by dozens, they were still being matched by the defenders.

The sun by now had risen high over the treetops on the plain southeast of the river, and that sun was dimmed by smoke from the burning town. Flakes of burning bark, and sooty swirls from blazing thatch roofs, rose on the heated air. Embers from the fires had drifted into the autumn-dry woods downwind, and the forest was starting to burn along the south bank. Something had also ignited the ancient timbering of the bridge, and it was blazing with a roar and crackle that could be heard even over the voices and blows of the battle. Still more smoke was boiling from a portion of the castle roof, which was shingled with riven wood slabs more than a century old.

Wind Made by Wings fought on and yelled exultantly for his warriors to be strong. His oiled body had squirmed so often from the grasp of enemy soldiers that the black and red of his body paints were smeared into each other, and he was smudged and spattered with blood. His sword hand was sticky with blood; his right hand was so cramped from gripping and swinging the stone ax that he probably could not have straightened his fingers.

So many warriors and soldiers had fallen along the narrow parapet that one could not move without stepping on the dead and dying. Wind Made by Wings would batter and slash his way through four or five Euchee warriors to get at one of the white soldiers, because in his fevered mind any one of them might be the king. And Wind Made by Wings lived by his dreams, and he had dreamed that he would kill with his own hands the murderer of the old good chiefs.

KING ALENGWYNED LOOKED DOWN ON THE BATTLE FROM A CRENEL in the castle tower forty feet above. He could scarcely believe what the savages had done, even though he was seeing it with his own eyes. The castle roof and the wooden bridge were all roaring flame. The towns on both sides of the river were ablaze.

And directly below him, shrieking native warriors were climbing the supposedly impregnable wall like ants over a doorsill.

The king had called for archers and crossbowmen to come up onto the tower, and the wooden staircases inside the tower thundered with their running footsteps. Gruffyd, his most able and trusted thegn, still had not arrived to aid in the defense of the tower, and no one knew where he was.

This tower being the castle's beacon, it supported a great iron brazier which was always burning, and there were kettles of oil and bales of barkfiber tow kept here for use by the beacon tenders. And in the decking of the tower there were trapdoors with iron pull rings, which could be opened to allow defenders to shoot or drop missiles on anyone below. These machicolations had been built in the time of kings who had still known the science of fortification, which Alengwyned and his thegns knew not. There had never been occasion for their use, but their purpose had always been apparent. And so now the king, eyes bugging in rage and desperation, ordered his soldiers on the platform to open the trapdoors; others he told to build up a blaze in the brazier and heat oil.

The wood of the platform and trapdoors was badly worn and weathered with age, so some of the pull rings simply came loose; others pulled up a few powdery, punky planks as the trapdoors broke apart. Still, it was only a few moments before all the machicolations were open and Alengwyned and his thegns could look straight down at the combatants on the parapet, and could likewise observe the stairs inside the tower, by which their compeers were still tramping up to join them.

Alengwyned grabbed the shoulder of a frightened-looking thegn and yelled at him: "Set the archers to killing those natives down below! When the oil is hot, pour it down on them! Use the tow! Pour fire on their heads! They have wrought an awful folly in attacking my kingdom, and they must be cooked alive for it!"

The thegn looked down through one of the trapdoors and wondered how archers or fire throwers could hit the natives without shooting or burning the defenders with whom they were grappling. But of course he did not argue with the king.

WIND MADE BY WINGS WAS AIMING A BLOW AT A EUCHEE WHEN AN arrow seemed to sprout from the top of the Euchee's head. As he slumped, eyes bugging and a bloody gurgle in his throat, Wind Made by Wings realized that an arrow striking a man that way must have come straight down. And he saw that other arrows were showering down; some were striking the flagstones with their iron tips, making sparks, splintering and bouncing, but most were sinking to the fletch in the bodies of men already fallen, who by now virtually covered the parapet. It was as if Creator were sending down a rain of arrows. Only then did Wind Made by Wings look up and see that the tower of the castle, so closed and mute at the start of the battle, was alive with archers and shouting hairy-faces. A part of the tower that projected from its high wall now had openings that he had not seen before, and through those openings he could see men and weapons moving, silhouetted against the smoky sky. Brave and furious as he was, Wind Made by Wings flinched at the deluge of arrows; gasps and screams told him that his warriors were being hit. Something hummed past his right ear and burned along his back, clanged against a flagstone behind him and spun off into the air. He did not know it was an iron bolt from a crossbow, but he knew he was hurt. He took a deep breath, and seemed not to have been hurt inside. But he knew that the most terrible danger yet was now being presented by that high place and the Alengwyneh soldiers up there. . . .

The high place! *Ai!*

The high place in his dream!

Wind Made by Wings knew suddenly that the dark stone tower that loomed above him raining death on his warriors must be the place where his enemy the king was at this moment. Somehow, he knew, he would have to go up there to kill that king. In his dream he had already seen it happen, and knew that it must, though he did not know yet how to get up there.

And now a ball of fire came tumbling down from the tower, and then another and another; in a moment it was raining fireballs as well as arrows. Burning wads stuck to men.

Wind Made by Wings glanced around frantically. He saw that there were arrows going up, too. His warriors still out on the ground beyond the parapet were now bending their bows and sending flights of arrows toward the top of the tower.

Wind Made by Wings yelped with pain. Something boiling hot was searing his head and shoulders. Men everywhere around him had stopped fighting each other and were cringing, swiping at themselves with their hands, and were contorted in what looked like a wild dance.

He knew at once from the smell that hot oil was being poured down from the tower. His own skin was blistering. But that was only pain; pain could not kill him, and he could ignore it. But he had to get up the tower somehow and get the king.

With both oil and burning fiber being flung down from the tower now, many of the dead and wounded men on the parapet were beginning to burn. The white men's clothing was catching on fire; hair was being singed off. The wounded ones writhed and shrieked as they burned.

The king and his men on the tower, it seemed, did not care that their fires and missiles were falling on their own soldiers as well as the attackers. There was so much panic and confusion that virtually no one on the parapet was fighting now; most were reacting only to the deluge of pain from above.

Wind Made by Wings, still carrying sword and war club, made his way through the carnage to the great wooden door through which he and his bodyguards had earlier charged out of the castle onto the parapet. Several of the big white soldiers were trying desperately to push the doors shut, but the threshold was clogged with corpses, and Wind Made by Wings gutted one of the soldiers with the great sword, then hewed the flesh off another's shoulder. Some of his bodyguards had come following him, calling others to follow, and with him they stormed through the big double doors, shoving them wide again as they went through, and slaying the rest of the soldiers there.

This side of the tower had no entry. Wind Made by Wings led his warriors along the base of this wall, battling a few confused Euchee soldiers as they went, then rounded the corner to the west side of the tower. Here they found Euchee soldiers and armored Alengwyneh running up a sloped ramp that led to a door in the tower wall and going inside. Wind Made by Wings saw at once that this was the entrance to the tower. He turned to two of his followers and told them to go back to the big fight outside and lead as many warriors as they could to this door. "Their king is up there," he said. "I am going up to kill him. I will need help to go up there. Hurry, and bring me more warriors!" He was all smears of red and black paint, and blood. His chest and arms were cut in several places and blistered with burns. Some of his straight black hair had been crisped and frizzled by fire, and down the muscle of his back, just alongside the spine, was a long furrow in the skin where the crossbow bolt had creased him. His chest heaved from the exertions of the battle. But now he knew where King Alengwyned was, he was certain, and he felt so strong and so eager with purpose that he could scarcely contain himself.

With a fierce howl he sprinted for the tower door, his warriors right at his heels. The Euchee soldiers were swept away like leaves before a whirlwind, and three or four of the armored men near the doorway were simply flattened by the onrush. As they tried to get up, they were clubbed senseless. He and his warriors flung themselves at the soldiers and Euchees who were on the first flight of wooden stairs.

But here they faltered. They had come upon something entirely new to most of them: stairs.

It had looked like a steep slope leading up in the dim interior of the tower, with the enemy running up the slope. But the warriors' feet met not a sloping surface, like a hillside, but flat stair steps. This was so totally unexpected and unfamiliar that for a moment most of the warriors were stumbling and falling, then trying to climb up on all fours, which, with weapons in hand, was almost impossible. Even Wind Made by Wings, who had climbed some staircases before in his attacks on the river towers, was thrown off balance momentarily and tottered. The Euchees and the soldiers on the stairs, hearing the commotion below and seeing the mass of stumbling, crawling natives, turned and charged down at them with their pikes, swords, and battleaxes. Wind Made by Wings quickly righted himself and began flailing at them, but not before they had hacked several of his bodyguards down.

Now the old wooden staircase inside the tower became still another battleground—a cramped, steep, narrow, thundering, reverberating, dusty battleground where no more than four or five men could actually strike at each other at any moment, while those above and below crowded at them and pressed them so tightly that any moving weapon could not miss flesh. Soldiers up on the next flight of stairs, meanwhile, began hurling pikes and spears down at the native warriors who were crowding behind Wind Made by Wings. Several of his bodyguards thus fell wounded back down the staircase, or keeled over and plunged to the stone floor below. The shouting, howling, thumping, and clatter were deafening, and the gloom inside the tower, relieved only by faint daylight from the open trapdoors far above, created a frightfully unfamiliar oppressiveness upon the spirits of the native warriors.

Wind Made by Wings had expended more of his strength already this morning than he ever had on any other whole day of his life. His arms and legs and torso burned with exertion, and his breath rasped. Everything about him hurt and stung, and he felt pressed in and trapped at the very cutting edge of this melee, hardly able to move a foot forward or back, fending and thrusting at an endless succession of blows struck at him by shouting, grimacing, stinking men wearing metal and leather armor. But his strength kept swelling in him as fast as he spent it, and now and then an enemy would fall dead or wounded on the stairs, and Wind Made by Wings could climb one step toward that place above him where he would face his great evil enemy as in his dream, and execute him for murdering the good old chiefs. His body protested that he could not go on fighting any longer, but his spirit kept rising.

The battle on the stairs continued, on and on, and seemed as if it would never be finished. But eventually Wind Made by Wings and his followers had killed and pushed back enough white soldiers to attain the first flight of stairs, and then the second. More warriors had been coming in from the parapet, following his bodyguards. They were relieved to be sheltered from the rain of arrows, fireballs, and hot oil. And although the din and turmoil in this great, square enclosure was strange and intimidating, at least death was not spattering down on them like a rainstorm. They clambered up the stairs over the bodies of their own brothers and the enemy alike, and the higher they climbed up the precarious heights, the louder and hotter it became, and the rain of spears and other hurled missiles grew more intimidating. Every few moments some combatant or another, or two enemies locked in a mortal struggle, would fall into the abyss of the stairwell and thump on the stone floor far below, bodies broken.

It was while fighting on the last flight of stairs that Wind Made by Wings became aware of a particular great voice from the top of the tower. It was a resonating, loud, grating voice, obviously from someone with an immense chest, and something told Wind Made by Wings, even while his whole body and soul were concentrated in combat, that this was the voice of the Alengwyneh king himself. The voice seemed to be shouting commands and scolding people. Wind Made by Wings was almost maddened by that voice, knowing he was within a few paces of the king but still having to spend his strength hacking at these soldiers who blocked his way. The top of the stairs rose to a large trapdoor that opened onto the tower deck, and now and then Wind Made by Wings would get a glimpse of sky up there, and dirty smoke, and the figures of men moving about on that roof, a head wearing a helmet with antlers, a bearded face.

There were flights of arrows always crossing that patch of sky, as many, it seemed, as the great flocks of birds over the river. . . .

Suddenly now the great voice above was bellowing with such urgent ferocity that it seemed to overpower the whole din of the battle. The soldiers still fighting at the top of the stairs began to retreat, to clamber desperately backward up the stairs, to squeeze through the trapdoor opening onto the deck above. Wind Made by Wings charged after them, his warriors right behind him. And then the way was clear; there was the bright sky, the billowing smoke, the arrows sailing over . . .

And the king!

The moment Wind Made by Wings saw the huge figure in shiny armor looming above him, not three paces away, he recognized him: it was the king on the high place, standing just as Wind Made by Wings had seen him in the dream. Now the time had come to kill him! Wind Made by Wings had never been shown the end of the dream, but he knew it already: he had reached the place where the King of Alengwyneh stood, and he knew that nothing could save that evil giant now; he would die this day for his murders and his arrogance in a land that was not his!

At that moment the king stepped aside and two men staggered into view, carrying something heavy between them—a great kettle of iron. And just as Wind Made by Wings sprang up the last few steps, they dumped the kettle.

Boiling brown oil gushed out of it. Wind Made by Wings was drenched by it from the waist down, felt the greatest pain he had ever felt in his life, felt his skin frying and blistering, incredibly searing pain that seemed to cook him to his bones. His warriors on the steps just below him were sloshed with it from head to foot and stopped where they were, screaming in agony, then toppled and went falling down the stairs.

But Wind Made by Wings did not fall. He could still see and could still move and there was nothing he could fear that would be worse than the pain he was suffering now. He sprang from the stairs onto the platform. With sword and club he killed the two men who still held the overturned kettle. It tumbled, banging, down the stairwell, and one of the soldiers, his hand still gripping the handle, went down with it.

There were perhaps two dozen armored men and Euchees on the tower platform, many of them around the crenels or tending the roaring fire in the brazier, heating more oil and lighting wads of tow, and a dozen archers and crossbowmen shooting down through the machicolations at the combatants far below. But Wind Made by Wings saw only the king. Through the red veil of pain and fury he perceived only that figure, just as he had perceived him in his dream: the one giant evil man on the high place—and he went straight at him with a tremolo cry pouring from his throat, swinging his long-handled, blood-soaked war club right at the king's temple. The king was so astonished to see this apparition of blood, soot, and burned flesh coming at him that he failed to get his guard up, but he did recoil quickly enough that the club missed his skull. The bear claw on the tip of the club ripped Alengwyned's nose from his face. That shock blinded the king for just an instant and he staggered back toward the brazier. Instantly, then, he shook his head to clear his vision, spraying the blood that was gushing from his face, and drew back his sword to strike the warrior. Wind Made by Wings had not paused, and with the sword in his left hand he swung a horizontal blow that caught the king on the breastplate, not cutting the armor but denting it, the blow staggering the king again and the clang of metal on metal ringing in the air.

This personal combat had erupted so quickly that most of the Alengwynehs on the roof, already caught up in their own roles in the battle, had not seen it yet, and did not even notice yet that one of the savages was among them on this high place. A grizzle-bearded old thegn paced to and fro on the other side of the brazier, giving orders to crossbowmen. Other thegns of the king were running about and yelling, mere shapes in the pall of smoke that poured from the brazier and rose from the burning roofs of the castle buildings below. The first soldier to see that somebody was attacking the king was a fire bearer who had been lighting wads of oil-soaked tow to throw down as fireballs on the natives below. This soldier, holding a long set of iron tongs with a fireball flaring in their grip, now saw the screaming savage flailing at the king and rushed at him with the blazing bundle. It caught the warrior chief full on the flank—but his pain was so general already, and his rage so intense, that he hardly felt the burn. The fireball fell from the tongs and rolled along the wooden decking, which was slick with spilled oil. The soldier then jabbed at Wind Made by Wings with the hot tongs themselves, but was unfortunate enough to be within the arc of a sword blow that the king had aimed at the savage. The soldier, nearly decapitated, careened aside and fell near the stairwell, and there his body lay as the oily flooring began to burn around him.

Alengwyned was nearly twice the size of the hideous savage who was attacking him, and was outraged, but was afraid as well, for he had never in his life been confronted by such a demon. His whole face was stinging and throbbing with intense pain and he had no idea how badly he had been hurt, but he knew he was gushing blood and that his vision had been so affected by the blow that he could see little but the mad eyes and white teeth in the wild face before him. And so Alengwyned, sword gripped in both hands, swung and stabbed at that face.

One of his blows caught Wind Made by Wings on his left wrist. Hand and sword turned in the air and fell separately on the burning floor. Seeing that his hand was gone and that blood was pumping copiously from the stump, the war chief uttered another pulsating scream and swung his war club again at the king's head. The blow of the club shattered one of the decorative antlers and sent the helmet spinning away. The king's scalp and right ear were gashed by the edge of the helmet as it was knocked loose, and he stood tottering, stunned. By this time the old thegn had seen the attack on his king, as had another thegn and a pikeman, and they all charged at the red-and-black demon at once. The pike passed through his waist and came out the other side. Someone's sword laid open the warrior's left shoulder, and another sword stabbed him in the kidney. Even then Wind Made by Wings was able to throw one more blow of his club at the king, shattering his teeth and knocking his jaw out of its sockets. The motion of this final blow broke the haft of the pike off in the pikeman's hands. And at last Wind Made by Wings sank to the deck.

He knew he was dying. He was ready now, because the pain was too great even for him to bear and his blood was pouring out. He had hoped to see the enemy king lying dead, but in his dream he had not seen the end of it. Wind Made by Wings had done his best and he could not even move now. And he did believe that this would end with the king dead; he had believed that about his dream all along.

But it was bad to be down and to see the king still standing above him.

Fire and smoke were rising all around. The giant king was fading behind a veil of black and red as Wind Made by Wings began to succumb to a great weakness, and he looked up at the king's bloody, featureless wreck of a face, and sang his death song.

Creator, Great Good Spirit
Hear me sing
See me coming
I come I come
Back to the Beginning
When I was in your hand
And you create me
Now
Creator

Alengwyned the King, shaken through with pain and horror, looked down at the bloody red demon who lay at his feet singing.

Alengwyned's whole head and face stung and ached, and his vision was swimming; blood from his face was drenching his hands and arms, his whiskers, and his clothing. But he did not feel that he was mortally hurt, and it appeared that the attack from the tower stairwell had been repulsed with the boiling oil. Even though the sky was still full of flying arrows and the din of battle still rose from below, Alengwyned still stood alive on his own feet, apparently invincible as he had believed, and there were still plenty of able-bodied defenders up here, and surely down below, too. Perhaps the day might yet be saved. . . .

It was then that Alengwyned became aware of the rising heat, and began to cough from the acrid smoke.

His heart plummeted. He now understood what was happening:

Flames poured up from the tower stairwell. The oil had caught fire below and the old timbers were blazing. From the cracks between the old gray flooring planks, white smoke was seeping up everywhere. His soles were searing. This whole tower deck where he and his defenders stood was burning from underneath.

The stone tower was now like a giant chimney flue, sucking an updraft to fan the burning, and this structure of ancient, dry timbers was the fuel.

And there was no way down. The staircase was already an inferno.

"Your Majesty," an old thegn gasped, "we are doomed. Farewell . . ."

The great weight of the brazier and its stone fire pit started the collapse; the masonry sank through the flooring with a crackling, creaking noise, and flames roared up through the broken deck around it. The brazier tipped, kettles swayed, then toppled, and gallons of hot oil spilled into the holocaust with a roar. A ball of flame exploded over the top of the tower. The masonry plunged through. Coals, ashes, kettles, oil, and bodies plunged through the flaming hole, and as they went down, the updraft through the tower intensified to a pulsing roar. Stairs, posts, and beams were consumed; even the limestone masonry was exploding. Alengwyned, his thegns, archers, everyone on the tower, breathed searing heat. Eyebrows, beards, and hair vanished. Alengwyned's last thought was of the thundering falls of cool water far below; he imagined himself leaping, falling into it. . . .

But he was already dead, lung-scorched, when the blazing floor gave way and he and all the rest spilled into the inferno. Their tower of defense was their funeral pyre.

THE FIGHTING ON THE PARAPET HAD ALMOST CEASED. SOLDIERS AND natives ran to keep from being crushed by huge falling chunks of the battlement, and most of the soldiers just kept running. Other burning roofs of the castle buildings were collapsing and flaring up, and the rooms and corridors echoed with the screams of trapped Alengwyneh and their Euchee servants.

Across the river and below the falls, the other castle was blazing, too, the castle where the old Weaver Queen had lived long ago. In the town around it, the Iroquois were executing the hundreds of Alengwyneh and Euchee they had captured. There had been virtually no fighting in that castle or village; the Iroquois had simply overrun everything, and rounding up the people, hacked and speared them whether or not they resisted. All through the smoke-filled valley, shrill screams and the roar and crackle of burning could be heard over the timeless rush of the Falling Water. Soldiers, workers, women, and children were fleeing. The warriors of the Lenapeh and their allies would have to hunt them through the valley and kill them all. For nearly two hundred years these hairy-faces and half-bloods had troubled the peoples and disturbed the Spirits of the Ancient Ones in this sacred Falling Water Place. They had proven themselves unfit to live among the true Children of the Creator, and they could never be permitted to come here and start growing again.

It was as Wind Made by Wings had said.

SWEETGRASS SMOKE CAME AWAKE GROANING AND WHIMPERING from a dream in which men were holding her down and hurting her, and she thrashed and struggled against the restraint. But when she opened her eyes, she saw that the strong arms that were holding her were those of her father, Stonecutter. His face was a grimace and his eyes shone with tears, and he was lifting her onto the padded bench at the edge of the pool. She hurt everywhere, especially below the waist. She felt as if her loins and bowels had been scoured raw with gravel. Every joint in her body ached, and every move caused white flashes of pain to shoot through her head. When Stonecutter laid her supine on the bench, her head lolled, and between the bursts of pain she saw the flickering lights and the pale daylight from above, and heard the running water, and remembered that she was in the Rain Room, the place of terror.

Then she began to see the bloody bodies everywhere, the bodies of the thegns and soldiers who had been hurting her so badly, and waves of whiteness swirled through her, and she fainted away from the pain and the confusion for a while, into a wide, yellow, treeless land where a wind blew and blew. When she opened her eyes and returned, her flashes of pain were in the places where Stonecutter was touching her and pouring warm water over her. In the half shadows of the cave his face was a changing mask of emotions. He looked angry and he looked afraid, but he was weeping, too. She had never been touched by her father in the places where he was touching her now, and he had not seen her all naked since she was a little girl, but she realized that he was gingerly washing blood and mess off of her. She saw the metal of the precious dipper glint in the light.

When she spoke, her voice startled him and he dropped the dipper. "Father . . . did you kill those men?" Quickly he loomed over her face, looking in her eyes. Her vision was blurred by tears or water and one of her eyes was swollen almost shut. She groaned again; she had been choked so severely that it had pained her to speak.

"I?" he said. "Kill them? Oh, daughter, no! When . . . when I came to find you, they were all like this. . . . The Lenapehs must have killed them. Two warriors lie over there. Daughter, was it the Lenapehs who hurt you so? And where is our king? I brought his Sacred Bundles for him, but find him not here!"

She was swept by a flood of tears and horrors, and wept so violently that every hurt place in her body twitched in agony. Then, after she had grown calm again, she began to tell her father what she could remember.

The telling took a long while because each memory choked her, but at last Stonecutter knew—whether he could believe it or not—that it had been the king himself who had used her so brutally and then had thrown her to his thegns to finish off.

Stonecutter was no bold man. Though his work had hardened his body into brawn, sinew, and callus, he had never served as a fighting man, nor even as a hunter for his family; his strong body was a tool, not a weapon, and he was not used to thinking of violence. Sweetgrass Smoke tried to hold her senses together and make sense of the things her father was saying in his quaking voice as he treated her bruises and abrasions with the Rain Room's balms and salves. She could barely hear him over the splashing water and the ringing in her head. ". . . perhaps safe here . . . for a while . . . Lenapeh running in the castle . . . castle is burning . . . but if we stay and those warriors return . . ." Then he exclaimed:

"Surely you do not mean the king hurt you like this! What did my daughter do, what did you say, to anger the king?"

"No, no, no! I tried to do as he wished, as Grandmother instructed me! Still he hurt me. As if he likes to give pain!"

Stonecutter shook his head and sighed. Yes, he knew that to be true; he had seen that before. He put his head in his hands and finally looked hard at her, then looked away and said something that made her heart twist. "You bleed from behind. Did you let men disgrace you there?" She realized one of the awful things he was thinking: that she had *let* herself be made a No-person!

She sobbed until she could answer: "They held me, and the king did that! I could not stop him!"

Stonecutter clenched his hands before his face in disbelief. "Can this be?" He shook his fists at the ceiling. "The king is a No-person?" He slumped and fell to muttering.

She asked him to get her tunic from where it hung, and with excruciating pain she put it on. The effort exhausted her and she had to lie down again. She drifted in and out of her pain and shame as the water relentlessly trickled and hushed.

"It will soon be night," she heard Stonecutter say. She opened her eyes. The light from the fissure where the water poured in had grown faint. She remembered how it had brightened in the morning, and it seemed as if she had been in here forever. Stonecutter said, "At this time of the day I would be going home to the village. . . . You and your mother and grandmother would feed me. . . . I have been wondering if the Lenapeh attacked the villages as well as the castle!"

And finally after a while he said, "I cannot bear to hide here and know nothing! I fear for our family, our People! Daughter, can you walk?"

She dreaded to try, but strained to rise. When she had lowered her feet to the floor and was sitting, so many severe pains exploded through her hips and bowels that she almost fainted again. She stood up slowly, stiffly, stooped like an old, old woman, and she felt warm blood oozing out of her and cooling between her legs and on the backs of her thighs. Every breath she took was a gasp.

The fire in the Rain Room had gone down to embers and it was becoming cold, and only one lamp was still burning.

Stonecutter looked out the Rain Room door. The corridor was unlit. He took a torch from the wall and held it over the last lamp until it was burning, giving off oily smoke. By its light Sweetgrass Smoke saw him gather some leather things from a ledge and put them under his left arm. He said, "These are the Alengwyneh Magic Bundles. I should . . ." He shrugged. "I do not know what I should do about them. I should keep them safe until we find the king or . . ."

Then it was that Sweetgrass Smoke rose above her whimpering misery and cried, "The king? The king is a No-person!"

Stonecutter nodded. "Yes . . ."

They now crept along the corridor toward the castle, up the slope, the girl waddling and gasping, stopping every few steps to brace an arm against the wall. Her father peered anxiously ahead into the limits of the flickering torchlight, and as the watery sounds of the Rain Room and the rumble of the falls faded behind them, Stonecutter listened ahead for the sounds of conflict. But there was no noise. As they turned into the main tunnel of the castle, he smelled the dense odors of burnt wood and, he thought, scorched meat. He was very hungry, he realized; his fear-dry mouth suddenly filled with saliva.

They emerged into the Great Hall of the castle and stopped, stunned by what lay before them illuminated by the twilit sky overhead, the feeble light of the torch, and by licking flames everywhere.

The castle was roofless. The floor of the Great Hall was a jumble of smoking, charred roof timbers and rubble of limestone, and the air in the unroofed space was hot and smoky.

Sweetgrass Smoke gasped and stood swaying, staring at something on the floor.

It was a person's leg protruding from under a burnt timber, and the leg itself was so burnt and crisped that only a sandal on the partly burned foot showed that it was somebody's limb. And as she and her father glanced about, they began to see hands, heads, and legs everywhere in the rubble, all charred. She clung to her father's elbow to keep from passing out again. Off to their left was a blackened skull, in a copper helmet that had melted partly out of shape. Stonecutter realized that the fire in the room must have been as hot as a kiln to soften the helmet like that. The scorched meat they had smelled was the flesh of burned people. The limestone walls were half fallen, and pieces were still crackling and dropping.

"We cannot pass through here," he said. "We must go back through the tunnel." He realized, too, that the room of the Sacred Bundles must have been destroyed, so it was no use trying to put the bundles back there.

No one knew the plan of the castle better than its stonemasons. He led her back through the tunnel, past the mouth of the Rain Room corridor, then through a low, narrow passageway that had always been used to transport kegs and wineskins to the Great Hall. The ceiling was so low that he had to walk stooped. It had been built for slaves and Euchee servants to pass through, not the tall Alengwyneh who had never been anyone's servants. He thought on such unfamiliar notions as he led his halting, gasping daughter through the musty tunnel. There had been an order to things in this kingdom, going back to the times of his grandfathers, and he and everyone else he knew had been obedient, unquestioning parts of that order. In that order, the taller and whiter people had always been at the top and could make anyone else do anything; the smaller and browner the others were, the harder their lives. At the bottom had been the slaves, captured from faraway tribes, the slaves who could be used by anyone in any way.

This day, that whole order of things had been shaken apart in Stonecutter's mind. Wild Lenapeh warriors had run through the castle, threatening and killing. The king had shown himself to be a No-person. And Sweetgrass Smoke, the daughter of an esteemed artisan of the castle, had been used like a slave by useless, brutal thegns who were only one step above him in the order of things.

At the end of the passageway was a stout oaken door, barred from the inside. He put an ear to the door, heard nothing outside, carefully lifted the bar, eased it down, and pulled the door inward. Fresh cold air rushed in, stirring the festooned cobwebs and whipping the flames of the torch. The air was rank with smoke and damp with the spray from the Falling Water, which rushed loudly beyond the courtyard and hedge garden a few yards away.

Clutching the Sacred Bundles to his chest, Stonecutter snuffed out the torch against the ceiling, then eased out to stand in the courtyard, studying the skies, the walls nearby, and the distances. The sun had long since set, and there was only a tinge of sunset glow along the horizon downriver. A quarter moon was high in the sky, but it was again and again obscured by clouds of smoke.

Through that smoky pall the whole vast river valley seemed full of dull, ruddy fire glow. The brightest fire was across the river, and he knew at once it was the old Weaver Queen's castle. He could make out the shape of it now and then when smoke and mist blew aside, its low, black profile under flames that rose and fell and reflected off the turbulent water below the falls. There were also curragh ships burning at the wharf on that far shore, it appeared to him.

Points of firelight and long, wide lines of fire were burning along both riverbanks. He knew this valley well, having lived his whole life here, and it was easy for him to see that the big villages on both sides of the river were burning, and all the fishing camps, the tannery, the boatyards. And tongues of flame were glowing on the steep, wooded bluffs and in the ravines on the north bank of the river. Enough dull fire glow from everywhere was diffused through the shifting smoke and river mist that one could see one's way without a torch to draw attention. He turned back to the door. "Come, daughter."

She stood shivering with pain and weakness in the dank air. Even in her shame and misery she had noticed something that made her heart shrink. In all her life the Falling Water Place had never been without voices—the voices of the hundreds of villagers—even over the rush of the water. Sweetgrass Smoke now had noticed the ominous quiet out in the night. She had heard no voices. Not even cries.

CHAPTER 13

Near the Falling Water Place
Autumn 1404

They found not a person alive on the castle island, though they stumbled over countless bodies in the dark shadows along the castle walls. Their feet grew sticky with blood. On the ground and the parapets, twisted and mutilated corpses sprawled, misshapen dark lumps in the lurid fire glow which sometimes glimmered on a piece of armor or a burnished shield. Stonecutter clung to the Sacred Bundles and led his dazed daughter limping across baileys and gardens so littered with arrows that it was like walking over the dead twigs in a woods. Though it was an autumn night, the old castle walls were so full of hot rubble and wood embers that the air seemed dry and hot, and was dense with the smells of blood and excrement.

The castle gate and portcullis had collapsed into blackened ruin, and the short bridge from the castle gate to the south bank had burned and collapsed, so they had to wade through the cold current while clutching at charred pilings to keep from being swept downriver. Stonecutter balanced the bundles on his head and held them there with a free hand until he could climb ashore on the bank and help pull his daughter up. Their bodies were streaming with water, but they were not cold because here the burning of the town had baked the ground, and huts and woodpiles, pole fences and mounds of roof thatch, still flared and smoldered. The air was thick with soot, sparks, and thick smoke. The town had been made of poles, bark, thatch, and reed mats—no stone—and it was totally leveled. There were far more corpses here than there had been on the castle island, and most of them had been scorched. Dogs were tearing at their flesh; fortunately, the gloom and smoke were so deep that this could be seen only dimly.

They made their morose way down the riverbank. Sweetgrass

Smoke was vaguely aware that they were going in the direction where their hut had stood, on the riverbank a few hundred paces downstream from the bridge. In her mind as she walked she would see the face of her mother, Moss on the Tree, and her grandmother's face; then she would step on an ember and recoil, and the lurch would send bolts of pain through her innards, and blood would gush from her orifices. Her eyes stung from the smoke and teared so badly that she had to keep wiping them with a finger to keep her sight from blurring. Her nose and throat were raw. The smoke was mingling with mist from the falls, which made its smell even more harsh.

Nothing was left of any house along the riverfront, but when Stonecutter stopped at a place and set the bundles down, she looked about and felt that, yes, this was where she used to live, in that other life, before she had gone to the castle as a Maid of the Rain Room. That had been another world, another time; it could not have been just yesterday.

But this was the place where she had lived, in that onetime happy life with her father and mother and grandmother; there was the path to the riverbank; by the red light of the burning castles and hillsides she could see where the path was, and the two big cottonwoods; though their leaves were all burned off, she knew the shapes of their trunks. But there were no voices. There had always been voices, in that life.

Her father was scuffing through the ashes. A bit of broken pottery, a wad of half-burnt hide that had been a bedcover, rocks of the fire ring in the center of the lodge, those were all the recognizable things that he kicked up.

There was a faint clink. Stonecutter stooped in the warm ashes and groped with his fingers, and soon turned up seven of his stone-cutting tools—clouring points and chisels, and the head of a hammer, its handle charred. They were old tools, having belonged to generations of stonemasons before him. He rolled them up in the patch of scorched leather and laid them by the Magic Bundles.

On his sooty, greasy face there appeared a wan smile. He had found here no bodies, no blackened bones of his wife or mother, and so he could hope that they were alive somewhere, hiding. "Perhaps," he said, "we will find people . . . and build again with these tools. . . ." His voice, the first she had heard in this desolation, was strange, startling.

"I want to see Mother, Grandmother," she groaned. What had been done to her in the Rain Room, as a woman, was the one enormous thing in her spirit, and she needed those women of her life to help her understand it. Only women, her mother or grandmother, could tell her if she was truly a No-person.

"We will hunt for them. Now we must find a place to hide and rest. The Lenapeh warriors would kill us, I think, if they found us."

She was swaying, hurting, faint; in the roiling fogs of her mind she saw a face painted red on one side, black on the other, eyes that gleamed like fire. She had heard her father speak of Lenapeh warriors, but had hardly understood what he was saying. She wondered if she had seen Lenapeh warriors, or if that, too, had been a part of the terrible dreamings.

He picked up the bundles and the tools and they started down the riverbank, limping across ashes and debris, through the bitter mists of the night, hearing nothing but the rushing of the waterfalls behind them and the distant hoots and wails of owls and coyotes, while a dull quarter moon tried to show itself through the drifting smoke above.

THEY SLEPT LIKE BURROWING ANIMALS IN DRIFTED LEAVES UNDER A limestone ledge on a creek bank that night, far back from the riverside paths where Lenapeh might travel. The girl whimpered often in her sleep, kicking her father awake with the spasms of her sharp-edged dreams. Over every bed in their home there had hung a small hoop interlaced with a web of cords, through which good and smooth dreams could pass while the barbed edges of bad dreams snagged and were held safely away from the dreamers. Because there was no Dream Catcher net here, Sweetgrass Smoke was wakened over and over by the piercing barbs of bad dreams. She would lie awake awhile, shift her painful, cold body on the stony ground until fatigue pulled her away again into more dreams, and then would waken again from pain. In one dream, vast, treeless hills were burning, lines of flame racing faster than a man could run, but she was not in danger because she was in a boat in the middle of a wide river, which, unlike the Beautiful River, seemed to flow away from the direction of sunsets instead of toward them. After the fire passed she walked on the ashy hills and ate the delicious meat of animals that had been caught by the fire and cooked.

When daylight came she awoke looking at a stone ledge above her head. Her father was not beside her. She craned her neck to look about for him, but her eyes were so swollen from bruises and smoke that she could see only vague, narrow bands of daylight. She remembered that perhaps she was a No-person, and was afraid her father had abandoned her. But the leather bundles and iron tools he had been carrying were still there; she realized he intended to come back.

It took her a long time to decide to try to get up, then still longer to do it. All her joints were bursting with pains, and her abdomen and bowels felt as if they were full of boiling water. Finally she was up, squatting in the leaves, her lower lip between her teeth, relieving herself with groans and gasps, her holes feeling scalded by the outpourings, and much of what she left on the ground was blood.

Gradually she stood and looked up to see smears of red-yellow, which she realized were autumn leaves in the treetops. Many dark little shapes were sliding in the gray sky beyond the treetops. She squeezed her eyelids shut tight and squinted again, and then could see that the things in the sky were vultures. She stood looking up, bemused even through her misery, never having seen vultures so thick in the sky, not even when bison herds crossing the river went over the Falling Water and their corpses washed up on the riverbanks. She had seen hundreds of vultures at such times, but now there seemed to be hundreds of hundreds.

Sweetgrass Smoke sighed. She wanted to lie down and perhaps let her spirit just slip over to the Other Side World. But she could not do that. Her father would be returning, and she would have to have something ready for him to eat. It was what a woman did in the mornings.

There were tall, straight hickory trees everywhere in this ravine, and the nuts were profuse on the ground. Squirrels were scurrying, gathering them. Sweetgrass Smoke could gather nuts and make *pawcohickory*; if she had luck, she would get a squirrel to put in it.

She gathered small wood and tinder first, gasping and walking stooped, picking up nuts also as she scoured the leaf-covered ground. Then, with one of her father's tools, she dug a hole in the ground. In the leather that had held the tools she carried water up from the brook at the bottom of the ravine and set the leather in the hole, thus making it a basin of water in the ground. This exhausted her, and she sat and rocked against her pain until she was strong enough to make a fire. That was the hardest work, twirling a stick in a groove on a log until smoke and a little ember started. She thought, All the world is burning, but here I have to make a fire. The thought actually seemed funny, and she smiled.

She made a hot bonfire and put rocks in it to heat, then went gathering more nuts. She stripped off her tunic and used it to carry nuts in. Two times she flung rocks at nearby squirrels, though the motion of throwing hurt her badly. The third rock she threw stunned a squirrel, and she scrambled to it and wrung its neck before it could move.

Back at the fire, she put on her dress and hulled nuts, pounded them between stones until she had a large pile of them broken, then dumped them into the leather-lined water pit. Using mason tools to carry hot stones from the fire, she dropped them hissing into the water, until it was boiling. The boiling separated the nutmeats from the shells and they rose to the top, where she could skim them off. Using the edges of rock fragments as knives, she skinned and gutted the squirrel and dropped its carcass in. When her father came wandering back up the ravine from his scouting to see whether she was awake, she saw the great surprise in his face because there was a fire and a good meal to eat. He reluctantly doused the fire, saying it might attract enemies, but she could see that he was very pleased with the food, and as they ate together, she saw in his face that he did not think she was a No-person.

They rested awhile, needing to let their stomachs get used to their first food in a day and a half. She lay in leaves under the limestone ledge while he dried the leather by the warm ashes and rewrapped his tools in it, saying nothing. Finally, after midday, he said, "Have you seen that the sky is full of vultures?"

"I saw them. So many."

He said, "I went to the place where this brook runs out of the bluff. Down there in the bottomland the ground is black with vultures. All the Alengwyneh, men and women and children, and all the Euchee, too, are feeding the vultures. I believe the Lenapeh warriors killed everyone who lived at the Falling Water. Everyone's skull has been smashed, all the same."

She had risen, and rocked on her heels and moaned. After quite a long time she said, "I would like to go there and look for Mother and Grandmother."

"No, daughter."

"Father, I must know."

"Daughter, you would never find them," he said. Then he told her what it had been like down there, about the broken heads, about the faces already eaten off by the birds. "I looked for them as long as I could do it. I did not see them."

She squatted and rocked and shook and wept, and she said nothing more about going down to look.

FOR ANOTHER DAY STONECUTTER AND SWEETGRASS SMOKE LIVED beside the creek, eating nuts and roots and crayfish, turtles and elm bark, a small turkey, moss and puffballs, and finally an opossum that Stonecutter surprised close to the camp early in the morning. He made a Dream Catcher to hang overhead that night, and they slept calmly, deep in leaves piled under the stone outcrop.

The next morning he opened the king's Magic Bundles to show them to her: the leaves of mysterious little marks, the pictures of animals. "Those are the stories of the Alengwyneh people and their animals," he explained as well as he knew how. "This bundle is said to be the story of their god. It is a sacred thing full of the most powerful messages. Someday priests are to come who can look at all these lines of specks and understand the messages. The king himself cannot understand them, it is said, though he pretends to." He thought for a while, then said, "If the Alengwyneh were all killed, and the king with them, then this"—he touched the nearest bundle—"this is all there is of them now. Think of that."

She asked, "What is in the third bundle, Father?"

"It is a thing used to cast spells on one's enemies, they told me," he said, unwrapping the old, old harp. "It is a most sacred thing, that was used long ago only by a great shaman-singer of the Alengwyneh. It seems to be a bow of many strings. I will wrap it up again. To look at it troubles me."

As the day grew warm, such a stench drifted off the killing field that they knew they could not stay this close for another day. So they gathered up the tools and the Magic Bundles, and Stonecutter led the way up over the hillocks toward the southwest, with the hope of getting upwind from the carnage. He had no idea where he was going or what they would do. Everything he had known in the world had changed in one day, and he and his daughter were alone in the world, and it frightened him to think about their tomorrows. So all he could do was walk and walk and hope to get away from the smell of the many deaths, and hope not to cross the path of any of the Lenapeh if they were still in this valley.

This course brought them, within an hour of walking, out of the woods onto the bank of the Beautiful River at a place where it ran southward for a long way before curving westward again.

They were now perhaps a league southwest of the castles, beyond any villages of size, and thus he could hope that the Lenapeh had not invaded this far down. Here there were only fishing camps in the bottomlands, he had heard, and beacon towers on the high bluffs, far apart from each other. He thought that if they could reach a beacon tower somewhere, the soldiers in it would be alive and they could tell him what to do.

They stood at the river's edge, and the wind that blew in their faces did not stink of death, but there was still the smell of smoke—and thus perhaps more danger. Frowning, he led her along the riverside path. After a few hundred paces they emerged from the brush onto still another scene of destruction: wisps of smoke drifting off the charred ruins of a cluster of fishing huts.

He said, "I fear the Lenapeh went the whole length of the river." His dread of the changed world had been growing in him, and now he knew that what he feared was his own ignorance. If there was no one left, who would do all the things he had never had to know? Because he had always been an artisan for the king, he had always been provided for by the castle. He was not a hunter; he knew little about snaring or fishing or fowling, or about the food plants or the medicine plants of the countryside. This was a bountiful land, for those whose spirits remained close to Mother Earth and her creatures. For generations such Euchees had brought the meat and the fish and the birds, the sunflower and maize kernels, the beans and squash, and edible roots and leaves, and those had been prepared for the tables of those who worked with skilled hands for the Alengwyneh. Stonecutter could build walls, make mortar, and shape cornices, but he could not feed himself or make clothes. Everything he had eaten since the day of the battle had been killed or gathered by his daughter, who was so sick and hurt that she could hardly move. If she did not get well, Stonecutter knew he might starve. Soon it would be winter.

He remembered a bear cub the king had owned. For amusement, Alengwyned had kept it in a cage or on a neck chain. After it grew big enough to be troublesome, the king had had it released by the riverside. It had kept coming back to the castle to beg for food, and then to the villages, until it was driven off, and soon thereafter it had been found dead in a thicket, not having known how to take care of itself. Stonecutter realized that he was like that bear, and therein lay his dread. What good was a stonemason if there was nobody to need castles?

While he was looking at the smoldering camp and thinking those forlorn thoughts, Sweetgrass Smoke uttered a small cry and pointed.

Drifting into view from behind a screen of willow came a ship—one of those hide-covered curraghs of the king's trading fleet.

It was not under sail. It was not even being rowed. It was just drifting on the current, going sideways.

But it was not empty. Rather, it was laden with far more people than it was built to carry, so many that its gunwales were low in the water. Stonecutter knew little about ships, but he knew these wicker-frame curraghs sometimes came apart and sank when they were overloaded with stone or lime from the quarries.

Even from this distance he could see that the people crowded in the vessel were Alengwynehs and half-bloods—yellow-hairs, gray-hairs, a few with helmets—but predominantly women. Whoever they were, they were his People, not Lenapeh, and his heart soared. They must be some who had escaped the massacre somehow and had set off in the ship seeking safety on the river!

Now he saw that several coracles, about a dozen of them, were following the ship like ducklings behind a mother duck. They, too, were overloaded, with three and even four in a boat. Some had paddlers, while others were just drifting, and some were strung together with ropes. From this awkward flotilla came a murmuring and chattering of voices, and here and there the shrill crying of a child, in the hush of the cold river breeze.

"Thank our Creator," Stonecutter exclaimed. "We are not all dead!"

Sweetgrass Smoke, clinging to his arm with a shaking hand, said in a voice choked almost to a whisper, "Is Mother there? Grandmother?" Stonecutter, who had already presumed the whole nation dead, had not even thought to hope that. But now he ran down to the very edge of the river, waving and calling toward the vessels. Sweetgrass Smoke waddled painfully after him, lugging the unwieldy bundles and the clanking tools.

At sight of them, the people in the boats began milling and crying out, as if afraid they were being attacked. Then a man's voice, very piercing in tone, called out in the Euchee tongue, "Who are you there?"

"Stonecutter! A mason of the castle! With my daughter! I seek my wife, Moss on the Tree!" As the vessels drifted with the current, he had to stride along the bank to keep abreast. Stonecutter was speaking into the wind, and the people were making too much chatter to hear his words. The vessels were not a hundred yards off, though, and their occupants would recognize him if they knew him. If Moss on the Tree were among them, she would be calling to him.

Now he called out, "Come and take us on! We are your People!"

"What?" called the loud voice from the ship, and Stonecutter repeated his request more loudly. He prayed there were no Lenapeh near enough to hear all this shouting.

"No room for you!" the loud voice called back. "Follow us along!"

And so Stonecutter tried to keep up. For the rest of that day, with Sweetgrass Smoke stumbling and panting behind him, he tried to keep the drifting boats in sight. But when they had to cross creeks and swamps and thickets, the vessels receded farther and farther ahead downstream.

By dusk, gasping and stumbling with fatigue, they reached a place where the river bent westward after its long southerly course, and even in the waning light Stonecutter could see that the beacon tower on the bluff above was in ruins, and that the brush around it had burned; wisps of smoke still curled off the hilltop.

He was more sure that the Lenapeh had indeed ravaged the whole valley from end to end, the entire realm of the Alengwyneh. The ship and coracles had long since vanished from sight, and, as they probably would keep drifting through the night, he all but lost hope of catching up, of even seeing them again.

"We will have to climb on the burnt bluff here," he said, pointing up. "There is no bottomland here. Let me carry those bundles." She relinquished them gladly; her hands were cramping from carrying them all day.

Dusk faded to darkness as they climbed along the ashy bluff. Sweetgrass Smoke hitched along, moaning. She had walked too hard this day and bleeding had resumed, soaking the seat of her dress and drying to a crust on her legs. The evening autumn wind cut sharply at her here on this height, and she squinted and trembled. She wondered how her father could bear the cold wind; he had nothing but a loincloth, and all these days and nights in the autumn chill his skin had been tight over his muscle, and usually covered with gooseflesh.

"Daughter!" His voice came back on the wind. "The ship is at the shore down there! We can get to the people!"

Three bonfires burned close to the water's edge below and downstream. The moored ship was just visible in the edge of the fire glow. Coracles had been carried ashore and overturned to make little shelters, and indeed the little camp looked almost like a village, with the fires in the center.

Sweetgrass Smoke clenched a hand over her heart and listened.

Voices! Her own People's voices! Women's voices!

Stonecutter said, "How foolish to build such big fires! But they will help us find our way down. . . ."

To keep from startling anyone and being attacked by sentries, Stonecutter called down as he helped his daughter descend the bluff through the rustling leaves. He called out his name and that he was from the castle. Several men came cautiously toward him with their spears and clubs, and though he saw no one he knew by name, two were hunters he had seen before. Compared with the rest of them, Stonecutter was a very big man. Because of his stature, perhaps, or his mention of the castle, they approached him politely, with timorous smiles, though they kept their weapons sloped in his direction.

A few people came to look as he and Sweetgrass Smoke limped into the firelight, but most seemed too absorbed in their own miseries to pay much attention. He saw that some were wounded and some had been burned badly on their arms and legs. There seemed to be about a hundred souls here, in their varying states of misery.

So many of them were women, with the Alengwyneh traits: the light hair, the blue or gray eyes, tawny light skin. But there were not many men here with the traits of that race. Some of the armed men were mixed-bloods with auburn hair or blue eyes, but none of the yellow-bearded giant soldiers were in the camp. Hardly anyone wore armor. A few mature women came out to stare at Sweetgrass Smoke or to help her. Her tattered dress was a mass of blood and dirt. The people traipsing alongside were full of questions.

"Is the king dead?"

"What have you there? Is it food?"

"Tools," he said, "and the king's Sacred Bundles."

"His Sacred Bundles!"

"He has the king's Sacred Bundles!"

"Ai-a-haiee!"

"How do you happen to have the bundles, man?"

Suddenly afraid he might be suspected of stealing them, Stonecutter told the truth as he remembered it. "I was working in the Room of the Bundles when the attackers came. When the castle burned, I saved the bundles."

"You were allowed in the Room of the Bundles?" a wide-eyed man exclaimed.

"Yes. I am a king's builder."

"Ah! And is the king dead?"

"That I know not. I did not see him that day. My daughter was bathing him in the morning but he went out."

"Your daughter was his bather!" a woman exclaimed.

More and more people were coming, gathering around them by a bonfire, attracted by the excited talk, and Stonecutter began to feel that these people had no headman among them, and that he himself was being looked up to as someone of importance. A woman behind Sweetgrass Smoke said:

"Your daughter is bloody. Is she in her moon?"

"She was abused by the thegns," Stonecutter replied. "She is hurt inside. She—" He stopped without telling how they had hurt her in the bowels.

"Come, girl," said a woman. "My mother is a healer. She is over here." Sweetgrass Smoke looked up at her father, her eyes sunken and dark with pain and fatigue. She was ready to fall into caring hands.

"Go with them," he told her. He sat down on a driftwood log near the bonfire, laid the bundles and tools by his feet, and warmed his deep-chilled hands and legs. He sighed. "I smell food," he said. "What do you have here?"

"Fish, sunflower root. Rest, Okimeh, and I will bring you some." A yellow-haired woman spoke thus and hurried away, leaving Stonecutter to look after her in surprise. *Okimeh* meant "Our leader." It was the way the Euchee tried to pronounce *King*, and had come to mean "Leader." Stonecutter knew he was no leader. He had never even known an *okimeh*, because the Alengwyneh king had not let the Euchee have their old tribal or clan councils to govern themselves. For generations there had been no leaders but the Alengwyneh kings, and the word *okimeh* was only a remembered word, used by the old storytellers. Still, it was a good word with a strong meaning, and Stonecutter kept hearing it in his head, even though other people kept talking to him. A thin Euchee man with a leather helmet and a bow and quiver squatted before him and said:

"I believe the king to be dead. I saw him at the top of the tower while we were fighting the Lenapeh, and then the tower fell in, with a great fire going up into the sky. He has to be dead, the king does."

"Then perhaps he is," said Stonecutter.

"These other people do not believe it," said the archer. "We all argued about it on the ship. They do not believe the king could be killed. . . ."

"Did you see the king's dead body?" a man nearby said, with mockery in his voice.

"No," the archer said angrily. "I told you, that was such a fire that even bones would burn up. And then at once I was knocked out of my senses. I am surprised to find myself alive this day. I could not be looking for the bones of a king."

"What you are not saying is that you fled," said the mocker.

"Who did not?" retorted the archer.

"The vultures are feeding on those who did not," somebody said. A moment of silence followed, but soon the mocker's voice again came out of the shadows. "No one else saw what you say you saw. Are we to believe what one little man says on the death of the great king?"

Stonecutter did not know whether to believe or not, but he did remember how the castle had looked after the fire, and remembered the burnt bodies, and no living people in the castle.

In any case, he thought with a certain malicious satisfaction, Alengwyned is either dead or a No-person.

The yellow-haired woman came back with a gourd full of food and handed it to him, smiling in a very becoming way and saying, "Eat, Okimeh." She squatted on the ground near his feet, looking up at him, and her ways made him feel strangely strong and important. He picked warm fish and roots out of the broth with his fingers and chewed ravenously, but before the gourd was empty he paused and asked if his daughter had been fed. The yellow-haired woman nodded, and smiled at him. He thought he had seen her before, in the castle.

Stonecutter turned back to the archer and said, "You were fighting the Lenapeh? Will you tell me about that? And what else did you see besides the tower burning and falling? How did the Lenapeh get on the castle island?" He needed to see in his mind some of the great and terrible things that had happened so swiftly to change the world he had lived in. He had seen nothing that day but some Lenapeh warriors in a corridor, and then the long wait among corpses in the Rain Room. He wanted to hear what the archer could tell him about such a great conflict and how it had been to fight in it. He glanced at the pretty, yellow-haired woman and wondered what she had seen, too. And the other man, the mocker.

And everybody here, he thought.

If everybody tells the part he saw of it, then we might understand, and know what to do.

He wanted very much to know, among other questions in his mind, whether the Lenapeh had all gone away. And whether there might be more of the people who had escaped the great killing done by the Lenapehs in the bottomlands where he had seen the countless vultures.

He had a notion then, coming like a voice speaking inside his head, telling him that the things that many people said could be fitted together to make the whole understanding, as blocks and lintels and corbels of stone are fitted together to make a castle. He reached down and picked up the Sacred Bundles.

Stonecutter once had seen the king sitting in the Room of the Bundles with these same leather-covered things on his knees, his eyes closed while some of his thegns talked to him. He had wondered, then, whether the bundles helped the king to hear and understand, through their magic. And so now Stonecutter put the bundles on his lap and said to the archer:

"I ask you: Tell me what you did, and what you saw."

And the yellow-haired woman leaned closer to Stonecutter's leg, as if she were his woman, and said to the archer, "Yes, little soldier. Talk to this *okimeh*. People! Come and listen!"

And as the archer began to tell of the battle, Stonecutter looked curiously at the woman. She was a strong, big-speaking woman, not like his wife, and either she believed that he was an *okimeh*, or for some reason wanted the people to think he was.

"When they called for the archers," the man was saying, "the Lenapeh warriors were already at the wall, trying to climb up . . ."

ONE BY ONE, PEOPLE TOLD STONECUTTER WHAT THEY HAD SEEN. There were some who had escaped because they were away hunting and had come back to see everything afire. Some had been left for dead and crawled out from under corpses when the warriors left. Some had crawled to safety when their burning huts collapsed around them. Many had seen members of their families killed. The Lenapeh had been merciless, everyone agreed.

"But no," said a hunter. "They were Iroquois, the ones I saw." He told of being on the north bank and seeing them running down the path toward the village at dawn. Somebody else said, "Yes, I think they were Iroquois."

Someone said, "But the Lenapeh and the Iroquois are enemies of each other. Would they fight beside each other?" The listeners were confounded, and they all looked to Stonecutter, as if he might have some explanation. After a time, stroking the leather bundles on his lap, he spoke of a notion that somehow had come into his mind:

"Our king . . . he was cruel and haughty. He even named the land for himself, even the mountains that separate the Lenapeh and the Iroquois. Two enemies to each other could have said, 'That king at the Falling Water is a worse danger to us than we are to each other,' and they would have agreed to kill him." He did not know where this idea had come from, but it seemed to answer the question, and the yellow-haired woman at his feet looked up at him with intense eyes and said:

"Our *okimeh* the castle builder understands such things. Listen to him! See, he touches the Sacred Bundles and they tell him! Is that not so, Okimeh?"

He was bewildered again by being called that, but the way this woman looked at him and treated him made him feel strong, and he did seem to be at the center of the people's thinking. He did seem to feel the hum of power where his fingers touched the bundles. His thoughts were floating, and the fire before his eyes grew blurred, and he thought of the bundles and the way they made him feel. Then he jerked. He looked around and everything was as it had been, and he realized that in the warmth of the fire he had fallen asleep; even sitting up with his eyes open he had fallen asleep.

"We should all lie down and sleep," the woman at his feet said; she had seen him doze.

"We should sleep," Stonecutter agreed. "We should get in the boats at the earliest light. The enemy warriors are surely all about in this country. We should kill these fires."

"The *okimeh* is right," said the woman in an earnest tone. "These fires should be out. Why have none of you fools thought of that?"

"If the sentries give any alarm in the night," Stonecutter said, "we should all be ready to get in the ship and coracles and go out on the river. No place else would be safe."

Again the woman said, "The *okimeh* is right. Listen to him!"

Then she laid a hand on his bare thigh and said to him, "Three wounded men died on the ship today and we put them in the water. There is room aboard now for you and your daughter."

The people began banking the fires, and four hunters went out to guard the edges of the camp. As the fire glow diminished, Stonecutter began to feel the chill of the autumn air and remembered that he was virtually naked, as he had been for days. And here there was no niche full of leaves to burrow into with his daughter for warmth.

The yellow-haired woman seemed to know what he was thinking. She said, "Your daughter is warm, and sleeps already. Okimeh, share my robe."

Some of the people who heard her looked down and aside. Stonecutter opened his mouth to tell her that his own wife might still be alive, or that if she was dead, he should be mourning for her. But he did not say it. The world had been wrecked. Nothing remained. He did not believe his wife still lived.

He thought, It was a marriage by law of a kingdom that is no more.

Besides, Stonecutter could hardly even remember his wife. Believing her to be dead, he had tried to make her name silent in his mind, with no echoes.

And, too, there was a power in the eyes and the face of this yellow-haired woman who kept calling him *okimeh* and made him feel like a chief. It seemed to Stonecutter that she was a woman of uncommon force and good sense, and that much of what he would need to know she already knew. So he rose from his place by the fire with the leather bundles, and the people pretended not to see them go off into the shadows together.

While she gathered leaves and willow boughs to cushion their sleeping place at the base of the bluff, Stonecutter shivered in the autumn night air and tried to think of a way to protect the king's Magic Bundles from anyone among these people who might get the notion to steal them. He suddenly had the thought that perhaps this woman wanted to get the bundles. Maybe that was why she had befriended and flattered him. And so now as she got their sleeping place ready, moving in the darkness with a big bison robe a few feet away, with faint moonlight to see by, Stonecutter stood with the Magic Bundles hugged against his chest, and a suspicion of her began to worm its way into the curiosity and desire that she had already aroused in him. Stonecutter was so tired that he did not believe he could think well. He had never trusted his ability to think well even in the best of times, unless the thinking had to do with quarrying and masonry and tools. Now in his weariness nothing seemed very real, and he feared that this was a cunning woman, much wiser than he was; in truth, she seemed more cunning and wise than any of the other people here, and he was a little afraid of her. She seemed to be a woman who might make him do things he did not believe he ought to do, such as sharing a sleeping place with her while he was uncertain about the fate of his wife.

He feared her, but he believed that he needed her. She had brought him food that he had required, and now she was offering him the warmth inside her robe, and it was as if there were no other possible haven of warmth for his cold and exhausted body.

"Come in now, Okimeh," her voice said from the darkness. Awkward, nervous, he obeyed. He put the bundles in a nook between the base of the cliff and the bed of boughs, where one would have to reach or climb over him to get them.

The boughs and leaves rustled as she shifted on them, and he smelled her body, felt the warmth on the air, and knew she was holding the robe open for him.

He got in beside her and she closed the hide around him. She had made a pillow for him of her dress, which was a fine fabric, the kind the women in the castle wore. She was all naked and she pressed close against him. Both he and she were cold, and it was a while before either of them was generating any warmth in the robe. He lay shuddering, breathing her body musk and her breath and the moldering smell of the old bison-hide robe. His heart was beating rapidly and he lay absolutely still, hardly touching her; against his will he kept thinking of Moss on the Tree, who suddenly had returned to his memory, her face vivid.

The woman said, very low, "Lie close, Okimeh, and be warm. You are like the ice in the river in winter. I hope you will not melt away." She chuckled deep in her throat. Elsewhere in the camp there were few voices, except those of children fussing and the soothing voices of their mothers. The fires were down to embers and the only light was from the moon.

"Why do you call me Okimeh?" he asked her at last.

After a moment she said, not whispering, but in a murmur: "Did you not look at these people? Do you not look at yourself? Who else is here who could lead them? You are strong. You know of kings. You know more, and you build. And you have the Magic Bundles of the king. That is why I call you Okimeh. Only you could be their chief and lead them!" By the time she had finished these words, her voice was hissing with excitement. He grew more fearful.

"Lead them?" he said. "Lead them where? And I know nothing more than they know. I have been thinking how little I know."

"That is the best way to start," she said, "knowing that you know nothing. You are like a new field of snow without tracks in it. I will teach you. They will teach you. Listen," she murmured. "Tonight I saw you sit by the fire and listen to us until you knew all about the war, which you had not seen because you were in a cave when it happened. But now you know more about that war than even those who saw it. This is the way of a great *okimeh*!" She rolled slightly toward him on her side and laid her right leg across his thighs. Her breasts were large and soft and warm against his right arm. He was so aware of her now that he could scarcely think. All his sense seemed to be going to his loins, and it was a moment before he became aware that she was talking to him again, her voice soft as the breeze and the flowing river: ". . . seeds as we go down the river," she was saying. "We must stop in the fields and harvest anything the Lenapeh did not destroy. The maize, the beans, the squash. They will keep us alive through the winter, if we get enough. Then we must save all their seeds, and we will plant them next spring, so they will grow. As this mighty thing grows under my leg." She breathed laughter out of her nostrils and quickly reached inside his loincloth. Her touch nearly caused him to ejaculate, and he twitched, recoiling. She sniggered and said, "I think *that* is ready to plant seeds already, in the earth of my belly. Is it ready, Okimeh?" He could only swallow and nod. He was almost afraid of her; she was so much like an attacker. But he wanted desperately now to be inside her, even though his warming body was buzzing with weariness. Her fingers were at work on the knot in his waistband, and their touch made invisible sparks in his skin. The little garment fell loose, and now he was as naked as the woman was, and she seized his part with a strong, callused hand, making him gasp and squirm. "Then you will be our *okimeh*, and I will be your queen?" she murmured.

"You confound me," he said. "I am only a stoneworker. I do not believe that I could be an *okimeh*! I told you, I know little."

She seemed to contract from him, to grow cold, and took her hand away.

"You could be *okimeh*," she said. "If you were, I would be

yours, now and henceforth, and a help to you, as I know of such things as that. But if you were not *okimeh*, no."

Stonecutter wanted her to show desire again. He was afraid that she would grow tired of his doubtings and excuses and put him out in the cold. Exhausted though he was, he did not believe he could sleep until his desire for her was fulfilled. He whispered, in a thick voice, "Come close again. I do need you." He reached for her, but she shrank back, drawing the robe with her until he felt cold air on his back.

"If you say you will be *okimeh* and I will be at your side."

"How can a poor stonemason decide such a thing in a night?" he protested, in a voice almost whining.

"Dare not touch me until you decide."

Suddenly Stonecutter's frustration welled up into anger at this forward and ambitious woman. She had flattered him and lured him into her bed to lie naked with him and fondle him in the most brazen manner, and now she was trying to steer him by desire into something he did not want, and now denying him because he did not want it. In a surge of indignation he thought as he would never have thought before: he could take her anyway. He was very strong. She had enticed and provoked him. And so, with a ferocity that was entirely new to him, Stonecutter pressed a hand over her mouth and crawled upon her. She writhed and grunted. Holding her down with his weight, he forced his knee between her legs, then the other knee. He was wild in his belly and ready to spurt. In this darkness she was a paradise of nakedness.

She yielded. She was opening up like a flower and her hand was again reaching to his groin.

He felt an entirely new kind of exultation. Never before in his life had he won anything he wanted by taking it forcefully; it was like being a king. For the first time he exulted in his manly power and strength of will, and it made him feel so intensely alive that he could scarcely contain himself.

The woman's hand moved along his tingling organ as if to guide it into herself, but then she reached farther under and her hand encircled his scrotum. Her grip grew tighter.

And tighter.

Stonecutter gasped. He tried to roll away off her, but her strong hand twisted his bag and her fingertips separated his testicles and made him afraid to struggle. When he tried to move an arm to strike or choke her, she squeezed still harder and he stopped, helpless, gasping with his mouth open. His brief enjoyment of the feeling of power was gone. She hissed in his ear:

"You will be our *okimeh*."

"I will be," he gasped.

"I will be the queen."

"Ngh! You will be!"

"We will lead these people away from danger, to the other side of the Mother of Rivers, away from all Lenapeh. Do you promise that?"

"Agkh! I do!"

"You will keep this promise?"

"Yes. Yes."

"You will be glad, Okimeh. It is for the good of our people who are the Children of First Man. You will see. . . ."

"Please let go, woman."

"Honor your promise and you will be a great king and I will give you the greatest pleasures and help you every day."

"I . . . I will honor the promise," he groaned, although he did not know how he would feel about the promise after this pain was gone. He would never want to give her a chance to get him this way again.

She released her grip and he rolled off of her onto his back, teeth clenched, eyes rolling. For a while the release of the pain hurt as badly as the grip itself had hurt. He wanted to get his breath and then get up and away from this strange and terrible woman, who was beyond anything he had ever known. But she said now in a warm tone:

"Okimeh, lie with me now. We will keep each other warm. We will talk about what the *okimeh* will need to do."

"Not talk," he muttered, doubly exhausted now by what she had just put him through. "I need to sleep!"

Somebody nearby sighed loudly and said, "Yes. Do sleep!"

"Close your mouth, you!" the woman snapped back. "You are talking to our *okimeh*!"

Stonecutter rubbed his palm over his face and groaned with misery. *Okimeh?* he thought. Did anyone ever become an *okimeh* this way before?

Her hand touched his abdomen, and he nearly jumped out of the robe. But she did not seize him that way again, she stroked his groin and murmured, "Okimeh, I am your queen and I will give you pleasure."

"Be my queen after tomorrow. I hurt too much for pleasure."

She moved closer and her breath smelled like mushrooms. "I can change the pain to pleasure," she whispered.

And she did so, before the moon had set.

In their whisperings afterward, he learned that she had been the wife of a thegn called Gruffyd, for whom she had only contempt. "He was more married to the king than to me. Alengwyned was a shitting dog and Gruffyd was his turd." She did not know whether they were dead, but joyously believed they were.

She told him also that she had seen him often in the castle and had admired him for his strength and dignity. "I have neither now, after what you have done to me," he murmured, and she smiled.

Her grandparents had been Euchees and had named her Singing to Snakes. The grandfather had been a storyteller and singer in the castle, and she remembered most of his stories of the Ancient Days, including their story of First Man, Madoc, who had come from beyond the Great Sunrise Water. "The stories I know are the ones in those Sacred Bundles," she whispered. "Of First Woman being made from the side of First Man. Of a flood over the world, and First Man letting a dove go to search for the land. Of First Man being hung up to die for his people with two others hung up beside him . . . You see, the Creator brought us together in this place! Only *we* have the Story of First Man: you and I! With me beside you, you can truly be *okimeh* for these fleeing people as they seek a safe place to be, a new home, without a cruel shitting dog of a king! And like First Man, we go to that new land in a ship, from the east, do you see? You are the *okimeh* who will be the First Man of these people and I will be First Woman, at your side!"

It was a grand notion to consider as one went to sleep exhausted from days of pain and fatigue and now this great pleasure. He nuzzled close to her, wanting to believe her and knowing he never wanted to be far from Singing to Snakes, his queen. But as he drifted off he did wonder again whether anyone had ever become an *okimeh* this way. It was not something about which an *okimeh* would ever tell anybody.

CHAPTER 14

A Bluff Above the Muddy River
Autumn 1492

Man-Face Boy, whipped by the wind and squinting against the sun, draped the heavy bison hide over his shoulders and took his last instructions from Strong Leg, the Bison Decoy. Strong Leg's hair was white, but not because he was old. He was one of those Pale Ones, the tribe whose ancestors had come to the Mandan people long ago led by the great *okimeh*, Stonecutter. The Pale Ones had joined the People and lived with them, and eventually Stonecutter had become chief of all the Mandans, and Stonecutter's wife, Singing to Snakes, had been the Storyteller and the Keeper of the Bundles.

Of the Pale Ones who had come on that day, the only one still alive now was Sweetgrass Smoke, daughter of that great *okimeh*. Sweetgrass Smoke had lived more than a hundred summers and had been Keeper of the Bundles since the death of Singing to Snakes.

Now on this day of the *pishkun*, when Man-Face Boy was getting ready for the great danger, he was not very much afraid because he knew old Sweetgrass Smoke was praying for his safety; he could *feel* her prayers, even at this great distance from where she was in the village. To be a Bison Decoy was very dangerous, and Sweetgrass Smoke would not let him die doing it because she had chosen him to become the Storyteller and Bundle Keeper when at last her time should come to cross over to the Other Side World.

It was both an honor and a burden for a youth to be selected from among other youths for an important duty, and twice already Man-Face Boy had been selected, even though he had not yet lived fourteen summers. He was going to be a Bison Decoy because he was a superior runner and could think as an animal thinks, as his hunting skills had proven.

And he was going to be Storyteller and Bundle Keeper because the spirits had pointed him out to Sweetgrass Smoke. Since the spirits could see times to come, that assured Man-Face Boy that he would not be killed today in the *pishkun*, as Bison Decoys sometimes were, but would live to do what the spirits had selected him to do.

Now, though, he would have to do the brave thing that Strong Leg expected him to do, which was to help lure the bison herd over the edge of the cliff, where they would fall to death on the rocks of the riverbank below.

"They are almost here," Strong Leg said, pointing to the brow of the hill, over which dust from the moving herd could be seen. Man-Face Boy could smell bison, and also he could feel through his feet on the ground the tread of the herd, which would just now be coming slowly up, stopping to graze now and then but still staying warily ahead of the drivers who were gently herding them toward this bluff. Man-Face Boy could see neither the herd nor the drivers yet, but knew that soon the first of their dark heads and humps would appear beyond the waving grass at the brow of the hill. "Cover yourself now," said Strong Leg, "so they will see not a person but one of their own. Never lose sight of your marker on the cliff. Think like the bison. Pray for him to trust you and follow you. And when you hear the hunter shout, lead the herd to your marked place and go over. I go now to my place," Strong Leg said, drawing his bison hide over his head and stooping. "May Maho Peneta watch over your life, young brother!" he murmured from under the hide, and moved off to his place farther up the bluff. With his legs stained black and the hide's tail swinging, the woolly shoulder-hump hair of the robe high upon his head and its head held low in front of him, Strong Leg did indeed look like an old bull walking away, if one did not count the number of his legs. And of course the real bison would not be counting legs.

And so now alone on the windy hilltop, Man-Face Boy drew his own decoy robe up and made himself look like another old bull, and waited, praying. And in the wind he could hear the sound, though not the words, of Sweetgrass Smoke's prayer for his safety.

After a while the herd appeared upon the bluff, wandering slowly toward him, and some of them looked at him, without suspicion, and grazed, then raised their heads, came closer, and grazed some more. He sent bison-thoughts to them. *I am one of you. Trust me to know which way to run when danger starts you.*

This way. You see there are no two-leggeds over this way, only open space. He did not allow himself to think of the cliff while he was thus praying to them, because it might put the cliff thought in their heads and they would run in another direction, away from the cliff.

Man-Face Boy was wet with sweat in the bison hide, and his arms were burning from holding its shaggy head up in front of him. He had moved within fifteen paces of the edge of the restless herd and now was between them and the cliff, just the place where he needed to be. He could hear them ripping the tough grass with their teeth, could hear their ground snufflings, the bleating of calves, even the splatter of their dung on the ground, and the stamping of their hooves. Looking from under the edge of his hide he could see the legs and hooves of the nearer animals, and was keenly aware of the danger of those hooves.

The herd, numbering more than a hundred, was nervous, aware of the two-leggeds whose smell kept wafting to them from upwind; for days the two-leggeds had been ranging in the distance, their presence not very frightening, but enough to keep the herd drifting toward this place on the bluff. Man-Face Boy, thinking like the bison, could feel the nervousness of the herd.

He was aware, too, of his own nervousness, his profuse sweat, which, if the breeze shifted just a bit, they might smell this close to them and start stampeding back away from the bluff. He had bathed and purified himself in the sweat house, and rinsed in the river and rubbed his body with sage, all to remove his man-smell, but he knew that all this sweating was again making him smell like the two-legged he was, and he prayed that the flow of the breeze would keep the strong smell of the herd coming toward him, instead of carrying his to them.

And so for a time that seemed forever, Man-Face Boy prowled and acted like an old grazing bull between the herd and the cliff, waiting to hear the signal, keeping an eye on the place he had marked at the edge. When a decoy died, it was almost always because he could not find, or reach in time, the place on the edge of the cliff where he would escape. He kept checking it out of the corner of his eye; it was where a cluster of bitterweeds trembled in the wind at the brink of the cliff, dark green bitterweeds fan-shaped and stark against the hazy space beyond. That place was less than a hundred paces from where he now stood; his feet were eager to speed him there the moment he heard the signal shout from the drivers behind the herd. He licked salty sweat off his lips and tried to keep his two-legged's thoughts from getting into the bisons' minds.

I am one of you. Follow me when you get alarmed.

Then: the shout!

And then more shouts, rising into a vibrating howl. The herd tensed and began milling at once, eyes rolling, tails going up, heads tossing. Man-Face Boy, seeing that some of the animals were already swinging toward him, made the voice of a bull, spun, and headed for the clump of bitterweeds. The hide on his back flapped and swung, slapping his legs, and now he could hear the rumble of hooves growing loud behind him. They were coming, following him! Far off to the side he glimpsed Strong Leg running toward his own escape place on the cliff, and behind like a swift dark thundercloud came the stampede. Man-Face Boy's heart seemed to be pounding in his throat now. Fast as he could run, they could run faster. He desired to be far, far ahead of them, but as a decoy he must not get too far ahead or they might veer away and not follow him to the edge. Thistles and sedge whipped his bare legs. His instinct as a two-legged was to fling off the heavy robe, straighten up and run for his life. But it was the bisons' instincts he had to use now, not his own.

His eyes were full of sweat, blurring his vision just when he needed to see clearly. It seemed to him now that the bison were right at his back.

Then he was on the brink. Under his nose there yawned the empty bright air, the yellow-green river far below.

He dove through the bitterweed as he had done in practice, scrambled sideways, let go of the robe, dropped facedown onto a narrow stone ledge just below the lip of the cliff and clung to rock. Straight below him dropped the sheer face of the cliff, and, at its base, treetops of bright green willow. The crag upon which he lay trembled with hoof thunder. The bright sky above him was darkened by great dark bodies hurtling over. Man-Face Boy cringed on his tiny ledge, heartbeat slamming. He was pelted with dirt and rock fragments and shreds of bitterweed, and specked with bison drool. When he looked out and down he saw bulls and cows and calves, slowly turning in air, some head down, some belly up; he saw the dreamlike sight of bison floating down into treetops. At first the leafy trees shuddered and swallowed the bison, but soon all the limbs were broken down and he could see other bison falling onto the ones on the ground. Some lay still; others kicked and twitched and bellowed. Up from below swelled a storm of noise: thumping bodies, cracking trees, clattering rocks, shrieks and mournful bleatings, all lifted to his ears on a rising cloud of dust.

Along the bottomland below he could now see the hunters running in with their lances to kill the ones that had not died at once in the fall, and behind the hunters came the women with their butchering knives, poles, rope, and baskets.

There were no more bison hurtling over him. A few yards below, his decoy robe hung from a snag, swaying in the wind. The sun was on his back. He was alive, high above all the death. The women's voices trilled with joy as they waded in and began the butchering, working naked so their clothes would not be drenched with blood as they harvested Creator's bounty which he, Man-Face Boy, had helped deliver to them. They had days of hard work ahead of them from this: meat to cut, cook, and hang to dry; guts and stomachs to clean for use as waterbags and fat casings; tongues and back fat to cook for tonight's feast of thanks; skins to flense and cure for robes and tent covers and moccasins; hooves and cartilage to process for glue; sinews to dry, pound, and shred for making thread to sew with; bones to crack for marrow, tails for quirts and fly whisks, horns for spoons and ornaments, hair for stuffing, weaving, and padding—everything the People needed was there, and everything would be used. Man-Face Boy lay on his ledge with the sun drying the sweat on his back, and tried to bring the quiver of his limbs under control so he could stand up, thanking Creator for his safety and for letting him serve his People so well. Some of the hunters below were waving up at him and smiling, and he stood up on the ledge and waved back at them. He had done this brave thing well and had been spared from harm for the purposes of old Sweetgrass Smoke, and he felt the old woman's spirit thanking Creator for his life.

A shadow fell over him. He looked up. Strong Leg's figure stood on the lip of the cliff looking down on him, silhouetted against the sun, which gleamed through his white hair. Standing behind him were the many drivers who had herded the bison onto this high place. "Climb up," Strong Leg said in a happy voice, reaching down with his hand to help him. "I shall take you down and show our People a man, and they will give you the bull's skull that you have earned well. Come, Man Face."

He had noticed: Strong Leg had called him not Man-Face Boy, but Man Face.

* * *

THAT NIGHT AFTER THE FEAST, MAN FACE SLEPT VERY DEEPLY FOR a while, being exhausted from the hunt and the dancing. Sometime after the fire had died down to coals, he was awakened. He could hear his parents, brothers, and sisters all breathing in their sleep, and all was calm and dark inside the lodge, but even with his eyes closed he could tell that something was glowing white.

He looked and it was the white skull of the bull bison that had been given to him. In the darkness it was floating and glowing above his bed as a full moon glows, and it began telling him about things of his life, the most important things he could know. It did not tell him in words. Instead, it showed him two visions. They were like dreams, but in them Man Face could not only see but hear and taste and feel and smell.

In one vision he was the First Hunter of the Creation story of his People, being pulled up from under the ground. Light came from a hole above. In the story, First Hunter had climbed vines to reach the light, but the cords that pulled Man Face up were pinned in the flesh of his chest. When he thus rose into the light of the present world, he discovered the four-leggeds, and learned their thoughts and their languages, and how to hunt them.

In the other vision, Man Face was sitting astride the back of a beautiful beast something like *omepah*, the elk, but with no antlers, as the animal ran about with incredible swiftness and power. This Spirit Elk was not afraid of him, but took him where he wished to go, and it felt as if Man Face and the animal were one spirit. The vision ended with lightning, and the dark wings of the Thunder Birds shadowed him, and in the darkness the bison skull faded away like a moon vanishing behind clouds. He slept then, but remembered the visions in the morning, and got up to go and see old Sweetgrass Smoke. She would know about this. He had been shown something from his life farther ahead on the Circle of Time, something both after and before his present time. It was both after and before because everything comes back around.

The sun was just barely up over the hills across the Muddy River, and there was frost on the narrow pathways among the domed lodges of his People's town, but women were already up, working around the timber-pole porches of their lodges, hanging out strips of bison meat to dry in the sunlight, or on their hands and knees flensing fat from bison hides staked out taut on the ground, and those who saw him passing smiled at him and thanked him. He smiled back at them, but hurried on toward the lodge of Sweetgrass Smoke.

The lodges in the Mandan town were so close together within the stone walls that two or three persons abreast could barely pass among them. This was not like the open towns of other tribes on the plains. Sweetgrass Smoke had explained to him that this was the way her father, Okimeh Stonecutter, had built the town to make it safe, with a wall of squared stones to keep enemies out. Only in the center of the town was there an open space of any size. This round plaza was the place for the People's dances and ceremonies. The *okimeh*'s lodge and the shaman's lodge were two whose doors opened onto the plaza, and another was the lodge of Sweetgrass Smoke. In the center of the open place stood the Sacred Canoe, as it was called. It was like an upended hull, but made of riven planks, standing taller than a man, and in it were kept the Magic Bundles of First Man and the sacred relics of the Mandan People. The Sacred Canoe, it was said, represented the vessel in which First Man had crossed the Great Water, and had been made of wood from the ship in which Okimeh Stonecutter had brought the Pale Ones up the Muddy River to this place. The Sacred Canoe was like the hub at the center of the village. When a person approached within an arm's length of it, he could feel the vibrations of its power. No one could enter the Sacred Canoe and touch anything in it except the *okimeh* or the shaman or the Bundle Keeper.

As Man Face passed near it, he felt its power and still could hardly believe that someday he himself would be the Bundle Keeper.

Three tall poles stood in front of the *okimeh*'s lodge, silhouetted against the vast, bright morning sky. At the top of each pole hung a bison hide in the form of a human effigy, the top stuffed and bound in a rounded shape resembling a man's head, decorated with hair and feathers, the rest of the hide flapping below in the breeze like a loose garment. These, according to the teachings of Sweetgrass Smoke, represented the Hanging-Up-to-Die of First Man with lesser men hung up beside him, which had been a glorious and terrible event, countless generations into the past. Two of the hides were ordinary dark ones, but the center one was made from the hide of a Wunestu, or white bison. White bison were very rare; a man might live his life without seeing one. Any white animal was deemed to be the spiritual leader of its kind, and so First Man was represented by the Wunestu's hide. The *okimeh* of the Mandan People would make long journeys to the lands of other tribes to buy a white bison hide, if he heard of one, and would pay much for it—perhaps everything he owned. Then he would make it into the shape of First Man Hanging Up like this, and here it would remain, high in the rain, sun, snow, and howling winds, until it was rotted and ragged.

As the old woman's teachings said, a sacrifice of little value was an insult to the Creator. And, she would say, First Man had been pale as a Wunestu.

Man Face thought of First Man hanging up for the good of his people and then rising to a higher life, and remembered how in the vision he had been hung up and drawn above for the good of the People. Man Face believed he had had the visions at this time because he was coming to see Sweetgrass Smoke this morning.

She was sitting in the light from the smoke hole overhead, already waiting for him, leaning against a backrest of willow and reeds. Her white hair, thick and long, seemed to glow like mist in the beam of daylight from above.

Her eyes glinted within their pockets of wrinkles. Her breathing was full of rasps and gurgles. She signed for him to sit down near her. He saw that beside her the Magic Bundles lay stacked, the three packets of ancient brown leather.

She gave him a sprig of dry sage and a fan made of eagle wing feathers, and pointed at the little mound of embers in her fire pit. Man Face leaned forward, put the sage on the embers and fanned it, and when the white, fragrant smoke rose from it, he scooped toward himself with his hands and bathed his face, chest, arms, and thighs with the smoke. He gave her the fan then, and she slowly swirled smoke onto herself, then watched silently for a while as wisps rose through the light to the smoke hole.

She was quiet for a long while, just a small bundle of bones and wrinkles and breathing noises, but her silence was like prayer and he felt strength from it. Finally, she said in a voice as dry as rustling leaves: "You did well on the *pishkun*. They all speak of you. My heart is glad because you are safe."

"Grandmother, I thank you for your prayers. I felt them."

"Yes. They were strong."

"I have come to tell you what I saw in the night. Two stories were shown to me by the skull of the bison bull. They were stories in which I moved. The first was one of the stories of our People in the Beginning Time." Then he told her, carefully remembering every detail, the vision of being pulled up from under the ground. As he told it, he almost felt that he was in the vision again, because the inside of the lodge with daylight shining down was so much like the underground place from which he had risen, or the cave from which First Man had risen after death in that other story, and the smell of the earthen floor here was the smell of underground.

"Yes," the old woman said. "Yes, that is the way the People came into this world, long even before the flood. They climbed toward the light and got through the hole into this world. That is how it still is, to be born into this world. They climbed, one by one, until a great fat woman tried to climb up, and she broke the vines when she fell, so the rest could not come up. They are still down there. When we lay our heads down to sleep, they try to talk to us through the earth, and their words come into our dreams and tell us things they know."

"In the vision," Man Face went on, "I did not climb the vines with my hands. I was hung on them, and was drawn up by a power."

The old woman started, and her eyes glittered. "How were you hung up? Was it by sharp things through your flesh?"

"It was!" He was always amazed that she could know details of his dreams and thoughts.

She took several deep, gurgly breaths, slowly shaking her head. "That is how First Man was hung up, with sharp things through his flesh. Did you feel the pain of that?"

He thought of how to answer, remembering. "I *knew* of the pain, but was above it."

There followed another long time with no words. Finally, she asked, "What do you think will come of what you saw? There is one true answer."

He said, "It is a thing I will do. I was shown it, by the skull, and so it will happen."

"That is the true meaning," Sweetgrass Smoke said. "So it will be. You will hang up like First Man." After a thoughtful time she raised a hand, which looked like a rough-barked branch with twigs. She said, "First Man died by being hung up by his flesh, though he was stronger than any man. Do you believe you will die, being hung up?"

"In the vision I did not die. So I believe I am not to die from it."

"That is so, and that is good, for you are to keep the Sacred Bundles for the People." She moved her tongue inside her mouth, across her toothless gums, then said, "You told me the skull told you two stories."

"Here is the other one, old Grandmother." When he told her of sitting on the back of the Spirit Elk, she put a hand on her breastbone and breathed so hard she was almost panting. Afterward, she sat for a long time looking up at the light, her eyes very bright and glittery; by this he could tell that she was very moved, even though her face was so full of deep wrinkles that one could hardly read any expressions.

Her voice came then, like a rustling: "Have I opened the Sacred Bundles for you before and showed you the insides?"

"No, old Grandmother."

"Oh. Oh, oh!" She rocked back and forth. "It shows me I was not wrong when I saw you as the Bundle Keeper! Yes, the spirits said it is to be you, and there is no doubt of it!" Never had Man Face seen anyone of great age so full of shining spirit. "Now," she said, "I can open the bundles to you, because of what you saw in your dreaming!"

His heart raced the way it had while he was decoying the bison herd. He swallowed and breathed hard as the Very Oldest Grandmother reached to her side and picked up one of the leather bundles. It was heavy-looking and she was frail, but she picked it up so easily he thought it must be empty—or perhaps was full of light spirit that made it float.

"Untie that and fold it open," she said, placing it in his hands. To his surprise, it was heavy as a stone. "You will find leaves, many leaves one on another," she said. "Open it where a ribbon passes between the leaves."

He opened it as she had said, and a musty odor came up.

He gasped at what he saw: it was his dream-vision!

It was a picture of a man riding on the back of an animal like *omepah*, the elk. He stared at it, heart racing, and remembered how it had been in the vision. He pointed at it and said, "I sat like that upon it! It means it will happen! There are such beasts, and they will come here! They will let us ride upon their backs! Is that not so, old Grandmother?"

"Everything says it will be so. Now, fold it the way it was. There is much more in that bundle and you will come to know it very well, but you have seen what you were meant to see this day. Give it to me and open this one."

The second bundle was also very heavy, but from it he felt strength going up his arms. "Look inside," she said. "I shall try to tell you about what you will see."

He opened the cover. The inside was flat and smooth and light, the color of fine tanned doeskin, with darkening edges and brown spots. "They are like the leaves in this one, too. Fold back another." He began turning the pages, amazed at their thinness. Then on one he saw a beautiful design, such as the Mandan women sometimes made with quills and their blue beads, but not a picture of anything like the Spirit Elk. She signed him to turn more, and then he found himself looking at lines and lines of tiny marks, each as small as a gnat. There were so many of the marks and lines of marks that they seemed to shimmer and vibrate as his unaccustomed eyes stared at them. Quickly he leafed over more pages, afraid that too much staring at any one place would be bad medicine in his head.

Finally he looked in bewilderment at Sweetgrass Smoke.

"Those marks are . . . words," she began, trying to explain in her dry old voice. "They are like . . . pictures of words. The people called . . . ah . . . Alengwyneh, long ago they knew how to look at those marks and speak the words. Many of the words spoken one after another would . . . would sound like a story. It is a magic, but the magic is lost now; no people can do it. But the words"—she pointed a gnarled finger at a page—"the words are still there. A person who knew the magic could look at them and tell the story. Even if he had never heard it before!"

Man Face could only gape in amazement at the old woman, then at a page crowded with the little marks, then back to her. There were many kinds of magic in the world, and he had tried to think on some of them, but this was not like any of the kinds of magics he had heard of.

She continued, "The magic marks you hold are said to be the story of the Alengwyneh People before they came across the flood to this land. . . . It is said to be their story of Creator making the world . . . and of Okee-hee-dee the Evil God . . . of God's son First Man, who was born from no man's seed in his mother's belly. . . . it tells of the Flood. . . ." She paused, tired.

"But Grandmother," Man Face exclaimed. "*You* tell those stories to us! How can you do that, if you do not know the magic of these words?" It was known that she had much power and wisdom, much knowledge of the Pale Ones from the east, that she had even lain with a *maho peneta okimeh* of the old Giant Race, who were all dead now. "You must have the magic of the words, or you could not—"

But she shook her head slowly.

"I know the stories only by my ears. The old storyteller and Bundle Keeper, Singing to Snakes, who was a wife of my father

Stonecutter . . . she died before you were born . . . Singing to Snakes knew the stories. . . ."

"Then did Singing to Snakes have the magic of these little word marks?"

"Not even she. Nor her grandfather, a Euchee storyteller who taught her the stories. . . .

"She told me that the magic of those marks was lost even before her grandfather's grandfathers. Only the Alengwyneh ever had that magic in this land, but they lost it. . . . I am so sad." She rested her mind again awhile. Outside, women were still talking happily as they worked with meat and skins, and there were voices of children, cheerful as birdcalls, but all those voices were faint, muffled by the thick clay walls and dome of the lodge. Sweetgrass Smoke began speaking again:

"You have looked at that bundle and you hear no words. I have looked at it for my whole lifetime as a woman and sometimes I think I hear a word, but no. It is a lost power, one of the bad things that happen to a People . . . like grasshoppers eating all the crops . . . or grass fires that burn them up, or years when the bison never come near. There have been whole tribes dead of illness spirits. This is like that, a loss. When you are the Bundle Keeper, you may look at the words as long as you want, and if the words come to your ears, you will be very great. . . . But Singing to Snakes said that there is only one way the words will ever be understood again."

"How, old Grandmother?" Man Face was tingling with wonderment over all this.

"Only if other Pale Ones come from beyond the Sunrise Water. If they have not forgotten the magic of the marked words, they could look at these leaves and tell the stories." She sighed. "Oh, I am tired."

Man Face brightened suddenly, sitting up very straight and saying, "Ah, old Grandmother! Do not be sad about the loss! Listen: the Pale Ones will come, and then they can give us back the magic of the marked words! And they will come! They will come in my lifetime! We already know that to be true!"

She looked at him very hard, squinting so that her eyes were lost in wrinkled skin. "How do we know that?"

"The Spirit Elk!" he said. "Are not the Spirit Elk from that land? I saw that I shall sit on the back of a Spirit Elk, which they must bring! And that will happen. And when I meet them to get upon the Spirit Elk, I will show them the bundle and ask them, Say me these stories!"

After that she sat for a while wordless but seeming to glow, and once she made more sage smoke and fanned it over the bundles. "What you saw in the night will be important for the People. What is in these bundles is important. It is connected. You must always think of it and try to understand more of its meaning." He was already thinking of it; he was in a trance of thinking about it. It was all such a marvel in his mind that he had forgotten yesterday, he had forgotten all about decoying the herd over the cliff. Great as that had been, it now seemed like something of a long ago and lesser time.

Then he felt something in his hands. He saw that she had given the third of the Sacred Bundles to him.

Inside the hard leather case was something wrapped in a soft-cured deer hide and tied with thongs. He untied them and undraped a thing such as he had never seen before.

It was light in weight, made of polished, dark wood, two sides curved in a way that reminded him of bows, the third side wide but hollow. The bent wood sides were fastened with what appeared to be a row of bowstrings. He turned it this way and that in the light. It was a beautiful thing, and gave his hands the same feel of a well-carved weapon or toy, but he could not understand what it was for, unless it might be perhaps to shoot many little arrows at once. It felt strong, but at the same time light and delicate. He tapped the hollow side and it sounded like a gourd or a turtle shell, but gave off as well a strange tone, almost like a woman's voice calling from a distance. He tapped it again and heard the little voice again. The hair stood on the back of his neck. He looked at Sweetgrass Smoke. She smiled at him, a caved-in, toothless, but sweet smile, and then reached out with one hand and lightly drew her fingernails across the strings. The stillness inside the lodge suddenly was full of sweet voices, some as deep as a man's, some as high as birdcalls. They reverberated and echoed, like singing, and grew fainter until they lingered in his soul.

He exclaimed, "I never heard such a noise! May I hear it again?"

"Draw your finger ends across," she said, "but softly, for the strings are like sinew, very old. I have broken three by trying to tighten them."

He ran his fingers all the way across, making all the voices. But they were really not so much like voices as he had first thought; they were like both a voice and a drumbeat together. "May I touch one at a time?"

"With care."

He stroked one at a time, starting with long ones with their deep thrum, and ending at the short plinking ones. No string broke, for which he was grateful. "This thing is made only for the noise it gives, then?"

"I believe it to be," she said. "Singing to Snakes knew of this thing, and could make it sing. She said the Pale Ones in the great building where they lived would stroke it to add the sound to their voices when they sang. But only at sacred times. It is a sacred thing, this sound maker. Now, we must wrap it and let it sleep awhile."

"Old Grandmother," he said after a while, his heart feeling so swollen he had to swallow it down, "I have never known of such things. I have never had such a day. I will use my life trying to understand all this!"

"Man Face," she said, "I have waited many seasons for you. I should have crossed over long ago. A generation has come and grown since I was ready to cross over, but I have had to wait for you to be born, and to become a man. When you have done the Hanging Up that you must do, and I have taught you what I know about all these, then you will be ready to take the Sacred Bundles, and perhaps you will do more than I did with them. Then the spirits will allow me to cross over at last. Oh, I am ready!"

OLD SWEETGRASS SMOKE WAS TRULY READY TO CROSS OVER TO THE Other Side World. She could no longer sit up and was tired of the trouble and the effort of breathing. They had made a lying place for her in the shaman's lodge so she could be present at the ceremonies for Nu-mohk-muhk-a-nah, First Man. Each year First Man visited the town and asked for sacrifices to prevent another Flood. Outside the shaman's lodge the drums pounded and the People yipped and cheered all the dancing and pageantry around the Sacred Canoe, and Sweetgrass Smoke knew from every change in the drumbeats and voices just what was happening at any moment, because she had lived through more First Man festivals than anybody. But her remaining spirit was concentrated on the bright, blurred vision of the young man hanging halfway between ceiling and floor, all agleam with sweat and blood in the daylight from above. Man Face had been hanging there in silent agony for a long time, and the Very Oldest Grandmother believed that she had to stay on This Side until she knew he would live to be the Keeper of the Bundles. If he did not survive, then she would have to keep on living and keep on keeping the bundles until another person like Man Face was found and trained. And there just seemed to be no hope of that. Everything showed that Man Face was the chosen one.

Sweetgrass Smoke could only watch him and pour prayer into him and keep him in This World so that she could go to the Other. And so she was passing the remainder of her life into him, that was what she was doing. She had prayed and kept him alive on that day when he was a Bison Decoy for the first time, on a cliff far up the river beyond sight. Now at least she could see the precious life for whom she was praying, although the prayers still had to travel as far beyond as they had had to then. The circle of elders and shamans sitting below Man Face were looking up at him and praying for his life, too, and keeping the prayer smoke fire alive.

Sweetgrass Smoke tried not to let this become a selfish prayer, not just for release at last from her worn-out old body. She understood that this was a miraculous and holy thing happening here, that Man Face was becoming a person of the greatest sort of medicine, and that nothing would ever be the same in this Nation of People again. Man Face was giving the People an inspiration that would never be forgotten as long as they were a People.

She was seeing across time. She was seeing First Man suffering for all other men to make them better. And she was seeing even farther back, all the way to the Beginning, when First Hunter had been drawn up by vines from Under the Ground to lead the People into their creation upon this earth. She could see the vines upon which he hung, and the others below here in the cavelike gloom waiting for him to ascend.

Sweetgrass Smoke had lived long enough and seen the ways of men—she had outlived three husbands—that she was sure she would be the last as well as the first woman to witness this miracle. There would be repetitions of this ceremony for as long as the Children of First Man existed as a People. But the shaman had forbidden Man Face's mother to come in and see it, and the other women Elders, and so Sweetgrass Smoke knew that this would, like so many of the sacred things, become a thing of the men only. The women's part in it would be outside and around it, with all the work of it falling to them. It always happened that way. She had seen it over and over, from the time she was living in the green woods at the Falling Water Place, to the time when her father Stonecutter had become the *okimeh* of these people;

and Singing to Snakes, who had all the magic and all the wisdom that made him a great *okimeh*, stayed in the shadows around the edges and invisibly guided him. We women are the real power of life, she thought, and the men know that and are afraid of it, and so they take all the ceremonies into their own circles and keep us out in the shadows. . . .

But her mind had been wandering from the concentration of her prayer, and she was frightened that she would fail Man Face.

At that moment came a noise that sounded like one of the long strings breaking on the instrument in the Magic Bundle. The hanging figure lurched down, spun and bounced while the circle of men cried out, and then there was another of the dull breaking sounds, and the body of Man Face fell to the floor all asprawl and the ropes with their bloody skewers were dangling and dancing above, having at last torn through Man Face's taut flesh and released him.

She gave up a great, long sigh. Surely he must have died, as First Man himself had died from Hanging Up.

The men were all agitated, crying out, jumping up and moving around the fallen figure, and she could not see him anymore because men were in the way, as men always were, shutting woman's eyes from the center. The ropes with their bloodstained skewers kept swinging, in the light up among the cobwebs. The Very Oldest Grandmother could just barely see those, and only those, but she dared not close her eyes, afraid she might just forget to try to breathe, and drift off to the ease of the Other Side World. But she could not keep them open; they stung with tears, even though she thought her tears should have dried up long ago like all the rest of her.

"Beloved Grandmother," said a faint voice. She opened her eyes.

Man Face, or his spirit, stood at the end of her bed, gaunt, pallid, and yellow-skinned, streaked with his own gore. The torn flesh of his chest and shoulders still seeped fresh crimson. He looked so spent that the meat of his body seemed to hang between his bones. But in the dark, deep, and pain-tortured sockets his eyes glowed with a great, calm depth, and she knew he had seen beyond the sky.

"Now you may go on up," he said in a voice like the wind over the plains, "as you have been waiting to do. It is more beautiful than you could dream of, and you can see to the limits of the earth, and into the seas beyond. The big wing-boats from the other land are coming, as I said they would; I saw three of them far in the southeast, and someday they will reach us, bringing the people who can teach us to understand the Marking Language again. I will take the bundles and seek them, and try to learn that language from them. And from them I shall get a Spirit Elk and it will carry me upon its back. It is all as I was shown. I am here and I will keep the bundles well. Go on up."

In the Mandan tongue there was no word for farewell. She released her last breath and passed through the great warmth and light that surrounded Man Face. Her hands were young and strong again, and no longer full of pain, and with them she climbed the vines, up out of the darkness, more like swimming than climbing, into a brightness like the sun. She was like her name, like smoke going up. Like smoke she drifted and rose and dispersed into all the other smoke that had ever gone up.

When she looked far down and back to the village where she had last lived, there outside the stone wall she saw a scaffold in the Town of the Dead, and she knew that the little old body that had been hers was the one wrapped and sewn into a fresh bison hide and lying on that scaffold, her body's burial place. And Man Face, Keeper of the Bundles, with fresh scars on his chest and shoulders, was standing by the scaffold, looking up at the little swaddled bundle of bones. She could feel him praying her name.

Man Face, looking up at the silhouette of the wrapped body against the bright blue sky and remembering the Very Oldest Grandmother, detected in the sharp winter wind the faintest trace of the odor of burning sweetgrass, and he smiled.

"*Shu-su,*" he said. Good.

CHAPTER 15

In the Valley of the Mother of Rivers
Autumn 1541

There was smoke ahead, and Man Face was sure it would be them.

In the forty years that Man Face had been the *maho okimeh* of the Children of First Man, he had done many great deeds. Several times he had saved his People from defeat by the Pawnee, but eventually had led them to establish new villages farther up the Muddy River, away from those enemies. On that migration they had carried with them the bones of Sweetgrass Smoke, the first to go into the cemetery at the new site. Man Face now stood in the prow of his canoe far, far down the rivers from his People and peered ahead at the smoke rising from the shore of the Mother of Rivers, and he was sure that this he was about to do would be the greatest and most original deed he had ever done—even more important than inventing the Okeepah, or Hanging Up.

His eagerness had risen almost to an ecstasy. He was sure that the smoke rising from the shore ahead was the camp of the men who wore metal and rode animals, the men who could speak the Marking Language, the men who had crossed the Great Water in boats with wings: all those great things from his own visions. He had dreamed of these men all his adult life, and in search of them had traveled farther than any *okimeh* of his People had ever traveled except First Man himself, even through the lands of hostile peoples. Now the objects of his visions were no more than an arrow flight ahead! The paddlers in his long cottonwood dugout were tense with eagerness, too, for he had told them over and over about the importance of this meeting. "They are our brothers!" he had told them. "They are from the old land east of the Great Water, and that is where our own ancestor First Man came from!"

One year ago in his village far up the Muddy River, Man Face had begun hearing rumors of the presence of the men who rode on animals. Traders coming up the river to the Mandans had said such men were in the southeast.

The stories of these men were frightening and hard to believe. The traders said the men had more than two hundred of the riding beasts, as well as a herd of noisy short-legged animals that they slaughtered for meat as they went along, so that they did not have to stop long anywhere to hunt game. It was said that they had big dogs that were trained to tear apart people who resisted them or tried to flee from them. It was said that they wore metal shells on their bodies and heads that could deflect arrows, and that they shone like gods in the sunlight. They were frightful and terrible men, who enslaved the tribes and raped their women.

Those were the rumors spoken about them. But, frightening as the rumors were, each one after the other had excited Man Face more, because each made him more certain that they were the descendants of First Man's relatives in the far land. Sweetgrass Smoke had told him that the Alengwyneh at the Falling Water Place had worn such metal coats and hats. She had told him that they subdued and enslaved people, and that they forced themselves cruelly upon the native women; she herself had been assaulted by the Alengwyneh men when she was a girl—even by their *maho okimeh*, whom they had called King.

And the picture in the Sacred Bundle of a man from beyond the Great Water riding on an animal's back had looked just like what the traders described: a man in a metal coat and hat boldly riding the spirited animal. Yes, Man Face had thought, they are the ones!

The stories the traders told said that these men caused great trouble wherever they went, that they tried to force the tribes everywhere to worship their cruel god, and that they carried a kind of thunder with them that could kill people at a distance. Man Face as yet had no idea what that was, as Sweetgrass Smoke had never mentioned it. But he was not afraid of it, because he believed that those riding men would recognize him at once as a brother. The reason he trusted in that was because of one more thing the traders had said:

The riding men always carried before them a pole with an image of a hanging-up man on top of it!

And so now as Man Face stood in the prow of his long canoe, he stood under the pole from his lodge with the white bison hide hanging on it, representing the Hanging Up of First Man. They would recognize him the moment they first saw his canoe. Man Face firmly believed by now that these riding men had come across the Great Sunrise Water to find his long lost people who had sailed away from their country so long ago.

In just a few moments now it would happen, that long-awaited reunion between the riding men and the Children of First Man. Man Face could already foresee how it would happen, and he was fully prepared. The riding men would see his canoe coming ashore with First Man on a pole hanging high. Their *maho okimeh* would come riding forth on the back of his prancing beast, both beast and man smiling with friendliness. They would greet each other and their languages would be much alike; although the Alengwyneh language of the Pale Ones had become mixed with the old Mandan language in the last four or five generations, the riding men's chief would hear at once that this was not just another headman of another native tribe speaking, but a descendant of First Man. Then the *maho okimeh* of the riding men would take Man Face to eat in his lodge, and after that, Man Face would hand forth the Sacred Bundles and ask the other *okimeh* to teach him how to understand the Marking Language. And the other *okimeh* then would offer Man Face a chance to get upon the back of one of the Spirit Elks and ride it about, just as he had seen in his vision half a hundred years ago. Man Face was more than sixty summers of age now, and his hair was white, but he was still strong and limber and knew he would do well on the animal's back, because he had thought of it and dreamed of it so often through his life that he felt as if he were already familiar with it. He had never quite been able to visualize how one would get upon the animal's back, but he would be able to observe whatever trick the riding men used to get up, and he probably would not even have to embarrass himself by asking.

Man Face had dressed in his finest quilled tunic and leggings for this great meeting, and wore upon his head a cap made from the woolly forehead hair of a bison with its pair of horns sticking out on the sides and crested with the eagle feathers he had won for his many fights with the Pawnee and Dah-koh-tah and Arikara and other enemies. Such clothing from the windy plains was really far too hot to be worn on such a damp, hot day this far south, but this was the way a *maho okimeh* of the Children of First Man looked, and he was going to present himself proudly this way on such a sacred day. And so he wore his garb now, and perspired, constantly squinting his eyes shut against the stinging sweat that streamed down his face.

Now, standing proud in the prow of the dugout with his right hand gripping the pole of First Man Hanging Up, he pointed with his other hand to a clearing in the woods of the shore where the ground was covered with something yellow and gray, like wood chips. He presumed this was the landing place of the riding men's camp, because canoes were coming and going from there, both bark ones and dugouts, with men, women, and children of the river tribes in them, southern people who were almost naked and very brown. Those people looked with curiosity as Man Face's long dugout approached, and exclaimed and pointed. Probably those people were descended from the old enemies of First Man. But Man Face stood with his greatest dignity and ignored them.

He searched the riverbank for his first sight of the *okimeh* of the riding men. He heard knocking sounds, like drums.

But what he saw on the shore was disappointing and confusing. The yellow material on the shore was indeed wood chips. Onshore among the canoes were some new wooden boats of large size, and some still being made. The beating sounds Man Face had heard were not drums, but cutting and hammering tools being used on the boats. Most of the boat makers were southern tribesmen with short black hair, clad only in shreds of skin or cloth, very dirty and wretched-looking. Among them there were a few strange and ferocious-looking men whose faces and bodies were hairy. They were half clad in ragged clothes of remarkable dirtiness. Some of these strange men were using tools, but others held lances and long shafts with points and blades that seemed to be weapons. These men looked angry and seemed to have a bad darkness in their faces that made Man Face think of Okee-hee-dee, the Evil Spirit. Such faces he had not expected, and he had difficulty maintaining the dignified and kindly expression on his own face, especially when they noticed his approach and craned around to glower at him. In the faces of his own People, or even the other tribes he had fought, he had never seen such a look of meanness. It gave him a cold feeling even in this steaming swelter. These, he hoped, were not the true riding men. The one pictured in the bundle was not hairy-faced.

His long canoe nosed in to shore. It bumped bottom harder than Man Face had expected, and if he had not been holding onto the White Robe Pole, he might have pitched face first into the shallows. He straightened up quickly for the sake of his dignity, but some of the mean-looking men had seen him tottering, and uttered derisive, harsh laughs like the barking of dogs. Man Face's warriors muttered angrily and grew tense, but he calmed them with a motion of his left hand, and with a step very light for a man of more than sixty winters, he sprang ashore onto the shavings and glanced pleasantly at them. He turned then, grasped the White Robe Pole with both hands and lifted it out of the hole where it had been braced. It was top-heavy and unwieldy with the big robe hanging high on it, and required much of his arms' strength to keep erect. Taking a few steps up the bank, Man Face then stopped and rested the butt of the pole on the ground. Dogs with floppy ears, and deer-sized dogs with standing ears like those of wolves, were prowling, panting, scratching with their hind legs, or lying asleep everywhere, but a dozen or so came slinking forth with ears back to appraise the scent of Man Face, and he was wary of them; he had never seen such large dogs, not even in the pictures in the Magic Bundle.

Man Face stood still, looking around, as his warriors debarked and pulled the canoes ashore, and he was annoyed that no *okimeh* had come forth to greet him, and that the filthy men just stood insolently frowning at him without giving the least sign of recognition to the First Man Hanging Up on his pole. Surely, he thought again, these are not the great riding men, the relatives of First Man!

When his warriors were all ashore and standing tall behind him with their decorated lances and shields and bows, Man Face raised his left hand high and said in a strong, clear voice:

"We standing here are Si-poska-nu-Maq-Muk, the Children of First Man. We came to this land hundreds of winters ago, and we are the People you seek. Now we have found you instead!" The filthy men up on the bank just looked at each other and scratched, smirked, and shrugged, pretending, perhaps, that they did not understand him, even though he believed they must know the same tongue, for they, too, he believed, had come from across the Great Sunrise Water. He resumed his words:

"My name is Man Face. My People, the Children of First Man, chose me to be their *maho okima*. When I was a young man, I was a nimble and fleet Bison Decoy, and they agreed, too, that I should be the Keeper of the Magic Bundles of Maq-Muk, which you see here!" He turned aside and pointed to the three leather packages, which were being held by a gray-eyed young warrior whose black hair was oiled and slicked back to hang to his heels. "These Magic Bundles," Man Face said, still searching the mean faces impatiently for a sign of courtesy or understanding, "these Magic Bundles will prove to you that we are your brothers from the land you come from, as I have told you. Here above me is Maq-Muk, the First Man, Hanging Up as he did to die for the good of all his children. I, Man Face, was the first man since he died to hang myself up like that for the good of all the People! Now, many of our young men do it each year. You see that all these with me have the scars, which prove that they are above pain because they have hung themselves up." He pointed around at their scarred chests, which the strange men eyed curiously.

Again Man Face paused and waited for a response, but the dirty men showed no comprehension. One of them was picking his nose, one scratching his crotch, others turning back to work with their hammers and adzes on the big boats. The tangy smell of green cut wood was strong in the air, very fresh compared with the stench of their dirty bodies. Somewhere in the distance there was one of the thunderclaps that had mystified Man Face and his warriors since the day before, those isolated thunderclaps under a clear sky, the echoes rolling: the thunder that these People from beyond the Sunrise Winter were said to carry with them.

Man Face, now having to control his irritation at the discourtesy of these people, said:

"Tell me which of you is *okimeh*! We came far to find you, so you can cease your search for us. We came to learn to speak again the God-words pictured in the Magic Bundles. And I came to ride on the back of one of your friendly beasts. . . ." He told the youth behind him to open the picture bundle. Soon the young man was holding it open, and Man Face looked at the nearest man and put his finger on a picture. The man edged closer, clawing at his armpit, head tilted, squinting at the picture. He smelled like long-dead meat and old urine. He raised his eyebrows, then grunted, and said, not to Man Face, but to his own men:

"Hnh! Es caballo . . . jinete. Hnh!"

Man Face was disappointed by those words. Did not these men from across the Great Water speak the tongue from across the Great Water? Some of the other dirty men were edging closer to look at the picture of the man on the back of the beast, and Man Face then put his finger on the page of text, asking:

"Can you look at these pictures of words and say them? You must teach us! That is a matter of greatest importance to us!"

"Es libro," the nearest man remarked to the others. They looked at each other, then, with bored eyes and pursed lips, looked at Man Face. They began to inspect his clothing and ornamentation, the clean, soft leather, the intricate quillwork. They began to crowd around his clean-limbed, proud-standing warriors, peering most intently at their bows, lances, and war clubs. These men seemed to care nothing about the Sacred Bundle or even the pole with First Man Hanging Up, but only for the weapons.

"Far Eyes," Man Face said to one of his young chieftains, "let us see if these men know the language of the hands." Far Eyes came forward and stood close beside Man Face. "Ask them where is their *okimeh.*" The young man rotated his hand in a circle. Then he closed his fist and extended his thumb toward the men. Then he extended his forefinger and brought it forward in a high arc, to end pointed down. Then with his palm up, he flicked up his first three fingers several times to show "fire," and finally brought the hand back to his right shoulder. It meant, "Is the fire of your chief near?"

The white men had watched this with leering amusement. Then the closest one made his left hand into a loose fist, stuck his right forefinger into it and jabbed several times, while his companions laughed hard and slapped their legs. Man Face's eyes went hard and narrow; his lips shut in a firm line. They were mocking his earnest effort to speak to them of important things. To Far Eyes he said, "You had better get your weapons. Thank you for trying."

When the hairy-faced men saw the young warrior turn and pick up his weapons, they jabbered in alarm and edged back a few paces, and some put their hands on the hilts of their knives. One turned and shouted, *"Soldados! Soldados! Peligro! Vengan aquí!"* The others kept backing away, some drawing their knives. Some, with their long pikes, came slowly out from among the hull frames and woodpiles, tentatively brandishing the weapons, but looking back over their shoulders. The workmen in the boats were holding their tools like weapons and taking up the shouts of alarm.

Man Face tried to calm the hairy-faced men. He handed the Sacred Pole off to a warrior and stepped toward the nearer hairy-faces, holding both hands before him with the forefingers laid alongside each other, pointed up, signing friendship. This sign did not calm them at all; they seemed not to know this language, either. Man Face felt desperation. He did not want this long, searching, sacred mission to collapse into pointless bloodshed just because of the stupidity of these men. Man Face was not afraid of fighting, but he was desperately afraid that this would end as a fight and the wonderful questions would never be answered. He was almost afraid to make a hand signal of any kind for fear that it would be mistaken for a hostile move by these fearful, ill-mannered strangers.

He was thinking of getting his warriors back into the canoes and staying just offshore until some way of talking could be established. He turned and took the Sacred Pole from the warrior who had been holding it, and as he did so, he became aware of a sound he had not heard since the buffalo hunts: the beating of hooves. He heard them, and he felt the ground trembling. And he heard rattlings and jingling sounds, and shoutings, all growing close.

Man Face knew, even before he turned, what he would see there, and his heart began racing.

What he saw was the most splendid vision his living eyes had ever beheld; only his dreaming eyes had seen this before, and they had seen it just exactly like this. Yes, here came the great, powerful, beautiful beasts, prancing in among the boat builders, and each beast had a shining man on its back. Man Face could hardly think fast enough to perceive all this. In his life he had learned that when a vision from the dream eyes comes before the real eyes, it becomes smaller and less colorful than before. Now this was not so. Even as he looked with his real eyes, his dream had to grow to meet the splendor that now swirled before him.

The beasts were much taller than in his dreams; the men sitting on them seemed to have their heads in the treetops. The beasts had a kind of dancing grace in their movements that even the elks and forked horns did not have. Their eyes flashed and sparkled with spirit, pride, and sweetness; in an instant Man Face knew certainly that somewhere in the long journey of his soul he had looked into the eyes of such animals and they had gazed back into his eyes with love. Man Face also had not expected the riding beasts to be of so many colors. In the hunter's world, all the animals of a kind were colored alike and marked alike. But some of these were tan, and some were dark as bison, some the color of smoke-cured deer hide, some as silvery as the hair on an old man's head, some were speckled with colors.

The men riding on the backs of these magnificent creatures seemed splendid and warlike. Here again Man Face's dream vision had to expand, because the men were not like the round-faced, friendly, round-eyed man in the picture bundle. Their dark faces were covered with thick, black hair; their eyes were fierce, but almost hidden beneath their shiny headdresses, which fully encased their heads except their lower faces, even covering their necks and ears. Their torsos were encased in the same shiny material. The rest of their clothing was vividly colored, though dirty and ragged. They carried lances and long axes, and some carried what appeared to be long clubs which gave off wisps of white, sharp-smelling smoke. Man Face and his warriors watched in amazement as these spectacular men controlled their powerful animals; so much were the movements of the men and beasts coordinated that if he had not known about them already from the picture bundle and the legends of the old storytellers, Man Face would have perceived each beast and its rider to be one creature with two kinds of heads. His heart pounded with joy and admiration. He was inexpressibly happy that his lifelong dream-vision had come to be true.

These, he thought, must indeed be the Shining Men who came across the Sunrise Water to find us; those others must be a lesser tribe they use to build boats for them. And so, presuming once again that his people's language would be understood, Man Face raised his hand toward the closest of the riding men and said in his strongest voice:

"We standing here are Si-poska-nu-Maq-Muk, Children of First Man, from across the Great Water like you! Our ancestor Maq-Muk came here in a great sacred canoe hundreds of winters ago! Here we stand before you! Your long, brave search for us is over. Tell me which of you is your *maho okimeh*! I want him to teach me to say the pictured words in our Sacred Bundle. And I want to ride upon one of those very excellent beasts!" Standing with the Sacred Pole in one hand, the other hand raised in grand greeting, and a smile of the greatest joy on his face, sweating in his buffalo headdress, Man Face waited for the answer.

One of the riders brought his animal so close to Man Face that he could smell its clean sweet breath and the shiny sweat on its black shoulder. The riding man stared down at Man Face, touched himself on his breastplate with his knuckles, and said, *"Soy Capitán! Yo hablo!"* He held a knife as long as his arm.

Man Face, again disappointed, frowned and squinted. He shook the Sacred Pole, trying to make the riding man pay attention to it, feeling that he surely must know of the Hanging Up of First Man, even if he did not know language. The dingy old white buffalo robe flapped. The riding man flicked the hide with the point of his long knife, growling, *"Cómo se llama esto?"*

Man Face snatched the Sacred Pole back, his eyes suddenly ablaze with anger, and scolded the riding man: "Do you want to provoke Creator? Do you want to darken your own path? This is the pole of First Man! See it and be respectful!"

The riding man, obviously understanding not a word, just stared down at Man Face, while using ropes in his left hand to control the beast, which wanted to dance. Man Face could sense that the animal was frightened; perhaps it knew that its stupid rider had insulted First Man. Man Face often had seen that animals were more reverent than men. Man Face's warriors had pressed forward, too, an ominous murmur in their throats. The situation was not getting any better. Man Face's vision of this glorious reunion of the peoples from across the Great Sunrise Water was shrinking far down to match what his real eyes were seeing.

"The Land of the Alengwyneh!" he cried out in frustration. "Is there not a man here who speaks the tongue of the Land of the Alengwyneh? Far Eyes," he called back. "Come and speak to *this* man with your hands!"

Again the youth came and made the signals. Man Face's warriors were now fully surrounded by a wall of riding men on their mighty, dancing, blowing beasts, and all the riding men now had their weapons pointed down at the warriors. Probably some of the warriors were afraid. But they were not showing any fear of the weapons; they were young men who had been hung up, and they were above pain. Still, it was frightening to be here in the midst of such a great misunderstanding, stared down on by fur-faced men who sat high on these wondrous animals. And one of the most mysterious and intimidating things the warriors perceived was the strange-smelling smoke that kept wafting off the club sticks of the riding men. Never had the people smelled anything like that. They had burned sage, sweetgrass, tobacco, cedar, and willow to make prayer smoke, but all of those smelled good. This had an evil smell, like the black rock in some of the hillsides far up the Muddy River, when the grass fires would start the black rock to smoldering. If this evil-smelling smoke was the riding men's prayer smoke, perhaps they prayed to Okee-hee-dee, not to the Great Good Spirit. Maybe that was why they scorned First Man Hanging Up.

But at least, Man Face noted now with a little hope, the chief riding man seemed to be paying some attention to the hand signs of Far Eyes. He was making no move to answer, but he seemed to realize that the young warrior was trying to say something, and there was evidence in the riding man's face that he was thinking.

At last this chief riding man said to Man Face, *"Venga conmigo. Solo!"* He made a motion with his head that Man Face understood to mean "Come this way," and felt a flood of relief. Now perhaps he would be going to see an *okimeh* who would talk in language, a round-faced, round-eyed, friendly man who would understand the glory and importance of Man Face's mission! He prayed that this would be so.

The chief riding man now shouted some words to the other riding men, who suddenly moved their animals about. Some cut in between Man Face and his warriors, separating them, prodding the warriors with their sharp pikes.

"Okimeh!" Far Eyes shouted above the noise. "What shall we do?"

Man Face, feeling jostled and pressed, was alarmed, but did not believe he or his warriors were going to be harmed. He did not want to be separated from his bodyguards, but above anything he wanted to talk to the leader of these riding men, and was willing to go alone to do so. He called back to Far Eyes:

"Stay, my son! Be peaceful but not afraid! Fight only if they hurt or insult you. . . ." He thought of the worst that might occur, and shouted to the youth: "If I can talk to their *okimeh*, I will send for you to bring the Magic Bundles. But if I do not return, take the bundles and go home! Will you do that?"

Through the dust and noise he heard the young chieftain answer yes. He looked up at the chief riding man, smiled and nodded, and began to walk, holding the First Man Pole erect before him with both hands. Now this was like a sacred procession, he felt, as it should be; he was going in dignity with First Man before and above him, going up through the cleared way from the river to the place of their *okimeh*'s fire, and surely he would be met there in solemn dignity and ceremony by a great and wise chief from the Land of the Alengwyneh, and after all this confusion and misunderstanding, he would be able to fulfill his mission, and all would be united in joy. His heart sang and the sky and treetops of the world looked beautiful. Sweat had been stinging his eyes, but now he felt tears of happiness washing out his eyelids, and everything blurred. He felt the kindly strength of the great animals that walked beside him, and would have reached out to touch one of them if the Sacred Pole had not required both his hands. There was a riding man on either side of him, and the chief riding man was just ahead of him. Man Face paced along, admiring the beautiful walk of the black beast, the whipping of its tail as it whisked flies; he looked in amazement at its hooves, the first animal hooves he had ever seen in his life that were not cloven in two parts. When the animal whisked its tail aside, Man Face saw that it was a female, and the shapeliness of its haunches reminded him of the shapely women of his People, and he remembered them with an old man's delight. Man Face was keenly happy; his heart was full of all the feelings of his long life, even the painful ones, and his old heart seemed to be swelling so big that he could scarcely get enough breath. This was a sacred time which, he felt, he had been living for all through his long life, and one he would have to spend the rest of his life remembering. In the eye of his mind he was already painting the picture of this day on the robe that recorded the history of his life: the *pishkuns*, the battles he had won, the Hanging Up in the Okeepah that he had first done and shown the men of his People how to do, to make themselves superior to pain, to make themselves strong for the good of the People. . . . Yes, he, Man Face, had done many things for which his People would always remember him and be grateful. But this that he was doing on this day would be the longest remembered. He could already see his painting on the robe: himself walking with the Sacred Pole, behind one riding man and between two others; as he walked he heard the pleasant soft drumming of the beasts' hooves on the earth and the rhythm of their steps and their breathing, and he wondered how he could tell his wives and grandchildren about the sounds of this day. . . .

Thith ta thoth ta thith ta thoth ta . . .

That was how he would sound it out for them; he must remember that; it was almost like another language, a new language for telling people the sound of something they had never heard. He remembered how he had first heard the sound of the instrument of many bowstrings from the bundle that Sweetgrass Smoke had opened for him. . . .

So many things he had been the first of his People to see and to hear and to do! Man Face thought that perhaps no one but First Man had ever done so many first-time things.

While Man Face was thinking and feeling all this, and trying to imagine how he would paint the *okimeh* of the Shining Men whom he had yet to see, and wondering how he would paint himself sitting on the back of one of these great animals, while he was thinking and wondering about all this, the black horse in front of him raised her tail and turned it aside. Her black anus stretched open, larger and larger, and expelled pungent brown droppings which fell on the dusty grass in front of Man Face. And as he stepped over them, his eyes played a joke on him: the haunches of the animal looked as if they were the hind part of the man riding above, and that the droppings had fallen from the man. Man Face in his wonderful state of happiness thought that this thought of his was the funniest thought that had ever come into his mind, and before he could stop himself he was laughing out loud, laughing from both high joy and low humor, and when the chief riding man turned his surprised face to look at him, he did not look like a man who was in the least pleased to hear laughter; instead he looked like a man who has just embarrassed himself by dropping his waste before someone's eyes, and when Man Face thought of that, he laughed even harder. The riding man shouted something at him and turned his animal, and threatened him by raising his long knife.

Man Face managed to get his mirth under control. The meanness of the chief riding man was like a shadow, and Man Face thought he might tell the *okimeh* about how unpleasant this rider was. He needed to be made more polite.

Soon they were passing through an ugly place where many trees had been cut down and bark and branches littered the ground. The air was hazy with smoke, and many shabby, poorly made huts stood about in the mess, perhaps a hundred of them, put together from poles and bark. In this place were many dirty, naked brown children, but they were not lively and happy like the children of his own People. They sat on the ground or stood outside the huts, sucking their fingers. Most were so thin he could see their ribs through their skin, and their faces looked old. They were sick, Man Face realized with a shock of sadness. He had never seen more than one or two children sick at the same time. A few wretched-looking women stood or squatted by cook fires in front of the huts, and they, too, looked sick. They were naked except for little aprons of grass, and their faces were drawn in pain and misery. Man Face wondered where the men of this village—if it could be called a village—had gone. He remembered something then, something he had almost forgotten in the long years of his life, a thing that the ancient woman Sweetgrass Smoke had told him when he was a boy: that in the times of her childhood, the *okimehs* at the Falling Water Place had captured people of some tribes and had forced them to work. They had made them cut stone from the ground and carry it to places where they built walls. Sweetgrass Smoke's own father, Stonecutter the Okimeh, had sometimes had captive men working for him, she had said. Man Face remembered this now, and wondered if these riding men used the men of this village for work. He remembered that he had seen native men today working in the boat-building place beside the river. And off in the woods now he could hear blows that sounded like trees being cut down. Man Face was troubled by the thoughts of this. The notion came to him that his own warriors might be overpowered and forced into such use, and he worried about them, and about the Magic Bundles he had left with them at the riverside. His urgency to meet the *okimeh* of these people increased with every step. In the meantime, his arms and back were burning with fatigue from carrying the Sacred Pole, and his sinewy old body was trickling sweat. The air in this southern country is like the steam in a sweat lodge, he thought. He was all but gasping for every breath. But of course he could not put down the Sacred Pole, or give it to anyone else to carry. The mere pain of carrying it he could bear; that was less than the pain of the Okeepah. But he did fear that the want of fresh breath might make him too faint to go on.

Beyond the village of huts there stood a palisade of pointed poles, and through an open gate he saw some better-made houses. At either side of the gate stood a man with a long pike, and the two men wore the same kind of shiny headgear and body covering as the riding men. Man Face saw that he was being led to that gate.

As they drew near, the leading rider shouted a few words, and one of the standing men disappeared inside the gate, calling out. Within a few breaths he reappeared, and beside him there walked a person whose appearance startled Man Face. Somewhere he had seen this person, he was sure. He squinted the sweat out of his eyes, staring, trying to remember. The man was dressed in a black garment that hung from his neck to his ankles, with a rope tied around his waist. His face was round, with white hair growing only on his chin. There was no hair on his head, except some white wisps over his ears.

Man Face realized that he had seen this man—or a man of this sort—in one of the pictures in the Magic Bundle, and he was suddenly flushed with the excitement of hope. Surely the presence of this man further proved that he had truly found his own people from across the Great Sunrise Water!

The man came forward, peering at Man Face, his white hands clasped at his abdomen. He did not look healthy as he came closer. His brow was white as snow, his cheeks and nose very red and splotched with bright crimson sores. But his eyes were alert and not arrogant like those of the riding men.

Suddenly the leading rider swung his leg over his animal's back and let himself to the ground. It was a startling sight to Man Face. On the ground, this unpleasant man was small, a head shorter than Man Face.

Holding his animal by the ropes to its mouth, the man talked rapidly with the man in the black robe, sometimes pointing at Man Face without looking at him. The black-robed man kept looking at Man Face, nodding and squinting, making little throat sounds. A few dark-haired men with furry faces were wandering out of the gate, looking on curiously, and some naked young native women came skulking out and squatted on the ground to look on. One had a great bruise on one side of her face, and another's thighs and arms were marked with bruises large and small. The other two riding men got off their animals, and one held both beasts by their mouth ropes while the other went inside the gate. He returned in a moment with a container of some kind and offered it to the leading riding man, who stopped talking long enough to drink from it. Then the other riding man drank, and took it to the man who was holding the animals. He gave the empty container to one of the standing men at the gate. Man Face watched as one of the riding men put his left foot into a loop hanging at the beast's side, grasped the animal's shoulder, and raised himself up onto its back, then rode away. So, Man Face thought, that is how they get off and on! Now when their *okimeh* lets me use one of their beasts to ride on, I will not have to ask how to get on it. I will just put my foot in like that and get up, like a man descended from other animal riders. Man Face sighed with yearning, then turned back to watch the conversation between the riding man and the black-robed man. The black-robe had just spread his hands in some sort of gesture, and for the first time Man Face saw here among these people one of the visions he had been searching for most of his life:

Suspended from the belt of the black-robed man was a little carving of First Man Hung Up!

For just a moment Man Face gaped at it speechless; then he exclaimed to the black-robe:

"There it is! Here is the same thing, upon this Sacred Pole I carry! It is First Man! Then you *are* of my People from across the Great Sunrise Water! Brother, let us speak to each other in our own tongue!" He pointed from the belt to the pole.

At this outburst, the black-robe recoiled slightly.

The lead riding man simply threw up his hands and rolled his eyes toward the sky, then, shaking his head, took the opportunity to lead his beast away and leave the voluble native with the priest. He slung its reins over a post by the gate and stood for a moment eyeing the naked women. Then, keeping behind the black-robe, he crossed to the cluster of women, twisted his fist into the hair of the prettiest one, raised her to her feet and propelled her through the gate and into one of the huts inside.

Man Face was not long in realizing that even this black-robe did not comprehend or speak the language of the People, and he felt the greatest weariness from this new disappointment. The problem, he decided at last, had to be in the language itself. All the evidence was that these truly were people from across the Great Sunrise Water, that they did indeed know of First Man. Perhaps the reason they could not understand anything he said was that the language had changed in the hundreds of winters since First Man had crossed the waters. Man Face was aware that language changed; he had forgotten how Sweetgrass Smoke had pronounced some words, and the tongue of the Pale Ones was mixed with that of the Mandans.

But if I make them know we are long ago from the same land, they will be joyous, and then we can learn to talk together. The Old Grandmother told me the Marking Language does not change. But I must show this black-robe elder that we are not strangers!

Resting the Sacred Pole on the ground, Man Face held it upright with his left hand. He pointed at the First Man Hanging Up that the black-robe wore, then up at the white bison robe on the pole, back and forth, until he was sure the black-robe must see what he was trying to show him.

Then Man Face put two fingers in his mouth, took them out and pointed them at the black-robe's mouth, the sign that they had eaten together at the same breast and thus were kin.

At that, a glimmer of understanding lit the black-robe's eyes. The black-robe held his right hand in front of his mouth and extended his thumb and forefinger several times toward Man Face, and Man Face knew he meant, "Let us talk." Man Face nodded eagerly, made the sign for "Good," and again made the "kin" sign and pointed to the big First Man Hanging Up on his pole and the little First Man Hanging Up on the black-robe's belt.

For some reason that made the black-robe frown. It was either something he did not understand or something he did not like. But Man Face insisted, nodding vigorously and continuing to point between the two things.

If I could just put this pole aside and use both hands, Man Face thought impatiently, I could really make him understand, for this elder does seem to know the language of hands. I wish Far Eyes could have come. Man Face beckoned for the black-robe to follow, and carried the pole to the picket wall, near the tethered riding beast, and leaned it against the wall. Then he turned to the black-robe with a bright smile and began talking with both hands.

Are you *okimeh* here? he asked.

No, the elder answered. Our leader is in there. He pointed to a building inside the palisade.

Take me to see him, Man Face signed excitedly, meanwhile thinking how rude it was for an *okimeh* not to come out and greet the *okimeh* from another place who comes to visit.

No, the black-robe signed. He is very sick, dying.

Man Face showed his sadness, then signed, I can make well.

No, the black-robe signed. Many shamans, many tribes, all made him sicker. He will see no more.

Man Face sighed with frustration. He wanted very much to see these people's *okimeh*, to see if he remembered the language of First Man that everybody else seemed to have forgotten. He signed, Speak for me the name of your *okimeh*. Man Face had an idea for a way to see the *okimeh*.

The black-robe said, *"El suyo nombre es De Soto."*

Man Face tried in vain to remember and make the name with his lips, but it was too long and strange. He could not even make some of the lip and tongue sounds. Man Face had thought that when he learned *okimeh*'s name, he would just shout it until the *okimeh* answered. But Man Face could not even begin to pronounce the name. What a problem was this matter of languages! His dreams had not prepared him at all for this obstacle, nor even warned him of it. It was quite plain that the black-robe was not going to take him in to see the *okimeh* of these people. So Man Face sighed, and made the question sign, and signed: "Did you come from that way, very far, across the Sunrise Water?"

The black-robe thought, then nodded yes.

"Just alike did my ancestors!" said Man Face, making the signs as he talked. He expected the black-robe to be very delighted with that knowledge, and to show wonderment in his face. But there was only a frown. The old man looked weary and bored, and Man Face began to wonder if he was stupid, like the riding men and the boat builders.

"Listen!" Man Face said, and he made signs quickly and emphatically, saying:

I must see your *okimeh*. I have come two moons down the Mother of Rivers and the Muddy River to see him. I have Magic Bundles full of God Words for him to see! Have you not been seeking us, the Children of Maq-Muk? Here I stand! Fan the smoke from your eyes and unplug your ears! What I am saying is important to your *okimeh*! My People are the ones you seek! I question: What do you seek?

The black-robe stuck out his lower lip with the effort of hard thinking, then he began signing:

We seek the seven great towns of . . . He paused, then spoke a word: ". . . Cibola."

Man Face thought, then signed: Are the people in those towns the Children of First Man? We are the Children of First Man!

The black-robe waved his hand impatiently. He signed: We seek no people. We seek . . . He held his right hand up in front of his shoulder with the thumb and forefinger apart about the width of a nut, and said a word: *"Oro."*

Man Face repeated the sign and the word. "O-ro." Then he shook his head and made the question sign, indicating that he did not know of oro. The black-robe sighed impatiently and held up his left hand, upon whose forefinger he wore a gold ring.

"Oro," he said.

Man Face was confused. He signed, What you look for is on your hand?

For some reason, that seemed to make the black-robe very angry. His mouth puckered and his eyes bugged, and he raised his fists and shook them. Then he turned and stalked through the gate, muttering to the guards. Man Face, still on a mission that so far had achieved nothing, was not yet ready to lose the only man here who could converse, however poorly, so he followed the black-robe, exclaiming:

"I will go to my boat and get the Sacred Bundles! You will see the words pictured in them! Then you will understand! Wait and listen, Old Black Robe. . . ."

But at the gate, the two standing guards crossed their long pikes in front of Man Face, stopping him.

Astonished, he put his hand on one of the pikes and tried to move it, but the guard held it firm. "I am *okimeh* of my People," he exclaimed to the pikeman, "and I am talking with the black-robe! Open my way!"

The guards pushed him back. The women giggled; some by-standers laughed.

At last the rudeness of these people struck a fire in Man Face. His heart pounded in anger as it had never done except in battle. His face hardened. He looked around. There was his Sacred Pole, leaning on the palisade, beside the tethered riding beast.

Suddenly Man Face knew what he should do.

He stepped over beside the beast and took its mouth ropes in one hand. He put his foot into the hanging loop as he had seen the riding men do, and with swift ease, feeling that he had been on these beasts many times, he got astride. He was on a Spirit Elk! As he had seen in visions, he was on a riding beast! His heart soared like an eagle. The two guards from the gate were running at him, shouting with astonishment and anger, but they seemed so small and far below that they did not matter. "A-hai-eee!" Man Face cried, a great smile splitting his face, his heart laughing.

The animal, because of the whooping stranger on her back and the two shouting pikemen dodging around her, sidestepped till her rump hit the palisade wall, then lunged forward. Man Face reached out and grabbed the Sacred Pole, which in his excitement felt as light as a spear. People were shouting all around. Man Face almost lost his balance on the dancing beast two or three times, which made it all more exciting, but recovered quickly each time and laughed with exultation. He had no idea how to guide the animal. His left hand held her mouth ropes but he did not pull on them to control her, because he had grasped her mane with the same hand, to steady himself. At last, terrified by the turmoil around her, she set off at a gallop down the path through the village of huts, causing women and children to dart out of the way.

The flight was taking Man Face back toward the river where his warriors were, and it was just what he had wanted. He wanted to get the Magic Bundles as quickly as he could and bring them up to Black Robe, or even to the *okimeh* of these people, so that they could look at the words and understand all the things he could not make them understand. That was what he wanted to do; that was why he had gotten on the animal; and now, to his great joy, he was sitting on the running animal just as he had always foreseen in his visions, and was going like the wind, so fast the ground blurred under him. Never had Man Face been so happy; he felt he had crossed to the better world of the Other Side, having no longer the weight of his old body. It was like flying! The more he yelped, the faster the animal went. He still had his left foot in the mounting stirrup, but the other was free, banging her flank; that and the flapping robe on the Sacred Pole fed her panic.

As the path left the shabby village and went among the trees of the woods, Man Face saw from the edge of his eye that two of the riding men were racing after him, one coming along each side, and they were shouting at him. But as the path grew more narrow through the woods they had to drop back and follow behind.

Speeding through the woods was even more exhilarating. The limbs and leaves swished by in a green blur; he plunged into sun-dappled shadow and out into patches of sunlight, then back into shadow, and he howled with the thrill of it. He had been born fated to ride the swift animal; he knew it! He loved this animal with a love that made his heart as big as the world.

Through the foliage ahead he saw the boat builders' clearing. He saw the river, bright and vast, the riding men on their animals guarding Man Face's warriors beside their canoes, the boat builders standing in and around the unfinished hulls, everyone beginning to turn and look at him as he came yelping down into the clearing, the shouts of the two other riders behind him. His joy was brightened by the knowing that his warriors now were seeing him riding the back of the beast of his visions, as he had prophesied to them. It was he, Man Face, who had been the first of the People to be Hung Up like First Man. It was he, Man Face, who had been the first man of his People to be both *okimeh* and Keeper of the Bundles. It was he, Man Face, who had been the first *okimeh* of his People to win defensive battles against the hostile tribes. It was he, Man Face, whose visions had formed his People's ceremonies and customs out of doubt and confusion. It was he, Man Face, who had first followed his visions and made this long, bold voyage down the Mother of Rivers to seek the Shining Men. And now, the warriors could see, it was Man Face who came racing into the riverside clearing, the first of his People ever to ride the back of a four-legged.

In his way, Man Face was another First Man.

When the riding men in the clearing began shouting and trying to catch him, his beast veered away and ran from them. She thundered among the boat hulls and down to the river's edge; there she spun and ran along the shore until she saw thickets ahead and turned again to gallop up along the edge of the clearing. Man Face whooped with delight and had no desire to guide her. He believed she was the fastest and the smartest of all the riding beasts; probably that was why she had belonged to the riding men's leader; he believed she was playing a game with them and would win it. Then—he did not much worry when or how it would happen—she would stop and let him get the Magic Bundles and take him back up to show them to the blackrobe or the *okimeh*. Man Face felt that he and this splendid four-legged shared the same spirit, and what he wished, she would help him to do. He so trusted her now that he did not even feel a need to hold on. He had released his hold on her mane and her mouth ropes; the ropes lay loose over her neck. He now held the Sacred Pole high with both hands and stayed on her back just by the grip of his legs and by a kind of balancing spirit inside him that knew when and how she would move.

Now his beautiful and beloved four-legged had dodged all through the boat builders' clearing with the others in pursuit, and again was bearing down on the place where Man Face's warriors stood laughing and cheering in delight and awe beside their canoes. Man Face caught a glimpse of one of the Shining Men standing not far from them with his smoking club. The man had been trying to point it at Man Face, perhaps trying to make its magic smoke stop the flight of the four-legged.

Then, as the animal veered past that man, so close that Man Face could almost have touched him with the end of the Sacred Pole, a thunderclap and smoke cloud appeared right where the Shining Man stood.

Man Face was jolted and the four-legged ran right out from under him.

From above, Man Face saw his warriors run and pick up his body from the ground and carry it to his canoe, and saw them bravely fighting the hairy-face Shining Men on the riverbank until they could escape into the canoe and start home carrying his body.

On this day Man Face had been the first of his People ever to ride a four-legged. And he had been the first of his People ever to be killed by a thunderclap stick of men from across the Sunrise Water.

In the sky, the spirit of Man Face rose and rose and began to detect the fragrance of sweetgrass smoke.

CHAPTER 16

Mannah Sha's Town on the Muddy River 1680

It is only one of those foolish notions men believe," said Squash Blossom's grandmother as she combed grease through the girl's thick yellow hair, and the old woman's voice had merry mockery in it. "You only need to laugh at it inside and look serious on your face, and it will amount to nothing. It is harmless. You do it to humor your husband. The old men only pretend they can still do it anyway. Mannah Sha has been a great *okimeh*, but his root is wilted."

"I love Bull's Tail Up but I do not want to do this for him," Squash Blossom muttered.

Her grandmother slapped her lightly on the haunch. "You will do it. Bull's Tail Up is a good husband. He believes he will be given some of the old *okimeh*'s wisdom and strength through you. Also you will flatter the old *okimeh* and make him happy, as he deserves to be. Men have been doing this ever since the long ago times when our ancestors lived on the other side of the Mother of Rivers, and they offered their wives to the one they called King. Stand up, Granddaughter."

Squash Blossom stood naked in the firelight and the old woman anointed her limbs and torso with fresh bear oil. The girl was still warm and clean from the sweat hut by the riverbank. Her grandmother chattered on, making light of it. "You will just walk over the red sticks and offer yourself to Mannah Sha. Then you will walk out into the bushes with him and wait for a time that seems long enough, and then when you walk back, your young husband is happy because he thinks the *okimeh* has given him power through you. What is so serious about walking a little, if it makes them so happy? Young woman in love with your husband! Ha ha ha! Now put the robe around you. I hear the drum and flute. It is time for their game to start. Your husband is impatient."

Squash Blossom was half hopeful, her dread eased a little by the secret her grandmother had told her about old men, but she still was not happy about it. "I wish I did not have to be naked before old men."

The old woman laughed. "Child, every man in this town saw you all bare for your first eight summers, and no one's loincloth swelled up. Now no loincloths will swell up tonight because there is no swelling left in a pizzle as old as Mannah Sha's. I tell you!"

Bull's Tail Up, the young husband of Squash Blossom, was waiting for them at the door of the lodge of Mannah Sha. The old *okimeh*'s name meant "tobacco." Above the door, the effigy of First Man Hanging Up loomed high in the light of the full moon. Also waiting at the door was White Horn, one of Mannah Sha's grandsons, with his young wife also wrapped in a bison hide. Music came faintly out through the door.

Squash Blossom's grandmother went in first, carrying the six red-painted sticks for the ceremony, and the tobacco, sage, and sweetgrass she would burn to purify the lodge. After a while she came to the door and told the young people to enter.

Mannah Sha and the other great old man to be honored, Laughing Turtle, sat on the far side of the lodge. The six red sticks lay on the floor in a line going past the fire pit and ending where the *okimeh* sat. The air was thick with fragrant smoke. A boy of about thirteen blew on a wooden flute, another thumped on a hoop drum, and a third was plucking gingerly on the stringed instrument from the Sacred Bundle. The old Bundle Keepers had figured out how to make new strings for it every few years from sinew, but it was still considered a sacred and delicate thing and was used only for a few ceremonies, so its sound was unfamiliar.

Bull's Tail Up went to the fire pit. Squatting there, he loaded a red smoking pipe and lit it with an ember, took it to old Mannah Sha, and with elaborate care and poise, gave it to him. Mannah Sha took it in both hands, turned the stem in a circle, drew a mouthful of smoke and, eyes closed, let the smoke slowly out of his mouth while inhaling it through his nose. Then he handed it to old Laughing Turtle beside him. Laughing Turtle, who had grown so fat that he did not have the wrinkled face a man of his great age should have had, puffed the pipe and passed it to White Horn, who puffed and returned it to Bull's

Tail Up, who then had to smoke it until it had burned out. He returned the pipe to the fire pit, cleaned out the ashes and put sage in the bowl, and returned it to its cradle of forked sticks. Then he went to Squash Blossom and stood at her side for a few beats of the drum. Standing in place, the young women began shifting from foot to foot in time with the drum. Squash Blossom kept her eyes down, not wanting to see anyone else's eyes now. Her husband touched her arm. Taking a quick breath, she opened her arms and gave him the robe.

She cast one indignant glance at her husband, but he did not see it. He was watching the *okimeh*, and his face revealed the pride he had in her naked beauty.

She danced forward to the first red stick and stood over it, then squatted down. Her clitoris, circumcised and stretched in the old manner of her People, hung far enough down to touch the red stick. Her husband murmured with pride and looked toward old Tobacco, who was smiling and nodding. She stood up, shuffled two paces forward to the drumbeat, and squatted over the second stick, then went on to do the same over the third and fourth and fifth. When she squatted over the last stick, she was within an arm's length of the old *okimeh*, her eyes on the same level and looking into his. He nodded and smiled at her, and she stood and shuffled back to Bull's Tail Up, who was smiling at her and saying very softly, "*Shu-su! Shu-su!*" Good, good! She had done that part of it, and was glad when her husband put the robe back around her, because the Mandan women were modest and this was not a comfortable thing.

Now White Horn's wife took off her robe. To the heartbeat of the instruments she walked the sticks and turned to smile at fat old Laughing Turtle. Now it was White Horn's turn to look proud.

LATER, SQUASH BLOSSOM WALKED OUT OF THE LODGE AND through the moonlit town with old Mannah Sha limping beside her. Neither said anything as they went down the riverbank toward the willow thickets.

Squash Blossom knew all about Mannah Sha, old Tobacco. He was descended by six generations directly from the legendary *okimeh* Man Face, the first and only one of the People ever to ride a Spirit Elk. He had been killed by the Men Who Wore Iron for doing it, but his descendants told and retold the story, which had been witnessed by Far Eyes, who had become the next great *okimeh*. Old Tobacco had always tried to be as great as his ancestor. He had traveled far on the rivers to see all the old places of the People's history, and had tried to keep as much of the ancient Knowing as he could, telling the Old Stories to each generation, telling them over and over. He had done very much also to increase the numbers of his People, now having thirty grandchildren and more than a hundred great-grandchildren.

Like all her People, Squash Blossom admired and respected the old *okimeh*, but he did not at this moment seem to be a great man. He was just a feeble and almost toothless old man, playing the men's pride game of pretending to want the wife of a young warrior, so that the young man could think he was being passed some of the old one's greatness. Now it did seem as harmless as her grandmother had told her, and a funny ritual. Now that the immodest part was over, it was, as Grandmother had said, just some walking around.

As they came to the edge of the willow, she slowed and said, "Here, Grandfather?"

"*K'hoo,*" he replied. Yes.

She stood, holding her robe around her, nibbling her lips, looking out over the river, looking up at the moon, just waiting for time to pass until they could walk back up to the lodge and pretend.

But then, to her surprise, he spoke: "*K'hoo*, I said, yes, this is a good place for us to lie down."

Now she was not gazing about anymore but right into his face, and the moon glinted in her astonished eyes. He pointed to the ground again. A dubious little smile appeared on her moonlit face, and she knelt and then stretched out on the ground, still wrapped in the robe. He knelt beside her on popping knees and cast her robe back to reveal her to the moon and his own eyes again. He looked from her to the sky for a moment, moving his lips as if he were praying.

Then Mannah Sha was untying the waist of his breechclout, and she came to believe that he was not pretending anything. He was old and bony but he was proving that some things her grandmother taught were wrong presumptions.

And later as they were walking back up the riverbank, Squash Blossom could not help saying, "Our beloved *okimeh*, you have surprised me. I believed we were only to walk."

"*Sook meha,*" he said, chuckling. "Girl, I know what old grandmothers tell you about old grandfathers. I am happy if I can surprise a grandmother." He leaned on her. She asked:

"E da ta hish?"

"Megosh, wah e da ta hish," he said, No, I am not tired. He panted from the climb, but his craggy old face was smiling in the moonlight. "Yes, it is good to surprise a grandmother. It is even better to surprise oneself!"

OLD TOBACCO HAD MADE THE YOUNG MAN HAPPY BY PASSING HIM some of his power. He believed, though, that he could give young men power more truly by sharing knowledge with them. Whenever he could get them away from their young-man pursuits, he sat with them in his lodge and told them of things he had seen and thought in his far travels and long life.

His son, who had been White Horn's father, had long been dead, killed in a fight with the Oto far down the Muddy River. Someday, when Tobacco passed over, his grandson White Horn probably would become *okimeh* of the People, and Tobacco wanted him to know whatever was to be known.

On this day he was smoking a pipe and telling White Horn and Bull's Tail Up about his long ago journey to the Falling Water Place in the east on the Beautiful River. He had gone there by canoe to see it because it was where the Ancestors of the Pale Ones of the People had been massacred by the forest peoples, more than ten generations ago.

"At that place, I saw crumbled walls of stone, great, long, thick walls. In some places they had been washed away by the floods, but it had been a stone lodge as big as this our whole village. And there were teeth there as big as my hand. . . .

"I found whole creekbeds full of skeletons. And skulls in metal headdresses, and also skeletons wearing old, old metal clothes as a turtle wears its shell.

"Grandson! Among those many skeletons the spirits of the dead were so troubling that many of my warriors became unable to walk or speak, and we fled from there.

"Listen, for those things I saw have a meaning deep in my heart: I saw hills that had been made by men, and earthen medicine wheels two hundred paces across. I saw the remains of towns ten times as big as this of ours. But there are not many people there now along that Beautiful River, not many more than are along our Muddy River. Who were the people there who were so many? Where did they go?" The young men's faces showed that they were truly awed and sharing his wonder.

"Here," he said, "is what is in my heart about those things: all that is a Lost Knowing, like the Lost Knowing of how to understand the rows of marks in the Sacred Bundles. Like all the other *okimehs* before me, I have protected the bundles in the Sacred Canoe, and pondered their mysteries, and felt my heart ache over the Lost Knowing." He raised a forefinger for attention. "I pray that no Lost Knowing is lost forever. By and by it should come around again on the turning of Time, as all things come back around: the seasons, the rains, the sunrises, the full moon. Did not First Man, white and hairy-faced, come across the Flood from the Sunrise long ago in the beginning, and then did not other hairy-face white men come again from the Sunrise in the time of Man Face?

"And listen now: there are now more white-face men in the country! Our men who went to the sacred red-stone cliff to collect pipe stone last year, they were told by hunters from the Stone Cooker People that more white men had passed not long ago, looking for trade. Yes, there are white men now in corners of Turtle Island, and news of them comes on the four winds.

"Sometime they will come here, and they will bring back the Lost Knowing. I, Mannah Sha, Tobacco, wanted to be the one to regain the Lost Knowing, but I am old now and doubt that it will happen in my life. Perhaps, grandson, it will be you who meets them. If so, you must be hungry to know the way I have been hungry to know. The yearning must be in your heart, so that you always think of it and look for it. If not, it is like the hunter who sleeps beside the game path, and the prey pass by him unknown, and he gets nothing to feed his family.

"Tell me, grandson, that you will listen for their language if ever you meet the white men in your lifetime. If they say any word that you know, they will surely be your relatives from long ago, from that far land. Take their hand peacefully and tell them we are the ones they seek. They can return the Lost Knowing to us. They can bring us the friendly four-leggeds such as our ancestors rode upon in that old land, as you have seen in the picture of the bundle. We will want those animals, and must learn their ways. There are tribes south and west of us who already have gotten the four-leggeds from the Men Who Wear Iron. There will come a time when those animals come into our country, and you must not be sleeping beside the trail when that happens, either, or they will pass by you, and your People will not have the use of their power.

"Listen, grandson: what we have lost, the Knowing, may not come back around to us in a lifetime. We have waited for this since before the time of Man Face. From grandfathers to grandsons many times over we have said these things and kept watching. If you think a life is long, go look at the old stone walls and the great heaps of earth made long ago. We live just a moment, any man does, but the People live on as Time turns and comes back around to them. It is for the People that we must keep watching for the Knowing to come back around."

White Horn's eyes were bright. "I will never forget this, Grandfather. You give me power by this great story."

Bull's Tail Up was likewise in a wondrous state. He said, "Great Okimeh, with your words you make me strong, as you made me strong through my wife not long ago. My heart is rich from the wisdom and greatness of my elder."

The old *okimeh*'s eyes glittered with the remembering of that night. He wondered if Squash Blossom had told this young husband how he had surprised her. Old Tobacco had spent his life looking for Knowing, but knowledge of such secrets as that, a man was better off without.

He chuckled. He did hope that she had told her grandmother.

SQUASH BLOSSOM WAS GATHERING FIREWOOD IN THE DEEP SNOW near the hunting camp when she heard the distant shout and stood up to listen and look. The camp was only the hide-covered little tipi lodges in a clearing among sandbar willows, beside a curving little creek, several days' long walking from Mannah Sha's Town.

The voice was her husband's. He had gone out northward early in the morning on snowshoes, vanishing into the snow-dusted wind. Squash Blossom smiled when she saw Bull's Tail Up coming, shouting; he was coming downslope toward the camp as fast as she had ever seen anyone move on snowshoes, and now she could hear his words.

"Roo hoo tah! Roo hoo tah! Ptemday!" Come, he was calling the hunters, I have found bison!

They answered with joyous cries and began dashing about, getting their snowshoes, bows, and lances. He came panting in, eyes shining, smile bright. Squash Blossom ran to greet him, her yellow hair blowing in the wind. They hooked their arms together and he pulled her close and touched his forehead to hers. She cried out, almost squealing, "You found them! Are they many? Are they far?"

"Many! They are huddling in a ravine of deep snow, hiding from the wind." He called out to the hunters' wives, "They are far that way! Break the camp and follow after us!" It was easier to move the light camp than to carry great loads of meat and hides back here. In moments the six hunters were gliding after him on their snowshoes into the whitened wind. They were hardly out of sight before the wives were following them with the entire camp, poles, firewood, rations, everything on toboggans or on their backs.

Squash Blossom was thanking the Creator for letting her husband be the one who had found the prey. Bull's Tail Up had been enjoying good fortune in everything in the moons since old Tobacco had passed him his powers through her. She herself had come to believe that, and to disbelieve her own grandmother's mockery of it. It was as Bull's Tail Up said: Creator intended a Coming Around of everything, with life always rewarding life so that one received what his own generosity made him worthy of receiving. Bull's Tail Up had been generous with Mannah Sha, and now he was being rewarded with one blessing after another. Squash Blossom waddled through the snow, a little behind the others, pulling a toboggan with a tent cover and some firewood on it.

One of the blessings coming to Bull's Tail Up was that Squash Blossom was soon going to bear a child.

WHEN THE HUNTERS' WIVES REACHED THE TOP OF THE THIRD HILL, following the tracks of their husbands' snowshoes, they could hear their shouts and the bellowing of the bison not far ahead. And so they hurried down that slope and up the next, plunging along in the deep snow. Reaching the top of the next rise, they looked down into a ravine, and there was the good hunt he had promised, and it was just as he had said. The bison, about fifty of them, were floundering shoulder deep in the snowdrifts, hardly able to move forward, while the hunters on their snowshoes ran swiftly on top of the snow, up beside the lunging beasts, and very easily lanced or shot them through the heart. The snow in the ravine grew red. As the women moved close and set up the butchering camp, about twenty of the herd, those in back, split off and made their way up a slope that had been blown almost bare of snow, and those got away from the slaughter.

But the hunters had killed about thirty, and that many of them were enough to make the women's arms tired and bloody from butchering. They worked in the bloody snow until the sun went down and wolves began howling, and even the men butchered.

To butcher in the snow was to suffer, for hands and arms and legs grew wet and numb, and sometimes the meat froze hard even before it could be cut. But a good thing about winter hunting was that there were no flies, and the meat did not spoil.

THEY HAD COME THREE DAYS' TRAVEL WEST OF TOBACCO'S TOWN before finding the herd, and the next day they started back, carrying the meat on their backs and pulling it on the toboggans with the hides on top. It was a slow, hard trip with all the weight, and when night fell, they were on a windswept plain blown almost clear of snow. They set up the shelters as lean-tos facing each other and made a bonfire between them to throw some heat in, then crowded in close under fresh hides and tanned robes so their bodies could warm each other, and slept. They did not leave anyone out as a sentry because of the intense cold.

Squash Blossom awoke needing to make water. She did not want to get out from the warmth between her husband and the husband and wife who were sleeping on the other side of her. The fire was down to flickerings, and the moon was setting.

Squash Blossom needed to make water often at night, now that she was growing a baby inside. She pressed her hands here and there on the slight swelling of her belly, smiling. Her husband, Bull's Tail Up, was proud that he was going to be a father. But sometimes in her private thoughts Squash Blossom would joke with herself about whether this might be instead the seed of Mannah Sha, old Chief Tobacco, who had so surprised her on the night of Walking the Sticks. Some men of great age kept fathering children when they got young wives, so it probably was possible that she might have gotten Tobacco's seed that night. Maybe she would never know whether this child was from him or from Bull's Tail Up. But what delight it might be for old Tobacco at least to think it was his!

In a strange way, Squash Blossom almost hoped it was Tobacco's, because he had pleased her and made her come down inside—something that Bull's Tail Up had never done because he always spurted the moment he got inside. Her mother once had confided to Squash Blossom that sometimes elder men were better because they were slower.

"Either that," she had said, "or have your husband get several other wives so they can slow him down for you by keeping him busy!"

It was so amusing to Squash Blossom to hear what women said about men, and what men thought about women, when they talked among themselves. "Oh, a man is a creature of some uses," her grandmother would say, "but a dog will carry a load, and might come when you call him."

Her grandmother was amusing. Squash Blossom would never forget the look on her face when she had told her of old Tobacco's surprise!

Squash Blossom would have liked to lie in the warmth and just think about grandmothers and men and babies and dogs, instead of having to slip out into the terrible cold to make water, but she had no choice. Your baby could drown in there if you don't go soon, she joked to herself.

Not wanting to wake the others by thrashing around for moccasins or leggings, she just slipped out from between the robes naked, hurried through the biting cold down to the thicket and squatted on the snow. She could stand to be cold for as long as it would take to pass the water. When she got back in beside her husband, of course, he would probably cringe away from her cold skin and feet, but very soon everything would be warm again. She shivered and listened to her water hissing in the snow, smelling it in the icy air.

Squash Blossom heard something that sounded like bison running, the beating of hooves on frozen earth, getting closer and louder. Her heart jumped in alarm. She had heard stories of herds stampeding at night and overrunning camps, hurting and sometimes even killing sleepers. Maybe she should run up and awaken the camp. She started, her bare feet squeaking in the moonlit snow.

Then she stopped where she was, stunned by what she saw.

A dark mass of moving, big forms was coming across the snow very fast, but it was not a bison herd. She saw men coming into the fire glow, but they were far taller and bigger and louder than men were supposed to be. Suddenly whooping and trilling, they overran the little sleeping camp. They were men riding on the backs of what must be Spirit Elk! From high on those animals they were shooting arrows and stabbing lances down into the little shelters of the sleeping people.

It was not something that could be happening. But she could hear the screams and groans of her own People as well as the war cries of the attackers. The beasts these attackers rode were dancing and trampling around the fire, almost in it. They had blazing, wild eyes and huge, quick bodies.

Because this could not be happening, Squash Blossom stood

stock-still in the thicket, growing colder and colder on her skin but with a frightful heat rushing inside her.

Soon some of the men were jumping down off the backs of the animals and were clubbing and stabbing where she knew her People were lying. Her husband!

Yes, it was happening. Devils riding in on beasts had charged into the hunting camp just before morning and attacked the sleepers, and now they were taking everything, the meat and the hides. Squash Blossom's soul was quaking and shrinking. She squatted back down, hugged her knees, shut her eyes, and tried to become unseeable. And she prayed and tried to make the rest of her heat go inward to warm the baby inside.

WHEN SQUASH BLOSSOM LIMPED INTO TOBACCO'S TOWN FIVE DAYS later, wrapped in a scorched half of a hide, wearing one woman's moccasin and one man's and clutching the bloody shaft of a broken arrow, she was barely alive and could not talk. Some of her fingers and toes were frozen black, and the little finger of her left hand was gone. The families of the hunters and their wives kept up a clamor to know what had happened to their People, not knowing whether to grieve or go out searching for them. Fed marrow and meat broth, she slept from one noon to the next, and when she woke, she was able to say in painful whispers that she would talk to Okimeh Mannah Sha, and she was carried to his lodge.

She showed him the broken arrow that she had taken from her husband's body, and he saw that it was of the Shienne. That troubled him. What it meant was that those people now had the Omepah Peneta, the Spirit Elks, to ride, and were using that new power to hurt their neighbors, and were ranging far to do so. She told him the attackers had burned everything they did not take, including the bodies and clothes. When they had left at sunrise, she had come out of the snowy thicket and warmed herself at the terrible fire. She had worked hard a whole day trying to bury the charred and scalped bodies in the frozen earth so the wolves would not eat them, but she worried that they were not deep or covered enough. Then she had started trying to walk home to the town. It was a very hard and cold and hungry way. She had had no blade to cut off her little finger in mourning for her husband, so when it froze brittle, she just broke it off. That was all. There was vast grief in Mannah Sha's Town, for the lost hunters and their wives had been related to almost every family.

Squash Blossom told the *okimeh* of the baby she was going

to have, if it survived the suffering she had done. "Maybe," she told Tobacco, "you are its father."

That was how Squash Blossom, the fifteen-year-old widow of Bull's Tail Up, became the youngest wife of Tobacco, who so admired her that he taught her to be the first woman Keeper of the Sacred Bundles since Sweetgrass Smoke. She bore a son named Fat Legs, who was the delight of Tobacco's last years. Though Squash Blossom was Tobacco's wife, he never did get upon her again; she kept Fat Legs at her breast for three years, and by the time he was weaned, Tobacco was just too old and weak to surprise her again.

He Passed Over, very peaceful and contented, a very old and honored *okimeh* with a very young son. He had seen much of the world in all Four Directions, and had kept the Stories of the People from being forgotten. And he had even outlived Squash Blossom's grandmother, so she could not tell little untruths about him after he was gone.

A YEAR AFTER MANNAH SHA DIED, HIS GRANDSON, WHITE HORN, whose wife had died in childbirth, came to Squash Blossom and declared his love for her. Soon they were married, and the People simply had to overlook the curious fact that White Horn was marrying his own grandfather's widow. But there were some who liked to joke that White Horn was a husband of his own grandmother, and that he was older than his own grandmother, and that his stepson was his uncle, and many variations of such gossip. When he became *okimeh*, the joke died quietly because he and his bride were very much respected.

Whatever people had thought, White Horn and Squash Blossom, both yellow-haired, were very good for each other, and they believed that no one had ever been so happy. The sadnesses behind them made their happiness more intense. Often they lay in the firelit stillness of their lodge long after copulating, and talked of their great need for each other, and about the long turning of Time and the brevity of lives, such things as old Tobacco had taught them to think on, and sometimes she worried about being separated by death if something happened to one of them before the other. One night he assured her, "We are sure to find each other on the Other Side. Creator brought us by long and crooked paths to find each other and would not let his work be undone."

But she said, having certain memories, "It seems to me that death must be like the winter wind blowing all the yellow leaves away off the trees. How would two leaves that had been together on the same twig ever find each other after such scattering? How would our two spirits find each other after being scattered to the Other Side World? I am afraid of that. I do not ever want to be without you again."

White Horn lay in the firelight holding her and thinking about that for a long time. Finally, he said:

"Listen. It does not matter that the two dead leaves are scattered from each other after they are blown away. They will become part of the same earth. And as everything goes around and returns, the earth will feed that tree. And on the same twig where they grew that last summer, two new leaves in the new summer will grow side by side, and our same two spirits will live together again in those new leaves."

IN THEIR FIFTH SUMMER AS MAN AND WIFE, WHEN WHITE HORN HAD been *okimeh* for only a short time, three hunters trotted in from the parched plains. They told White Horn they had seen, on a distant ridge, ten Shienne warriors riding on the backs of Omepah Penetas. Being only three, and on foot, the hunters had not followed the riders, but had hurried back to tell of them.

At once White Horn called forty warriors together. His eyes were ablaze when he came into his lodge. He painted a streak of ocher across his nose and cheekbones and gathered his bow and lance. He squeezed Squash Blossom's wrist and said:

"Shienne have ridden into our country, as they did when they killed your husband and the hunting party. I never hoped I could avenge those murders, but the Great Spirit, Maho Peneta, has put this chance into my hands, and means for me to take it!"

Squash Blossom tried to hide the dread she felt. She did not want him to go, even to avenge the terrible thing that had happened to her. She pleaded, "How can men on foot catch men on the riding animals? Husband, I saw how they can run!"

"As we hunt the swift deer and the forked horns. We shall track them unseen and catch them in their sleep. We will get the revenge we have awaited. And"—his eyes were so wild they frightened her—"we will bring back their riding animals!"

She was almost whispering in her breathless fear. "I beg you not to go, beloved husband!" She was thinking of two yellow leaves scattered by wind.

But he was too inspired to listen to warnings. He wanted the Shienne to die for the sufferings of Squash Blossom, of which he was reminded whenever she touched him with the stubs of her frozen-off fingers.

And he also was inspired to be the first of his People since his ancestor Man Face to have the Spirit Elk and ride upon its back.

She watched her husband and his forty warriors run away into the far hills, guided by the three hunters who had seen the Shienne that morning. She knew they could run all day without tiring, and that they were the finest warriors. But they had not ever seen the way men could be when they were riding on the tall and mighty animals.

She took the Sacred Bundles into the lodge that evening and prayed with them all night. Her son Fat Legs got out of his bed twice during the night, disturbed by the fervor of her praying, and finally she asked him to pray with her, and he did so until the last darkness before morning, when he grew too sleepy to continue.

At dawn Squash Blossom went out onto the wall of the village and prayed to the sunrise across the river, then she stood and watched the hills in the southwest for White Horn's return. The day grew hot very early. There had been no rain for almost a moon. Every day there had been Rain Makers on the roofs calling for the Thunder Beings.

In the middle of the forenoon a hopeful Rain Maker mounted one of the domed roofs in a far part of the town and began his imprecations, aiming his bow at the sky and calling for clouds to come. Some people watched him and prayed with him, but more came up to the wall to watch with Squash Blossom for the return of their young *okimeh* and his warriors. The sun beat down and the only sound besides their murmuring conversations and prayers was the wail and chant of the Rain Maker.

In the afternoon someone near Squash Blossom exclaimed, "Look! He is bringing rain clouds!" She saw a dark cloud building along the western horizon.

The people watched the dark cloud for a long time and listened for thunder. At last someone said, "Look at it! Smell it! That is not rain coming! That is great smoke!"

"K'he cush," a man said. Bad. "The grass is burning again." Already in this hot season they had seen the plains burning on the other side of the river; the long, crooked lines of fire had filled the nights with red smoke. Now it was burning on this side of the river. Hunters were watching it and trying to foretell which way it would drive the forked horns and the bison.

Soon the dark smoke was into the roof of the sky, and the sun was a dim yellow circle trying to see through it. Squash Blossom prayed with all the power of her soul, for the thing that no one had spoken was that White Horn and the warriors were somewhere out there. The smoke stung her eyes and throat. Grass soot was drifting down from the sky like black snow.

That night the sky was red. But the fire was still beyond the hills, and no flames could be seen from the town.

Squash Blossom stayed on the parapet of the wall and kept praying until she was praying in her sleep.

She was awakened by cold rain pelting her. A strong, ashy-smelling wind howled over the town, followed by a downpour that flooded the streets faster than it could run off. The night was black; there was no glow anymore from the grass fires. Voices were jabbering and laughing about the beloved rain and praising the Rain Maker; their voices came in fragments through the rush of rainfall as Squash Blossom climbed stiffly down, her clothes and hair sodden, and splashed home to her lodge.

In bed, she prayed with the bundles while Fat Legs slept. As the fire burned down to a dim glow, the raindrops through the smoke hole hissing in it and making puffs of steam, she again fell asleep praying. She dreamed of a wind blowing through trees. She saw two yellow leaves on the end of a twig, shaking and waving in the wind, but clinging. . . .

And then the wind tore one of the leaves from the twig and it flew away in a yellow cloud of blown leaves.

The next day, hunters went out, looking for the forked-horn antelopes and bison and rabbits and deer that were often driven in large numbers toward the river by fires.

The hunters were seen coming back on the second day. As they came closer to the town, they were singing mourning songs.

They had gone out onto the burned part of the plains. Following the spiraling vultures, they had found the charred bodies of the warriors and hunters and their *okimeh*, White Horn. There had been no sign of Shienne or riding animals. White Horn and his warriors had no arrows in them, no wounds.

No one could outrun a high-grass prairie fire.

Squash Blossom, Bundle Keeper of the Children of First Man, little beyond twenty summers of age, for the third time was a widow, and there were many other young widows in the town.

CHAPTER 17

Village on the Muddy River, West Bank
December 3, 1738

The old woman clutched the buffalo-hide robe tighter at her throat to keep the wind from blowing it away, leaned on her walking stick and spoke to the dog:

"Yes, yes, bring it along! If you want to eat, you must work!" She chuckled. "Why, I used to carry that much on my back!"

The dog, looking like a brown-haired wolf, seemed to be grinning, its lips slightly drawn to show the points of its white teeth, its eyes closed almost to slits against the cutting wind, and pressed forward into the harness of leather straps, clawing at the ice to get traction. The toboggan, heavy with its tied-on pile of firewood, slid forward on the gray ice.

The old woman, Squash Blossom, was about halfway across the frozen river. She was in her seventy-second year, long widowed from White Horn. Hundreds of times in her life she had walked across the frozen Muddy River like this, carrying firewood on her back, or leading the dogs that pulled sled-loads of firewood. In those moons when the river was not frozen over, she had paddled across in her little round leather-covered bullboat, towing rafted bundles of wood and driftwood behind. The town had been here so long that there was hardly any wood on the west bank. Across the river there were still groves and thickets in the ravines and bottomlands, and, too, there were places where the nature of the river's current was such that it deposited driftwood on that shore more than it did on this. She thought of the river as she hobbled across its frozen width. It was said that this river started in the Shining Mountains, so far to the west that hardly any of the People had ever seen them. Some of the buffalo and beaver hunters had walked far enough up that way, many sleeps of travel, to see the tops of the Shining Mountains in the distance. But Squash Blossom never had. No woman ever had. Still, she could feel the wondrous long river when she walked on its ice, just as she could when she floated on it in a boat, just as she had when she had been young enough to swim across it. In those days she had been like an otter or a fish, as much at home in the river as on shore, and her old body, though now full of relentless aches and stiffnesses, could still remember the wonderful lightness of floating and swimming, the strange feeling of being a part of the river flow. Under her feet this very moment, below the thickness of ice upon which she walked, the river was flowing just as it always had and always would. There were fish living under there even now. This river was as much a part of the lives of the Children of First Man as were maize and bison. The People would never starve or be unhappy as long as they could live beside the river.

The keen wind tore at the buffalo robe, blowing across her face the part that she had pulled up over her head like a cowl. Out of the side of her eye she saw other people and dogs with sleds, creeping across the ice, going both ways. Far up and down the bend of the river other columns of people could be seen, people of the Mandan towns that sat on both riverbanks. Those distant people looked like summer's ants, going along in busy lines. Sometimes the wind blew enough snow along the ice that those faraway people would vanish in frosty whiteness, and even the great, high river bluffs would fade out of sight.

Now that she was old, Squash Blossom could be frightened by the terrible cold of this land in winter. Every blast of wind could make her bones hurt. In her youth there had been a fire inside her, so great a fire that she could swim among the ice chunks when the river was thawing and hardly quake inside, but since the time she had so nearly frozen, after the murder of Bull's Tail Up, she had had no such inner fire. Her People were very tough, full of the fire, and they could thus live in this harsh land of short summers and long, windy winters. By being able to live here, they were able to keep space around them. Squash Blossom had heard that far downstream to the south and east there were so many peoples living that they were often in wars with each other.

Maybe it would be good to live where the winters are not so hard, she thought. But surely the cold of winter is not as bad as the heat of war.

She recalled that terrible time, more than half a hundred years ago, when the Shienne had swept into the hunting camp and killed everybody, including her husband, and only she had escaped. War is worse than cold, she thought. "Hurry along, dog," she cackled. "Don't you want to get into our lodge and lie by the fire? I certainly do!"

Yes, war is worse than cold, she thought. Cold can make every part of you hurt except your heart, but war makes the heart hurt. The pain of cold goes away when summer comes, but after war your heart never stops hurting.

Squash Blossom plodded on, keeping a careful footing on the ice. Sometimes when she fell on the ice it required all her strength and many efforts to get back up, unless someone came along and lifted her to her feet. As she went along she remembered a dream that she had had many times since she had been the Keeper of the Bundles. The dream was of white-faces walking toward the towns of her People, carrying a tall pole with a banner on top. In the dream she had gone out on the prairie to watch them come, and had talked to them about the Ancient Language of the People of First Man. They had not understood, so she had told them of the Marking Language in the Magic Bundles. Then in another part of the dream she had seen herself going far down the Muddy River with those Magic Bundles. She wondered about those visions. She had lived more than fifty winters seeing those same dream-pictures, and she would not live very many more years probably, and yet none of the things in the visions had happened yet. How would there be enough time left in her life for them to happen?

Of course, as she knew, sometimes the dreamed things did not happen in the dreamer's own lifetime, but later.

Squash Blossom remembered that the dreams had started after she had been chosen to be the Keeper of the Magic Bundles. Old Mannah Sha before his death had honored her by giving her that responsibility. He had been perhaps the greatest of all the *maho okimehs* since First Man himself, and she was glad to have been a part of his life once. He had left much honor with her. She remembered the night when Bull's Tail Up had her walk with the old chief, the night of Walking the Red Sticks.

That was only one of so many ceremonies that were all blurred together in her memory. When women or men reached new age levels, they held ceremonies to buy the next-higher age society from their elders, and there was a different ritual for each one: the Skunk Women Society, the Goose Society, the River Women Society, the White Buffalo Cow Society. And the men of all ages, too, they had their secret societies, from the Kit Fox to the Half-Shaved Heads Society. Since each women's society was allied with at least one men's society, the men and women were often in each other's ceremonies. At the time of any ceremony, it was the most important and vivid event in a person's life, but when an old woman or an old man looked back over a lifetime, it could be hard to keep all the memories detailed and sorted out. One certainty was that all those society events, added to the yearly religious ceremonies in the Medicine Lodge, kept the lives of the People rich and interesting, and one was suddenly old.

Old Squash Blossom was full of the memories of her whole People. They flowed through her mind and soul all the time, just like this great Muddy River on which they had dwelt for hundreds of years. Like the river, which she had drunk and swum in, her memories were both within her and containing her. Inside her head she could see herself as a younger woman remembering what she had had to remember then.

Now along her river of memories were the hundreds she had outlived.

Her son Fat Legs was still alive, a lean and skinny-legged man who was now *okimeh* of the whole nation of Children of First Man. One of her many grandsons, Arrow Feather, was now *okimeh* of the village farthest downriver. Yes, the long spirit of old Squash Blossom was itself a river, flowing through generations. She was important.

Still, she went out in the hard weather to gather and bring firewood. She chose to do it because she did not want to be useless. She had noticed that when she did nothing but stay near the Sacred Canoe and think about the Magic Bundles and about her old dream-visions, she would almost go crazy from the strangeness of her thoughts. It was better to do something every day that required the efforts of her physical body, because, at least until she Crossed Over into the Other Side World, she was living in a body that was meant to be doing things. And so every day she gathered wood, or walked out to visit Tobacco in the Town of the Dead, or helped her granddaughters and the wives of her grandsons dress buffalo hides or make pots. Squash Blossom might be full of memories and a part of the People's memory, but she was not ready yet—and did not ever intend while she was still alive—to be merely a memory.

The old woman was near the shore of her own town, not a hundred paces from the snowy bank, when a harder gust of wind whipped the cowl back off her head. Turning her back to the wind and grappling to pull the robe back up, she saw a robe-muffled man making his way across the river much faster than any sensible man should try to walk on ice. He was obviously in much hurry, and that caught the old woman's attention. Then she recognized the man's profile. It was a man from the town of her grandson, Arrow Feather. This man was half Hidatsa; there were several Hidatsa half-breeds since a tribe of the Hidatsa had settled near the towns of the Children of First Man. This one she knew, and she called him; her shrieky old woman's voice carried to him. "*Roo-hoo tah!*" Come here!

He veered from his course and came near. His face was full of impatience, but she was, after all, the grandmother of his village chief, and he could not ignore her after she had called him. His eyes were squinted almost shut and his dark, broad, bony face was a grimace against the cutting wind. "Old Grandmother," he said, beginning to walk beside her, carrying his lance and trying to hold his robe shut with the same hand, "your grandson Arrow Feather asked me to give you his greetings."

She glanced at him with doubt. "He sent you here just to say that to me?"

The Hidatsa grunted. "I come to tell Fat Legs something. But your grandson said I should give you his greetings while I was here." He glanced ahead, eager to hurry on. She said:

"Ah, as I thought. And what did you come to tell Fat Legs?"

He replied, "This: that hairy-faced men are coming!"

Her hand shot out and caught his robe. "What! Hairy-faces?" She was remembering her old dream-vision. She could see the vision as she had first seen it. "Are they many? Are they on foot, or are they riding on Omepah Penetas?"

"They are not riders. A hunter came in from the north and told Arrow Feather. They march from the north across the plain, guided toward our country by a large number of the Stone Cooker People. That is all the hunter said. Now, Old Grandmother! I must hurry to your son and tell him!" He hastened on ahead, and in a few minutes was off the ice, running at full speed up the steep path to the town.

The old woman's heart was racing, and she quickened her step as much as she could. "Dog!" she cried. "Hurry along! They need the firewood, and I must remind my son that I have dreamed and dreamed of these men coming!"

OLD SQUASH BLOSSOM WOULD NOT ALLOW FAT LEGS TO LEAVE HER behind, but she was not able to walk very far, and so they wrapped her up in furry robes, strapped her on a loaded toboggan, and harnessed it behind three pulling dogs. Fat Legs had with him about forty of the proudest warriors of his own town, and several women came carrying bags of maize and bundles of fine furs and some parfleche bags containing pipe-smoking mixtures, decorated feathers, strings of the beautiful blue beads the Children of First Man still knew how to make after hundreds of years, and quantities of clay-dye powders.

It would not be good to go out and greet important strangers without gifts, Fat Legs had said. And if there were many of the Stone Cooker People, they surely would want to do some trading, and probably some gambling, too. Fat Legs was plainly nervous about the coming of the hairy-face strangers, knowing they probably were the object of his mother's old visions. Fat Legs's party crossed the river ice just before dusk and walked along the northeast riverbank to Arrow Feather's town. There they would stay until the next morning, and then go on out onto the plains with a respectable number of the warriors from that town, and walk until they met the hairy-faces, whom the hunter had first seen about two long days' walk from the river. "Surely," said Fat Legs, "we will meet them in the high part of the day tomorrow."

Arrow Feather said, "They must be a strong people, to have traveled so far in this hard season, against this wind which has not stopped in the past moon!"

The wind had diminished by next morning; it was still strong, but not whistling. The sky was of unbroken, black-bottomed clouds, crawling low over the snow-dusted dead grass plain. As Fat Legs and Arrow Feather left Arrow Feather's town with about a hundred warriors, and with old Squash Blossom being pulled along on her toboggan, thirty warriors were sent out ahead with several bags of multicolored corn in the ear, and a few hands of tobacco wrapped in furs, to offer as gifts to the travelers. They vanished over the brow of the bluff, waving overhead their feathered lances and whooping with excitement.

Squash Blossom this morning had insisted with haughty crankiness that she did not want to ride the toboggan facing backward, but would lie propped up on it facing forward so that she could see where she was going instead of where she had been. She wanted to see these hairy-faced men as they approached, to see how they matched the dream-vision she had had of them so many years ago. And so now she rode that way, sitting back against a bundle of hides and firewood, and did not complain that most of what she could see with her old eyes was the tail ends of the sled dogs. That proved eventful, for the dogs, within the first part of the morning, got into several snarling fights with each other, stopping the march till they could be separated.

Her son Fat Legs and her grandson Arrow Feather walked close by, each wearing a headpiece made of bison skull wool with horns still on. The two men looked like the same man at two different ages, they were so much alike. As she rode along over the immense plain, her mind sometimes drifted to images of their childhoods, and she remembered waiting in pity, fear, and agony during their respective ordeals in the Okeepah. But such memories were only momentary. She was trying to concentrate upon her memory of the dream-vision of the coming of the hairy-faces. She would gaze ahead at the horizon, expecting at any moment to see the dark line of walking figures in their strange dress. She would shut her eyes and see the remembered vision, then open them and expect to see the strangers there. But it was a long, long jolting ride before she at last perceived anything in the distance. Several times she dozed off to the sound of footsteps, people talking, gusts of wind over the snow, anxious voices, the rattle of weapons and shields, a muffled cough . . .

And then she was aroused by the sound of men's voices gone intense with excitement.

Old Squash Blossom opened her eyes and stared ahead, raising her head to see over the pulling dogs.

It was not clear at first what she was seeing. But there was a smear on the white horizon, a blob of darkness her old eyes could just discern. She kept staring at it as the sled moved forward. She could feel the tension in the men, saw them squinting ahead nervously. Her son Fat Legs looked back and down at her from where he walked, as if to see that she was awake. With his horned bison hat on and his robe pulled high on his shoulder, he looked like a bison with only two legs. She nodded at him, looked ahead and waited. Fat Legs told his warriors to stop here and build a fire. They unloaded sticks and tinder from Squash Blossom's sled. Then, with a pot of embers they had carried from the town, they quickly kindled a good blaze for the meeting place.

The dark line in the distance grew larger and began to spread and separate into mist-blurred fragments, and then the fragments took form as oncoming runners, growing clearer as they grew bigger and closer. The first ones were dressed like her own people, and Squash Blossom realized they were the ones who had been sent ahead, and that they had met the strangers and were returning now, leading them back. These men raised their lances and bows and came sprinting back, whooping and yipping, running so light-footed that their moccasins hardly seemed to touch the snow.

The main body of people in the farther distance remained clumped together and moved slowly, but she could see that they were a huge crowd, several hundred men on foot. Squash Blossom struggled to get her stiff old body up from the sled, wanting to be standing when they approached.

Now the runners had reached Fat Legs, and they were all trying to talk to him at once. They said the hairy-face men were led by a strong, gray-haired chief in a dark robe that was not made of hide, that he had about fifty hairy-face men with him, two of them being his sons, and that about three hundred of the Stone Cooker People, mostly warriors, but with a few childless women, were marching with them. One of the runners said:

"Where we met them, they had twice as many of the Stone Cookers with them, more than we could ever feed. And so we offered to let them join us in fighting the Dah-koh-tah, and at that, they had a council and decided not to come farther. Those Stone Cookers are not brave."

Fat Legs chuckled. "That was a smart thing to say. We cannot feed all the Stone Cookers. But you say three hundred still come on?"

"The chief of the hairy-faces said he is no coward and will come on. He has the sticks that kill far off with thunder and lightning, and he has given those to some of the Stone Cookers, too. So some of them decided to come with him."

"The Stone Cookers have the killing sticks, too?" Fat Legs exclaimed in astonishment. "Those Nakodabi people have the sticks?"

"That is bad to know!" Arrow Feather breathed.

Fat Legs stood frowning. He murmured, as if talking to himself, "Tribes to the south and west of us have the riding animals, that they got from the hairy-faces who dress in iron. Now there will be the Stone Cookers not far to the north of us, who will have the killing sticks given to them by the hairy-faces up there! We are between two dangerous things! I do not like this! Though I have looked with joy to meeting these hairy-faces, I wonder if they will be bad for us!"

"But, my Father, listen," said Arrow Feather. "If the Stone

Cooker People have those weapons, we can soon have them, too! It might be that the hairy-face chief will give some to us, as he gave them to the Stone Cookers. Why would he not?"

"That might be true," mused Fat Legs, squinting into the distance toward the great crowd of approaching marchers. "Yes, perhaps you are right, my son. I would hope he would be fair like that."

"And," Arrow Feather added, "as you know, Father, the Stone Cookers are such fools in trade and in gambling that if they come to our towns with their killing sticks, many would probably leave without them, and go home carrying not those weapons but feathers and beads and tobacco and pretty things made by our women's hands. You know those people are mad for blue beads."

Fat Legs nodded and now he was smiling shrewdly. "Ha! Yes, that is true about them! I have never seen one of these killing sticks, and might not like them. But if our neighbors have them, we should also, to protect our People." He nodded hard, affirming, and grunted, and then studied the slow approach of the strangers. "But," he said after a while, "when somebody has a thing of power, he will not trade it off so easily as a thing of mere usefulness or beauty. You know, the tribes with the riding animals keep them very close to themselves. When we have tried to trade for them, they would not ever agree to do so."

Squash Blossom, while the chiefs talked, had raked hot ashes and embers around a pot of food, to warm it. It was a paste of maize meal and dried-tuber flour cooked with sweet pumpkin and seasoned with currants. The pot contained enough only for the chiefs of both parties to eat—just a ritual meal at first meeting. Real feasting for everyone would begin later, when the party of strangers went down to Arrow Feather's town. Squash Blossom peered at the distant people and tried to guess whether the food would be warm enough when they arrived. They were coming so slowly. But they were close enough now for her to see that they were not so strange as to be monstrous. In fact, they were beginning to match perfectly the image of the dream-vision she had carried so long in her mind.

What she recognized first was the white flag fluttering from a pole being carried by one of the men in the front and center of the crowd. In her dream she had seen that, but, not knowing of any such thing as a flag, she had seen it as a white buffalo skin on a pole, like that which hung on a long pole atop the lodge of a *maho okimeh.* The banner was being carried with difficulty, being quite large and whipped hard by the prairie wind. The man carrying it was big and strong-looking, appearing as burly as a bear in his thick garments, but he was struggling with it. Soon another burly man came to him and relieved him of it, and that one, too, had to carry it with strong arms in the wind.

"See," Arrow Feather said to Fat Legs. "There must be their *maho okimeh*." Fat Legs nodded, and held high his long lance with its red-dyed streamers and its full comb of eagle plumes fluttering in the wind. "Now lay the robes around our fire," he said, "for our visitors will be here soon."

They came trudging down the last long stretch of snowy slope, looking tired but still formidable; their faces were just people's faces, yet with a difference in their way of looking ahead, as if they were looking for something that neither the Children of First Man nor the Stone Cookers with them knew to look for; yes, they were different somehow in the eyes. Squash Blossom's spirit was singing, because they were just as she had foreseen: a people with faces like her own people instead of the faces of the other tribes. True, many of these men had hair growing on their chins, but in their eyes and the color of their hair, she saw a sameness with her people.

She looked at the banner they carried and could see that it was not a white buffalo robe, but rather a material of extreme lightness and smoothness, and not just white as it had seemed to be, but marked with three bright yellow designs like lance points. She looked at the face of the man carrying the banner, expecting him to be their chief, but no, he was a young man with something of a stupid and frightened look in his eyes. The other man who had been carrying the banner pole before was also young and stupid-looking. And then Squash Blossom, and her son and grandson, all determined at the same moment that neither of the banner carriers was the chief; rather, it must be the older man who marched between them.

This man's eyes were heavy-lidded, sleepy-looking, and, as he carried his head tilted back, they seemed to look down along his fleshy, red nose. His mouth was wide and thin-lipped, and the thrust of his chin made his lower lip close outside the upper. His face was dirty-looking and grown with stubble, but unlike most of the others, he did not have a hairy face. His skin was neither white nor brown, but rather a mottled gray, almost the color of snow-bearing clouds. On his chin was a grizzled tuft of whiskers that reminded Squash Blossom of the chin whiskers of a bison. The man wore a muddy, dark brown cape that reached his knees, and his legs and feet were encased, up to the middle of his thighs, in thick leather boots with pointed toes. When his cape blew open now and then, a glinting of metal things could be glimpsed, things he was wearing on his clothing. But he was not, or did not appear to be, all clad in iron like the cruel hairy-faces who dwelt down on the Mother of Rivers.

On his head was a most remarkable headdress, made of heavy black material handsomely folded to give it three corners, and on its left forefront was a sort of shiny white ornament, out of which grew a thick white plume almost as long as a man's arm, and the plume rippled and whipped and shivered in the wind. That plume arrested the chiefs' attention as much as the flag had; it was a beautiful thing to see upon a man's head.

Behind that hairy-face chief came his hundreds of followers, and they were a spectacle to amaze the eye: short, squat men with faces as woolly as bull bison, carrying on their backs such thick bundles that they looked like the bisons' humps. Many of these men were ugly, uglier than anyone Squash Blossom had ever seen, grimacing with jagged, dirty teeth, some scar-faced and one-eyed, some looking like stooped-over demons. But there were some with strong, handsome, pleasant faces, some boyish and wide-eyed, smooth-faced and obviously afraid.

Most of these men carried what appeared to be staffs, but did not lean upon them as they walked. They were not lances, either, or bows, and they were too long to be war clubs.

All the rest of the people were, judging by their dress and ornaments, the Nakodabi, known as the People Who Cook with Hot Stones, a people who lived and hunted far to the north beyond Turtle Mountain, twenty sleeps of travel from the Muddy River. They had long been friendly with the Children of First Man, traveling the long distance to trade for the leathers and decorated tunics, the pottery and blue beads the People made so beautifully. For those things, the Stone Cooker People had been bringing, in the last few trading seasons, metal things they had obtained from the hairy-faces: metal awls and needles, iron choppers and knives, iron cooking pots that could be put directly upon fire without cracking, and shiny metal knives that were much stronger and easier to use than flint. They had also brought curved metal strikers which could be knocked against flint to make sparks for fire building. The women of Fat Legs's nation loved the metal items, which made their lives easier. As the great crowd of hairy-faces and Stone Cookers drew up a short distance away, called to a halt by the plumed man's clear voice, Fat Legs and Arrow Feather glanced at each other, both noting that many of the Stone Cooker warriors did indeed carry the curious-looking sticks.

For a little while no one moved to close the distance between the two groups. The flag fluttered like a white flame in the wind; garments and feathers were blown about. The chief hairy-faces spoke softly to one another and to a few of the Stone Cookers in the forefront, and back in the crowd some of the women could be heard yelping as they separated their snarling, fighting pack dogs.

Then the gray-faced chief of the hairy-faces and the two banner carriers came forward toward Fat Legs and Arrow Feather. With them was a tall, elegant Stone Cooker man who had been to the towns of the Children of First Man several times in years past and could speak their tongue. This man stopped in front of Fat Legs and stepped aside. He glanced back and forth between Fat Legs and the gray-faced chief and said something in a language Squash Blossom had never heard. She kept listening for words of the ancient language that had been taught with the passing of the Magic Bundles, but as yet heard none. Surely, she thought, if these are indeed the people of our ancient forefathers, they will speak some of the words of First Man!

Mannah Sha said to listen for words we know, she thought. Listen!

Then the translator said to Fat Legs in the Mandan tongue:

"Father and friend, Fat Legs, first chief of the Mandan people, greetings. With the help of Creator, this great chief and his people have walked for two moons in this hard weather to come and find you in your country. He brings fine things to trade, and prays that you will help him to learn about your country and places toward the setting sun. He wishes to take your hand and embrace you."

Fat Legs peered hard at the gray man. Then his mouth worked for a moment without words, and broke into a smile. He stretched out his hand to touch the gray man's hand. For a moment they clasped their hands tight, feeling each other's strength. Then each leaned toward the other and reached around to embrace with one arm, and the gray-faced man put his mouth against Fat Legs's right cheek, then his left. Fat Legs almost recoiled at the smells that enveloped him from the man's mouth and body. The man smelled worse than a long-dead corpse. Fat Legs leaned back, breathed some fresh air, and then said to the translator:

"Tell this man that Fat Legs, *maho okimeh* of the Children of First Man, is full of joy because he comes here. That my People will feed and shelter him and his People. That we will answer, as well as our knowing permits us, whenever he asks anything. Now you please tell me, first, what is the name of this strong man who has come so far to see my People?"

The translator thought about the question and smiled weakly.

"You ask me this man's name? It is hard to say. He is . . ." The translator licked his lips and pronounced carefully: "Lah-va-lehn-da-ee."

The gray-faced man touched his own chest and said, *"Je suis Pierre Gaultier de Varennes, Sieur de la Verendreye."* The words rolled and twanged and gurgled out so voluptuously that Fat Legs leaned back farther, afraid the man was about to vomit. Then the man stood looking down his nose at Fat Legs, as if he did not approve of what he was seeing.

Fat Legs, wanting very much to remain polite until he could judge how to treat this strange, stinking, but important stranger, smiled and gestured to the robes spread on the snow by the fire. "Say to him that we will sit and eat, and smoke, and when he is rested, we will turn and go to the town, where there is food and shelter for all his People."

The Stone Cooker translator went to work with hand signs and strange noises, and although he could not make the same sick noises in his throat, he somehow managed to convey the message; the gray-faced man and the two with him sat on a robe and stretched their hands toward the fire. The wind blew smoke into their faces. Fat Legs and Arrow Feather sat opposite them. Squash Blossom gave Fat Legs a large scoop made of the horn of a mountain sheep. He stuck it into the hot grain mush with the handle pointing toward the gray-faced chief and signaled him to eat.

The man at first nibbled cautiously at the edge of the spoon. Then his expression bloomed into surprise and pleasure, and he soon cleaned the spoon of its steaming contents. Then Fat Legs smiled and signed for the others to eat. Then he and Arrow Feather ate. All the time, the chiefs and the strangers were studying each other's faces with great curiosity, though trying not to stare too rudely. When the pot was empty, Fat Legs took his long leather pipe bag out from under his robe, drew the wooden stem and the redstone bowl out and fitted them together. The bowl was stuffed with sage. He took out the sage and sprinkled it over the fire, fanning its fragrant smoke over the strangers—though the icy wind was already doing that—and then he began filling and tamping in a mixture of tobacco, red willow bark, and bearberry leaves, which he lit with a coal he snatched out of the fire with his fingers. He sucked on the stem until smoke came, and then he shut his eyes, turned the stem to each of the Four Winds, up to heaven and down to earth, and then passed it to the gray-face.

It was evident at once that the gray-faced chief did not like the tobacco; he made a disgusted face and passed the pipe on. Fat Legs was both annoyed and fearful. He wanted to please this powerful stranger, but thought he was rude. Meanwhile, all around, Fat Legs's warriors were mingling with the Stone Cooker People, laughing, signing, sharing, and trading. It was a visit of great conviviality, even though it was taking place on a bleak, snowy, windswept slope without horizons.

They sat for a long time. The translator did his best, and a vague notion of the strangers' mission gradually began to form in the mind of Fat Legs. The gray-face was of a people called French, who had come across the Great Sunrise Water many generations ago and now had towns east of the big freshwater lakes. They had been coming westward for more than a hundred years, establishing trading posts in the nations of many peoples, and now had reached this far. The gray-face chief said he was looking for a waterway to the Sunset Sea, and that he was making pictures of the lands and hills and waters, so that others of his people could find their way in these great grasslands. It seemed to the gray-face chief to be a very difficult task, and Fat Legs thought that indeed it must be, if it had taken a hundred winters just to get this far. Fat Legs told the translator to explain to the gray-face that there were trails and peoples all over the whole land, and that the peoples all knew how to get from anyplace to anyplace else. "Did you not come to us by the northern carrying place, and the Stone Cookers' Trail, and around Turtle Mountain?" he asked. The translator said that they had. "It is all very easy," Fat Legs said. "If the Dah-koh-tah are not your enemies, why can you not go anywhere you please? I do not understand why a people would need a hundred winters to cross a land that can be crossed in two years even if you bring your women and children."

The translator thought for a while, being stared at by the gray-face, and then expressed something to him in a jumble of words and gestures, which the gray-face did not seem to understand.

To old Squash Blossom, who had been hovering near the fire, scraping out the empty food pot and listening, all this seemed to be going nowhere. If these far-coming strangers were indeed descended from the great tribe beyond the Sunrise Water, it should be stated now that they were all brothers. Squash Blossom had begun to doubt both the ability and the intentions of the translator. She had been listening to the words of the gray-face, and although she had never heard such strange noises from a human mouth before, she now and then thought he said some word that echoed in her memory of the talk of the Ancient Times. But when she heard such a familiar word, she could not remember what it was supposed to mean. She could remember practically nothing, it seemed, because of her age, and that frustrated her.

But suddenly, as she was passing near the seated strangers, looking at the bright, shiny emblem and the long plume on his hat, she remembered the word that meant "beautiful."

"Prydfa!" she cackled, pointing at the ornament. *"Prydfa! Prydfa!"* She almost danced with glee. The strangers, startled, swiveled about to glare at the old woman. She stopped, dumbfounded. "What? They do not know that word? They do not know their own word for 'beautiful'?"

The translator, obviously embarrassed, jabbered and waved at the visitors for a while, and suddenly they all began laughing. The chief white man touched himself on the chest and exclaimed, *"Qu'est ce qu'on dit? La vieille me juge beau? Ha ha!"*

One of the younger men laughed and nudged the gray-face's elbow. *"Peut-etre elle veut coucher avec toi, Papa!"* They all laughed and snorted, and the older one shook his head. Then after a pause, he grumbled:

"Il fait froid! Allons au ville!" He began getting up, very stiffly. The chiefs, too, in confusion, began to stand up. Squash Blossom, dismayed, tottered among the big men, reaching for sleeves. She could not believe that they did not understand a major word of their own tongue. Only then did the doubt set in. She thought:

Perhaps it is not their tongue! Maybe these are not the other Children of First Man, after all!

They seemed to be getting ready to proceed on to the town. Squash Blossom thought:

The Magic Bundles! The language of First Man is in the bundles! They did not understand the word because I perhaps did not know how to say it their way. Yes, it has been hundreds of years. Perhaps words are not spoken the same as they were long ago. But surely the ones written on the leaves would not change with the passing of the years! Sighing, she climbed back on the sled for the ride back to the town. Perhaps she could cross the ice tomorrow and bring one of the Magic Bundles for the strangers to see. Now she was very tired, and not very happy with the way this first meeting with the strange men had gone.

Some people were happy, though. Here and there were men of her own people trotting along through the snow with bright smiles on their faces. They were carrying the strange long clubs that were believed to be killing sticks.

Always more clever and persuasive than the Stone Cooker Nakodabi, they had already gotten some of these important possessions away from them, either through sharp trading or gambling. Fat Legs saw these and he smiled.

WHEN THE MARCHERS CAME ONTO THE PLAIN ABOVE ARROW FEATHER's town late that afternoon, hundreds of the town's inhabitants came running out joyously across the snow, yelping and trilling, accompanied by countless excited dogs. Even more people were crowded along the ramparts of the palisade and the dry moat outside, perhaps as many as a thousand, all in buffalo-hide robes painted, quilled, and feathered, carrying staffs and lances festooned with bright, fluttering ribbons, a profusion of colors against the snow, the gray sky, the clay-colored dome houses. Still more hundreds of people were perched on the roofs watching, despite the icy winds.

Within a few hundred paces of the palisade, the French leader halted his crowd and had all those with killing sticks—perhaps a hundred hairy-faces and Stone Cooker warriors—line up in a single straight rank, shoulder to shoulder. One of his subchiefs stepped out four paces in front of the center of the rank and stood with the pole of the white-and-gold banner planted on the snow at his feet. With shouts, the gray-face directed the hundred to raise their sticks to their shoulders and point them at the sky. His voice was strong enough to be heard over the howling of the onrushing villagers, who were now coming within a hundred paces of the line. Squash Blossom and her son and grandson, the chiefs, were between the banner and the oncoming villagers, and she, on her sled, was watching the happy and excited faces of her People come toward her when the thunder erupted.

It was the loudest noise she had ever heard. It was so loud it struck a pain in her head and she even felt the air itself shake with it. It was a cracking, sputtering boom, dwindling into more sputterings and the whooping of the Stone Cookers.

Her people reacted as if they had been struck by the mightiest Thunderbirds. Some fell down. Some stopped. Others collided with each other. All screamed with utter terror. In a moment some were running back toward the town, while some lay in the snow writhing and sobbing with their arms wrapped around their heads. At that moment, her ears still ringing and her heart nearly flying out of her breast, Squash Blossom saw smoke roll across the scene before her, smoke with a sharp, thick, bad smell. Her son Fat Legs and her grandson Arrow Feather, being brave and self-controlled men, did not fall down or run, but stood in dignified and alert postures, but their faces were wrenched with fear.

The French gray-face chief was shouting again and waving his arm. All the people along the line had their killing sticks down in front of them and were doing something to them. After a few moments they began pointing them at the sky again. Many of these men were laughing at the fright and mayhem that the smoky crash had caused among the hundreds of villagers. Even the people on the ramparts and in the distant village were milling and howling; some were even falling off the roofs.

At another shout from the gray-face, the thunder roared again, and a hundred long showers of sparks flew into the air, and the stinking smoke again roiled through the crowd. The People again writhed in the snow and covered their heads and wailed. Some who had been standing in shock now turned and ran back toward the town. The dogs tied to Squash Blossom's sled had been whimpering and howling since the first crash; this time they all bolted as one, running after the fleeing people, and the old woman hunched down, gripped the sides of the sled and hung on for her life. Never had she gone so fast in her long lifetime. The ground blurred. The dogs sped past running people, and the wildly slithering sled hit several on their legs, knocking them down. Squash Blossom's pounding heart was high in her throat. Snow was spraying in her face and veiling her sight. She had passed half the running crowd when she heard the third thunderclap go off, now so far behind that it did not hurt her head.

When she saw that the veering dogs were about to swing the sloughing toboggan into the wall, she let go and rolled off. She skidded and tumbled along the snowy ground until she came to rest against the body of a screaming fat woman who had just been upended by the careening dogsled. Squash Blossom lay still for a while amid the howling mayhem of the frightened villagers, and finally deduced that her old body was not broken.

THE TERROR HAD DIED DOWN, AND THE VILLAGERS WERE ALMOST delirious with excitement. Never had they had such delightful fright without any destructive or sad consequences. Now the hairy-faces had come down to the village to be admired for their strange clothing and their strange smelliness, and the People of Arrow Feather's town crowded close in on them, looking amazed, looking coy, looking amused. The village was a din of voices and drums and barking dogs. The sky had cleared, and a golden-red afternoon sunlight made the domes and poles of the village glow, and sunbeams slanted through the haze of smoke and dust. By custom, the gray-face French chief was carried on the shoulders of warriors to Arrow Feather's lodge. The lodge was big and spacious, but so many people crowded in that it was hard for anyone to breathe or to hear. Arrow Feather and Fat Legs, being pressed against the hairy-face chiefs, had to breathe through their mouths to keep from being overwhelmed by the stench of their mouths and bodies. For a while the gray-face chief could not even make himself heard to his Nakodabi translator because of all the excited voices, but at last he had him ask Arrow Feather to clear some of the people out, to give his Frenchmen some room and allow them to put their baggage down where they could guard it, because it contained valuable gifts for the Mandan people. When he finally understood this message, Arrow Feather shouted and shouted, pleaded and pushed until at last there were only ten of the strangers and their translator, three chiefs, Squash Blossom, and two of Arrow Feather's wives left in the lodge. When the lodge had been thus emptied, the gray-face suddenly began darting around in the lodge, waving his hands and shouting, and in a moment all the other visitors were doing the same. Fat Legs and Arrow Feather looked at each other in bewilderment, not knowing why their guest was displeased.

At last the translator managed to convey the cause of it all: the bag in which the hairy-face leader had brought presents was missing. The carrying servant who had brought it in had set it down and taken his eyes off of it; it seemed then that someone among the departing villagers and Stone Cookers must have snatched it up and carried it out when they were driven out of the lodge. It was full of valuable things, cried the translator—

full of great treasures! The leader's face had gone from gray to purple, and the translator and the Stone Cookers who were still in the lodge began crying about rascals. One said he was going to have a search made among his own People at once, and darted out. Another tried to berate Arrow Feather for letting his People steal from a visitor the moment he arrived. Arrow Feather's eyes grew angry. He shouted that the Children of First Man were not thieves. "Only your Stone Cooker People could have known that was a valuable bundle!" he cried. "Only they would have thought to steal it! Did not your own man run out just now to look for it among them?" His eyes full of the fire of indignation, he then asked the old French leader: "What will you do now, since this unhappy thing has thrown a shadow over us? Do you mean to leave us in anger? Do you mean to hurt my people with your storm sticks? Please, do not hate us or distrust us because this has happened! You need not give us gifts to make us welcome you here! We want you to stay among us to talk about the things you came so far to speak of. We will feed you well and give you whatever you want. You do not have to pay us with presents!"

While the translator was relaying those words, Arrow Feather and Fat Legs stood looking as dignified as they could, despite the fear and mortification in their hearts. They leaned close to each other, father and son, and Arrow Feather asked:

"Should we search the town?"

"No," replied Fat Legs. "No. I think the Stone Cookers took it, not our People. If we search our own People, this Stinking Chief will think we do not trust our People's honesty. We must refuse to search for his bundle, but make his heart restful here in spite of what happened."

Fat Legs glanced at the translator, who was jabbering busily, and said to Arrow Feather: "Look at that one and listen to him make mouth-wind! And we do not even know if he is telling the Stinking Chief what we told him to say! *Keks cusha!* Very bad. We were so eager to see these hairy-faces arrive, but such trouble they bring at once! I wonder if we will be sorry they came!"

"Father," said Arrow Feather, "whether their visit proves good or bad, at least we now have some of their storm sticks that our warriors got already by trading and gaming. We will be glad they came, if only for those. Look, now, Father. The old chief of the hairy-faces does not look so unhappy now. Perhaps this Stone Cooker word-changer has really told him what we meant! How strongly I pray that he will be easy among us!"

The translator began, using his grandest gestures and aware of his own beauty and importance. "Lah-va-lehn-da-ee hears you with his ears and his heart. He has pity on you and your people, and despite the theft, he will stay among you and talk with you for a while this winter. My people, too, will stay here with you, for we love and fear our Father Lah-va-lehn-da-ee, and we do not want to leave him."

Squash Blossom heard this, and saw the relief upon the faces of her son and grandson. Though she ached everywhere from her tumble off the toboggan, she too felt warm and happy with relief. For if the hairy-faces stayed awhile, surely there would be a chance to show them the Magic Bundles, and, with time, perhaps the forgotten part of the language of First Man might be relearned.

But at the same time, she thought:

How will our People feed these hundreds of Stone Cooker People for the winter, and ourselves as well?

THE CHIEFS KNEW THEY COULD NOT FEED ALL THE STONE COOKER People even with all the food they had stored in their towns on both sides of the river. And so they plotted to spread the word among them again that Dah-koh-tah had been seen by hunters nearby and might attack at any time.

The ruse worked. By the next day the leaders of the Nakodabi had made up their minds to take their People back to the north where their women and children were encamped, and then to go on from there to their town far beyond the Turtle Mountain.

Not wanting the hairy-faces to flee with the Stone Cookers, Fat Legs and Arrow Feather needed somehow to tell the gray-face chief of their ruse. They could not tell him through the translator, because he was a Stone Cooker himself. It was a delicate matter. But at last, using hand signs and shrewd facial expressions, and one of their own hunters who knew a little of the Stone Cookers' tongue, they made the French chief understand that there were really no Dah-koh-tah nearby. They thought they could read in his face that he saw their plight and that he approved of their shrewdness. Fat Legs told him, with much difficulty, "We can feed your people, and they are welcome here, but we cannot feed all these Stone Cookers."

And so, when the French leader sat down in council that day with the leaders of both tribes, he put his hands on the heads of both, and told them that he was not angry with anyone, neither for the loss of his treasures nor for the Stone Cookers' decision to leave. The lodge was filled with shouts of joy and relief. Now at last it all seemed to have been worked out to the very best advantage. The Frenchman's interpreter would stay here with him, as well as five brave Nakodabi warriors who would stay to guide the French back north when they did decide to go. Four Frenchmen would go back north with the Stone Cookers. They would take back to the French towns in the northeast the news that the French people were wintering here. All such arrangements having been made, everyone settled down for an evening of feasting, trading, gambling, and flirtation with the beautiful young women of Arrow Feather's town. That night, under the whistling winter wind, there were the muffled sounds of laughter, giggling, flutes and drums and rattles, and the shouts and murmurs of intense bargaining and betting. It was as happy a night as anyone could remember, and old Squash Blossom in particular was suffused with joy because she anticipated sharing the Magic Bundles with these men from afar, those Magic Bundles that she, like generations of Bundle Keepers before her, had been guarding in anticipation of the prophesied arrival of the other descendants of First Man.

And that night many a Frenchman discovered, to his amazement and amusement, that some Mandan husbands offered their wives in hospitality, and that many of the women had between their thighs a strange and titillating appendage they called the Little Tongue, in which they and the men found delight.

Very late, there was a music of excited voices outside the lodges. Naked men and women got up from their sleeping places and by fire glow wrapped themselves in buffalo robes to go outdoors. They looked up at the night sky and gasped and exclaimed and prayed.

Most of them had seen it before, having lived their lives here in the cold land, but they had not seen it often, and it was certainly a sight given them by Creator, to remind them to revere him. Some even thought it was the Creator himself, waving his vast White Buffalo Robe in the night sky. It shimmered like starlight, folding and unfolding and rippling, and sometimes seemed to change from greenish-yellow to pearl; now and then it seemed faintly blue at its top, faintly red along its lower edge, like the hem of a white robe when its wearer has walked over red dusty earth.

After seeing it, some people felt good, and others felt bad, depending on how they felt about other things.

When it was gone and the people went back to their sleeping

places, many of them dreamed about it, or lay talking in soft tones about what it meant, having come during the visit of the bearded men.

OLD SQUASH BLOSSOM SET OUT AT FIRST LIGHT TO WALK ACROSS the frozen river to Fat Legs's town, to get the Sacred Bundle that contained the word markings. She thought her son was too busy with the French leader to go with her, and everyone else in Arrow Feather's town was too busy with the presence of the strangers to think of going over to Fat Legs's town. In fact, people from Fat Legs's town kept coming across the river to Arrow Feather's town to see the hairy-faces and to trade with the Stone Cookers. And so, in order not to be an old woman bothering younger and busier people, Squash Blossom walked out, stooped and leaning on her walking staff, her bones aching from age and weariness and the tumble from the toboggan, down the slope to the bottomland where she could walk sheltered a bit from the wind of the plains, and there she plodded through the drifted snow and the willow thickets, upriver toward the river bend where she would cross the ice to Fat Legs's town. It was hard walking, but not too much for a woman who had made the same trek countless times in her long life, usually carrying great loads of firewood or hides on her back. Up on the bluff she could see groups of wind-buffeted people walking along the high path toward her grandson's town, and now and then families passed her on the bottomland path, going in that direction. Most of them greeted her and expressed surprise at seeing her going the other way, but they were plainly in too eager a haste to stop and talk. That was all right with her. She was in her own eager haste. Walking home, then returning to Arrow Feather's town with the Magic Bundles, was certain to take her all day, so she did not want to be delayed by talkers. Still, they asked her things. So she would simply tell them, "The Stone Cookers are leaving today." And the People would hurry on, not wanting to miss a chance to sell them a few things before they set out.

Squash Blossom pushed onward along the snowy path, along the great river whose frozen surface looked like polished flint.

At last she reached the crossing place and walked onto the ice of the river. It took her a long time to cross. She climbed the hill to her son's town, stopping often to rest. She tottered among the houses to the Sacred Canoe. The town was almost deserted, the few people in it being in a rush to cross the river and go down to see the strangers. Wind sang around the Sacred Canoe.

She untied the knots that secured the forbidden door, set the door aside and went into the musty gloom, where the familiar bundles and bags lay upon their scaffolds. She picked up the two leatherbound Word Bundles, feeling as always the vibration of their mystery. Then she went out, set them on the ground while she secured the door again, picked them up and started back through the town. She passed her own house and wanted so much to go in and rest, to eat something. But there was not time. To walk back to Arrow Feather's town would take the rest of the daylight.

She went down and recrossed the river and hobbled along the way she had come. Already the blown snow had covered her footprints. Now and then a shout, diminished by wind and distance, would come to her through the rushing noise in her head, that rushing noise that seemed to be the sound of her spirit flowing through her like the river, and such a voice would be as faint and wordless as a birdcall. Compared with forever, her husband once had said to her, the life of a person is surely as brief as the life of a tiny bird.

And, she thought, our voice is just a chirp.

Her foot hooked on a willow branch in the snow and she fell forward. The fall was cushioned by snow and boughs and did not hurt even her stiffened old frame. She smiled, chuckled. How nice it was not to hurt. She hugged the Word Bundles.

She felt as if she were in a warm bed, too tired to get up just yet. She sighed into the whiteness of the snow around her face. Oh, never, never had she been so weary.

The Magic Bundles pressed against her ribs, as if telling her to get up and go on quickly before it was too late to show them to the hairy-face chief. But for now she had simply forgotten that task, and was instead lying comfortably here, as she often had in her bed for so many years, thinking about the word markings on the leaves in the Magic Bundles. Sometimes when she had looked at those markings she had thought she could hear voices saying strange words—unfamiliar words, but words she nearly understood. She thought of *prydfa.* Vaguely, she remembered how that word had always meant "beautiful" in the special language of the Bundle Keepers, the ancient language, and she remembered that sometimes, while looking at the word markings on the leaves of the Magic Bundle, she had heard a voice—or if not exactly a voice, a birdcall—saying *prydfa*, as if to tell her: Those are the markings that mean "beautiful." Sometimes it had seemed that she was so close to the Knowing of those markings!

So close!

Canu: singing. *Tefyn*: the stringed thing in the other bundle. *Canu* and *tefyn*. Those words were so often in her mind together. She understood why. It was like singing and drums; they belonged together.

She wished the Stinking Chief had understood the word *prydfa* when she had spoken of the great feather on his headdress.

I must get up and go on with these Magic Bundles, she thought, so that he will understand that we, too, are the Children of First Man. Once I almost froze to death. I must go on.

But when she thought of going on along the river the rest of the weary way to her grandson Arrow Feather's town, she dreamed that she was doing it, and thus thought she was, even though she was lying unconscious in the snow.

And the snow blown by the wind was covering her up, while she dreamed of going along, not as a walking person anymore, but as a yellow leaf blown off a tree.

FAT LEGS WAS BEWILDERED. THE GRAY-FACE FRENCH CHIEF WAS IN a bad mood, and was getting ready to leave and go away, back north, even though he had said he would stay for the rest of the winter and talk with the chiefs.

It was an awful disappointment to the chiefs, because they had hoped to talk with the French chief and prove to him that they were related to him through First Man, far back in the Early Times.

Fat Legs and his son Arrow Feather talked this over with great worry. Arrow Feather said:

"Father, I know he is not pleased with us. He expected to find us living in great towns like the ones he came from, and wearing the woven clothes like his, and having many possessions such as his People own. That was what he expected, and he is disappointed in us. This is what his man said to me, the one who talks between us."

"But," Fat Legs protested, "even so, he was going to stay with us and let us tell him about the lands and the peoples down that way." He pointed toward the southwest.

"Yes," Arrow Feather said. "That he was going to do, he said. But he has changed his mind."

"Why is he angry with us?" Fat Legs fretted. "If we are not as like his People as he expected, I do not think that is our fault." He sighed in misery. "I do not understand this. I want to know more.

"My son," he said, his face suddenly brightening, "let us send for his man-who-talks-between! If we spoke to him of what we want, perhaps he could make his French chief understand more clearly than we can that we truly want him to stay."

Arrow Feather looked in surprise at his father, and the fire-light from below made his surprise show clearly, in his round mouth and wide eyes.

"Father, did you not know about that man-who-talks-between?"

"What do I not know about him?"

"That he is gone!"

"What? He is gone? The very one who talks between our tongue and theirs?"

"Father, yes. He ran away with the other Stone Cooker People who were afraid the Dah-koh-tah would come and attack. He is far away. That is why the French chief has not come to talk with us since the Stone Cookers went away."

"But that man is needed! How can we talk without him?"

"Yes, Father, and yet he left, even though he had promised that he would not leave the French chief's side. Mostly that is why the French man is full of thunder."

"Then he is angry at him, not at us! That is good! I am happy to learn that at least!" His face was suffused with a benign expression of relief.

"Yes, Father, but even though he is not angry, he will not stay with us for the winter if it gains him nothing. And without his man-who-talks-between, he cannot gain the land-knowing that he came for."

Fat Legs nodded. "That is so." He sighed. "But we ought not to let him march out to the north in this the coldest season. Let us tell him he should stay here until the warm winds."

"Yes, Father, but he has already thought of that, and chooses to go while the ground is hard. He said one cannot walk in the mud in those northern lands where his People live."

Fat Legs looked gloomy again, at that news. Then he took a deep breath, sat up straighter and said, "We ought to go and get the Magic Bundles for him to see. We have no way to talk to him now that his talking man is gone, and we do not remember how to speak the Ancient Words. But if his people are truly from beyond the Great Sunrise Water, he will be able to understand the words drawn on the leaves of the Magic Bundle, and to make music come out of the *tefyn.* Heh! It is as my mother said! The Magic Bundles should be brought here for him to see before he leaves us. Then perhaps we will be able to learn to understand each other and he will choose not to leave us! She is so wise. Where is she? I have not seen her since the Sacred Light was in the sky."

Arrow Feather raised his eyebrows and stuck out his lower lip, his sign that he didn't know. "Did she not already go home?" He turned and summoned one of the youngest of his wives, who had been sitting close behind him, pulling quills between her teeth to flatten them for weaving into designs. "Go inquire among the women and find out where our grandmother Squash Blossom has been sleeping. When you find her, ask her to come here." The young woman slipped moccasins on her feet and pulled a buffalo hide over her shoulders, hair side in, and went out through the door flap into the town. Fat Legs and Arrow Feather shared a pipeful of the tobacco the French gray-face chief had given them on his arrival. Compared with their own mixture of homegrown tobacco and barks and leaves, it was terribly potent, so pungent they could hardly bear to inhale it, but it made their heads and fingers hum and tingle, a feeling they rather liked. Arrow Feather said after a while:

"Five of my warriors traded with the Stone Cookers and got their killing sticks. They call them by a French name: *tvu-zee.*"

Fat Legs nodded. "Three of my warriors got some of those *tvu-zee* also. The Stone Cookers showed them how to use them. There is a kind of black dust that burns. You have to have some of that or the stick is only a club and will not make its thunder or throw lightning."

"I have seen that to be so," said Arrow Feather. "It is not a Magic Power, but just a trick they have made."

"If there is Magic Power," Fat Legs mused, "it is in the black dust, not in the stick. But even the black dust that burns might be a trick they make. Do we ourselves not know of black stone in the hills that burns after a prairie fire has passed?"

"That is true. We have seen that with our own eyes. Probably those hairy-faces just make their dust that burns and it is not Magic Power at all. It is said that our Ancient Grandfathers, the Children of First Man, could burn stone and make a white glue that stuck rocks together for high walls." He pointed toward the southeast where earlier towns of the People had been, many generations before. There were still such stone walls down there, so strong that the stones could not be pushed or lifted out. "But," he went on, "even if one had no more of the burning dust left, the *tvu-zee*s could be useful, for fire-sparking."

"Yes," Fat Legs admitted, thinking of the flintlocks, which had been demonstrated for his wondering eyes by La Verendreye. "Never have I seen anyone strike sparks so well. If a woman had one of those, she could make a fire at once, whenever she needed it." Most of the People still used bow drills of wood to make fire, though the chiefs and the Bundle Keepers had sometimes used the tools of the ancient stonecutters to strike sparks from flint stones for special ceremonial fires.

The problem had occurred to Fat Legs that the killing sticks would be useful to hunters and warriors only as long as there was black burning dust, and since the hairy-face men had the secret of the burning dust, a chief would want to make a long friendship with them. And so it was a deep worry for Fat Legs that the French chief was getting ready to leave. It seemed that the hope now lay in the Magic Bundles with their ancient words. Squash Blossom, being the Bundle Keeper, should be taken over to the other town to get them. When she was found, he would send warriors to take her on a sled, to hurry the mission.

Fat Legs shifted impatiently. Arrow Feather was impatient and told another wife to go after the first and ask around. But at that moment the first came back and told Arrow Feather:

"People saw your grandmother walking to the other town. That was the day after the Sacred Light in the sky."

"Ah! Then," Fat Legs said, "at daylight we will send people at once to bring her and the Magic Bundles. That will be even quicker." He said to the wife, who had slipped out of her robe and sat down to her quills again, "Thank you for going."

She said, "The chief of the strangers is sick."

"What?"

"The women at his lodge say he is very ill and has not sat up since yesterday."

Fat Legs was at once alarmed for the visitor's health, afraid that somehow it might be blamed on his People. Still, a gleam of hope came into his eye. "Then the French will not leave, if he is ill!"

"Come, Father," Arrow Feather said, rising from beside the fire. "We cannot let our important visitor lie ill in our town! Let us go to the lodge of Spotted Snake the Healer and take him to the French chief. It would be to our People's disgrace if this important traveler should sicken and die here, and never learn of our Magic Bundles!"

* * *

WHEN THE MESSENGERS CROSSED THE FROZEN RIVER TO FAT LEGS'S town the next morning and learned that old Squash Blossom had not been seen there for days, they turned and hurried back to Arrow Feather's town without even thinking of the Magic Bundles. They found Fat Legs and Arrow Feather both in distress over the French leader's refusal to be treated by their healer, and by his insistence upon starting back north as soon as he could stand and walk. But when they told the chiefs that Squash Blossom was not in the other town, either, the anguish in their faces was so great that the French strangers might as well not have existed.

The chiefs called out everyone in the town, men, women, and boys, to comb the paths between the two towns. The recent drifting of snows had erased all tracks except new ones, so no one knew which way the old woman had gone. No one was really sure that she had even started back from Fat Legs's town. Trackers were sent out to range in widening circles around Arrow Feather's town. They searched the Town of the Dead, the copses of willow and cottonwood down in the bottomlands and gullies, and the windswept slopes in every direction. Some ran for half a day in the direction the Stone Cookers had gone, thinking it possible, though not likely, that somehow she might have gone away with them. But the trail of the Stone Cookers had been obliterated by snow, and they had been so many days gone that that search was abandoned as the afternoon light faded.

The low path along the river was almost invisible. Here where the winds from the west swept along the curve of the river, all snow that had fallen on the river ice had been drifting into the thickets and was waist deep, sometimes chest deep. The men and women waded through these thickets, breasting the wind-sculpted snow, almost shoulder to shoulder, but they could only search the ground with their feet. And their feet were growing numb with cold.

Arrow Feather was among these searchers on the low path, because he knew it was his grandmother's favorite path in winter, out of the way of the wind. Fat Legs was among the searchers on the upper path, whom Arrow Feather could see far up there in the golden light of the sinking sun.

The searchers had come so far now that night would find them near the crossing place. Arrow Feather could see the roofs and palisade and cook-fire smoke of his father's town across the river. He pushed his weary, wet legs forward through the snow, which was to his waist, and felt the unseen path with his half-numbed feet. Now and then his moccasined foot would come down on a branch hidden under the snow, and the branch would yield and then lift up, or would break under his weight with a snow-muffled crack.

Now he stepped on another limb. It gave under his foot and he plowed on, his breath clouding in the evening air. That last limb had been the thighbone of his grandmother, old Squash Blossom, but he did not know it.

THE SNOW COVERING OLD SQUASH BLOSSOM'S BODY DID NOT MELT until the next spring. By then the French explorer and his party had long been gone, but their chief's illness had spread and had killed hundreds of the People. There had been many funerals and much grief. But at last spring came, bringing its renewal of hopeful spirits. The thick ice on the Muddy River broke up and moved grumbling and crunching downstream. For a while the People still crossed the river between the towns on ice, hopping nimbly from one floe to another, but eventually the water was clear enough of ice that the fragile little hide-covered bullboats could be used without danger of being crushed in ice jams. That spring a large number of bison carcasses came floating down the river, the beasts having drowned in a bank cave-in or an ice breakup somewhere upstream. The People exuberantly raced out onto the river, leaping from ice chunk to ice chunk or paddling their little boats, to get ropes on the carcasses and bring them to shore. These carcasses were deemed a generous gift from Creator, and although their meat was not fresh, it was not spoiled beyond all use, and the hides, horns, hooves, and bladders could all be used. The butchering parties worked along the riverbanks, singing and laughing, harvesting this unexpected bounty, and sometimes people passed within a few yards of the place where Squash Blossom's thawing corpse was beginning to be visible in the melting snow. At any time it could have been found, for the scavenger creatures had already started coming to it, and the early flies. But vultures and flies were already everywhere because of the butchering, so the thicket of willows with its few scavengers at work did not attract the attention of the People.

Then came the spring rains, and the river, already swollen by snowmelt, rose to swirl among the willows on the bottomland, and one rainy night the cold water worked the little cluster of clothing, bones, rotting flesh, and Sacred Bundles loose from the roots, turned it this way and that, and finally rolled it into the current that the old woman had so often thought of as being like the current of life.

And thus she who was the Bundle Keeper of the time when the hairy-faces first came, old Squash Blossom, started down the long river up which her People had come so long before. Her sons and grandson, the chiefs, never knew what had become of her. They mourned, though there was no grave for her in the Town of the Dead.

When the Sacred Canoe was opened to get out the sacred relics, the water drum, and the altar for the Okeepah ceremony, the Word Bundles were not there. It was an enormous catastrophe, but there was no explanation for it. It was known only that Squash Blossom the Bundle Keeper and the Word Bundles themselves had vanished without a trace. It was a shameful and ominous thing, and the shamans feared it might bring years of misfortune for the Children of First Man. One shaman had a dream that told him the People would all be dead in a hundred years, that the ones who had died of the hairy-faces' illness were just the beginning.

The tribal council decreed that from that time on, no woman would again be the keeper of the rest of the valuable things in the Sacred Canoe, and that the name of Squash Blossom would not be remembered by the People.

Wherever she was, she would be without a name.

CHAPTER 18

Slaps the Water's Town
1750

Through a veil of blown snow the forty Shienne horsemen looked down at the walled village in the river bend below and prayed for strength and good fortune in the attack.

The Shienne were hungry and far from their homes. Spring had begun, bringing them out northward, but then winter had turned back on spring and caught them here in the land of their enemies, the strange people called Mandans. Though they had ranged far on their lean horses, which they called *ka vah yoh*, the Shienne had found no bison. Snow had covered the sprouting spring grass over these endless plains and the *ka vah yoh*s were growing weak. There would be grain in the Mandan town for them, and meat for the warriors.

It would require great daring and surprise for forty men to invade a town. But a large number of the town's men had been seen leaving on a hunt, so the town would be lightly defended. Also, the Mandans had no horses, and horses were a great advantage in war. So was desperation, and the Shienne were desperate. They could strike, loot, and leave the Mandans behind, as they had done to Mandan hunting camps in the past. To attack a whole town would be a great risk, but to succeed would be a great glory. Of this, their leader had persuaded them, and the Shienne warriors were eager, or at least seemed to be.

But the young warrior called Man on a Horse was not eager for this attack. He had questioned the leader, "Must we raid a town of women and children just to feed ourselves? If we went down there under a peace sign and asked them for meat and grain, they would feed us, just as our People would feed any strangers who came hungry."

But the leader, a man hungry for war feathers, had looked hard at him and argued, "No. The Mandans have been enemies of our People too long to welcome us. We will *take* what we want!" Then he had asked Man on a Horse if the cold and hunger were making him feel like a coward and a beggar. With everyone's eyes upon him, Man on a Horse had replied:

"You know well I am no coward. I only ask that we pray for wisdom and then decide which to do. If all wish to raid that town, I ride among you, perhaps before you, into the fight."

Under the challenging eye of their leader they all had voted for the attack. The leader pointed down a draw that would conceal their approach until they were a short dash from the town's palisade wall. He showed them the open gap in the wall where the Mandan hunters had gone out. There were no guards at the gate. The Mandans expected no danger in snowy times. The only villagers that could be seen moving about were a few down on the riverbank, where they were gathering driftwood and tending fires by their sweat huts.

And so the Shienne warriors prayed for a quick victory, and then began riding down the draw through the swirling snow. Man on a Horse thought about the people he was going to attack, thinking of them as a hunter does about the soul of his prey. These Mandan people were a kind unto themselves. Their place on the great Muddy River made them a center where tribes came far to trade with each other. They were often persecuted by their neighbors the Dah-koh-tah and the Rickaree, but were tenacious and strong in their walled towns. Having no *ka vah yoh*s, they still hunted bison in the old ways, with drives and surrounds and *pishkun*s, and were very skillful in those ways, and prospered. These were the Pale Ones, many of whom, it was said, had white and yellow hair even when young. Man on a Horse had seen some of their light-colored scalps in the lodges of his grandfathers. Among animals, white ones were those with special spirit powers, and he feared that such might be true with these people. That was all he knew about them, except that unlike the Shienne, they were a people who had not yet obtained horses, and that would be good today. But he wondered if, unlike the Shienne, these people had any of the thunder-stick weapons. Man on a Horse was one of his people's best horsemen and he was no coward. But he wondered, every time he rode on a raid, if he would be faced by the legendary thunder weapons. He prayed the Mandans would not have them.

If they have them, he thought, their hunters probably took them when they went. May that be so!

* * *

Snow Hair, a great-granddaughter of the lost old woman whose name was no longer spoken, squatted on the riverbank in a place by the fire pit where she got warmth from it without smoke stinging her eyes, and waited for more stones to get hot. The wind sweeping down the wide valley of the Muddy River blew stinging snow against the side of her face. She would have preferred to be helping her mother in the lodge, where there was no wind. The wind in this season rarely stopped. This day the sky was hidden by ragged, dark clouds that sped above the town, and the river was gray and choppy, looking like flint. Broken sheets of ice still piled up on the far side of the river bend. Though there had been a few greening days of spring, the ground of the riverbank was now frozen and dry again, so that the snow did not melt, but skittered along and drifted into low places. The wind made the ash swirl above the fire pit and fanned the embers so that they glowed with yellow heat, and that was good for heating the stones.

The wind whipped Snow Hair's hair about her face. Though she was of only fifteen winters, her hair was white. It always had been. Her eyes were as gray as the cold sky. Snow Hair had a most pleasing face and smooth, tawny skin, and her mother and father had told her to be proud of the white hair, which meant that her Ancestors had been the great *okimeh*s in the Old Times, but she was not happy about it. She envied the glossy black tresses that most of the women had. There were young men in the village who were so ashamed of their light hair that they spent much of their time blackening it with soot and oil. If the braves themselves did that, she often thought, why should I believe that white hair is good? When the black-haired people greased their hair, it shone, but when the light-haired ones did, it just looked dull yellow and dirty.

Her father was coughing in the steam hut nearby; the sound was muffled by the hides covering the hut and by the hissing wind, but she heard him. He would suck the sage-scented steam through his nose and his open mouth until he could not keep from coughing, and would cough and wheeze until he could stop. He did it to cleanse and purify his lungs.

The steam baths were said to be a tradition from the Ancient Ones, that First Man had brought the tradition from beyond the Flood when he came. They were used to relieve aching bones and joints and sinews and congested chests of a people who lived hard in a cold land. But her father, Slaps the Water, was never sick, and he used the steam just to keep himself purified, and to pray in, and for luxury.

She heard him call for more heat. With green-wood tongs she poked in the embers and lifted out a round stone the size of her head. Smoke whipped off the tongs where the hot stone seared the wood. Lifting the bottom of the flap door with her foot, she slid the hot stone into the steamy darkness, then she pulled out one of the stones that had cooled, dropped the flap, carried the stone back to the fire pit and put it deep in the embers. After putting two more hot stones in the hut, she laid some more driftwood on the fire and squatted as close as possible to get some of the heat. A few other family steam huts along the riverbank were in use. After her father had finished, Snow Hair would use it, taking advantage of the fire and hot stones.

Her father was the village chief, a good and self-contented man who was proud of his direct descent from Man Face, a legendary chief of long ago, the only Mandan who had ever ridden an Omepah Peneta and had been killed by a thunderclap—which, people understood now, probably had been a *tvu-zee*, such as the French had brought a few years ago.

The present *okimeh* of the whole People was Fat Legs, a grandfather of Snow Hair. Through the Stone Cookers of the north, Fat Legs still now and then obtained some of the black burning powder that made the *tvu-zees* work. Snow Hair had been told that her father Slaps the Water probably would become the whole People's *okimeh* when Fat Legs was no longer able, and then he probably would be the one who would trade for the burning powder. But there were only a few of the *tvu-zee*s left in the tribe. Most of them had been broken, and only the hairy-face men knew how to fix them.

Snow Hair's mother, Follows Dog, was one of the three living wives of Slaps the Water, but not his favorite. He liked the two black-haired ones better, though Follows Dog was the hardest worker. Snow Hair presumed it was natural that he would like the gray-haired wife Follows Dog least.

Slaps the Water now came crawling out of the steam hut, naked. He ran down to the riverbank, steam whipping off his heated body, his long muscles moving under his flushed brown skin, long wet hair slapping against his back, and dashed into the icy gray river, dove in and disappeared. A moment later his head appeared, far out in the stream. He blew loud breaths, turned and swam back to the shallows and then walked out of the river, every muscle tense against the chill. She met him on the bank and wrapped his bison robe around him, woolly side in. He thanked her through clenched jaws and set off at a brisk walk up the slope toward the village and his lodge, where he would then nap by the fire in the robe.

Now the steam hut was hers, and, quick with eagerness, she hauled out the cooled stones and replaced them with hot. She stripped off her dress, ducked into the hut and closed the flap behind her, shutting herself into the hot darkness. With a gourd she dipped water from a pot and sprinkled it over the red-glowing rocks, so that a dense, sage-scented steam filled the cramped darkness, so hot and wet her pores seemed to sting. Then she climbed into the wicker bed that lay on a platform above the stones, and laid herself back on it with her eyes shut, skin tingling, cough starting, sweat beginning to pour, carrying away the tightness of her muscles, which had been cramped against the cold. She lay asprawl with her knees up, trickling with sweat. Here in this dim heat she might have been in her mother's womb or in a burial shroud, at either end of the time of life, or where life met death on the turning of Time. Sometimes when she dreamed here, it was as if she herself had a memory of the Ancient Times before the People had climbed from the darkness under the ground.

Thus lost in pleasures and womb-dreams inside the little thunder sound made by the wind blowing on the hut's skin canopy, Snow Hair did not hear the shouts and screams and hoofbeats as the Shienne attacked her father's town on the bluff above.

Slaps the Water, aware of hoofbeats even in his deep sleep, dreamed of hunting bison at the *pishkun*, of driving them over the cliffs.

He was awakened by screaming, and as he flung off his cover, heart racing, he was still hearing hoofbeats, feeling them through the floor. They felt and sounded as if they were right in the village.

He clambered to his feet, still naked from his steaming and his plunge in the river. He had been so deep in sleep that he was confused, but these truly were hoofbeats, and women really were screaming, and his name was being called. Then, as he turned for his clothing, he heard something that made his blood feel as cold as the wintry river:

It was the trill and yip of warriors in the full cry of attack—and inside the walls of his own town! The commotion and yelling outside his lodge rose to a terrifying din.

There was no time to dress himself. He could only grab his bow, quiver, and knife from the post on which they hung, put his shield on his left arm, and dart for the door of the lodge. At that moment the door flap flew open and a silhouette and pitiful scream burst in on him.

Follows Dog, his white-haired wife, fell in through the doorway, tumbled to the floor and lay there gagging, blood gushing from her mouth. An arrow was through her torso, so deep that only its fletches protruded from between her shoulder blades.

And in the moment that the door flap was open and daylight showing, Slaps the Water saw a brown beast, as tall as a bison, stamping and turning just outside.

But it was not a bison, and there was a man on its back! It was Omepah Peneta, the Spirit Elk! Slaps the Water was so stunned that he could not move for a moment.

But he was a warrior, and his People's *okimeh*, and he had to defend his People, no matter what he had to face. He charged out the door despite his fear.

The sight that met him outdoors was beyond belief. Warriors on beasts milled everywhere, giving off power like thunderstorms. Many men and women and children were lying on the frozen ground, bleeding, some bristling with arrows. People of the tribe dashed about in the snow swirls, everywhere in the wide plaza around the Sacred Canoe, screaming, some falling, rolling on the ground, covering their heads with their arms. Some men had climbed onto roofs to get out of the way of the riders on their mighty, snorting animals.

The riders, he saw at once, were Shienne. They rode the beasts as if they were a part of them, turning and goading the animals without effort, keeping their hands free to use their bows and lances and clubs.

And how high and powerful and dangerous they looked, those men! From up there they could see and strike down on other people. And the wild eyes and the slavering and snorting, and the earth-shaking hoofbeats of the animals, made them still more frightening. It was no wonder that the People of his village were in such panic.

But all those thoughts had flashed through his mind in an instant. He was not their *okimeh* just to stand with trembling knees while his wife and his People were slain in their own village. With a whoop of rage, he whipped an arrow from its quiver, nocked it and let it fly at a rider who was trying to spear a fleeing woman. The arrow flicked through the rider's waist. He lurched and dropped his weapons, clutched his middle, leaned, leaned farther, and then fell on the ground a few paces from the Sacred Canoe. With another arrow already fitted, Slaps the Water shot it into the chest of one of the animals, not knowing whether it would affect a Spirit Elk or not. The beast reared up on its hind legs, causing its rider to fall off backward, then tumbled back on him with its thick haunches and rolled over, legs thrashing. The rider lay there looking broken, and Slaps the Water sent another arrow into his throat.

"My People!" he bellowed as he fitted another arrow. "Stop running! See! They can be killed! Be strong! Fight them! *Roo too hah!*" Come here!

Now the Shienne warriors had seen and heard him. Two or three turned their animals to come at him at once. He shot one off his mount, hit another of the beasts in the breast as if he were shooting elk, and was just reaching for another arrow when a lance flung by one of the riders swished past his temple and ripped his left ear loose. He spun sideways and fell to his knees, then shook his head to clear his senses and nocked another arrow. A rider was bearing down on him with a lance. Raising his left arm, Slaps the Water deflected the lance point with his rawhide shield. The beast thundered past Slaps the Water so close its winter-thick hair brushed his skin; its rider, howling through a grimace, came sliding off its near side grappling for Slaps the Water, and bore him to the ground as the animal veered past. Slaps the Water and the Shienne thrashed on the hard ground for a moment, clutching and gouging. In an instant the warrior was on top of him, pressing the edge of his own shield against his throat. He was a very strong young warrior with square jaws and an intricate stripe tattooed across his nose and under his eyes. For a long time, it seemed, Slaps the Water, unable to breathe, looked at the tattoo and struggled in vain and thought that perhaps the last thing he would see in this life would be that curious tattoo. Slaps the Water was not a young man, and he had drained his vigor in the steam hut such a short time ago. . . .

Suddenly, something jarred the man who was on top of him, and the man's face began bleeding, the blood trickling down over the tattoo. Another blow made him grunt, and Slaps the Water felt the warrior's strength leave, and he began struggling to shove him off.

It was then that he saw what had hit the warrior.

Follows Dog, staggering, the arrow still protruding between her breasts and her gray hair hanging in bloody strands down both sides of her face, hovered over him, looming against the gray sky. In both hands she clutched a stone corn-grinding pestle. As she tried to raise it for one more blow against the warrior who had attacked her husband, her eyes rolled back and she staggered, the stone slipped from her grasp and she crumpled to the ground.

With a sob, Slaps the Water rolled the stunned warrior off, snatched up an arrow that had spilled from his quiver and jabbed it into the Shienne's throat, then leaped to his feet. His heart felt crushed. He had but a moment to look down at Follows Dog. She lay apparently beyond her last breath. Her breasts and torn tunic were soaked with blood. Somehow, mortally wounded, this least-favored wife had risen from the pool of her blood to try to defend her husband. *Moor-seh!* he thought. Oh, *wife*! Then he had to turn away and fight the riding warriors. The air was full of snow and din.

I must rally my people and give them heart to fight, he thought. Most of his warriors were away hunting for bison, he knew, but he had shown that even riding warriors could be killed. He gathered up arrows from the ground. He saw that several of the Shienne warriors were lying on the ground. He saw three of their big animals lying down, and one on its rump, propped up on its forelegs, making a shrill noise of pain.

And he saw that some of the town's boys, the brave youths with fresh Okeepah scars on their chests, were on the rooftops with their bows and lances, and that they were past their first fear and were shooting the enemy warriors off the backs of their great beasts.

Slaps the Water, still stark naked in the snowy wind, was on fire inside; he ran forward at a crouch, arrow ready to release at its next target, and yelled encouragement. He was beginning to believe that Shienne on their terrifying animals were not going to conquer his village after all.

Perhaps we might even capture some of their beasts, he thought, and ride them as Man Face first did!

He howled with exultation and shot another arrow. Another Shienne riding-warrior fell to the ground behind his beautiful running beast, and a Mandan woman darted out to where he lay and slashed his throat with a flint knife.

A ROCK THROWN BY AN ENRAGED WOMAN STRUCK MAN ON A Horse so hard on his ribs that it knocked breath out of him and almost unseated him. There was a splintered arrow shaft scraping his arm under his shield where it had wedged, and he was bleeding from one thigh where a small boy had gouged him with a lance as he rode by. Man on a Horse guided his speckled mount this way and that, trying to chase the Mandan villagers who darted everywhere, throwing things at him, trying to thrust poles between his horse's legs to make her stumble.

He had tried to tell his leader not to attack a town of women and children because he had felt pity for them. Now he knew that another good reason was because they were as numerous and furious defending their town as a nest of hornets.

At first they had run screaming and hiding, so easy to knock down, and for a while the Shienne horsemen had thundered through the village whooping and terrifying everyone. But now the invaders were being crowded closer and closer into the open space in the center of the town, being shot by arrows—even the little bird and rabbit arrows of small Mandan boys—thrashed and pounded by people with sticks and poles, snared and thrown down by thrown loops of rope, jarred by stones and every other kind of throwable object, and pierced by the arrows that rained down upon them from the domed rooftops all around. Now some of the Shienne mounts were galloping around the plaza with no one on their backs, neighing in panic. There were more Shienne warriors lying on the ground than villagers. Man on a Horse had nearly been slashed open by the knife of a naked, sinewy man he had tried to ride down; his tunic had been laid wide open by the blade. Here in the smoke and blown snow in the center of the village, Man on a Horse flinched and ducked flying arrows, pots, hatchets, stones, and clubs, and he could not have ridden to escape through the infuriated crowd of people even if he could have remembered which way it was to the gate. Man on a Horse had been right and the leader of his party had been wrong, and now the Shienne were trapped; it did not look as if any would get out alive. A naked woman ran in front of him and shrieked and waved a smoking firebrand that made his mare whinny and rear. Something caromed off his shield and something else bounced off his forehead, making his vision a yellow flash for a moment.

One of the few Shienne still alive and mounted was the leader who had led them into this trap. He rode by a little way off, surrounded by a throng of snarling, yelping women, trying to beat them away with his club. Man on a Horse at that moment heard what he had always dreaded to hear: the thunderclap.

Right before his eyes a shower of sparks flew and a ball of

dark smoke billowed, and the clap of sound hurt his ears and made his head ring. As his horse neighed and sprang sideways, the Shienne warrior saw his leader fling out his arms, arch his back, and fall.

After that Man on a Horse could not see another of his comrades still riding anywhere. Now and then as he tried to push through the crowd he would see a Shienne on the ground being kicked, pounded, or stabbed by women and boys. He felt hands continually grabbing at his leggings and feet. One young woman had his mare's tail in both hands and was hanging on, screaming in fury till spittle clung to her lips. She was as frightening to him as almost anything in this chaotic trap, except perhaps the thunder stick.

Now another of those crashed near him, seeming to split his head. He had lost his bow and his lance. He had nothing to fight with except his quirt; with its whistling, stinging leather straps, he slashed at faces and arms.

He saw a gray, open area ahead through the snow. Few people were in front of him at this moment. Whipping his mare, digging in his heels, he drove her toward the opening. It was not the gate the warriors had entered, but it was a gap between the lodges and overlooking the river. Countless missiles bounced off his back and shoulders as he urged the maddened mare onward. She could hardly trot with the big young woman hanging on her tail; she would lunge forward, falter, lunge forward again, her strength almost spent. She could not get ahead of the screaming crowd, but she was starting down now, down a steep slope that led toward the riverbank, drawing part of the murderous crowd along with her, and her rider kept kicking her, kept the bloody quirt whistling left and right, left and right, gripped the mare's sides with his sinewy legs to keep from being pulled off and rode for life toward the unpeopled riverside. Even as he struck at his clutching tormentors alongside, he could not help admiring their barehanded ferocity.

What a People! he thought. What a People!

SNOW HAIR HAD STEAMED IN THE SWEAT HUT UNTIL SHE WAS WEAK; she lay there needing to breathe deeply, and the breathing of the sage-scented steam caused her to cough over and over. Finally she could lie quiet again. The wind was still buffeting the skin cover of the steam hut, and even whistling around it, making sounds which, with the ringing in her ears, reminded her of people singing or screaming. She lay on the bed of sage pouring forth sweat, preparing herself for the run through the cold wind and the plunge into the river.

But she felt very strange. She felt somehow as if she were not alone. In the yellow-red clouds that drifted behind her eyelids she saw the face of her mother, Follows Dog, and her mother seemed to be trying to talk to her. But the voice was not just her mother's voice, it was also the voices, it seemed, of countless women beyond her mother: her grandmother, whom Snow Hair could clearly see in her memory, and her great-grandmother, whom she could barely remember, and then a long succession of others reaching farther and farther back into the mists and steam, all with their mouths open and urgently speaking. But there were no words she could understand; there was only the drumming and moaning of the wind, and the singing and screaming. And there in the foreground of her thoughts was her mother, with her dirty-looking gray hair and her gray eyes, trying urgently to say something. Eventually the face of Follows Dog vanished, and so did all the others, and Snow Hair lay wondering, that so many spirits had come to her in her dreaming. Slowly she began to get up, stopping and coughing, bracing herself with her arms and keeping her head low so she would not faint. Stooping then, she lifted back the door flap, and though the day was still cloudy and gray, the sudden light made her sneeze, sneeze, and sneeze again. Then she snatched up her tunic and ran staggering down to the river's edge, dropped her garment there and made a shallow dive into the water, keeping her head above the surface, gasping at the shock of its cold on her overheated body. Every breath was a wheezing gasp, and she moved with the swiftness of a scared forked horn, to get cooled enough without chilling through. After springing and floundering in the shallows for the duration of about twenty breaths, squinting and shaking her head violently, the naked girl splashed ashore, swiping the cold water off her body with quick hands, and slipped her tunic on over her head, heaving for deep breaths, thoroughly exhilarated and, as usual, nearly bubbling into laughter from the sheer tonic of it. The wind was colder than the water had been. Snow Hair started running up the shore toward the village, where she would dart into her family's lodge, wrap in a robe and nap by the fire. She tossed her head once more to swing her wet hair out of her eyes.

It was only then that Snow Hair realized that the screaming sounds she had been hearing were really screams. The whole village, on the bluff a little way above her, was aswarm with people running, shouting, screaming, trilling, and throwing things.

And, running among the People, there were beautiful animals, as big and graceful as elks, as if she were seeing a dream. Snow Hair stopped where she was, and her slamming heart almost stopped in her bosom.

One of the beautiful beasts, with a handsome and wild-eyed young man on its back, came out of the town, down the riverbank toward her. Boys and women were chasing them.

Snow Hair was astonished to see the People of her town running after this mighty creature, not away from it. One woman even hung onto its tail, her knees dragging the ground. They were all coming down toward Snow Hair. She turned to run away from the oncoming beast as fast as she could move. She threw herself on the cold ground behind a pile of driftwood and covered her head with her arms, thinking this must be a dream from the shock of the great heat and the sudden cold.

She heard hoofbeats coming and going, toward her and away, then close again, and the angry screams of the People were everywhere. Sensing eventually that the man on the beast was too busy saving himself to hurt her, Snow Hair peeked out from under her arm just in time to see the People surround the riding warrior and haul him down from the back of his animal. They pounded on him with hands and sticks for a few moments, then lifted him from the ground and half dragged, half carried him back up toward the town, all bloodied. His great animal, meanwhile, seemed to have become very docile after all the rush and clamor of the pursuit; it shook its head, gave a loud, snorting sigh, went to the river and drank, then ambled among the onlookers and finally bent down to snort away snow and try to graze, even though it was encircled by a murmuring crowd of curious People.

Bewildered by all this, and entranced by the sight of the great tame animal, Snow Hair got up and crept, shivering, toward the crowd. She saw that the animal had been painted in several places with pictures: here a hand, there a sun, here a quartered hoop. Some kind of covering had been tied on its back to give the rider a place to sit, and a rope of braided thong was tied through its mouth and around its lower jaw. In the long hair along its neck were tied some hawk feathers. The beast had a speckled coat, flecked with much blood.

As Snow Hair turned to watch the rider being hauled up toward the town, she felt a hand on her arm. It was Red Berries, who lived in the nearest lodge. The girl's long black hair blew about her face, but Snow Hair saw a fearsome look in her eyes that made her feel cold inside. Red Berries put an arm around her waist and started leading her toward the town.

"Red Berries! Tell me what has happened."

"Sister, how can you not know?"

"I was in the steam hut. What has happened?"

"They came, many riding on these beasts into our village. They killed and hurt some before your father led us to fight them back. He made us win. We killed all but that one." Red Berries now was looking out of the sides of her eyes at Snow Hair in a pitying way, and she said, "Then you do not know about your mother?"

Snow Hair shuddered, her heart chilled. The two girls ran stumbling up the slope, past dead beasts and warriors and the bloodied bodies of people of the town. Terrible sobs were shaking Snow Hair's breast. She remembered how her mother had come so strongly into her reveries when she was in the steam, and the older women all behind her; now she knew that Follows Dog's spirit had come to her as it was leaving to pass over to the Other Side where the Ancestors were.

"Your brave mother," Red Berries was saying, "saved the life of your father so he could win against the riding warriors. . . ."

MAN ON A HORSE WAS PREPARED TO DIE. THESE MANDAN PEOPLE were ferocious. They had killed all his fellow warriors, and now they had him alone in their hands. They had every justification for killing him by torture or burning.

They had no way to know that he had spoken out against attacking them. Even if he knew their language to tell them that, to say it would only sound like a coward's plea. And had he not ridden in and struck women and elders like the rest of them?

He was bruised and bleeding all over and covered with their spit, and the wind on him now was like a knife of ice. When they dragged him up in front of a lodge with bison-hide effigies hanging high above it on poles and stood him in front of a handsome, severe man with a ripped-off ear, he remembered having seen this man in the battle. Yes, this was the naked one who had darted in close and slashed at him with a knife. He was wrapped now in a bison-hide robe painted with pictures of war deeds, and held in his right hand a decorated lance. This man, obviously a headman, had been pointing about and giving directions to the boys who were rounding up and leading in the several horses that had survived. When Man on a Horse was put before him, this headman stopped and turned his full attention upon him, and the young Shienne for the first time in his life found himself looking into eyes that were the color of the bright sky. The closeness of death was familiar to Man on a Horse, but in the color of this man's eyes there was powerful menace. Still, Man on a Horse dared show no fear, and he stood erect, ignoring his countless hurts, and looked straight back into the blue eyes as the clamor of the crowd grew still.

The headman pointed to the ground beside the door of the lodge, where a white-haired woman lay with an arrow protruding from her bloody chest.

"*Ea Moor-seh,*" he said, and his eyes now swam in tears even while blazing with ferocity. Man on a Horse believed he understood that this had been the headman's wife, and his heart ached with shame and regret, but there was no way to respond.

Then the blue-eyed man pointed at a Shienne warrior who lay nearby, his head so badly bludgeoned that Man on a Horse could not tell who it had been. The headman signed, She killed him. The crowd murmured and yipped, an ominous, fearsome sound.

The man made more hand signs to Man on a Horse, saying, Many of our women and children killed Shienne warriors this day. It was the wish of Creator, for what you did.

"*Shu-su! Shu-su!*" the People cried. But in other parts of the village, voices were wailing and trilling with grief for their dead. Man on a Horse saw two young women slip in through the edge of the crowd. He recognized the light-haired girl as one who had been wading naked out of the river when he had fled down to the shore. She dropped to her knees beside the bloody corpse of the headman's wife to tear at her wet hair and work her mouth in a voiceless scream. When he looked up at the headman, those blue eyes were blazing at him. Man on a Horse did not know what showed on his own face; he was trying to reveal nothing. But his heart was crumbling. He had a mother and a sister far away southwest in his Shienne village, and he suddenly felt what it would be to see either of them killed by intruders in a cruel and pointless raid like this. At once his heart was so gripped by grief and remorse that he had to swallow and swallow to keep from moaning aloud—and, shame of shames, he felt tears making cold tracks down both sides of his nose. The chief of the People he had helped attack was standing an arm's length in front of him, watching him weep.

Now Man on a Horse did hope they would kill him, and

quickly. He had disgraced himself this day, first by attacking an undefended village, then by being captured by women and children, now by betraying the weakness of his heart.

The blue eyes continued to drill into his quaking soul, while the wailings and shouts and hisses of the Mandan People flooded over him. The leader said something to the people around him. Some responded with cries of *"Megosh! Megosh!"* or *"Shu-su! K'hoo!"*

Then Man on a Horse was seized by merciless hands and hauled away amid howls and babbling. He was lashed tight to a pole near the center of the village plaza. People spat on him. He expected them to start stacking firewood around his feet.

But they did not. They left him there, in the cold, left him tied, to shiver, encrusted with dried blood and spittle and his own tear streaks in the war paint of his face, with the war-horses of his dead comrades tied across the plaza from him—twelve horses including his own—and there he stayed, shivering, starving, and heartsick, for two days in the bitter cold wind, while the Mandans prepared their own dead for burial but left the Shienne warriors lying scattered in his view, where the dogs of the village began gingerly eating them.

THE CAPTURED SHIENNE WARRIOR WAS KEPT ALIVE, AGAINST HIS own desire, at first.

Slaps the Water had made a name for himself that would be remembered, being the first Mandan *okimeh* to defeat mounted warriors and to capture some of the riding beasts. Now his People finally had twelve of them.

Slaps the Water now proved himself to be as prudent and wise as he was brave. He knew that the Shienne captive could be very useful to the Mandan People, and so he treated him kindly, after his first two days of punishment. He spent some time counseling with the Shienne. They talked in hand sign, with some help from an old Mandan who knew some of the Shienne tongue. He let the Shienne take care of the twelve riding animals, since he knew them well and seemed to have a great love for them. And he let the People watch him take care of them, and see how he handled them.

Eventually Slaps the Water held a council with an old woman present. Her son had been killed in the raid. Man on a Horse was given to that old woman's family. They could choose whether to kill him for revenge, make him their slave, or adopt him to replace the lost son.

They chose to adopt him, which was what Slaps the Water had hoped and expected. Now Man on a Horse could be trusted to teach the Mandan warriors everything he knew about the riding beasts. The Mandan warriors were quick, strong, and bold, and very soon they became superb horsemen.

The young warrior had a true respect and admiration for the Mandan People, and he learned their language, though it was a very difficult tongue and much different from any other. In the tribe he was named Nu mohk p' Ka Vah Yoh, which meant, as his Shienne name had meant, Man on a Horse. He said the Men Who Wear Iron, the Spaniards, called the animal *ka vah yoh.*

The next Day of First Man, Man on a Horse was hung up in the Okeepah ceremony, which he had chosen to do because he wanted to be a true man of the Mandan People.

Then one day he came to the lodge of Slaps the Water to talk. After they had smoked, Man on a Horse said, "In my head and my heart there are matters for your ears."

"With interest I listen," said Slaps the Water, and he leaned on a backrest made of willow wood and woven reeds.

"Our animals are a great gift to us, Father. They are of very great use. But we have only the twelve of them that were captured when the Shiennes came and attacked." He spoke of the Shienne now as if they were others, for in his heart he was now a Mandan. "And as you have seen, all the twelve we have are females."

Slaps the Water nodded as if he had known that, though in truth he had never given it a thought. He had not thought of these splendid creatures in the way one thinks of bison or forked horns, in terms of bulls and cows, bucks and does, but rather as animal gods, not something that breeds and calves. "Speak more," he said. "Tell me why it was that the Shienne should have ridden here to make war on us on only female animals."

"The answer is a plain one. If male and female *ka vah yoh*s are on the trail together and the female ruts, the male, who is very fierce and strong, loses his head with desire. He is hard to control and makes too much noise and too much trouble. Riders can get hurt. They are very lusty, those *ka vah yoh.*"

Slaps the Water thought hard about this knowledge, and finally he said, "That means, then, that the females only can be used, and the males are useless to men?"

The young man shifted his weight as he sat and answered, "The males can be made to behave around the females, by cutting off their seed balls from under the man-parts."

"What!" Slaps the Water practically jumped where he sat. He flinched and squinted at the thought.

"That cutting makes them tamer than the females," Man on a Horse said, "so they, too, can be used on the trail for hunting and war. But the best of the males are kept with their seed balls on, and those are used to breed the females."

Slaps the Water nodded. "Of course." He lit the pipe again with an ember and passed it to his guest, who thoughtfully puffed on it a little while, and then continued:

"The *ka vah yoh* are obtained by the Shienne in two ways. One is by trading for them with the A-pah-chi, who steal them from the Spanish men. The other is by catching runaway *ka vah yoh*s that have run wild. There are many of those in the south, and they always increase."

"That is good," said Slaps the Water. "I would rather get a *ka vah yoh* that was running loose than go near the Spanish men. My ancestor Man Face was killed by those men just for borrowing one of their *ka vah yoh*s, not even stealing it!" The *okimeh* was enjoying this meeting, learning many things. "Tell me more of what is in your heart and head," he said.

"Father, you should understand that the twelve female ones are not enough for this tribe to have, for hunters and warriors alike to use. You have seen that the Mandans from the other villages grow envious and want them. As you have seen, the *ka vah yoh*s are easy to kill in battle, big and strong though they are. They also get killed in hunting the bison.

"Even if our twelve female *ka vah yoh*s were never killed in a hunt or in a war, they would not live forever. They die at half the age of a human being. If their legs and hooves are hurt, they are useless because those do not heal. Father, a People like ours should have not twelve *ka vah yoh*s, but twelve hundred—both females and males with their balls on. And thus they can become more and more numerous. Every man and boy should have at least two."

"Every man and boy does have two," said Slaps the Water.

"I mean *ka vah yoh*s, not balls."

Slaps the Water laughed. Then he took a deep breath. "Twelve hundred *ka vah yoh*s!" he exclaimed. He would never have thought in such numbers! He looked at Man on a Horse with a much intensified interest and respect. Here was a young man who brought wide visions into his head with just his words. Here was a man who did not think in the little and old ways. But now, pretending not to be as awed as he was, Slaps the Water said, "Then perhaps fifteen hundred *ka vah yoh*s would be even better. You know that we have fought the Dah-koh-tah peoples for many, many years, and will have to keep fighting them, whenever they grow arrogant. And so too the Rickaree. *Ka vah yoh*s would help us defeat them."

The young warrior nodded. "Someday, everyone will have them. I have seen that to be so, there in the south where my . . . where the Shienne live. The peoples who have none trade for them with those who have, or raid for them. The Spanish men did not want any of the tribes to have *ka vah yoh*s, but it started, and has grown. All peoples will have them. And . . ." He paused. "Someday, all peoples will also have the thunder shooters, such as yours, but many more."

Slaps the Water felt the hair prickle on the back of his neck. This young man kept saying things that he never would have thought of. He lit the pipe again and handed it to the young man, and then kept his hand on his wrist and asked him:

"Are you a prophet?"

The young man looked very surprised. Then he smiled and shook his head. "I have never thought I was a prophet. I think only a shaman is a prophet, and I am a warrior, not a shaman."

Now the young man seemed to become nervous. He looked at his hands, then at Slaps the Water, then up toward the smoke hole. At last he said, "My okimeh, I have not yet spoken of the matter for which I came to you."

"There is more than all these important matters? Tell me, then."

"You have the daughter, with white hair."

Slaps the Water cocked his head and waited.

"I have thought," the young man said, "that she would be a fine wife. I thought it would take boldness to come to the *okimeh* and ask for her, since I am new among the People."

"So, then. You have decided to be bold?" This was delighting Slaps the Water more than he would dare to reveal. Snow Hair had never had a suitor. There were so few men and so many women in the tribe. Now here came a handsome and bold and far-seeing warrior who certainly would become an important man. Slaps the Water hid his high feelings by gravely refilling and lighting the pipe. He smoked, then gave it to the young man and said, "What would you bring to me and to her family in return?"

"*Ka vah yoh.*"

Slaps the Water looked at the young man intently. "But you

have only the speckled female one, and you are the best rider. I would not want you to be without yours. As husband of my daughter, you should keep yours, the better for you to hunt and provide food—"

The young warrior put forth his hand, shook his head and smiled. "No, Father. I do not mean to give you my own. It is as I have said to you just before: if our People are to have enough *ka vah yoh*s to be strong among the tribes, there must be a male one here who can father more among our twelve. With a male *ka vah yoh* here, just one, our twelve could become a hundred or more in a few summers. Do you see, then, what I mean to do?"

"Tell me. I am not sure I see tomorrow as you see it."

"I mean to go far to the south and get a strong male with balls and bring him here. I will give him to you for your daughter. Then he, the father *ka vah yoh*, would start a tribe, and I would start a family."

Slaps the Water took a quick breath. To think that a man would do such a bold thing to win a wife and help the People grow strong! Slaps the Water had no sense of how far away south was, but he and his warriors had walked for many, many sleeps across the great spaces and had never reached the south—at least not the south from which this young man had come. It was almost too great a deed to believe! "How would you do that?" he asked.

"I would ride by the way the Shienne warriors came. I remember it well. Then I would get a male one, in some way, and ride him back here."

"Would you not be afraid on such a journey alone?"

"Father, I have hung in the Okeepah. I fear nothing."

"But would you not want some of my warriors to go with you, to watch your back? You would pass through people hostile to us."

The young man pondered, looking down at the fire pit. "I do not understand why you ask that, Father. It is I alone who would bring you the *ka vah yoh* in return for your daughter. Why should other Mandan men be put at risk in lands they do not know? I am the one who wants your daughter."

Slaps the Water was beginning to have what he feared was an unworthy thought:

Would this young man be a deceiver? Was he plotting to go back to the Shienne who had been his People? The more Slaps the Water thought of that, the more he disliked himself for thinking it. This was a very noble and brave young man who would be an excellent son-in-law and who seemed eager to do service for the Children of First Man—and yet Slaps the Water was suspecting him of wanting to betray the People. He did not want to think this way. But why did Man on a Horse insist on going alone? Slaps the Water sighed. He did not like the feeling of being suspicious. He sent the young man away without an answer. Then he called in the Elders to ask whether they thought the young man should be allowed to go alone.

He had never asked the Elders a question like this. There had never been such a circumstance.

First to give his opinion was old Bone Cracker, an uncle of Slaps the Water. Bone Cracker looked at him in disgust out of deep, wrinkled eye sockets. "It is small of you to doubt what this brave young man wants to do. Is he not now one of us, who hung up? Is that not enough to make you trust his words? Let him go and do what he promises!"

But then Mossy Horns, the oldest man in council, who was a doubter by nature, said, "Can you not see that this Shienne just wants to escape and go home? If you let him go south, send warriors to watch him!"

The old men had not helped him. In their words they had only repeated the two sides he had had in his own mind.

But better counsel came to him in his sleep that night. He saw the face of Follows Dog, she who had been his wife, and her spirit voice said to him:

"Listen. There could not be a better husband for our daughter. This will be an *okimeh* someday. If he wished to desert us, he could just go. Our daughter sits beside my grave in the Town of the Dead every day and tries to speak to me with her heart. She needs this man. So do our People, who need the animals to ride. Say yes to him, husband! He is a gift from Creator to our People!"

And then her face was gone and he woke up. He called Man on a Horse into his lodge the next morning and said, "Go bring him."

MAN ON A HORSE RODE SOUTHWARD FOR TWENTY DAYS ON HIS EXcellent mare. In a pouch slung over his shoulder he carried meal of parched maize and sunflower seeds, several thin sheets of dried buffalo meat, and a cluster of dried wapato roots. But he did not really need those. There was always fresh meat to be shot along the way, and the rivers he crossed were full of fish and watercress and cattails. He caught turtles and rattlesnakes, found the eggs of geese and ducks, stampeded a small buffalo herd to kill a calf, once shot a young forked horn who came to see what he was, and one day on a plain of short grass he chased a jackrabbit until it was so weak and confused that he could lean down from his galloping mare and grab its ear with his bare hand.

One evening as he approached a river from the north he saw that the sun was setting in a smoky haze, and when he reached the riverbank he saw that the prairie on the other shore was burning, perhaps from a lightning strike, for as far as he could see. It was a slow fire in short grass, with little breeze to chase it along. The flames were no more than knee high, and the burning grass smelled good. He made his camp on the north bank of the river and sat into the night watching the long, crooked, flickering lines of fire crawl eastward through the darkness, yellow-red lines extending away into the night until they faded into the smoke. He thought it was as beautiful as a sunset. He lay on the grass looking up at stars that showed faintly through the haze, while his mare, with forelegs hobbled, slept standing nearby. The warrior thought of Slaps the Water and Snow Hair, and remembered how he had ridden up this way the year before with the forty mounted Shienne warriors, all feeling invincible and strong because they were mounted on the mighty beasts in a land where everyone else still went afoot.

But we were wrong, he thought. The Children of First Man were stronger and braver than we thought they could be.

He thought of the people of his birth nation, and wondered what they had thought, what they had suffered, when not one of the forty had ever returned home. He thought of the families of the warriors. Each warrior had been a son, a brother, to someone. At least three that he could remember had also been fathers. They, too, were a strong and brave people; he had loved them.

And now I am one of the Children of First Man, he thought. They are a strange People, he thought.

No, *we* are a strange People.

Young people with white hair. People with yellow hair and blue eyes. People with brown hair and gray eyes.

He thought of Snow Hair, for whom he was making this long journey back to his homeland—making this long journey as a stranger. And then he had a thought that troubled him so that he rose on an elbow and lounged there with his eyes wide open.

What will happen when I reach the land of my birth People? They loved me well. They would want to welcome me back among them. Surely they believe I am dead. My blood father and my blood mother and blood sister still think of me, I am sure.

At this moment, in fact, he believed that he could feel their sad hearts yearning for him, yearning to see him come riding back. He thought he was feeling their prayers pulling him.

Now Man on a Horse, who had little fear of anything, was full of a cold and turning fear.

Where do I belong in the world? he mused.

I was hung up like First Man and became one of his People, he thought. But then he reflected:

I was born a Shienne. My blood is the same.

He tried to envision the faces of his parents.

Instead he saw the face of Snow Hair, so young and beautiful, yet so strange with the white hair. When he went to sleep, the flames of the prairie fire blurring in his heavy eyes, he believed he was of the Children of First Man.

The next morning he swam the river. He rode all that day through burnt grass, the animal's hooves stirring black dust and crumbling wisps that floated on the air; his mare grew black to her shoulders. Eagles, hawks, and vultures wheeled high in the shimmering sky. Most animals had been able to travel ahead of the grass fires, but here and there lay a scorched rabbit, a singed coyote, a charred magpie, and the sharp-beaks were coming down to eat cooked food.

Late in the day he came to the edge of the fire. It was creeping through the low grass, a thin veil of smoke drifting above it. To continue on his way south he would have to cross the fire onto the unburned prairie, and he wondered whether he could make his animal cross the flaming margin; she was nervous and fearful, and grew more so as he rode toward the fire.

He tried twice to ride her through. The first time, she stopped and would not move until he reined her to the right, away from the fire. The second time, he got her running parallel to the fire line, then tried to turn her to run through or jump it. But she stopped so suddenly that she nearly threw him over her head, and when he prodded her to move again, she reared.

Man on a Horse slid off the animal's back. Holding her by the rein that was tied around her underjaw, he looked into her eyes to see what she was thinking. With a sigh, then, he took off the sash he wore over his shoulder and tied it to cover her eyes.

Thus blinded, she was very nervous, and sidestepped and kicked, and pawed the ground with a forehoof. Once she tried to throw her head back and rear, but he kept the jaw rein tight, and she gave that up.

He stroked her muzzle, talked softly to her, and began walking her one way and another. Then he started trotting, and she trotted along obediently as he tugged lightly on her jaw rein. Finally he veered to his left and ran quickly across the creeping edge of the fire. She followed and was across the small flames, through the curtain of smoke and on the unburned grass before the smoke in her nostrils and the heat on her hooves reminded her of her recent fear. She tossed her head a little, but he held her firmly and talked to her. He stopped her about thirty paces beyond the fire and took the sash off from her eyes. She arched her powerful neck and glanced about with frightened brown eyes. When she saw that he was leading her away from the smoke and fire instead of toward it, she snorted, dipped her head and shoved his shoulder with her forehead. He laughed. He put his sash back over his shoulder, remounted, and rode off at a trot toward the hazy blue plateaus that marked the southern horizon. And that evening, when the fire was miles behind, he camped in a low plain where the grass still had a tinge of green. There the good animal grazed after her day of hunger in the burnt prairie. And her rider, rolled into his robe, smiled and went to sleep looking up at the stars. He dreamed of being the only man in the vast world, as he was beginning to feel he was, but later he dreamed of sitting in a lodge beside Snow Hair, who was feeding him.

UNDER A SCAFFOLD IN THE TOWN OF THE DEAD, SNOW HAIR SAT and mourned loudly, as she had done a part of every day since her mother's death. The woman's body, wrapped and sewn into airtight layers of rawhide, lay on a lattice of willow sticks at the top of the scaffold, just high enough to be out of reach of man or beast. When Snow Hair raised her head to look upward, the body of Follows Dog was silhouetted against the bright sky. On one of the scaffold poles, Slaps the Water had attached a long ribbon of berry-dyed antelope skin. This red ornament honored her bravery in striking a Shienne warrior to save her husband's life. Most of the hundreds of burial scaffolds had no ornaments on them; only the graves of chiefs and brave warriors were usually marked with such honors, and here and there in the maze of scaffolds, such tokens swayed or flapped in the wind.

About eight or ten of the scaffolds in the Town of the Dead were new, holding the bodies of villagers killed by the mounted Shienne. A few were still newer, for some persons had died later of their wounds, and there had been the usual natural deaths in the village. Under most of the recent burials there lay mourners, crying and lamenting, some cutting and scarring themselves to signify their loss. Snow Hair herself had cut off the last joint of her little finger in lament of her mother's death; the tiny stump was healed slick now, but still ached even after all these moons.

Hundreds of older scaffolds stood in the Town of the Dead, which was outside the walls of the village and up the slope from the river. On some of the scaffolds there still lay the old mummified bodies in their stiff, crumbling rawhide shrouds, and all the bodies lay with their heads toward the sunset, feet to the sunrise. Scores of the scaffolds were in states of decay and collapse, their bodies long since removed, bones buried in the earth and skulls placed in the skull rings beyond the Town of the Dead. When Snow Hair sat up and stopped crying to rest her voice, she could see her father, Slaps the Water, sitting in the midst of one of those distant rings of skulls, where he was conversing with the spirits of some of his forebears.

Now Snow Hair sat with the wind cooling the tears on her face, gazing at her father in the distance. The weeping had calmed and satisfied her heart, and she could feel the vastness of the world and the great roundness of time. When time and the world seemed this immense and bright, one's own losses and worries were smaller and lighter, and the will of the Creator was easier to understand. Now things seemed to be properly connected.

Her father had at last honored her mother. He spoke often of her bravery and her goodness, now that she had died for him.

She thought of the warrior who had killed people and then had been adopted. She wondered about his desire to be the husband of a light-hair. It was odd. Maybe he just wanted to be married to the daughter of the *okimeh*, she thought sometimes. There were men who thought that way, she had heard it said.

In the meantime, she thought often of the young man and wondered how far away he was, and how long it would take him to go so far—however far that was, and she could not even imagine—and she wondered whether he would even come back.

A young man of the village had raised that doubt to her. He had said, "I think Man on a Horse does not mean to come back here. He is only running back to his own People. Would he want to marry a light-hair, when he has never seen them before?"

She had replied, "He is of our People now." But the doubt had been planted in her mind, and she did wonder if he had asked for her only to get her father's leave to go away—probably forever.

To Snow Hair, the idea of passing the horizons and going on and on in one direction was like the idea of Passing Over, as her mother had done, into the Other Side. It did not seem that one could go out of sight beyond the far hills on this side of the Muddy River or on the other side, or go to the upper end of the river or down to the lower end, and still return. She had never been out of sight of her People's village; it was the center of the world. Hunters would go out of sight, that was true, but they only went out in widening circles around the People's town, looking for game, or trying to herd the buffalo toward a *pishkun* somewhere not far from the town, and when those hunters went out, the village was still the center of the world and they were drawn back to it. But to go and go, for days and days in one direction, that, it seemed to her, would make one lose his hold on the center of the world, and he could then only go to the Other Side.

Surely, she thought, the country of the Shienne, where he is going, must be as far distant as the Other Side World.

She thought, I am afraid he will not come back.

She sighed and got up off the ground. Her thoughts had quit the mourning of her mother for now. She still stood in the shadow of her mother's corpse, but now Follows Dog was being silent in Snow Hair's thoughts, and so it was time to leave the Town of the Dead for this day, to go and do something else. Without speaking words, then, she bade Follows Dog goodbye, waved to her father, who was still kneeling in the skull circle, and went down around the town walls to the riverbank where all the women and girls bathed and swam in the summertime. She was hot and dusty. She anticipated the feeling of the cool water, and being naked in it, and swimming like a fish. The river water was as important in her life as the town and the People and her family, and the earth and maize and sunflowers. When she was in the water, she was like a little animal, like the otter or muskrat or beaver, and did not have to think about such things as whether a man would go out of This Side of the world and not come back.

* * *

FAR, FAR SOUTH, MAN ON A HORSE, WHILE RIDING ACROSS A SEEMingly endless lowland of sand, spike grass, and yellow-flowered prickly pear, saw a swift shadow pass over the sunbaked ground and looked up, shading his eyes with his hand. Against the glare of the sky in the southern quarter there flew an eagle, not very high. It veered in a wide, westerly curve. As he turned to watch it, the eagle swung northward, then came about and glided toward the sun. It looked as if it would hit the sun, which stood in the very top of the sky. For an instant the white burning of the sun winked as the bird passed between it and the young man's eyes. Then the eagle continued straight southward, its shadow on the ground flickering through the scrub. Then it veered slightly westward again. The young man, though almost stupefied by the still, dry heat, watched the eagle as long as he could see it. Having cast its shadow on him twice, it was surely a Messenger. The last place where he could see it was above a slight break in the shimmering blue horizon in the southwest—a place where a pass cut through a long mesa. The rider understood the guidance of the eagle: he was being told to ride to and through that distant pass. It appeared to be a day's ride ahead, and was to the west of the way he had been going, but a Messenger was not to be doubted or ignored.

And then, as he leaned his trudging mare off into that direction, a harsh whistle penetrated his ears from high above, and was repeated once. Shading his eyes again, he looked toward the sun.

What he saw against the blue now was only a speck; the eagle had climbed and climbed into the dazzling sky. But it had called down to him, to show him that it was returning toward the north. He craned his neck and watched it go back that way until it had vanished in brightness.

He camped that night by a shallow, sluggish pool, below the pass the eagle had directed him to, and here he killed and roasted a ringtail, the only animal he had seen all day besides the eagle. The ringtail was not much food, and was tough and strong-tasting, but its meat gave him strength.

His *ka vah yoh* rubbed him with her muzzle when he was tying on her leg hobbles. Soon, when she urinated, he saw that the urine was not clear and yellow but cloudy. She held her tail aside and displayed her female part, and it kept winking open and shut. He knew what this meant. His mare was in heat.

"Too bad," he said. "You are very alone. Like me."

The Evening Star disappeared behind the edge of the mesa,

and a breeze sighed in the delicate foliage around the pool. The warrior lay wrapped in his robe to keep the mosquitoes off his skin, though it was much too hot inside for comfort. Unable to sleep, he thought over and over about the message of the eagle. Clearly, it had directed him this way. Then it had flown back north, whistling in triumph. It could only mean that by going this way he would obtain what he had come for, and then he would hasten northward in victory.

In his mind at last he saw Snow Hair as he had first seen her, coming out of the gray river. Then he went to sleep.

Screams woke him. He lunged up, heart pounding, trying to remember where he was.

His good mare was fighting with another *ka vah yoh.* They were whinnying, rearing, whirling, kicking, raising dust, and trampling vegetation a few paces from where he lay, and now their contest brought them so near that he had to scramble out of his sleeping place to avoid their mighty hoofsteps. He leaped to his feet, gasping, watching.

The mare, being hobbled at the forefeet, was in trouble. She could scarcely kick or pivot without fear of falling. Her ears were laid back, her eyes white with wildness, mouth open and flecked with foam, teeth bared to nip.

The warrior skipped and hopped about, trying to stay out of their thundering, screaming, snorting way. Was this a dream-vision? Where had this tawny, black-maned, lathered, and lean-muscled animal come from to arrive here without warning at sunrise, many long travel days away from any known place?

And just then the warrior noticed two things that made his heart leap up from bewilderment to joy:

The strange *ka vah yoh* was male. And the frenzy of the two animals was not a fighting frenzy but a mating frenzy. The male was biting at the female and trying to climb onto her. She, apparently, was fighting her hobbles.

This male animal must have been sent here by Creator, who had led him and his mare here by the eagle's message. He had prayed for his travels to lead him to a male father *ka vah yoh*, and now here was as fine a one as ever he had seen, and it had arrived just when his female was in her heat. A prayer had been answered.

Now the warrior knew he must act at once. Because of the power of the animals, the female might be hurt if he did not cut her hobbles.

And because he had come south to get a father *ka vah yoh* for *all* the females, he must catch this strong beast and take him back to the town of Slaps the Water.

Dodging the trampling beasts, he got to his sleeping place and snatched up his knife sheath with one hand and his coil of rope with the other, then darted away as they came back through, stamping his robe into the dirt. He drew the flint blade out of its sheath and began stalking the animals, trying to get close to his female without drawing the notice of the rampaging male to himself. She stumbled close to him, her whinnying voice piercing his ears. He stopped quickly and with one quick slash of the blade cut the hobble between her forelegs, then leaped back out of the way.

At once she realized she was free. With joy and fierce abandon she led the male in a spectacular mating dance in and around the campsite, her tail up and aside, while he reared and pawed after her. At last she arched her neck and backed toward him. Biting and screaming, he mounted her and found entry.

While they were engaged in their magnificent coupling, snorting, whistling, and raising dust clouds that billowed in the slanting morning sunbeams, the warrior made a slipknot in his rope. Then he stood, crouched, watching, awed by their power and passion, thinking ahead to the coupling he would have with the girl named Snow Hair when he returned to the north with this mighty Father of Beasts.

He wondered when he should rope the great animal. Not yet. He wanted its seed in his female *ka vah yoh*. He would let them finish. He breathed deeply in a strange sort of excitement, at the same time praying that the male would create life in her. And sometimes he felt like laughing, because the male animal so comically lost all his great dignity in this copulation, foaming at the mouth, wild-eyed and shrieking, groaning and snorting, humping and staggering. To the Shienne People among whom he had been born and raised, people in copulation were a source of amusement and joking, except, of course, the ones who were doing it; they were always so serious. It was the most important thing people did, being the creation of life, and thus was too great to think about in a serious way. And so if people were seen doing it, much fun was made of how silly they looked. Now it was the same way with the father *ka vah yoh*. He was in his big moment now. He snorted, grunted, and convulsed, tossed his head just as the female was doing, and then slumped, too weak even to hold up his head, which he let lie along her back in a tender-looking way for a moment before sliding off and letting her walk out from under him.

Now, the warrior thought. Now I must rope him! He is weak for a moment. Soon he will be able to think about something besides her and he will realize that a two-legged is here and try to flee!

It was true. In that moment the wild stallion's eyes cleared; he had smelled the warrior and was looking to see him. He was turning and looked ready to bolt away.

With the coils of the rope loose over his left arm, Man on a Horse flung the slip noose over the stallion's head and prepared himself for the explosion of power that would come next.

Feeling the rope around its neck, the animal shuddered and flew into a panic. It reared to spin away. The warrior yanked the noose tight, bracing himself and leaning back, and nearly toppled the lunging beast. But it did bolt away, up the slope away from the creek, and the warrior, not having enough strength actually to hold the beast, had to sprint after him, paying out a little rope as he followed, but keeping the noose tight enough to hinder the animal's breathing.

Putting just this much drag on the running animal required all the strength, breath, and nerve that Man on a Horse had. His feet scarcely touched the ground as he raced after the animal, keeping the rope tight but not too tight. Each step drove prickly pear needles into his feet—tiny spears of pain—but he knew that if the animal pulled him off balance and dragged him, he would have the spines everywhere in his body, not just in his feet.

The beast circled back down the slope toward the creek, bucking and flinging his head, giving choking, wheezing noises at every breath. He plunged into the shadows of the willows. The warrior knew he could stop the animal by getting the rope around a tree. But he also knew the stallion could break rope—or its own neck—by fighting in panic against a fixed tether; he had to keep easing off on the rope.

Meanwhile, the mare was becoming excited again by the running struggle, and as the male tore back out onto the open prairie, she whinnied and came galloping after him. She passed by the warrior and ran alongside the male, shrieking, nipping at him, and threatening to get afoul of the rope.

And so they all ran about in this desperate and noisy manner for so long that the warrior thought his lungs would burst or his arms would pull out of his shoulders. Never in his years of catching and breaking *ka vah yoh*s had he held to such a swift and strong one. In the wild herds, the best ones could always outrun their mounted pursuers. This was one of those best ones, and if he had not smelled out the rutting female and come to mate, there would never have been a chance to get a rope on such a creature.

He is a gift from Creator, the warrior thought.

Creator, help me be strong and quick, or I will lose your gift even before I have it! he thought.

Eventually the animal showed signs of weakening. It slowed, straining for breath through the noose, then stopped, spraddle-legged, facing its captor, and the warrior walked toward him, making soothing noises but keeping the rope tight. He flicked the loose end of the rope at the mare, driving her out of the way at least for a while, and kept the noose tight on the male as he took up rope and moved in.

Exhausted though the great beast was, he tried again and again to rear or spin away, but with the rope shortened now, the warrior could keep him from throwing himself over backward, which he probably would have done in his panic. His eyes were wild, their red-tinged whites showing, and his mighty body was covered with lather. He yanked repeatedly but in vain at the rope, but it was so tight at his throat he could scarcely draw a rasping breath. Every muscle on his great lithe body was twitching and quivering.

When he was within arm's reach of the animal's head, Man on a Horse suddenly made a noose on the loose end of the rope and slipped it into the animal's open mouth, thus lassoing the underjaw. This so vastly increased his control over the animal that he could hold him still with one hand while using the other to untie the neck loop and hobble the forefeet. Still quivering with near-fatal fright, the beast was now virtually helpless, drooling and foaming at the mouth, snorting and nickering. Through the intervention of good spirits, or so it seemed, the female remained at a little distance and was calm, sometimes watching, sometimes grazing, but not in the way.

"Now it is time for us to talk, Father Ka Vah Yoh," he said to the animal in a soothing voice. "I too am called by a name you would know. I am Nu mohk p' Ka Vah Yoh. If you will listen to me and be my friend, we will ride together to the north and I will give you many females to mount. . . ." As he talked, he removed his breechcloth, showed it to the beast, then swiftly draped it over the animal's eyes, blinding him, and held it there.

After one immense spasm of fright, the animal stood still, and the warrior kept talking to him:

"Brother, I know how your kind are. You will not move unless you can see. Oh, how afraid you are! But, brother, here, smell the breath of your new friend. I, truly, need you and will never hurt you. We will go together on long voyages and hunts and wars, and we will always trust each other."

With his hand holding down the animal's muzzle, he blew his own breath into the animal's nostrils, once, twice, and by the third breath the animal was perfectly calm. The warrior felt the Fear Spirit leave the animal, and felt his own spirit enter. He slid the end of the breechcloth down and let the animal breathe the odor of his body, then gradually uncovered his eyes.

Now the animal looked at him without fear. Holding the rope with his teeth, the warrior put his breechcloth back on. "Come with me now," he said, tugging gently, and the animal stretched its neck until the rope was tight, then stepped forward to follow.

Limping on his bloody feet, he led the stallion about. He took it closer to the creek. He veered away, and the animal pulled hard, wanting to go to the water. But the warrior gave the rope a sharp tug and made him come away, still talking to him. "You can have water when I let you. You must cool off first, for you have been on fire inside. Good *ka vah yoh*, come along. Look, she follows. She wants to be your wife again. That will be soon. First, I will teach you to carry me on your back."

When the animal's lather had dried, the warrior stopped near the trees and stood awhile in the shade, then led him to the water's edge and waded in. The animal stopped and drank. Man on a Horse bent down, cupped his hands and drank, too. Then he pulled the rope and led the animal farther out into the creek, until the water was to its shoulders.

"My good brother," the man said, "do not be afraid." He passed part of the rope over the animal's withers and tied it to the side of the jaw halter, thus making a rein on either side. Then, grasping the rope and a hank of mane, he waded to the animal's left flank and threw himself belly first across its broad back. The animal tensed to buck, but instead merely turned where it stood and tried to toss its head. The rider at once controlled its head with the rein, swung his right leg over the rump and sat up astride. He was glad he had caught this mighty stallion near water; he knew that a *ka vah yoh* is afraid to leap or buck when it cannot see its footing. One could teach a new horse to carry a rider on dry land, of course, but in water it was easier and less dangerous. And cooler. With his feet in the creek water, the young man's spine-tortured feet did not sting and burn, but only stung. He talked to the animal, reined this way and that, stroked it, let it stop and drink, rode it out of the creek and then back in, and then back out onto the dry ground, where he urged it to a trot, halted it, urged it to a trot and then a canter, then back to a trot, and finally lashed it into a full and thrilling gallop with the female following desperately, whinnying after them. With a couple of quick, merciless adjustments on the jaw rein, Man on a Horse cured his new mount of any notion of heeding her.

The male *ka vah yoh* had awakened him at sunrise with its assault on the female. By the time the sun was halfway up the morning sky, the warrior had caught and tamed him, taught him to obey, to run, to halt, to turn by rein or by leg pressure, and to stand still while being mounted or dismounted. Man on a Horse had, for perhaps the hundredth time in his life, proven himself worthy of his name. Now he let the animals mate again, and at last settled down by the creek to pull stickers out of his feet and doctor them with creek mud. And he was very happy. He loved this fine, strong breeding male he had caught for the People . . . or perhaps better to say, that Creator had given him to take to the People.

And Slaps the Water would love this fine father *ka vah yoh*, which would increase the People's wealth and strength.

And Slaps the Water would let him marry Snow Hair.

"Great, good four-legged," he said, "plant your seed in her today. And tomorrow we will start going north, to a place where the wind always blows, and where the bison are so many, they say, that you cannot see the ground between them. And you and I, my strong friend, will be important to the People and will strengthen them. We will strengthen them even more, for they are a strong People already."

But as he thought of the Children of First Man, he heard deep in his soul a song of the Shienne, the People whose blood had flowed in his veins since his birth. He knew that he was not far from the villages of the Shienne. He was ten or twenty times as far from the village of the Children of First Man.

How easy it would be not to ride north, but just turn up this creek and go past its source and then down the far slope, to the creek that flowed the other way, toward his first home.

But his one true home, he knew in his heart, was north, far to the north. He had been hung up like First Man in the

Okeepah. Now it would be impossible for him not to be one of the Children of First Man.

Tomorrow he would ride north.

THE SKY WAS GREEN AND FULL OF RAIN, AND THE TWO *KA VAH YOH*S, male and female, were full of bad spirits. They were as jumpy and fearful as rabbits, as hard to handle as when the female had been in heat in the early days of the return journey. Now she was pregnant, and the male left her alone, discouraged by her biting and kicking, and most of the long trek back toward the Muddy River had been plodding and uneventful, with Man on a Horse riding either animal and leading the other. But this weather had put dark spirits in both the beasts, and, through them, in their master as well. He knew that the *ka vah yoh*, though it was a servant of man, was tame only on its surface, with the heart and eye of a game animal, and that it could see and hear things that no person can detect, however hard he may look and listen. If there was anything to fear, horses sensed it soon.

Even the warrior himself had troubling spirits within. During the last few days of his approach to the town of the Children of First Man, his heart had changed from pride and happy eagerness to a kind of dread. The air had been hot and damp for days, with some kind of a force in it that had made his skin prickle and his heartbeat quicken. Then, this morning, as he came within a short day's ride of the town, thunder had begun to rumble in the west, and tall, shining clouds had climbed to the peak of the sky, then passed on to darken the sun, and under them had come damp winds and seething, low, dark clouds spitting cold rain. For a while he had ridden in that cold rain with his hide robe over his shoulders, pinned shut with a piece of bone, both hands busy controlling the animals by rein and lead rope. Low overhead the black clouds had roiled and swirled, and the wind had flattened the short grasses. Then had come such mighty cracks and rumbles from the skies that he had seen the great black beating wings of the Thunderbirds, and the white fire from their eyes had sizzled to the ground, almost blinding him. Both animals had reared in the flashing light, and in order not to be pulled off the back of the male, he had had to let go of the female's lead rope. After getting his mount under control by severe use of the jaw rein, he had chased off after her through the sheets of rain, often losing sight of her entirely. But the stallion had never lost her, even in the howling obscurity of the storm, and by his superior strength and speed he soon overtook her and ran head to head with her until his rider could stretch out and catch the lead rope. Eventually, when both animals were near exhaustion, he had got them under control and kept them thus despite the continuous flashing and crashing of the sky's Thunderbirds.

Then he had pressed on through the storm, knowing he was close to the town he had come to think of as his home, the town of Snow Hair and Slaps the Water. On he had ridden for a long time in the rain, though he could gauge his direction only by the wind and the slope of the prairie. After a while he had noticed that the mare kept tending to pull toward the left. Realizing that she had come from that village and the male had never been there, he dismounted, retied their ropes, and got on her back, to let her instincts lead them home. Man on a Horse felt more tired than ever before.

It was while they were plodding along this way, his water-soaked leather robe so heavy on his back that he could scarcely sit up straight, that the sky began to pale and look green. The rain diminished, almost stopped, for which he was thankful, but the wind was rushing and howling so fast across the ground that he felt he would be blown off his mount. Sodden though his robe was, it fluttered and flapped and tugged at him, almost strangling him with its pull and frightening the stallion. So he unpinned it, yanking out the bone, and the robe sailed away in the wind. As he turned to watch it, he saw behind him such a thing as he had never seen in his life, but only in his dreams.

It appeared to be a writhing, twisting, gray-green snake, but so enormous that its head was in the clouds and its tail was whipping the ground. He opened his mouth to yell, but in the wind he was speechless.

In the oldest legends of the Shienne people there had been stories of a great eagle or thunderbird that had flown down from the sky and snatched up a powerful serpent of the earth. In some of the stories the thunderbird had eaten the serpent, and in others the thunderbird and the serpent had fought so furiously that they became one, a serpent with wings. Some old sages said that either way, the story was the same, for what is eaten becomes one with that which eats it. But every Shienne child had dreamed of the thunderbird with the snake in its talons, the rattlesnake whose chattering tail made such a fearsome noise; and now at this moment, alone on a vast plain, Man on a Horse, near the end of a long, long journey in which he had talked to no one but animals for days and days, cold and wet and tired almost to death, was truly seeing that great vision, the battle between the Sky and the Earth. It had been a quest for a great stallion to father the herds of the Children of First Man, and he had found that, but now he had found a vision as well, an even greater vision than that from the Okeepa Hanging Up.

Man on a Horse, who should have been full of fear as the mighty twisting power came toward him over the plain, the great rattles roaring and churning up the sod, the black cloud wings of the thunderbird beating overhead, was not afraid, but full of a great, thankful joy, because he was now a man of two visions!

Yes, he was a man of two visions, and his heart was joyous with the knowing of that, and he was not afraid. But the two *ka vah yoh* did not know about the two visions, and they were afraid. They were in a state of growing terror and were becoming hard to handle again. He tried to keep their heads turned away from the vision. But they could hear the great rattles getting louder. And *ka vah yoh*s, being prey, could see almost all the way around themselves even if not allowed to turn their heads, and they could see that the great power was coming along behind them, growing closer. It was coming across the plain, it seemed, about as fast as a man running, the rattle tail of the serpent seeming to chew up the ground. And its huge, twisting, rippling body, in the grip of the thunderbird, was racing even faster across the sky; it was almost straight overhead now. Man on a Horse could not control both the frantic animals any longer. They wanted to run, and he was beginning to agree with their judgment. It was one thing to be reverent about a vision, but another thing to ignore the messages of four-leggeds. And across the wide plain, he could see, other four-leggeds were in flight. He saw forked horns running, and in the far distance, deer. Something small came spinning down from the air above him and glanced off his shoulder, and when it tumbled on the ground ahead of him, he saw that it was an animal bone. Bits of grass and root were stinging and pelting his bare wet shoulders and back. Something pale hit the ground off to his left and he saw that it was a hairless baby rabbit. And so when the horses insisted on running, he said, "Yes! let us go!" and kicked his heels into the flanks of his mount, and she sprang forward at a gallop, and the male lunged forward, too, and soon was racing so fast ahead that Man on a Horse could not keep the end of the rope in his hand and had to let him go. The river valley opened below to his view.

He was now where he had been, in that other life, when he and the Shienne had first looked down upon the town. The ground now was sloping away toward the river, and the running was downhill, headlong. He looked back over his shoulder and saw the terrible snake tail coming on. It had risen off the ground, as if the thunderbird were carrying it skyward, but pebbles and bits of material were still raining down. When he looked forward again he could see the poles on the top of the chief's lodge, and the hides hanging from them were flapping straight out in the strong wind. As he galloped down the curve of the hill then, he saw the dome roofs of the lodges, and the palisade, and the scaffolds of the burial ground. The scaffolds were so shaken by the wind that the corpses on them seemed to be alive. People were running. The surface of the curving river was gray and running with whitecaps.

In the town, things were tumbling and flying in the wind. The little round hide-covered bullboats and the toboggans that the people kept on their roofs when not using them were being blown over and around the lodges and some bounced into the river.

Man on a Horse saw all this in a glance as he sped at full tilt down the slope. But then his thought was taken away from the town, this town he had ridden so far to reach, because the stallion had veered away to the right, apparently having seen the town and wanting to get around it. He was tearing along the bluff downstream from the town at full gallop, mane and tail flying in the wind, the rope lasso dragging or sometimes streaming in the wind. From the sides of his eyes as he galloped after him, Man on a Horse glimpsed some of the People, who were fleeing for cover and had turned to look back; some of those were looking at the thunderbird and the serpent in the sky looming over their village, but a few of them had seen Man on a Horse himself speeding by in the rain, clinging to the back of his female mount and chasing another beast they had never seen before. They were squinting and their mouths were open in screams that were inaudible before the rattling roar of the snake's tail and the shriek of the chaff-laden wind. Even in this frantic rush, Man on a Horse had an instant of wonder: Could they see only him, or could they also see his vision? Had he actually led his vision to where others could see it? Never had he known of anyone's vision being seen by others at the same time. . . . But there was no time to think of this now. Perhaps even the town was a dream and only his pursuit of the stallion was truly happening.

The beautiful beast was now galloping down on the riverbank, running alongside the shore, and the shore curved back toward the right. The warrior knew that his tired mare, with him on her back, could never catch the male in a straight line. But he realized that if he rode straight down the slope while the male was making his curve along the riverbank, he could meet him there, perhaps even head him off. He kicked the mare and tore headlong down the slope, forgetting the vision, forgetting everything but the pursuit.

If I had another rope! he thought. I could throw it over his head and catch him as I did the first time!

But the only rope was the one that was already streaming from the fleeing animal's neck. If he were to catch the beast at all, he would have to do it by getting hold of the rope that was already on him.

And he knew that was what he would do, if he could.

Recklessly he tore down the treeless slope and into the animal's path. He glanced back only once, and saw that the great serpent from the sky was thrashing into the edge of the town, flinging up palisade poles and house timbers, mud and boats, corpses and scaffolds from the graveyard, and enormous clouds of dirt. He did not pause at the sight. He was at the animal's shoulders now; the ground below was a blur with the speed of the chase. He leaned to the left and snatched at the flying rope, once, twice, three times, always missing. At last he leaned forward, hugging his mount's neck with his right arm, reaching out so far and low that he could touch the breast of the great male beast, and here he caught the rope, snatching the muddy, wet cord just below the slipknot. And then as the terrified animal pulled ahead of the tiring mare, the warrior began letting the rope out, meanwhile righting himself and regaining his seat.

For a long way he followed the stallion, keeping the noose tight enough to tire him and hinder his breathing but not enough to increase his panic, and the constant pull on the great stallion's right side at last drew him away from the riverbank and in a wide arc up onto the slope. By the time he was worn down to a walk, the great snake tail of a storm had jumped across the Muddy River and risen into the sky, becoming a blackish swirl in the dark clouds, as if the thunderbird had eaten him. Poles and chunks were still dropping from above and splashing into the river, and through the roar of the wind came the wailing of many voices. Far up the slopes some of the town's other eleven horses were racing around loose, still frightened. People were beginning to creep out of the wreckage of houses and rise from the ground where they had been thrown. From what Man on a Horse could see, more than half of the houses had been crushed or blown open; nothing remained of some but the round pits in which they had been built. Every piece of ground in and around the town was strewn with trash: parfleche bags, broken pots, burst baskets, clothing, arrows and tools, robes, sticks and bones, mummies, bison skulls, ropes, chunks of clay, sunflower seeds, and the red, yellow, and purple grains of maize. So terrible was the devastation that the people of the town seemed not even to see Man on a Horse coming in with the great beast, though his departure on the long quest for it had been one of the most important events in the memory of the People.

He saw that by some wonderful chance the Sacred Canoe in the middle of the town had not been damaged. And though the house of Slaps the Water had been broken in two, the part of its dome still standing held up the First Man Hanging Poles, which he had seen bending in the wind earlier; all had been stripped bare except First Man's own, which even now flew a few rags of its white buffalo hide. This surely was a sign of the Creator's mercy.

But now as he rode into the edge of the town leading the nervous animal, Man on a Horse saw the bloody legs of a child sticking out from under the edge of a collapsed roof, and he realized that the Creator might not have been so merciful after all. As dazed and crying people staggered and ran from place to place across his path, not even seeing him, his exhausted heart quickened again:

Snow Hair! he thought. Only now was his head becoming clear enough from the vision and chase and fatigue to realize that the girl he had won as his bride might well have been hurt or killed in this awful devastation of the serpent's tail.

He rode through the smashed town looking for her, calling her name amid the cries of other searchers and the screams and moans of the hurt ones and the bereaved. He kept leading the new stallion because he could not think of anything else to do with it, though it was growing fretful amid the confused milling and wailing.

It was the grandmothers who first began doing something to help the hurt ones. Grandmothers were always the first helpers and healers. They were now helping the limping ones, tending to cuts, gathering wood for splints, fanning fires to heat poultices and brew broths and herb teas. It was the same here as it had been among the Shienne, his birth People: the old women were always the best of the People in times of pain and trouble. And soon they had the younger women helping them, and then boys and men. The town was a chaos of mud, wreckage, windblown smoke, and busy People, half of them naked and bloody. Four warriors walked toward the Sacred Canoe, carrying between them a mummy that had been blown in from the Town of the Dead. They wordlessly laid it on the ground in front of the Sacred Canoe, and one of the men looked up just as Man on a Horse rode by. The man's name was Laughing Thunder. He was one of the warriors whom Man on a Horse had taught to ride.

Laughing Thunder's eyes widened and he exclaimed: "Brother! I saw you come chasing a great *ka vah yoh* ahead of the Devil Wind, but I thought it was a dream! Is he truly the father *ka vah yoh*?" Laughing Thunder was quickly looking over the great new animal, captivated by its magnificence despite the profusion of pain and misery around him.

"It is he," replied Man on a Horse. "I went nearly to the Land of the Sun in search of him, and then he came to me. But now, tell me, where is our *okimeh*?"

"Ah! He is somewhere," Laughing Thunder said, swinging his arm in a vague arc. "The Devil Wind blew away his dead wife from the Town of the Dead. Now with his other wives and his daughter, he hunts for her bones, everywhere out there, to return them to their resting place."

Man on a Horse's heart leaped up. Snow Hair and her father were alive! He dismounted and handed the rein of the weary mare to Laughing Thunder. "Take her," he said, "and start rounding up the others that are out on the hills, will you, brother?" He swung onto the back of the great stallion, much to the admiration of Laughing Thunder, and before riding off, he said, "That one now carries the seed of this one!"

"*Shu-su!*" cried Laughing Thunder, waving after him. "Good, my brother!"

THE MANDAN COUNCIL SAT IN THE LIGHT OF A BONFIRE IN THE ruined town two nights later and considered the future of its People. All the clouds and storms that had brought the Devil Wind were gone, and stars were intense in the sky. The village *okimeh*, Slaps the Water, stood in the firelight elegantly dressed in his painted robe with a bison-horn headdress, and old Fat Legs, *maho okimeh* of the nation, stood beside him. The Sacred Canoe was behind them. Some of the People were seated on the ground; others were on the roofs of the lodges that remained standing. The air was so still that all the hundreds of People whose ruddy faces reflected the fire glow could hear everything said in the council. The council pipe had already been passed and smoked and had been returned to its resting place on two forked sticks before the fire. Slaps the Water sat down.

Fat Legs, wizened and stooped, held in one hand the feathered lance that was his staff of leadership. Fat Legs's voice was raspy but strong, and he began:

"My People, Children of First Man, hear me with your ears open so that my words may echo in your hearts.

"We are heavy with sadness. Many times since our Ancestors came from beyond the Flood, our People have been smashed down and driven away from the good places they built. Many times before, it was enemy peoples who struck us and killed our People. This time it was the Devil Wind.

"The Devil Wind," he went on, looking and extending an arm toward the west, "has hurt us before. Our hunters have sometimes been caught in the open and sucked into the sky. Our towns have been damaged before. Sometimes we rebuilt our towns and stayed there for another generation. Or until another People pushed us. Or until the game left. But as you know, my People, down the river from this town, all the way to the Mother of Rivers, there are old stone walls and marks in the ground to show where our towns were. We are an old People, and many troubles we have known.

"But we will always be this People, the Children of First Man. Always we have our Ancient Relics in the Sacred Canoe in the center of our town, and thus we are always the People."

The old leader paused, turned to face the Sacred Canoe, and spread his arms toward it, lifting his *okimeh* lance. Then he faced the fire again. "In this council," he said, "we will make our choice whether to stay here and rebuild our homes here or go farther up the river and make new towns. There are some here in council who want to stay here and repair our towns, here where most of us now living were born.

"There are others here in council who would like us to move to a new place farther up the river. We will speak on both sides.

"I, Fat Legs, your *maho okimeh*, will first tell you what is in my heart on that matter.

"I believe we should go farther up. Here is why I say that: The wind is a messenger. Like the four-leggeds and wingeds, and swimmers and crawlers, like the movements of smoke and water, like the visions that come in our dreams, the wind is a message bearer. When the Devil Wind came this time, it not only struck our houses, it struck also the Town of our Dead. It moved many of their bones. Some of their bones were found, but others were not. The skull of my own grandfather was blown away. Many of you do not know anymore where the bones of your fathers and mothers are." Many of the listeners nodded; some covered their faces with their hands.

"A People does not like to leave the place where its forefathers' bones lie. When a wind scatters those bones, and they do not lie there anymore, that is a message from the Wind, saying that it is a good time to move on, to new hunting grounds, away from old enemies. I think the Devil Wind has told us that. I have no more to say now." He sat down, his old knees popping. Slaps the Water came forward.

"In my heart echo the words of our *maho okimeh*. My thinking is as like his as the moon shining on still water is like the moon shining above. But I have other reasons to say we should change our place." He turned and pointed to the slender warrior who stood near him. "You know Man on a Horse. He taught us to ride. He then went alone far toward the sun, and brought back a powerful father *ka vah yoh* to breed our females. Some day we will have fifteen hundred. I am proud of what he has done. You know that my daughter will be his wife. Maybe they will increase to so many."

The People around the council fire whooped and laughed. The laughter sounded and felt good; it was the first that had been heard since the Devil Wind. Slaps the Water so liked the sound of it that he wanted to make more of it, and so he strayed from the point he had been making and said:

"I have talked with my daughter about the marriage and it makes her happy. She has promised that she will be a good wife and keep his man-part shiny, like that of the father *ka vah yoh*." The people loved bawdiness, and this made them howl and laugh even more. Snow Hair, close to the fire, bit her lips to keep from smiling and looked at the ground, so that her husband-to-be would not see her eyes.

When the laughter had died down, Slaps the Water returned to what he had been saying before. "But this man is not just a fine warrior who does well for our People. He, too, is a bringer of messages. Hear me:

"Did we not see him come racing the great father *ka vah yoh* and leading the Devil Wind? Who has seen such a thing if it was not a dream-vision?" He paused and let them think of that. Those who had seen it were remembering it vividly, and those who had only heard of it could see it just as well. Man on a Horse himself was remembering it as it would have been seen by the People, rather than the way he had actually seen it while chasing the great stallion. And he was seeing it in his mind even as he looked at the awed and thoughtful faces of all the people in the firelight. It was indeed like a dream vision, and the warrior knew again, as he had known when it was happening, that it had been a moment of great power and of messages still to be understood. Though he knew now that the Devil Wind often came through this part of the country, it was, to him, still the thunderbird carrying the terrible Earth serpent, and still an important vision-message. He looked at Snow Hair's face and saw that she was looking at him with admiration and fear and great love.

Now Slaps the Water resumed speaking, breaking the reverent silence.

"I have thought of this vision that Man on a Horse brought us, and here is what I think it tells us:

"The *ka vah yoh*s will make our lives different. We will be better hunters and will never lack meat and skins for our food and clothing. We will have so many hides of the bison that we can trade them to the tribes that have no *ka vah yoh*s, and for all the sorts of fine things they have. Tribes that have been our enemies will come and be friends, both because they will fear us and because they want to share in our plenty. It is our son Man on a Horse who taught us to use these animals so well, and it is he who went to the Land of the Sun to bring us the father of their race, a journey farther than any of our People ever made since the time when First Man crossed the Flood to come to this land. I tell you that this man is great to us as First Man was great! And that is why the Devil Wind pursued him! It is a sign of his importance to us. Man on a Horse and his race with the Devil Wind spoke of our change to a greater People. Many of us saw the sign with our own eyes; it was not just to one the sign was shown. My People, that is what I have to say. Now I stand back to hear what others wish to say about these things."

"*Ho! Shu-su!*" many exclaimed in approval.

Bone Cracker, Slaps the Water's old uncle, was the first to rise and speak then. He rose with difficulty and stood leaning on a staff, because his right foot had been broken in the destruction of the Devil Wind. His voice was resonant but cracked with age:

"Sons and daughters, my People, Children of First Man. I have awaited a chance to speak about this warrior called Man on a Horse ever since he rode in with the Devil Wind at his tail. If he had not led that wind here, I could stand here on my two feet without a stick to hold me up." He pretended to glower at the young man, and brought laughter. Then he went on:

"We Elders, called upon for our wisdom, counseled with our *okimeh* on whether this man should go to seek the male *ka vah yoh*. I, Bone Cracker, spoke in his favor. I believed his heart was true and he would return to us with the great animal he was going to get. Another person in that council—" he cast a mocking glance at Mossy Horns, who sat a little way to his left, then continued—"that person warned us that the warrior was plotting to trick us and run away to the south, and take that one *ka vah yoh* and never come back to us. But you can see he came back—and now my foot is broken!" That made the people laugh again, and Bone Cracker smiled and said, "But I am glad I spoke for him! By and by I will be able to walk well enough on both my feet . . . but all our warriors and hunters will be able to ride on our many *ka vah yoh*s. And so you see, I was right. My People, try to remember the times when I am right."

They were laughing as Bone Cracker, helping himself with the shoulder of a nearby boy, sat back down. While he was getting down, Mossy Horns was getting up, which took him just as long because of his ancient joints. He gave Bone Cracker a sly look and said:

"My People, you know me. I am the oldest man here, and thus the wisest." People smiled. "In my long years, I have been right more times than Bone Cracker has yet to be." Again laughter, and he continued, "And so, it does not make Bone Cracker wiser than I just because I finally was wrong . . . *once*!"

Even Bone Cracker laughed loud then.

"It makes me happy," said the old man, "that I was wrong about this warrior. I doubted before, but he has proven himself in a fine way. Now I, too, believe this riding man is of much importance. I believe he will become a great *okimeh* when we are a riding People, in the new land up the river."

The crowd cried out its approval, and Mossy Horns turned as if to sit down, but then turned back around as if he had just remembered something, and raised his hand to point at Bone Cracker, saying:

"I tried to keep him from going away only to keep you from getting your old foot hurt."

To an uproar of laughter, Mossy Horns slowly eased back to the place where he had been sitting. Man on a Horse, feeling full of honor and happiness, looked around at the faces of the People, their laughing faces in the firelight, so many handsome and beautiful faces, so many old and wrinkled, but all of them turned toward the fire that was their People's center, all of one heart laughing and smiling so soon after the wreckage and pain of the Devil Wind, and he loved them so much as his People now that his eyes blurred and he had to swallow. His gaze moved beyond the fire to the glimmering eyes of Snow Hair, and caught her staring at him. He remembered the first time he had seen her, coming naked out of the river in the snow.

Shu-su, he thought. It is good!

Part III

1804 — 1837

I have, for many years past, contemplated the noble races of red men who are now spread over these trackless forests and boundless prairies, melting away at the approach of civilization. Their rights invaded, their morals corrupted, their lands wrenched from them, their customs changed, and therefore lost to the world; and they at last sunk into the earth, and the ploughshare turning the sod over their graves . . . millions of whom have fallen victim to the small-pox, and the remainder to the sword, the bayonet, and whiskey; all of which means of their destruction have been introduced and visited upon them by acquisitive white men . . . yet, phoenix-like, they may rise from the "stain of the painter's palette," and live again upon canvas, and stand forth for centuries yet to come, the living monuments of a noble race.

—*George Catlin, 1832*

CHAPTER 19

Near Mih-Tutta-Hang-Kusch, a Mandan Town October 1804

The boy named Mah-to-toh-pah, Four Bears, a fourteen-year-old grandson of the renowned Man on a Horse, was squatting in the pit under the eagle trap, watching up through the lattice of boughs toward the gray sky, when he thought he heard shouts from the camp of the Eagle Hunters.

Through much of the afternoon he had been patiently and keenly watching the sky, trying not to think songs or otherwise let his mind stray, waiting for an eagle to come down for the dead rabbit bait so he could reach up through the lattice and catch it by its legs. But now those wispy shouts in the moaning wind had caught his attention, and he was alarmed. The conduct and ceremony of eagle hunting were very strict. Shouting in the Eagle Hunter camp must mean something was very wrong.

Four Bears listened hard to hear whether they were calling for him or to each other, or were perhaps warning that they had seen Dah-koh-tah or other enemies, but when the cold autumn wind was blowing down the valley of the Muddy River, it was hard to hear voices from the camp down in the willows. He could not hear what they were shouting about, only that they were excited.

Four Bears, tawny-skinned, slender, and fine-featured, raised the edge of the lattice, stood up in the pit, and looked about the vast valley. His trap was dug into the slope of a grassy draw high on the bluff, and his vision was so sharp that some men said he could see as the eagles themselves saw.

Up the river there was nothing alarming. The boy squinted into the hissing wind, toward the distant Hidatsa towns across the great river, at the mouth of the Knife, half a day's walk away. There was nothing unusual to be seen up there, just the usual clusters of low, domed lodges under wisps of windblown wood smoke.

So the boy peered across the river toward Mih-Tutta-Hang-Kusch, his own People's town, and ran his gaze across the wide field and the great hillside beyond it, a slope covered with rippling yellow grass and rising gently to the plains above the broad valley. If enemy war parties came, they usually appeared first at the top of that long slope and could be seen at the edge of the sky, ready to ride down and catch anyone who was outside the town palisade. When bison herds came along that side of the river, they usually moved along that vast slope. But he saw no enemy horsemen, no herd of bison. All looked peaceful, the bend in the wide, gray-green river, the wind-whipped water, the willow leaves blowing off in the bottomlands, a few bull-boats out near the far shore with the tiny figures of women or fishermen in them, some towing bundles of driftwood to be used for firewood, the town on its stone cliff, protected on three sides by water and on the land side by its long palisade of pointed logs.

But the roofs of the town were swarming with people, as if it were a summer day. This time of year when the winds blew cold, the people usually did not stand or lounge on their roofs. They were all looking and pointing downriver at something.

Being in the gully, Four Bears could not see what they were pointing at far downstream. He knew he was not supposed to abandon his eagle trap, but felt that he must see what was happening. So he slipped out from under the edge of the lattice and replaced it, and began running up until he was out of the draw above the Eagle camp and on a high, grassy bluff from which he could see far down the curve of the river.

His mouth dropped open. He had never seen such a sight, except the three times when he had dreamed of First Man.

In the middle of the wide river below the bend there was a boat that looked as big as a house, with a huge white wing over it, and it was coming up slowly against the current. Beside it came two smaller wood canoes, one red and one white.

The boy Four Bears stared at the big canoe and he could only believe that he was dreaming of First Man again, dreaming even though his eyes were open and cold wind was blowing his hair around his face.

First Man, said the Grandfathers, had floated to land after the Great Flood in a huge canoe like this, driven by a white wing on top and many paddles on either side, and led by a bird. The boy could see the paddles moving even from this distance.

Yes, surely this was the dream of First Man again, and although the boy did not feel as if he were asleep, he had not felt he was asleep the other times, either, though he had been.

So now he was happy and no longer afraid, safe in a dream, not thinking of enemies. He could see the others running from the Eagle camp down toward the shore, shouting, and he would run down after them, and when the Great Canoe came close to shore, he would again see First Man, who was pale-skinned and had yellow hair on his head and even on his face. Just so the Grandfathers said First Man had looked, and just so had First Man appeared in his dreams before. Four Bears ran fast down the long slope, the cold wind at his back, toward the river.

WITH THE OTHER MEN AND BOYS FROM THE EAGLE HUNTING CAMP, Four Bears stood on the riverbank and watched the white men come shoreward in their red and white canoes, and what was happening was real after all, but more exciting even than the dream of First Man.

The Great Canoe had somehow been stopped in the water offshore with its white wing folded up small. About thirty men could be seen standing on it.

The men paddling the red and white canoes looked little different from the French and British traders who came and stayed in the nearby towns, and the boy looked them all over for the one he hoped to recognize as First Man. This still seemed so much like a dream.

At the top of a pole in the white canoe there was a fluttering cloth with a pretty design of white, blue, and red, all very bright. All the men in the canoes had shiny guns. Guns were rare and formidable things here; the boy had seen only a few that the traders sold to Mandan men for furs.

The men in the canoes were carefully watching the men and boys on the shore, and Four Bears could see and feel that his own People were likewise wary. The river waters were choppy from the hard wind. It would not be easy for the white men to land without help from shore.

As the canoes came nearer the shore, a short, one-eyed man in the front of the red canoe carefully stood up. He pointed to one of the Mandans from the Eagle camp, then to himself, then held his forefingers up side by side, indicating friendship. The Mandan responded likewise, and smiled, and the one-eyed white man smiled, then picked up a loop of rope and made a motion as if he would throw it to the man on shore, and the man nodded. So the white man tossed the rope, and the man on shore caught it with a laugh and pulled. Two others took hold of it and helped, and everyone was laughing and nodding. Four Bears liked this and felt good.

When the white canoe came closer, a big man in front boldly stood up with a coil of rope and gestured to another man of the Eagle camp, nodded, and threw it. It was blown by the wind and came closer to Four Bears, who caught it in the air and held on until the other man grabbed it and pulled with him. The boy was smiling, happy to help. Just then the wind blew off the big white man's hat, making him laugh and grab for it with one hand, but it fell in the water. Four Bears let the other man have the rope and waded into the cold water up to his waist and got the hat. Cold water was nothing to a Mandan boy. When Four Bears waded ashore with the hat, the big white man was just leaping from the prow of the canoe onto the riverbank, a very agile leap for a man so large, and Four Bears went toward him with the wet hat and got a good look at the big man.

He was astonished. Never had he seen a face more to his liking.

This was not exactly the face of First Man as he had seen it in his dreams, but it was a face equally to be remembered until another dream.

Unlike First Man, this white man had no hair on his face. His skin from his eyes down was reddish brown from sun, but his forehead was high and very white, and his hair red as a mallard's breast. His eyes were blue as sky, a deeper blue than the gray-blue of those in the Mandan nation who had blue eyes, and were the happiest eyes the boy had ever seen. His teeth were very white and straight as he smiled, and when Four Bears gave him the dripping hat, the man laughed and said something in a great, deep, and warm voice that the boy could feel inside. Here was a man perhaps as great as First Man!

So it seemed to Four Bears.

THE WHITE MEN TALKED BY HAND SIGNS TO THE LEADER OF THE Eagle camp, and told him many amazing things and asked for his help. They gave him some twists of tobacco to take as gifts to the chief of the village, and asked if the chief could come to see them here.

The red-haired man was very good with hand language, and he told the Eagle Hunters that his great boat brought men from the great Council Fire of a nation in the east called the United States, that these men were on their way to the Great Water where the sun sets, and that, with winter so soon coming, they wanted to build a place here to live until spring, as neighbors and friends of all the people hereabouts, the Mandans, the Hidatsa, the Minetaree. They even said they had counseled with the Dah-koh-tah tribes downriver to be friends with these tribes here, who had always been their enemies. The Eagle Hunters gaped and listened and hoped they could carry such incredible messages to their chiefs Kagohami and Coyote.

Bring your chiefs across the river to talk to us, said the great-voiced Red Hair in hand language, and we will make with them a friendship that will make your People rich and happy forever.

The boy learned to pronounce the name of the Red Hair, though it had a sound in it that he had to teach his tongue anew to make: *Clark.*

The Eagle Hunters went up the river to where they kept their bullboats, and they set off across the cold, wild, pounding river in the little round skin-covered vessels to take these complex messages and the gifts to their chiefs.

The boy Four Bears looked back to the far bank of the wide river and watched the white men taking things ashore from their Great Canoe to build themselves a winter village.

It still seemed like a dream, like something that would somehow change everything, even like the long ago coming to land of First Man.

"THERE!" EXCLAIMED HA-NA-TA-NU-MAUH, THE YOUNG WOLF, "there is Okee-hee-dee, the Devil! I told you!"

Four Bears looked up toward the gate of the fort the hairy-faces had built. He and Young Wolf had crossed the river and hung around outside the fort for three days to see the famous black-skinned giant, but so far had not caught a glimpse of him.

But now there he was! He was standing in the open gate in plain daylight beside the Red Hair Chief of the white people, and his face and hands were indeed as black as soot from a pinewood fire. He was as tall as the Red Hair Chief, and, like him, was dressed in a fringed coat of hide, but his body was as thick and powerful as two men put together. Four Bears stood with his mouth open and his heart racing. Never had he seen such a thing. He said, "Perhaps he paints himself black, with soot and grease, like the man who is the Man of Night in the Okeepah."

"No," Young Wolf said with his usual haughty certainty. "My grandfather and many of the elders have seen him and rubbed his skin, and the black will not come off. And the women who have lain with the black one all agree that even his behind and his man-part are black. They all talk of it to each other, and none disagrees with any other."

"Then it must be so," replied Four Bears. "But it is wrong to call him the Devil, I think. His face is kind and happy, as you can see yourself. Do the woman who lie with him say he was good and kind, or like the Devil?"

"They say he is good and kind," Young Wolf admitted. "But does that prove he is not the Devil? Any man would be good and happy when he is doing that with a woman."

"I have heard that some of the French traders are mean and angry when they do it to their wives."

"Perhaps *they* are Devils," said Young Wolf. "Some people say so."

"Look," Four Bears said. "Your grandfather comes up."

The Red Hair Chief and the black man had raised their hands in greeting to someone coming up from the river. The man coming up was Shahaka, or Coyote, chief of the town called Mih-Tutta-Hang-Kusch, the town closest to the white men's fort. Coyote was a fat man who was always happy and talked too much. He was descended from the First Man People and had a round, jowly face. Though his hair was not light like theirs, his eyes and features looked like theirs. He was waddling up the snowy slope now, wrapped in a decorated bison-hide robe with a beaver skin crown on his head and a big smile on his face, one hand raised to greet the Red Hair Chief. Coyote spent much of his time in the white men's fort; he was said to be helping them draw a picture of the lands to the west, showing where the river came from and where the great Shining Mountains were. It seemed that all the white men who had ever come here were interested in the lands toward the sunset. When the first hairy faces, the French, had come, almost seventy winters ago, they too had been interested in learning how to go west to the end of the land. It was curious, how they all wanted to go there.

Following the fat chief were the usual members of his retinue. There was the swaggering French trader Jussaume, who lived near the Mandan towns, and his surly-faced wife; Jussaume could speak English and Mandan, and was interpreter when Coyote was with the white men. There, too, was Charbonneau, another French trader and a beaver-skin broker. He was a loud-mouthed and smelly man who molested women, even though he had a lodgeful of young wives of his own. A friend of Jussaume, he was said to be clamoring to join the white men as an interpreter and guide. Behind them, just coming past the place where the white men's great canoe was frozen fast in the ice at the riverbank, were two small women with huge bundles on their backs. The older of those two women was Yellow Corn, Coyote's favorite wife. The other was a slight, scrawny girl-child, the youngest wife of Charbonneau. Charbonneau had won her in gambling from a Hidatsa warrior of the Knife River town upstream, whose slave she had been. She had been born in the Snake tribe of the Shining Mountains, and captured in a raid east of the mountains when still a little girl. Her name was Sakakawea, meaning the Bird. She was very pregnant.

Four Bears knew all this about these people from Young Wolf, whose grandmother was one of Coyote's older wives. He knew that the black man was the servant of the Red Hair Chief. Young Wolf insisted that the black man must be Okee-hee-dee. But Four Bears did not believe that the Devil would be a servant to any man, and especially not to a good, kindly, cheerful man like the Red Hair Chief.

The fort of the hairy-faces was a place of great fascination to Four Bears, who had never seen people work so much. A Mandan town might be busy in winter, with people going from lodge to lodge visiting, with children playing in the snow, with men going down to the steam huts for their baths, but a Mandan town was otherwise calm and lazy. This fort of the white men was always loud with hammering, chopping, and hewing, and with the ringing sound of metal hammers striking metal. That had become a new and finally a constant sound in the valley. There were men in the fort who could make any kind of thing out of iron. They made iron axes and tomahawks, arrow- and spearheads, spoons, hoes and scrapers, awls and spikes—all the kinds of tools and weapons that the Mandans usually had made of stone, bone, and horn—and they repaired the hunters' old French guns and their broken beaver traps. These metal things they gave to the People in return for meat and grain, and sometimes for women's love. They also had needles of shiny metal to trade, wonderful, strong needles that did not break when women sewed leather with them, and they had pendants of metal with tiny pictures of their Great Chief upon them, the head of their Great Chief in the East, looking to one side. All the important men of all the towns had been given these flat metal pendants, and they wore them on thongs around their necks, like important trophies. Coyote wore his proudly all the time, as if he wanted to be the favorite person of the white-face chiefs. They usually called Coyote by the name Big White, flattering him by making him believe he was much like them, and he devoured their flattery the way a starving man eats meat. The white men were befriending all the chiefs up and down the river, not just those of the Mandan towns, but also the Minetaree and Hidatsa whose towns were clustered nearby. They were trying to win their trade away from the British traders, the rumors said. Okimeh Coyote was jealous of the proximity of his town to the fort, and lavished attention and generosity upon the two young white leaders, whom he called Red Hair Chief and Long Knife Chief. He was so attached to them, in fact, that he was planning to travel back with them someday to their Great Council Place in the East.

When the river thawed, they said, the white men would continue up the Muddy River to the Shining Mountains, and then down the other side of the mountains to the Sunset Water. When they came back, they would take their devoted friend Coyote back east with them so that he could befriend their *maho okimeh*, Jefferson, who was pictured on the pendants the chiefs wore. From that friendship, they promised, Coyote would obtain wealth and power for his Mandan People. This promise had become a great dream in the head and heart of Coyote, and he talked of it constantly when he was with his family and village councilmen. The planned voyage plainly filled him with both eagerness and dread. Fortunately it would be a year or more before it could happen, so he did not have to do anything yet but talk. Coyote preferred talking over doing, as everyone knew.

Young Wolf feared it. He was afraid his grandfather would go so far away with the Black Devil that he could never return.

But Four Bears did not have that bad suspicion. He had never forgotten the day he had first seen the Red Hair Chief and rescued his hat from the river, nor had he forgotten the wonderful smile on Red Hair's face. Even now, when he looked upon Red Hair standing in the gate waving to the approaching *okimeh*, Four Bears could not help thinking of First Man. He felt connected with Red Hair as if in a vision that passed through the whole Circle of Time; sometimes he dreamed that Red Hair was his Ancestor of Ancient Times, First Man, who had stepped from the other side of the Circle of Time to meet him and smile at him on this side.

And so now a great swelling came up in the heart of Four Bears as he looked at Red Hair and his black man, and he suddenly was ready to do the thing he had longed to do for so many days. Coyote and his followers were still at a distance down the riverbank slope, slow to climb because of Coyote's fatness and the heavy loads of food and hides the two small women were carrying. There was still a little while to do that which he meant to do. His friend Young Wolf did not know he was going to do it, and probably would not approve of it. But the heart of Four Bears was full. He had something to give to Red Hair, something that had the power to protect him.

He ran quickly to him over the snow. The Red Hair Chief heard Four Bears's feet squeaking on the hard snow and turned to see him coming, and, though he had seen him only once before, he again smiled at him as if he recognized him. Four Bears stopped directly in front of Red Hair. He opened his hand to show him what he had brought.

It did not look like much. It was only a white, clean piece of bone, no longer or thicker than any of his fingers, but he had smoothed and hollowed and drilled it in the old way. And he said to the Red Hair Chief, even though he knew he could not understand his words:

"This I made for you from the wing bone of an eagle I caught before the first day I saw you. Listen to it." He put one end between his lips and blew two long breaths through it, and its sound was exactly the sound of the scream of an eagle. "The eagle watches over good people," he said to Red Hair, whose blue eyes had widened at recognition of the eagle's voice. "If you are in danger sometime, blow this and the eagle will fly over and protect you. I, Mah-to-toh-pah, Four Bears, one of the Children of First Man, give you this!" His heart was pounding with the excitement of this bold thing he had done, and with love for the Red Hair Chief with his good face.

Red Hair took the whistle and said something in his strange tongue, in his deep voice. And before Four Bears could turn and run back, Red Hair took his hand in his own mighty hand and held it, and turned and said something to the black man, who turned and went in through the gate. Four Bears felt a good power flowing from Red Hair's hand into his own, and stood waiting, even though his *okimeh* Coyote was now coming up and was only a few paces away, frowning at him.

In a moment the black man returned, and he gave something to Red Hair. Red Hair said something to Four Bears in a kind voice and put into his hand something hard and flat and round that flashed in the light. At first Four Bears thought it must be one of the Great Chief pendants. But when he held it in his palm and looked at it, he saw an eye. Not a picture of an eye, but a living eye, an eye with an eyebrow. When he turned it slightly a nose appeared, and then another eye! This seeming magic so startled him that he jerked his hand, and in the disk then he saw the sun flash, then blue sky.

He was almost afraid of the thing; it had so much magic in it he was fearful that it might burn his hand. But the Red Hair Chief had made him a gift of it, and it would not be good manners to pitch it on the ground and run. And, too, it was obviously a great treasure. And so, closing his fingers over it, he nodded twice to Red Hair, and again to the smiling black giant, and backed away; then he turned and trotted to where Young Wolf stood nearby scowling with his upper lip between his teeth. "Come!" he said, his heart still racing. "I must show you something!"

And as the two boys started away across the snow, Four Bears heard the voice of an eagle screaming, very close by. He turned and saw the Red Hair Chief with the whistle in his mouth, and Red Hair Chief blew the eagle cry again, and smiled and waved at Four Bears, just as Coyote and the French traders came walking up to him at the gate.

YOUNG WOLF, AS FOUR BEARS HAD EXPECTED, SCOFFED AT THE gift. He called it a thing of little worth, saying that the white men's soldiers often gave these little things to young women in return for body pleasures. "It is just a looking-at-self stone," he said. "White men make these. I have seen several."

"But you do not have one," Four Bears said.

"I do not have one, and I would not want one," Young Wolf said, in such a haughty tone that Four Bears knew he was writhing with envy.

The boys went down the path, which had been trodden by so many feet that it was shiny. The path led down to the place where most people crossed the river ice to and from Coyote's town. The path led within a few paces of the white men's big boat, which was frozen in the thick ice at the shoreline, as fixed in the river edge as a lodge was fixed on land. Whenever Four Bears had come near the big boat, he had gazed at it and studied it, but now the foremost thing on his mind was the looking-at-self stone the Red Hair Chief had given him, and he scarcely glanced at the boat. He stepped into a hollowed place sheltered from wind by willows and warmed slightly by the low and distant winter sun. Here he squatted, and Young Wolf squatted beside him.

"Now," Four Bears said. "I must look at this gift to me from the Red Hair Chief. You may wish to go away and not look at it, since you say it is such a common and slight thing."

But Young Wolf did not leave. Four Bears opened his hand and examined the gift.

"I saw eyes in it," he said. "Look. They are mine. This is like looking down into a pot of water and seeing your face, but it is so small you can only see an eye or a nose."

"All I see is sky."

"I will turn it toward you."

"Ah! Now I see my mouth talking." He smiled. "I see my teeth. Now I see my eye."

"It is like ice, hard like ice. But you cannot see yourself in ice. This is strange and wonderful," Four Bears exclaimed. "I wonder if it melts when it is warm."

"The women say they do not melt. They are more like a metal. Do you remember the polished metal looking-pieces the French traders gave the women to look in?"

"I never did see one," Four Bears said. He was turning the little mirror to and fro, and saw that it sent a little, quivering spot of sunlight dancing across the snow and across the robe of Young Wolf. He moved it so that the spot of light glared on Young Wolf's eye and made him squint.

"Yes, you did see one," Young Wolf said, blinking hard. "When the Hidatsa chief Black Moccasin came to see my grandfather, he was wearing one that hung on his chest. Remember how the light blazed from it? We spoke of that then."

"As you speak, I do remember." Four Bears turned the little mirror over. Its back, a material looking something like rawhide and held on by a metal rim, had a tiny picture painted on it, in red and blue, of a butterfly. That in itself was beautiful to look at, and Four Bears's heart swelled with gratitude for the kindness of the Red Hair Chief, and he said to Young Wolf:

"I shall always be a true friend to Red Hair and his People. They are very good!" Then he added what had been a most private thought, though he knew that the arrogant Young Wolf might scoff at it:

"I believe the Red Hair Chief to be the spirit of First Man, coming back among us!"

Young Wolf did not mock. His dark eyes widened. He turned his head, looked up toward the white men's fort and stared at it, his breath making frost clouds in the frigid air, and he did look like a wolf, a wolf just beginning to try to name a new smell that has appeared on the wind.

"Then," Young Wolf said at last, "I shall try to like them, too."

CHAPTER 20

Mih-Tutta-Hang-Kusch
July 1806

Young Four Bears was so full of vast thoughts he sometimes felt that he must hold onto his head with his hands or it would fly away in all four directions at once.

His soul had been this way ever since the chief Red Hair had come through with his soldiers, going west. Those People had made his mind different.

Four Bears was lying on the roof of his father's lodge, feeling the good sun on his body. He could have dozed, as some People were doing on the roofs of their houses, but his mind kept him awake with all its pictures, and all the different pullings of his thoughts.

Much of the time his mind was pulled upriver toward the west, the way the white men had gone, and he always believed they would come back down the river in their long canoes. He watched for them.

They had said they were going to go up the river to where it started in the Shining Mountains, and go across the Shining Mountains, and down the far side to the Great Sinking Water where the sun sets. What a notion! And then they had left, as if they really meant to do such a thing, and they had been gone for more than a year, but Four Bears did not know what would happen to them. Surely they could not have done what they thought they were going to do.

Of course, there were Shining Mountains far to the west; that was known. Bison hunters from some of the tribes had gone far enough in that direction some summers to see mountains shining with snow on top, though the boy himself did not know anybody who had ever seen those mountains. And it was known, too, that far down on the other side of those Shining Mountains there was a Great Water. In his own father's time, chiefs and hunters from that far side of the mountains had come over with things to trade, and they had said that, yes, there was a Great Water at the far end of the land out there. But the boy himself had never seen those People from out there, he had only heard his father talk about them. But that was enough to make him know it was true.

Four Bears stretched lazily in the sun, feeling the sun-hot clay of the roof under his back and the sunshine on his front, hearing the constant murmur of his People's voices in the town all around him, hearing a flute being played somewhere, hearing laughter, hearing the hot wind whisper around him. He half opened his eyes and saw the deep blue of the sky, and above him and to the right he saw the three bison hides flapping in the wind on their tall poles above Okimeh Coyote's lodge. Each robe was tied with a bulge at the top of the pole so that it looked like a head, with the rest hanging loose below. The hide on the middle pole was that of a white bison that had been bought at great expense from Blackfeet hunters. Whenever such a rare white hide could be obtained, it was put on the middle pole, and there it would hang in the wind, rain, and snow for as many seasons as it would last, as a tribute to Creator. The three hides were said to be ancient signs of three men hanging on poles, the middle one being a man of shining whiteness, Mohk-muck, the First Man. Only the shamans claimed to know what the three figures meant, and it was rumored that even they did not really remember the old story. It was something that had happened long ago to First Man who had come in his Great Canoe across the Great Water of the Sunrise, something that was still sacred, though nobody really remembered.

A Great Water toward the sunrise. The boy now was thinking of that. None of his people now living had ever seen such a Great Water, any more than they had seen the Great Water toward the sunset, but there was said to be one, that it was known that First Man had come across it in a boat. The white men who had been here in Mih-Tutta-Hang-Kusch last year had seen the Great Sunrise Water in their own lifetimes, or so they had told the *okimeh*s. Some of them had even been on that Great Water in boats, or so they had said, and they had been believed, for they were far travelers.

So there was said to be a Great Water where the sun came up and another Great Water where the sun went down, and yet when the sun rose every morning out of the faraway Great Water, it was still on fire, and the boy now thought of that, feeling the hot sun baking his skin, and he thought that the sun must indeed have greater power than anything, that it must indeed be the Eye of Creator, and maybe the explanation was that Creator shut his eyelids when he sank into the Great Water and kept them shut until he rose next morning from the other Great Water.

Creator must therefore swim under the land every night from the west to the east, Four Bears thought.

Ai! Such thinking could make your head hurt!

But the white men had said they were going to go to the Great Sunset Water, and it had been more than a year since they went up the river, and perhaps they had done what they meant to. Certainly they were wonderful men of great power. That first winter they had built themselves a village in just a few days, down there where Four Bears had first seen them, and they had lived in it through that winter, and some of them had come across on the ice of the frozen river and visited Mih-Tutta-Hang-Kusch, talking with the chiefs, lying with some of the village women, making music with strange instruments, doing strange, funny dances—there had even been one man who had danced on his hands with his feet in the air, a trick that many of the Mandan boys had been trying to do ever since—and trading pretty things for food. Those white men had made good medicine for the people of Mih-Tutta-Hang-Kusch and the other towns. They had cured frozen feet and hands and made coughing go away for many sick people. Those soldiers had been remarkable hunters, sometimes going out onto the plains for days at a time when the cold was so deep it made trees crack and when the snow was blowing so hard you could not see five paces ahead, and then coming back carrying meat on sleds they had made themselves while they were out there.

They could make anything, or so it seemed. They had made themselves four more log canoes from willow logs across the river, big canoes to carry all the things they had brought on their big wing-boat. Some of them had sailed the big boat back down the river the same day most of them went on up in the paddle canoes. And the thoughts of the Mandan People had been a little different ever since they left. People still missed them and thought about them, still remembered their music, still remembered the sounds of their guns echoing in the wide valley, still remembered their big man who was the color of charcoal and looked like Okee-hee-dee the Devil and could dance on light feet even though he looked as big as a bison bull.

Yes, certainly they were men of great power. They had

changed the thinking of many People. They had inquired about the light-hairs, asking if they had had an ancient ancestor named Madoc—but no one remembered hearing of such an ancestor. There were babies in the towns now who had been fathered by the white men. It was said that some of them probably would grow up with light hair and skin and blue eyes, like the people in the tribe who were already like that, the ones who were considered to be the Children of First Man.

Four Bears basked in the sunlight and thought of those white men and of how they had caused him to think more and more about the size and the shape of the world, even though he personally had never had time to talk to any of them. He had never even had a chance to see their other chief, called Lewis, except from far off through a crowd. But he still saw every day in his mind the wonderful face of the red-haired one, the one he thought must be so much like First Man. He thought of his face now and smiled, and practiced pronouncing his name.

"*Clark,*" he said.

And just then he heard a commotion beginning, the rising babble of many voices in the town, and someone shouting the exciting words that made him spring to his feet and look up the river:

"The white men's boats! See them! Red Hair returns!"

IN THE SUMMER THERE WERE ALWAYS PEOPLE SWIMMING IN THE great river, and many were on the water in the bullboats. As the boy Four Bears ran down the shore to dive into the river, he heard gunshots, and saw white smoke billowing off the white men's canoes. For an instant the shots frightened him, making him stumble, but then he heard joyous shouts, and remembered that the white men used to celebrate and say hello and farewell with bursts of shooting, and he realized that they probably were just acting that way now. So he dove into the river and began swimming toward the boats, as were dozens of other men, women, and children. His people, who had so long lived among the great rivers, were among the best swimmers anywhere, and Four Bears was one of the fastest and strongest of them all. He swam with a powerful crawl stroke and churning feet, keeping his head low in the water and breathing only under his left arm on every fourth stroke, and soon he was even passing the bullboats that were being drawn upstream by strong paddlers.

In a few minutes he was alongside the white men's canoes,

floating and laughing, smiling up like an otter as he looked them over for a glimpse of their Red Hair Chief called Clark.

Now he saw him, bareheaded in one of the big canoes, grinning happily, and the Clark Chief looked even more like First Man. His face hair had grown, and his hair was all lightened by the sun. He was sitting among bundles near the stern of the long canoe, shouting happy words to the hairy-face men who were paddling. Also sitting among the bundles was the little young woman called Sakakawea, who had gone on the voyage with the white men. She had her little boy in the crook of her arm and was looking ahead toward the town with a very happy face. As that canoe glided by, one of the white men in it shouted and shot another gun into the air. It was the closest Four Bears had ever been to a gunshot, and it hurt his ears.

Now the other canoes were going by, and he turned in the water and swam swiftly downstream alongside them, among the skin-covered bullboats and the whooping people, back toward the landing beach below Mih-Tutta-Hang-Kusch. The noise of voices was growing ever louder, and it was plain that there was going to be a great and exciting welcome in the town for his People's friends, these white men. As for Four Bears, his mind was boiling over with the question he wanted to ask but could not because they did not know his language:

Had they done it? Had they gone beyond the Shining Mountains and down to the Great Water of the Sunset?

THE ANSWER WAS YES, THEY HAD. THE WORD OF IT WENT AROUND the town for days while the white men were visiting. Everyone was talking about it, though it seemed to be beyond the comprehension of most of them even as they spoke of it. They heard of mountains so tall that you could not see a man from the top, and of tribes of fat people who ate nothing but fish, and of a forest near the ocean where the sun never shone and it rained for ten and twenty days without stopping, and they heard of a great fish that had gone up on the shore of the Great Water, a fish that had been longer even than the big wing-boat in which the white men had first arrived here.

About then the Mandans began listening to the tales with glazed eyes and wandering off in disappointment. Before, they had always thought these particular white men could be believed, and they now felt let down. Then when the woman Sakakawea said it was true and that she had seen it herself—at least the skeleton of it—and explained that it was a special giant fish called a "whale," and that whales are commonly that size, big enough that a man could live in one's stomach, and had done so in the white men's ancient stories, the Mandans politely stopped listening to the tales, and some lamented that it was bad that a woman of their own race, perhaps through too long an exposure to white men, had learned to tell their kind of silly stories. Some even began whispering their doubts that the white men had even gone to the End of the Land.

But there was at least one person in the Mandan town who was willing to keep believing the stories.

It was Four Bears, he who had spent so much time thinking of the white men during their absence. He did not get a chance to hear the white men themselves tell the stories of where they had been and what they had seen, but when they were repeated around the fires in the town, he did not laugh with the rest of the People about those stories. He was not only able to believe in a fish that big, he had even seen such fish.

He had seen fish that size in his dreams of First Man. And he believed in everything he had seen in those dreams.

THE TIME HAD COME FOR COYOTE, THE *OKIMEH*, TO GO WITH RED Hair Clark and Long Knife Lewis to the Great Council Town in the East. He could no longer just talk about it, as he had been for more than a year; their canoes were ready and this was the day they were setting out.

Four Bears and Young Wolf squirmed through the excited crowd as Coyote and his wife Yellow Corn walked down toward the riverbank with Red Hair and Long Knife. Both Four Bears and Young Wolf looked distraught as they tried to keep close to the chiefs. Four Bears knew that Young Wolf was afraid he would never see his grandfather Coyote again. Four Bears himself was close to tears because he was afraid he would never see Red Hair again.

It was a hot day with wind blowing. Coyote's long black hair blew over his shoulder. The silver cones hanging on rings in his ears jingled as he walked, and the fat on his body jiggled as he walked downhill toward the boats. Behind him and Yellow Corn was Jussaume, who was going with Coyote to be interpreter.

Four Bears had told Young Wolf he should not be sad or afraid, but honored because his grandfather had been invited to travel so far to meet the Great Father of all the white-faces, the man called Jefferson whose picture was on the medallion. If Young Wolf felt the honor of it, he did not show it. All he showed was agony, and he showed it even though he was trying to look manly and brave about it.

Four Bears and Young Wolf kept moving along the edge of the clamoring crowd with Four Bears's little brother at their heels, watching them take what surely would be their last walk down the bluff out of Mih-Tutta-Hang-Kusch. Red Hair was returning to his own world, and Four Bears was trying to put every detail of him into his memory.

At the water's edge where the boats waited, there were long delays for embracing and praying and weeping. Young Wolf slipped through the mob to touch his grandfather's hand one more time. Four Bears was a few steps from Red Hair and trying to catch his eye, hoping Red Hair would notice him and remember him and perhaps even shake his hand again. Then he found himself standing crowded close to someone who was watching Red Hair. She was Sakakawea, the Bird, with her fat, black-haired baby astride her hip. By the look in her eyes Four Bears could see that she too was filling her memory with Red Hair.

At this moment Red Hair was engaged in deep talk with Sakakawea's husband, Charbonneau. One of the tales of the far journey was that Red Hair had saved Charbonneau from drowning in a fast mountain river by swimming after him and pulling him to shore. That was such a story about Red Hair as Four Bears would believe and always keep in his memory. Red Hair was brave, as First Man had been brave; Red Hair was a far traveler and discoverer, as First Man had been. . . . Again Four Bears had that strong feeling that First Man's spirit had returned to him across the Circle of Time in the body of Red Hair, and Four Bears thought: If I could talk to him, I would tell him that in the next Okeepah I am going to hang up like First Man!

The Red Hair Chief and Charbonneau had finished talking. They held each others' shoulders and pressed their bearded cheeks together, left side and then right, while Coyote the *okimeh* stood nearby saying farewell to relatives, including Young Wolf.

Four Bears tried to will the Red Hair Chief to look in his direction. He wanted to wish him well with his eyes. He would have liked to go and touch his hand, even touch faces with him in the strange way the Frenchman had done, but his manners would not permit him to do that. He had not been among those whom the white-faces had visited; he was just another of the hundreds of boys of the towns who admired Red Hair. Still, he wanted Red Hair to see him and recognize him, and at least smile at him, and so he sent him his thoughts as hard as he could. But Red Hair's eyes, when they came around, stopped instead on the Bird and her baby, and they were an intense sky-blue, and he was looking at her and at the baby with such power of attention that Four Bears knew he could see no one else. She walked toward Red Hair, who smiled at her and said something, and then she lifted the little boy off her hip and handed him to Red Hair. With a look of pure joy on his face, Red Hair held the child under the arms, tossed him into the air and caught him as he came down, then did it again and again, while the baby chortled and shrieked with laughter. Then Red Hair handed the baby back to the Bird, while people all about laughed and exclaimed about what they had just seen. As Red Hair settled the baby in its mother's arms, he laid his big hand gently on her cheek and she squeezed her eyes shut.

Four Bears was astonished by that unexpected gesture of tenderness, such as he had seen only rarely, only between husbands and wives, and in their own lodges. But it made his heart swell up, and he thought how fine it was for a great man to be so kind to a small woman with a half-blood child, a woman who had in fact been a slave of the Hidatsa. And thus even that small gesture increased Four Bears's sadness about the departure of the Red Hair Chief.

And soon, with unexpected swiftness after all the prolonged farewells, the boats were loaded and everyone was aboard, and they were being shoved into the current of the Muddy River. Four Bears was swept by a great urgency then, a feeling that he personally must say farewell to Red Hair somehow, or he would always regret that he had not.

So Four Bears ran along the shore. He was only one among many who were running, running to wave and shout farewells to the white-faces as well as to their *okimeh*. Four Bears ran and ran. Eventually, his little brother grew tired and slogged to a stop. The boats were still not far from shore, and Four Bears could see that Red Hair was near the other captain, the one called Long Knife, that he was kneeling by him and talking, and only now and then glancing back toward the village. It looked hopeless now; Four Bears thought he should have gone to Red Hair and touched him while he was on shore, regardless of manners.

And then he remembered something. He remembered the little disk of looking glass the Red Hair Chief had given him two winters ago. He took it out of the little hide bag in which he had always carried it. He held it up and made its bright reflection of the sun on the ground before him, then tilted it until the bright spot darted out across the water toward the boats. Then he wiggled the mirror, making it flash the sunlight toward Red Hair's boat.

He saw some people in the boats look back toward him.

And then he saw the Red Hair Chief raise one arm and wave, and saw him put his other hand to his mouth.

Then, from across the water there came the shrill cry of an eagle, blown on the whistle he had given Red Hair.

Four Bears, his heart swollen with admiration and joy, stood on the riverbank and waved.

The Great Red Hair Chief had remembered him!

And I will remember the Red Hair Chief always, Four Bears thought. If ever I know there is something he wants, which I can do, I shall do that.

He told his little brother, as they walked back toward Mih-Tutta-Hang-Kusch, "I shall always be a friend of Red Hair and his People!"

CHAPTER 21

MIH-TUTTA-HANG-KUSCH
AUTUMN 1808

IN THE TWO YEARS OF COYOTE'S ABSENCE, FOUR BEARS AND Young Wolf had been hung up in the Okeepah. The torn-flesh scars on their chests and shoulders were still fresh and red.

The cry went through the village that a boat of the fur trader Chouteau was coming, and that Coyote and Yellow Corn were in it. Everyone in the village ran through the streets and down the slope to the landing place to meet their long-gone *okimeh*. When he had tried to return the year before, the boat had been turned back by an attack of the hostile Arikara, and Coyote and his wife and Jussaume had spent an extra winter in the city of St. Louis at the mouth of the Muddy River. In that city their friend Red Hair now lived as warrior chief and agent for all the tribes west of the Mother of Rivers, and Long Knife Lewis was *okimeh* of all the western territory they had explored. That knowledge had already preceded the fur company boat up the river by a long time, and now at last the boat was here.

Mooring lines were thrown ashore and tied, and the Mandans stood eagerly awaiting their beloved *okimeh*.

The first people to come down the gangplank were a fat man and woman in strange and ridiculous clothing.

Four Bears and Young Wolf looked at the man and woman, then looked at each other. The crowd had grown utterly still. Four Bears saw the fat man look eagerly from one person on shore to another. No one moved. The man looked at Young Wolf, and Young Wolf looked down.

Four Bears stood and watched. He saw the fat man's face go flat, all eagerness disappearing. He saw the People looking past or through the strangely dressed pair. Then they watched others, traders and crewmen, come off the boat.

The fat man reached up and tilted his three-cornered hat, and the woman opened a little thing that looked like a roof on a stick, and held it above to make shade for herself, and then with her hand on his arm they started strolling up the hill. The fat man had a brown thing that looked like a stick in one side of his mouth, and a longer stick with a curved handle hanging on his other arm. He reached into the front of his clothes and pulled out a shiny thing that looked like a medallion, glanced at it and put it back.

The people turned cautiously to watch the two fat people go up the hill toward the *okimeh*'s house. The woman's dress trailed in the dirt. The man's black coat had two black tails hanging down to the backs of his knees.

Then the People, still very quiet, turned back to the boat. Their faces brightened when they saw Jussaume coming down. He was dressed as he always dressed, in deerskins with a sash around his waist, and the People crowded close and greeted him. They had a question for him: Was not their *okimeh*, Shahaka, the Coyote, supposed to be on this boat?

With a snort, Jussaume replied, "What? Are you blind? He just walked past you! There he goes up the hill with Yellow Corn!"

"We saw no one," said Young Wolf.

"No," said others, "we saw no one."

And Four Bears saw that they believed what they were saying.

Four Bears approached Young Wolf in the center of the town several days later. Here the white-face traders were surrounded by husbands and wives who were trading beaver pelts and tanned bison and antelope hides for awls and needles, mirrors and fire strikers, kettles and tin cups and guns. It was a fine clear day with intense blue sky and a nipping breeze from the north, which heightened the aromas of roasting meats and burning tobacco that drifted everywhere. Everyone was talking and it was a time of greet cheer. But Young Wolf was surly. He looked past people's faces and appeared as if he were ready to shout or cry. He let his friend Four Bears stop him, however, and they stood basking in the sun next to the Sacred Canoe. Four Bears could tell that Young Wolf needed to talk to someone, and that that was the reason why he seemed not to want to talk to anyone. After they had said a few things about the goods of the traders, Young Wolf suddenly blurted out, with quivering chin:

"Coyote is a bag of lies!"

That was what Four Bears had been hearing, but he was shocked to hear it from Young Wolf. So he said nothing, just gazed at the bison hides swaying on their tall poles atop the *okimeh*'s lodge, and waited for his friend to go on. He did not look at him because he did not like to see a young man fighting back tears. Young Wolf had almost worshiped his grandfather, and Four Bears knew it must have been very hard for him to say what he had just said.

Soon Young Wolf spoke again. "When he went away on the boat with the white-faces two winters ago, I foresaw that my grandfather would not come back. I believe he has not! They have kept his spirit there and returned to us a bag of lies that looks like his body and face. You saw him, dressed in clothing that made him look like a huge magpie! Men would not have laughed at my grandfather, but they laugh at this magpie that has come back!" Young Wolf clamped his lips shut and breathed hard through his nose, still trying to keep from crying.

Four Bears decided to remind him of something, and said, "Do you not remember that sometimes men did laugh at him because they thought him a man who talked too much?"

Young Wolf turned blazing eyes on Four Bears and retorted, "But they never said he was a liar! And now they are all saying it! My grandfather was not a liar, and this man the white-faces brought back is a liar! I believe they have stolen his spirit and returned to us a fat magpie!"

"What does he say that they think untrue?" Four Bears asked. The boys were walking away from the center of the town as they talked, getting away from the noisy crowd of people. They strolled toward the part of town that sat on the bluff high above the riverbank. Soon they were looking down on the big moored oar boat of the fur traders.

Young Wolf pointed down at the vessel and said, "He told us that on a river in the east there is a boat as big as that one, and that he saw it going up the river without oars or paddles. That could not be!"

Four Bears thought, then his face brightened and he said, "A big boat could! Do you not remember that when Red Hair first came up the river, his boat had a wing on it that the wind blew on, to push it forward up the river!"

"I understand the wing-boats. But Magpie was not speaking of wing-boats. He said that boat on that river was driven by a great fire in its belly, that it grumbled and breathed smoke."

"Fire made it go?"

"That is what he said. And of course that must be a lie."

Four Bears agreed that that must be a lie. "What other things did he tell that seem not to be true?"

Again Young Wolf pointed to the fur traders' boat. "He said he saw boats ten times as big as that one, with such forests growing on their tops that a hundred men could stand in their limbs. And he said there are hundreds of such boats on one city's shore."

"Ai-ee!" Four Bears exclaimed. He remembered dreams in which he had seen great boats with trees on them. All he could say now was, "Might there be such boats?"

"No. Just lies," said Young Wolf. "Almost more than one's head can remember. He said that on a night in summer, all the people of a great town went down to the shore to watch fires burst in the sky. He said the fires banged like guns and whistled like eagles, and that they flashed like suns and bright smoke ran down across heaven's face like waterfalls. He said it was more bright than the winter lights in the northern sky. But most terrible about that lie was, he said that those lights were not made by Creator, but by the white men themselves, and that they did it for their amusement.

"He said also for their amusement they go into great lodges of high roofs where hundreds sit in rows while a few men and women stand high in front of them and scream at each other, and finally kill each other with long knives or short knives. . . ."

"What! Truly kill each other?"

"He said they sing their death song as they die! But then, when they all come out at the end, the dead ones are alive again!"

"Ai-ee!" Four Bears cried. "He, our own chief whom we must trust and believe, would tell such things to his People?"

"In the same kind of a great high-roof lodge, he said, many hundreds also sat in rows to watch twenty or thirty others use tools that made loud sounds. There were drums, and flutes, and bells, but there also were many with tools they scraped with switches to make noise. He said some of the noise was pleasant, but mostly it screeched or thundered until he wanted to get up and run out. But, he said, even that noise is no worse than the noises in the streets, and so it was no use to flee outdoors!"

Four Bears's scalp was prickling. If these things were true, the world of the white man was a horrible place; if they were untrue, Coyote had perhaps gone mad, maybe because the white-faces had indeed stolen his spirit. For the People here, that would be worse. It did not really matter so much if the white-faces so far away were crazy, but to have one's own principal chief be crazy was troubling.

"Listen," Young Wolf said, gripping Four Bears's upper arm tightly. "Coyote said that a man in one of the cities stood beside him and took his image off of him and put it on a flatness, and that when he looked at it, it was exactly like him! I have been thinking, that is perhaps when they took his spirit from him!"

That was a frightening thought, and Four Bears said, "That would be a bad kind of magic! One would not want to let a man do that. I ask you something I have been thinking about all these stories. Jussaume was with Coyote. Has anyone asked him if any of these awful happenings occur?"

"They asked him," Young Wolf said. "And he said they all happened. But of course Jussaume is a white man, and as long as he has been among our People he has always lied and acted crazy. He, too, is a bag of lies!"

Four Bears did not like to look at the unhappiness in the face of Young Wolf, so he gazed off over the top of the fur traders' boat at the sparkling waves on the blue-gray river, and remembered the first day he had seen Red Hair, and had gone into the cold water to get his headdress for him. "I wish Red Hair had come back here with Coyote," he said quietly. "We could ask him how much of that was true. He was not a man who lies. I am sure of that!" He remembered Red Hair waving to him across the water and blowing the eagle-wing whistle.

Young Wolf scowled at Four Bears. "You should not like a man so much who took our *okimeh* away from us and sent us back a bag of lies!" He snorted. "A man who said he saw fish so big that a man could dwell in its stomach? Ah! And this: "That man who used to be my grandfather, that magpie, he said he saw visions every day he was gone."

"*Keks-cusha!*" exclaimed Four Bears. "Very bad, that lie! A vision is a rare thing! Not every day!"

"They gave him a drink, very strong, and there would come the vision!"

Four Bears suddenly grasped Young Wolf's shoulder. "Ah, now! Then he is not crazy, nor does the East of the white-faces have fire boats and flame in the sky and dead returning to life at the end. You see? He drank their spirit water too much, and only *thinks* he saw such things! Your grandfather is not a bag of lies, then, is he? And did he say he met Maho Okimeh Jefferson?"

Young Wolf pushed Four Bears's hand down. "He said he did. But if he had the spirit water, maybe he only thought so."

CHAPTER 22

MIH-TUTTA-HANG-KUSCH
AUTUMN 1822

BEFORE DAYBREAK THERE WERE A FEW SHOUTS AND A RUMBLE OF hoofbeats out on the slopes beyond the Town of the Dead, and they were heard by no one but a girl who had gone out early to pray for the spirit of a deceased grandparent. She did not come back to say anything about the noises until after sunrise, when she looked up from her prayers and saw that the *ka vah yoh* herd was gone. Two of the boys who guarded the horses were found gagged and tied in a gully, with lumps on their heads, but alive. The third boy had been stabbed and his scalp taken. The two could remember only that the herd had become restless; they had not even seen the people who knocked them out of their senses.

Four Bears, now war chief of the Mandan nation, would have liked to believe the horse thieves had been the Arikara, old enemies nearby who had killed his brother a few years ago, but the Arikara had not done this. A saddled pony that wandered back in with strays was decorated with Shienne markings. The herd's tracks led southwestward.

Because hunters were out far and so many of the tribe's horses had been stolen, Four Bears and Young Wolf could gather only enough men and mounts for a party of fifty to go in pursuit of the Shienne, and because many of them had to come from other Mandan towns down the river, much of the first day was gone before the Mandans could set out on the chase. They rode hard, following the well-trampled trail.

In the middle of the second day the trail grew very fresh; the horse droppings were not even dry. The warriors adjusted their weapons. About half now had French *tvu-zee*s or American and British flintlock muskets.

Four Bears and Young Wolf always rode out in front, and

would cautiously scout over the top of every hill before summoning the rest forward. Early in the afternoon they rode over a rise and there, at last, saw their enemy below.

Four Bears, face to the wind, halted and raised his hand. The fifty warriors, eyes blazing with vengeance, looked down on the drifting dust and the sun-drenched multitude of Shienne and hundreds of horses on the open prairie below, and their ferocity dissolved. Young Wolf exclaimed:

"So many of them! They are three or four times our number!" Horse-stealing parties usually were small. Young Wolf, small-eyed, square-jawed, and fierce, with many coup feathers testifying to his bravery, now had caution, if not fear, written on his face, and so did most of the others.

"They see us," Four Bears said. "We must attack them or turn and run back. My blood is hot. The Shienne have murdered our hunters since the time of our Grandfathers. To catch up with them like this and then turn back would shame us. What will it be, brothers?"

Young Wolf was sweating as he watched the Shienne racing about the horse herd far below and beginning to form up a battle party. "We should avenge them another day," he said. "We would all die here."

Four Bears could see that the others agreed. Four Bears was the war chief of this party, and the lives of fifty warriors rested upon him.

But so did the honor of his People. He said:

"There is no time to run home and get more warriors. It is too far. Look, they are coming out for us." Then he shouted, "All stay here. There is a way with honor."

Then, to everyone's astonishment, Four Bears kicked his horse into motion and rode howling down the slope directly toward the Shienne. Halfway to their lines, he halted his mount and cast his lance straight down to stick in the ground. Then he made his horse rear and prance, rode in a tight circle and back to the lance. He slipped off the red sash he wore across his chest and tied it to the shaft of the lance, where it fluttered like a war banner, the bloodred challenge. Then, with this musket in his hand, controlling his horse by his knees, Four Bears rode back and forth before the oncoming line of Shienne warriors, his bison-hide shield always presented toward them.

Soon a bold and much-decorated Shienne came out and approached at a full gallop. He wore a splendid headdress of eagle feathers and carried a lance festooned with feathers and ermine furs. He was on a tall gray horse with black legs. He rode within shouting distance, reined in, and cried in his own language:

"Who is this? Who makes this challenge alone before all my warriors?"

Four Bears knew enough Shienne from his grandfather Man on a Horse to shout back: "Mah-to-toh-pah, Four Bears, war chief of the nation whose horses you stole, he stands before you! Four Bears, alone, will fight your war chief to win back our horses, and our warriors may all look on and not be hurt! Only one man need die today!"

The Shienne sat silent on his horse for a moment, pondering this extraordinary challenge. Then he shouted, "See here, hanging on my horse, the scalps I have taken as our war chief. Yes! I am the man you will fight!" He caused his horse to bolt forward, rode around Four Bears's lance, and thrust his own into the ground near it. His feathered headdress and scalp locks blowing in the wind, glittering eyes appraising Four Bears's broad chest and sinewy arms, the Shienne cried, "Here we fight, then! Who wins, the horses are his, and our brothers go home safe. I like this!"

"Your life for our boy you killed! This is good!" Four Bears replied. They signaled their warriors to make ranks facing each other.

The two war chiefs rode to opposite ends of the field thus laid out, and turned their horses toward each other. Four Bears powdered the priming pan of his flintlock, snapped the frizzen shut, and cocked the hammer. Squeezing his eyes shut tight, he pressed toward heaven a prayer of such intensity that he felt all the faintness and power and pain of the Okeepah shake him through, and when he opened his eyes, he could see like an eagle, and his flesh felt ready to laugh off pain. Vigor seemed to be coming up from the prairie ground to tingle in him and his horse. He felt a sudden surge of love and sadness about the horse, and knew that the great animal was going to die.

The sun was hot, the wind cool. Four Bears uttered his shrillest war cry. The Shienne chief's cry came back like an echo to his own. Then both drove their horses forward and came thundering toward each other, their muskets leveled at each other. When they approached the standing lances, both pulled triggers. A howl had gone up all along the lines of warriors; it was blanked out by the crash of the guns. Four Bears felt hot stings on his face and his left thigh, like bee stings, and felt a jarring tug as the Shienne sped by his left in the powder smoke.

But he did not feel that he had been hurt. He rode on a few more moments, looking back, and saw that the Shienne, too, was still mounted, and looking back at him. Four Bears wheeled his horse around and halted, and reached for his powder horn to reload his musket. The Shienne, in the distance, was doing the same, and all the warriors were yipping and shouting brave words. Even from this distance Four Bears could see the white teeth of the enemy chief bared in a joyous grin.

But the powder horn in Four Bears's hand was smashed and empty. The Shienne's ball had hit it. Four Bears had no powder for his musket.

Jerking the powder-horn sling off over his head, Four Bears held it up and cast it aside to show the Shienne that his gun was useless, and then threw his musket off into the grass, too, and reached for the bow and quiver that hung by his knee.

When the Shienne saw this, he threw his own musket into the air and drew his own bow and quiver. "Hah!" Four Bears exclaimed in admiration. This enemy was a man of honor as well as courage.

Down the line of whooping warriors they charged each other again, shields presented, arrows nocked. As they passed they let the arrows fly. The Shienne's first arrow glanced off Four Bears's shield with a splintered shaft, and instantly both riders wheeled, each with another arrow set, and rode at each other again, releasing them. An arrow pierced the top of Four Bears's thigh muscle. They swooped at each other again, and as they shot and passed by, Four Bears saw his arrow tear the Shienne's warbonnet off his head. On the next pass, the Shienne's arrow cracked off the rim of Four Bears's shield and slashed his cheekbone.

The two horsemen were soaring around and past each other like eagles spiraling in the sky. Their horses were strong and responsive. The Shienne was the finest kind of a rider and a man who seemed to exult in fighting; he looked as intent and happy as a man playing a dice game. At times the two passed so close that Four Bears could see the puckered scars on the skin of the Shienne's chest, and knew that he had proven himself in his own People's piercing ceremony, the Sundance. Another time when they thundered past, Four Bears saw that one of his arrows was in the muscle of the other man's calf, but his face was still fierce and happy; here, too, was a man above pain.

Four Bears had only three arrows left in his quiver. As he let one fly at the Shienne, he felt his horse stagger under him. The animal made a whistling noise and crumpled. Four Bears sprang from the saddle. A Shienne arrow shaft, only the feathers and the nock, protruded from the animal's left side just behind the shoulder—a perfect heart shot. The animal raised its head feebly, then let it fall; its sides stopped heaving, and the life passed from it.

Four Bears stood above the animal, gave a howl of grief and anger, and nocked his next-to-last arrow. Standing here firmly on the ground, he knew his aim would be good. He waited for the mounted Shienne to charge.

Instead, the grinning war chief once again gave away his advantage. He leaped from his horse, smacked it on the rump with his bow to run it away, and took his stance opposite Four Bears with his shield forward and bow at ready. He began walking toward Four Bears, and even the arrow in his calf did not hinder the stealthy grace of his stride. Drawing his bowstring as far back as his ear, he sent an arrow with such force that it punctured the fire-hardened bison hide, and its iron point gouged Four Bears's shoulder, biting an inch into the muscle. Four Bears then stepped toward the Shienne, the arrow through his thigh muscle making him limp slightly, and let fly his arrow with equal force. The Shienne slanted his shield and Four Bears's arrow whanged off of it and fell sideways among the Shienne warriors. Four Bears nocked his last arrow and walked closer to the enemy chief, who was doing the same.

Now they were close enough to shoot each other in the face. The trilling voices of the warriors on both sides were like a song from heaven.

The two chiefs released their last arrows at the same time. Each having his bow arm extended with its shield strapped on it, their bodies were both unprotected at that moment. Four Bears's arrow caught his enemy on his left eyebrow, but it was a glancing hit and just tore the skin of his temple open and passed through, carrying away the tip of his ear. In that same instant the other man's stone-tipped arrow passed through Four Bears's right hand entirely, jerking it back and numbing it.

All his arrows gone, the Shienne chief, his face bathed in blood from his forehead, cast down his bow and quiver and shield at his feet, drew from its fringed sheath a broad-bladed, double-edged steel dagger, with a claw protruding from the butt of its haft, and sprang at Four Bears.

With his left hand Four Bears struck a mighty backhanded blow that turned the thrust of the dagger and knocked the

Shienne off his feet. The warriors on both sides were yodeling with excitement and admiration for their own chiefs, and each others', but staying back out of the contest as they understood they must. As the Shienne scrambled to his feet, Four Bears threw away his shield and bow, determined to be as honorable as his opponent had been and keep the contest equal. But his right hand, still oozing and numb from its piercing by the last arrow, could not find his own knife sheath.

The Shienne flung himself at Four Bears again, knife raised high. Their blood-smeared bodies slammed together and they teetered, writhing, with Four Bears's unhurt hand desperately gripping the wrist of the Shienne, trying frantically to control the knife hand while, with his benumbed right hand, he groped in vain for his own sheath.

The Shienne's right arm was stronger than Four Bears's left, and little by little he pressed the huge blade down toward Four Bears's neck, all the while yanking his head back by pulling his long hair with his other hand. In this deadly embrace they struggled and sweated and bled for a long and timeless time, each looking into the other's maddened eyes, as intimate as lovers in their sharing of the center of life which was the edge of death.

When the knife was down almost to his throat, Four Bears knew he would need both hands to arrest the strength of the Shienne's one. He forced his right arm between himself and the enemy, his forearm across his throat, and grabbed for the Shienne's knife hand with his bloody right. Instead of the hand, he got the blade. Though both edges of its blade were cutting his hand, he twisted and pushed it, while straining at the wrist with his other hand. The Shienne yanked upward, pulling the blade out of Four Bears's fist, cutting his hand and fingers deeply. For that moment the knife was farther back from Four Bears's throat, but the Shienne pressed it down again with remarkable strength. Again Four Bears grabbed for the hand and got the blade. And as he twisted it, he pressed his sinewy forearm harder and harder against the other man's neck, shutting off his breath. As they struggled in this terrible embrace, each was trying to hook the other's leg with his own, to throw him off balance. But each was too nimble to let himself be thrown, and this apparent dance did not succeed in giving either one the advantage. Each had an arrow in one leg, and the ground under their skipping, stamping feet was specked and spattered with blood. The warriors on both sides had stopped whooping and now were watching the tight struggle with squinting, grimacing attention, some of them moaning as if in pain.

Then something happened that made them gasp.

Four Bears kicked the wounded leg of his enemy, breaking the shaft of the arrow that stuck through it and causing the Shienne to recoil in pain. Having him momentarily off balance, Four Bears wrenched his wrist and pulled on the knife blade, and in an instant the knife was his. He grasped its haft with his left hand, shoved his enemy back with his right arm, and said, "Great enemy. Go in happiness."

He stabbed up under the breastbone.

The Shienne's grip on Four Bears's hair loosened. His body, hard and tense as a drawn bow, loosened and grew limp. And as he began to slump, he looked up into Four Bears's face with the blaze gone out of his eyes. His face was as soft and serene as a woman's. He nodded, shut his eyes, and was dead before his body was on the ground.

Everything was silent as Four Bears grasped his fallen foe's hair and made two swift, curving cuts on the scalp. He yanked off the scalp and stood up, holding it overhead.

He swayed a little, and a blizzard of sparks rushed through his vision for a moment, then cleared. He turned toward his warriors.

"We have won our horses back!" he shouted. "Now let us all go home in peace!"

His warriors sat on their horses stunned, looking over the field. On the short grass lay a dead horse and a dead man, bows, arrows, guns, shields, a broken powder horn, a Shienne warbonnet. Two decorated lances stuck up in the middle of the space, and between them stood their sharp-faced war chief, Mah-to-toh-pah, Four Bears, who had won a war by himself. They, who had feared to fight, could not exult, not for themselves. Even the reckless Young Wolf had sat and watched.

But they could gaze with love and admiration upon Mah-to-toh-pah, their war chief, and each one was inspired. They would tell of his deed throughout their nation, and their sons and grandsons would know what Four Bears had done this day.

CHAPTER 23

Mih-Tutta-Hang-Kusch
Summer 1832

Four Bears, Mah-to-toh-pah, war chief of all the Mandans, and Old Bear, Mah-to-he-ha, the shaman, smoked together in the Medicine Lodge and prayed for rain to come. The cornfields were yellow and withering, dry to the roots, the women were despairing for their whole crop, and Rain Makers, one after another, had scolded and beseeched the bright blue sky in vain, day after day, from the roof of the Medicine Lodge. All had failed.

Now came Waka-da-ha-hee, White Bison Hair, carrying the old painted shield with which his father, White Bison, had brought rain long ago, when Four Bears was only a youth. White Bison Hair was one of Four Bears's favorite warriors, a fine archer, courageous, kindly, and honest. He had spoken for the hand of Antelope, a beautiful daughter of Mah-sish, old War Eagle, and Mah-sish had approved. A good life seemed to be ahead of these esteemed people. White Bison Hair sat down now with Four Bears and Old Bear, and, after smoking with them, he said:

"I have prayed, and at last the Thunder Beings came to my dreams last night. Their eyes flashed white light, and they told me they would bring rain tomorrow if I would call them." He touched the shield, upon which was painted a lightning bolt in red. "This will draw the flash down to our town, and show the black clouds how our women need rain. I shall shoot a hole in those clouds with my strong bow and from it the rain will pour. I ask, Fathers, that you let me go onto the roof of this lodge tomorrow, for I have been promised that I can bring rain for the corn and for the green grass the bison need."

Old Bear fanned a wad of smoldering sage on the altar with an eagle's wing feather. The men swept the purifying fragrance over themselves and breathed it, and Four Bears remembered that particular eagle feather; it was from an eagle he had caught nearly thirty years before, on the same eagle-hunting trip as when he had first seen the wing-boat of the great Chief Red Hair and Chief Long Knife. A bone of that same eagle he had made into the whistle he had given to Red Hair.

Four Bears still remembered Red Hair fondly. Red Hair for more than twenty summers had been living in the city called St. Louis, where the Muddy River ran into the Mother of Rivers, and was the protector and counselor for all the tribes. Whenever a boat came up from that city, Four Bears would try to talk to anyone who had seen Red Hair Clark, and he had never yet heard anything to disappoint him. Red Hair seemed to be the only honest white man. The Mandan People had remained friendly to the white people because they had promised Red Hair and Long Knife they would. But it was hard to do because few of the white men were honest or honorable. They had built a fur traders' fort within sight of Mih-Tutta-Hang-Kusch. It was called Fort Clark, but Four Bears sometimes said that was not a good name for it. He would tell Mr. Kipp, the trader in the village, "They should not name a dishonest place after an honest man. They price things too high and try to have their way with our young women."

Four Bears sighed, coming back from the musings where that eagle feather had taken him, and said to White Bison Hair:

"So, you climb above here tomorrow, and use your power to bring rain, and we will sit here beneath you and add the power of our prayers."

"I, Waka-da-ha-hee, shall do it, though others failed," the young man said, "for I believe the dream I have seen!"

At that moment Four Bears saw in his memory's pictures the fire-driven boat old Okimeh Coyote had insisted until his death that he had seen in the East. He remembered other unbelievable things the poor old man had said, and sighed again.

If the white-faces can do all the magic Coyote said they can do, he thought, like making thunder and lightning for their people to watch in their big towns, it would seem that those in the trading fort over there could make thunder and lightning and rain for our women's cornfields here.

WHITE BISON HAIR, DRESSED BEAUTIFULLY IN TUNIC AND LEGGINGS of soft, pale, mountain sheepskins trimmed with dyed quills and scalp locks, arrived at midmorning, and Old Bear purified him with sage smoke. Then Four Bears climbed with him to the roof of the Medicine Lodge, and for a while they stood together, gazing over the parched plains and the faraway hills that faded to blue in the shimmering air of the distance, over the great, gray, curving river, the dome roofs of the other lodges all around him, the palisades, the scaffolds of the dead beyond them. Downstream a little way and on the same riverbank was the squarish trading fort of the white-faces, with its banner flying above. At the hazy distance upstream at the mouth of the Knife River lay the smoke and huts of the People of the Willows, three villages of them, the Hidatsa band of the Crow who had come to trade with and live under the protection of the Mandans. Four Bears turned around and looked downstream again, farther down, toward the distant domes of Young Wolf Chief's town, under its sun-shimmering haze of cooking smoke.

Everywhere along the great, life-giving river, people moved: fishing, swimming, gathering deadwood and driftwood, launching their little round skin boats, which, it was said, had been invented long, long ago by First Man. On the plain outside the palisade a large group of warriors practiced the Ta tuck a mahha, the Eight Arrows game, betting on who could load and shoot fastest to keep the most arrows in the air at once. White Bison Hair was a champion at that; almost every time he could launch his eighth arrow before the first hit the ground. Four Bears himself in younger days had been able to do Ta tuck a mahha, and he might have stood here all morning watching the game, but he remembered that the arrow to watch today would be the one White Bison Hair would shoot into the clouds.

But first he would have to bring the clouds. The plain was so dry that only a dust cloud showed where the town's warriors were racing their best horses. All the Children of First Man were reveling in the sunshine, wearing little or no clothing in order to enjoy the blessing of the sun's rays. They loved the sun, their winters being so long and hard. But the sun was parching all life in the valley; even the Muddy River was a bit low, which seldom happened, and White Bison Hair the Rain Maker was right now the most important person in Mih-Tutta-Hang-Kusch. Many of the people within the town had gathered in the plaza and on their roofs to look at him and pray for his success. "See their faces turned to you," Four Bears told him. "They are as earnest as the thirsting plants for you to bring rain. Do well." Four Bears climbed down from the roof and stood watching him.

In his left hand White Bison Hair held his short, stout, sinew-backed bow, one arrow with an obsidian head and a tuft of white bison hair fixed behind the point, and a raven's feather. Taking the raven feather in his right hand, he flicked it into the air. Then he turned his back on the tumbling feather and cried out in his strong, clear voice:

"Children of Nu-mohk-muck-a-nah, the First Man! You see me! I am ready to ease your thirst and distress! Maize plants in the field and grass on the hills, you see me! Prepare to drink water from the sky!

"You saw which way the raven feather fell. All this day I shall hold this lightning shield in the direction from which the breeze comes! The great birds of thunder will come to it, wrapped in the darkness of their wings! Then this arrow I shall shoot into the clouds to make a hole.

"At my feet, too, is a hole! Up through it comes the sage smoke carrying our great men's prayers toward the Maho Peneta, the Great Spirit! That smoke will rise through the hole my arrow makes in the clouds, and Maho Peneta will heed our prayers and the rain will fall upon our crops and the grass of the plains!"

"Ho! Shu-su," murmured Four Bears, looking up at the young man, liking the pictures White Bison Hair was making with his words. The more clearly Maho Peneta saw such images, the more likely they were to come true.

But above the smoke hole, the sky was still all blue and clear, and White Bison Hair might be hoarse before he made any change in that sky.

The Rain Maker was standing wide-legged with his shield presented toward the breeze. "Spirit of the West Wind! My People are in distress! They want rain! Nothing has come down for too long!" He stamped his foot on the roof. "See my shield! It was made by my father, and he once brought rain with it! See the chains of red lightning on it! That lightning was taken from the black cloud my father summoned on that day, in his time! I am White Bison Hair, his son, and this is my time! I need rain for my People. . . ."

Thunder reverberated in the valley: a distinct *boom*, then rolling echoes. The murmuring and jabbering of the crowd dwindled to silence as they looked with amazement at White Bison Hair and listened, not sure they had heard what they thought they had heard.

Again the thunder rolled; White Bison Hair had stopped shouting and his mouth hung open. He took his decorated arrow in his right hand, ready to shoot it toward the clouds, but there were as yet no clouds; the sun still blazed almost overhead in the clear blue that stretched to the horizons. When the thunder boomed and echoed a third time, the crowd began to cheer and howl in praise of the Rain Maker, and out from the door of the Medicine Lodge came Old Bear, to join Four Bears in watching White Bison Hair.

It was on the next thunderclap that Four Bears realized that the peals were not coming from the west, but from downriver, and he could hear faint voices crying out in the distance far down the shore. Leaping onto the roof and looking that way, he saw a sight that seemed to have come out of dream memories:

It was like a fort or a white men's building, long and rectangular instead of rounded like a real lodge, but it was moving on the surface of the water, like a boat, and smoke, both dark and white, billowed from its roof. At the moment that Four Bears decided that it was indeed real, not a dream-vision, a cloud of smoke and a flash of fire burst from its side, and in the space of two heartbeats another thunderclap rolled up the valley.

Clearly, the great thing approaching, although it was not being rowed, or using the white wings called sails, was a boat! It was a bigger boat than Red Hair had come in so long ago, a bigger boat even than the ones the traders came in, but Four Bears could see it was a boat, not a fort. How it could be moving upstream without oars or sail-wings, he was too amazed to figure on, and at that moment more fire and smoke erupted from its side, followed by another rolling thunderclap. The Eight Arrow shooters and the horse racers on the far meadows had stopped their contests and were coming at full haste toward the town.

At last White Bison Hair, seeing Four Bears staring downriver, turned and saw the great smoky thing coming. His eyes bugged, but he quickly found words and cried:

"My People! Hear me! My power is great! I have not yet brought you rain from the sky, but I have brought a Thunder Maker boat! Look and see it on the river! The thunder you hear"—even as he said this, another peal rolled forth, even louder—"the thunder you hear is from its mouth! I have brought you a thunder boat, a thing such as no one has ever seen!"

Now the people were swarming onto their roofs, and they saw the huge thing coming up with its clouds of smoke and steam, and its rumbling, huffing sounds, like the noise of a bison herd in flight, could now be heard over the wind.

Four Bears saw and heard still another flash and thunderclap out of its side. He gaped at the apparition, and he exclaimed:

"I know that thing! It is what the old *okimeh* said he saw in the East—the boat driven by fire! And we called him a bag of lies!"

WHEN THE GREAT THUNDER BOAT HAD MADE TWENTY THUNDER-claps, it quit, and then, grumbling and hissing, turned shoreward and came to rest at the landing shared by the trading fort and the Mandan town. Some white men went out on the front and threw ropes over the pilings. Usually when a big boat came in, someone from the village would be on the riverbank to take the ropes, but because of the monstrous size and the seething clouds and the noises of this boat, Four Bears called everybody into the village and had the warriors arm themselves for defense on the palisades and around the brow of the bluff. Everyone, warriors, chieftains, medicine men, women, children, and elders, peered down from the bluff or the rooftops at the great, smoking thing. After a while it gave a great sigh with white clouds, then fell still. A few men moved around on it and laid a gangplank across to the bank. This, the People knew, was to permit walking between the boat and the land, and was a friendly sign, but Four Bears was not yet ready to let his People be in danger, and told them all to stay inside the town. Soon somebody on the palisade wall shouted that Young Wolf Chief was coming across the prairie, and in a few minutes the pickets at the gate were opened to let him gallop in, at the head of fifty of his own horsemen. Young Wolf Chief wore a bonnet of black feathers trimmed with red. His square jaw set and small eyes intense, he leaped off his horse and said in a quick, low voice to Four Bears:

"Is it not the thing my grandfather spoke of so long ago, the boat driven by fire?"

"I believe it to be that. We should not have laughed at him."

Young Wolf Chief switched his quirt against his legging. "This thing passed my town, then it began to make thunder. I saw it was coming to your town and rode up to help protect your people."

"Thank you. As you see, it is lying still. . . . Ah! *Etta hant tah!* Look there! At that door. Is that not Sanford, the Red Hair's agent to our People? It is. They are friends, then. We must go down and welcome them."

Young Wolf Chief licked the corner of his narrow mouth. "Yes." It was plain he did not want to go near the thing, but it was proper for him as principal *okimeh* to welcome anyone who came to his nation, particularly on such an important occasion as this seemed to be.

And so, soon, Wolf Chief and Four Bears, in their feathered bonnets and carrying lances and pipes, walked down the steep path from the village, followed by the shaman, Old Bear, and almost everybody else, except White Bison Hair, who had been the center of attention but was now all but forgotten. What was to have been his day of thunder had been stolen by a boat of thunder. The People did not seem to credit him for bringing it. Their voices droned as they went down, encouraging each other to be careful and speculating whether it would boom again when they were close to it. Gray smoke still rose from what appeared to be tree trunks on top, and Four Bears deduced that the great wheel of slats on the side, which had stopped turning, must be the paddle that moved the boat. How the fire inside drove the paddles, though, he could not imagine.

With Sanford the agent stood Kipp, the fur buyer who lived in Four Bears's town. He had been gone downriver. Now there he stood. Kipp was a fairly good man, not too dishonest for a white-face, was married to a Mandan woman, and could speak the Mandan tongue, and Four Bears was glad to see him back. Surely he could explain some of these marvels. Standing with Kipp and Sanford were other white-face men in their odd-looking garments and huge, black hats; most of these men were fat and short and soft-looking. They looked so small. The thunder boat looked so big, it seemed as if it could be a town, a town built on the edge of the water where before there had never been anything but people fishing or swimming. Four Bears looked down at the river water running around the boat, which reminded him that it was indeed just a boat, not a town, and that like all other boats the white men had ever brought here, it would float away sometime, probably on up to the white men's next fur-trading fort upstream, the one at the mouth of the Yellow Stone River. The thunder boat was piled with the things the white-faces called "barrels," which Four Bears feared would be full of spirit water. Four Bears knew that Red Hair tried to keep the trader boats from carrying spirit water into the tribal lands, but the traders always brought it. Four Bears would not let it be drunk in his town, and Young Wolf Chief had forbidden it anywhere in the Mandan nation. But at the trader fort up the river at the mouth of the Yellow Stone River, where many tribes of the Plains gathered to trade, it was used by the tribes whenever a boat came up. Four Bears did not like to see these barrels. Only days ago, he had heard by a messenger, Dah-koh-tah at the mouth of the Teton had slaughtered fourteen hundred buffalo and brought their tongues in to trade at the fort for spirit water, leaving the carcasses to rot. That story had hardened his anger at his old enemies the Dah-koh-tah, who had let the white men's spirit water corrupt them into a sacrilegious act. He thought their chiefs who had let them do that should be killed for it. He also thought that the sellers of spirit water should be killed, but the old *okimeh* Coyote had long ago promised Red Hair and Long Knife that Mandans would never kill any white-faces. And they never had, even when the white men cheated them.

Now, just as Four Bears prepared to step on the gangplank and go up on the thunder boat, he saw another face that struck his heart just as that of Red Hair had done so long ago. Four Bears stopped where he stood and looked at the man, who was staring at him, looking at him with the same cheerful, open, and kindly expression that Four Bears had seen in the face of Red Hair. It was as if he were seeing Red Hair himself after so many years—but only because of the expression.

This was not a great tall man, or big in the shoulders, nor did he have the warrior look that Red Hair had had. This was a smaller and more finely made man, without Red Hair's large features.

But in his lean physique and direct, blue eyes, Four Bears saw some uncommon power and goodness; he felt drawn to it. It was the calm glow that Four Bears had seen in rare men who were true to their own hearts. This plainly was not one of the chiefs or the wealthy white men, not one of those self-important ones, as he seemed to linger at their edge; none of them were talking to him except Kipp, the trader. It seemed to Four Bears that the other white men might not know how important he was. Since so few of the white men had that glow on them, they probably could not see it on others. But Four Bears had been as moved by the glow on this man as he had been by the thunder and smoke of this thunder boat, and only now, as he felt Young Wolf Chief pressing him from behind to move on up the gangplank, did Four Bears remember where he was. He smiled momentarily at the blue-eyed man, and then, steadying himself on the narrow gangplank, he started up.

Kipp took a long time introducing Four Bears, Young Wolf Chief, and Old Bear to the white-faces, talking in both languages to translate their politenesses and waiting for everybody to shake hands. The trader had to explain to the white men that Young Wolf Chief, rather than Four Bears, was the head chief of the Mandan nation, and Young Wolf Chief now and then looked sullen, his tiny eyes hard. Therefore Four Bears took it upon himself to give a long speech, which Kipp translated, telling them of the great bravery and the many exploits of Wolf Chief, until they were duly convinced of Wolf Chief's stature as a leader. Then Wolf Chief himself made a short and simple speech:

"That was long in telling. If I were to speak of all the brave deeds of Mah-to-toh-pah, Four Bears, the war chief of my People, who stands here beside me, it would take twice as long. His history is painted on a bison hide, and fills every corner of it even though it is painted in very small figures. Perhaps he will let you see the robe and hear the stories, if you stay awhile. He painted the pictures himself, and I know they are all true, for I was with him many of those times, and my warriors who were with him the rest of them agree they are true also."

Most of the white faces seemed to be only half listening to this, but the man with blue eyes was intent. When Kipp directed Four Bears to this man, Four Bears took the man's hand, which was strong and hard and warm, and the two looked very deep into each other's eyes. Kipp said, "This man is called Catlin."

"Cat-lin," said Four Bears. "Is Cat-lin a chief?"

"Not a chief," said Kipp in Mandan. "But he is a good friend of Red Hair, and he is a maker of pictures. He is a Shadow Catcher, who can put a man's true face on a piece of cloth."

Something stirred in the memory of Four Bears. He remembered another of the unbelievable tales of Coyote's long ago journey. First a thunder boat, and now a Shadow Catcher! Were all of Coyote's tales to be proved on this one remarkable day? Four Bears said to Kipp:

"Tell Cat-lin that Four Bears likes him, and would like to show him the painted robe upon which Four Bears has caught the shadows of his deeds."

But Old Bear spoke up now, with urgency, to Four Bears: "*Naga! Naga, Maho Okimeh!* No, great chief! You do not want a Shadow Catcher to come in our town! It was one of those, a Shadow Catcher, who stole the *peneta* of the old *okimeh*, making him *megash*!"

"Did ye hear that," one white man exclaimed to another. "If that old bogey didn't speak Welsh, sir, I don't know my own father's tongue!"

The man called Catlin heard that remark, and looked momentarily surprised, but Four Bears did not understand it, nor did Wolf Chief or Old Bear. Four Bears had paused in his greeting, still grasping Catlin's hand, and quickly told the shaman: "Be still, old one! This is a man of good power and I want to make him welcome."

Kipp now translated Four Bears's invitation, then Catlin's reply. "The boat is going on up the river to the fort at Yellow Stone River, but this man Catlin will come back down in one or two moons and then would like to stay awhile with Four Bears and his people." Then Kipp explained: "The boat stopped here to buy some wood to burn, for it runs on fire. It will proceed up the river at once. This man Catlin has come up this river to make pictures of all the peoples, of their chiefs, and of how they dress and how they live. At the Yellow Stone he hopes to make paint pictures of the Crow and Blackfeet who trade there. But he will come back soon. That is his promise."

Four Bears nodded, understanding that much, but his mind was racing with questions as to why this man would want to make so many pictures. The pictures on his robe would show him how battles were fought, but why would anyone want pictures of ordinary living? He would have to ask him those questions when he came back to stay, though, because a great deal of confusion was beginning to build on and around the boat.

Now that their chiefs were on the boat, all the people seemed to have become unafraid and were crowding the shore. Boys were already in the water, swimming around the huge vessel as if they had never been afraid of anything, although they had been in sheer terror so short a time before. Some adventurous ones had already found the huge paddlewheels on the sides wonderful devices to climb on, and were swarming on them, climbing, laughing, falling or jumping back into the water. Some young women had slipped discreetly through the willow thickets to the river's edge downstream, left their clothing onshore and, using immersion for their modesty, were surrounding the thunder boat like playful fish, to the delight and amazement of crewmen and traders, who were nearly falling over the rails to gawk at them. Up in town, meanwhile, White Bison Hair had resumed his rain-calling.

The traders on the boat offered spirit water to Four Bears, Wolf Chief, and Old Bear. Four Bears's eyes flashed with anger, but he kept his refusal polite. "It is our way not to decline, or to refuse, any hospitality. But Kipp should have told you that we will not drink that, because we know it is not good to do. Share a pipe with us while wood is put on, and then you may go on up."

When that was translated, the man called Catlin cried, "Bravo!" Four Bears did not know the meaning of the word, but the approval in the man's face was unmistakable, and Four Bears's heart was glad.

Looking past Catlin, Four Bears noticed that a dense, dark pile of thunderclouds had risen and was coming rapidly eastward, flickering with lightning. Nobody around the boat seemed to have noticed it, but suddenly Four Bears heard the distant cries of White Bison Hair grow more shrill and loud:

"Now it comes! See me draw the great cloud toward me by my father's shield! Soon I will pierce it with this arrow, and our corn will be wet with the rain from the sky!" People began turning to look. They saw the cloud looming over the town, and joy shone in their faces. Their attention strayed from the great novelty of the thunder boat to the rumbling of real thunder, and they were exclaiming about it, adding their many voices to that of the Rain Maker, who was screaming:

"Come, Tche-bi, Spirits that ride the Wind! Come closer over me and I will give you this arrow, fringed with the white bison hair that tells you it is mine!"

At that moment the leading edge of the storm cloud passed under the afternoon sun, throwing the whole town under its shadow. A gust of cold, damp wind swept over, lightning flashed, and a peal of real sky-thunder shook the boat and rumbled down the valley.

"Now!" White Bison Hair's voice sang out, "I shoot a hole in the cloud!" At once there flashed a white blaze of lightning and the sky cracked so loudly that the smokestacks of the thunder boat reverberated. The dark surface of the river was suddenly churned white by a sheet of cold, hissing, wind-driven rain. The afternoon had grown almost as dark as night, relieved every moment by sizzling, blinding lightning, which seemed to be striking everywhere but upon the thunder boat itself, and everyone on the boat crowded through doors to get out of the slashing downpour. The people on the riverbank began swarming up the slope toward the town, slipping on the suddenly muddy path, helping each other up, laughing and squealing with delight.

THE TORRENTS THAT WHITE BISON HAIR HAD BROUGHT FORTH continued without letup into the evening. The skies flickered constantly, and the boat shuddered with the impact of thunderclaps.

Because of the great storm, the boat could not depart to go on up the river.

Four Bears hid his nervousness behind an unwavering smile of politeness, but Old Bear the shaman and Young Wolf Chief were visibly nervous about being in this strange vessel with all its rocking and creaking and the rain drumming on its walls and roof. The boat's big room, in which they were crowded with the white men, was a square room, a room with corners, which seemed unnatural and made them uncomfortable, but most distressing were the openings that Kipp said were called "windows." These were like doorways, through which the chiefs could look at the river or the shore outside and see the flickering lightning; but, through some magic, no air or rain passed through these openings. Kipp tried to explain these, and invited the chiefs to touch the openings. They jerked their hands back when their fingers encountered what seemed to be hard air. He explained *glass*, which they had seen in looking glasses the traders brought, except in *windows* one could see through to the other side. "Ah," exclaimed Four Bears, reaching inside his tunic and pulling out the little looking glass Red Hair had given him almost thirty winters ago, and which he wore hanging next to his skin on a thong passed through a hole in its rim. Old Bear in particular was upset by the *windows*, and kept looking at them, and trying not to look at them, all the time.

The room was dense with tobacco smoke and reeked with the whiskey and body smells of the white men and the oil of lamps that were fixed to the walls. It was not bear oil, and Kipp explained that it was oil from a huge fish called a *whale*, an ocean fish as long as this thunder boat. The two chiefs looked at each other, remembering an old, old doubt, and then Four Bears told Young Wolf Chief, "You see? Red Hair never did lie!"

The white men in their strange clothes talked loudly, ever more so as they drank their whiskey; only the one called Catlin seemed to be respectful enough to listen to what the Mandans had to say. When he was not looking intently into their faces and listening to Kipps' translations, he was making swift markings on what Four Bears knew to be a book of leaves, such as those in which the traders recorded counting. Catlin asked Kipp if the chief would mind showing him the remarkable dagger he wore in a scabbard made of grizzly head fur.

"Ah, that!" Kipp exclaimed. "And let's have him tell about how he obtained it, by winning a battle single-handed! It's another of his astounding deeds I'd started telling you of, and one of the best. . . ."

By nightfall Young Wolf Chief and Old Bear were growing ill from the bad air, the rocking of the boat, and the confusing din of the drunken white men's voices, and insisted on going up to the town, even through the downpour. Four Bears told them to go on; he was going to stay and learn more about this Shadow Catcher. "It is important that he has come," he told them, though he was not yet sure why it was important. Protesting that he should not stay on this bad medicine boat alone with so many white men, but unable to stand it any longer themselves, they finally went out into the black downpour and made their way up the path by the lightning flashes.

Four Bears learned that the Shadow Catcher had been born in a part of the East known as Pennsylvania, the fifth of fourteen children born to his mother. That fact alone made Four Bears's eyes grow wide, for there was hardly ever a woman of any tribe who gave birth as many as four times. "A tribe, from one mother!"

"We were just about a tribe," the man replied with a smile. To help his father feed so many brothers and sisters, Shadow Catcher had planted and harvested crops, and hunted and fished in the woods near his home. As Kipp translated the story, Four Bears tried to envision this man as a boy on a horse, chasing bison, or perhaps even as a Bison Decoy on a *pishkun*. Catlin when grown up had gone to a city to learn a trade called *law*, which, Kipp finally managed with difficulty to explain, was something like doing counsel on the problems of his People.

But Shadow Catcher had found that he liked something much better than law, and he had trained himself to make images and paint faces, and then for several years he had earned a living in that way. But even then, he said, he had known that he was destined to use his abilities for something more important.

Always in his heart, he said, there had been a great love of the red Peoples. A hunter from one of the eastern tribes had been his friend when he was a boy, but that hunter had been murdered by white men who had never been punished for it. In the city called Philadelphia, where he had worked as a painter of faces, Shadow Catcher had seen many of the groups of red men who had been brought to look at the white men's cities, and he admired them so much for their beauty and their dignity that he could not stop thinking about them.

Four Bears nodded, and he wondered whether this Shadow

Catcher might have seen Coyote when he was taken to the East. But the Shadow Catcher kept on with his story:

"I could see that all the tribes in the East had been weakened and scattered and ruined, by whiskey and disease and lost wars. The government of the white men grows ever more ruthless toward the red men, so much that I am ashamed. I am afraid that the coming of my race into the West will ruin all the tribes here, as it has done there already."

His face was so grave and full of anguish as he told this that Four Bears felt sorry for him. He put a hand on Shadow Catcher's arm and said to Kipp:

"Friend, tell this Shadow Catcher that such terrible things will not happen to us in this part of the land; he needs not be sad for us. Long ago, my People made a friendship with the great soldier chief Red Hair, when he was young. That friendship remains strong. Red Hair is now the chief who looks over all the tribes between the Mother of Rivers and the great Sunset Water, as you know. Tell him that friendship will never be broken. Tell him that Red Hair knows our People have never raised a hand against any white man, and never will, and so there is no reason for your country to do us harm."

Catlin listened to this being translated, and nodded sadly. Then he replied, "Tell Four Bears that Red Hair is indeed his friend and protector and that he loves the Mandans and all the peoples. Tell him that I stayed a long time with Red Hair in St. Louis and painted portraits of many chiefs who came to visit him, and that I painted a portrait of Red Hair himself. Tell him that Red Hair is a powerful chief and uses all his power to protect the tribes, and tries to keep the whiskey sellers from coming into the country. Tell him that Red Hair hopes to send doctors who will vaccinate the people, so that the white man's diseases will no longer sweep through their towns and kill everyone as they have done to so many. . . ."

Kipp said, "With all due respect, Mr. Catlin, you're asking a lot, for me to try to explain vaccination to the chief. I'm damned if I half understand it myself."

"Then let's try," Catlin replied. "It could be the most important thing we could ever tell him. Smallpox and the other diseases have already killed ten times as many Indians on this continent as all the wars together have done, and, yes, even more than whiskey and rum, too!"

And so they tried for a long time, through lightning flashes and thunderclaps, and interruptions by the hard-drinking fur merchants, to explain inoculation to Four Bears. At last the handsome chief, with a patient smile, answered that his People already had doctors, like Old Bear, who knew how to cure any sickness or injury, and he said that although Red Hair's kind intentions warmed his heart, it would not be necessary to bring "little death in a bottle" to protect the Mandans from big death.

"I am trying to warn Four Bears," Catlin said, "that even all the strength and kindness of Red Hair cannot stop what is coming. The Red Hair Clark is directed by his government in Washington. That government is not concerned with red men, and Red Hair often has to struggle alone to protect you. Listen: I have seen the People of many tribes, from the eastern sea to this place. Here you are still the way your god made you. You live on the gifts he gave you, and you are healthy and strong and honest. But those other tribes in the East were once like you. They thought they could stay the way their god made them, but if you saw them now, drunk and sick, starving and begging and lying, and all their honor lost, you would know that even Red Hair cannot stop what is coming."

Four Bears thought long and hard after the translation, then said, "Red Hair told us that your Great Father Chief had a good heart toward his red children. Was that not so?"

"The President then was Jefferson," Catlin said. "Explain to him, Mr. Kipp, that the present leader is a different man, and that Mr. Jackson has no concern for the red men but to get them out of the way of the white men."

"If that man is so bad for us," Four Bears inquired then, "why does Cat-lin, a white man, come so far and speak of his People's badness? Is he an enemy of his own People, a cast-out from his own tribe?"

Catlin glanced over his shoulders at the other white men in the salon, then he said to Kipp:

"Try to explain to him that the pictures I paint, and the words I write, are to show the powerful people of my government that they are about to destroy something that is good—that the tribes are good, their people are good, their land is good . . . that they live well, and are free, and should be protected from the sort of things that were done to them in the East. Just tell him what I've been explaining to you all the way along this trip. . . . Tell him—well, just tell him that I am of one heart with Red Hair, and will try to help him with the power of words and pictures."

Kipp talked and signed for a long time to Four Bears, and when he had finished, Four Bears looked at the painter and said:

"Shadow Catcher, I knew you came for something important. When I saw your face, I knew you to be a friend.

"Now I have sat on this seat of sticks too long and my legs feel full of foam. I will have to stand up slowly, or I will fall down and you will think I have drunk spirit water."

Kipp chuckled. "I gather his legs've gone to sleep, Mr. Catlin. They aren't used to chairs."

George Catlin stood with Four Bears, who said, "I must go up to my town now, or Young Wolf will come down with fifty warriors to get me.

"I will think hard upon what you say. I never knew that your country was against me, who have always been a friend to your country. I never want to fight against your country, for we promised peace forever with you. I will pray that you show what should not be done to us, and stop it before it gets here. I always did know that images made with paint could be strong messengers. One of our young men today called this storm to us with a shield painted as lightning. And when I show men my robe upon which I have painted my battles, they see what happened and believe, as you will see when you return to visit with me.

"Thank you for what you try to do, Shadow Catcher. I will look eagerly up the river for you to come back, and I will help you then."

Lightning flashed again as they shook hands, and Four Bears stepped out on deck into the downpour.

FOUR BEARS HAD CLIMBED THE MUD-SLICK PATH IN THE RAIN, SEEING by lightning flashes, and entered the town, soaked clothes hanging heavy upon him, all the while pondering the disturbing words of the Shadow Catcher, when he felt a terrible strange tingling all through him. In an instant a whiteness brighter than the sun burst directly in front of him, and the lodge of old Mah-sish, War Eagle, burst into white sparks and brilliant smoke. Four Bears was knocked breathless by the hardest blow he had ever felt.

Then he was looking down from a high place into his lodge. He smelled the putrefaction of death and heard the deepest silence he had ever known. He was floating toward the smoke hole in the roof of his lodge, feeling pulled up as if by the ropes in the Okeepah rite. Below him was his body, all blackened and spotted and befouled, crawling with flies, a horror of a sight, looking like a corpse already decaying. And with a crushing grief he saw also that his wives were dead and rotting. He passed up like smoke through the roof, and saw that there were bodies everywhere on the ground among the lodges, rotting bodies, many being pecked and shredded by vultures and ravens. The lodges were burning and caving in, and a foul smoke rose with him toward the heavens. As he rose higher, the fires went out, and he saw his town, Mih-Tutta-Hang-Kusch, and Wolf Chief's distant town, as nothing but groups of round pits in the ground beside the curves of the great Muddy River. And in the wisps of smoke now rising all around him were the faces and forms of all his People.

Cold rain and frantic voices woke Four Bears. Some men of his town were lifting him from the mud, their hands under his arms and chest. His body felt full of sparks in every part. But he was alive, and the cold rain was still pelting his skin and soaking his leggings and running into his eyes, and the thunder was still cracking and booming, and the lightning was still flashing. In the wind and rain around him, men and women were yelling and sobbing, most of them gathered around the smashed and smoking lodge.

"Father!" cried one of the young men holding Four Bears's arms. "Okimeh, you live!"

"What has happened?" Four Bears cried in the rush of wind and rain. "Did I see lightning go into the lodge of old War Eagle?"

"It struck there! Yes!" the youth answered in a strained voice.

"Ahhhh!" Four Bears groaned. "Is he hurt?"

"War Eagle was burned and cannot talk sense, Father. But he breathes and is not dead, and his wife is not hurt, though she wails for her daughter. Many are in that lodge over there, weeping for Antelope."

"She was harmed?"

"The girl was struck dead. Her mother said she shone like the sun and then fell to the floor, giving off smoke, and the roof dropped upon her, all afire."

"*Keks cusha!* My heart hurts! And what of White Bison Hair? Does he know it happened?"

"Yes, Okimeh. He cries that the blame is his, for bringing too great a storm."

Four Bears's legs were still full of sparks, but he felt that he could walk now. "I will go in and speak to the wife of War Eagle. Go and tell White Bison Hair that I will talk with him in the Medicine Lodge. Have Old Bear be there, too."

I wonder how long I was dead from the lightning? Four Bears thought as the youth ran off through the rain.

Oh, my heart hurts! I believe I have seen my People die, all the Children of First Man!

In the eye of his mind Four Bears saw the face of the Shadow Catcher.

Yes, he thought. Somehow it is important that he is here!

CHAPTER 24

Mih-Tutta-Hang-Kusch
Summer 1832

There was tension in the Shadow Catcher's lodge. Four Bears could feel it. He could feel Shadow Catcher's intense power of concentration. In Wolf Chief, who was standing erect in the overhead light from the smoke hole, Four Bears could sense resentment, fear and pride, and an intense suspicion. Though Four Bears had explained several times to Wolf Chief why the man named Catlin wanted to catch their shadows, it was plain that Wolf Chief did not fully believe this was a safe or proper thing to do, and his square jaw was set, and his little eyes stared unwavering at the painter. Because he was the nation's *maho okimeh*, or principal chief, Wolf Chief had the honor of being the first to have his shadow caught. Then it would be Four Bears's time to stand and be portrayed.

In the meantime, Four Bears sat beside Kipp the interpreter and smiled and smoked red willow bark in his pipe, trying to ease the tightness in the air. Without wanting to seem impolitely curious, he tried to see everything the painter was doing. He watched him dip a little brush into a tiny pot of brown liquid he had just mixed from a powder. That was perfectly understandable, no mystery, for Four Bears had done that himself sometimes when drawing his war history on the hide of a bison. Then Catlin quickly and surely made little strokes with the brush upon a piece of white cloth stretched tight over a four-cornered wooden frame, similar to those upon which the Mandan women stretched furs to be worked. The frame stood upon three legs of wood and was about as high as the upper half of his body, and it was turned so that only the painter could see the side he was working on. Wolf Chief stood haughty and straight on the other side of it, and Catlin glanced repeatedly at him between strokes of his brush. From where Four Bears sat, he could see only the edge of the frame, and although he was squirming with curiosity, he was too polite to ask if he could move over and look. And for all he knew, if he did look to see the image, it might break the magic and cause something bad. If Catlin had anything to say about the doing of this, Four Bears presumed, he would say it.

Then the artist stopped using the brush. He knelt by a box, took out little things and squeezed them over a paint-smeared thing that looked something like a small shield, and a strange, pungent odor filled the lodge, something musky and unnatural. He worked over it with a little knife, and Four Bears saw colors forming, beautiful colors, shades like dried blood, like vermilion, like night sky, like day sky, like marrow fat, like cloud-gray and cloud-white. It was amazing how quickly and surely he made these little blobs of color with the knife, all the while glancing at Wolf Chief. Then he set the knife down in the box and lifted a bigger brush, dipped it in one of the colors, and began making big, swift strokes. As he worked he began to talk, saying to Kipp, "Tell the Wolf Chief that he has a fine look about him, and it is an honor and a pleasure to do this." The words made no visible impression on Wolf Chief, who might as well have been frozen, but he did yield a small, sighing grunt from his throat.

Four Bears took a long draw on his pipe and let the smoke rise from his lips into his nostrils, and then he asked Wolf Chief, "Do you feel anything?"

"Nagash," Wolf Chief replied.

"And so you see, nothing is being taken from you? Enh?"

Wolf Chief unfroze only enough to shrug, but said nothing.

"Mr. Kipp," the painter said, having paused with brush at rest, "that word the Wolf Chief used—*nagash*—does that mean 'no'?"

"It does, sir."

"It does in Welsh, too, if memory serves me."

"Hm!"

Catlin looked to Four Bears, touched himself on the chest with the handle of his brush, and said, *"Mi."*

Four Bears smiled, touched himself on the chest, nodded, and said, *"Mi."*

"That's Welsh, too, Mr. Kipp."

"Hm. It's also English, too, ain't it?" He touched himself on the chest and said, "Me."

Catlin pointed his brush around to indicate everybody and said, *"Ni."*

Four Bears indicated the full circle with his pipe, nodded and said, *"Niew."*

"That means, 'we,' " Kipp said.

"It does in Welsh, too," Catlin said. Then he pointed his brush at Wolf Chief and said to Kipp, "How do they say Wolf Chief?"

"Ha-na-ta-nu maho."

"*Ha-na-ta* is wolf?"

"Yes sir."

"*Mawr* is chief, or greatest, in Welsh," Catlin said. *"Maho . . . Mawr."* And how do they say, 'greatest chief'?"

"Well," said Kipp, "*maho peneta*, or sometimes *maho okimeh*."

"In Welsh, *mawr penaithir* means 'sovereign,' or 'greatest lord,' if I'm not mistaken," Catlin said. Then he resumed his work, brushing and glancing at Wolf Chief while soundlessly mouthing words.

Kipp, bemused, asked, "Are you Welsh, sir?"

"Oh, no. By Heaven, though, I wish I were right now, so I could compare more of the words with theirs. It's thought by many a scholar, you know, that these people descend from Welshmen. Governor Clark, for one, thinks it so."

"Clark!" Four Bears exclaimed. "Red Hair!" He smiled.

"Yes," Catlin said, smiling and painting. "Let's talk about this. Those little round boats of theirs, they're just like a Welsh coracle. Only the Mandans have them, of all the tribes in this country. And they have their legend of the Great Flood, and sending out a dove from the ship to find land. Ask Four Bears . . ."

And so the work and the talk went on. Wolf Chief, holding two long-stemmed pipes in his left hand, and his right arm akimbo with his wrist resting at his waist, had not moved a muscle. He was a perfect model. On his head was his circular crown of raven feathers tipped with red fluff, and his knee-length tunic was profusely festooned at shoulders and hem with ermine and other furs, while one tiny ermine skin hung down from his forehead and between his eyes. While the painter worked, Four Bears told of what had happened the night of the great storm weeks ago when the thunder boat had first come up. He told of the death by lightning of one of the tribe's most beautiful girls. White Bison Hair, repentant for bringing too mighty a storm in his zeal, a storm that killed his own betrothed, had made a gift of his three best horses to the girl's family, and now was a respected medicine man, though he stayed much alone with his sorrow, and often went onto the hills for days at a time in quest of Helping Spirits.

"He is on the hills now," Four Bears said. "When he comes down, you will see him."

"I should like to see him make rain," Catlin said. "But just rain, not such a violent storm."

"Nagash!" Four Bears exclaimed when Kipp had translated. "One calls rain only once, and proves his power. Then he does it no more, and leaves it for another young man to call rain and prove himself!"

Soon the painter put down his palette and wiped his brush. "Mr. Kipp," he said, "would you tell them the Wolf Chief's portrait is finished now. They can come around and look at it, but please ask them not to touch it because the paint's not dry."

Four Bears rose and came around to face the picture, and Wolf Chief came around from the other side.

Their eyes grew wide in astonishment, but they said nothing. Each placed his palm over his mouth and they stood gazing at the picture.

"What's wrong?" Catlin asked Kipp, imitating their pose.

"They're dumbfounded," Kipp said. "It's their way. They cover their mouth to keep from saying anything wrong until they have their senses back. By God, sir, that's good! It's him to the littlest detail, and every bit as snooty!"

"Proud's a better word, Mr. Kipp."

"Aye. Proud's what I meant, sir."

At last the chiefs took their eyes off the painting, removed their hands from over their mouths, looked at Catlin, then at the palette on the floor with its smears of paint, then back to the artist again. Then both came close to him and in the gentlest manner they each took him by the hand in a firm and warm grip.

"Te-ho-pe-nee Wash-ee!" Wolf Chief murmured to him, looking down in what seemed to be bashfulness. Then he stepped aside and Four Bears likewise held his hand and looked down, and said the same words. Then they moved off a few feet and turned to stare at the portrait.

"What did they say?" Catlin asked Kipp.

"Te-ho-pe-nee Wash-ee," Kipp replied, beaming. "They've named you 'Medicine White Man,' Mr. Catlin. Congratulations!"

* * *

THE NEXT MORNING WHEN FOUR BEARS AND WOLF CHIEF approached the lodge where Catlin was staying, the painter, standing in the doorway with Kipp, gasped in admiration. This day, Four Bears came looking as much like a king as Catlin perceived him to be, striding grandly, using as a walking staff a seven-foot lance with a red blade and a shaft hung all along its length with eagle feathers and red-dyed horsehair. Women and children thronged around him as he came, greeting him and calling his name in musical voices, the little ones darting close to touch him. On his head was a magnificent bonnet of white buffalo scalp hair with the horns attached, a dried magpie skin behind each horn, and from its crest hung a comb of red tufted eagle feathers, half a hundred of them at least, reaching to his heels. He wore a fur-fringed tunic dyed red on his right side but natural tan on the left, with an intricate emblem of quillwork circles over his heart, and a handprint in yellow paint at his waist. He was not aloof from his covey of admirers, but turned this way and that, speaking pleasantly to them as he came on.

"They love him, don't they, Mr. Kipp?"

"Yes, sir, indeed they do! Wolf Chief is the nation's chief by heredity, but in the People's hearts, Four Bears is their man."

Four Bears stopped in front of Catlin, smiled, called him Te-ho-pe-nee Wash-ee, and shook his hand. Catlin was agog at the splendor of his subject, his proud, happy, keen-eyed visage as well as his beautifully made costume.

"Yes, oh, yes!" he exclaimed to Kipp. "If I can even half do justice to this wonderful fellow, Americans will look at his picture and realize it's a crime against Heaven to destroy such a People as these!"

FOUR BEARS TRIED TO FEEL WHETHER ANYTHING WAS BEING TAKEN out of his spirit by what the Shadow Catcher was doing, but the draining of his vigor could just as well have been from the strain of standing absolutely still for so long. He held the red-tipped lance in his left hand, its shaft resting on the floor, and his right hand hung at his side, most of his weight on his right leg, the left foot slightly in front. He kept his facial expression immobile, looking the way he hoped he would look in the picture when it was done, strong but not severe. He was not like Wolf Chief and did not want to look like Wolf Chief. It was hard to believe how this Shadow Catcher had created the very person of Wolf Chief on the cloth. It was as if there were now two Wolf Chiefs! No matter where you stepped in front of the picture, the little hard eyes of Wolf Chief seemed to follow you. You would think that if you walked around to the left, as when you walk around a standing person, you would soon be looking at the side of the face, and the eyes would be looking where you were before, but from every direction, Wolf Chief's eyes appeared to be following. Four Bears really could not have assured anybody at this time that the Shadow Catcher's image of Wolf Chief did not have life in it. The picture was now leaning against a post beyond the center of the hut, well lighted by the daylight through the smoke hole above, and Wolf Chief was seated in a place where he could stare at it when he needed to. He was plainly still mystified by what had been done to him yesterday, and uncertain whether it had been good or not to let the Shadow Catcher do it.

"At least," he had said this morning to Four Bears before they started walking to the painter's lodge, "at least I am still alive!"

There was hardly any talk in the artist's lodge this morning. He was working with such an intense concentration that it was almost like being near a fire, Four Bears thought. From outside the voices and noises of the People filtered in. There seemed to be many of them near the lodge. Although they did not know what was being done in here—the chiefs wanting to see first what would come of it—the People were obviously very curious and uneasy about their chiefs being hidden away in a lodge with Mr. Kipp and the newly arrived white man, who had shown up yesterday in a dugout canoe with two French paddlers from the fort up at the Yellow Stone. It was a secret thing going on in this lodge, and Four Bears thought about his People sidling all around the lodge, consumed with curiosity, probably listening as hard as they could for a few words from inside that might give them a hint of what was happening. Four Bears smiled when he thought thus about his beloved, lively People.

But then he felt a little sadness and fear, remembering that dream he had had when the lightning knocked him down, the dream of going up toward the Other Side World with the spirits of all his People floating there with him.

I do not want all my People to stop being, he thought.

But it seems to me that this Shadow Catcher also does not want my People to stop being. And if he thought that taking our images would make us stop being, then surely he would not be here taking our images as he wants to do.

He is important, Four Bears thought, and I believe he is good.

Four Bears looked at the painter's face, which kept glancing between him and the work. He looked at the kind and keen blue eyes. He looked at the strong, sinewy, well-shaped hands. The artist's sleeves were rolled to his elbows, and the ropelike muscles in the forearm of the brushing hand moved and flicked under the thin white skin. This Shadow Catcher was not a large man, but he evidently was full of compact strength. The more Four Bears saw of him, the better he liked him. Looking into Shadow Catcher's kind face, Four Bears began to have a question, and he asked it through Kipp:

"Has this Medicine White Man ever been a warrior?"

The answer came back. "Mr. Catlin has never been a soldier, and has never fought any man."

Four Bears said, "When I see the deep scar under his eye, I wonder."

Catlin laughed. "When I was a boy, another boy threw a tomahawk that glanced off a tree and stuck in my cheekbone. We were having a contest. No war. But it festered, and I nearly died. One doesn't have to get in a war to die." He laughed again, and returned to his painting as Kipp translated the tale.

"I would like to know," Four Bears said, "if a man of your People can gain honor without being a warrior."

"Yes, there are many ways. One can be a healer, or a wise counselor, or a great singer or actor. . . ." He realized that he would have to start explaining what some of these people were, so he stopped and said, "There are many ways. You have a man who gains honor by calling rain. We have no one like that, but we do have priests and other spiritual leaders, and they have honor."

Four Bears thought on that while holding his pose. Then he said, "In the big boat you came on, there were men who seemed to admire certain other men. What had those other men done, that they were so admired? Had they done things of honor in their country?"

Catlin clenched his teeth. He knew that Four Bears was referring to the fur merchants. He began explaining:

"There is one thing among the white men that makes them give each other a kind of false honor. I regret to say that white men are more admired for the getting of money than for anything else. It does not even matter that they get it in a dishonorable way. The more they get it, the more they are honored for it, even if they get it by ruining red men with spirit water and stealing their lands and their furs." Catlin paused and let Kipp translate all that, which was a task for the trader, then he said:

"I have seen that the red man dwells within sacred circles. The world is a sacred circle. The seasons go in a sacred circle. Living goes in a sacred circle from birth to death and back around, and life gives to life." As he spoke, he made circles in the air with the paintbrush, while Kipp translated as well as he could.

"Indeed that is true," Four Bears replied. "All the world is like that, as you describe it. All the circle is sacred, and all is in sacred circles. I like the way you say it. We go on and on around and it is always the same, and that is good because that is how Creator made it to be." He nodded and then assumed his pose again.

"But the white man does not know these sacred circles," said Catlin. "To the white man, time goes in a straight line like an arrow or a bullet, from one place to another place, and whatever it passes through is never the same again. Do you believe the bison are beyond number? They are reborn faster than your few people can eat them, and as fast as all the predators can eat them.

"But, my friend, listen: East of the Mother of Rivers, where there were bison without number a hundred years ago, you will no longer find even one. And now on this side of the river, the merchants are buying their hides, more than two hundred thousand a year, from hunters who take only the hides and leave the meat to rot. Every year that number will grow until there are no bison left. That is what I mean when I say that the white man's straight line goes through the red man's sacred circle and nothing is the same anymore." His eyes were flashing.

"Slow down, Mr. Catlin," Kipp said. "I'm still trying to figure out how to say 'two hundred thousand.' *Ee sooc mah hannah ee sooc perug*," he said to Four Bears, and then held up two fingers. "Far as I know," Kipp said to Catlin, "their biggest number-word only goes to a thousand." Then he finished translating into Mandan what Catlin had said, sighed, and asked the painter, "Should you be telling him this sort of thing? His people have always liked whites."

"If a friend of yours was about to be killed and robbed by someone he trusted, wouldn't you try to warn him? I'm just trying to warn my friend."

Four Bears had been thinking. He said, "Why would white men kill all the bison when they know the bison are the source of our life?"

"Two reasons," Catlin answered. "If the bison all die and the Indians all starve, they won't be in the white man's way anymore. The other reason is that there is money to be made from bison hides, and if the white man has a sacred circle, it's the coin!"

Four Bears appeared to be growing sad as that was translated to him. He asked, "Is not Red Hair truly our friend?"

"Mah-to-toh-pah," Catlin replied with fervor, "Red Hair and I might be the only friends you have!"

THE PORTRAIT OF FOUR BEARS WAS FINISHED IN THE MIDDLE OF THE afternoon, and the chiefs' response was just as it had been the day before. After they had stared at their two portraits and at each other and talked rapidly and low to each other, they shared a pipe with Catlin, shook his hand and called him Te-ho-pe-nee Wash-ee several more times, then left the lodge together, again mobbed by Four Bears's admirers. Catlin and Kipp were left to sink down in weariness and study the two beautiful paintings. Kipp kept staring at the picture of Four Bears, shaking his head in amazement.

"By God, you're right, sir," he exclaimed. "There's the picture of a king if I ever saw one!"

"Listen!" Catlin said suddenly. "What's going on?"

Every part of the lodge seemed to be creaking, bumping, murmuring, rustling, and whispering, as if it had come to life. The light seemed to change every moment. Kipp looked up and started and swore. Catlin glanced up and saw at least half a dozen faces looking down through the smoke hole in the roof, the dark heads silhouetted against the sky.

Kipp grinned, put his forefinger over his lips, rose swiftly and darted on tiptoe toward the door of the lodge and jerked up the door flap. Voices squealed everywhere, and the whole lodge erupted with scurrying sounds. "*Keks-cusha!*" Kipp cried. "*Roo-hoo-tah! Keks-cusha!*" In less than a minute he was back in the center of the lodge, grinning and shaking his head. The noises had ceased, except for the twittering and cooing of women's and children's voices fading away. "Like bees on a hive!" Kipp exclaimed, chuckling. "Girls and boys and little tads all over this old rotten lodge, and it's a marvel the roof didn't fall in on us! Hey hey! I'll tell ye, sir, they're a-burnin' up with curiosity. If Four Bears doesn't satisfy their curiosity pretty soon, they *will* cave this hut in on us!"

THE TWO CHIEFS WERE BACK AGAIN THE NEXT MORNING, BOTH dressed again in all their finery, both looking somber and full of purpose. They gripped Catlin's hand warmly, went to look at their pictures, sat to smoke with Catlin and Kipp, and then asked, "When can those be touched?"

"Why," Catlin said, "this afternoon. They're nearly dry now." He had learned to paint dry and thin on the canvas when in the field, not having the convenience of a studio or enough permanence of place to protect wet paintings very long. And the arid air of the Great Plains helped in quick drying.

"Good," Four Bears said. "In the afternoon we will show them to the People. Before then, we will tell them that they will get to see them. We will tell them what the Te-ho-pe-nee Wash-ee has done with us here. We will tell them that he wishes to catch the shadows and make images of other important people of our nation, and of the things we do in our days. We will ask the People to be kind and to give help to the Te-ho-pe-nee Wash-ee, and tell them that he is our important friend and is here to do us good."

"Ah!" Catlin exclaimed. *"Dy-awf!"* He had asked Kipp to teach him the Mandan word for "Thank you," and had found it close to the Welsh. Four Bears and Wolf Chief both smiled openly when they heard Catlin say it in their tongue.

By afternoon the news of the Medicine White Man's work had spread through the village, and once again the lodge was creaking under the swarm of children, while every opening and crack in the dilapidated hut revealed a glittering eye. Whenever Catlin peered out through such a crevice, the eye beyond would widen and then be gone, and he would see that the whispering, murmuring throng outside in the plaza had increased to hundreds. But they were all women and girls and small boys. Only at the far edges of the plaza were there any men, and they were all gazing about, looking everywhere except at the hut, elaborately feigning lack of interest. Catlin filled his eyes with the sight of these beautiful people, and his hand virtually yearned to draw them. Only the Crow and Blackfeet men upriver could surpass these warriors for grace and good looks. Most wore their long black hair greased and mudded into red-dyed, ribbonlike strands an inch wide, laid back over the head and behind the ears to hang almost to their heels, and stood as erect as palace guards. Their physiques were supple and athletic, more heavily muscled in the legs than in the arms and shoulders, and they kept their skin gleaming with bear grease, which they applied afresh daily after their steamings and river baths; according to Kipp, there could not be any other People on earth so dedicated to personal cleanliness. The women kept their long hair glossy with oil and combing, always parting it in the center and filling the part with vermilion or red clay. If their tresses were not hanging free, they were in a pair of perfect braids, one hanging behind each ear. Both sexes paraded in garments of beautifully dressed skins, some antelope, some mountain sheep, some deer, soft and pale almost as cotton, and artfully decorated with feathers, shells, porcupine quillwork, fringes, blue beads, fur trim, and long streamers of hair.

The Red Hair General William Clark, in his frequent talks with Catlin in St. Louis, had often gone dreamy-eyed in recalling the beauty of the Mandan women, and Catlin had allowed some of it as an old man's hyperbole, but now he could see that Clark had not exaggerated at all. The young women's faces were so softly modeled and fine-featured they caused him heart twinges, and even the matrons had the smooth brows and carved features of Egyptian queens. Most stunning, though, was the sight of so many with oval faces, skin as creamy as his own wife Clara's, blue, gray, and hazel eyes, and cascades of chestnut, auburn, even wheaten hair. It was as if a third or a fourth of these Mandans were not Indians at all, but Angles or Northern Europeans. "I swear, Kipp," he murmured, "if I let my hair grow to my waist and put on their costumes, I could mix among these folk and never be noticed! I've just got to find leisure to query Four Bears about the old history of these folk. They simply *must* be the lost Welsh! There's no accounting for it otherwise!"

"Well, yonder he comes now, Mr. Catlin, but I doubt y'll have much time to talk history, judging by the crowd on his heels."

Following the chiefs as they approached through the throng were several mature and handsomely dressed men, whom Catlin presumed to be chieftains or clan chiefs, and perhaps a dozen tall warriors carrying feathered lances. By now the crowd in the plaza was mixed, including the men who before had loitered in the distance pretending to be aloof from curiosity.

When the chiefs came in this time, the whole population tried to squeeze in with them. Quickly Four Bears set his warriors at the door with their lances across the doorway to bar it, and requested that no one come in except those who were called, as the hut obviously could hold only a few. The subchiefs and a few important warriors and medicine men were admitted, and all shook Catlin's hand, meanwhile trying to peer into the shadows of the lodge and see the now-famous and mysterious pictures.

But Catlin had turned them face back by his bed, and only the backs could be seen.

Four Bears asked him to turn them around and hold them up where the men could see them. Again the astonished murmurs, hands over mouths; even though these chieftains obviously had been told what they would see, they were unprepared to see their chiefs doubled in life. They moved obliquely this way and that in the lodge, and again the most usual exclamation was that the eyes moved in the pictures.

While all this was going on, Catlin was being introduced individually to all who had come in, by name, and they called him Medicine White Man. One small, powerfully built and handsome warrior caught Catlin's eye not only for his impressive appearance, but also the extraordinary beauty of the quillwork on his leggings and on a bandolier he wore over his shoulder. This young man was introduced as Waka-da-ha-hee, or Hair of the White Bison, and Catlin realized that this was the man who had called the rain, and that was surely the reason why he had been admitted for this first showing. Through Kipp, Catlin asked White Bison Hair if he could paint his picture.

The response was surprising and disappointing. The youth drew back, his face full of fear, and cast his glance down and aside. Catlin had Kipp ask him again, but White Bison Hair said he was afraid something bad would come of it.

Catlin resigned himself to the refusal; it was, after all, the young man's own private person, and he felt he needed to protect it. But Catlin had one more request. He said to Kipp, "Ask him if he will sell me those leggings, for my collection." He had been purchasing weapons and articles of particular beauty throughout the West, to help show the American public the artful accomplishment and skills of the supposedly primitive peoples, and those leggings were an exquisite example.

"*Hoh-shee,*" Kipp said. "This Te-ho-pe-nee Wash-ee will pay you very well for those *hoh-shee*, which he finds most beautiful."

But the young medicine man kept looking down and shook his head.

The noise of the crowd outside now was growing louder and more insistent, and now Four Bears came before Catlin and said, "We believe we must now show your medicine to our People, who have heard of it and have thought of nothing else. May we show them the two images you have made of us?"

"Certainly. How do you want to do it?" He thought the chiefs might let the People file through the lodge and look, as white audiences did at museums.

Instead, Four Bears asked Catlin and Kipp each to take one of the paintings outside the door of the lodge and hold it up to the People's view. So Catlin took the one of Four Bears, and Kipp the one of Wolf Chief, and they stepped outside into the daylight, before the pressing crowd of Mandan People, the two chiefs beside them, and raised the portraits overhead.

For just an instant the crowd was utterly still as they stared at the paintings for the first time. As Catlin gazed over the multitude and glanced at individual faces, he could almost feel the terrific upheaval of their perceptions.

At once then the stillness exploded.

Hundreds began yelping as if their souls had burst. Many began weeping with distorted faces. Others sang. Most of the men in the crowd clapped their hands over their mouths and stared with amazed and glittering eyes, but some, with apparent indignation, leaped up with curdled screams and thrust their lances into the ground, and a few spun like dervishes with their bows over their heads and launched arrow after arrow into the sky. The angry ones then charged out from the crowd and disappeared among the lodges.

It required several minutes for the wild uproar to subside to a general hubbub. The people who had stayed in the plaza had somehow got themselves reconciled to seeing their chiefs in duplicate, or perhaps had merely spent their emotions. Now, it seemed, they were turning their curiosity to the man who had made the miraculous images. The paintings were passed back into the guarded lodge, and Four Bears took Catlin's arm and gently led him into the midst of the throng. At once he was hemmed in by lovely, musky-smelling women, gazing at him in wonderment, smiling coyly and shyly, by brawny warriors and leathery old men who reached to shake his hand, and by an absolute swarm of boys and girls who struggled through the crowd to touch his face and arms with their fingers. Catlin felt as if he were wading through a neck-deep river of caresses. And below his waist, up and down his legs like the nibblings of little fishes in that river of humanity, were the fingertip touches of the very small children who were creeping among and between the legs of the adults. The eagerness and admiration of the People swirled over Catlin and engulfed him in what seemed to be a warm glow of love, a powerful infusion of delight, totally unlike the fearful pressure and sense of suffocation he had felt when caught in city crowds of white people. He would indeed have enjoyed a total rapture in the embrace of these People, had it not been for the anger he had seen expressed by that small part of the crowd a short time before. He could not quite forget that.

And Catlin had been aware all day of the absence of the old medicine man Mah-to-he-ha, Old Bear, who originally had always seemed to accompany the two chiefs. Even in the midst of this crowd's fervent adulation, Catlin remained a little uneasy.

By the next day several of the older chiefs had agreed to sit for their portraits, and one old one was actually in the lodge and posing when Catlin became aware of a new sound from outdoors—a mournful, keening sort of chant, which came close and then receded and came close again—not one voice but several. He was mixing paint on the palette, and so sent Kipp to look out and learn what was happening.

Kipp was gone for a considerable time, and now and then Catlin would hear his voice, and the voices of women, then voices of men, engaged in earnest conversation. When Kipp finally returned, he looked troubled and a bit angry. He explained what he had learned. "It seems, sir, that some of the ladies of the town have got fearful of you, and they're going around lamenting."

"Fearful of me?"

"They're saying that you're a most dangerous man and should be put out of the town at once. They've got a few of the old quacks on their side."

"Good heavens! But . . . but what about Four Bears? Why doesn't he talk with them?"

"Well, sir, he's been in and out of council much of the morning. You're being discussed good and proper, apparently. As ye saw, most of the town thinks you're a fair marvel. But some of the biddies are trying to raise an opposition to you. They're trying to warn everybody that when you put somebody on the canvas, you must be taking part of him to do so. They're saying that those you paint will be dead. Or that you'll take their spirits with you when you go away to the white men, and they'll never sleep quiet in their graves. They're afraid that if you take everybody's image, there'll be no spirits left here. Granted, that's just a small part that feels that way, Mr. Catlin, but these are a people easily swayed by their superstitions."

"This is dreadful, Mr. Kipp! Tell me, when you said that

about 'the old quacks' . . . where does Old Bear stand in this, I wonder? I haven't seen him about."

"Oh, him, sir! Well, he's been out there a time or two, howling and whispering that same kind o' warnings. But he's half-hearted at best, I'd say. Like a politician. He's making a little bit o' protest so that if the doomsayers win, he can say he was with them."

Catlin sighed. "Well, well! Tell me, Mr. Kipp. Is there a chance that I could get invited to their council and make my own case?"

Kipp grinned and rubbed his palms. "My guess is, Four Bears would be real relieved to have ye do that, sir, as he's had to do most of the arguin' himself and could use a little help. A chief can't be very influential if he isn't popular, and you can get unpopular if you argue a lot."

"Then see if you can arrange me an audience. Meanwhile I'll try to ignore their caterwauling out there and get this old gent painted before they spook him out."

THE COUNCIL NEXT DAY WENT MORE EASILY THAN CATLIN COULD have hoped. Four Bears set Catlin at his right, and after the council pipe was passed around, Four Bears told the gathering that the Te-ho-pe-nee Wash-ee had come to speak for himself against the bad birds that were flying about the village. With Kipp translating, Catlin made a brief speech:

"You are kind to call me a medicine man, but I assure you that the pictures I make have no great medicine or mystery about them. I am a man like you, and any of you could learn my art and do it as well as I, if you would practice it as long as I have.

"I believe that your chiefs Mah-to-toh-pah and Ha-na-ta-nu-mauh understand my heart. They know I have the kindest intentions toward you and all your People, that my affection is true and that it grows more fond every day I spend among you. When I have to leave you and return to my own People, I will carry your spirits with me only in my heart, as parting friends do. I will not carry them away in my pictures. My pictures are nothing but paint on a cloth. Your chiefs have seen me work, and they know that I do no more than brush paint on cloth.

"I have often told Four Bears why I do this. I want to show the distant white men, the powerful ones, what a handsome and happy people you are, so that they will not let bad things happen to the Mandans. I have talked often with your old friend Clark, the Red Hair Chief. That man and I are of one heart. We love you and we want to protect you. Now I want to say one more thing:

"It seemed to me yesterday that most of your People do not fear me. They gave me their hands with warm hearts and smiling faces. It seems to me that the dark wings of fear that make shadows over this village today are those of only a few women. In my country, where I lived, brave men never allowed unhappy women to frighten them with their foolish whims and their dark gossip. I think you are a nation of brave men. *Dy-awf!* I thank you for letting me come into your sacred council circle and speak to you."

"Ho!" the men of the council exclaimed, all rising immediately to shake Catlin's hand. *"Shu-su!"* With a few more words among themselves they were soon heading out the door. Four Bears came over grinning so wide it looked as if his cheeks would crack, and his eyes were glittering. He said, "They are going to get dressed in their best garments, for you to make their images. You spoke well, my friend!"

Kipp kept chuckling as he and Catlin walked back, followed by admirers, toward the lodge. "Smart man, smart man!" he exclaimed.

"You mean Four Bears?"

"I mean you. Tellin' 'em not to be scared by hen talk! Heh heh! You're smart, Mr. Catlin. A true medicine white man!"

THE PORTRAIT PAINTINGS PROCEEDED FOR SEVERAL DAYS WITH LITtle trouble. Several of the young subjects lost their nerve under the gaze of the chiefs' portraits and rushed out of the lodge with their robes drawn up to hide their faces, and would not come back. But there were plenty to take their places. White Bison Hair, the handsome little rain-caller, came to sit one day. Catlin posed him in such a way as to show his beautifully made leggings in detail and was about to sketch a full-length portrait when White Bison Hair suddenly put his hands over his face.

"Tell him I can't paint him if he hides," Catlin said to Kipp.

Kipp told him, but White Bison Hair mumbled from behind his hands that he was sorry, he could not bear to have his eyes painted so that they would be alive on the cloth.

"I cannot picture a face without its eyes," Catlin told him. "Please let me proceed. It will not harm you." At the same time, he began hearing a familiar voice outside, haranguing and howling. It sounded like Old Bear the shaman.

But Catlin could not be bothered by that now. White Bison Hair, whom he so wanted to paint, was trying to leave, protesting and apologizing as politely as he could, even while trying to make his way out of the lodge with his hands over his eyes. Catlin sighed. "Very well, Mr. Kipp. Help him make a graceful exit, and tell him I'd like him to come back if he ever changes his mind. By the way, ask him again if he'll sell me those leggings."

But he wouldn't.

Catlin went to the door to watch White Bison Hair leave, and the sight that greeted him was that of Old Bear, stalking around the plaza, wailing and blabbering to anyone who came by, and pointing with some kind of medicine stick toward Catlin's lodge. "What's he saying, Mr. Kipp? I can't help guessing that it pertains to me."

"Good guess, Mr. Catlin. He's telling them that anyone who comes in here to be painted is a fool and will soon die."

Old Bear, now seeing Catlin standing in the door of the lodge, made several aggressive steps toward him, snarling and whooping and making jabs in his direction with the medicine stick. Suddenly Catlin strode straight out toward him. Kipp, surprised, trotted along with him, asking, "What are you doing, Mr. Catlin?"

"My father used to tell me, 'When a dog comes at you, whistle to him.' "

Old Bear had stopped prancing and shouting at Catlin's approach, seeming not to know whether to puff up and growl or to run, but fully confused. Catlin stopped right in front of him, stuck out his right hand, and smiled. "Mr. Kipp," he said, "tell our old friend Mr. Old Bear here that I am very happy to see him. It has been days!"

Upon hearing that, Old Bear looked even more confused, but a tentative half smile flickered on his lips, and he looked warily between the two white men.

"Mr. Kipp, tell him that I have had my eye out for him, that I have queried about his deeds as a shaman and found them most admirable. Say that I have liked the look of him since the day I first saw him. . . ." As Kipp conveyed all this, Old Bear's expression changed from suspicion to intense interest. Catlin went on: "Because of his character, and his looks, and his standing in the tribe, tell him I have resolved to ask him to sit for his portrait. Say I would have asked him sooner, but my hand was stiff from paddling down from the Yellow Stone and that I wanted to loosen the stiffness for a few days by practicing on the other pictures. Tell him I now feel that I could do him justice, and am prepared to begin this very day, if he'll do me the honor to come in and sit."

The shaman sucked at the inside of his cheek for a while, glancing around to see who might be looking, and when Catlin began strolling off toward his lodge, he trudged along with him. Inside, he went from one to another of the paintings that hung on all the roof posts, wandering about absorbed, in such a way that reminded Catlin of the first time he himself had wandered as a youth through Peale's Famous Museum and Art Gallery in Philadelphia, stunned by its wonders.

When Old Bear had completed his tour, he came to Catlin, stared at him earnestly and then took his hand.

"I believe you are a good man. You are a great medicine man, and your medicine power is great, but I believe now that you would do no harm to anyone. I go now, to my lodge, where I will eat, and in a little while I will come, and stand here, and you may go to work." And he was gone. Kipp shook his head and smiled, and soon was chuckling and finally laughing aloud.

Catlin smugly cleaned his brushes and palette and whistled away the rest of the morning, and shortly before noon stretched a canvas over a frame and set it upon the easel.

"Think he'll really come back, don't you?" Kipp gibed.

"Well, we may have time for a pipe of tobacco before he gets here, but . . . Ah, no! Speak of the Devil!"

The door flap swung open and Mah-to-he-ha, the Old Bear, stooped to come in, followed by a half-dozen younger medicine men who were introduced as his apprentices. Old Bear obviously had spent the forenoon at toilette, daubing and streaking his face and body with colors and attaching all the talismans and potions of his profession into his hair and on his waistband. Black feathers and some light-colored sort of a plume sprouted in all directions from the back of his head; he had hair pipes and beads and fur tufts knotted into the hair across his brow, and a necklace of heavy beads around his throat. His face from the nose down was blackened with bear grease and charcoal. He was bare to the waist, but wore a gruesome apron made of a badger's skin, with forepaws and claws and head and teeth all intact. Tufts of dried sage and sweetgrass protruded from the apron, and a luxurious foxtail trailed behind each moccasin. In either hand he grasped a red-stone pipe decorated with a fan of feathers and hung all over with scalp locks and tufts of down, holding them at his sides as if the feather fans were his own wings to fly with. Without further ado, he took his place in the center of the room, facing Catlin, began waving the feather pipes and singing the medicine song he sang over his ailing patients.

Catlin just as enthusiastically threw himself into his own kind of medicine, peering, squinting, bobbing and weaving, mixing and daubing, humming and whistling, and thus the two looked straight at each other and did their respective kinds of magic for much of the afternoon. Catlin presumed that Old Bear was doing his chants as much to protect himself from harm as to be authentic in his posing. But by not having to talk with his subject through the translator while painting, the artist was able to concentrate in the way he loved to do, and soon the full-length picture was done.

Days later, Catlin sat writing his latest article as correspondent for the *New York Spectator*. Smiling, he penned:

> . . . His vanity has been completely gratified . . . he lies for hours together, day after day, in my room, in front of his picture, gazing intensely upon it; lights my pipe for me while I am painting—shakes hands with me a dozen times on each day, and talks of me, and enlarges upon my medicine virtues and talents, wherever he goes; so that this new difficulty is now removed, and instead of preaching against me, he is one of my strongest and most enthusiastic friends and aids in the country . . .

FOUR BEARS WAS NOW SATISFIED THAT THE SHADOW CATCHER WAS in Mih-Tutta-Hang-Kusch as a special gift from the Creator, and that the purposes he had explained were true and worthy purposes. Four Bears was delighted with the white man's way of winning Old Bear's affection and loyalty and dispelling the fears of the doubters. "This is a wise and affectionate man," Four Bears told everybody he talked to. "He does love and respect us, even as Red Hair did. Make him welcome everywhere. Let him take the images of everything he wishes to see, for I am sure that he does all this as a true tribute to our People. In this way he believes he can protect us from bad things, and he is working very hard to do that. He is a sort of storyteller, as we see now; his pictures tell the story of our People, just as the pictures on our robes tell the stories of what we have done, and always, storytellers have been a most honored people among us, yes? So I ask you to honor him and protect him."

And so, George Catlin the painter, Te-ho-pe-nee Wash-ee, began to enjoy the purest and sweetest hospitality he had ever known. He was never allowed to go hungry or to want anything. He was allowed to go anywhere and set up his easel, and to make sketches or paintings of every kind of activity in and around the village. He painted pictures of chieftains and family groups, of archery contests and games and dances, of buffalo hunts, of the burial grounds and the skull circles, of the manufacture and use of everything from weapons and pottery to houses and bullboats. Wherever he went, he was escorted and guarded unless he expressed a desire to be alone. The Mandans were amazed to see a man work so hard, all day every day. When he was not painting or drawing, he was doing what he called *writing*. He made countless lines of tiny markings on sheets of strange white material he called *paper*, and he explained that it was a way of talking to people far away, a kind of sign language that distant people could look at and hear him talking. This was too great a medicine to be believed; although some of the older men in town could remember that old Coyote had spoken of such a thing, they had presumed it to be another of his big lies. But now that their beloved guest the Shadow Catcher was doing it right before their eyes, they could believe in it.

This *writing* language was a thing that haunted Four Bears. He knew the old stories that said First Man and his people in the Ancient Times had known how to use a Marking Language, by which they could talk across distance and time. He remembered the legend that there had used to be some Magic Bundles in the Sacred Canoe, bundles in which there had been much of the Marking Language, and that the Bundle Keepers for many generations had waited and watched for white peoples to come from the old Land of First Man, peoples who could tell them what the marking words in the old bundles meant, and perhaps even teach them to use that language themselves again.

But those Magic Bundles had been lost. Sometime before Four Bears's grandfather had been born, an old medicine woman who was then the Keeper of the Bundles had disappeared with those bundles of marking words, and from her time on, only men had been permitted to guard the relics in the Sacred Canoe. That had happened while the first Seeking White Men, the French from the north, had been visiting the nation. That had been almost a hundred years ago, and after those Magic Word-Bundles had disappeared, there had been very little thought about the Marking Language. Sometimes Four Bears would be sad, thinking of its loss, but since it was not really a thing that was needed, it should not matter so much. Most people loved and needed the sound of voices, and so why should a silent language be important? In the very Ancient Days, it was said, man had known how to talk directly with all the other kinds of animals, but through certain sins they had lost that knowing, and *that* was a loss worthy of remorse—far worse than the loss of a Marking Language. Perhaps a Marking Language would be very important to a man like Shadow Catcher Catlin, who was very far from his own People, but it was not important to a People like the Mandans, who were always together.

Four Bears was very happy that Shadow Catcher had left his own People to come here. Whenever he thought of him and saw his face in his mind, he was happy. He tried to see him at least once every day, usually to see if there was anything he needed. Once, while mourning a dead relative, Four Bears asked if the Shadow Catcher would paint another image of him, and the painter had been happy to do it. That second time he had painted him not in full length and full dress, but bare-chested, just his face and shoulders. While he was being painted that second time, Four Bears had asked Catlin if there was anything he would like to have that he did not have yet. "Yes," the painter had said. "There are two things. I wish to collect some of the fine garments and pottery and decorations that your People make, so that I can show my own People how skillful you are. For example, I have been trying to buy those beautiful leggings that Waka-da-ha-hee wears. Never have I seen such beautiful quillwork. But he answers that he cannot sell them because they were made by his grandmother, who cannot make them anymore because her eyes have gone bad."

"Do not ask me to make him sell them," Four Bears said. "I would not tell a man to do anything he thinks is wrong. If I did, I would not be a good chief."

"Oh, no, I'm not asking you that! I am only saying, that is the kind of thing I would like to collect and take east to show. If you could let people know that I want to buy such things, I will be grateful."

"I will tell them you want such things. And what is the other desire you have, my friend?"

"The women here are so very beautiful," Catlin said. "I should like very much to have certain ones come here so that I can make pictures of them."

Four Bears's keen eyes flashed with interest, but not particularly with pleasure. He was used to having fur traders and other white men ask for pretty women to sleep with or marry; Kipp himself had a Mandan wife. But this was a more complicated request, and Four Bears paused a long time before answering: "My friend, you have made many pictures. You know that the men who have sat here to have their images made were selected because they are chiefs and notable warriors. You remember that when you started to paint one of the Fancy Men, you were asked not to do it because he was neither a warrior nor medicine man, but merely one of those pretty men who loaf around the town to be looked at. The good warriors and chiefs told you that if you painted that Fancy Man, you would have to destroy all their pictures at once."

"Yes, I remember that day," Catlin replied, flushing with embarrassment. It had been one of the few mistakes he had made here, and it had been quickly forgiven after the fop walked out.

"You see, my friend," Four Bears went on, with Kipp translating, "the people you paint here are important men. We would not have you use your magic on unimportant people, and take back to your country pictures of people who are not important."

Catlin looked in puzzlement at Kipp, and asked, "Is he saying that women are not important enough to paint?"

"That's probably his drift, Mr. Catlin. I'm afraid so."

"Well, now, let's just try to change his outlook, shall we? Tell him, will you: in all the white men's countries, portraits are painted for two reasons, for prestige and for beauty. Tell him there are as many women painted for their beauty as there are men painted for their importance. Tell him that a man has to be rich or important to have his portrait painted—and so does a woman, if she's homely—but that a woman's beauty is importance enough in itself. Tell him that if I went back to my country with pictures of Mandan men only, they would ask me, 'Are the Mandan women so homely, then, that you wouldn't paint them?' Ask him if he wants the white people to think such a thing!"

Four Bears tilted his head and thought very hard as he heard Kipp translate that argument, and he said nothing more about it as his portrait was finished. He left without mentioning it.

But the next day there appeared in front of Catlin's lodge an exquisite copper-skinned girl with delicate features, gray eyes, and flowing brown hair bleached by the sun. She said her name was Mint, and that she doubted that she was pretty enough to be worthy of a portrait, but that she had been encouraged to come and offer herself. Catlin painted her with delight, and she was the first of many.

ONE EVENING WHEN CATLIN HAD FINISHED CLEANING HIS BRUSHES and was standing in the doorway of his lodge watching the hills soften in the golden light of sunset, Four Bears came strolling toward him, dressed in his fine tunic and smiling. They shook hands. Then Four Bears put his arm gently through Catlin's, pointed toward the other side of the plaza and said, *"Roo-hoo-tah."* By now Catlin knew that meant "Come."

They walked arm in arm through the town, among the narrow passages between lodges, and came at last to a large lodge, forty or fifty feet in diameter, with a pole arbor in front of the door. Extending a hand toward it, he said, *"Ote Mah-to-toh-pah."* Home of Four Bears.

He led Catlin in. The interior was roomy and very clean. The floor was of earth so well-trodden and swept that it had almost the gloss of tiles, and in the center under the smoke hole was a sunken fire pit lined with stone. A nearly smokeless cook fire glowed therein, and a wonderful aroma of roast meat filled the room. On the floor around the fire pit were laid a few reed mats, a tanned buffalo robe of uncommon size painted with horses and human figures, and a carpeting of smaller and plainer hides. Upon one of those sat Kipp, who raised a hand in greeting and said, "You're his dinner guest of honor, Mr. Catlin, and he asked me to be here to help you talk."

Four Bears led Catlin to the decorated robe and indicated that he should sit there, and then he seated himself cross-legged on a mat within arm's reach. He lit a pipe quite solemnly and passed it to Catlin. It was a mild mix, mostly red willow bark, a little tobacco, and a thin sprinkling of powdered buffalo dung which made it keep burning and gave off a pleasant grassy smell. As they smoked and nodded and smiled at each other, saying nothing as yet, Catlin noticed that they were by no means alone in the big lodge. The periphery of the room was divided into eight curtained sleeping places, and in the recesses between them were numerous women and children, playing, coddling, or reclining, all conversing in such subdued voices that they hardly made a murmur. Some of the women and all of the children were naked, but they stayed discreetly back in the shadows, while the ones preparing and tending to the meal were modestly dressed. They were very pretty women. Four Bears was known to have seven wives, the eldest and most esteemed one being about forty years of age and the youngest a coy and pregnant fourteen-year-old with silvery hair and blue eyes, who was one of those attending the cookery. All the wives looked cheerful, and the children, some ten or eleven of them that Catlin could see, were contented and well-behaved. He remembered the constant hubbub in his parents' household of fourteen children, and marveled at the harmony in a household of seven wives. Putnam and Polly Catlin, his parents, would have been stunned speechless by this arrangement.

Four Bears, using only hand signs, directed the women to serve the honored guest, and watched him dine on the rack of roasted buffalo rib, and the pemmican buttered with marrow fat. Four Bears watched him solicitously, directing the women to keep his platter full of the hottest and most succulent meat. They moved with a quiet grace, kneeling and rising smoothly even with their hands full, and Catlin could not help yearning for the comforts and services of such marvelous creatures. Any number of Mandan girls could have been available to share his nights if he asked, he knew, but he kept forcing up in the forefront of his mind, at such times, the face of his beloved and trusting wife Clara.

He had a hard time getting used to eating while the chief and Kipp sat back, but he had already learned that it was the custom in most of these tribes for the host to attend his honored guest instead of feeding his own appetite. Kipp, though a guest, too, was not the honored guest, and he would eat later. After eight years of life with the tribe, he knew the protocol and was not insulted. Catlin ate and ate, while Four Bears looked after him, meditated in what apparently was the greatest contentment, and slowly and deliberately recharged the smoking pipe for its use after the meal.

At last Catlin set his platter down and sheathed his knife. "*Dy-awf,*" he said. "*Shu-su!*" It meant, "Thank you. Very good!" Then, as Four Bears smiled fondly at him, he added, "*Mah-to-toh-pah e numohk k'shese k'tich.*" It meant, "Four Bears is a great chief."

The host bowed his head shyly and proceeded to light the pipe. Though it would have been easy to take a coal from the cook fire to ignite it, he instead brought forth flint and a steel striker, with which he deftly struck sparks into the pipe bowl. The powdered buffalo dung on top was a perfect tinder, and in a moment the smoke was going strong. Four Bears turned the pipe stem in a circle to acknowledge the Four Winds, pointed it up toward Creator and down to Earth Mother, and handed it to Catlin. Then it was passed into Kipp's hands. Now was the time to talk.

Catlin praised the calm and harmony in Four Bears's house, and said, "It is no wonder you are a happy man. You have many beautiful wives and children to surround you."

Four Bears evidently knew that most white men believed in having only one wife, because he took a little while to talk about his large family. "Every woman who wants to have a husband should be married, do you not agree? But you have noticed that there are so many more women than men in our nation. The Dah-koh-tah and Arikara make war on us in our own country, and the Shienne and others when we ride far out to hunt. So many of our young men die, in the hunt and in those fights, that we have four or five women for every man.

"And a chief, especially the *maho okimeh*, must always have a good house and much food, for his guests are many. A man with a number of good wives can have more crops to feed his guests, and more well-made gifts to give his guests, and a cleaner house."

"I see the sense of that," Catlin replied.

"So many of our young men are killed," Four Bears said, returning to the topic natural to a war chief. "A chief must do everything he can to keep the warriors and hunters from being killed. He must encourage them to learn how to ride and shoot better than their enemies, and to harden themselves so they are not made helpless by hardship. That is why you see my young men always practicing with their bows and racing their horses, and running footraces with each other. And swimming. And wrestling. And in the Okeepah, they learn to bear more pain than any enemy could give them. And so they are fine warriors. Fewer fine warriors die than ordinary warriors, when they have to protect their People. Yes. A war chief must do all he can to keep his warriors alive."

"I have heard," said Catlin, "that you fought an enemy war chief with your own hands and let your warriors stand back safe, so they would not be killed. It is a widely told story."

"It is a story told in pictures, on that robe where you sit. I shall tell the whole story to you now, for no one else can tell it fully. . . ." Catlin sensed that the whole conversation had been building up as an opportunity for Four Bears to tell the story. He was glad to listen. It was a thrilling and inspiring story, and as he heard of the repeated headlong charges on horseback, he thought of the storybook jousts of the medieval knights; when he heard of the chiefs throwing down this weapon or that so as not to have unfair advantage, he thought of a chivalric code such as he had read of only in idylls.

Of course, he thought, we are presuming that this man descended from Madoc, who was after all a medieval knight and prince of the Welsh . . .

But then, he thought, where did the Shienne chief come by *his* chivalry?

And as he listened to Kipp's translation of the story and pictured the duel in his mind's eye, there returned to him a notion that he had entertained ever since he had been in the Plains, painting the noble, wild, courageous chiefs and warriors of the Dah-koh-tah, the Blackfeet, the Crow, the Sac and Fox, the Cree, the Ojibway: the notion that these proud and free and honorable horsemen were by their own tradition true knights, not a whit less than any who ever clanked around in shiny armor in Europe. He was rapt with that thought when Four Bears concluded his story by holding out his broad-bladed, two-edged dagger, saying, "This was his knife, which I put in his heart."

Catlin did not have to feign his admiration, and so Four Bears felt encouraged to go on. He told a suspenseful, hair-raising story about his single-handed revenge upon an Arikara warrior named Won-ga-tap, who had mutilated the body of young Four Bears's brother on a battleground and left his signature spear in the corpse. For four years that atrocity had screamed for revenge in Four Bears's heart as he carried Won-ga-tap's spear with him, but they never met in battle, and at last the frustrated Mandan warrior had set out alone on foot for the Arikara's town two hundred miles away. Half starved, he had slipped into the town at nightfall. Keeping his face in shadow, he had entered Won-ga-tap's lodge after the Arikara warrior had retired to bed, and sat by the embers of the cook fire, eating from a pot of meat left by the coals, and then had smoked a pipe that Won-ga-tap had left by the fire ring. Once he heard the Arikara's wife ask, "Who is that eating by our fire?" and Won-ga-tap had muttered to her, "I do not know, but if a stranger comes hungry, we must let him eat." Finishing the pipe, Four Bears had then stirred the coals with the toe of his moccasin until enough light flickered to show him just where Won-ga-tap lay. Rising silently, Four Bears had stepped to the bed of his brother's murderer and thrust his own spear through his body. Then with Won-ga-tap's scalp in his hand he had darted through the screaming uproar of the Arikara town, vanished into the night, and run home to Mih-Tutta-Hang-Kusch, hiding by day and traveling by moonlight, praying thanks to Creator for the perfect revenge.

Catlin shuddered, and that encouraged Four Bears to continue. "On that robe upon which you sit, I have painted the story of each of the battles in which I have killed my enemy with my own hand, all honorable fights, as my People will attest. There are fourteen such stories. I have told you two of them. Here, smoke some more, and I shall tell you the rest, one by one . . ."

Late in the evening, when the last bloody detail had been recounted and Catlin was sure he had heard the most incredible life story ever lived, Four Bears rose, took Catlin by the hand and helped him stand, and looked close into his eyes, a slight smile parting his shapely lips. Catlin had never felt such a sensation as when he looked into those intense, wolflike eyes, which, at this moment, were brimming with tenderness. Here was both the wildest and most civilized man Catlin knew or could ever have imagined.

Four Bears bent down, took up the beautiful painted history robe by its corners, folded it, and said, "I brought you here this evening, my good friend, to give you this present, for you said you want fine things to remember us by when you have to leave us." He laid the robe over Catlin's shoulder, hooked arms with him as before, and walked him back to his painting lodge under the stars, shaking his hand once more in parting.

The sky was cold with the hint of fall, and in George Catlin's throat there was a lump he could not swallow. He shivered violently, and turned and went into a darkness dense with the smell of pigment and oil, the lonely workplace of a Shadow Catcher, in the heart of a doomed civilization.

CHAPTER 25

MIH-TUTTA-HANG-KUSCH
AUTUMN 1832

HIS NOTEBOOKS WERE FILLING WITH SWIRLING, HASTY SKETCHES; the active and complex lives of the Mandan People kept him on the run from one place to another, and he could scarcely keep up with all the spontaneous occurrences: the coming and going of hunters and war parties, the horse races, the carouses and dances of a dozen fraternal and religious societies, the idyllic riverside scenes of fishing and swimming and bullboating, all the daily alarms and accidents of a vigorous and reckless People, their rolling-hoop games and arrow games, their farming, their butchering, their preening, their ceaseless gatherings for story-swapping and joking in the plaza and on their rooftops; never had he seen such a happy and vigorous and curious People, and he sketched them and wrote down everything he could learn about them whenever he was not in his studio-lodge painting their portraits. He kept poor Kipp busy almost every hour translating his interviews with the adults and his joshings with the children. In every conversation, he tried to probe their knowledge of their myths and legends, in particular those that might hint at their connection with the ancient lost colony of Madoc the Welsh prince. Most gave no clues at all; others had vague notions about someone called Nu-mohk-muck-a-nah, the First or Only Man, having come out of the Great Flood on a big boat and finding the shore of this land by sending forth a dove. Most of the People were aware that their Ancestors had come upriver, from some land where some sort of pheasant birds—turkeys, he presumed—lived. They referred to themselves as See-pohs-kah-nu-mah-kak-kee, the People of the Pheasants. Some of them in speaking of First Man would gaze toward the buffalo-hide effigies hanging atop the poles high above the Medicine Lodge. And if Catlin mentioned the name *Madoc* to see if they recognized it, they sometimes would correct him: *"Nagash: Mohk-muck!"* Some told him that the Magic Bundle of the People contained a thing like a short bow of wood with many strings, which made strange music when stroked with the fingers. They had never seen or heard it, but their grandfathers and grandmothers had told them of seeing it played in secret ceremonies long ago. When he asked if he could go and talk to those old grandmothers and grandfathers, though, he was informed that they were all gone over to the Other Side World. When he asked Four Bears or Old Bear about the so-called bow, which he was sure must be a harp, they would only smile and tell him politely that the contents of the bundles in the Sacred Canoe were not to be known. Once Catlin drew a small ink sketch of the crucified Christ and showed it to some of the people he was interviewing. Their eyes widened at first; then they looked down from it and murmured, "Nu-mohk-muck-a-nah." Exasperated, sometimes he would ask, "Do you recognize the name 'Jesus Christ'?" Most shook their heads, but now and then somebody would reply: "The white men at the fort say those words when they are angry."

"As ye may imagine," Kipp remarked with a smirk.

"Think of it," Catlin groaned. "They have—I am sure of it!—forgot the very name of their Savior!"

ONE COOL MORNING AS CATLIN AND KIPP WERE EATING BREAKFAST in the trader's hut at sunrise, they were startled by an outburst of women's screams and the barking and howling of dogs. Thinking that the town must be under attack by Dah-koh-tah or other enemies, Catlin sat for a moment wondering where to go and what to do, until Kipp sprang up from the table, exclaiming:

"Now we have it! Drop your fork and grab your sketchbooks! The Okeepah is starting, and this is what you've been waiting for! You won't want to miss the beginning, because First Man is coming!"

Within a minute Kipp and Catlin were in front of the Medicine Lodge. Catlin's heart was racing, goaded by the frantic tension and the piercing screams and howls. Virtually everyone had climbed onto the roofs of the lodges to gaze toward the prairie slopes. Catlin clambered onto a crowded roof and stared in the same direction until he saw the object of their attention. *"Nu-mohk-muck-a-nah!"* was what they were screaming, he realized. A mile away, coming in a swift walk directly toward the town, was the figure of a man, white as chalk against the green prairie. Catlin's scalp crawled.

Now the crowd scurried and acted as if putting themselves in a state of defense. Horses were rounded up on the prairie and brought inside the palisade; warriors were blackening their faces and stringing and twanging their bows, and the howling grew ever louder and more shrill. The white figure came on steadily, closer and closer. Soon he was out of sight outside the palisade and then he walked in through the gate and made his way among the lodges into the plaza and walked straight toward the Medicine Lodge, with people leaping in front of him and then darting out of his deliberate way. He was naked except for a cape of white wolf skins and a headdress made of two raven skins, and carried in his left hand a decorated pipe. His entire body and face were covered with white clay.

Catlin sketched and craned as this figure went to the front of the Medicine Lodge, where he was met by Four Bears and Old Bear and most of the chieftains Catlin had painted. They all greeted him with handshakes, each repeating his name.

Then the white figure entered the Medicine Lodge as if it were his own, and the screaming of the crowd subsided.

"Now," said Kipp, "the First Man will have the Medicine Lodge swept out, and then he'll hand over his medicine pipe to the shaman who's been chosen the Okee-pah Ka-se-kah for this year—that means he gives him the authority to conduct the ceremonies in there—you know, the torture. The Hanging Up. You won't get to see that, Christ be thanked; they don't let anybody in there but the medicine men that's involved, and the lads they're going to string up. No white men, that's for sure!"

Catlin nodded weakly. "I don't have the stomach for torture."

"No. And never mind; there'll be more going on out here in the next four days than ye've got ink or paper to draw. The Bull Dance, the Okee-hee-dee business, the Last Race—"

"Okee-hee-dee? That's the Devil, isn't it?"

"Aye, the Evil Spirit. A lewd and riotous show he makes, what with his big cock and all! You'll see, Mr. Catlin! You'll get pictures you'll scarcely dare to show to genteel folks back East! Ha ha!"

CATLIN VIRTUALLY DID HAVE TO BE IN SEVERAL PLACES AT ONCE TO keep up his sketches and notes in the next three days, for the whole town was caught up in the festival. He went from place to place in the excited crowd with his notebooks, shouting questions to Kipp and cupping his ear to hear the shouted answers.

After the First Man had ordered the preparation of the Medicine Lodge, he then spent the rest of the day going to the door of every house, and wailing and haranguing until someone came out and put something in his hand, at which time he would go to the next house and resume his lamentations.

"He's gathering cutting tools," Kipp explained as Catlin sketched the strange pale figure. "He tells them that he was the only survivor of the Flood that covered the earth, that he landed his boat on top of the mountains over there, and that if he doesn't collect an edged tool from everybody, there can't be boats made to save the People from the next Flood."

"Remarkable," Catlin exclaimed, pausing in his drawing to scribble a few words. "What if somebody wouldn't have a tool to give?"

"They always have a spare one in the house when this time of year comes around."

"And do they get their tools back after the festival?"

"Oh, no! At the end of the four days all those tools are sacrificed to the Flood Spirit. They're all pitched off the cliff into the river, with the whole town as witness."

"Truly? Why, hard as blades are to come by, I'm surprised," Catlin exclaimed.

"Well, sir, they figure that a sacrifice that doesn't hurt much doesn't amount to much!"

That first night, a dreadful silence prevailed over the town. First Man was still in the village, but no one knew where he was sleeping, so everyone stayed indoors, and even kept their dogs inside. The next morning Kipp led Catlin trotting to the plaza, where they found the crowd already assembled on the rooftops, keening and crying as the fifty young volunteers for the Okeepah tortures were led into the Medicine Lodge by First Man. All the youths were naked, and covered with red or yellow or white clay, and each carried his shield, his bow and quiver, and his medicine bag.

For a while nothing happened in the plaza; the strident voice of First Man could be heard from inside the Medicine Lodge. Then his whitened body appeared in the doorway and he called to an old man who was waiting near the Sacred Canoe, his whole body and face painted yellow. As the man moved toward the Medicine Lodge, Catlin exclaimed, "Why, that's Old Bear!"

"Yes, sir," said Kipp. "So it is." First Man had begun a

speech to Old Bear, and Kipp translated. "He's passing him the medicine pipe . . . tells him good-bye, says he's going back to the mountains and will be back next year to open the lodge again. He says he's told the boys to trust the Creator for His protection during the ordeal, and Old Bear is now in charge."

Even as Kipp spoke, the white figure of First Man was striding across the plaza through the crowd, and going out through the palisade gate, and for a long time the murmuring crowd on the rooftops watched him make his way back across the green prairie the way he had come, until he was lost in the distance. Old Bear, in his yellow paint, had vanished inside the Medicine Lodge. Catlin stood looking at the big lodge, which seemed fairly to vibrate with mystery and dread. To think of the agonies that were soon to be endured under that clay dome roof was almost more than he could bear.

But then he thought of Four Bears, of the extraordinary controlled wildness in his face, and he thought:

Part of what made Four Bears was what happened in there when he was a boy like those.

And he, and they, chose to do it.

He shook his head, turned a new page in his sketchbook, and turned his back on the Medicine Lodge.

FOUR AGED DRUMMERS PAINTED RED SAT NEAR THE SACRED CANOE, pounding with drumsticks on bladders full of water, in rhythm with rattles shaken by the dancers, and their voices looped, soared, and sobbed in the song of the Bel-lohck nah-pick, the Bull Dance, which was to call the bison herds close for the coming season. Eight dancers with the entire skins of bull bison draped over their backs, horns and hooves and tails still on, were dancing and stamping, bent forward from the waist and looking out through the eyeholes of the hides as if through masks, imitating the moves of bull bison while shaking rattles. Their leg muscles grew turgid and ropy with the exertions of their dance, and they kept a cloud of dust kicked up all around the Sacred Canoe.

Among them, doing the same steps and shaking rattles to the same time, were two dancers representing day and two representing night. The day dancers were painted from head to foot with vermilion, with white streaks running vertically to represent the night ghosts that the morning rays chase away. The night dancers were painted entirely black with charcoal dust and grease, with spots of white clay all over to represent the stars in the firmament.

The entire nation seemed to be the audience for this keening, thumping rite, giving a deafening shout of approval each time the drums and dancers stopped. Then the pounding and wailing and rattling would resume just as before. Fortunately for Catlin, it was being repeated over and over, because, even as master of the quick sketch, he was trying to record a scene nearly overwhelming in its myriad details, and they were all totally unfamiliar details. Besides the dancers, there were countless other painted and costumed performers acting out their parts of the drama. Two men wearing full grizzly bear skins complete with heads and claws were growling loudly, ponderously waving their paws and threatening to devour everything and everyone, including the dancers, and in order to appease them, women kept rushing in and setting platters of meat before them. But sometimes those offerings of meat were snatched out from under the bear men's noses by other men with blackened bodies and whitened heads, representing bald eagles, who would dart in with outstretched arms and carry the meat out through the crowd and onto the prairie. They in turn were pursued by about a hundred small boys with white-painted heads and yellowed bodies. "Those are the *ko-ka*, the antelopes," Kipp explained. "As you see, they will get the meat away from the eagles and eat it, because the Mandan believe that Creator's gifts at last fall to the innocent." Catlin's head was pounding, his hand cramping from the tension of handling his drawing instruments over this profusion of details and making word notes for what he would later have to write. "I feel," he shouted to Kipp over the drumming and singing, "like someone trying to stuff a whirlwind and a symphony into a bag!"

"Well and good, Mr. Catlin, but save a bit of strength and a lot of ink, for when Okee-hee-dee roars in with his giant cockstand, because they've been challenging him all day to come!"

BY THE FOURTH DAY OF THE FESTIVITIES, CATLIN HAD FILLED SHEETS and sheets of sketchbook paper with the bizarre scenes, had scribbled thousands of words of notes, and was beginning to sense the order that really did underlie the apparent chaos. On the first day, he realized, the Bull Dance had been given once to each of the Four Winds; on the second day, twice to each; on the third day, three times to each direction; and now on the fourth day it was being given four times to each of the Four Winds. Thus what had seemed to be only an increasing frenzy and abandon was actually being governed by spiritually significant numbers. Catlin had just jotted down this observation as the fourth dance was concluding, the whole townful of spectators being in a state of exultation and hilarity, when the mirthful tone suddenly escalated to a heart-quaking screech of terror, coming from the people on the roofs. All the hundreds of people up there had turned to face the west and were staring into the distance, shrieking as if to tear out their vocal cords. Many women jumped down from the roofs and crowded into the plaza, where the dancing and drumming had just ceased. Catlin clambered onto a roof and stared off to see what had precipitated this frenzy. Kipp had got up beside him and pointed toward the slopes, grinning. "Right by the schedule, Mr. Catlin! Get your brushes ready, for here comes the Devil himself!"

The figure now running down the slope toward the town was black. He was running at full tilt, pushing and waving something ahead of him, but darting this way and that as he came, like somebody chasing a butterfly. He was a swift runner, and even with his erratic detours, he was closing on the village fast, causing the spectators' dreadful screaming to grow even louder. Then he entered the palisade gate at a full run and charged into the crowded plaza, shrieking and snarling like a mad beast.

At the sight of Okee-hee-dee, Kipp jabbed an elbow in Catlin's ribs and threw his head back in laughter, and the artist himself burst out in hilarious laughter, even though everyone else in the town was still screaming in terror, either real terror or mock terror.

This devil, a big man, was black as ebony with bear grease and charcoal powder, with long white fangs painted from his lip corners to his chin, and white circles were painted here and there on his torso and limbs. Except for his coat of paint he was stark naked. But the most grotesque feature he displayed as he charged into the crowd was a black wooden phallus with a bright red ball of a glans on the tip of it. He held this in front of him with both hands, and it projected some eight or nine feet out in advance. Sometimes he held it up and waved it like a giant erection, but usually he slid it along the ground ahead of him as he chased this way and that toward the Sacred Canoe, still shrieking and snarling. As the crowd recoiled and fled from Okee-hee-dee's demented charge, Catlin realized that almost everyone in his way now was a woman or girl; except for the dancers and drummers still milling about the Sacred Canoe, there was hardly a male on the ground; most of them had taken the females' places on the roofs and were howling and laughing as the black monster chased into the squealing horde of fleeing girls. They screamed for help and protection, and stumbled over each other and fell in their frenzy to get out of his reach, while he thrust the tremendous organ at their bottoms and tried to get it under the skirts of their dresses, all the while grimacing, rolling his eyes and lolling his tongue as in a fit of lustful depravity. Catlin, still too stunned to put a mark on paper, remembered what Kipp had said about genteel readers back home. The women and girls seemed to be in an extreme of terror, so much so that Catlin had to remind himself that this too was surely one of their charades . . .

But suddenly everything stopped in an instant, even the screaming, even Okee-hee-dee himself, who had gone stock-still. There was a moment of deathly stillness as the girls squirmed and crawled and ran out of his reach, and only then did Catlin see what had stopped the Devil's attack:

The shaman, Old Bear, covered with his yellow paint, had materialized as if by magic directly in front of the black giant, and was holding the sacred medicine pipe before him, and Okee-hee-dee was immobilized by the pipe's benevolent charm. Okee-hee-dee now looked so awkward and ridiculous standing there with his wooden penis jutting from his groin that the entire audience burst into hooting, delighted laughter and shouts of applause, and the redheaded staff slowly sank from its erect slant until the tip rested on the ground, and the mirth grew still more hysterical. Okee-hee-dee's expression of malevolent power dissolved before the glaring eyeballs of Old Bear.

At last, seeing that the women and girls were out of harm's way, Old Bear gradually withdrew the medicine pipe from the monster's path, and Okee-hee-dee was gradually able to move again, at least enough to rub the penis tip on the ground a bit and growl a little, upon which Old Bear thrust the pipe toward him and immobilized him once more. The moral was obvious; all good hinged on the powers of the pipe that First Man had brought, and the Devil himself was immobilized by its presence. This time when Old Bear withdrew the pipe, Okee-hee-dee slumped, looking tired, and turned and began to slink and stumble back over the way he had come, past the bent-over bull dancers. As he went, he jostled one of the bull dancers, seemingly by accident, and he looked at him, and his dragging stick at once rose off the ground. Reanimated, to the whoops and laughter of the spectators, Okee-hee-dee thrust his staff between the legs of the dancer and mounted him, thrusting and bawling with lust. Then in quick succession he did the same to three more, while the crowd howled with delight and encouraged him, and prayed to the Great Spirit to make many, many bison and bring them near in the coming season. Catlin, trying to start sketching, kept chuckling and shaking his head, even though he could feel his face flushing at this extravagant bawdiness.

When Okee-hee-dee withdrew from the fourth dancer, he was staggering and bobbling his head upon his neck, and his rose-tipped rod was not only on the ground but dragging behind him. And now that he was so spent and weakened, the women and girls he had been terrorizing began to advance on him in emboldened groups, taunting him and teasing, while he sighed and rolled his eyes and tried to weave away from them. One young woman squatted and scooped up two handfuls of dust, sidled up to Okee-hee-dee and flung it in his eyes. Blinded, howling, he reeled about for a moment, and then began to cry like some huge baby, while other girls scooped dust and flung it all over him, making his greasy blackness fade to mere dirt, and when he was in this most abject state, a sturdy woman snatched the phallus from his hands, broke it over her knee and flung the pieces at him, bringing such a cheer from the crowd that Catlin cringed with the pain in his ears.

Now the morality play was nearly over. Okee-hee-dee in total defeat bolted for freedom, racing back toward the palisades and darting through with piteous howls. Not by accident, there were about a hundred young women and girls waiting for him there, and they chased him for a half mile or more out onto the prairie, kicking him, switching him with willow slips, and pelting him with clods and stones and contemptuous epithets, until he outdistanced them and went howling and sobbing back where he had come from. And Catlin, under a hasty sketch of Okee-hee-dee, scribbled a notation:

> In midst of their relig. ceremonies, Evil Sp made his entree for purpose of doing mischief and disturbing their worship—but was held in check by superior virtue of First M's medicine-pipe, & disgrac[d] was driven out of town by the very ones he came to abuse—a beautiful moral tho p'haps too crudely made for the fastidious!

"Well, sir, what did ye think of old Okee-hee-dee?" Kipp asked laughingly. "Think your readers in the New York parlors will get some titillation out of that?"

"I'll just say, I could argue with our old family preacher back home who used to advise us, 'Turn your back on Satan!' "

Kipp bent over laughing, slapping his knee. Then he said, "Do you know sir, Okee-hee-dee didn't used to be black. Old folks tell me that until Captains Lewis and Clark came through, the Devil was just painted a gray color."

"Odd! Why did they change it, I wonder?"

"They say it's because of that big Negro they had with them. That he was such a randy big devil they changed their Okee-hee-dee to look like him!"

Catlin looked at him askance. "York his name was. Well, well! Do you suppose that story's true, Mr. Kipp?"

"I don't know, sir, but that's how they tell it."

Catlin shrugged and shook his head. That was not encouraging. If the People's legends and lore could be changed that whimsically, it was no wonder they couldn't remember the name of the Savior after six hundred years; it was no wonder they were so vague about Madoc!

Now that the Bull Dances were over and the uproar of Okee-hee-dee had died down, a sort of apprehensive sadness hung over the whole town, the people now perching on the roofs and talking softly, often gazing toward the Medicine Lodge. The water drummers had left the Sacred Canoe and gone inside the lodge, and Old Bear, too, was inside; his voice could be heard crying to the Great Spirit on behalf of the young initiates inside who had been fasting and sleepless these four days and were now about to be pierced and hung up. Catlin's own sympathies were turning back now to those fifty boys inside. The Medicine Lodge had just now begun to pulsate like a heart with the thumping of the water drums.

"Hear those?" Kipp said, tilting his head toward the lodge. "Bags of water make funny drums, eh? You know they say those bags hold water from the Great Flood itself. That it's been in those bags ever since, and was given to the Mandans by First Man. They keep it in the Sacred Canoe with the other relics. What I don't understand is why it doesn't freeze and burst the bags. . . ."

A young messenger had come from the Medicine Lodge and taken hold of Catlin's sleeve, saying, *"Roo-hoo-tah."* He also took the sleeve of Kipp, who said:

"What's this now? He wants us to go to the Medicine Lodge."

Four Bears met them in the doorway, shaking Catlin's hand solemnly and talking low. Kipp turned amazed eyes upon Catlin.

"You're invited in! Old Bear wants you in because you're a great doctor! Good God, what an honor!"

Catlin was swept with a feeling of dread. "I . . . I really hadn't wanted to see this—"

"Hush, Mr. Catlin! No white man has ever seen this! Back down and I'll never speak to you again! And just you try to make sense o' this town without me!"

OFTEN IN THE NEXT TWO HOURS, CATLIN'S EYES WERE SO BLURRED with tears of pity that he could hardly see his sketches. Sometimes he grew so close to vomiting that he thought he would have to quit his privileged seat and run out.

But he stayed, and did the best work he was capable of doing in such a turmoil of mind and stomach. He had come to the Plains, despite the warnings and protests of all his friends and family, to try to record in words and pictures the very essence of the lives and beliefs of a doomed race, and he had been given this matchless opportunity to witness the innermost mystery of the best People he had ever known. He was in this sanctum because he had won the trust and respect of Old Bear, who had been formerly opposed to his taking of images, and now he was being allowed to take the most sacred of images, this ceremony that no white man had ever been allowed to attend. If he meant to understand the hearts of the People he had dedicated his life to understanding, he would have to endure the spectacle of their most crucial trial and triumph, the moment in which they were closest to their god: the Okeepah ordeal. He remembered his notion of that recent night, when he had looked into the piercing eyes of Four Bears, the man he admired more than anyone, the notion that if he could understand this, he could understand the man's very soul.

And Four Bears was sitting not fifteen feet away from him, occasionally glancing over to study him.

No, Catlin thought. If I fail to face this, his heart will turn from me. Even though he knows I am not a warrior, he believes I have his kind of strength. I cannot disillusion him.

The worst moment, but also the most sublime, occurred as one of the last four youths was being cut for the insertion of the skewers, late in the afternoon. Forty-six of them had already been hung up and taken down; Catlin had already seen more physical agony then he had ever dreamed of, more dribbling blood, more severed fingers, more fainting, more faces distorted by incomprehensible pain; it was like a subterranean Golgotha with the skylight flooding down on the twitching, jerking, shuddering crucifixions, a Golgotha repeated over and over; each scream of anguish drained more of his strength, while each refusal to scream drained him even more. Forty-six had already been hung from the ceiling by the ropes attached to the skewers in their flesh, pushed and spun by attendants using poles; all those forty-six had hung until they passed out and dropped their medicine bags or until the skewers tore through the flesh and let them fall, and all forty-six had been taken out of the Medicine Lodge to run the Last Race around the Sacred Canoe, that excruciating Last Race whose screams and howls could be heard outside even now. Catlin's hands were shaking so badly he could hardly draw a line, and the quaverings seemed to be even in his very heart. He was not sure he could endure one more groan, one more drop of blood, and was trying to keep his eyes mostly on his sketch pad instead of looking at the final group of victims, who were just now being stood up to be pierced, when he heard a mellifluous voice saying, in sweetest tone:

"Te-ho-pe-nee Wash-ee waska-pooska! Et-ta hant-ah!"

Even through the turmoil of his pity and nausea, he knew those words. Someone was saying, "Medicine White Man, Shadow Catcher! Look here!"

Catlin looked up. The youth speaking to him was the one nearest by, a clean-limbed, broad-shouldered boy of seventeen or eighteen. Old Bear had already pinched up the flesh of his pectoral and was thrusting the jagged blade through it, and even as Catlin heard the knife rip through the flesh, the youth raised his hand toward his face and said in Mandan, "Shadow Catcher, look at my face." As the knife tore the flesh above the other nipple, the youth was smiling upon Catlin with the sweetest, most pleasant expression, like that of a saint. He kept smiling that way as the skewers were inserted and the ropes drawn to lift him toward the ceiling, keeping his eyes upon Catlin until the artist seemed to feel the blade in his own breast, and tears filled and overflowed his eyes, making the skylight shimmer around the head of the youth as he rose skyward. The image was far beyond the artist's skill to capture, to even try to capture. It transcended dirt and blood and earthly place, and was a vision.

Four Bears looked across at Catlin's uplifted face and his

glistening eyes, and he nodded and thanked the Great Spirit for showing his friend at last the true heart of his People.

In its own way, the Last Race was as ghastly to see as the hanging inside the Medicine Lodge had been, but it was out in the stark daylight where everyone saw the suffering, where the initiates spent the last dregs of their fortitude and strength under the eyes of their families and countrymen. Here was the final proof. That Hanging Up in the Medicine Lodge had been a secret and holy trial, a matter between the medicine man and the tortured; but this was public and profane and brutal, a preenactment of any suffering these future warriors would meet on the battlegrounds of their future lives, and, like the ordeal of the battleground, it was played out in dust, din, sunlight, bloody flesh, and fatigue. For the four days of the Okeepah, the young volunteers had been denied food, drink, or sleep; then they had been hung up by their own pierced flesh with weapons, shields, and bison skulls pinned into the meat of their arms and legs; then each had had a finger chopped off. And now they had to run around and around the Sacred Canoe until the weight of the weapons and skulls jerked those last pins out of their limbs.

Catlin sketched this scene as well as he could with his trembling hands: the boys stumbling around and around the course, faces death-gray, the blood and sweat on their bodies caking with yellow dust, the heavy skulls bumping and banging and jerking at their legs, running and staggering until they dropped on all fours, when pairs of young men from the crowd would dart in and grab them under the arms and force them, even drag them, around the course again and yet again and again until the weights tore loose. All the while the crowd screamed at the top of its lungs to drown out the ghastly sounds of suffering, and occasionally a bystander would throw his weight upon some tenaciously dragging skull to help yank it loose. Catlin glanced at Kipp and was glad to see that the trader, brash fellow that he was, had grown as green and peaked as he felt himself.

At last, shortly before sunset, when the last of the fifty youths had crawled or limped unaided out of the plaza to go home and tend his wounds, Old Bear and his attendants gave a last prayer to the Creator for protecting the lives of the young sufferers, then closed up the Medicine Lodge, carried the load of edged tools First Man had collected, in several leather bags, to the cliff above the river, and pitched them all into the deep water below as a sacrifice against the return of the Great Flood.

Catlin stood on the cliff watching the red afterglow on the cold river until the first stars appeared. When he turned around, shivering with cold and exhaustion, there was not a person in sight. Cooking smoke drifted above the domed huts. The town of Mih-Tutta-Hang-Kusch was still. The Okeepah was over for another year. Fifty superlative new warriors had been conditioned to bear what they might have to bear to protect their People, the See-pohs-kah-nu-mah-kah-kee. The young men had triumphed and were worthy. In their eyes henceforth there would be a glint like that in the eyes of Four Bears.

CATLIN'S DUGOUT CANOE LAY ALONGSIDE THE RIVERBANK, LOADED with his rolled canvases, easel, paint boxes, clothes, sketchbooks, weapons, and the bundles of treasures he had been able to obtain from the Mandans: knives, clubs, beadwork, pots, leatherware, and, most treasured of all, the history robe of Four Bears's life that the chief had given him as his personal gift. The two hired French paddlers stood on the bank waiting for Catlin, gazing up wistfully at the beautiful women in the crowd that had come down to say good-bye to the Te-ho-pe-nee Wash-ee waska-pooska, who had given them a new way of perceiving the world. Old Bear the shaman held him by the hand in his "doctor's grip" and smiled and nodded at him until his chin began trembling, and quickly turned and walked away. Then Four Bears, with his robe drawn over one shoulder like a toga, appeared on the path above them, coming down. Kipp shook Catlin's hand, blinking.

"Godspeed," he said. "Don't know what I'll find for myself to do, without you to look after. Just run my store, I guess."

"Thank you for everything," Catlin said. "Deepest thanks."

Four Bears came through the crowd and stopped at arm's length from Catlin, where he stood looking at him with those intelligent wolf eyes, clasping his hand. Catlin could feel power pulsating into his arm. Four Bears tilted his head back a little.

"Shu-su, ne," he said. There was a slight smile on his mouth, but his underlip was trembling.

"Shu-su, ne," Catlin replied. *"Nu-mohk k'shese k'tich."* You, too, are good. A great chief. He glanced at Kipp. "What's their word for 'good-bye'?"

"I've never learnt it. Never want to. Don't think there is one."

Catlin had been determined not to leak tears in front of Four Bears today, but Kipp's remark made him have to clench his teeth to keep from it. He and Four Bears were gripping their hands so firmly that their arms felt hot. At last Four Bears took a deep breath and let it out shuddering, nodded and turned away. He stood with his back to Catlin and his head down. Catlin could not stand to see that and so he climbed into the canoe's bow and told the Frenchmen to get in and shove off. Beautiful women with auburn and silvery hair and blue and gray eyes followed a little way along the shore, smiling and languidly waving, then stopped and gazed as the canoe went downstream.

Clara, he thought to his faraway wife, be glad I'm getting out of here when I am. I'm in love with about a thousand girls. He watched a few more women going upstream in their coraclelike bullboats, and they stopped paddling long enough to wave.

"By God," he muttered, "they're Welsh or I'm Chinee."

"Pardon, m'sieu?" said one of the paddlers.

After a while Catlin turned for a last look at Mih-Tutta-Hang-Kusch atop its cliff over the river bend, a cluster of clay-colored domes, pickets, and the effigy poles above the Medicine Lodge. Then he squinted.

A man was running along the bluff, twenty feet above the shore, a swift and nimble man in only a breechclout and moccasins, carrying something in his right hand as he chased after the canoe. As he caught up, Catlin saw that it was the Rain Caller, White Bison Hair. When he was directly above the canoe, he flung the bundle he had been carrying. Just as the Frenchmen looked up in surprise at the man on the bluff, Catlin caught the bundle in both hands and waved. White Bison Hair stood on the bluff. Catlin untied the thong and folded back the elkhide wrapper.

Inside were the perfectly quilled *hoh-shee*, the leggings that White Bison Hair had always refused to let him buy. When Catlin looked back up, the Rain Caller was no longer there.

He could hardly have seen him anyway. Everything was blurred.

CHAPTER 26

Mih-Tutta-Hang-Kusch
June 28, 1837

Four Bears was on a parapet of the picket palisade, gazing over the prairie for signs of hunting parties or Dah-koh-tah raiders, when he began to hear the distant rumbling noises that told him the thunder boat was coming, the steamboat called *Yellow Stone*.

Every year now it came and went. Its arrival was always a time of excitement for his People, but the visits did not make Four Bears happy anymore. The *Yellow Stone* often brought badness.

The first year, it had been a great novelty, and it had brought his heart-brother, Catlin the Shadow Catcher, and that had been so good that Four Bears had been eager to see the boat the next year.

That second year it had brought another Shadow Catcher, one called Bodmer, and a word-writing man who had been a Prince of Europe, from across the Sunrise Water. Those two had stayed at the trading fort nearby, and had painted many of the same things Catlin had painted, and asked many questions. But they had not become the kind of friends Catlin had been. Four Bears had been disappointed. Other white travelers had come, full of curiosity; they had stared at the Bull Dance, the Green Corn ceremony, and even the Walking Over the Sticks, but no white since Catlin had been honored by an invitation into the Okeepah.

In five summers the steamboat had brought various kinds of badness, some of which could be seen directly with the eyes, some of which could only be felt. The main trouble it brought was simply too much of everything and too many white men. The white men came up, as Catlin had warned, to make everything into money. They bought beaver pelts and they sold spirit water. They had built another trading fort still farther up the

Muddy River than the one at the mouth of the Yellow Stone River. In at least one of those forts up there they had made a building in which they could produce spirit water of their own, so that it did little good anymore for Chief Red Hair down in St. Louis to forbid white men from bringing spirit water on boats up the river. Now there was spirit water upstream, and like anything upstream, it came downstream easily. Bad stories came down about Blackfeet and Cree, Atsina and Crow and Nakodabi Assiniboin, becoming crazed on spirit water and hurting or killing each other. Those bad stories came down, and so did white men who wanted to sell spirit water to the peoples in this region, the Hidatsa and Mandan. So far there had not been any Mandan men known to have drunk spirit water, and the Mandan council had forbidden any use of it, but it would be hard to keep everyone from trying it, because it was said that a young man could attain spirit-vision with the greatest ease just by drinking it.

Something else the steamboats were bringing too much of was guns. Tribes would buy guns and then would have advantage over their neighbors who had none, and push them from their hunting grounds. Then the victims would want guns, too, and would pay too much to get them so that they could have revenge, or so that they could push aside still another neighbor that did not have guns yet, and that sort of mischief was getting very bad everywhere. These were the kinds of trouble that Catlin the Shadow Catcher had warned of, and likewise was another trouble caused by so many guns: it was easier to kill the bison with guns. White men at the forts would want great numbers of bison hides to take down and sell in the East for money, and so they would promise a certain quantity of spirit water for a certain number of hides, and there were hunters who would go out and shoot and skin hundreds of bison, and leave their meat for the wolves and vultures, and trade the many hides for the spirit water. And then when they had lost their good sense that way and had broken their sacred circle, they could be encouraged even more easily the next time to do the same kind of evil again. Yes, many of the warnings that Catlin had made only five years ago were proving to be true, and so Four Bears was not so happy to see the steamboat coming as he had been at first, and it was hard to be a friend of the whites with all his heart anymore. When Four Bears watched great boats go down the river loaded with more bison hides than his People had taken in his lifetime, and stacked to their roofs with beaver pelts, he remembered Catlin's unbelievable warning that someday those countless animals would all be gone, and he was beginning to think that perhaps that could happen after all.

All the beavers had been killed out of some of the creeks and small rivers, and the trappers had deserted those rivers and gone farther up toward the western mountains. The trappers were not missed very much, but as there were no more beaver towns to build their dams in the creeks, the rains sometimes caused terrible rushing floods where there had been no floods before. Four Bears knew of hunting camps where floods had come so quickly that children had been washed into the water and drowned.

The steamboats, which ran by fire indeed, burned up much wood so they not only bought or took deadwood from the villages along the river, they also stopped sometimes and sent men ashore to cut down trees so they would be seasoned enough to burn the next year. That had been done to one little island that Four Bears knew about, not far downstream. It had been a beautiful little forested island covered with shade all his life, but now there were only stumps there and most of the island had been washed away by floods. Sometimes Four Bears would go to sleep thinking about such things and would have dreams about the return of the Great Flood. You could take all the knives and hatchets First Man gathered up and sacrifice them to the river every year, but the world of First Man had been a world with plenty of beaver dams and plenty of trees on the riverbanks, and maybe those sacrifices would not work in a world without them. In a dream, Four Bears had seen a red circle, a sacred circle turning around and around in his thoughts, and that was the sacred circle of the world of the Peoples, and then a white line had gone through the circle, straight through, breaking it, and the red circle had been changed and could not be made whole again. It reminded him of things Catlin the Shadow Catcher had said to him five years ago, or so he seemed to remember. The straight white line must be the people who come on the steamboats, Four Bears thought. They are changing things, and their changes are not so good.

The many white men traveling on the Muddy River in the last few years had sold many, many guns to the Arikara and Dahkoh-tah who lived farther down the river, and so now those tribes grew ever bolder and more aggressive. They raided the Mandans' hunting grounds now, much more than they had dared to do in the past, before they had so many guns. In the last three years they had even brought war parties up into view of the Mandan towns, and raided for horses, and killed Mandan hunters. Already this spring, parties of bison hunters from Mih-Tutta-Hang-Kusch had had to flee from large parties of Dah-koh-tah, and Four Bears was aware that right now there were so many gun-bearing tribes close around that it was dangerous for hunters to go out of sight beyond the hills, even if they went fifty or a hundred together.

It was for such reasons as those that Four Bears lately spent so much time every day looking out over the palisades toward the surrounding country and feeling surrounded by danger. In just the last few years, it seemed to him, the freedom of his People to go where they pleased and do what they pleased had been tightened down. And in one way or another it seemed to be the fault of the white men who kept coming up the river on their steamboats, the steamboats like the one he could now hear coming.

His People down in the town were beginning to notice its distant noise now, and were bestirring themselves. Four Bears gazed at the river, but could not see the steamboat yet.

Soon it will be in sight and start booming its big thunder guns, Four Bears thought.

But no longer do my People ever think those noises are thunder brought by the Rain Caller, he thought with a sad smile, remembering the first time, five years ago. We are getting used to things that we once thought were magic.

It is just now one hundred years, he thought, since the white men first came to our towns, the French white men who walked down from beyond Turtle Mountain and scared us with their guns. No one is alive anymore who saw them come, but my grandfathers saw them. Now we know that guns are not magic.

It was more than thirty years ago that Chief Red Hair and Chief Long Knife came here and I ran down from the Eagle Hunter camp and got his hat out of the river. It is since then that so much has happened to change us. They say Red Hair still watches over us from where he lives by the Mother of Rivers.

I would like to go down the river and see Red Hair, Four Bears thought. Many chiefs have gone down to counsel with him, and they came back and said he is so good to us.

I wonder if it would be wise for me to go down the river and talk to Red Hair myself and tell him some of the bad things that are happening. I ought to speak of that in council next time. How I would like to see Red Hair again!

He is an old man now. I ought to go and see him before he

Crosses Over. Perhaps he still has the eagle whistle I gave him. I still have the looking glass he gave me.

No, I should say my wives have it.

I would go to Red Hair and I would say, "Greetings, old friend Red Hair! Let me hear you blow the eagle whistle, as you did the last time I saw you!" And we would laugh.

And I would say, "Let us go over and see Shadow Catcher Catlin, who is your friend and my friend, too!" And we would go over and see Catlin, too, if he lived not too far from Red Hair. It would be so good, the three of us sitting together to smoke and eat and talk. Catlin said that he painted the Red Hair Chief, and he has painted me, too. And maybe we would say, "Now, Catlin, we will sit side by side, and you may paint us together, as very good friends!" Four Bears smiled at that thought.

Catlin told me that Red Hair is now all white hair, but that his hair still shakes with the greatness of his laughter.

Four Bears smiled at those fond thoughts. And then the first of the thunder guns of the *Yellow Stone* boomed, and people of Mih-Tutta-Hang-Kusch began hurrying in the streets. Four Bears climbed down from the parapet by a pole ladder and started toward the river with the crowd.

He always liked to go aboard the steamboat when it stopped. It was something that the chief of a town should do, a respectful thing, to greet travelers.

And, too, there was always a little hope in his heart that he might climb aboard as he had that first time, and that there would be Catlin, come back to see the Mandans again!

CATLIN WAS NOT ON THE STEAMBOAT. FOUR BEARS SAW SOME OF the fur company agents, and some merchants who tried to give him spirit water to drink. Kipp came aboard, and a fur trader named Chardon from Fort Clark, and a few subchiefs from Wolf Chief's town down the river. White Bison Hair came aboard for a little while. But the captain of the steamboat was in haste, and wanted to stay only long enough for the Fort Clark trader to make a few transactions. The boat was so full of merchandise that there was hardly anyplace to stand. Four Bears and White Bison Hair edged back into a passageway to make room for men who were carrying a crate along the deck, and they smelled something putrid in the gloom behind them. Turning, they found two men lying in bedding on long crates in the passageway. One had a hand up and seemed to be saying something. Four Bears leaned close. He saw White Bison Hair take the man's hand in greeting. Suddenly the warrior released the man's hand and stepped back. "There is something wrong with that man!" he told Four Bears.

Four Bears leaned down close to look at the reclining man, wondering if he should send for Old Bear the medicine man. Then he, too, started back. It was not just the man's repugnant odor, but the sight of his face and his upreaching hand.

The man's eyes were swollen shut, and pus was oozing from them. His skin was bumpy as a frog's back, and slimy-looking, and he was giving off a terrible body heat. He groaned, and said something, and groaned again.

"Come," Four Bears said to White Bison Hair. "Let us talk to Kipp."

Kipp went back to the passageway and took a look at the two men who were lying there, and when he came out, his face was very pale and his mouth and eyes were full of anger. "Get all your people off the boat, *now*!" he said. "Those men are very sick!" He talked rapidly to the man called Chardon from the fort, and Chardon hurried around helping Four Bears round up the Mandans and take them down the gangplank. Four Bears, a man who feared nothing, felt almost frantic. There was some kind of an evil in the way all the white men were acting. Kipp was scolding the steamboat captain and the fur company agent in a fast, hissing voice, and they began shouting at him, their faces growing red. Four Bears's feet were no sooner on the shore than the steamboat began to rumble and hiss, Kipp and Chardon leaped ashore and threw off the mooring lines, and the great boat's sides churned the water white as it moved out onto the current. A crowd of men and women from Mih-Tutta-Hang-Kusch, waiting on the shore for presents, moaned in disappointment. But then they saw the expressions on the faces of Four Bears and Kipp, and when their chief told them to go back up to the town, they turned and went.

Four Bears had many dreams that night. By morning he had forgotten most of them, but he remembered one dream because it reminded him of something he had either dreamed before or really heard before.

Then he remembered.

He remembered the night he had first met Catlin the Shadow Catcher, when lightning had struck the lodge of Mah-sish, old War Eagle, and killed Antelope and momentarily had knocked Four Bears out of This Side World. He remembered the vision he had had then, of all his People lying dead and rotting.

And he remembered, too, a dream that somebody else had spoken of; he could not remember who. But it had been a prophecy that all the Mandan would be dead a hundred years after first meeting white men.

Four Bears was afraid.

FRANCIS CHARDON, THE RESIDENT FUR TRADER AT FORT CLARK, pressed a knuckle against his upper lip, scooted his lamp an inch toward him on his desk, spread the pages of his journal and dipped his pen in the inkwell. He wrote *July 14th,* and then paused and listened. Very faintly from the Mandan town he could hear the beating of the drums, which had been going on all day and into the night. And the shrill voices he had been hearing just over the wind were not the usual happy singing voices of the Mandans.

He penned under the date:

> A young Mandan died to day of the Small Pox—several others has caught it.

Old Bear, in the lodge of the family of White Bison Hair, waved his feather-fan medicine pipes like flying wings, and stamped and whirled and sang, bending over now one, now another, of the young brothers and sisters of White Bison Hair, who were lying on mats on the four sides of the fire ring. Their faces and bodies were grotesquely swollen. Their mother sat on the floor nearby, rocking back and forth with her eyes closed. She had torn her hair out of its braids and let it hang wild around her face, which she had smeared with soot, in mourning.

Old Bear sang, and the sage and sweetgrass smoke curled up carrying the prayers of his songs, and he fanned the incense burner with the feather fans to keep them burning, but he could not feel that the prayer-song was rising to Creator. He kept trying, till sweat was running down his body, but he had little hope. This sickness was not like anything his People had ever had.

On this very day, between sunrise and noon, White Bison Hair had become thirsty, and swelled up, and died in a speechless agony. His body had scarcely been cleaned and dressed for burial before his younger brothers and sisters had started swelling. It was a very discouraging sign, for White Bison Hair himself had been a man of strong medicine, a Rain Caller, but he had hardly had a chance to pray before he was gone.

* * *

KIPP PACED IN HIS HUT, HIS TEETH CLENCHED. HIS YOUNG MANDAN wife sat by the fire, her face full of fear, her eyes rolling every time she heard a scream from outside.

"Husband," she whimpered, "I am afraid for us! You were on that boat with those sick men!" She had cringed every time Kipp came near her today.

"You don't need to be afraid for us," he said. "Don't you remember when we went down the river and a doctor at the fort down there scratched our arms and made the itching place? We will not get sick, because of that. But the rest of these poor souls!" He started in English now, because the Mandan tongue did not have the words he needed. "God damn those pompous bastards on that God damn steamboat! God blast their greedy souls for stopping with poxed men on board! All to make a few more filthy dollars at every town! God damn, God damn it, God damn them! And it's going through here like a prairie fire. Burn in Hell, you plagued sons of bitches! I hope your scummy poxy boat hits a planter and goes down and drowns every scurvy one of you! To Hell with you, and to Hell with your boat, too!"

He stopped in the middle of the lodge and he could hear the wailing of people in the night air. He would have advised the villagers to flee the village and go out and live in the untainted hills until the pox had run its course in the town. But they couldn't go out and live in the hills because the countryside was full of enemies with guns.

Kipp raised his fists toward the stars he could see outside the smoke hole, and shouted: *"God damn them!"*

MINT, NOW A BEAUTIFUL YOUNG WIFE, HAD A SON PAST NURSING age and an infant. The boy was swollen and about to die. With her lip between her teeth she prayed for Creator to understand what she was doing and why she was doing it. She picked up her husband's war club, which had a heavy wooden knot at its end with an iron spike sticking out. Her husband was out in the center of the town by the Sacred Canoe, dancing desperately with dozens of other young men who were trying to make the evil go away by dancing and drumming.

Mint could feel herself getting sick, getting hot. She remembered that when she had gone to get her image painted by the Shadow Catcher five years ago, an old woman had caught her dress and hissed at her:

"He will take your spirit and soon you will be dead, and there will be nothing of you anymore but that image of paint!"

Mint cried out, clenched her teeth and let out the scream of frenzy that was in her soul. Then she raised the club and drove the spiked head down and smashed the skull of her suffering son. Then she snatched up her infant, and, still screaming with every breath, she ran out of the lodge. It was almost dawn and the sky in the east was paling. As she ran toward the edge of town where the cliff stood high over the river, she saw other people running and screaming, or shouting at each other. She ran to the place where the medicine men always threw the knives down the cliff into the water. Without pausing, still screaming, she dove over the cliff with her baby onto the rocks far below.

FOUR BEARS HAD BEEN THE MOST HANDSOME AND COURAGEOUS and admired man of his People, but now he lay all rough with slimy bumps that were too sore to touch, and which broke open and seeped, and everything about him was hot and stinking. His children were all sick in their beds around the great lodge, swollen and whimpering and crying, and most of his wives lay with them, also too sick to rise up. Old Bear the shaman had danced over them until he was exhausted, and now just stood looking sadly at Four Bears. Kipp stood beside him, and Chardon from the fort had come. They stood nearby, with a few of the Council Elders of the town. Four Bears took a long breath and spoke.

"I have been in many battles, and often wounded. But today I am wounded by whom? By those same white dogs I have always considered and treated as brothers.

"I do not fear Death, my friends. You know it. But to die with my face rotten, that even the wolves will shrink with horror at seeing me! The wolves will say to themselves, That is Mah-to-toh-pah, Four Bears, the friend of the whites!"

Kipp bit his lips, clenched his fists and thought how good it was that Catlin did not have to see and hear this. Four Bears continued:

"Listen well to what I have to say. Think of your wives, children, brothers, sisters, friends, and in fact all that you hold dear; all are dead, or dying, with their faces all rotted, caused by those dogs the whites. Think of all that, my friends. This is what we are given, who have never raised a hand against them!"

THE JOURNAL OF CHARDON IN FORT CLARK WAS BEING DONE IN hasty scrawls.

July 27th, The small pox is Killing them up at the Village, four died today . . .

July 28th, Two splendid dances, they say they dance, on account of their Not haveing a long time to live, as they expect to all die of the small pox—and as long as they are alive, they will take it out in dancing . . .

August 8th, Four More died today—the two thirds of the Village are sick . . .

August 9th, Seven More died to day . . .

August 10th, 12 or 15 died to day . . .

August 11th, I keep no a/c of the dead, as they die so fast that it is impossible . . .

August 13th, The Mandans are dying 8 and 10 every day—an Old fellow who has lost the whole of his family to the Number of 14, harrangued to day, that it was time to begin to Kill the Whites, as it was them that brought the small pox to the Country . . .

August 14th, A Mandan chief came early this morning and appeared to be very angry—telling me that I had better clear out, with all the Whites, that if we did not, they would exterminate us all . . .

August 16th, Several Men, Women and Children that has been abandoned in the Village, are laying dead in the lodges, some outside of the Village, others in the little river not interred, which creates a very bad smell all around us . . .

Chardon put down his pen after that entry and drank down a glass of watered rum, then put a wet handkerchief against his nose and mouth to try to minimize the smell of death that drifted down from the Mandan town with the incessant drumming and wailing. Chardon's round face was black with stubble; he had not shaved for days.

There was a rap on his door and he said, "Yes, come in!" He slipped a flintlock pistol off the top of his desk and put it down between his legs out of sight as three of his French employees and an American clerk entered. Their eyes were wild and sunken. They were as unshaven and sweat-sheened and rumpled as he was himself. No one could sleep. He took the handkerchief down from his face and said, "Well, Messieurs, what is it?"

The three Frenchmen looked at the clerk. He cleared his throat and said, "Sir, we came to tell you we want to set out."

"Want to set out, you say?"

"Yes, sir. We'd like to take the pirogues and get away from

this Hell pit. Sir, there's Mandans coming to the gate all day begging us to shoot them. We'd oblige, but they'd lay there stinking if we did. We want out of here, sir."

"How many? Just you four?"

"Everyone's talking thisaway, sir."

"Well, you can go tell everyone," said Chardon, "that they're all staying here with me until this is over. There's a fortune in fur company property here, and we're not going to leave it to be looted or burned by savages."

"All due respect for your opinion, M'sieu Chardon, but we think they'll burn the place down anyways, with us in it."

"You are wrong. They make threats, but they don't have the strength or the brains left to do anything. They can't even bury their dead." He made a vague gesture with his left hand to indicate the stench.

The clerk looked at his fellows and said, "The men are saying they'll go with your permission, or without it."

Chardon raised the pistol from behind the edge of his desk, cocking it and pointing it at the clerk's face. "Boy," he said to the startled clerk, "tell them I've locked up the armory, so there's no way they can shoot me, but I am able and willing to shoot the first man who tries to desert me, and the second, and on down. Now, go have yourselves a grog, and set your teeth, and wait this out with me. It'll all be over soon enough. Every one of those poor rascals in that village will be dead in a few days and there'll be no more trouble. They're dying at the lower town, too. Wolf Chief himself has passed over, they say."

FOUR BEARS, ALWAYS THE STRONGEST OF MEN, HAD RISEN FROM HIS deathbed. His beautiful lodge was full of his dead wives and children. He had been too weak to carry them out for burial, and everyone else still alive in the town was too crazed or sick to help him, so he had just gotten up, covered each mottled corpse with a buffalo robe, and left them inside, and had shut up the lodge and blocked the door with a bullboat to keep dogs from getting in. The dogs were eating the bodies that had been left in the streets, and those of the people who had gone outside the pickets to die on the prairie. Four Bears had always had a respect for dogs; even though they were not free and wild like the other animals, and were, as citizens of a town, not very well disciplined, they were useful and, he had thought, good friends of their human masters. But now he had seen them tugging with their teeth at the erupted skin and swollen flesh of their own masters, even the babies they usually guarded and played with, and he suddenly came to despise the dogs. They are less than the wolves, their cousins, he thought. They have pretended to be our friends so we will feed them, but when we are too weak and sick to give them scraps from our meals, they do as their cousins the wolves do around the herds, and pull down the sick and devour the dead.

Wolves, he thought. One of the traders from the fort had told Kipp that Wolf Chief had died down in the other town. Four Bears trudged through the town, burning with fever, shaking his head in misery. How many battles did we fight beside each other, Wolf Chief?

He remembered how, when they were boys, Wolf Chief had refused to like Red Hair and had been suspicious of all the white men.

Four Bears thought, Maybe Young Wolf was right!

Then he grimaced. No! he thought. Red Hair *is* good! He would not have let this happen to us if he could have stopped it!

He remembered that Red Hair once *had* tried to prevent this. He had encouraged the chiefs of all the Peoples along the Muddy River to have a scratch on their skin which would keep them from getting this disease! Yes, Red Hair had tried that, and had sent soldier doctors everywhere to make the scratches. Kipp and his wife had done it, and now they were not even sick.

But most of the chiefs had not trusted the soldier doctors. They had warned their Peoples that the doctors were probably bringing death in little bottles, to kill the Peoples and get them out of the way. The chiefs had all learned not to trust the white men or anything they said and did.

Four Bears himself had forgotten his trust of Red Hair and had not let his People go and get the scratches. Now, he thought, we will all die because I forgot to trust Red Hair!

Four Bears howled with his remorse, but his howl was just another one in the village, where howling had not stopped for many days.

Red Hair, I am sorry I did not listen to you!

He took the thong that hung around his neck and pulled up the little gift that Red Hair had given him more than thirty years ago. For a long time he had let his wives use it, but when they all died, he had taken the little mirror and put it back on himself, suspending it by the thong around his neck. Now he raised it up, remembering those happy days of health and hope, remembering in particular the day when he had given Red Hair the eagle whistle and Red Hair had in return given him this. As used to be his habit, he turned the mirror to look at his eye in it.

But now what he saw in the mirror, a puffed and gummed eye surrounded by rotten flesh, yes, even with flies walking on his eyelid, made him bellow in anger and disgust and yank away his hand. He took from his bearskin scabbard the wide dagger he had wrenched from the hand of the Shienne war chief so many years ago, cut the thong that held the mirror and dashed the mirror to the ground. It did not break, but lay there flashing the sun up at him. He dropped to his knees, growling and snarling. With the point of the dagger he stabbed furiously once and the little mirror shattered into splinters.

He stayed on his hands and knees in the plaza until he had strength to get up. There were bundles of rotting bodies all around, and flies were so thick everywhere they were like dark smoke, and they droned and whined like the murmurings of Okee-hee-dee.

Four Bears slowly got to his feet. I must not go crazy like the rest, he thought.

I will go up on the hill where the wind is clean. I cannot bear to die down here.

Leaning on his red-pointed lance, he limped away from the splinters of the mirror, went toward the pickets and through them, and started over the sweet green grass toward the hills. He had gone only a few steps when he saw the twisted shape of old War Eagle coming toward him, coming from the direction of the Town of the Dead. Mah-sish had been a twisted man since the night five years ago when lightning had shot down into his house and killed his daughter.

War Eagle seemed excited, and there even seemed to be a smile on his face, though it was so swollen and corrupt and covered with eruptions that it could have been a grimace instead of a smile, and should have been.

War Eagle stopped in front of Four Bears and jabbered, making awkward gestures with his hands. No one had been able to understand his words after he recovered from the lightning burns. Everyone thought he had been given a new language by the lightning, perhaps the language of the Thunder Beings.

Old War Eagle jabbered in his strange tongue and pointed down toward the river, then to himself, then to the river. Maybe he was saying that he was going to go down there and jump in. So many had done that. Four Bears asked him:

"Is your wife sick, too?"

War Eagle's smile went away and he pointed to a little ragged corpse on the ground. Apparently he had tried to drag or carry her to the Town of the Dead and his strength had given out. He muttered something in his unintelligible tongue, then turned away and continued toward the river. Four Bears sighed, looked up toward the clean slopes and began to limp along.

OLD MAH-SISH, THE WAR EAGLE, SQUATTED BY THE FIRE PIT NEAR his sweat hut on the riverbank, and with the green willow tongs he took another hot stone out of the fire, and brought it to the steam hut and set it under the platform. It exhausted him, but he needed two more stones, and so he limped and gasped back to the fire pit and got another one in the tongs and took it to the steam hut, and then, staggering, he got the last one and put it in. He hated to look at his arms and hands as he did this. They were so swollen and bumpy with pustules and seeping sores, he had to pretend that they were not even part of him, even though he knew he was like that all over.

War Eagle was preparing his own sweat bath because there was no one left in his family to do it for him. In the old days before he had a daughter, his wife had heated the stones for him and put the sage over the heat. Then his daughter Antelope had helped him sometimes. But then the lightning had leaped into the house and killed her the night of the great storm when the thunder boat first came. And so she was gone, and two days ago War Eagle's wife had died of this disease the thunder boat had brought to Mih-Tutta-Hang-Kusch, and so War Eagle had no family anymore. Even the best friend of his family, White Bison Hair, had died, and War Eagle was alone in the world. Few people had liked him after he was hit by the lightning, because it had made him somewhat crazy, they had thought. Just because it had made it hard for him to talk and they could not understand what he was trying to say, they had decided that he was crazy from being hit by the lightning. But he had always been able to think and see clearly; he just hadn't been able to stand straight or talk clearly.

Now that this disease had come, nobody could stand straight or talk clearly. They were all screaming crazy. They were killing each other because they could not stand to see how rotten their loved ones had become, and they were hanging themselves in lodges, not hanging by pins as in the Okeepah, but with knots around their necks, until their necks broke or they choked to death. They kept throwing their children off the cliff onto the rocks so they would not suffer anymore, and jumping off the cliff after them. There were vultures and dogs all around the base of the cliff all the time now; he could see them from here, vultures and dogs eating the same rotten bodies.

Old War Eagle shook his head in sadness and disgust. His whole People had gone crazy with fear, as if getting a white man's disease were a harder fortune than being hit by lightning! Even Old Bear the medicine man had gone crazy and did not know what to do, and just stamped around in the Medicine Lodge and cried beside the Sacred Canoe and waved his feathers, none of which had helped anybody get well.

Yes, even Four Bears was confused. Four Bears must be the strongest man in the world, the way he kept walking around and trying to understand and to help his People even though he himself was so horrible with the sores that it made one weep to look at him. War Eagle had said to Four Bears, "Get in the steam hut! That will make the poison boil out and you will be well! I am going to do that and I will be well!" But of course no one had been able to understand War Eagle since he was hit by the lightning, so Four Bears had not been able to understand him and had just staggered away, limping with his red-tipped lance as a walking stick, gazing up toward the hills as if he could not stand to look at the dead people lying everywhere anymore.

And it seemed that no one else had thought of the obvious cure, either. There was no one down here on the shore among the sweat huts except War Eagle.

Probably it is because they are so burning hot inside already that they can't think of heating themselves further, War Eagle thought. I myself am full of fire so that I can hardly stand it. But I can bear more heat because I was once full of lightning.

He crawled naked into the sweat hut, closed the flap to keep all the heat in, and with his last strength crawled up on the bed of crushed sage and flopped over on his back. For a while he lay gasping in the rankling smell of the sage, until he had enough strength to reach down at his side and find the handle of the gourd. Swinging it under him, he dashed water on the red-hot stones, which sang and hissed and popped and filled the darkness with powerful, choking, stinging steam. He coughed over and over.

Sweat was gushing from him now and trickling down over his rotten skin, making him itch almost more than he could bear. But soon that will pass, he thought, and I will get well.

He dashed more water over the stones, and after a while he could hear the prayers the stones were singing. He moved his lips with the words.

> Great Good Spirit who created this beautiful land and placed us here to live upon it: Hear me!
>
> Great Good Spirit who breathed life into my body and the body of my wife and the body of my daughter: Hear me!
>
> Great Good Spirit who made the ancient stones that sing with my prayer, make me pure again and well!
>
> Great Good Spirit who has drawn the breath of living out of my old wife, give me my strength back so that I can take her body and wrap it properly and make a scaffold to put it on in the Town of the Dead, up where wolves and dogs cannot reach it!
>
> O Great Good Spirit whose exhaling gives us the breath of life and whose inhaling draws it back out of us and into yourself. O give me enough strength to bury her body properly so that she will return to you whole and beautiful as she used to be, instead of rotten and ugly as she is now!
>
> O Great Good Spirit this is the prayer I and the ancient stones sing to you now! Hear me! Hear us!

War Eagle thought, and then began singing again.

> O Great Good Spirit make me strong, and I will bury all the others, as long as I can lift my arms!

It had been a huge promise to make to the Great Good Spirit, for there were, he thought, as many as ten hundred dead in the village by now. But was it not what a warrior was for, the care of his People?

Now, Mah-sish the War Eagle thought, the sweat has washed all the poison out of me and I am pure. Now I will swim in the river, then go to rest a while, and the strength will come back and I will go and make a scaffold to bury my wife on in the Town of the Dead.

Then I will start burying all the others, he reminded himself.

He crawled out into the light and stumbled naked down to the river. He was too weak to spring with his legs and dive, so he waded.

When he was in the river to his chest, he was seized by a terrible chill, and there was a mighty cramp in his heart, a blow like that of lightning. He slid down in the water. He gasped, and water poured into him.

The War Eagle rose out of the water and circled in the air above it, and as he looked down, he saw his body turning slowly just under the surface.

The War Eagle soared off toward the sun. The town of Mih-Tutta-Hang-Kusch and all its screams and flies and vultures grew smaller and smaller below him. Far away on a green slope he saw his chief Four Bears slowly going up toward the hills.

War Eagle did not have anything to do on the ground anymore, or with the burdens of a two-legged's body. Vultures were circling far below him. He was free.

ON THE HILL THE WIND WAS CLEAN AND THERE WERE NO FLIES AND no screams. Gasping for breath, Four Bears stood and looked back down at Mih-Tutta-Hang-Kusch, where he had lived the entire half century of his life. There in the bend of the river it was a beautiful place, standing high on its bluff with the sunshine on its domes, with the gray-blue river behind it, making its colors stand forth bright, and beyond the river were the bluffs on the other side, and the gap down through them where the path to the crossing place ran. Still farther beyond, the far slope of the valley rose up and up, in undulating slopes of prairie grass that grew from bright green to blue as they diminished into the distance, and over them there moved slowly the clouds' shadows. A soaring eagle climbed above it all.

It was beautiful, and Four Bears's heart ached with the seeing of it. This was the way he would remember Mih-Tutta-Hang-Kusch when he crossed to the Other Side World. Perhaps Mih-Tutta-Hang-Kusch would be there in the Other Side World; it was believed that everything on This Side World was over there, too, but without any troubles or flaws. Over there, there would be no cloud of vultures drifting above the town, or above Wolf Chief's town down the river. And there would not be a Fort Clark standing nearby, as there was in the valley below now, because Fort Clark had been built by the fur company people, who could not build in the Other Side World. The whites could not build over there because the Other Side World still belonged to the original Peoples, and was as it had been for ages before the whites had come up the river, even before they had come across the Sunrise Water, to break the Sacred Circle of Life with their Straight White Line.

The wind blew around Four Bears like the breathing of the Creator, blowing the echoes of the constant screams out of his ears, bathing his soul as the river water used to bathe his body.

He did not feel so hot now.

Something inside him said that he had passed the worst part of the disease and that he might even live. Kipp had said that sometimes people got well after the smallpox, and that if they did, they would never get it again. A few very strong people did live through it; Four Bears had seen white men with scarred faces, and had been told that those were men who had lived through the smallpox.

But Kipp had admitted that he did not know of any Indian who had lived through it.

Kipp had told Four Bears those things when he was trying to encourage the Mandans to get the medicine scratches from the white doctors. And so Four Bears had not believed his words to be wholly true. Even a good white man like Kipp told only part truths.

If any white man had ever told Four Bears the entire truth, it must have been Catlin the Shadow Catcher. Everything he had warned about seemed to be happening. Shadow Catcher had warned very strongly about the white men's diseases.

Four Bears looked down at Mih-Tutta-Hang-Kusch with its cloud of vultures above it. He was surprised how well he could see, how far he could see. This was the way eagles looked down on the world.

He saw a moving speck on the long slope between his hilltop and the town, and he could see that it was a man riding a horse, coming up. He watched it for a while and saw that it was Kipp. Kipp was coming up just the way Four Bears had come up, except riding instead of walking.

He follows my track. He looks for me, Four Bears thought. After a while Kipp looked up and saw Four Bears standing on the high slope, and urged his horse, and soon he was standing next to Four Bears. He dismounted.

"I saw you climbing up," Kipp said in Mandan tongue. "I came to ask why you come up and leave your People below."

"I want to die up here. That place is no more."

"You should not leave your People," said Kipp. "You are their *maho okimeh*."

"Friend, my People have not seen me or heard me even though I walked among them. Since this illness came, they are blind and can see nothing but the fear inside them. Your intentions are probably good, but you should not come up here and tell me what I ought to do. My People are already lost to me and I am already lost to them. They do not know I am alive, and so it is as well that I am up here, closer to my Creator. Listen! Do you not love summer wind?"

Kipp gnawed the corner of his mouth. Then he said, "No one else would have had the strength to climb up here. Do you know that you might be getting well?"

"I have thought that I might be getting well from the disease, but I am not going to live."

"What! What are you saying to me?"

"I told you, friend, that I came up here to cross to the Other Side World. Once I had a dream that when all the spirits of my People passed over, I was with them. Most of them have passed over, and I must go with them."

"I beg you, Mah-to-toh-pah! Come down! My wife and I are well. We will take care of you until you are no longer sick at all!"

"Friend, go back down. Enemies are around us, and you should not be out here this far."

"You should not be, either!"

Four Bears smiled. He could feel the pus and itching everywhere on his face, and knew that his smile must look terrible, and admired Kipp for his ability to look at him and talk to his face. This Kipp was a good man to have known. Four Bears told him, "If an enemy come, they will see my rotten skin and flee in fear. If they find me in the evening when it is too dark to see me, I will use this lance and I will cross over to Other Side World with several of them skewered on this lance like meat on a cooking stick. But if no enemy come, I will cross over quietly. I came here with no food or water, and so in a number of days, I will float over, as light as an eagle on the cloud." He saw himself that way as he said it, and it was so beautiful that he was impatient for it. "Now go back down, Kipp, and leave me to this peace. I have walked until all troubles and heaviness are below me. Your presence here is the only thing still clinging to me. Let me go, or I shall have to put this lance through you to get rid of you. I would not want to have to do that."

Kipp was blinking and his lips were tight and white. "Then I will go down. But my heart will stay here." He turned his horse in the blowing grass, and then Four Bears called his name. Kipp turned back.

Four Bears lifted over his head the thong that crossed over his shoulder and suspended his dagger in its bearskin scabbard. He extended it toward Kipp, and said, "Our friend the good Shadow Catcher would want this for his collection of things. Find him someday and give it to him. Remind him it is the knife I took from the Shienne chief, in that fight that is pictured on the robe I gave him. It will be good for him to have those together, the picture story and the knife. Promise me that you will try to find him and give it to him. I know it is a big land, and there are many white men, but promise me you will try to do that."

"I promise. He won't be hard to find. He has become famous in the East."

"*Shu-su!* Now go, Kipp."

Kipp looked at Four Bears one more time, and his eyes were brimming. Then he turned and rode back down the long green slope.

It was like dwelling in heaven.

Four Bears watched the sun go down, sitting on the grass with the wind in his face. He watched the stars appear above the afterglow. He thought of his wives one by one and his children one by one, and was impatient to float over like an eagle and be with their spirits once again. His body was full of heat and pains and itchings and tinglings, but he had learned in the Okeepah how to hover above pain. He looked at the stars and watched the moon go down. It went down beyond the horizon after turning from white to yellow and then red. Sometime before morning he slept, and then awoke to watch the rays of sunrise touch the hilltops upriver. He watched the sunlight brighten the far slopes and cast the shadows of willows in the river valley. Far upstream he could see the Hidatsa towns on the mouth of the Knife River, and he wondered if the Hidatsa, too, were dying.

Again the sun went down, and he watched the stars most of the night, then slept without dreams until daylight woke him again. His mouth was parched and his stomach was full of pain, but he knew he had a long way to go yet before he could leave his body here and float over.

On the evening of the fourth day on the hill, after sunset, he listened to wolves singing their song of twilight, and it seemed as if he could see their intertwining voices, all slightly different, some rising while others were falling, like strands of light hair being braided. He thought of his youngest wife and remembered the sight of her braiding her hair. She had been one of the light-hairs in the tribe. Four Bears remembered just how she felt when they were joined in copulation. It would be so good to meet her again on the Other Side.

He spent much of the next day pondering the matter of the light-hairs and the light-eyes among his People. Catlin had asked so many questions about them that Four Bears had pondered the mystery of it over and over in the last five years, even though it was something he had hardly thought about before. For as long as Four Bears could remember, there had been some light-hairs and light-eyes among his People, though perhaps less than a fourth of them were. Four Bears himself had light eyes.

He tried to remember things that Catlin's questions had disturbed in his memory. The name *Madoc* that Catlin had used for First Man. Though Four Bears had not remembered ever hearing that name himself, it made an echo in that part of him that was connected to the great Circle of Ages, just as the first sight of Red Hair Clark had made an echo and made him see him as First Man.

Four Bears remembered that when Coyote had come home from the whites' country in the East, he had told of being at a great falling-water place on a westward-flowing river and knowing that his ancestors had been there and that it had been a very important place in their times. There was a part of any man, Four Bears knew, that remembered what the man himself had never known. But much was forgotten as the generations were born and died, and because living was so full of new things that outshone the remembered things, the remembered things were always fading, no matter how often they were spoken of.

The white men have a great power, in their Marking Language, he thought. If they teach their new generations to understand the Marking Language, each new one can look at the oldest markings, and all the memories of their people are there!

He thought of the Word Bundles that had been in the Sacred Canoe for so long and then had vanished. He remembered hearing that in one of those there had been pictures of men riding horses, so that his People knew of horses even before they saw them. The people who had made those Marking Language bundles had had horses, but then there were no horses here until we got them from the whites. That was amazing, what could be known just from a picture; it must be even more amazing what can be known from the Marking Language!

Catlin the Shadow Catcher put my People in both pictures and Marking Language. As the women warned, there is nothing left of us now except what Shadow Catcher put down! It was good that we let him do it! At least there is that left!

And there is nothing left of my battles except what I painted on the robe. So! I was a Shadow Catcher, like Catlin! *Shu-su!*

The sun set and rose and set and rose and set and rose, and the mind and spirit of Four Bears grew lighter and more vast.

He did not know how many days and nights he had been here on the hill, hovering above his dying body, when he began to see through his mind instead of through his eyes.

He began to see water, but not the water of the Muddy River curving below; instead, he was seeing water as if he were swimming in it and there was no shore. It was bright blue-green water, and warm.

For a long time he saw only water. He would open his eyes and turn his face so that he should be able to see the river and Mih-Tutta-Hang-Kusch below, but he would see only water.

I am about to cross over, he thought. But I did not expect this about the water.

That night he slept just above his body, and his wives and children floated up to him. They cried. They said that they had been swimming and could not find the shore of the Other Side World.

He woke up suddenly with the sun on his face.

They cannot find the shore of the Other Side World because they have not been buried! he thought.

And then he knew that he had been wrong in leaving their bodies in Mih-Tutta-Hang-Kusch and coming to the hill to die. That had been a wrong and selfish thing for him to do, and he knew that he would have to go back down and get them into the Town of the Dead, or they would always be floating.

Four Bears had wasted so far in his body that it was harder to walk down the hill than it had been to walk up it before. His red-pointed lance was almost too heavy to lift, but he needed it to lean on. He fell often, and crawled much of the way down, and the rotted skin on his hands and knees sloughed off on the ground. He saw no vultures over the town now, but he began to smell the death and decay even before he was down on the level ground.

He walked very slowly through the pickets. There were bundles of bones in the passageways and in the plaza, all stinking and covered with flies, but the scavengers had eaten all they wanted and were gone.

Four Bears went to the Sacred Canoe, and saw that nothing remained there but a pile of ashes.

In the doorway of the Medicine Lodge he saw a skeleton with Old Bear's two medicine pipes lying beside it, and nearby was part of the badger skin he wore in his healings.

So that skeleton must have been Old Bear. He looked at it for a while and gathered his strength to walk on.

When he reached his own lodge, it required all his strength to move the bullboat out of the way of the door so he could go in.

The smell of his family's bodies was so dense that he could hardly bear to enter. The scavengers had not been at them and they had been decomposing under their buffalo-robe shrouds all the while he had been on the hill. The odor so weakened him that he staggered and fell down beside one of the bodies.

I will have to rest awhile before I can do anything, he thought.

While he was lying there, he saw the water again. It was all a beautiful blue-green water.

He saw that he was not swimming in the water, but was standing on a big boat.

It was a long boat with a crowded deck and a striped square sail.

He was young and strong, bearded, burned by blazing sun.

He held up a little cage made of reeds, wiped his forearm across his brow to wipe away his sweat, and opened the top of the cage. He tapped it on the bottom and a pigeon flew out on fluttering wings, and vanished into the hot glare of the afternoon sun.

"Go," he said. "Fly away and find us Iarghal."

EPILOGUE

NEW YORK
AUTUMN 1838

Mr G. Catlin, Esqr, Artist
Dr Sir:
In hopes that you will remember me, I seek an audience with you as soon as your convenience permits. I have tracked you some 3000 miles to bring you items and news from M'Kenzie & myself. Please reply by this messenger, who will wait.

KIPP
American Fur Company

"Oh, yes! God be praised! Wait." Catlin, his smock spattered with paint from his constant touching-up and refinement of his Indian Gallery paintings, shoved a stack of his manuscripts over to give himself a few inches of writing space on the writing desk of his studio.

KIPP!
I am paying y^{r} messenger to bring you here at once! If you need a conveyance for what you bring, hire it and bring me the reckoning. Plan to be MY guest for a change!
Await^{g} the sight of you I am y^{r} affectionate friend,

G. CATLIN

After a back-pounding embrace and much gazing into each other's misty eyes, Catlin and Kipp hoisted the smelly crate from McKenzie off the back of the carriage and staggered into the house with it, while Clara Catlin and the two small daughters held doors for them. "Like everything from the company," Catlin laughed, "it reeks o' beaver gland."

"Can you be hungry in an hour, Mr. Kipp?" Clara asked.

"Indeed I can, ma'am. Thank ye!" His face was brown as an

Indian's, except his forehead, which was white above the hat line. "Fine lady!" He looked around the crowded studio, seeing many familiar faces in the portraits, and by the time Catlin had poured him a brandy, his eyes were brimming and his chin was crumpled and trembling. The two men clinked their glasses and emptied them.

"I've read a little about the epidemic," Catlin said. "Precious few details, though. What can you tell me?"

Kipp shut his eyes and shook his head. "More than you could stand to hear, I'm afraid."

"Four Bears?"

"Gone. Last to die. He was so strong, ye know."

"Ah, God!" Catlin closed his eyes and hung his head. He could not stand to look at either of the two portraits of Four Bears, which looked down from their prominent places on the studio walls. "Wolf Chief?" he muttered.

"Him, too."

"And White Bison Hair?" Catlin remembered his last sight of him on the bluff throwing down the precious leggings.

"The first one to go."

"Old Bear?"

"To save us a lot of names, sir: anyone you name is gone."

Catlin stared in tear-filled disbelief. "Are you implying the Mandan are . . . extinct?" *And the lost Welshmen as well!* he thought.

"Not implying, sir. Just saying it. A flat fact. There was maybe thirty that got captured by the Arikarees and might still be alive. But yes, sir, *extinct* is a good word for it. One exception: my wife. I'd had her inoculated, ye know."

Catlin was sitting in an armchair with his hands steepled and his chin resting on his fingertips, brow wrinkled, eyes swimming in tears, looking all about the ceiling. "No sweeter, no happier a people!" His chest shook with voiceless sobs, and Kipp remembered how glad he had been that Catlin had not been there to see Four Bears cursing the whites.

After a long while Catlin said in a small voice, "The papers said, what? Twenty or thirty thousand wiped out on the Upper Missouri in just a couple of months?"

"That's about it by Mr. McKenzie's reckoning, though as ye know he tends to underexaggerate on figgers. Hidatsas, Crees, Blackfeet, Shienne, Crow . . ."

Catlin let out a long sigh. "You know, Kipp, I get so sometimes I dread to paint another portrait."

"Oh! Mustn't stop, sir! It's a God-given talent few's got!"

"Kipp, I painted Osceola. He died the next day. I painted Black Hawk, then he was gone. Thunderer, the Osage, killed next day . . . Tenskwatawa the Shawnee Prophet . . . Now Four Bears and Wolf Chief and every single Mandan I painted! And then who knows how many of those poor Blackfeet and Crow and Shienne the smallpox got were ones I'd painted. . . ." He shook his head and buried his face in his hands, from where he murmured, "I painted General Clark, too, you know. And he died this year."

"Aye, he did," Kipp mused. "They say he up and died of heartbreak, because all his Indians refused to take his advice and get vaccinated. They'd always listened to him on every other matter. . . ."

"Oh, God, Kipp, this is just terrible!"

Kipp leaned toward him, stretching out a brown hand. "Look, old friend. Ye mustn't put it on to yourself like that. Everybody dies, whether he ever gets painted or not. . . . I see your own picture over there. Isn't that by your own hand?"

"Yes . . . self-portrait, when I first started painting. . . ."

"Well, and see, you're still alive. You didn't commit suicide by painting yourself!"

Catlin looked up at Kipp, a strange smile on his tear-wet face. "Funny joke, Kipp." He drew out a large handkerchief and wiped his eyes, then blew his nose. Then he shook his head and looked as if he were about to start weeping again. "Remember how those Mandan women—and even Old Bear himself!—warned that everybody I painted would die? And there wouldn't be anything left but their images on my canvases?" He shuddered. "Prophetic! How did they know?"

"Well, but I remember, too, what a pleasure Old Bear got after you *did* paint him! Remember how he'd just lay there all day and admire himself? Heh heh! I reckon he don't regret it."

The two old comrades sat quiet awhile. Catlin poured more brandy, sipped, then smiled and said, "What kind of a council is this? We didn't start with a pipe!" He reached over his desk toward his clay tavern pipes and tobacco urn, then paused. He got up and went to a shelf in a corner, and brought back a long-stemmed Mandan pipe with a red-stone bowl. "Remember when we smoked this one with Four Bears? This'd be more appropriate, don't you think?" He pulled out the wad of wild sage he kept in the bowl when it was not in use. "Wish I had some *kinnikinneck* instead of tobacco. . . ."

Kipp held up a finger, reached into a side pocket of his ill-fitting store-bought frock coat and pulled out a small, quilled bag. "Kinnikinneck," he said.

As he filled the bowl, Catlin said, "In 'thirty-six, do you know, I went up to the Pipestone Bluff where all the tribes quarry this red stone. Damned near had to fight my way in, because the Eastern Sioux said it was a holy place and no white man had ever been there. My friend Wood and I just about had to fight twenty or so of 'em, but we finally talked them into a peaceable state and rode on to the quarry. . . . It's a funny thing. The stuff's called 'Catlinite' now, because I was the first white man to find the place. Why don't they call it 'Indianite,' for all the red men who've used it for a thousand years? In fact, the Great Spirit is said to have told all the tribes on the Continent to use it for their peace pipes because it *is* their red flesh. But now it's 'Catlinite,' which I guess shows you how important the Indians' thinking is in this country. Hnh! And now, as you know, Andrew Jackson—may God forgive me for uttering the name!—is pushing the last ones out of the East, and doing all he can to deal doom to the whole race! Thank God William Clark won't have to work under this administration any longer. *That's* probably what broke his heart!"

"Well," Kipp said, "it's better to see you raving mad than all melancholy. Now what do you say we have that pipe?"

Catlin lit it and presented the stem to the four points of the compass, and then to the sky and earth, and for a while they savored the scents of red willow, sage, tobacco, and sumac, and Catlin felt the reverence and calm, the bittersweetness and spaciousness that those old familiar scents evoked in his soul. "I'm having a hard time living in square rooms in stinking cities, where you have to lock your house, where every move is made for the love of money."

"I don't envy you," Kipp said, " 'spite of all your fame and success. For which, by the way, congratulations."

"Congratulate me when I've finally produced one shred of benefit for our red brothers. Not till then."

There came a gentle rap on the door. Clara pushed it open a little way and said, "Supper will be on the board in fifteen minutes, if our guest would like to wash off the road dust."

"Thank you, Mrs. Catlin, I will." As he got up and went to his saddlebags, he paused and touched his forefinger to his temple. "Ah! Mustn't forget this!" He reached into one of the bags and drew out an oblong object enfolded in the soft skin of a mountain sheep. "This keeps a promise I made to our good friend Four Bears, God rest his soul."

George Catlin unrolled the heavy bundle. What he saw first inside was the yellow-brown hair of a grizzly. Then the gleaming curve of an old bear claw. Now he recognized it.

"Ah, Kipp!" he groaned, a knot growing in his throat. And he drew from the grizzly-skin scabbard the item that had long been deemed the strongest medicine in the great bend of the Missouri.

It was Mah-to-toh-pah's dagger, tarnished by the lifeblood of his enemies, as well as his own.

Catlin held it in his right hand, not by the haft, but with his fingers around the double-edged blade. Eyes shut, the lingering sage and tobacco smoke recalling the vast plains of Four Bears's world, Catlin squeezed on the blade till his hand was wet with blood and his eyelids wet with tears, feeling a pain that Four Bears, the brother of his heart, had felt one glorious day long ago.

AUTHOR'S NOTE

For two centuries or more, scholars have been divided over the legend of Madoc and his lost Welsh colony in the New World.

This novel was not written to advocate the legend. This is a work of fiction and imagination. Nevertheless, I researched it as diligently as if I had been trying to resolve the dispute. Where documentation was available—the fratricidal wars for succession to Owain Gwynedd's throne in twelfth century Wales, medieval voyages, and expeditions of La Verendreye and Lewis and Clark, the activities of George Catlin, the plague that wiped out Four Bears's Mandans—I used such documentation conscientiously. I studied all the arguments pro and con.

Some of the arguments in support of the Madoc legend, ironically, lost credibility in the 1790s simply because they were told too well. Edward Williams, a Welsh literary man and Madoc theorist who used the name Iolo Morganwg, the "Bard of Liberty," was not content to relate only the actual information he had obtained. In regular Saturday night meetings of the Society of Gwyneddigion, he embellished his historical and literary knowledge with considerable fabrication, creating scholastic confusion as yet untangled.

Presently the controversy grows even more wondrous as Welsh and American scholars compile a theory that a different Madoc, brother of the legendary King Arthur, came to North America in the *sixth* century—500 years earlier.

I set out to tell this tale upon the following set of popular assumptions: that in 1169, Madoc, son of King Owain Gwynedd, did discover the East Coast of North America, then on his return the next year sailed his fleet under the Florida peninsula into the Gulf of Mexico and landed his colonists at Mobile Bay; that he worked his way overland to settle in the Tennessee Valley and thence explored up through the Ohio Valley to the Falls of the Ohio, site of present Louisville, where his followers eventually were destroyed; and that survivors eventually mingled with the Mandan tribe and migrated slowly up the Missouri (Muddy River) to the Dakotas, where they were encountered by the Frenchman La Verendreye just one century before their extermination by smallpox in 1838. There has been plentiful physical evidence to support that itinerary, and it also explains the oral traditions of many Native American Peoples.

George Catlin's map of the Welsh and Mandan migrations presumes a simpler route right up the Mississippi to the Ohio, but that would not account for the ruins of stone fortifications near Chattanooga and Manchester, Tennessee, and a tribal memory of the Cherokee that their ancestors warred with Welshmen and drove them out of the Tennessee Valley hundreds of years ago.

The sudden decline of the Mississippian Mound Builders Culture lost its mystery for me when I realized that Europeans possibly had entered their realm at just that time, with their ship rats and their myriad Old World diseases. The ordinary suppositions made by archeologists had always seemed to me too feeble and farfetched to explain the catastrophic demise of such a mighty civilization. Epidemics would account for it very well, as evidenced by the later great waves of disease brought upon the natives by Spaniards, Englishmen, and Frenchmen in the centuries after Columbus's arrival.

In the oral traditions of most tribes I have studied, there are references to a "white tribe" or to "white giants with beards" or to "pale men from beyond the sunrise sea" who were defeated and massacred by an alliance of tribes on the dark and bloody ground of Kentucky, long before Columbus came. The ghosts of those white men, in fact, were supposed to haunt Kentucky so powerfully that no tribes would make their homes there; Kentucky was not a place of tribal residence, but only a hunting ground shared by several woodland tribes.

Other findings that kept the Madoc legend alive in the Ohio Valley were ancient fortress walls made of quarried and squared stone, brass and bronze armor found near the falls, great quantities of apparently Caucasian skulls and bones scattered about as on a battleground, iron tools unearthed from beneath the roots of trees centuries old, and the frequent occurrence of Welsh words and numerals in native tribal vocabularies.

And some scholars of the matter believe that the word "Allegheny" derives from the name of Owain Gwynedd, Madoc's father, after whom they believe the region may have been named. You can almost see them roll the syllables over their tongues as they compare.

Such intriguing clues do not satisfy those who scoff at the Madoc legend. Those who do believe cite them as irrefutable proof that the great Welsh Mariner Prince was indeed an American pioneer.

If he was, the land and the natives and the adventures he and his descendants found here would have been, I think, much as I have envisioned them in this story. Here were Peoples in transition between the great Mississippian Mound Builder Culture and the independent hunter-gatherer-farmer societies found here in historic times.

Most haunting to my imagination is the notion of European people being gradually absorbed into a so-called "primitive" culture, bit by bit, until their literacy and their Christian religion are lost.

And if indeed Madoc's Welshmen, through typical Eurocentric hubris, did bring the natives' wrath down upon themselves, that conflict would have been a harbinger of the violent conquest that began three hundred years later when the white men began coming again. If the newcomers had ever respected the natives' ways and treated them as equals, there never would have been a violent frontier. This land was already occupied by richly civilized societies who were almost all hospitable by nature. Europeans, unfortunately, have long been afflicted with a mental condition which makes them think that only their beliefs can have validity, and so they have wrought irrevocable damage on every continent on earth.

The natives of all those continents have had precious few triumphs to celebrate. If Madoc's Welshmen truly were wiped out by a confederation of natives at the Falls of the Ohio, as the native legends aver, then the Native Americans might take some satisfaction from that. As one old Ojibway man recounted from tribal memory, while being interviewed by linguistic scholar C. F. Voegelin early in this century:

> Well, my friend, I will tell you one story now as I sit here at this university where I talk foolishly. I'll tell about what must have happened. An unknown number of years may have elapsed since then: It has always been supposed that the In-

dian at first lived here in the Big Knife Land [America] . . . After a while the whites arrived, settling here in the Big Knife Land. Then they greatly humbled the Indians. After a while, however, those began to realize how they were being treated by the whites. Then those Indians told them, "If you do not stop doing this, we will put out your fires."

However, those whites annoyed them again, more and more. Then the Indians told them, "You will not do this to us again." Then when they had told them for the third time, that's when they put out their fires for them: where they did away with all of those whites.

The reason I believe this story is that now white people on this side of the world find very many things of long ago . . . These things are unusual looking, which you used. Then also those white people are inclined to believe it. Those who are called Whites must have been in the Big Knife Land.

Well, I myself believe it. Well, it's unknown what all of you think: I do not know you. That's the way I heard it, my friend.

When I read that old Ojibway's words, I can imagine his sly, bittersweet smile.

What he said doesn't prove anything one way or another. But I imagine his story referred to the fate of Madoc's Welshmen.